The

J.M. Hewitt is a crime and psychological thriller author. Her work has also been published in three short story anthologies. Her writing combines the complexity of human behaviour with often enchanting settings. In contrast to the sometimes dark content of her books, she lives a very nice life in a seaside town in Suffolk with her dog, Marley.

Also by J.M. Hewitt

THE
DREAM
JOB

J.M. HEWITT

CANELO

First published in the United Kingdom in 2024 by

Canelo
Unit 9, 5th Floor
Cargo Works, 1–2 Hatfields
London SE1 9PG
United Kingdom

A CIP catalogue record for this book is available from the British Library.

Print ISBN 978 1 80436 509 0
Ebook ISBN 978 1 80436 510 6

Cover design by Lisa Brewster

Cover images © Shutterstock, Depositphotos, Alamy

Look for more great books at www.canelo.co

Printed and bound in Great Britain by Clays Ltd, Elcograf S.p.A.

1

For Tracey Jordan

With love

1

ALINA, FRIDAY

Alina Arpels watches as the ten-foot-tall sculpture begins to sway.

Until then, at the pre-opening night at the gallery, she had been slightly bored. This is more like it. Fascinating. She marvels at what these artists do nowadays. Back when she was a child, just Sofia's age, galleries were all portraits and marble busts. There needs to be a reveal these days, something that sets the artist apart from their contemporaries. Or a backstory.

Or a history.

She thinks of her parents. Of how long it has been since she saw them. How long it has been since she even spoke to them. She wonders if they visit museums and galleries, their joy so easily raised, their hearts struck by a simple painting. Or if they sequester themselves behind high walls and electric fences, a life lived in fear because of the choices they made.

What would they make of this? The ten-foot-tall, blade-constructed pile of metal. It is called Lucifer, although it doesn't resemble any depiction of the demon she has ever seen.

'A gimmick,' her father would retort, crossly.

'How novel!' her mother would exclaim.

Alina's thoughts drift further. Part of her mind hovers on the realisation that her daughter is no longer at her side, while the other half wonders whether to have one more glass of champagne or take her girl somewhere for a late dinner. Or they could even just go straight home, cajole Willem into rustling something up in the kitchen.

He's at home tonight – Willem, her husband. And they're both so damn busy with their respective lives that when they are both in the same place, it's a treat. Even fifteen years and one child later, she still loves being in his company.

She nods to herself, decision made. They'll go home. Have dinner, put Sofia to bed together, then maybe, because Willem is leaving tomorrow night for Antwerp, they'll open a bottle and spend all night on the terrace of their Richmond house, drinking Russian vodka and playing cards. Enjoying the hot summer night as though they're any other couple, and not millionaires.

The gasp from the crowd pulls her back to the here and now. She looks up. The demon is more than moving now. It is rocking manically.

She can feel something prickling over her skin. She listens to her body, to her inner self, and understands.

The demon is not supposed to be moving.

What drama on an otherwise boring Friday night! For a moment, she's perked up again, her interest heightened once more.

Her half-thought of seconds ago bites at her, commanding she take notice.

Sofia is not at her side.

It's a recurring nightmare, one that Alina has had since her daughter was born. *Natural*, Willem used to say, soothingly – a mother's instinct.

It's not a maternal thing, though. It's born of her heritage, of the way she herself was raised. With fear, with the threat of the outside world drilled into her from before she could even walk or talk.

She covers it well. Not a single soul knows the thoughts that play on Alina's mind *all the time*. Her husband believes her to be laid-back and casual. He doesn't know that her fears plague her, of how she wants to scream if she loses sight of Sofia for a few, heart-stopping moments.

Like right now.

'Sofia!' The word is short and snappy, the accent she lost a long time ago coming back to lie heavy on her tongue, as it only does in times of stress or excitement.

She looks left and right, cranes over the heads in front of her, annoyance rising at the bodies that surround her, impeding a clear view of where her child has gone.

The man in front of her steps to his left. Through the gap, Alina sees her daughter.

She is crossing the floor in front of the sculpture, not even appearing to notice the crowd's collective second gasp, the mounting, rising, panicked chatter, or the monstrosity of sharpened metal that tilts and undulates behind her.

Sofia is in the firing line. The first blade is already slipping from the structure; the other however many hundreds look set to follow swiftly, her daughter in their deadly trajectory.

Her own scream shocks those around her into a moment of silence. She frightens herself, the way she sounds, the way she feels. The freeze that swallows her whole is appalling. She fights back against it, thrusting out her arms. Her hands, curled into fists, batter against those who stand close to her. She doesn't care, her focus

3

is solely on her girl, on reaching her, *shielding* her, taking those blades into herself because that's what a mother does.

She would die for her child. She would kill for her. Exchange her own life for that of her daughter's.

The first blade slides down Lucifer's form, the gentle chime concealing the danger ahead. The noise changes when it hits the concrete floor. The rattle is startling, signalling the oncoming danger.

Alina is too far away. She struggles, hemmed in, moving her shoulders to barge against the unmoving crowd.

These people are not intentionally obstructing her, she knows that. They are panicked, seeing it unfold too. Just like she was moments ago, they are frozen in place.

Alina uses her elbows and legs; she kicks out her feet and screams like a banshee directly into the ears of her neighbours. At the commotion she has created, they begin to move, but still far too slowly.

A seemingly well-meaning older gentleman sees the danger she is intending to rush into. He takes a hold of her arm to keep her back.

Alina punches him without hesitation, a sharp jab to his ribs. Her father's lessons from childhood a muscle memory within her.

The man who had only good intentions exhales into her face, a whoosh of champagne-flavoured air. He doubles over, releases her arm.

It has cost her precious time.

Everyone parts for her now, as she forces her way through.

All the time, she hears her own voice inside her head.

It's happening. Everything she has feared for all the eight years of Sofia's life, all that doomsday thinking, is actually happening *right now*.

A flash of movement through the shoulders of the people in front. Someone else is moving, fast, head down like a sprinter, aiming for Sofia.

They are close to Alina's child, nearer than she is.

Their intentions are good, she can see that by the frenzied, fast way that they move.

Alina urges them on with a prayer.

Another scream comes – maybe from her, maybe someone else – as the figure reaches Alina's girl, splays out her arms, dives on top of her.

This stranger, this unknown blur of speed, covers Alina's daughter. Shields her. *Protects* her, just like Alina intended.

Lucifer's steel blades fall faster now, punching the air. A wail rings out from somebody as a thin fountain of blood spirals upwards.

Not Sofia's, Alina begs internally. *Please, not my girl's blood.*

She breaks through to the front. Dizziness catches her as she sees the spectacle on the floor. Sofia's saviour is a woman. Smartly dressed in a lightweight blazer, blonde hair, small in stature but big enough to cover Sofia's body entirely. It strikes Alina that this woman, from this view-point, looks like some kind of SAS soldier as she clings like a limpet to the small girl's body and crab-walks her across to a cluster of people, doing her best to avoid the fallen blades that surround her.

The stranger escorts Sofia bodily to a place of safety, out of reach of the remaining, falling steel.

As the last Japanese blade crashes to the floor, and Lucifer lies crumpled in a pile of metal, the crowd lets out one, final exhalation. Silence descends once more.

The woman is removed from Sofia's form. Alina recognises the man who lifts the stranger. He is Jerry, has worked here in the gallery since its opening night decades ago. He is a big fan of telling people that, all the visitors and staff and patrons who come here.

Alina bypasses both him and the woman who saved her child's life. She aims straight for her girl.

Sofia is sitting up, wide-eyed, shocked. There is a graze to both of her knees. Not a cut from the metal that rained down on her, but a consequence of being moved along the rough, concrete floor.

A miracle, thinks Alina.

Immediately, she dispels this reaction.

Not a miracle at all. Sofia came out of this unscathed because of the selfless actions of a stranger.

She needs to speak to the woman, but right now, she simply gazes at her girl. She can't take her eyes off her. Can't even speak to ask Sofia if she is okay.

But she is, she tells herself. She is sitting up, she is breathing, she is not bleeding. Apart from the grazes to her legs, which are commonplace on little girls the world over, Sofia is fine.

The staff of the Momotaro Gallery surround her, bowing and scraping, and offering apologies and tears, tissues and water.

Alina glances past them, looks right through them as she sinks to her knees in front of her girl.

The woman is leaving. She's being practically carried up the stairs by two people that Alina doesn't know. Faithful Jerry is heading up the rear. A trail of blood

6

follows the route they have taken. It's so red. It looks obscene against the off-white concrete floor.

Tate, the artist – the person responsible for the bladed installation – is still here. In a crouch beside his revolting Lucifer. He looks not at Alina, nor Sofia, and not even at the woman trailing a blaze of claret behind her. He stares at the pile of metal that rained down like hellfire upon the people who paid him handsomely to come see his work.

His face is ashen.

Just like her own. Just like Sofia's face.

Alina clenches her teeth so hard that her jaw hurts.

There must be something in her face, because when she glances around again, the room is startlingly empty.

Alina stands up.

She will deal with the artist later.

She will locate and thank the stranger later.

Right now, it's time to go home.

She picks Sofia up. Eight years old and the girl still fits against her like she did when she was a toddler.

The remaining onlookers – a few staff, a few patrons – surge towards her.

Alina glares at them.

They fall back. This time, the crowd parts for her without hesitation.

–

'It was fucking terrible.'

They are home, Sofia seated at the dining-room table, Willem crouched in front of her.

He has the vodka out, just like she'd planned, but is using it on the grazes on Sofia's knees.

He darts her a look in response to her language. She softens a little at the glance he throws her way. He has that effect on her. It is why they work. He is the calm to her storm.

The soft side to her steely parts.

Willem is Dutch.

Alina is Russian.

Willem is the owner of a company specialising in lab-created diamonds.

Alina is the heiress to a shipping empire.

By society's standards, their roles are reversed in every way.

Somehow, it works.

'And what sculpture was it?'

She shudders. She will never forget the grotesque atrocity as long as she lives.

'The structure is – *was* – ten feet tall. It was supposed to be a shimmering, glinting depiction of Lucifer, entirely constructed out of metal.'

'Was supposed to be?'

Alina jerks her shoulders angrily in a shrug. 'It was conceptual, I suppose. It didn't look like Lucifer. It was just a hulking great pile of blades.'

Willem frowns. 'Blades?'

'Actual blades! Japanese steel!' she hisses at him, scandalised, feeling fury again at the memory.

'And it collapsed.' Willem sets his jaw, strokes the cotton swabs on Sofia's knees. He turns his full attention back to his daughter. 'Sofia, how are you feeling? Apart from these, I mean. How are you feeling in here, up here?' He taps a gentle finger on her chest, where her heart beats, and on the side of her head.

Both Willem and Alina watch her reaction carefully.

'Okay.' Sofia gives him a smile. 'I liked the fairy before she fell down.'

'It was a devil,' snaps Alina. 'And he's a *man*. And it didn't even look like a devil or a man.'

Sofia shrugs. 'I liked him. It made me sad when he fell over. All that artist's hard work.'

Alina's chest heaves. She is close to tears. Not rage, not this time. That has passed, though it will return. No, this one is for her daughter's sensitivity. She's sad for the literal fallen angel. Sad for the hard work that Tate put into his sculpture.

The girl is Willem's child, that's for sure.

Willem has his hands in Sofia's hair now. Feeling for lumps, bumps, head traumas that might come back and bite them in the middle of the night. Alina imagines it. Waking to check on her… No, not waking, because Alina won't sleep at all tonight. But going into her room, finding her little girl, blue face, no breath, zero heartbeat.

All her nightmares coming to life.

She stands up. 'We will take her to the hospital,' she announces.

Sofia squirms on her chair and wriggles under her father's hands.

'I'm fine,' she protests.

Willem removes his hands from her hair, places them either side of her face, and plants a gentle kiss on her forehead. 'She is fine,' he says to Alina.

There's a tiny red mark on the girl's chin. The woman, the stranger, the *saviour*, leapt upon Sofia as she hurled her to the ground. Subsequently, Sofia smashed her chin on the concrete. Tomorrow it will bloom into a bruise.

But a banged-up chin doesn't equate to a head injury, nor the death that could easily have occurred.

'Bedtime.' Willem lifts Sofia to standing.

The girl stalls like she always does. Seeking cuddles from Alina, searching for special pyjamas which she absolutely must sleep in. She drags her feet, delaying the inevitable bedtime.

Alina is relieved. Shock and trauma would impact the girl's normal routine.

And this is totally normal.

Willem herds Sofia up the stairs, clapping behind her, shrieking manically. Sofia's giggles echo around the house. It sounds just like any other night.

But it isn't. It's the night Sofia could have died.

Alina reaches for the vodka when her husband returns to the room.

'You'll find the woman who helped her.'

It isn't a question he is asking, merely a statement.

'I'll speak to Jerry,' she says, pouring them both a hefty double measure. 'I saw him helping her on the way out.' She remembers the trail of blood.

She had passed it when she left with Sofia. She had stepped carefully around it. Sofia had tried not to look at it, whereas Alina had been unable to drag her eyes away.

'And the bloody artist,' Willem continues. 'You'll look into him, find out what happened, speak to the gallery.'

'That *fucking* artist,' she mutters.

'You'll handle it,' he says.

They both know what he means when he says that.

2

HANNAH, FRIDAY

She's bleeding all over the floor. It's kept pristine, normally. Shined to perfection daily. Hannah has never seen so much as a discarded piece of litter upon it. No shoe scuffs, or muddy footprints.

She clings onto her arm, trying to prevent it from dripping further, but it's no use. The bleed is a stream from her torn flesh.

Outside, she shivers with the sense that she is being watched. She glances around at the people who are moving up and down the high street, going about their own business. Some of them catch sight of her, blood still dripping. They stare openly.

Jerry personally escorts her to an urgent-care facility, down the street from Momotaro, and Hannah hesitates at the automatic doors, looking upon the reception area that's full to bursting. A cacophony of bloody noses, a coughing chorus, moans and cries. The silent ones are the worst. Their eyes blank as though this is death's own waiting room, and they've accepted that fact.

She backs away. 'Jerry, I'm fine, I really don't need—'

'Yeah, Hannah, you really do,' he replies.

She blinks at the tone of his voice. Subservient Jerry, the epitome of professionalism, of cool and quiet and brimming over with respect. He steers her through the door, taking care not to touch her anywhere near her sliced shoulder.

'I've got healthcare,' she tells him, desperation in her voice, thinking of the private hospital that's within walking distance.

'That's good. These guys can stop the bleeding, patch you up, and tomorrow you can check in somewhere else.'

He's right in that she is still bleeding. A river that starts at her upper arm, running down her side to join the flow in the wound at her ankle.

There is a brown, bristly mat at the entrance to the centre. The red pool that's collecting is fascinating and nauseating in equal measure.

Jerry steers her through the room and deposits her on a hard plastic chair.

'Wait here,' he commands. He hurries in the direction of the reception desk.

'Who shall I call?' he asks when he returns.

'Nobody,' Hannah says.

His hands flutter anxiously. His eyes never leave her arm. As another audible amount of blood plops to the floor, he whips a tightly pressed handkerchief out of his pocket and applies it with pressure to her shoulder.

The material, a crisp, bright white, is claret within seconds.

'We really need help over here!' Jerry cries. He holds up the hanky, a scarlet flag demanding assistance.

'I'm quite tired.'

There is a hint of surprise to her voice. Hannah doesn't get tired. She's like a machine. She keeps herself nutritionally fed and watered. She exercises regularly. Her life is busy. There is no time for fatigue.

It's an odd feeling that she has now, as she leans against him. She thinks of his nice shirt, of how smart he always looks, of how the dry-cleaners won't be able to make a dent in this stain she's imprinting upon him.

'*No!*' Jerry's shout is loud in her ear. 'Anyone!' he shrills. 'Come *on!*'

—

Later, after the tired-looking doctor has put a gruesome row of untidy stitches in her arm, bandaged up her leg and fired questions accompanied with narrowed eyes about this apparent knife attack, she is allowed to leave.

It is after midnight, and the waiting room is even fuller than it was when she arrived a couple of hours ago.

She attempts to stride to the doors, walking in her usual manner, testing her ankle. Weight-bearing or speed seems to have no detrimental impact on it, so Hannah decides she should be okay to walk home.

Home.

Her mother, Marie, will be waiting anxiously. Marie is used to early-evening gallery openings and exhibits that turn into late-night networking parties, but the two of them are as close as two people can be. Her mother will have sensed tonight's drama in her bones.

Marie is a worrier. Hannah is her only child. A mother always knows.

Out of the doors, on the still-warm street, it is as busy as it was when she arrived earlier – more so, if possible, just like the medical-centre waiting room. London nights, as vibrant and action-packed as the daytime.

She shudders as the doors swish closed. She vows never to enter the place again. Tomorrow, she will go to the Royal Chelsea and ask that they redo the ghastly stitches.

13

Then, the doors open again. Amongst the muted conversation within, she hears someone call her name.

'Hannah!'

The voice is low. Hannah turns, surprised to see Jerry still there, a woman at his side.

She blinks at the pair of them. Warmth floods through her at the realisation that her mother is here. Did her mum know, summoned by some maternal knowledge, that her daughter was in danger?

She switches her gaze to Jerry. He had asked who he could call for her. *Nobody*, she'd told him, not wanting her mother to get that dreaded telephone call late at night.

There is a look on his face, a curious mixture of guilt and defiance.

Jerry called her mother.

Hannah visualises her home, the place where her mother mostly stays, confined in near-luxury, her duty as a grandmother one she takes very seriously as she keeps a watchful, eagle eye on Hannah's two-year-old son.

'Oliver is fine,' says Marie, even though Hannah hadn't asked the question. 'I called Nita to come over.'

Nita from next door isn't Hannah's favourite person. She's struck up a more than neighbourly friendship with Marie that Hannah finds stifling.

'We should go home, then, let Nita get back,' says Hannah.

Marie says nothing. Her face, stricken and pale, speaks for her. Jerry, on the other hand, can't seem to stop talking. Half-explanations and apologies spill from his mouth.

Hannah waves him off impatiently. She can't believe that placid and professional Jerry would be so bold as to take her purse and find her address from her driving licence, which he holds out to her now. She wonders if he went to her home to break the news to Marie in person.

'Thanks, Jerry,' she says wearily.

The night has caught up with her, and Hannah sways. Barely noticeable, but her mother sees it, as only a mother would. She catches her daughter's arm, holds her steady, and much like the way Jerry steered Hannah into this place, Marie escorts her away from it.

Hannah protests against getting a taxi; the mews home that she shares with her mother and her son is a mere twenty-minute walk away.

Marie, for once, argues. Jerry nods, siding with her, and before Hannah can refuse, the two of them are tapping on her phone, summoning an Uber.

Marie offers for Jerry to share the ride, but he's going back to the gallery.

'I'll be expected to be part of the clean-up crew.' He winces.

Marie stares at him and Hannah realises she doesn't fully know what happened yet.

'I'll fill you in,' Hannah says quietly to her mother. She wishes Jerry good luck with the massive pile of deadly blades that await him.

He shrugs. 'I might not be needed yet. They'll want to investigate, look into the accident...' He trails off, and Hannah knows he is revisiting the event again in his mind.

'An investigation?' Marie's voice is sharp. Her eyes are narrowed slits as she stares at Jerry.

Hannah flaps her good arm at her. 'I'll fill you in later,' she repeats.

They move to the kerb as Jerry walks off back towards Momotaro. Seconds later, the Uber pulls up.

Hannah looks out of the window on the short drive home, into the London night that is always as bright as day.

She can feel Marie's eyes on her, silently questioning, wondering, watching all the time until they reach home. As Hannah walks into the hallway, she bypasses Nita and her faux concerns and well wishes. Leaving the neighbour to Marie, she heads upstairs.

The murmur of hushed conversation fades into the background as she goes straight to her own bedroom.

Marie trots upstairs, stands in the doorway as Hannah lays her handbag on the bedside table and peels off her clothes. Marie's eyes travel the length of Hannah's body as she undresses, narrowing at the sight of the two bandages.

'It was a child,' Hannah says, 'at the gallery. The install-ation collapsed; razor-sharp pieces of metal were raining down.'

'Jesus.' Marie pales even further, her cheeks a cold, marbled grey.

'The girl's okay.' Awkwardly, Hannah pulls on a vest and climbs into bed. 'I'm okay, too.'

'Do you need anything?'

Hannah reaches out her arms. The motion is childlike, something Oliver does all the time. Obligingly, Marie bends down and allows Hannah to wrap her arms around her.

'Good night,' Marie whispers.

Vaguely, Hannah remembers the painkillers that the doctor handed to her. Prescription ones, industrial strength. Awkwardly, the stitches pulling as sharply as the blades that sliced at her earlier, she reaches into her bag on the side table and pulls out the bottle, dry swallowing two.

She relishes the fatigue as it covers her like a blanket.

3

ALINA, SATURDAY

Alina is up and about super early, before either her husband or daughter are even out of bed.

From her bathroom, she calls the curator of the Momotaro Gallery, requesting Jerry's telephone number. Ignoring the man's simpering and apologising, she hangs up as soon as she has the information she needs.

She imagines him – the curator – finding out that the girl who had almost died at his gallery was Alina and Willem Arpels' child.

The fear he will now know.

It is a small consolation for her.

When she calls him, Jerry suggests a pre-breakfast drink at The Members Club, Kensington. Alina approves of his choice. It tells her that although they are only on nodding terms, he knows exactly who she is, and that she will have no problems contacting the place and ensuring they will open up five hours earlier than normal for her and her guest.

She messages Merle, the French owner, telling him she needs a meeting in one hour at his establishment. Alina and Willem count him as a close, personal friend, and he responds immediately. He will open now, he says, and he will get his haute chef to prepare anything Alina and her guest require, should they decide to extend it to a breakfast meeting.

Alina edges into Sofia's room and stands over her girl.

The bruise is coming out in full force on her chin now, a mark so purple that it is almost black.

A small price to pay. So small, so insignificant in the grand scheme of things.

She imagines how it may have been last night; how, in another universe, or a parallel one, Alina would be standing over a bed that is empty, the little girl who should be in it elsewhere, in a morgue, in a space that is frozen in order to preserve her until a burial.

Her body is liquid. Her knees suddenly give way, and she sinks down to kneel upon the thick carpet.

'Mama.' The voice is tiny, ever so slightly fearful.

Alina, head low to try and get some blood back to her faint self, glances up.

Sofia is awake, peeping over the bed at her.

Alina slips her wedding ring off and holds it up. 'Dropped my ring, silly Mama,' she says with a forced grin.

Sofia frowns.

As well she might. Alina is being fake, pretending, and Sofia is clever enough to know.

Alina kisses her daughter on her chin, near to the blooming bruise. 'Go back to sleep,' she whispers. 'It's early.'

Alina summons her driver, Lucas. He is always on call, always ready for her.

He gives her a concerned look. She wonders what she looks like. If it is apparent that she's not slept, if her distress is written all over her face.

She gets into the passenger seat of the car and directs him into Kensington.

The journey is silent from her side. Unheard of for Alina. Lucas pretends not to notice. He keeps up a steady stream of chatter, mostly inane remarks about the traffic and how hot it is, even though it's still so early.

Alina leans her head on the window and watches London pass her by.

Jerry is waiting for her, prompt and punctual. He looks as dapper as always in a crisp, white shirt and jacket, and his shoes have been shined to perfection. She doesn't know his history, where he came from, but has always admired that he takes his position as security guard at the Momotaro Gallery above and beyond.

'I appreciate you meeting with me, so early,' she says, giving his hand a firm shake as Merle leads them to their table.

'Anytime, Ms Arpels,' he says, eyes lowered respect-fully. 'May I enquire how Miss Sofia is, after last night's…' Here he hesitates, seemingly seeking for a word that shows he knows how serious the situation was, but maybe not wanting her to flare up.

'Fuck-up,' Alina says, snapping the linen napkin and laying it across her lap. 'Let's not beat around the bush, Jerry.'

He bobs his head to the left, to the right, and nods in understanding.

Merle arrives with tea, coffee and a selection of light, delicate pastries. After he has placed everything on their table, he crosses to the door, turns the sign around so that it pronounces The Members Club closed.

'That's by the by, anyway,' Alina says airily. 'I want to know about the woman who helped Sofia. Name, address, that sort of thing.'

'Of course. I suspected as much.' Jerry smoothly takes an envelope out of his inside jacket pocket and slides it across the table to her. 'Miss Hannah is a regular at the Momotaro. A real lover of art. An expert, I'd go so far as to say. Indeed, she works in the Harman Gallery herself.'

The Harman Gallery is not far away. Alina knows it well; one of her oldest friends owns the place.

'Is that so?' Alina takes the envelope and puts it in her handbag without looking at it. 'I assume she got medical attention last night?'

Jerry nods and raises the cafetière questioningly.

Alina demurs.

Jerry pours himself a coffee into a tiny cup. 'Yes, I stayed with her. She had stitches in her arm and got her leg patched up. I asked her mother to collect her and then I saw them into an Uber home.'

'Her mother?' Alina is surprised.

Jerry ducks his head. 'Miss Hannah lives with her mother and her son.'

The coffee smells more than good. It is more than inviting, suddenly, a necessity.

She glances to her left and Merle is there in an instant.

'Can I get a bigger cup, please, Merle?' she asks. Her tone is one of dog-tiredness.

Merle obliges. Alina thanks him and pours the coffee into the new mug, filling it to the brim.

Alina didn't sleep last night. Willem and Sofia did. Willem snored beside her, irritating her, even though he wasn't particularly loud and sounded the same as he did every night.

She'd got up at midnight, hurried along the landing into Sofia's room. The girl was snoring too, sounding just like her father. Alina pulled a blanket from the chair, wrapped it around her shoulders and sat beside Sofia's bed.

Hours passed. Several times Alina thought about getting up and going back to bed, but it was as though her legs wouldn't work. Her body wouldn't allow her to move away.

She leaned forward, concentrating on Sofia's soft little snores.

Best to stay here, she'd thought. If a breath failed to materialise, she could leap into action. If she went back to bed, and that breath didn't come, she wouldn't know until it was too late.

It was nearing dawn when the door was pushed open. Willem filled the doorway, his eyes flickering between his wife and child. He held out a hand to her.

With her fingers in her husband's grasp, her legs worked once more.

He led her down the hallway, steered her to their bed. He offered her coffee, tea, something stronger. Some food, because she'd barely touched the plate he'd made up for her last night.

She declined it all and reached for him. Sustenance, the only kind that truly comforted her.

All the time she lay with Willem, the thoughts swirled around her head: her need to thank the woman who saved Sofia's life, but even more importantly, the need to know why it had happened in the first place.

Now, in the light of the day after, Alina drains Merle's coffee and taps the side of her handbag. 'I assume her address is in here?'

'Of course, Ms Arpels.'

'Great. Thank you for your assistance and for meeting me so early. I'm sure you had a very late night.' She stands, putting a hand up as Jerry rises too.

'Please, stay.' To Merle, hovering behind the counter, she says, 'Please serve Jerry anything he wants from the menu. Charge it to me.'

With a goodbye to both men, she sweeps out of the restaurant and into her awaiting car, idling at the kerb.

4

HANNAH, SATURDAY

Oliver is up when Hannah wakes; she can hear him downstairs, his laughter competing with the clash of bowls. Breakfast time.

Hannah rolls over to the empty side of her bed, where her husband would sleep if he were still here.

He's not. Marie is, and so is Hannah.

The little girl from the gallery is still alive too. Hannah closes her eyes and hears the noise that the blades made as they fell. Like piano music.

She thinks about Tate, the artist, and the way he looked after the thing collapsed.

He didn't look at Hannah, nor the child. He definitely didn't look at the girl's mother.

She had never imagined he could be the way he was last night, that cool, serious man. Like he was about to have a stroke or something. But the fronts that people put on can be notably contrasting to their true selves.

Her gaze falls upon her arm, to the ugly stiches that are concealed underneath the white bandage. She reminds herself that she has to do something with those. The doctor who stitched her last night had looked exhausted. As a result, his work was substantially under par. She wonders how many people he saw last night, how many stitches he did before his shift finished.

There's a tap on the door. It's pushed open before she can sit up.

Her mother, a cup of tea in one hand. She puts it on the table next to Hannah's bag and slides an envelope onto the duvet.

'A messenger dropped it off, just now,' she says.

'Thanks.'

'Oliver is waiting for breakfast. Pancakes. I'll bring some up for you.'

Hannah doesn't tell her not to bother, like she normally would. Her breakfast every day is a green smoothie, one that she drinks on the way to work. Once there, she'll have another one. Lunch is avocados, and dinner is the one meal she occasionally allows herself to go to town on.

But today is Saturday and pancakes sound amazing.

'I'll come down,' she says as Marie leaves the room.

Once Hannah is alone, she picks up the envelope. It's not from a bulk stationery order – that much is obvious. It's cream, excellent quality, and on the back seal it has a little mark in the shape of a gemstone with the initials W. A. S. A.

Carefully, she opens it.

> *A car will be sent for you at 4 o'clock this afternoon to bring you to my home.*
> *I would very much appreciate the opportunity to thank you in person.*
> *Sincerely, Alina Arpels*

Hannah draws in a breath and reaches for her tea. It's hot and sweet, and she can't even remember the last time she had a sugary tea.

Today is an exception.

As she makes her way down the stairs, Marie looks at the envelope in her hand.

'The mother of the girl from last night.' Hannah passes it to her mother to read.

Marie runs her finger over the wax seal. 'W. A. S. A.?'

'Willem, Alina and Sofia Arpels,' explains Hannah.

Marie looks up sharply. 'You know them?'

Hannah shakes her head. 'Nope. I know *of* them.'

'Sending a car...' Marie glances up.

'She's very rich. Very influential.'

Marie stares into the middle distance. Hannah knows that her mother doesn't get the different levels of wealth. She thinks that Hannah and, by association, herself are loaded because they live where they do, in this Kensington mews house, set back from the street in a lane where cars don't go. They are not wealthy. The house is theirs thanks to the life insurance policy. They wouldn't live here without it.

'Eat your breakfast,' instructs Marie as she hands the letter back.

As she idles in the kitchen, Hannah wonders what happened at the gallery after she left last night. When will they start the clear-up? The blades and the blood were terrible; would the police have been called, or will the gallery handle the incident in-house? She knows the curator well enough to understand that he will want last night's debacle swept under the carpet. She wonders if his job will be at risk, and who might step into his much-desired role.

She allows herself a rare daydream that it's her who fills his place. The vision spreads and grows until her mother leans over her, taps her fork against her plate.

A reminder to eat.

Hannah looks at the pancakes. They smelled amazing before, but now they are cooling. The batter in the middle looks uncooked, white and stodgy.

Appetite gone, Hannah pushes the pancakes away. Ignoring her mother's stare, she retreats upstairs to get ready.

She's out of the house before Marie can protest, walking the streets she knows so well.

She takes her normal route, down the small mews lane, straight out onto the high street. Automatically, as always, the distaste hits her. To come from her immaculate home – in the pretty, flower-lined, private road, beyond the peaceful, green park – into *this*. It is always an assault on Hannah's senses.

But that's London life – invisible borders crossed in a split second – and Hannah wouldn't swap it for anything.

Here, unlike in the mews, she is careful to watch where she steps. Road sweepers are always out in force, but they fight a losing battle. The wreckage of these streets can never be fixed.

Outside the gallery, everything looks the same as it always does.

She pushes open the door, moves inside. She pauses as always, ready to inhale the special scent that the Momotaro is known for.

An interruption, before she can even breathe.

'Hannah!'

Faithful Jerry is here, at her side, kind eyes full of concern yet again.

'Good morning, Jerry. I'm fine,' she tells him before he can ask. Her voice is tremulous, hesitant. She knows he sees it. Jerry sees almost everything. 'I thought I should revisit. I… I need to.'

Jerry tilts his head and studies her.

'This place is… my haven,' she goes on. 'I can't let what happened last night spoil that for me.'

He nods as though he understands. 'They're in there now, sifting through it,' he informs her.

'So soon?'

He shrugs. 'No time like the present.'

She'd thought she'd be there before the clean-up crew. Before they started poking around in poor Tate's pile of broken metal.

She looks towards the stairs. 'Can I…?'

Before Jerry can answer, Grantham sidles up to them. He's the curator of the Momotaro. She doesn't like him. Doesn't feel he's the best fit for such an important job. She knows that if she was in his position, she'd put this gallery firmly on the map. She'd have fresh ideas and make the Momotaro a hotspot, a place to see and be seen at.

If Hannah worked here, last night's drama would never have happened.

'I'm so glad to see you, Hannah,' he says.

His expression tells a different story, however.

'Hi, Grantham,' she says. 'How are you?'

His mouth twitches. 'Fine, busy. More to the point, how are you?' His stare drifts to her arm, bandage on full show.

'Okay.' She looks at the stairs again. 'I was just telling Jerry that it was all very shocking, what happened last night. I can't stop thinking about it. I'm just going downstairs, hoping the view of it will… make some of these feelings subside.'

Grantham looks unhappy. 'I can't let you in.' He utters a short laugh, a bark really, which betrays his true feelings. 'The top brass won't even let *me* in.'

Hannah nods thoughtfully. 'Maybe later, then,' she says.

–

Back home, she takes another painkiller, just the one, because she doesn't want to feel as muffled as she did before she went to sleep last night, not if she's meeting Alina Arpels later. She sits on her bed after choosing her outfit and skims through her phone, looking for any mention of last night's incident on the art pages that she follows religiously.

She finds nothing. The post advertising the opening night has been removed from the Momotaro's page.

Her eyes grow heavy. She sets an alarm on her phone to wake her up at three o'clock.

She falls asleep, her slumber filled with dark dreams of razors and children.

Later, she dresses carefully. This is not an exception. Hannah dresses like this every day, even if she is just going for a walk down the high street, or to the shop. Smart. Professional. In control. She wants to move up in rank in her chosen field. It is important to be prepared for any such chance that may arise, at any time.

From somewhere in her room, she can hear the vibration of her phone.

She smooths her hand through the duvet, finding her mobile underneath her pillow.

The number that flashes up on the screen has no name saved. A cold chill runs the length of her body as she hits the red button to send the call to voicemail and turns back to the mirror. She scrutinises her reflection one last time before heading down.

Through the kitchen window, she watches her mother and son playing in the courtyard. Nita is there again. Hannah observes all three of them. Eventually, as if she can feel Hannah's eyes on her, Nita makes her goodbyes and leaves through the back gate.

The car comes for Hannah at exactly one minute to four. It rolls quietly into the mews street where she lives, ignoring the fact that it is a no-vehicle zone. It negotiates the bollards, rolling to a stop outside.

Marie, watching from the front window, darts a panicked look at Hannah.

Hannah laughs. 'Don't worry, Mum. People like Alina Arpels don't get parking fines.'

'It's a man,' Marie says. 'Where is she?'

'Waiting at home, I imagine. That's her driver.' Before her mother can reel off any further questions, Hannah opens the door. 'See you later.'

'Wave goodbye to your mother, Oliver,' says Marie.

Hannah glances up. Her son is crouched on the landing, quietly watchful. As Hannah waves to him, he drops his gaze and scoots back towards his bedroom.

The driver introduces himself as Lucas. He holds the rear door open for her, gets back behind the wheel and drives carefully out of the mews.

The big car glides down the high street, past the Momotaro, past the park and the eyesore of a hostel, the only real blot on the landscape of Hannah's neighbourhood. The big museum casts a shadow upon the car, and then they're travelling through Hammersmith, skimming the Thames on their left.

The scenery changes, grey to green. They almost reach the river again at its turn, before the driver angles away, into the leafy, clean residential streets.

The Arpels' house is detached, four storeys, red–brick, stately. All clean lines and sharp angles. Its simplicity reeks of money.

Hannah fingers the bandage on her arm. Despite the square padding, she's sure she can see the outline of the ugly, bulky stitching. She pulls down her sleeve, far over her wrist.

As she prepares to alight from the car, she sees a woman standing in the doorway of the big house. She's wearing a green, weird boiler-suit ensemble, with strange rubber-looking slippers on her feet. Her hair is pulled back, some of the dark strands escaping to frame her youthful, delicate face.

Alina Arpels.

Hannah takes a deep breath, waits for the driver to open her door, and swings herself out and up the stairs towards the woman who is waiting for her.

5

ALINA, SATURDAY

The young woman is very… poised, thinks Alina as she ushers her into her home.

And she doesn't seem overly impressed by the Richmond place. Alina reminds herself that this woman has a mews home in Kensington. While it is not Richmond, it's still a huge deal for someone who lives with her mother and apparently fatherless child.

Maybe the mother has money, she thinks, as she surveys Hannah. And she is still intrigued as to where the father is. Both fathers, Hannah's and her child's.

Hannah Barker looks normal, although a bit overdressed for a Saturday. She appears just like any other young woman who enjoys art and galleries, and exhibit openings. There's a giveaway on her wrist, though: an Audemars Piguet watch, the left sleeve pushed up just enough to show it off. Even Alina, who could buy several of them, is impressed.

The right-hand sleeve of the woman's jacket is pulled far down, almost covering her fingers.

'You live in Kensington?' Alina asks politely as she leads Hannah through the huge, gleaming white kitchen to the glass house.

'Yes, that's right,' replies Hannah politely.

'We're practically neighbours.'

She'd looked at the house in Kensington on the internet when she sent Lucas to collect Hannah. She might investigate Hannah's finances to see how she can afford it; it's unheard of for a young woman who works in a lesser-known gallery across town.

Just to be nosy. Alina likes learning about others. Where they came from. How they got here. What their stories are.

Belatedly, so caught up in her own musings about this stranger, she realises there is an awkwardness here, something that needs to be dispelled before she goes any further with what she plans to do.

She does an about-turn, striding back past Hannah towards the hallway.

'Come with me,' she says. 'I want to show you something.'

She opens a door set into the wall, the one that leads to the basement, and gestures for Hannah to follow her.

They walk down, the lights coming on automatically thanks to the motion sensors that Willem spent a fortune on.

When they reach the bottom, they are in a room much like the one they shared yesterday evening. There is enough space for fifty people down here, but it's only Willem and herself who come here.

'Our own exhibit,' she says, standing against the wall, trying to see it for the first time, the way Hannah is seeing it.

It is sparse. Not quite a concrete room, not like the one underneath Momotaro. A grey marble, walls and floor, expensive and soundproofed. Along one wall are four large, white metal structures with a computer monitor attached. A giant furnace, currently unlit, sits in the centre, attached to a chimney breast, metal teeth bared.

'You know what my husband's business is?' Alina asks.

Hannah shakes her head and looks around the room. 'Construction? Design?'

Alina smothers a smile. 'Of sorts.' She walks to the side of the room, touches a panel in the wall which springs open.

'My husband creates laboratory-made diamonds.' Alina lets her words hang in the air.

'Oh.' Hannah comes closer to the wall and peers in. 'I don't know much about lab-created diamonds. These look like the real thing.'

Alina slides the panel closed, annoyed. 'They are the real thing. Willem uses the same process as nature. These are physically and chemically identical to mined diamonds.' Alina slides her eyes to look at Hannah. 'Without destruction, to the land or to lives.'

Hannah meets Alina's gaze before looking away. 'You know a lot about it. Do you get involved in creating these?'

Alina smiles. 'I mostly just wear them.'

It's not true. Alina loves nothing more than joining Willem down here. Over the years she's learned from him and knows enough to play around creating her own stones. Not just diamonds, either. Alina likes working with the more potent gems, like cinnabar and torbernite, the ones where you have to use full hazard suits before the heating starts and the radioactivity or mercurial properties seep into the air. Sofia is forbidden from the basement, with no exception. Willem doesn't like Alina down here alone, but he knows better than to attempt to force any restrictions on her.

Somewhat disappointed with Hannah's reaction to the veritable goldmine in the basement, Alina walks back to the stairs and starts up them. It's freezing down here, always is when the furnace and Willem's machines are not blasting out heat.

'Willem has a bigger lab in the city, but this is where he does some of his work. I play around with them, occasionally.' She gestures down at herself, at her outfit. At the godawful shoes that are really ugly but comfortable as hell. 'That's what I was doing before you came. I'm not opposed to getting my hands dirty.'

Hannah's voice floats up the steps behind her. 'In making your own diamonds? Is it a dirty business?'

'I mean I'm not opposed to it in any way.' At the top of the stairs, Alina turns once more. 'I took over my father's company. I could have handed it over to the heads of departments. I didn't. I learned it, all of it, and I'm an integral part of the machine. What I mean to say is, there is nothing in this world that I would hand over to someone else without being prepared to do it myself. Do you understand?'

'Yes.' Hannah's voice is grave, serious. 'I think I do.'

Alina closes the basement door and, with a click, it locks into place. She leads Hannah through the hall, turning left into a large glass house.

She sees Hannah glancing around. Alina wonders if she is musing on the absence of people in this big house.

'My husband is getting ready for a business trip,' she says, by way of explanation.

'And your daughter, she's okay?'

Alina utters a laugh. 'She's doing better than me. She's out at a class she takes on Saturdays, in Kensington, the school there.'

Alina's face darkens. The Momotaro Gallery is practically across the road, and Alina's insides have been churning at the thought of Sofia being in such close proximity to the awful blades that nearly finished her the night before. Ridiculous, really, but the feeling is there nonetheless. Alina hadn't wanted her to go to the Italian lesson today, wanted to keep her close by. But Sofia loves the classes, and Alina had given in, reluctantly.

'Oh, what language is she learning?' asks Hannah, politely.

Alina looks at Hannah dead on, alarmed by the other woman's ability to seemingly hear her thoughts.

Hannah rushes on to explain. 'I know the school you mean, I know the classes they do there. I looked into them myself, when I was working on Greek art history.' She gives a little laugh, a slight shrug of her shoulders. 'I never actually got to booking the classes, though, so good for you. Good for Sofia.'

Alina offers a nod as she tells herself to relax. She's still on edge, after last night. Everything a perceived threat, every word spoken she's turning over in her mind, looking for the dark side.

She shakes herself off and stands taller.

'We'll talk in here. Hannah, what would you like? Tea, coffee, mimosa? Anything, please.'

Hannah sits down in a chair. 'Whatever you're having is fine.'

Alina gives her a long look before turning to a cabinet. 'Coffee,' she says, 'with a side option of Tia Maria.'

She sets the machine whirring, pouring two shots of the liquor into separate glasses. She arranges everything on a tray which she carries over to the coffee table that sits between the two chairs.

36

Alina takes a seat opposite Hannah and pours.

A beat of silence while Hannah sips her coffee, *sans* Tia Maria for the moment.

'You're a regular at the Momotaro.' It's a statement from Alina, rather than a question.

Hannah nods. 'It's my favourite space to be. I love art, especially the kind the Momotaro puts out there. One day, I'd love to work there.' She fixes Alina with a steely stare. 'It's my career goal.'

Alina sniffs. 'I'm sure you'd do a better job than that buffoon they've got in charge at the moment.'

Hannah smiles, politely. Neither agreeing nor disagreeing, Alina notes with interest. There is a professional air about this woman that she appreciates.

Time to move on to the reason Alina invited Hannah here today. She takes a deep breath. 'How can I thank you?' Alina asks.

In response, she gets the funny, British platitude that she had expected.

'Oh, there's no need,' Hannah demurs. 'Anyone would have done the same.'

'But they didn't.' Alina's throat feels raw as she replays the previous night's events.

She is not surprised by her emotion. It doesn't show itself, not normally, but this was Sofia. Alina's family are the only ones who raise her to passionate proportions. 'There were fifty people in that gallery. All gasping and showing horror on their face. Nobody moved to help. Only you, Hannah Barker.'

Hannah shrugs. 'Instinct, I guess. I have a child too—'

'Half the people there have children,' Alina snaps, her fury on the rise. She takes a gulp of scalding coffee. The burn does the trick. She continues, slightly calmer now.

37

'This isn't an empty offer, Hannah. You've heard of the phrase "an eye for an eye", yes?'

Hannah looks faintly startled. 'Yes, of course…'

'I come from a place where this is a real thing. We also appreciate the other side of the coin. A kindness, a good deed.' Alina snorts, a humourless laugh. 'That undersells what you did. To be clear, you saved my daughter's life.'

She sets her coffee aside, all business now. 'I can give you whatever you want, Hannah. For what you did last night, I can grant you anything your heart desires.'

She anticipates a long pause, a wait while Hannah tries to find a polite way of asking for as much money as she can possibly get away with.

A million, two… It's pocket change to Alina. Sofia's life is worth all the money in the world, twice over.

Hannah clears her throat and puts her drink to one side. She sits back, stares at Alina.

'You will give me anything I want in the world?'

Alina nods. Now they are getting somewhere.

Hannah looks around the room. Alina imagines she is seeing the riches it holds. Perhaps she is reflecting upon the diamonds in the basement. Hannah works in an art gallery. She wears an Audemars Piguet watch and those famous, red-soled shoes. She knows what things are worth.

She knows, just from this house and the items it holds, that Alina is seriously wealthy, even if she doesn't fully know the Arpels' background.

'It doesn't have to be money?' Hannah clarifies.

Alina blinks, surprised. 'Of course not.' She sneaks a look around her own room, her eyes travelling the path that Hannah's own just took. God, has she seen something

38

in here she wants? Or is it the gems in the vault below their feet?

It doesn't matter, she thinks with relief. There is nothing in here that she wouldn't give away in return for Sofia's life.

She thinks of Hannah's statement of just moments ago, her desire to work at the Momotaro. That's doable. Alina has made a promise to provide anything Hannah desires. To put her in a position at the gallery would be a piece of cake.

Long moments tick by. Alina narrows her eyes as she studies the other woman. Hannah looks as though she's on a soul-searching mission, but Alina can tell she already has a prize in mind.

Hannah shifts in her chair before locking her stare onto Alina. 'If you're really serious, I want you to get someone out of my life.'

At Hannah's words, Alina's fingers twitch, anxious to reach for the liquor shots. Ridiculous. Alcohol has never been a crutch for Alina. Hell, she's never needed anything to lean on, to reach for.

She assesses her body, her emotions, coolly, calmly.

She is intrigued, she finds. She expected to part with money today, but this is something altogether different.

A boyfriend or, more likely, an ex. A hassle to Hannah. She has ditched someone; he does not want to let go.

It's a small price to pay. A pittance. And actually, far less time-consuming than money, and bank transfers and all that. An errant man, a coercive figure, can be dealt with by a mere flick of Alina's hand.

And this is a desire that Alina understands. Not from now, with her husband, not even from boyfriends in her youth, but from the trappings of blood binds, and the constraints and expectations of DNA. Before Willem came along. Before she escaped with him.

She wonders if Hannah will clarify. Alina wants all the juicy details. Does Hannah want the man to be given a warning? A threat? Or cash to disappear?

Alina leans back in her chair, relaxed now – quite pleased, actually, that someone has asked for something other than money for once.

Not that she wouldn't have paid. She would bankrupt herself for Sofia.

No, this is just… exciting. New. A small thrill in a city where nothing much happens.

'Tell me about him,' Alina commands now.

But Hannah is silent, her eyes drifting to beyond Alina, settling on the doorway.

Alina doesn't turn around, but she tunes into herself once more. She feels the connection of a presence, as clear as if the cord were still attached.

It's Sofia. Back from her stint at the language school, collected by faithful Lucas.

She smiles, beckons with a flap of her hand without turning around. 'Come in, Sofia.'

The telltale padding of her little girl's feet. The girl's familiar aroma: lemon-fresh hair, flesh that holds a scent of the soap that Alina used in her own childhood. There is a swish of a breeze as Sofia comes to stand beside Alina.

'Do you remember this lady?' she asks her daughter.

Sofia looks down at the floor. 'Mama said you saved my life,' she says quietly.

Hannah regards her. 'I don't know about that,' she says, modestly.

'You did.' Alina's voice is sharp. 'I know that. Sofia knows that.'

'Thank you,' Sofia says.

So polite. Willem has instilled that in her.

Alina tries to teach her child that sometimes it is okay not to be polite.

This isn't one of those times, though.

'You are very welcome,' says Hannah. She shifts forward on her chair, gestures to Sofia's knees, bare in her cut-off denims. 'Do they hurt?'

Sofa runs a finger over the plasters that Willem applied. 'Not much,' she says.

The little girl looks at Hannah's arm, hidden underneath her sleeve. 'Did the thing hurt you?'

Hannah's fingers go to her arm. She touches where the bandage is, through the material. 'A little bit,' she says.

'Did you go to the doctor?' Sofia asks.

'I did. They just… patched up the cut. Put a plaster on it.'

Alina snorts. Hannah looks at her, clearly startled.

Alina takes Sofia's hand. 'The blades that hurt Hannah were deadly, like the Sakuto knives that Daddy uses when he cooks for us. The doctor would have had to stitch her skin together. She lost a lot of blood, Sofia.'

Sofia nods seriously. 'I know. I stepped in it on the way out.' She looks at Alina, fidgets and squirms. 'Can I go upstairs, now, Mama?'

But Alina is elsewhere, back at the gallery, thinking about that blood… Nausea hits her again. She swallows and swallows, and finally it dissipates.

Hannah clears her throat and changes the subject. 'I'm glad you're okay, Sofia, and I hope your knees heal soon.'

'Small price to pay,' remarks Alina. 'The chin, too.'

The bruise is coming out now, a mark on the girl's otherwise flawless skin.

41

Hannah, as though noticing it for the first time, puts her fingers to her mouth. 'Oh, no,' she says. 'I did that, when I—'

'When you saved her life. Yes.'

She reaches out for Sofia, but the girl darts out of her reach and trots from the room.

Hannah inhales shakily. 'I saw your daughter, just before it happened,' she says.

Alina tilts her head to one side. 'What do you mean?'

'I… She was standing there, and she was just the cutest little thing.' Hannah drops her gaze to the floor. 'Our eyes met, I waved at her.'

Alina watches in horror as a single tear tracks its way down Hannah's cheek.

'What if she thought I was calling her over for some reason? She walked straight into the path of that awful pile of metal.' Hannah puts a hand to her lips. 'Now she's got bruises, cuts to her legs…'

Alina leans forward and shakes her head. 'My girl is overly confident. She's sociable, too much sometimes…' Alina frowns. The Sofia who was just in the room with them isn't the daughter she knows so well. Maybe last night's incident has impacted her more than she or Willem thought.

She turns her attention back to her visitor, to the reason she is here. 'The bottom line is that you saved her life. I will pay any price. And you were just about to tell me what that price is.'

Hannah stands up, so abruptly that Alina sits back quickly in her chair.

'I… I have to go. I'm just happy that your daughter is okay,' says Hannah. 'I… I don't need anything. That she's safe is payment enough.'

Alina rises from her chair, flailing a little at the abrupt change of direction. 'I'm not from here. I mean, I wasn't born here. I was raised with an entirely different view of how life works. Where I come from, someone does you a good turn, you do what you can for them. Whatever they need. If they need nothing, then offer whatever they *want*.' She tilts her head to one side. 'You started to tell me your desire. I don't know if it is something you want, or something you need. Sit down, please, and continue.'

'I... I need time to think. Is that okay?'

Alina stalks towards Hannah, her crazy, awful shoes slapping on the polished floor. 'Please don't rush off. My driver will—'

Hannah has reached the front door now and clasps her hand around the doorknob, pulling it open and tripping down the steps in one, fluid motion. 'No need! I'm fine! Thanks again and take care. Sofia too.'

The heavy door closes behind her.

Her daughter's saviour is gone.

She goes upstairs, in search of her husband, annoyed that Hannah has gone before she even had a chance to introduce them. She finds him in their large bedroom suite.

'I don't understand,' Alina says plaintively, after explaining the strange encounter.

Her voice is whiney, the sort of tone she wouldn't stand to hear from Sofia, and yet, she can't seem to stifle it.

Willem is packing for his trip to Antwerp, the diamond capital of the world, to meet with several high-flyers about his lab-created gems.

It won't be easy to convert the Flemish from their 500-year-old rule over the diamond trade. Or maybe it will. After all, the old guys are gone now. The ones in their place are young and hungry, open and curious to new ways of doing things. Just like Willem.

He'll fit in too. He speaks their language; they speak his. The two nations are great allies. Their cultures are similar. They love their neighbours, these new bloods, and hold none of the rivalry of their ancestors.

'Maybe you frightened her,' remarks Willem now, after listening to Alina's story of how Hannah fled from both her home and her offer.

Alina flounces across the bedroom to fling herself in the chair by the window. 'I didn't frighten her.'

'What exactly did you say to her?'

'I offered her anything she wanted. I granted her a wish,' she says.

'Like a genie?' He rolls his eyes.

Alina frowns. 'What?'

'Well, Christ, Alina. It's a bit intense. Can't you just send her a fruit basket, or a hamper or something? You know, like a *normal* person.'

Alina fixes her husband with an ice-cold stare. 'You think our daughter's life is worth a *fruit basket*?'

Willem laughs loudly. He doesn't take offence at her tone or her strange ways. 'How about one of my diamonds?' he suggests.

She thinks abouts this. 'She didn't seem very impressed with them, to be honest.'

It is his turn to frown. Now his feelings are hurt. She hurries to pacify him. 'Maybe she doesn't value gemstones. Maybe she's not interested in expensive things.'

But she doesn't think that's true. Alina saw the watch Hannah was wearing. The shoes that cost as much as one of Willem's smaller stones.

'No. She wanted something else. She almost told me, but she lost her nerve,' Alina concludes. 'It wasn't anything I said. I didn't frighten her.'

Willem abandons his case, sweeps her up and places her carefully down in the middle of the bed.

'You frighten me, sometimes,' he says. 'But I wouldn't have you any other way.'

He kicks the case off the bed to make room for himself.

Alina matches his grin, surrenders to him, the only one she relinquishes herself to.

Thoughts of Hannah leave her mind.

She offered.

The woman declined.

End of story.

6

HANNAH, SATURDAY

The driver is still there as she walks smartly down the steps of Alina's Richmond house.

She avoids his eye, moves past the idling car and out onto the road. She lingers just to gather her bearings and pulls out her phone to find the best route home.

It's too far to walk, even for Hannah, who stalks round London and uses the exercise as her cardio.

She loiters for a beat of a few seconds, giving it just long enough for Alina to chase out of the house after her.

But the door to the big house remains closed.

Maybe it's not too far to walk, she thinks, as she starts down the footpath beneath the lush green trees. Perhaps she will just go as far as she can in her heels, then call an Uber if she starts to wilt in the summer evening heat.

Hannah wonders if she did the wrong thing by running off like that.

The offer that she's turned down.

The woman is a veritable fairy godmother.

Exactly how many wishes would Alina grant her?

Because Hannah knows exactly what she wants to ask for.

She doesn't know what stopped her.

Yes, she does.

She didn't want to seem overly eager. Didn't want to state her desire and have it come across as rehearsed.

Of course, she had known a little about the Arpels, Alina especially. Had heard whispers about the power the other woman wields. But to witness it, to be a recipient of it...

Does she want to be indebted to someone who holds that kind of power and standing?

But she wouldn't. Hannah's brain argues with itself. Alina is the one who will be repaying a debt. Right now, she's the one who owes Hannah. Once Alina pays up, in a way of Hannah's choosing, the debt will be cleared.

She growls, frustrated, and glances behind her.

She's far enough away from the house to know now that nobody is running after her. No big black car trailing her down the street.

She looks at her phone again, pinpoints her location and sets up the route home. Two hours. Six miles. She will cut through the park, she decides, then cross over and walk by the Thames.

She will also stop for a late lunch. She glances at her watch. It will actually be an early dinner. She missed out on the pancakes this morning and didn't even make her usual smoothies. Just the coffee at Alina's, and now her stomach is empty and tight, roiling like a tide.

Her neck prickles. She looks back once more, sure she can feel eyes on her. Cars travel up and down the road, but she can see no people, no dog walkers, not a person in sight.

She grips her bag tighter, puts her head down and walks quickly towards the area of Chiswick Park.

On the main street, she ducks into a fancy bistro, pleased to get a table and ready to go to town on the

French fayre. She figures that because she's skipped all of today's nutrition, this dinner is well-earned and needed. She will swallow down and eat up her worries and anxiety.

Hannah has never minded dining alone. She doesn't need a book or a newspaper or her phone to hide behind. These times of solitude are for thinking. For planning, usually about her work. For plotting ahead, also job-related, on how she's going to get out of her role at the tiny gallery and make that elusive, big step forward into the Momotaro.

She thinks about it all the time. Daydreams and desires. The Momotaro is a rich gallery who pay their staff an incredibly generous salary. And Hannah needs the money that they pay.

Not for herself, of course. But Marie is getting older, and Hannah wants nothing more than to see her mother taken care of in the manner that she deserves. Not relying on state pensions or benefits. Marie deserves to live like a queen, for the rest of her life.

As she eats the starter salad she ordered, it occurs to her that she could likely go to the Momotaro, make it known that she wants the curator's job. After all, at that gallery, after last night, she's a hero, isn't she?

Of course, Alina could also make it happen.

But you walked away from her. You refused her. And she didn't chase after you and insist, like you thought she might.

The voice niggles at her again.

Hannah shrugs to herself as her soup is placed in front of her.

Alina's offer didn't come with a time expiry stamp.

Did it?

And Hannah didn't decline her; she simply requested time to think it over.

By the time she is presented with her tartiflette, the stitches in her arm are pulling painfully.

Damn. She had meant to go to the Royal today to get them removed and redone. She could have done that this morning, before her impromptu gallery visit, or after, instead of spending the empty time sleeping. She could have done it an hour ago, instead of heading here to gorge herself on a three-course meal that will do her no good whatsoever.

There is an ache in her ankle now too, and she curses herself for being so stupid as to wear her heels to walk across London. She abandons her fork on her plate, rummages around in her handbag and comes up with one of the industrial-strength pain pills. She washes it down with the last of her Château Ausone, and nods to the waiter to refill her glass.

Hannah is surprised to find that dusk has fallen when she staggers out of the restaurant. She leans against the wall, squinting at her watch.

She can't see the numbers on it, and she's fearful as she pulls out her phone in order to look at the slightly bigger digits.

It's gone ten p.m.

She blanches, fumbles with the mobile and just manages to catch it before it drops to the pavement.

How is it night-time? She's certain it was daylight when she went into the bistro. She recalls the wine, the carb-laden dishes, the pain pill. The worries, the fretting – about her job, about the woman who will grant her any desire, about—

Her mobile rings and she looks at the screen, still in her hand.

Hannah slides the phone back in her bag without answering the call. She pushes herself off the wall and wills herself to make it home.

On she marches, more on her own territory now, rather than the unfamiliarity of Richmond and the middle ground between the neighbourhoods. She moves into the park, aware she's not as steady as normal, hesitating on the pathway, wondering whether to get back on the street and summon a lift for the remainder of the way home.

God.

This is unthinkable. This… mess. The hours she has lost. The state she is in.

For the briefest moment she considers whether Alina put something in her coffee, has spiked it. But the very notion of that is ridiculous.

The night air will clear her head. She doesn't want to reach home still feeling so… undone.

Doesn't want Marie to see her like this. Her mother will worry. And Hannah hates when her mother has something to worry about.

She cuts across the grass, crisp and yellow underneath her feet.

And stops.

A footstep behind her. Not unusual, not for a city-centre park on a hot London night.

But…

She starts to walk again, listening carefully now, and just as abruptly, she comes to a halt.

So do the steps behind her.

She ups her speed this time, swearing quietly. All the years she's lived here, she's never met a mugger yet. She has walked the capital a hundred times over and never felt a threat.

The thought is wrong. Lately, she's sensed something, someone… waiting, watching.

Normally, she would run. But not in these shoes. Not the way she's still feeling, off-balance and not herself. Foggy, because of the damn painkiller she took and the dull ache in her ankle.

She walks faster, and up ahead, maybe fifty metres away, she can see the silhouette of lamp posts, the reassuring glow which, even though it's just a sickly yellow hue, is better than this pitch-black open space.

Hannah surges onwards, tripping in her haste to reach sanctuary and safety.

She's down on one knee before she even realises it, crying out as her already-injured ankle complains.

The footsteps behind her are hasty now. In a mere second, she feels a hand on her upper arm.

Her injured arm.

She's not sure if it is shock or pain that has her cry ripping into a scream.

The person – man, woman, she can't tell as the mixture of painkiller and wine sends a fog over her vision – darts away from her.

Her ankle sends a searing pain through her foot, up into her knee, and she clutches at her bandaged arm as she forces herself upright. She moves away as fast as she can, stepping off the path onto the lawn, bag swinging on her wrist. The sprinklers have been on, and her heels sink into the damp soil.

She chances a glance up, towards the person who has followed her, who has grabbed her.

A hooded figure, getting smaller the further away they get, ducking out of sight in the shadows of the horse chestnut trees that line the route. Their canopies are so wide that no moonlight casts a glow on the stranger.

From the gates at the end of the path comes the ringing sound of laughter, chatter – people like her, just on their way home.

Not like her. Not so stupid to walk alone at night. They are in a group. They are sensible.

The clamour of their voices breaks the odd moment. She glances towards the gate, then back again at the place where her persecutor disappeared. He or she is no longer there.

Hannah turns on her heel, as well as she can manage in the damp lawn of the park.

She swallows down the tears and the scream that threaten, and heads towards the voices, to the sound of laughter, towards other people that equal safety.

She breaks into a jog despite the pain, back on the path now, not even pausing as she lifts first one leg, then the other, and wrenches her shoes off.

Hannah. Hannah!

It's just the sound of the wind, suddenly picking up, swirling through the leaves and the long grasses near the fence. The traffic is closer now, volumes of people on the other side of the railings. It's just the bustle of London life, she tells herself. Not her own name she hears in amongst the cacophony of sounds.

The traffic lights stand two abreast, before she realises that they are single lights. Double vision, she tells herself, from the strong pill.

Across the road, under proper streetlights now, safety in amongst the other pedestrians. Still, though, her heart refuses to return to a normal rate.

She resolves not to think about it, about the near-miss mugging, about what might have happened. She blanks out of her mind that it's not the first time she's felt like she's being watched. It's the first time they've got so close to her, though.

She slips her shoes back on, still feeling nothing like herself the closer she gets to home. She concentrates on the sound of her heels click-clacking along the high street.

The noise beats out a staccato rhythm that her mind has tried to stray from – about whoever it was who touched her, who looked at her.

Following me. Watching me. Chasing me.

It spins around in her mind, making her feel just as dizzy as she was earlier. She runs the last few hundred yards down the high street and into the mews entrance. She slams into her house, leaning against the wall, panting hard. Trembling, she pulls her shoes off and looks ruefully at the filthy heels and soles. Her feet are black too, crusted with damp grass and tiny pebbles.

She hears low chatter from outside, and she spins round, flicking the chain on, slamming the deadbolt across. Belatedly, she realises the sound is coming from the rear of her house, the courtyard.

Marie is out there.

She moves through the house, slips outside. The warm night does nothing for the chill she feels.

'Are you okay?' Marie asks.

'Hi, Hannah, late night!'

The voice comes from the shadows, making Hannah jump.

It's Nita. Here *again*.

In the strange silence that ensues, Nita picks up her glass, drains it and stands up.

'Best get home,' she says.

There is a flurry of goodbyes, mostly between Nita and Marie, who sees her friend down the hall, out of the door, and waves her off.

In the courtyard, Hannah slumps into a seat and surveys the almost-empty wine bottle and glasses on the table.

'Had fun?' she asks when her mother returns.

Marie nods, drags a chair over and clutches Hannah's hand. 'Are you okay, Hannah? You seem—'

'What?'

'Fraught.'

Hannah sits up in her chair and gazes at Marie.

'Mum...' she starts. 'Do you ever hear from anybody from... before?'

Marie frowns. 'Before?'

'From before we moved here.'

Marie is suddenly far away. Hannah can see it in her face: a dreamy, almost wistful, look.

Hannah wants to shake her. Marie misses that time, back then, when they lived in a mid-terraced house. When their family held more members than it does now.

Look around you, she wants to yell. *Look at where you are now!*

As if sensing her daughter's thoughts, Marie's face reverts to normal.

'I don't speak to anyone – we've all moved on, haven't we?' Marie pours the remainder of the wine from the bottle. 'Why do you ask?'

'Never mind,' Hannah answers.

They slip into silence. A common occurrence between the two of them these days.

'How was your meeting with the fancy lady from the gallery?' Marie asks, when the quiet has stretched on a little too long.

'Good.' Hannah nods at Marie. 'She just wanted to thank me, gave me a nice lunch and then drove me home.'

Lies.

All lies.

Hannah stands abruptly. 'I'm turning in.'

'Oliver's asleep, don't wake him.' Marie turns her face so her daughter's kiss lands upon her cheek. 'Night, Hannah. Sleep well.'

Hannah leaves Marie outside, reflecting, perhaps, or maybe reminiscing.

As she turns to head upstairs, a new photo on the table in the hallway catches her attention. A silver frame, a black-and-white print. Hannah and her husband on their wedding day.

'Why is this out?' Hannah calls through to the garden.

Marie knows what she's talking about. Her face is that of a child, defiant, provoking.

'It's a lovely photo,' she answers. 'I don't know why you don't want it on display. It's not like you divorced, is it? And besides, Oliver will want to know about him.'

Too much to unpick there.

She resists the urge to tell Marie that she, Hannah, bought this home that they live in, and she'll decide what to have on display in it.

It's fruitless, anyway. Marie knows that Hannah has designed this place. Minimalist in its furniture, fixtures, fittings. Hannah doesn't have room in her home or her heart for sentimental décor.

She pauses at the bottom of the stairs, and makes sure Marie is watching as she turns the picture face down.

Now she is the one who is childlike, petulant.

'Maybe I find it painful,' she says. 'Good night.'

She drifts up the stairs, thinking about Marie's face in the moonlight, her expression knowing, as though she suspects that Hannah doesn't find the loss of her husband painful at all.

–

Hannah dreams of Clark that night. It is a rare occurrence.

At first, he appears the way he was: suave, gentlemanly, handsome. Good-natured, too. All the qualities that Hannah wanted replicated in a child of her own.

The child that became Oliver.

They didn't live in the Kensington mews house then. They were in a semi, out in Barnet. Marie down the road in Edgware.

Hannah yearned for London life, always had. The noise, the lights, the non-stop action. She found it soothing. It quieted her mind.

She had a great plan to move the family to the city centre. Her mother included.

Marie looked slightly horrified when Hannah opened the dialogue.

'I've lived here for ever!' she exclaimed. 'Besides, you don't want your old mum cramping your style.'

But Hannah did, and she suspected Marie knew it. She dropped the subject, for the moment.

A few months after Oliver was born, things changed.

They were still in Barnet, Marie still in Edgware, visiting as much as she could.

One day, Hannah made the trip back to her childhood home.

'Clark's depressed,' Hannah sobbed to Marie. 'He can't explain what's wrong because there's nothing wrong. He's clinically depressed.'

Marie surveyed her daughter, her brow furrowed with confusion. 'Since when? He's always seemed fine when I've been with him.'

Marie loved Clark. She worried over him like she was his own mother. Now, she picked up her bag, ready to travel back with Hannah to the Barnet house.

Hannah stopped her. 'It's pointless. He puts on an act in front of people. He's made me promise not to tell anyone. He won't even go to the doctor.' Hannah blew her nose, put her head down on the Formica table that had been in the house since she was a child, and wept, waiting for her mother to gather her up and console her with a maternal, loving embrace.

Two weeks later, Clark was gone.

These days, Hannah doesn't dream or think of him.

Apart from tonight.

In her dream he morphs backwards, into a teenager, then a child. Finally, he is a baby, not a year old. Even in her sleep, she knows that now she's not dreaming of Clark at all, but of somebody else entirely.

She wakes with a start, her breathing loud and fast.

The pain pill is to blame.

She reaches out for the bottle on her bedside table and hurls it across the room. The motion stretches the cut on her arm. Pinpricks of blood nestle alongside the ugly stitches.

She stifles her cry by burying her face in her pillow.

7

ALINA, SUNDAY

On Sunday morning, Alina wakes and stretches. She slings her arm over Willem, finding nothing but a cool sheet.

She remembers. Willem is in Antwerp. Sofia is at a friend's house, showing off her scarred knees, retelling the story of Friday night, no doubt.

Alina doesn't want to hear her girl's point of view. The replay that's on a continuous loop in her own head is enough.

Still, she thinks, if Sofia is happy to recount the tale, hopefully it means there's no lasting mental damage. Minimal trauma.

She recalls how Sofia was yesterday, in front of Hannah. Anybody else wouldn't have noticed Sofia was uncomfortable, but Alina did.

But after Hannah left, Sofia seemed fine. Maybe the girl isn't affected, and it was just the sight of Hannah's own bandage that made Sofia quiet and sombre.

Alina doesn't like to think about the impact of things. She had enough of that when she was a child herself and had to picture the stories that her own friends shared with her about Alina's parents, about what they did, who they were.

Of wars and retribution, of politics gone sour, bombs and dirty fighting.

Memories of men outside her childhood home.

Nightmares of those same men who managed to get into their house.

It's leftover memories from her childhood that have made her question whether Friday night's incident was, in fact, an accident.

It rolls over and over in her mind. Probably because she's alone. Willem, her voice of reason, is away. Sofia, her physical proof that everything is okay, is also out.

Alina dresses quickly, slips her sockless feet into her plimsolls and heads outside.

Lucas is there, as always, and he snaps to attention as the heavy door closes behind her.

'Where to, Alina?' he asks.

'Momotaro,' she replies, darkly, as she slides into the back seat of the car.

'Going to cause some trouble?' His blue eyes meet hers in the rear-view mirror as he crawls along the streets.

She smiles and winks at him. Willem may be away, but Lucas is here, her dearest friend. 'Oh, you know me, Lucas.'

It conjures another memory: Clementine, a friend Alina met through Willem's connections in the gem industry. Clementine's husband was a trader, and the two women became close after running into each other several times over the course of a season.

They were in the Scottish Isles, sourcing amethysts and sapphires. A fun holiday for both women. When they tired, they took Lucas and went off on their own, a drinking mission, a then five-year-old Sofia wedged in the back seat between them.

They arrived in a bustling city centre, Alina pulling on Lucas's arm, forcing him to join in, if not with the drinking, at least with the merriment.

Clementine pulled Alina aside later to address the way Alina treated her staff.

Alina laughed in her face. 'Lucas isn't "staff",' she said. 'He's fucking *family*.'

And he is. Lucas has had her back more times than Alina cares to remember. Like her, he would die for Sofia.

Or kill.

Bonds like theirs are a greater motivator than money, she's always thought.

Though, of course, he's paid handsomely – over the odds, and deservedly so.

'I'd better come in with you,' Lucas comments as he slows the car to a stop outside the gallery.

Alina shrugs but doesn't argue.

She'd thought she might be incensed, walking back in here, but there's something exceptional about the Momotaro. At total odds with the outside world, with the street's crap and trash and sleeping bags and noise and stench. Hauling open that door and stepping inside blocks out everything on the pavement outside.

The gentle fragrance of the Momotaro sweeps over her. Lavender, cypress trees and cherry blossom, with notes of bergamot and citrus.

She loves it here, normally. Everything inside the gallery is selected with a dedicated care. Even the name, Momotaro, alludes to a specific meaning. She'd enquired about it, when she first started visiting here. 'Peach Boy' is what it translates as. Peach Boy is a folklore tale, whose moral has become the pinnacle of Japanese conduct. Transcribed, it's a directive to live bravely, but most importantly, in an honest fashion. Alina has loved the fable since she became aware of it.

The upper level of this gallery is filled with interesting *objets d'art*, some for sale, some for show – all of them causing an emotion. Some stimulate, some soothe. All of them please.

She thinks of the statement that Hannah made yesterday, of how she wants to work here, and she nods to herself, approvingly.

Hannah would fit in here. From first impressions, Hannah is cool, calm and professional.

Maybe Alina will make that happen for her.

But first, she's got other business to attend to.

The exhibition room where Sofia almost met her end on Friday night is downstairs, in a large, concrete windowless area, minimalist to show off whatever installation or offering is on to its fullest potential.

Now, Alina sweeps past the desk that serves Japanese teas. Normally, she would get one. In fact, she can't remember ever coming in here and not buying one.

But they, like the scent here, are calming, and Alina wants to keep the elastic of her nerves and her gently simmering fury once she goes down those stairs.

Grantham, the curator of the Momotaro, sees her. A tiny, grey-haired, nervous-looking man whose age is indeterminate. Alina has never clicked with him, finds his bowing and scraping to people of her calibre off-putting. She can't explain why. After all, Jerry is respectful and subservient, but doesn't come off as a boot-licker like Grantham.

Across the room, Grantham tugs at his wiry hair and takes a step in her direction.

Alina looks up at Lucas, keeping close beside her.

'Do not let him approach me. I will not be held accountable for my actions.'

Lucas nods, breaks away from Alina and plants himself in the walkway, effectively blocking Grantham's path.

Alina tosses her head and makes her way to the stairs that wind down, down, down into the bowels of the building.

It's quiet down here, cooler too. Without the heady scents and sounds of upstairs, Alina's anger simmers again.

She sweeps along the corridor, past the two fishbowl reading rooms, entirely constructed of glass. Ahead of her, two women man the cloakroom area.

One of them offers Alina a smile, seems about to pipe up with a chirpy greeting. Her colleague obviously recognises Alina. She digs her friend subtly in the side before lowering her head in almost reverence.

Alina passes them without comment, and swings through the door to the exhibit room.

The place is in near darkness: none of the usual spotlights on, only the emergency floor-level lighting giving the space an eerie glow.

But even in the dimness, she can see it's still there. Lucifer, or what's left of him: a mountain of steel, untouched. Uncleared.

Alina swears viciously, her curse bouncing off the walls, echoing back at her.

She hears a sharp intake of breath, a soft, meek, 'Hello?'

She marches into the room, to the point where she was standing two nights ago when hellfire rained down upon her girl.

He is there.

The artist. Tate.

Sitting cross-legged on the floor, mournful, his rotten piece of art in front of him.

She sees the moment he realises who she is. The freeze that grips him.

The fear.

To be fair to him, he overcomes it fast. He lunges to his feet. In his haste, he stumbles on a stray Japanese blade as he comes towards her. The blade makes an awful scraping noise on the concrete, like nails on a chalkboard.

He winces, moves it out of the way, towards the rest of the pile of metal.

'Ms Arpels,' he gasps. 'I'm so glad you're here. I'm so sorry, I'm so awfully sorry. I don't know what to say. I can't say anything that will reverse this tragedy. But I can tell you this: you can do anything to me that you see fit. I promise you that, I'll take whatever punishment you want.'

Alina resists rolling her eyes. Artists and their flair for the dramatic.

But she's glad. Pleased that he's not trying to worm his way out, happy that he is holding himself accountable.

She eyes the pile of metal. 'Tell me about your sculpture.'

Tate takes a deep breath, fumbles into his back pocket and comes up with the flyer that has been on display at the Momotaro for the last few months. He holds it out to her, beseechingly.

She waves it away, impatient. 'I've seen that. I want *you* to tell me about your work. From the beginning.'

'I create structures and installations out of unusual materials. I started with recycled stuff, literal rubbish, trash, discarded items.' Here he pauses, holds up his phone. 'I can show you my other work, the older samples—'

63

'No. I want to know about this one.' She points to the floor, to the work destroyed.

'I've immersed myself in Japanese culture for the last five years. I've been living near Akita, learning from swordsmiths. I wanted to create something beyond anyone's expectations. By this I mean in size, material, detail.' Breathless suddenly, Tate emits an audible sob.

He covers his eyes briefly with the palms of his hands, shoulders shuddering.

Alina's nostrils flare. 'Have you ever had any dealings with any Russians?' she asks him.

He blinks at her through his fingers. 'Russians?'

'Do you have any Russian friends, contacts, anything?'

He drops his hands to his sides. 'No.'

She nods once, sharply. 'Carry on.'

He gestures to the pile of blades, openly weeping still. 'That was it, that was the outcome of my idea. I wanted to test my skill and my ability.'

'How was it held together?' She circles the pile, wanting to get away from the direct line of Tate's emotion. Alina doesn't have time for his tears. She is here for facts, not feelings. Tate can cry when she has gone.

'A weld. A small, welded joint.' He stoops, carefully picks up the blade he tripped on before. 'See, here?' He points out a slightly raised ridge on the steel. 'Think of them as feathers. They have movement, but they'll never come apart from the body they are attached to. Do you see?'

She does not. She thinks of all the feathers she finds in her garden, in the park, lining the pathways where she walks.

'But your "feathers" did come apart from the body, didn't they?'

64

Tate drops the metal. It clangs on the floor. Alina just about manages to stop herself from wincing.

'It was all set up correctly, so nothing could shift any of the parts,' he says, miserably.

Alina tilts her head. 'How so?'

He gestures to the middle of the room, the yellow tape still on the floor. A square, six feet in diameter. 'We did tests, had all the guys stamping their feet, using noise and sound vibrations. Nothing shifted any part of him.'

Alina almost gags as he refers to the demon structure as *him*.

'I wore gloves during the creation, the installation, but still got nicked and cut. I knew how lethal it could be, so we were real careful when we set it up here. The curator… He didn't want anyone near it, getting nicks in their fancy clothes, or accidentally cutting themselves.' His voice is pleading now. 'It was safe, *secure.*'

'And yet, it fell anyway.' Alina narrows her eyes. 'How many blades exactly are there?'

'Forty thousand.' Tate's reply is a whisper.

Forty thousand blades raining down upon her girl. Alina feels quite faint, suddenly. She gives herself a mental shake, straightens her shoulders.

'And what have they said?' she asks. She raises an eyebrow. 'I assume there has been an internal investigation?'

Tate nods, his face full of misery. 'They want to take it away piece by piece, examine everything to see why it collapsed. Maybe once they do that, they'll know why it happened.'

She fixes him with a look. 'They'd better,' she says. 'Though it might be in your interest if they don't find out why.'

Mean. She knows it. She's put the fear of God into him.

A thought strikes her as she looks him up and down, taking in his clothes, his thin beard that wasn't there Friday night.

'Have you been home?' She frowns.

He shakes his head. 'I don't know when they're going to start sifting through it. I don't want to miss it.'

She narrows her eyes. 'I assume you won't be assisting in the clear-up and investigation?'

He catches her drift, looks aghast. 'No! I'd never try and... do anything. Cover up, I mean. That's not me, I promise. I just want to know why it happened.'

She's tired of him now, and she wants the chance to look at Lucifer's remains without Tate breathing down her neck, irritating her further.

'Go and find my driver, Lucas. He's upstairs, fending off that awful man, Grantham. Get some tea, something to eat, for God's sake.'

He doesn't want to leave, but there's no way he's going to argue with the mother of the girl that his statue almost killed. He bobs his head, up and down, practically bowing as he backs out of the room.

Alone, Alina crouches down before the mound of metal. It's not as scattered as it was two nights ago. Someone – Jerry? The investigators? – has come along with a broom, swished everything into one, giant heap.

Shivers wrack her body as she studies it. A sour taste fills her mouth. It was bad when it was happening, but here, today, up close, the sharpness of these blades is bloody awful.

She knows that she won't rest until she finds out *why* this happened.

Alina understands how things work. Due diligence, health and safety, process and attentiveness are paramount everywhere, but none more so than in a place filled with members of the public.

Alina stands up. She takes her phone out of her pocket and slowly walks the perimeter of Lucifer, snapping continuously. Back on her knees, she switches to video, taking her time as she heads back the other way, zooming in, making sure to miss nothing.

The light is terrible in here, she realises, belatedly. The flash has come on on the phone, but Alina wants all the spotlights on, like they were on Friday.

The door swishes open and she turns, expecting Tate or Lucas.

Grantham, the curator.

His face is red, his eyes worried, his wire-brush hair standing on end where he has no doubt been pulling it in his unease.

She holds up a hand, a command for silence.

'Turn the lights on, please. On full, ceiling and spotlights.'

He hesitates by the door before snapping to attention.

'Ms Arpels—' he begins.

'Nope. You say nothing to me.' She glares at him over her shoulder. 'I'm not ready to talk to you yet.' And just in case he doesn't get it, doesn't quite know who he is dealing with, she adds, 'You'll know when I'm ready to speak with you.'

He's unsure whether he is dismissed, so he switches all the lights on and hovers around the doorway.

'You can go,' she says, without looking at him.

The door slaps quietly closed.

Alina resumes taking photos.

8

HANNAH, MONDAY

When Hannah wakes up to a new day, a new week, it is still dark. She curls into herself, foetal-like. Last night, she had the same dreams as she had on Saturday night. Her unconscious is thinking of those long gone. They linger fresh in her mind.

Yesterday was a nothing day. Marie took Oliver to the park near their home. The thought of going to the park, even though it wasn't the same one as she'd been in on Saturday, freaked Hannah out so she stayed home. Loitered by the windows, feeling the walls closing in on her.

Later, desperate to feel nothing for at least a little while, she took a pain pill and slept through the afternoon, evening and night.

Now, the pill has worn off and she is wide awake.

She picks up her phone, sees the missed call on her screen.

Hannah shoves the phone off her bed. It lands to sit beside the painkiller bottle on the floor.

She blinks into the darkness before throwing back her thin sheet and shuffling over to the window.

She pushes it open, and the room is immediately flooded with London sounds. A far-off lorry, emptying a bottle bank into its bowels. Shrieks of laughter. It will be from people heading home after an all-nighter, not going to work. People leaving for work pre-dawn do not laugh. They make their way through the streets, heads down, travel cup clutched in their hands like a life aid, bleary-eyed and yawning.

Hannah thinks of Alina, wonders what she is doing right now.

Anything. That's the answer she comes up with.

Alina Arpels seems to be some sort of anomaly.

Hannah gets the impression that Alina doesn't follow the rules of normal society, a bit like Hannah herself. Only, Alina is much, much more open about it.

She would probably be up before the sun, having not been to bed the night before. Hannah can imagine Alina laughing, shrieking, cursing, shouting. Heading out into the darkness, whether she's going to work or somewhere else. Or sitting in her basement, looking at the diamonds her husband creates for her.

How does Alina fare, with Willem Arpels? Are they like ships that pass in the night, counting their millions and raising their daughter jointly?

Does she miss him when he's not there, or does she embrace her child, and enjoy their time, just the two of them?

Has Alina been back to the gallery yet?

Hannah suspects so. She wonders what she found. If she hunted down Tate. What she said to him. What she *did* to him.

She sighs. Her mind is racing a mile a minute. She could go back to bed, try to sleep for another hour or two. Or she could just get ready, grab her smoothie, join all those commuters with their travel cups, head down on the walk to work, and get her day started.

She leans on the window ledge, looking left, right, down the lane.

It is so early that the streetlamps are not even on yet. She remains where she is, her eyes adjusting in the darkness.

She sees the figure then, standing in the lane. Doing nothing. Just… being there.

Hannah's mouth goes dry, very suddenly.

It's the person from the park, she's sure of it. The one who followed her, who pushed her, who frightened her.

The hooded one.

The one she's sure called her name.

She thinks of the missed call on her phone, the one she has ignored, like the majority of calls and messages that came before it.

She slams the window shut and slides down the wall to sit upon the plush carpet.

Her heart beats fast, so fast, too fast.

–

The person in the lane is gone the next time she dares to look.

By that time, hours have passed. The sunshine is out in full force, another sticky, London day.

She should get ready and head out for work, but today she doesn't want to. And Hannah *never* doesn't want to go to work. She could easily *not* go, because she still needs to get herself to the Royal Chelsea and get her stiches sorted out, though she might have left it too late. They are itching, the skin healing around them.

They could go to the park on this fine summer day. Her, her son and Marie. Take a picnic, a bottle of rosé for

Marie. She could spend a whole day with her mother. In a park that is far away from people who lie in wait for her.

The mews house is a haven, normally. Somewhere they can shut out the city noise, protected behind the closed doors, her family safe in one place.

Now, someone knows where she lives.

As if her thoughts have conjured it up, a message pings through on Hannah's phone. The number unknown, unsaved.

> Hi, how are you today? Do you fancy meeting up later?

Hannah turns the phone face down and looks out of her bedroom window again.

The street is no longer quiet and still. People are out there, using the land as a cut-through to the high street, chatting, jogging, hurrying.

Her watcher is not there.

But they could come back.

The house is not somewhere to be sequestered in today. They *will* go out, and they'll leave soon.

Hannah dresses quickly, forgoing a shower, dragging a brush through her hair. As a last-minute thought, she rummages around in the airing cupboard on the landing, finds a baseball cap that she never wears – she can't even remember where she got it from. She pulls it on.

'Mum,' she calls, as she rushes downstairs. 'Come on, we're headed out for the day.'

Marie is in the kitchen, and she pokes her head around the door. She looks frazzled, thinks Hannah, perturbed perhaps by this sudden turn of events. She likes her normal days where she knows what she's doing in advance. They both do. None of them are a fan of shocks or surprises.

'Nita's grandson is visiting her, and I promised her we'd do something. The park, probably. Are you coming with us?'

Hannah shakes her head, impatient. 'Oliver can spend the day over there. Today, I'm taking you out.'

Marie hesitates. 'We can take Oliver over to Nita's when we get back, maybe? It's a bit early to drop him off there now.'

'Fine.' Hannah clenches her fists while Marie packs for an unexpected day out.

Like Marie, Oliver is flustered, confused by the change of plan. In Hannah's house, routine is key. He senses this, as young as he is.

Marie says nothing, does not protest. The only sign of her displeasure is her mouth, downturned slightly, puckered with an unvoiced concern.

When they are finally ready to leave, Marie pauses at the door, catches Hannah's arm and draws her aside.

'Are you okay?'

At her mother's hand on her arm, Hannah feels warmth flood through her.

'Oh, Mum. I'm fine, honestly. I just… want to spend the day with you.'

Marie frowns and opens the door. 'Come on, then.'

Marie catches Oliver's hand as he toddles along the mews. At the end, Hannah makes them wait.

She always walks everywhere in London. She rarely gets on the Underground. But today, everyone is walking, enjoying the sunshine. Beneath the city streets, the Tube will be less filled with people. She will see more down there, see if anyone is trailing her, trailing *them*.

She thinks quickly as she marches them down the road. She wants to avoid her usual haunts, although that didn't pan out too well before. She came from Richmond, for heaven's sake, a place she *never* goes to, and yet, that man was there, in the park. Then later, outside her home.

She herds her mother and son along the crowded pavement, slipping down into the Underground, fumbling with the cards for the train fare, pushing them through the turnstile while keeping one eye on her phone, locating the Tube maps and working out the route.

They get off the Tube, back out in the now-searing heat. Oliver grizzles, sticky and too warm after being on the Underground.

Marie frets over him. She is red-faced and breathless herself. 'I should have brought a drink for him,' she says. 'Can we get a bottle of water somewhere?'

Hannah is aghast at her own irresponsibility. Horrified by the journey, which should have been simple, but has taken it out of her mother.

They don't normally do this, Marie especially. She doesn't hop on and off the Underground. She finds it too loud, too confusing, all those westbound and eastbound decisions to make. Easier to avoid it altogether. Better to stay within the confines of their courtyard, or the little park next door.

She sees a van selling hot dogs and confectionery across the road. Darts over to it, buying water and sweets. She shoves twenty quid at the man and doesn't wait for her change.

When she gets back to Marie, Oliver has settled. He points at the tower across the road, his blue eyes wide. He has forgotten the uncomfortable ride, the heat, and barely looks at the water Hannah passes to him.

'He wants to go in there,' says Marie.

Hannah looks around. They are at the Tower of London, a landmark that she would never dream of visiting. The dungeons, the ravens – they send cold waves down her body.

But being cool would be a good thing today. Inside, they will be out of the heat. They will do something different, away from the crowds in the parks and out of sight of prying eyes.

Hannah pays for their tickets and drifts along behind her mother and her son, as they ooh and ahh over everything. The white tower, gleaming in the sunshine, the chapel, the line of kings. Oliver stares wide-eyed at the armour, and Marie reads each plaque patiently to him.

Neither Hannah nor her mother wants to go into the Bloody Tower.

They move instead to the Crown Jewels. They make her think about Alina, of those gems in her vault, of the basement where her husband creates them using the skills that only belonged to nature before now.

She wonders if she will have contact with Alina again.

A part of her, an unfamiliar piece of her make-up, hopes so.

Another part of her knows that she *needs to*.

The ravens at the gate are their last stop. They perch on their bars, watching the people who admire them. They seem to look at Hannah intensely, and she shivers and turns away.

Oliver has started whispering to Marie about his play-date with Nita's grandson.

Marie gives Hannah a glance. 'It's been arranged for a while,' she says.

Hannah is irritated. She didn't know about it until that very morning. Oliver is her child. What if she had already made plans for her son? Or wanted to take him somewhere on a whim, which is exactly what happened.

She can't really protest. Marie has practically raised Oliver.

'But I don't want to get on the Underground again.' Marie shudders and draws Oliver close to her. 'Can we get one of those Uber cars, like we did the other night?'

If Hannah were alone, she would walk it, she thinks. A couple of hours, no rush, just taking in the sights and sounds of her city.

But that's what she did when she left Alina's, and look what happened there.

'Yes,' she tells Marie. They'll get a car. Oliver can see his friend, but Nita needs to bring him to their house: Oliver isn't going to Nita's.

It is a compromise, but Hannah can feel Marie's questioning eyes on her.

Her mother, however, says nothing.

Later, once Oliver and Bobby, Nita's grandson, arc playing in the courtyard, she can tell that Marie is getting up the courage to ask something.

Hannah raises her eyebrows at her mother, daring her to voice whatever is on her mind.

'You like Nita, don't you?'

Hannah contemplates her reply.

'Where did she come from... Nita, I mean?' Hannah asks. She skirts around her mother's question.

'Brentwood, originally.' Marie, preparing a light salad supper, skins a cucumber. 'Why do you ask?'

Hannah, Marie and Oliver have lived here in the mews house for a little under a year. Nita turned up a couple of months later. Hannah had looked at her: this single, older woman, who, according to Marie, spent her mornings walking in the park and her afternoons watching quiz shows on television.

What would it take to turn Nita's attention away from neighbourly friendship to something more… sinister? Not money, because, as Hannah knows, you don't get a mews house unless you've got a hefty chunk of cash.

Excitement, perhaps. Leaving the doldrums of everyday life to one side. A project to break up the monotony of the long days.

'Hannah?'

Marie's voice, sharp, concerned, brings her back to the here and now.

She blinks, back in the room, here with her mum who is making them dinner, putting enough in the large, wooden bowl to make sure Nita's grandkid has a decent meal.

Hannah rolls her shoulders. They creak with the tension she's holding.

'Miles away.' Hannah smiles, reaches across the counter for the vegetable knife and drags a pepper towards her. 'Let me help you, Mum.'

Marie sweeps the knife back to her side, reaches out for the pepper. 'No need. You relax, you've done enough for us today.'

Hannah does as she's told.

'I'll walk Bobby home, after dinner,' she tells her mother.

Marie stares at Hannah. 'We'll walk him home together,' she replies.

9

ALINA, MONDAY

Alina wakes far too early on Monday morning. Like Hannah, she did nothing of interest the day before, apart from her visit to the gallery.

She came away with none of the answers that she was seeking.

Or, she thinks, maybe she did, and they just haven't revealed themselves to her yet.

Sofia is still sleeping. Alina makes her way down to the basement. There, she hooks her phone up to the big screen and scrolls through the photos she took at the gallery.

Her mobile rings, and she swears as she tries to answer the call without losing the pictures from the screen.

When she sees it is her husband calling, she abandons the photos.

'Willem!' She breaks into a smile, the first genuine one since the night he went away.

'How are you, how's Sofia?' he asks.

'Good, she's still sleeping. I'm in the basement.'

'Admiring my work?' He laughs.

She joins him, delighted that he's on the phone, reminded of just how much she misses him when he's gone.

His joy, his laughter, his voice of reason.

'I went to the gallery and saw that horrid little man – the curator – and the artist too.'

'And?' he asks.

'The curator makes me want to vomit. The artist seemed devastated.'

'You've never liked Grantham,' he remarks. 'And what will you do about the artist? Do you think he is at fault, his construction of the installation?'

Alina fumbles with the remote control, zooming in on the pictures of Lucifer in his crumpled pile.

'I don't know. I keep thinking about the woman, too. She didn't want anything. No reward… Well, she did, but then she changed her mind.' Alina shrugs to herself as she relives the odd meeting with Hannah. 'Anyway. That's by the by. She'll come back, or she won't. Whatever, I offered. What are you doing? How's Antwerp and the old boys' club?'

'Fine. Nice lot. Not too many old boys left now. The new ones are open, curious. Put Sofia on, wake her up so her old papa can speak to her.'

Alina does as he asks, traipsing up the stairs, careful to lock the basement door behind her. As she treks up to the highest level of their home, Alina and Willem exchange whispered words that alternate between deep love, genuine friendship and their sometimes off-kilter passion.

In Sofia's bedroom, she pokes at her daughter, waving the mobile at her. Sofia grins with delight and takes the phone.

Alina sits beside Sofia's bed, on the floor where she spent the night of the accident. She listens to Sofia fill

Willem in on everything she's done since he's been gone. She smiles at Willem's exclamations and laughter.

When they hang up, Sofia hands back the phone and burrows back inside her duvet.

Alina makes her way back to the basement and unlocks the door. The files are still on the big screen, and she studies the pictures and the video she took until her vision begins to blur.

She told Willem that the artist was devastated, that Grantham was useless and weaselly. What she hasn't yet shared with him is the niggling feeling she's got that Friday night's drama wasn't an accident.

She has no proof and doesn't know what's leading her emotions in that direction.

She has her own paranoia, of course.

And perhaps that's it. Her maternal instinct, combined with the fear that has never gone away, is what is making her feel this way. Maybe the accident was just that: an accident.

She's about to turn the screen off when something catches her eye.

That! What is that there?

Alina zooms in again, exclaiming with frustration as the pixels grow and blur the image.

She switches to her phone, squinting at the photo. There is something there, something dark in colour, standing out amongst the silver blades. It could be something on the floor, she supposes, but it is unlikely. Momotaro's interior flooring is flat, matt, light grey concrete. There are no plug sockets embedded in it, no trailing wires or anything that may detract from whatever is on show.

Alina switches off the screen, shoves her phone in her pocket and makes her way upstairs.

She finds Julia, her assistant, making coffee in the kitchen.

Julia, like Lucas, is more than an employee. She's a nanny, a sounding board and, most importantly, Alina's closest friend.

'Sofia's still in bed – keep an ear out for her, will you, Jules?' Alina asks. 'Can you get her ready for school if I'm not back by then?'

Julia nods towards the planner on the wall. 'Teacher training day, no school for Sofia.'

'Oh. In that case, will you stay with her until I return?'

Julia raises her coffee cup in agreement.

Outside, Alina closes the door behind her. Lucas springs up at her side. 'Where to, Alina?'

She gives him a wry look. 'The gallery. Where else?'

He sees her into the passenger seat and walks round the car to the driver's side.

'Do I need to come in?' he asks, tongue in cheek. 'Or just be ready for when they call the police on you?'

Alina laughs long and hard. Lucas joins in. The thought of it is inconceivable. Alina has always thought that when they finally come for her – the authorities, her father's enemies, the government – it won't be official. It will be with a bag for her head and a noose for her neck.

They laugh about it, all of them, Alina especially. She must, because if she doesn't laugh, she will fear.

And Alina has enough of that fear already. She's squashed it down, as far as she can, so much so nobody would ever know the anxiety and spikes of concern that prod at her.

She's been here so long now, and it has been even longer since she's been connected to her father, that it's an almost normal life, now.

Until the night when Sofia faced near tragedy.

They take the drive that she's fast becoming accustomed to. Normally, she avoids going into central London so many times in as many days. But this thing with Sofia has shaken her more than she would admit to anyone. Even Lucas, her most faithful friend. Even her husband.

In amongst a cacophony of blaring horns, Lucas pulls up at the kerb outside the Momotaro.

'You can wait here,' she tells him. 'I'll be out when I'm finished.'

She sweeps in again, head high, as she did yesterday. It's busier today, being Monday, and there's no sign of either Jerry, who she wouldn't mind seeing, or Grantham, who she definitely *would*.

She takes advantage of the crowds milling around and heads smartly down the spiral stairs, into the depths of the building.

The girls are manning the cloakroom space, as they were the day before. Today they are armed with too many coats and tickets to spare her a glance. Alina moves speedily down the sectioned-off hallway and into the installation room.

It is empty. No sign that Lucifer ever existed is in here at all. The floor is clear. Smooth concrete from wall to wall. No chairs, no podiums, no blood stains. No set-up at all.

Alina backs out of the room, slams the door and marches up to the cloakroom girls.

'Where has the fucking installation been moved to?' she snaps, pushing in at the front of the line.

One of them studies her, recognising her instantly. The young woman bows her head.

'The investigation is ongoing – everything relating to the sculpture has been moved into an empty room.' The woman glances up, nods to a door set in the far wall and clasps her hands in front of her. 'Our curator has the key. Unfortunately, he is out right now, but is due in shortly.'

'Thanks,' says Alina, roughly. She will find the woman again later, explain why she spoke harshly, slammed doors and swore. She won't apologise, but she'll ensure this staff member knows none of it was aimed at her. 'Please contact Grantham. Tell him if he's not here in exactly one hour, ready to unlock that door, I'll arrange to break it down myself.'

The woman nods demurely. 'Certainly, Madam.'

Alina raps her knuckles on the desk. 'Just to be clear, that will make it ten o'clock. I'll be here, and Grantham will be here with a key.'

She leaves, swishing back upstairs, out of the door, and is rapping on Lucas's window. He winds it down.

'I'm waiting for that idiot to turn up. One hour. If you see him arrive before, you ring me.'

He raises an eyebrow archly. 'And you'll be…?'

'In the park. Walking. Enjoying the fucking sunshine like I should be, instead of gallivanting all over the city cleaning up other people's mistakes.'

He nods, winds his window back up and faces forward.

Alina walks across the road, mindless of the cars that honk at her. They will stop for her.

She spits out an almost manic laugh. Maybe one day they won't.

She always gets like this. Reckless, when Willem is away, when Sofia is not with her. When her thoughts start to crowd in on her.

The two of them make her a tripod of stability.

She moves into Hyde Park, walking fast down the path, headed at a diagonal towards the Serpentine. She walks beside it, soothed by its grey–silver surface, mirror smooth.

'Excuse me?'

She turns, frowning at the man who has appeared beside her.

'I'm so sorry to bother you. I was at the gallery, the Momotaro, Friday night. If I'm not mistaken, your daughter was involved in the terrible accident. I couldn't stop thinking about it.' The words of this stranger pour out of him.

Alina studies him. His eyes are heavy with... With what? Something that looks unmistakably like grief. His hair is mostly covered with a hat, just his pale orange sideburns giving away his colouring. His eyelashes are pale, like his face, but two spots of red are seared high on his cheekbones.

'She's okay, your daughter?' the man presses her.

Alina nods. 'Yes, she will be fine, thank you. Just shock, mostly.'

It wasn't really true. After all, Sofia had bounced back practically as soon as they'd left the gallery. Alina is the one who can't let go.

'*I* was shocked,' Alina admits. 'More than her.' It's not like her, telling a stranger something so confidential.

The man nods, his expression grim. 'And the woman who helped your girl, have you seen her? Did you *know* her?'

'Like you, she was attending the opening. Right place, right time, I suppose. Though of course, she was injured, so maybe it was a case of wrong place, wrong time, for *her*.' Alina grimaces, recalling the blood on the floor, the bandage around Hannah's arm the next day.

'Injured?' The man blinks at her. 'How so?'

The back of Alina's neck prickles.

She's back there, that night. She can feel the horror coming off the crowd in waves. The aftermath, the whispers as they all watched Hannah being helped from the gallery, the trail of blood, the other people in attendance spread out, looking at it all.

If this man had been there, like he claimed, he would have seen it.

She smiles, but it is as hard as one of the diamonds in her vault.

'I'm sorry, what did you say your name was?'

He looks worried. 'I... I didn't—'

Alina cuts him off. 'Or rather, I should ask, which newspaper are you from?'

He is shocked, or at least does a passable impression of being so.

'I... No, that's not—'

Alina glares at him. He stops talking.

She turns on her heel and stalks back the way she came, out of the park, furious that her pleasant few moments have been pissed on by the press.

At the gate, she pulls out her mobile and dials Julia.

She answers quickly, launching into a spiel about the breakfast she and Sofia are enjoying. Alina cuts her off.

'I was just accosted by the media in the park. Did they call you?'

'No!' Julia clicks her tongue and sighs. 'They should know better by now. Who was it?'

'I didn't recognise him. He didn't say, either. He was sly, making out that he was just a bystander.'

'What was he asking? About you, about Willem?'

'Nothing like that. He claimed to have been at the gallery Friday night, acted concerned, then launched into his interview.' Alina is cross again. More about the fact that he pretended to be a concerned citizen, rather than the ambulance-chasing newshound that he is.

'Don't worry, Jules, he rattled me, is all. Look, I'll be home soon, once I've finished up at the gallery. Let's sack off work for the rest of today and do something fun with Sofia.'

She smiles as Julia relays the message to Sofia and hangs up.

As soon as her loved ones are off the airwaves, the fury returns. She spins around, looking towards the Serpentine, but the riverbank is empty, the man nowhere to be seen.

They were standing by the edge of the river. She should have pushed him in. Laughed as his microphone or hidden wire got soaked.

But he has vanished.

She can't direct her anger at him, at that stranger – and, she admits to herself, he is not really the source of her discord anyway.

Alina crosses the road, crooking her finger at Lucas as she sweeps back through the doors of the Momotaro. He follows on her heels as she storms down the stairs.

The cloakroom women look at her, wide-eyed, as she points out the door to the room where Lucifer's remains are stored.

'Madam, you said one hour. Our curator is on his way – he will be here by ten o'clock, like you requested.'

Alina glares at her. 'I changed my mind,' she says. 'I want that door opened *now.*'

She looks to Lucas, who nods. 'Back in a second,' he says, and stamps his way back up the spiral staircase.

The women busy themselves with the coat- and bag-taking, working double time now, probably in order to clear this space of customers before it descends into a fully blown drama.

There are only the three of them when Lucas returns, in seconds as promised, with a crowbar clutched in his meaty fist. He gives an apologetic glance at the assistants, inserts the bar into the gap between the door and the frame, and heaves it with his weight against it.

Something splinters, the frame cracks, the door pops open.

'Thank you,' Alina says to Lucas. 'You can wait back in the car.'

She looks pointedly at the crowbar. Lucas ducks his head, slips it inside his coat and slopes off back up the stairs.

Alina moves into what is essentially a storeroom, about the size of Sofia's built-in closet at home. She flicks the light switch on.

No shelves adorn the walls; the room is as empty as the showcase gallery was, apart from a heap of metal towards the back wall.

The sight has a visceral effect on Alina. She swallows, tasting the bile that has risen.

She takes her handbag off her shoulder, pulls on the hard-wearing gloves she uses when she's messing about with Willem's gems back home and gets to work.

She sits cross-legged in front of the metal pile. One by one, she picks up a blade, examines it and throws it into the opposite corner.

At times, as she inspects each part of Lucifer, a tear escapes her eye. Up close, these blades are even worse than she remembered. Even more awful than when she glanced at them yesterday. Deadly. It's the only word she can come up with to describe them.

That one word is enough.

It says everything.

Forty thousand blades. She works faster, pulling out a handful at a time, sending them spinning to the side once she's confirmed they are plain silver.

As the pile gets smaller, she moves chunks of blades with her feet, not looking at them as a singular anymore, but just searching for that one, single, piece of black something she saw in the photo.

She checks her phone again, locates the picture, zooms in. It's there. Something is there, on the shot, clearly shown against the grey concrete floor and the shiny blades.

The ground of this storeroom is the same silvery grey as the other room.

There is nothing black here. Nothing plastic-looking.

Alina kicks at the metal pile.

Nothing. There is nothing here.

There are murmurings outside the storeroom. Alina opens the door, coming face to face with the two women who work the cloakroom. Beside them stands Grantham, the idiot.

Clearly, he has been berating his two staff members for the damage to the door and frame. Alina can imagine it: them, trying to explain; him, not even giving them a chance to speak.

'Oh, Ms Arpels,' he cries, his face changing in an instant. 'I didn't realise you were here, um, inside… uh, there.'

She sweeps her hand behind her, gesturing to the pile of what can now only be described as scrap metal. 'This is all of it?' she asks. 'There's nothing else from the install-ation?'

He edges closer, peering into the room, his expression telling her this is the first time he's seen this.

She burns. 'You didn't oversee the investigation?' she asks. 'You didn't stay on-site the whole time they were looking at this?'

His face is red now, at her shaming him in front of his staff.

He turns to the cloakroom girls. 'Go and take a break,' he says. And then, with something approaching despera-tion, '*Please.*'

They hustle away. Alina is sure they must be laughing.

She wonders how many times this awful little man has shamed *them*.

'The investigators are professionals; it wouldn't have been right for me to stand over them and insist—'

'This is your gallery,' Alina hisses at him. 'You are in charge; you can insist upon anything you like.'

She can't stay here a moment longer. She fantasises about picking up one of those razor-sharp pieces and slashing at him.

Instead, she sweeps past and is almost at the spiral stair-case before she turns back to face him. 'I said this *is* your gallery,' she says. 'That was my mistake. I should have said this *used to be* your gallery, Grantham.'

She hurls herself into the car, slamming the door with more force than is necessary. 'Take me home, Lucas,' she sighs.

10

HANNAH, MONDAY

She is in the lounge, staring at nothing, the room pitch-black, when she hears her name being called, an urgent whisper.

Hannah! Hannah! Hannah!

She moves to the hallway and starts up the stairs, stumbling into Marie, who catches her.

'I can hear something,' Marie hisses, her voice pitched with panic.

'What…'

'Shush, listen.' Marie holds Hannah's arm in a vice-like grip.

She hears it herself then. A thin wail. It sounds just like a baby's cry.

Marie whispers, 'I think it's outside.'

Hannah rubs at her upper arm. The stitches are feeling tight tonight.

'Outside,' she echoes Marie.

'A fox?' Marie is hopeful. In the gloom of the night, the whites of her eyes shine very bright.

They've had foxes before, many times. Urban London, it's their home now.

But Hannah knows this sound isn't coming from a wild animal.

They go back downstairs, side by side, and Marie checks the chain is securely on the front door before she opens it and puts her ear to the gap.

'I can't hear it as well out here,' she says, after a moment of listening. 'It's out the back.'

Marie checks all the locks are firmly secured before she goes down the hall into the back of the house.

She keeps the lights off, moving up to the glass of the patio door and cupping her hands around it.

Marie is right. The keening noise is louder back here.

Marie's hand settles on the handle, but she doesn't turn the key to unlock it.

'Mum?'

Marie lets her hand drop to hang limply at her side. 'It's so late. Why were you downstairs? Where have you been?' she asks. Her voice is sullen, as though she's cross with Hannah.

Hannah blinks at her. 'I... I couldn't sleep,' she says. 'Look, it's just a fox, we can go back to bed.'

But Marie darts her a glance like she knows different. Bravely, she steps back to the door, twists the key, pushes down on the handle and lets it swing open.

The cry is an assault. Louder now, desperation bouncing like an echo.

Marie doesn't step outside, but she reaches forward, her fingertips brushing the door handle. Then, she slides the door closed.

She wants to ignore it, thinks Hannah. She would rather stick her head in the sand as usual than face whatever may or may not be out there.

It is Marie all over. Avoid it, ignore it and it will go away.

Hannah takes a step towards the hallway, intent on going to her room, to her bed. After all, Marie is right, it *is* late.

'Wait!' Marie is galvanised into action now, her house-coat billowing behind her as she stumbles around the counter, pulling open various cupboards until she locates the torch.

She moves back to the door, no hesitation this time as she opens it and steps outside into the warm night.

The light casts a wide beam on the courtyard.

Their garden is simple. It's not huge, and the furnishings are minimal. A table, four chairs, an eyesore of a slide in the corner. A scattering of plots where Marie's flowers bloom. It is surrounded by walls, made of grey brick.

There is nothing, nobody, in their courtyard.

But the wailing sound continues.

Hannah stays where she is, just inside the door. Marie drags one of the chairs to the wall, clambers onto it and aims the flashlight over the other side.

She starts, lurching backwards, the chair shifting dangerously under her weight.

Hannah rushes forward, arms outstretched, putting one hand on Marie's spine, the other planted firmly on the chair back.

Marie dashes her daughter's hands away and climbs off the chair.

'It's Bobby,' she says. 'It's Nita's Bobby.'

It is as if panic has gripped Marie now. She runs back through the door, Hannah following. Then through to the front, unlocking the door, removing the chain. On the front stoop she turns back to Hannah. Her eyes are dark, flashing with… With what? Fear? Fury?

'Come with me,' she commands.

Hannah swallows and trails after Marie as she runs down the short path, down the mews lane.

'Close the door,' Marie says. 'Oliver will be fine.'

Hannah reaches inside, removes the key and locks her door from the outside. She grips the key in her palm and follows Marie up Nita's path.

'Try the door.' Marie lets Hannah move ahead of her.

Hannah does as Marie asks, yanking on the handle. It is locked.

'The back,' gasps Marie, shooing Hannah in front of her.

The passageway opens into a courtyard, identical to Hannah's own. Nita's isn't as simple, though. Pots filled with colourful plants compete for space alongside garden ornaments, Bobby's toys, a sunlounger and a deckchair, folded up and leaning against the far wall.

It is from behind the deckchair that the cry is coming from.

'Check it,' says Marie, her eyes on Hannah as she moves forward.

Hannah grasps the chair, pulls it away from the wall.

'Bobby!' Marie rushes forward, gathers up the little boy in her arms. 'Bobby, where is your nana?'

Bobby can't speak. His face is puce, wet with tears and panicked sweat. His breathing is a continuous sob, broken up only by an occasional hiccup.

Marie looks over her shoulder at Hannah. 'Try the patio door,' she says, her voice wavering, her plea almost a wail.

'It's locked,' Hannah calls.

Marie, with Bobby on her hip, steps to the door. She peers down at the frame that runs along the bottom and looks to Hannah. 'Not locked,' she says, indicating a green, plastic Lego base. 'Just jammed.'

Hannah hesitates, before reaching down and pulling the toy out of the frame. With the obstruction gone, the door opens easily.

Marie holds the still-quaking Bobby in her arms. Over Hannah's shoulder, she squints into the kitchen area.

'Nita,' she says.

Hannah feels her mother's body beside her as it turns liquid. It is Marie she can't take her eyes off, not the inert form of Nita, slumped on the floor.

–

Nita is tearful, confused, frightened when she touches her temple and sees the blood on her fingers. She reaches out for her neighbour, her friend. Marie, with Bobby still clinging to her, helps the older woman up and guides her to a chair.

Marie is strangely silent as her friend gathers herself. The child's mother is called, and arrives within minutes, a blustering whirlwind as she comes through the back door. She takes a hold of her mother and her son at the same time.

Hannah watches Nita, whose head is bowed. She is probably thanking some deity that she doesn't normally believe in that she has escaped a London burglary relatively unscathed.

Nita's daughter, Kara, asks out loud the one question that nobody has voiced so far.

'What happened?'

None of them, not even Nita, answers her.

Nita objects against calling the police. She glances at Marie, a strangely apologetic look on her face.

'You're coming to my house,' Kara says. 'We'll call the police from there.'

Marie and Hannah follow them out, down the path, to the end of the lane where Kara has parked her car haphazardly on the pavement.

They watch as Kara assists Nita into the vehicle, a trembling Bobby in his car seat beside his grandmother.

Marie trudges back up to their own house, pausing at the step for Hannah to catch up.

'You didn't see anything, when you took Bobby home earlier?' she asks, her voice husky, pleading, almost.

'No, nothing,' she replies.

'I should have taken Bobby home, like I said,' says Marie.

Hannah stares dizzily at her, wondering why they are not going inside their own home.

She remembers locking the door, and she opens her hand, surprised to see the key on her palm, the imprint burned into her skin where she has gripped it too tight.

11

ALINA, MONDAY

Willem would have scolded her for threatening the curator's job, had he been here.

But he's not, she thinks, churlishly, so she can threaten whoever she wants.

She invites Lucas in when they get home. Julia is still there, baking, with Sofia.

'Just in time!' she says, greeting Alina with a hug.

'What are they?' Alina asks, flinging her bag on the counter, studying the wares her friend and daughter have cooked. 'Actually, I don't care – as long as they are sweet and disgustingly unhealthy, I want one.'

'Cookies,' Sofia tells her proudly, giving a flamboyant gesture to where they sit on the cooling rack.

They eat them all, Sofia and Alina more than the other two. As Lucas entertains Sofia with card tricks from a deck that he pulls out of his back pocket, Julia gives Alina the rundown on the day's activities at the shipping line.

It runs itself, her business. Or, more accurately, the department heads run it, but Alina likes to be kept in the loop.

The company is far from failing. When Alina took over the business, over a decade ago, she wanted to go in under the guise of a personal assistant or secretary. However, all those men had known her since she was born. Instead, she found Julia, a woman Alina instantly connected with, and sent her in undercover.

Julia had done well. All the old boys who were corrupt, who were skimming off the top, she got them out straight away. All the other employees, who had been faithful and loyal to Alina's father, were also let go. Only, those ones got a healthy pay-off, and an even healthier pension pot.

Yes, the company is in good hands these days. Now, just as she had suggested to Julia earlier, they sack off any remaining work for the rest of the day. She retrieves a cocktail-making kit, makes mocktails for Lucas and for Sofia. Jules and she get hammered.

Alina plucks the deck of cards from Lucas. 'Poker,' she announces.

The day rolls into night. Sofia is put to bed, and Alina stands in the bedroom doorway as her girl falls asleep with a smile on her face.

Sofia is happy.

Sofia is safe.

With her, Julia and Lucas around – and Willem – Sofia will always be safe.

Except she very nearly wasn't. And on that occasion, Alina had been *right there* with her.

They switch to coffee when Alina returns downstairs. No sign of the night ending yet. Lucas and Julia don't care. When they came to work for Alina, they knew there was no such thing as a nine-to-five in her world.

She shows them the photos of the mass of metal she took the day after the accident, points out the mysterious black object as the coffee machine roars into life behind them.

They study it, zooming in, out, squinting. All the things Alina has been doing since she saw it.

'It's not there any longer, whatever it is,' she tells them. She informs them of the broken Lucifer's new living quarters, in the storeroom, and that that morning she sifted through forty thousand pieces of metal – and that's all there was.

Metal.

'Maybe you should let it go,' suggests Julia, gently.

Lucas flashes her a warning look.

Alina cocks her head. 'Let it go?' Her tone is light, but the look in her eye is unmistakable.

Julia backtracks, realising her error. She is always attuned to Alina's moods and emotions. This afternoon, the cocktails and the sense of merriment have knocked her off balance.

'I don't mean to say actually let it go,' she explains, hurriedly. 'I mean, the investigators will find anything that wasn't supposed to be there.'

'If they're independent,' comments Lucas.

Alina looks at him, alarmed. 'What do you mean?'

'Are they independent, or do they work for the gallery?'

Alina slams her hand down on the hard marble counter. 'Son of a bitch!' she exclaims.

Something else to investigate. She will have to go to the gallery again. She'll get that man – the awful, snivelling Grantham – and she'll tell him she's bringing her own people in.

–

She calls the gallery the next day, over and over, getting the answering machine that tells her she is calling too early for her call to be answered.

Stubbornly, Alina refuses to believe that there is nobody there yet. She imagines grey-haired Grantham, staring at the ringing phone, knowing it is her, too scared to answer.

Alina sighs. She doesn't want to go there again. Not yet. Today, she wants to chill out. Julia is in the main office, overseeing. Sofia has gone to school. Willem is still in Antwerp, though he'll return later this afternoon.

Today, Alina wants to spend the day doing absolutely nothing.

But she wants her own people on the case, looking through the metal. She's not stupid, far from it, but she can't believe she trusted that the gallery, that awful Grantham, would *do the right thing*.

She imagines telling her father of her oversight, that it took her driver to point it out to her.

He would pinch his lips together, shake his head. He wouldn't say anything. He wouldn't need to.

But she won't tell him. She can't even remember the last time she spoke to him.

Willem. Lucas. Julia. Sofia. They are her family circle now.

She dials Julia's number and waits for her to pick up.

She hears a tap at the door. It is Lucas; she recognises his form through the frosted glass portion.

'Hey, what's up?' she greets him.

'Visitor,' he says. His eyes dart to the right and she looks outside.

Hannah Barker.

Well, well, well.

She suppresses a little secret smile and swings the door open.

'Hannah, how nice to see you. Please, come in. I won't be a moment.'

The ringtone shifts to Julia's voicemail.

'Jules, I know you're at the office for me today, and thank you for that, my darling. Please can you keep trying the gallery and have them ring me? Cheers, Jules, love you.'

She hangs up. 'My assistant,' she says. 'Actually, Julia is so much more than that. She's a nanny, friend, confidante, drinking partner.'

She observes the young woman standing in front of her.

Hannah is looking different today. Alina tries to put her finger on it.

Determined, is the answer she comes up with. A woman on a mission.

Alina checks her watch. It's nine a.m. She hasn't even had breakfast yet. She regards Hannah carefully as she leads her down the hallway, and makes a snap decision.

'Have you eaten?' Alina asks.

Hannah gives her a small smile, opens her shoulder bag and angles it for Alina to see.

Alina glances inside, sees the tall, glass bottle, filled with something that looks remarkably like algae.

Alina shudders. 'Jesus, really? I was thinking of eggs, bacon. Something that is tasty.'

Hannah looks like a deer caught in the headlights.

Alina hates this ideology in people. Mostly women, she finds. The strange need to punish, to self-flagellate and deny oneself one of life's greatest pleasures.

She runs her eyes up and down Hannah's form. The woman standing in front of her has no need for such strict control. She is slim, not an ounce of fat on her. She is wearing a dress today, and her calves are toned, no curves anywhere.

Alina feels compassion, sudden and swift – an unusual emotion for her. She nods to herself, decision made.

'Yes, eggs, bacon, bread,' she states. 'Some potato things, maybe. You will eat with me.'

Alina calls Lucas in, tells him of the breakfast plan. He joins them in the kitchen, and with practised movements he begins preparations for their feast.

'Did you hear anything from the gallery?' Hannah asks.

Alina snorts. 'They're useless.' She shakes her head. 'That's not right. The curator is a prick.' She narrows her eyes as she regards Hannah. 'You want his job?' she asks, only half-joking.

Hannah's eyes burn with an unmistakable desire. 'More than almost anything,' she replies.

Alina cocks her head to one side. 'You're qualified for it?'

'More than qualified. I've worked in the industry since I gained my degree. I've arranged exhibits for years.' She sits up straighter in her chair, and Alina notes the look of determination on her face. 'Many of them – some of them you've probably been to and admired. I know you love the art world, like me.'

Alina frowns, wondering how Hannah can claim to know that. Friday night was the first time she's ever crossed paths with Hannah… wasn't it?

'I mean, I've seen you at the Momotaro, I'm sure,' Hannah says, her words coming out in a rush, the only slip of that cool, calm exterior that Alina has witnessed. 'And,' Hannah adds, 'your reputation precedes you.'

She says it with a smile, a small laugh, and Alina knows she's not ass-kissing like Grantham.

'What do you think of the Momotaro's exhibits, then?'

Hannah shrugs. 'They're fantastic, so different to what a lot of the galleries put out.' She raises her chin, defiant and confident once more. 'I could make them better, though. And I wouldn't let any installations go ahead without vigorous testing. Safety first, right, otherwise we might as well quit with the installations and go to a bloody theme park instead.'

Alina nods, thoughtfully.

'That's what you want, then? From me, I mean. That's the wish you want me to grant you?'

The time for beating around the bush is over. If that's what Hannah wants, Alina will arrange it.

In the silence that ensues, Alina thinks back to Saturday, when Hannah was on the verge of asking for what she wanted.

I want you to get someone out of my life. Those had been Hannah's words, before they had been interrupted and she had subsequently lost her nerve.

Hannah drops her gaze. 'It's… complicated,' she says.

'Your current employer?' Alina flaps her hand, dismissively. 'I can smooth that over, it's not a problem.'

Hannah shakes her head. 'No, it's… something else.'

Alina allows herself a small smile. So, Miss Hannah wants *two* things.

'Go on,' she commands.

Alina is excited to find out if the other woman is going to trust her this time, with that other thing she wants.

'You said you'd grant me anything,' Hannah speaks finally. Her chin is raised, as though challenging Alina to keep the promise she already made.

'Yes.'

'But what if you say no?'

Alina frowns. 'What do you mean?'

'I mean, if I tell you what I want, and you refuse. What happens then?'

Alina can feel Lucas watching the exchange with interest. She darts a glance at him. He covers a smile, returns to the eggs that he is breaking.

Alina clears her throat. 'I can't refuse you. You did me a service, one that wasn't expected – you didn't work for me, you didn't owe me anything. You didn't even know me, but what you did for me was...' Alina trails off. *Huge* doesn't cut it. She can think of no other word that accurately describes the enormity of Hannah's actions.

Everything. What Hannah did, saving Sofia like that, was *everything*.

Alina locks eyes with Hannah, her face deadly serious. 'I can't refuse you, is what I'm trying to say. I *won't* refuse you, whatever it is.'

Hannah takes a deep breath. 'I'm being followed, and harassed. I want it stopped.'

This is more like it. Alina sits up straight and reaches for a slice of raw potato to nibble on.

'Someone is following me. When I left here, on Saturday, I walked home—'

'You walked home? To Kensington, from here?' Alina sneaks a look at Hannah's muscled calves again. 'Wow.'

'I went through a park, it was dark. I was... I wasn't myself; I'd taken the painkillers the doctor prescribed me and they made me woozy. Someone was following me.'

Alina finds she is holding her breath. 'And?' she asks, sharply.

Suddenly, Hannah sags, as though defeated. 'I don't even know if it's a man or a woman, but I have my suspicions. They wore a hoodie, and… they kind of grabbed me, I think. Pushed me. I fell. I don't remember much, I got away. But when I woke up, yesterday morning, I looked out of the window and I'm certain I saw the same person from the park. Outside my *home.*'

London, parks, night walking – it's a danger faced by everyone. Man, woman, child.

Alina drops the piece of potato onto the counter. 'But you can't identify them?'

Hannah appears to think deeply. Seconds pass, the only sound in the kitchen the bacon jumping and spitting in the pan.

'I've felt like someone has been watching me.' Hannah swallows and her voice drops to a whisper, so quiet that Alina has to move closer to hear her. 'Someone has been watching me for a while now. They were outside my home. It's probably not the first time, and it won't be the last.'

It's not an answer to Alina's question. Suddenly, it's very clear. Hannah *can* identify this person, but for some reason, she won't.

A trickle of disappointment covers Alina.

Why doesn't Hannah trust her?

12

HANNAH, TUESDAY

Alina is silent for such a long time that Hannah starts to feel awkward.

What is Alina pondering, so deep in thought?

Does she... Is it possible she doesn't *believe* Hannah?

She opens her mouth to tell Alina of last night's drama, with her neighbour, Nita. Surely that story will imply that whoever went into Nita's home was searching for Hannah, but somehow got into the wrong house in the mews lane.

But Lucas interrupts, placing cutlery and warmed plates gently down on the counter.

She stares at him, her thoughts scattered now, wondering how Alina's employee can be so at home in her kitchen. Doesn't it bug Alina, the way it irritates Hannah when Nita is over at her place all the time?

She switches her gaze to the other woman as Lucas returns with silver trays lined with rows of bacon, sliced fried potatoes, and perfectly poached eggs. Alina pounces on it, blows a kiss at her driver.

Hannah frowns at the food. It looks delicious, worthy of one of the five-star restaurants Hannah goes to when she feels she's earned a decent meal, or when her life is out of harmony. Now, she's sure she can't stomach the food.

She looks at Alina apologetically. 'I feel sick,' she says. 'I can't eat it.'

Alina pushes a plate a little closer to Hannah. 'You can, you will and you'll feel better once you have.' She smiles, surprisingly kindly. 'I will handle whoever is hassling you. I promise you. Now, eat. You too, Lucas.'

To Hannah's surprise, Lucas slips onto a stool at the other end of the counter.

Hannah watches as Alina and Lucas dig heartily into their food. She scoops a tiny piece of potato onto her fork and nibbles at it.

The taste explodes in her mouth. 'Oh my God,' she says. 'This is really good.'

Alina smiles, reaches over and pats Hannah's hand.

The touch is almost maternal, somehow electric, filled with a warmth that Hannah realises is so sadly lacking in her life. When Alina takes her hand away, Hannah feels suddenly cold, and empty.

–

She visits the bathroom before she leaves, staring around at all the marble. She opens the cupboard over the sink, looks at all of Alina's things in there. Her tastes swing wildly, from basic and cheap supermarket moisturisers, to products that Hannah knows cost high in the hundreds.

She's feeling a bit better this time, as she leaves Alina's house. Not like she did Saturday. Then, she was frightened, unsure of whether she was taking a huge risk on not moving forward with Alina.

The food helped, without a doubt. Comfort food, Marie would have called it. A good old-fashioned meal. She knows her mother would love to have a dinner like that. She wonders if she does, sometimes, when Hannah is out at work or schmoozing with gallery-goers for her job.

Maybe when Marie is hanging out with Nita, that's what they do.

Hannah's mood darkens at the thought of Nita, of last night. She should have mentioned it to Alina and Lucas.

'You want a lift, Ms Hannah?' Lucas calls her, poised by the Merc at the end of the driveway.

She turns around, shakes her head. 'No thanks, I'm fine.'

And she is, she tells herself. It's daylight, her mind is not blunted by a prescription drug today. She has eaten, and eaten well, so she's not dizzy, nor light-headed.

. As if to mock her, Hannah's phone vibrates in her purse. She pulls it out, the familiar hammer of her heart dashing away all the good feelings.

The unsaved, unwelcome number flashes on the screen.

She stares at it, her chest tightening uncomfortably, until the caller rings off.

She's about to put the phone back in her bag when a text message comes through.

Hannah reads the invitation, her heart sinking. She can't put this off for ever. She has stalled too long as it is.

> Hyde Park, the round pond, tomorrow, midday?

The punctuation denotes that it's a question. But Hannah knows it's not. There really is no choice.

Reluctantly, she types out an agreeable but short reply.

Her mind and body feel heavier than ever as she starts the long trek home.

13

ALINA, TUESDAY

'She didn't want a lift, she's halfway down the street,' says Lucas, as he comes back through to the kitchen where Alina is still chomping her way through the food he cooked.

She grimaces. 'She probably feels the need to work off your carbs.'

Lucas nods sagely. 'She was walking at a fair old clip.'

Alina sniffs and helps herself to another poached egg. 'How sad.'

'What about this person following her, then?' Lucas claps his hands together, ready to get to work. 'We've not got much to go on.'

Alina thinks deeply. 'What she said, that she's been watched – followed – and she's felt like that for a long time…'

Lucas slaps his hand on the counter. 'There is your answer. If we go where she is, this person might be there too.'

'Her home.' Alina nods with approval. 'We'll go tonight.' She sighs deeply, and Lucas gives her a questioning look.

'I just wish she'd trust me. She knows who it is. But she won't give it up. I don't understand. I've given her all the assurances that she needs.'

'And there's the risk. We rock up and come across some unassuming, innocent person and give them a good hiding.' Lucas frowns.

'We'll go tonight,' Alina repeats. 'We will just observe, and if nothing comes of it, I'll get Hannah to trust me.'

Lucas matches her sigh of only moments earlier. 'It's a long shot.' He curls his lip. 'It's like game playing.'

Alina fixes him with a hard stare. 'You don't need to come, I'll go alone.'

Her tone is unmistakably frosty. His words were a slight on Hannah, and she feels a need to defend the girl that she barely knows but who saved Sofia's life.

'Of course I'll be there,' Lucas backtracks, his voice apologetic. 'You want me to call Julia to stay with Sofia?'

She shakes her head. 'Willem will be back later.' She feels a thrill at this, her irritation gone in an instant. Only four days he's been gone, yet it feels like a month.

Lucas slides the last of the potatoes onto Alina's plate and carries the tray to the sink.

'Later, then.' He ducks his head and moves out of the kitchen.

–

It's a rush that evening, and an effort for Alina to find the motivation to get up and go to Kensington with Lucas.

Willem is home, excited about his trip, happy to see Alina, ecstatic to spend the evening with Sofia. They are in the snug, Alina's favourite room with its oversized armchairs that are big enough for two people; the curtains are drawn, and Willem has his music on. Alina finds his love of techno peculiar. Despite the thumping beat, the scene is one of cosy familiarity, and Alina doesn't want to leave.

She tells him as much.

Willem shrugs and tilts his coffee mug at her. 'So don't go,' he says. 'Go tomorrow night.'

Alina groans. 'And if something were to happen tonight, to her? I'd have failed.' She looks at Sofia, snuggled into her father. Even though his legs are bopping up and down in time to the music, Sofia's eyes are growing heavy.

The desire to stay here, in this room, with her family is fierce.

But what if Hannah had had the same hesitation Friday night? What if she'd not sprinted across the room, thrown herself on top of Sofia, taken those shards of metal into herself?

She looks crossly at Willem. He doesn't understand, not really. She doesn't mean about Sofia, of course. He is eternally grateful for her safety and wellbeing. But his 'reward' would be to offer a handsome sum or a nice trinket to Sofia's saviour, rather than whatever the woman wanted or needed.

'I have to go,' she says. She pushes herself up out of the chair, pulling on her lace-up boots.

'You just be careful,' says Willem. 'You let Lucas do whatever he needs to.' He frowns, rests his head on Sofia's. 'What is the plan here, anyway?'

Alina smiles, her annoyance dissipated. She kisses her husband and daughter.

'Since when did I ever have a plan?' she says, and with a wave, she's gone.

She thinks of Lucas's words earlier, that it's like game playing. She shrugs internally. Alina loves games, normally. The excitement, the anticipation. She admits, though, this game feels different. And to Hannah it's not child's play.

It's serious.

She pauses at the end of her driveway and looks back at the house. Warm and inviting. Her two most important people inside.

She wrenches open the passenger door and climbs in the back seat.

'Let's make this fast,' she tells Lucas. 'I want to spend the evening at home with my family.'

They pick a spot on the other side of the high street, opposite the mews opening.

Alina has been up and down this street many times, but she's never taken any notice of the little lane with the cluster of houses.

'How many homes are down there?' she asks Lucas.

'Half a dozen,' he says. 'Maybe fewer. There's a park at the other end of the cut-through.' He shifts in his seat, angles his head to stare out of the window.

For a while, they sit in comfortable silence, until Lucas's arm shoots over the seat and he slaps at her shoulder. 'Look, this guy, what's he doing?'

Alina sits up, thankful for the tinted windows of the car.

She sees the figure immediately. Lucas referred to him as a guy, but at this distance, in the darkness, Alina isn't so sure.

'Wait,' says Alina, as Lucas's hand goes to the door handle. 'Just… wait.'

Alina stares for a moment longer, waiting to see what this newcomer's next move is.

Slowly, the stooped, relatively small figure shifts along the wall – inch by inch, casting furtive glances around, nothing distinguishable under the hood.

The hood. Hannah mentioned it. A disguise, a very deliberate one. Something that wouldn't normally be worn on what is a hot summer's night. Her heart beats a little quicker as, eventually, the person pauses at the opening of the mews lane.

Alina makes a decision. She touches Lucas on his shoulder. 'Go,' she says, quietly.

He's out of the car in a flash, moving at a normal pace across the road. The street isn't as busy as it is in the daytime, but there are still people around. Lucas, somehow, manages to blend in with them.

When Alina switches her gaze from Lucas, she sees that the strange figure has vanished.

Where did they go? Down the lane, towards Hannah's home?

Lucas is standing at the entrance of the mews lane now, his head moving left and right. If Alina could see his face, she knows she would see a frown creasing his brow.

In the car, she swears quietly.

Whoever it was, they've lost them now. They've gone as quickly as they appeared. Like the whisper of a ghost.

Alina opens her window just a crack. The sound of the city assaults her ears. Music – always there is music, the source unknown and unidentifiable. Chatter, shouts, footsteps.

Alina winds the window back up and sits back in her seat.

Then, a sense of someone approaching. Lucas. Alina climbs through to the front passenger seat.

'Well?'

He starts the car, moves smoothly off the pavement and edges forcefully into the flow of traffic.

'Gone,' Lucas says. 'They were there, then they were gone.'

His hands clench on the steering wheel, and that frown she'd known would be there has deepened into a scowl.

Alina imagines the scenario had Hannah's persecutor not fled. Lucas, his hard words, his even harder fists. He doesn't like to play games, not like her. He's not interested in the whys or the wherefores.

She shivers at the thought of what might have been. For the first time, she wishes Hannah had asked for money.

Swiftly, Lucas changes gears.

Alina looks out of the window and watches as London passes in a blur.

14

HANNAH, WEDNESDAY

Marie is fretting, walking around the courtyard, her phone clasped in her hand.

Hannah finds her there on Wednesday morning, Oliver playing quietly beside her.

'Mum?' Hannah says. 'What's wrong?'

Marie shrugs and puts the phone on the table. 'Nothing,' she says, with a forced attempt at brightness that fails. 'Are you going to work?'

'Yes,' lies Hannah.

Outside, she closes the front door gently behind her, and looks both ways down the lane. Nita's place is empty; her neighbour has still not come home. Hannah doubts she will come back here, to the mews home that she loved.

She walks briskly to Hyde Park. She's more than two hours early for the meeting.

She goes out of her way to enter the park through Bayswater, glancing over her shoulder with every few steps. Once there, she moves around the perimeter. She bypasses the memorial, heading towards the Italian Gardens, keeping near to the trees. She finds a bench that gives her a view of most of the park, while still remaining in the background herself.

She sits down, drinking the vegetable smoothie that she made before leaving the house.

She feels invigorated but gets a sudden, unwelcome longing for the bacon and potatoes of the day before.

There is a heat in her face at the memory. That greasy meal that she had gorged on. Lucas had cooked it in lard. Lard! Hannah hadn't even known what the packet that looked like a block of butter contained. Surreptitiously, she'd read the packaging, and looked it up on the way home.

A semi-solid white fat product, derived from the fatty tissue of a pig.

She'd had to pause, lean against the cool brick of a newsagent and swallow back the vomit that threatened.

Hannah shudders as she drains her smoothie.

It is all the upset that has happened recently. Soon, things will be back to normal.

She can't wait.

She feels no eyes on her, nothing that causes the hairs on the back of her neck to prickle. Still, she scans the park, her eyes moving left to right, and back again.

When the sun is almost overhead, she packs away her travel cup and walks slowly towards the pond. It is surrounded by benches, most of them already taken.

She doesn't want to do this. It's not a case of being brave, or remaining strong, because Hannah is both of those things.

She just simply does not want this meeting.

Her steps falter, and she pauses behind a tree to catch her breath.

At least this time, she is prepared.

She won't ever be able to erase their first meeting from her memory. She puts her hands to her head and closes her eyes.

Ten days ago.

She was early for that meeting.

She was eager.

She was stupid.

It was at the Momotaro, of all places. The invitation had come by email. It said nothing of what the proposed appointment was about, but Hannah knew deep in her bones.

She had been headhunted, and by her favourite gallery, no less! Grantham was on his way out, and she, Hannah, was in the running for the curatorship.

That morning is like a sharp nightmare that she can't shake.

The memory of walking down to the reading room, of passing the posters of Tate's upcoming show. Of the care Hannah had taken with her appearance, even more than usual.

Faltering as she descended those steps deep into the bowels of the building, seeing someone already seated in the fishbowl-style room.

Her prospective employer wore a denim jacket, over brown slacks.

The sudden realisation before she got into the room that this was not a job interview. This was something else entirely.

The basement area of the Momotaro building, always quiet, had stung with a silence so ferocious, it was as though the world's heart had stopped beating.

She should have left then. Turned on her expensive heels and escaped back out into the shit-covered, stinking street. She curses the fact that her curiosity was piqued, that she was so secure in her lovely, safe life that she walked straight into a meeting with the person who then proceeded to turn her world upside down.

She knew, as soon as she looked into those startlingly green eyes. She had seen those eyes before and would never be able to forget them.

Now, her body's reaction is visceral. Hannah allows herself a few more moments to gather herself before stepping away from the tree.

She turns to face the pond. Hannah digs her nails into her palm. She relishes the sting. Needs it to force herself to keep walking.

She thinks of the things this person wants from her, as they have told her in no uncertain terms.

'Hannah!'

She hears her own name. It is like nails down a chalkboard. Hannah suppresses a shudder.

On their last meeting, the stranger had gone in for a hug. Hannah had frozen. She remembers that now: how, back then, she'd still thought there was a chance she was attending a job interview. She had gone in for a handshake.

Now, they both know this is nothing to do with a curatorship, and the hug is forced on Hannah today.

Hannah allows it, as much as she detests it. The arms that wrap around her reek of danger, threatening everything that she has fought so hard to maintain.

'You're early! How have you been? I've missed you.' The accompanying overfamiliarity jars.

The silence that ensues is expectant, wanting the same reply.

Tread carefully.

Hannah smiles. 'It's good to see you again. Life has been… busy, I'm sorry I couldn't arrange anything sooner than this.'

'Busy at work, or… at home?'

The word 'home' sends a sharp spike of pain down Hannah's spine. A warning. She pays attention to it, chooses her words carefully.

'Busy in every aspect. The gallery has me rushed off my feet. Tourist season.' It's a lie. The gallery where Hannah works is rather niche. It doesn't draw tourists. The visitors are regulars. Just another example of why Hannah feels she is wasted there.

But the lie won't be known here, at this meeting. Hannah gestures around the park, using the packed benches and green areas to make her point. 'Things will slow down towards autumn.'

A hand, pale and veiny, reaches for her and Hannah stares, horror thrumming inside her at the skin-to-skin contact. 'I hope I'm not going to have to wait until autumn to see you regularly. And to meet everyone else.'

'Of course not.' It's all Hannah can do not to wrench her hand away.

Instead, she thinks of yesterday, when Alina placed her hand on Hannah's. The warmth she felt, the connection.

The hope.

'And you're going to tell Marie about me?' The eagerness reminds Hannah of a puppy.

She's never been fond of dogs.

'Of course.' Hannah disentangles her hand and rummages in her bag for her sunglasses. She slips them on her face and stands up. 'Soon. I promise.'

'Wait, do you have to go?'

'I need to get back to work. I had a day off yesterday, I've so much to catch up on.'

Her words make no sense, she knows that, seeing as they're both here well before the meeting time. But Hannah can't stay here any longer.

She turns to walk away, a faux glance at her watch as though she's late.

Fingers, greedy and wanting, clutch at Hannah's wrist. It feels like a burn. Like she's been branded.

'I want to see you again. I want to meet Marie, and your son.'

Gone are the chipper, friendly notes.

Hannah stares into those terrible eyes, gets lost in them – those deep, emerald, depths that she knows from before.

She looks away.

The dream job has been relegated to her second wish. The threat here is urgent.

She needs Alina more than ever now.

15

ALINA, WEDNESDAY

'No work today,' Alina announces as she comes down to breakfast on Wednesday morning.

Willem is already there, as is Sofia. They are eating baked German sausages, a huge salad in a bowl between them.

Alina averts her eyes from the meal. All that green. It reminds her of that awful drink Hannah had in her bag. A lettuce smoothie that was supposed to keep the woman nourished and energised.

'Give me those sausages,' she says, dragging a stool to join her husband and daughter. 'And something starchy, none of this.' She circles a hand over the salad and grimaces.

Obediently, Sofia goes to the bread bin and comes back with a stack of fresh, white rolls.

'Perfect.' Alina plants a kiss on her head and gestures for the butter.

'What do you mean, no work, Mama?' asks Sofia.

'It means I want to take a day off. Your father too.' Alina points her fork at him. 'Day off, okay?'

'And no school for me?' Sofia is hopeful.

Alina considers it, but before she can reply, Willem issues a strict, 'No.'

Alina knows he is right. Is grateful for his firm hand when it comes to child-rearing. Poor Sofia, though.

'How about if your papa and I pick you up from school, and we'll go to dinner anywhere you want.'

Sofia cheers, her loss forgotten, happy about the gain.

'What if I have to work?' Willem asks, eyebrows raised towards his wife.

'Tough.' Alina smiles at him. 'I haven't seen you properly in days, and I've missed you. My life has been a chasm of drama lately, and I want a quiet day with my husband.'

They see Sofia off to school, and then spend a lazy morning at home before they haul themselves up and out. Willem heads to the car, towards the always-present Lucas, but Alina calls him back.

'Today, we walk,' she says, waving goodbye to Lucas.

It's nice, she realises, as they make their way down their tree-lined street. Being out in the open air, sunshine blazing, a slight breeze. All this greenery which she normally only sees whizzing past the car windows.

Having no destination, no plan, is rather fabulous too. It is an anomaly. Orderliness keeps Alina's and Willem's hectically busy lives on track. Today, they have nowhere to be, and no set time to be there.

Willem tells her about his Antwerp trip as they stroll. His voice is animated. She enjoys listening to him talk about his work. She is glad he loves it.

She would reciprocate, normally does, but she's been nowhere near her own company this week.

Instead, she finds herself doing what she'd promised she wouldn't today.

Talking about Hannah, and whoever has been following her.

'So, who is it, then, who is after her?' he asks, as he takes her hand and tugs her across the road.

Alina looks up and around. They have walked to Kingston. She can feel a burn in her legs now, but it feels good, and she muses upon maybe walking more often. Be more Hannah, she thinks, and sniggers.

She hasn't answered his question, but he seems to have forgotten about it anyway.

'Come on, midday drinks,' says Willem, spotting a bar up ahead.

They sit on the terrace, both nursing beers; Alina is perusing the menu when Willem brings up the subject again.

'So, you're still no closer to finding out who it is?'

She shakes her head, wishing the conversation would move on. Last night, she failed. And Alina isn't used to failure.

She cheers herself as she thinks of the afternoon ahead, with Willem, and the dinner she has promised Sofia. Then an evening at home, the three of them – a rarity.

They pick up Sofia after school. She throws herself at them, before looking around for the car and Lucas.

'We are tourists today,' says Alina, smiling at Sofia.

They decide to use the Underground. Neither of them travels by Tube. None of them know what stop they are near, and no amount of craning for the tall, red, Underground signs throws up anything. They cool their heels on the street corner while Alina finds the closest one on her phone.

Finally, she navigates them to a stop, and they ride all the way to Leicester Square. Alina is already excited as they arrive outside the jungle-themed restaurant they are dining in tonight.

Willem is less so. He is the peaceful one. A tinkling, background piano is his limit, which is why Alina is always surprised when he gets his stupid techno beats on. This place is an assault on his ears. It makes Alina and Sofia laugh.

The space is windowless, down in the depths of the building. It reminds Alina of the Momotaro room – a sense of no escape – and gradually, as the meal goes on, her mind wanders.

So many dangers. Even coming here, on foot and train, the obstacles and hidden hazards were everywhere. Just like last Friday's gallery showing.

This is what she gets for having Lucas drive her everywhere in her solid, secure car. So that when she comes out into the world, like a normal human, the fear is looming like rain clouds.

No. She inhales sharply. Her somewhat privileged lifestyle is not to blame. Nor are her haunting childhood memories of life under rule and threat. The fault lies with the gallery, and their lack of due process.

She gets crosser as the evening goes on. She doesn't show Sofia her sourness; she smiles and laughs and joins in with the chatter, the exclamations each time the mechanical animals bleat or roar. Willem knows, though. He can see every part of her.

At the end of the meal, she summons Lucas by text, unable to face battling the traffic and the hot night and the steaming trains underground.

Once they are home, Willem puts Sofia to bed and the sound of their normal routine – her child laughing, her husband shrieking – calms her heart a little.

Willem finds her in the study, once Sofia is settled. He pours her a vodka without asking and leaves her to it.

She logs on to her work system, pleased to see that everything is in order; nothing has lapsed in her absence this week.

But her mind keeps wandering back to the accident at the gallery.

Finally, she acknowledges her true concern: that Sofia was the true target. That it wasn't an accident at all and that whoever was responsible had come from her past. Not her own past, but that of her parents, and theirs before them. She recalls the fright she had when she learned the news of the Russian who had been poisoned in London, and another in the not-so-distant Wiltshire. The connection was enough to alarm her.

That had been her fear, a leftover grim reminder of her heritage.

She wanders off in search of Willem, finds him in the basement, cooing over his latest batch of gems.

She folds herself into an oversized armchair and watches him.

Something resembling peace comes, finally.

16

HANNAH, THURSDAY

She goes to work on Thursday, almost one whole week after the incident at the gallery.

Francis, the owner – Hannah's boss – has been covering for her and seems relieved she's back.

'All better?' Francis asks.

Hannah blinks at her. She wasn't *ill*. She'd been injured.

'Getting there,' replies Hannah. And then, just in case Francis is genuinely in the dark about what happened, she adds, 'I have to take a lunch break today; I need my stitches checking.'

Francis is already moving on. 'You're entitled to lunch, Hannah. *Every* day, not just the days you have plans.'

Hannah watches her go, clicking down the empty gallery hallway.

Is it possible that gallery owners don't talk to each other, and Francis has no idea of the Momotaro's night of terror? She wonders if it has been hushed up.

Maybe it's better if it has been swept under the carpet. Hannah doesn't need her employer knowing her business. Alina knows what happened. And she's the one who matters.

Hannah feels relaxed as she does her daily walk-through of the rooms. It soothes her, being here, amongst the art. Not as much as being at the Momotaro Gallery, of course. It's a whole different ball game over there.

She slides into a daydream, of going to work every day at *that* gallery. The ideas she has are so often quashed here. She imagines how she could elevate the Momotaro to make it even greater than it already is.

The cut on her arm starts to itch.

Hannah does her best to clear her mind of her strife and carries on with her morning's work.

She is glad to get outside at lunchtime. She lied to Francis; she's not going to get her stitches checked. She left it far too late; they are embedded now. To have them removed and redone by a doctor she trusts and pays for would only serve to leave an even uglier scar on her otherwise unblemished skin.

She takes her smoothie out of her cooler bag and carries it to the nearby public gardens.

Her persecutor will not bother her today. They have gone home, to Ireland, for a short visit. Hannah received a text yesterday, announcing their plans to return to London at the weekend, along with the address of the hovel they're staying in.

Hannah has a couple of days' grace. The slight optimism soon fades. Two days is nothing. It will pass in a flash. They'll be back, determined, anxious to *move things along*.

She thinks of those eyes and knows she can't stand to have to look into them ever again. Memories of the past reflected in them, a reminder not so much of *what* Hannah did, but *who* she did it for.

She attempts to gear herself up, to make a plan. She has to contact Alina and make her request. Alina won't look in depth into the details of Hannah's request. She has as good as told Hannah that it isn't necessary. That the terms of their agreement are simple. Hannah saved Sofia's life. Therefore, Alina owes her. She doesn't need to know the ins and outs or the intricate details of Hannah's reasons.

It is a contract, pure and simple.

No questions asked.

Hannah drains her smoothie and goes to put her empty cup on the bench beside her.

Her hand freezes, in mid-air. She is made of glass. One flick and she will shatter.

Her breathing has changed, quick and fast, panting breaths.

Over there, beyond the trees. That hooded figure again. In the distance, so far that Hannah has to squint, *but still here*.

They'd said they were going home.

But they're *still here*.

It must be the same person. After all, who else would be so absorbed with Hannah's daily life?

Hannah is frozen.

Fight or flight.

The latter wins.

Hannah's travel cup topples to the grass. She leaves it, walks smartly away in the opposite direction, down the path to the exit.

At the main road she doesn't wait for the lights to change in her favour. She doesn't even break her stride, just walks out into the four-lane road. Car horns blare at her, a chorus of mechanical fury. In amongst the cacophony, she thinks she hears her own name being called.

She runs then, fleeing from the demon that is on her tail, nipping so close at her, like wolves and their prey.

She's going in the opposite direction to the Harman Gallery, but she doesn't want to lead them to her place of work.

She makes an anguished sound. Who is she kidding? They know where she works, where she lives, where she walks and takes her lunch.

She is sweating, but oh so cold.

There is one place they surely don't know about. That awful, soft-play area where Marie has only recently started taking Oliver on Thursdays. She used to go with Nita, who, as far as Hannah knows, has not returned to the mews. Oliver loves it, though, and Hannah knows that Marie would never let him be disappointed by not taking him.

She ducks down the side streets, realising how close the play place is to her work. She could have come here anyway, she thinks, guiltily, instead of heading to the gardens. She could have spent her lunch hour with the most precious person in her life. If she had, she wouldn't have had this episode today, this person standing there, watching her, *haunting* her.

Lying to her about going home.

Stalking her.

It is the same person. It's got to be.

She can think of nobody else that she may have pissed off, or annoyed. Most people – work colleagues, casual acquaintances – tend to give Hannah a wide berth.

She tells herself that their coolness is because she's risen high in the ranks of her job, and she's currently in a position that garners envy from those on the rungs of the ladder below her. But she knows that's probably not true. Francis, her boss, is just as coolly professional as Hannah, but she's popular, surrounded by friends and ass-kissers.

No. People just tend not to like Hannah. And that doesn't matter to her. The only family she needs in her life is already in it.

She reaches the soft-play building. She can hear the racket from outside on the pavement. She goes inside, pays the extortionate fee to enter a place she already hates.

She sees them immediately – her mother, her son – seated at a plastic table, both with hamburgers and chips in front of them. Oliver is red and sweaty, his dark hair plastered to his forehead. Hannah scans the play area, the maze of inflatables; the heavy scent of rubber and shoeless feet turns the smoothie over in her stomach.

She moves between the tables and chairs, carefully, ensuring not one part of herself touches anything or anyone.

'Mum,' she says, when she reaches them.

He stares up at her, her boy. Shocked to see her in a place like this.

'Hannah!' Marie, too, looks surprised to see her daughter, as she well might. 'What are you doing here?'

Hannah can see Marie is comfortable here, in amongst the masses of ordinary mothers, the grandparents who relish time spent with their grandchildren.

Marie's face drops. 'Is… Is everything okay?'

Hannah laughs, an attempt to brush off the shock of moments ago and to dispel Marie's worries.

Marie is a worrier.

Marie is a mother.

They go hand in hand, the two things.

'I realised this place isn't far from work,' she says, picking up a napkin, brushing it over the seat and sitting down. 'I wanted to see you.'

'Did you want something to eat?' Marie asks, cautiously.

Hannah manages to hide her feelings on the grey burger and soggy chips that Marie and Oliver have in front of them. 'No, thanks.'

'Hannah.' A voice behind her, the scrape of a chair, another tray of disgusting food being placed on the table.

Hannah turns, blinking in astonishment at the sight of Nita, Bobby clinging to her legs.

'Nita!' Hannah stands, unsure of what else to say.

She studies Nita's face. There are no outward signs of the attack on her in her home the other night.

Hannah peers closer.

Yes, there are. Nita is always groomed and looking immaculate. Today, her hair is limp, brushed to one side, hiding – Hannah suspects – a bruise. Her skin is sallow, her face make-up free. Not the Nita she is familiar with, at all.

Hannah reaches out a hand, pretending not to notice when Nita openly flinches. 'How are you?' she asks.

Nita's eyes fill with tears. She sits down and glances at Marie. Hannah looks at her mother, too. Marie has busied herself with Oliver, wiping at his hands with a packet of wipes she has produced.

Nita stands up and reaches for Bobby. She picks him up, wincing as she hefts him onto her hip. 'I'm so sorry, we have to go.'

She barges her way through the maze of chairs, head down, ignoring Bobby's sudden wails at his fun play date being cut short.

Hannah glances at her mother, expecting her to call after her neighbour. But Marie's head is down, studying her plate of uneaten food.

The other woman doesn't look back.

'What was that about?' Hannah turns back to Marie.

Marie meets her eye, reluctantly, and shrugs.

Hannah once again feels ice cut through her soul.

There is something in Marie's look, something unfathomable.

Something like disappointment.

17

ALINA, SATURDAY

Alina is outside, talking to Lucas, when she spots Hannah walking up the driveway.

Alina is strangely thrilled to see her again. 'Hannah! How are you?'

She can't understand why she's so pleased to see the other woman again. Apart from their mutual love of art, they have nothing in common. Hannah seems a little uptight, not at all the kind of person Alina would normally choose to hang out with.

'I'm good, thanks.' Hannah's reply is a low whisper.

Alina notices that Hannah is sneaking looks at Lucas as they walk up to the house.

She wonders if Hannah is here to ask if he found her stalker. Or does she find it hard to wrap her head around the familiarity and friendship that the employer and employee share?

'Did you… Did you find out anything?' Hannah finally appears to get the nerve to ask as they reach Alina's front door.

'Not yet.' Alina doesn't tell her about the shadowy figure hanging around the mews entrance. Doesn't want to admit that they got away.

'Oh.' Hannah's eyes drop to the ground, disappointment casting a very obvious shadow over her.

Alina narrows her eyes. She wants to tell Hannah that if she explains who her stalker is, it'll make it a lot easier for Alina to deal with it. But today, Hannah seems almost fragile, and Alina changes tactics.

'You want a drink?' she asks, as she leads Hannah to the kitchen.

'No, thanks.' Hannah clears her throat. 'I saw them again on Thursday. It was near to my work. I was on my lunch.'

Alina tilts her head. She wants to ask Hannah why she didn't approach him or her. After all, it was broad daylight, not like the time she was alone in the park. She doesn't say that, though. She is thinking of last Friday night, when all those knives fell. Better than anyone, she knows the freeze that denies coherent thought. 'You know you can trust me, right?'

Hannah smiles and nods but isn't forthcoming with any further information.

Alina sighs. 'I will deal with it, Hannah. I *can* deal with them, I'll tell them my name, my husband's name. It usually works.' Alina frowns, that abject sense of failure upon her again. Wondering why she can't get through to this girl.

People are malleable, mouldable. Alina normally emanates a personality that invites people to trust her, to confide in her.

But Hannah isn't so pliable.

'Come on. I'm making myself a drink; you might as well join me.'

She turns to usher Hannah through the door, but the look on the other woman's face stops her in her tracks.

'What's wrong?' she says.

'You can't tell them your name. Nor your husband's name. It's… It would lead to all sorts of problems.' Hannah's face is red, her chest is blotchy.

Alina pats Hannah's arm, careful to stay away from the bandage which is on full display today. Alina's eyes linger on it, guiltily.

Hannah put herself in a life-threatening position to save Sofia, and here is Alina, so blasé and cool.

'I'm sorry,' she says, seriously. 'Please, come inside.'

She leads Hannah to the kitchen while she selects some pods for the coffee machine. Sweet and sickly caramel for herself; no-frills Americano for her guest.

Hannah sits at the breakfast bar, ramrod straight, stiff, staring outside at the cloudless sky.

Alina attempts to put her at ease. 'You live alone in Kensington, with your son?'

'And my mother,' Hannah replies. She drops her gaze. 'I don't feel safe there. I always used to, but not any longer.'

'You have no man in your life?' Alina cranks the machine and Hannah jumps as it leaps noisily into life. 'Or… a girlfriend, maybe?'

Hannah narrows her eyes. 'Why do you ask that?'

'Relax, Hannah, I'm just making conversation.' Alina removes the cup of coffee and slides it across to Hannah. 'What about your job, how's that going?'

Hannah grows quiet. 'I love my work. The gallery is my calm space, even when it's hectic.' She pulls a face. 'Not that it is ever hectic. It's… quiet and steady, but I want to move up in the world. I want to live the dream. *My* dream. And…' Here Hannah trails off. She looks down, a slight blush on her face, as though letting all her desires slip has embarrassed her.

'And?' Alina prompts her.

'I want it all for my mother. I want to give her the life she deserves to live. One of comfort, a life where she wants for nothing. It's my ultimate goal.'

Alina ponders upon it. She can understand that, somewhat. But in most cases, certainly in Alina and Willem's view, they're building their successes for their child, not their parents.

Everyone is different, though, she tells herself. Willem's and Alina's parents already have their own money, plenty of it. Perhaps Hannah's mother doesn't. She finds it strange, though, that Hannah didn't include her son's stable future in her ambition.

'And you need to move up the career ladder to achieve your goal.' Alina gives Hannah a wink. 'At the Momotaro.'

Hannah nods, very serious now. 'It's what I want, almost more than anything.'

'Almost?'

'I want to be able to walk around the city, or be in my home, without worrying about who is watching me.'

Alina sips at her coffee and takes aim. 'But you won't tell me about this person.' It's not a question, but rather a statement. Alina softens her voice. 'I know you know their identity.'

Two high spots of colour stain Hannah's cheeks. She doesn't answer immediately.

Alina sighs as the silence stretches on.

She's draining the dregs of her coffee, wondering where to go from here, and why this is so hard, and why Hannah is so private, when Hannah speaks again.

'You said… You said no questions asked,' says Hannah, quietly.

Alina is faintly surprised at the pushback. 'And that was true. I just need to know some bare details so I can actually deal with it. And…' She takes a deep breath, deciding to be frank with Hannah. If she's straight with her, if she can make Hannah see that it's something along the lines of a friendship deal she is offering her, rather than an owed favour, maybe it will draw her out of the steely armour shell she wears. 'Look, I'm just… curious. I like to know the facts.'

'But all of that doesn't matter,' argues Hannah.

Hannah's sudden attitude needles at Alina. Thoughts of friendship and gossip are gone. This game has dragged on long enough and Alina is beginning to lose interest in what she'd started to think of as her pet project.

Alina yawns, openly, rudely. 'I'm not going to lie, Hannah. I'm kind of bored, now. Do you know this person's name? Where they live, where I can find them? I'll sort it, if you want me to. If you won't give anything up, then we should forget the whole thing and get back to our normal lives.'

At Alina's tone, Hannah stands up. 'I… I changed my mind.'

Alina rolls her eyes. 'For heaven's sake, just tell me, I'll sort it out. Or not. Whatever.' She sounds ornery now. That spoiled streak coming out in full force.

Hannah shakes her head. 'Please, forget it. All of it. I shouldn't have asked. No hard feelings, Alina. We should leave it here.'

With that, Hannah picks up her bag and leaves the house, closing the door gently behind her.

Alina is shocked by Hannah's sudden departure.

She has never reneged on a promise before. She's never failed, no matter what she set out to do.

Not until now.

She picks up her coffee. Changes her mind, gets a new cup and pours a healthy slug of vodka. She slumps in the armchair by the garden doors.

Hannah was right. Alina had granted her a wish with no conditions attached. A no-questions-asked basis. And what had Alina done? She'd asked questions.

She can't help herself. She finds it intriguing, other people and their stories. She loves the scandal, enjoys the drama. But what is mere gossip to Alina is a very real problem for Hannah.

She sighs. She feels bad now. She wishes her family was here to distract her.

Willem is out. He has taken Sofia out before escorting her to her Italian lesson later. The child's idea, to become multilingual. So far, she speaks Dutch and Russian, obviously, and she is also fluent in Spanish. Now she's onto Italian.

It makes Alina's head spin. She doesn't know why Sofia is so keen on these lessons.

She comforts herself that with her family's wealth, Sofia could easily do nothing, have no interests; after all, she could go through life having everything handed to her on a silver platter. The girl has get-up-and-go, and that counts for a lot in Alina's eyes.

Suddenly, she misses her daughter very much. An unexpected pang in her chest, as though Sofia has been gone for days instead of only hours.

Restlessly, she jumps up and grabs her mobile phone. She can't sit here and dwell. Instead, she will act.

She scrolls through her contacts, finds the one she's looking for and presses dial.

It almost rings out before it is answered by a woman with a harried, harassed voice. 'Yes?' The upper-class London tone is clipped and sharp.

'Hi,' says Alina. 'Bad time?'

'Ugh, always.' A pause, and then, 'Unless you're inviting me to lunch, in which case, it's a very good time.'

Alina laughs. 'The Members Club, half an hour?'

'See you there.'

Alina only dresses carefully when she wants to. Today, she wants to. She wants to dine with an old friend and get some much-needed inconsequential gossip – and, she realises with delight, she'll be on the right side of town to pick Sofia up from her language lesson in a few hours.

She hums to herself, a Russian tune, breaking into song as she pulls on a pair of tailored black pants and a scarlet bolero jacket with a black lace trim.

She goes in search of Lucas. Finds him with Julia in the dining room. She's got her laptop out, and Alina sees her own company's logo on the spreadsheets.

She feels a spike of guilt. Julia has carried the company this week. Alina can't remember having stayed away from the office for this long before.

'All good?' she asks.

Julia gives her a thumbs up. 'Like clockwork,' she confirms.

Alina picks up the car keys and jangles them at Lucas. She gives Julia a kiss on her cheek as she sweeps past her.

'Things will be back to normal, very soon,' she promises. 'And you'll get a week off – paid, of course.'

Julia catches her hand as Alina moves away. 'You know that's not necessary. Your work is our work.' She tilts her head and gives Alina a meaningful look. 'Whatever work it is.'

Alina pats Julia's cheek. 'Thank you, friend,' she says, softly.

'Where to?' Lucas asks as he starts up the car.

'Kensington.'

He mock-groans. 'Again?'

Alina shoves him. 'The Members Club.' She laughs.

He grins back at her as he pulls onto the street. 'Good,' he says. 'Things *are* getting back to normal.'

She looks out of the window and nods as if to confirm it to herself. 'Yes, they are.'

She wonders if it is a lie.

–

Francis Dowd is already seated at the rear of the room when Lucas drops Alina off.

Alina sashays over to her, does the obligatory air-kiss and envelops Francis in a hug.

'How's the gallery?' she asks, as she shrugs her bolero off and sits down.

'Stressful. A new showpiece is being organised.' Francis tilts her head. A waiter is miraculously by her side immediately. 'We'll have two G&Ts, no ice, doubles.'

'And a tequila, each,' adds Alina.

Francis rolls her eyes.

'Shut up. You need it. Listen, Francis, tell me about one of your staff members, Hannah Barker.'

Francis sits back in her chair and crosses her legs. 'Do you know what I like about you, Alina? There's none of this "let's exchange pleasantries" bullshit. You just launch right in, don't you?'

Their drinks arrive. Alina raises her gin in a toast. 'Life's too short for bullshit, Francis.'

Francis leans over the bar behind her, picks up a straw and puts it in her gin. She sucks at it, noisily, until the glass is drained.

'One more,' she calls out to nobody in particular, but the server is at her side with a fresh drink practically before Francis has finished vocalising her request.

'Now, then.' Francis lifts one perfectly manicured eyebrow. 'Why would you be asking about my Miss Barker?'

Alina stirs her drink and contemplates Francis's question. Why is she asking about Hannah? Why does she have this irrepressible need to *know*? Why isn't she just sorting out Hannah's problems, like she promised?

Like she *owes* her.

She admits to herself that she finds Hannah fascinating. And it's only natural to want to know more about someone who has garnered her interest.

Isn't it?

'Her path has crossed mine, recently. Not in a professional capacity, or a working environment,' she hastens to add. 'I know she works at your gallery, and I'm interested as to how you view her. You obviously know her a lot better than me – what do you think of her?'

Francis sniffs. 'Not much, to be honest.'

Alina perks up. 'Really? Why?'

'There's just something… a bit off about her. She isn't popular with her colleagues.' Francis looks thoughtful. 'I can't explain it. She's brilliant at her work: she's got a real eye for detail, her knowledge of every area of our world is second to none, which is why I keep her on. If she were anyone else, I'd have worried about her being poached by another gallery by now.' Francis reaches across the table and pokes at Alina's hand. 'Come on, spill the gossip.

What on earth could you and my Hannah have to do with each other?'

'She saved my daughter's life,' replies Alina, honestly. 'I've seen her a few times since, and I wanted to know a little more about the kind of person who would risk their own life for someone else's.'

Francis's mouth is a circle of shock. '*Really?*' she asks. 'Hannah? Are you sure?'

Alina nods. 'Yep.'

'How?' she asks. 'And where? What even happened?'

Alina lowers her voice conspiratorially. 'Did you hear about what happened last weekend, at the Momotaro?'

'Tate's collapsing statue?' Francis puts her hand to her face. 'I heard something happened… I asked Grantham, and he said it wasn't as big a deal as some people were making it out to be.'

'He said *what*?' Alina thumps her fist on the table. The cutlery jumps; the gin slops over the edge of Alina's glass. 'That horrible cretin of a man,' she hisses.

Francis shushes her, glancing around at the other diners. 'Tell me what happened, then. I knew he was covering something up. You're right, Alina, he is an idiot, that man.'

Alina takes several gulps of her drink to calm herself.

When she is finally breathing normally, she tells Francis everything that happened that night at the Momotaro. 'The whole thing collapsed; the whole, horrible, ten-foot-tall thing came crashing down. All that metal raining upon my girl, like guillotines!' Alina feels faint; it's the first time she's told someone since she relayed the events to Willem. She signals to the waiter for a refill. 'A double, again,' she says, weakly.

'And Hannah helped?' Francis narrows her eyes. 'I mean… What, like, in a first-aider kind of way?'

'No! She dived in there, into the crossfire! She protected Sofia. She got hurt herself,' exclaims Alina.

Francis is agog. 'Are you sure you got the right name?'

'Yes, for Christ's sake, of course I am!'

'Do you know, I vaguely remember her saying something the other day about having her stitches checked or removed or… I don't know.' Francis lets out a slightly drunken giggle. 'I didn't listen, I admit it.'

Alina feels an ache in her chest. She imagines someone having this attitude towards Sofia, twenty years from now, working in a place where she is sneered at or ignored. Used purely for her knowledge in her chosen industry. A cog in a machine.

The pain is replaced by a thin streak of fury. 'You don't care?' she asks Francis. 'I'm not exaggerating – it really could have been a deadly accident.'

Francis must hear the edge in Alina's voice. She sits up, reaches across the table for her friend's hand. Alina pulls away, out of her reach.

'Of course, I care,' Francis protests. 'Sofia's a doll, and I'm a mother – I understand how frightening that must have been for you.'

Alina shakes her head. 'But what about Hannah?' she presses. 'Your employee. She was hurt, badly.'

Francis gives Alina a small shrug. 'But she's fine, she's been at work. I've seen her with my own eyes.'

Alina shakes her head. Francis doesn't get it.

18

HANNAH, SATURDAY

Alina is all talk and no action, Hannah decides as she walks home.

Alina has let her down.

She's spikey with annoyance, as well as strangely hurt. And she is irritated enough to actually deal with this herself.

She pulls her phone out and thinks about the interloper who so desperately wants to insert themselves into Hannah's carefully constructed life. The annoyance turns inwards, on Hannah herself. Why did she even let it get as far as it did? Why did Hannah try to be nice? Kind? After all, she never has before.

Because she thought she was being offered a bloody job, that's why. And not just any role, but her dream job. For Christ's sake.

She scrolls through her contacts and hits the number before suddenly losing her nerve.

Hannah cuts the call before it can even ring the other end.

She glances over her shoulder as she cuts through the cemetery and skirts around the golfing meadow. There are plenty of pedestrians on this warm, sunny day. They move in flocks, zigzagging across the road, swarming the pathways, heading towards her, around her, away from her.

She scans as many figures as she can, feeling her breathing quicken with the terrible anticipation of suddenly spotting someone out of place.

Internally, she feels herself screaming.

She can't live like this.

She ups her pace, feeling her calves stinging. She relishes it, pushes harder.

It works. By the time she has covered three quarters of her route, she is drenched in sweat, gasping for air.

She buys a bottle of water from a street vendor and sits in the shade of a tree in front of a private girls' school.

Her mind wanders back to Alina. She wonders whether she went to a school like this, all blazers and knee-high socks. Elocution and pressure to succeed, to win.

She thinks of her strange clothes, her unique style, and decides that if Alina was institutionalised in a private school, then she's kicking back against it now.

Not that there are any prim and proper schoolgirls around today. She squints at the school: it is open, even though it's a Saturday. The people going in are dressed in jeans and dungarees, skirts and shorts, their own chosen styles on show, just for the weekend. She lets her gaze wander to the other people milling about. Some are heading inside; some are just loitering.

None of them stand out. Not in this city.

She drains her water and pushes herself to standing, keeping her eyes on the stream of people, eager to spend their weekend learning, as they pile up the steps.

The walk here has done her good. The march has fired her up. She is ready.

She pulls her phone out again, hits redial on the previous number.

It rings, just once, before it is answered.

'Hannah!' The voice is overjoyed, and Hannah realises that this is the first time she has initiated contact.

'You just caught me; I'm heading out to the airport in a minute. I'll be back in London before you know it.'

'Don't,' says Hannah.

A moment's pause. 'What… What do you mean?' The tone changes, from merry to worry. 'Is everything okay? Is Marie all right? Is it Oliver?'

You have no right to ask about my mother!

Hannah bites her lip to stop the fury spilling over into a scream.

She needs to be cold and hard and clear.

She needs to be Hannah, how she used to be, how she *always* has been.

'Don't come back to London. There's nothing for you here. I can't see you anymore.' Her tone has a bite to it, the way she intended, but she should have used stronger words.

She takes a deep breath. And just in case she hasn't made herself clear enough, she concludes, 'I don't want to see you again.' Hannah snatches the phone away from her ear and hangs up.

She leans over, hands on knees. The constant fear that has coiled around her insides is dissipating. She can practically feel herself growing calmer.

She did it. And why-oh-why, she wonders, didn't she say those words straight away at the first meeting in the Momotaro Gallery? It doesn't matter. She's done it now. It is over.

Hannah sits back down, taking pleasure in the shade now. God, she feels light. Like she's walking on air. Who needs Alina, the supposed powerhouse? Hannah's got this, all by herself.

She leans her head back against the tree trunk, watching as a new group of people wind their way up the path to the entrance of the stately school.

A youngster catches her eye, the only child she's seen so far. The flip of a ponytail, ankle boots clopping along, a strange little skirt which is almost a tutu.

Hannah emits a snort of laughter.

She was wrong earlier, when she thought that nobody stands out here. This one certainly does.

She knows the girl. She recognises the girl's style, straight from her mother's wardrobe.

Sofia Arpels.

She seems to have suffered no ill effects from last Friday's drama at the Momotaro.

Hannah fingers the stitches on her upper arm. They are itching now, new red skin growing around the ugly threads.

A male voice calls out Sofia's name. The little girl stops. Hannah watches as a man jogs towards Sofia.

He is tall, well-dressed in a navy suit. Blond, foppish hair, longer than average for a man. It suits him.

So, this is him: Willem Arpels.

He takes out his wallet from his inside jacket pocket and plucks a note from it, hands it to his daughter. He puts a hand on her shoulder, though she's like a horse waiting to get out of the starting gate. He angles his camera at her, takes a photo.

He goes into a crouch and pulls her close. Hannah watches as her arms go around his neck.

She allows the embrace for a long moment, before pulling away and trotting up the stairs to the school.

'I'll pick you up at four!' he yells.

She replies with a wave. Then, she is gone.

Hannah stands to leave too. After all, her work is done. She can go home now.

A chirp and accompanying vibration draw Hannah's attention to her phone, still in her hand.

A text message.

> It doesn't matter if you don't want to see me. I respect your choice. But remember, Hannah, this isn't all about you. There are other people in this equation.

Hannah feels the blood drain from her face.

Her intuition was correct, even though she'd pushed the feeling aside.

It's not over.

Not yet.

19

ALINA, SATURDAY

'Stay, have another drink,' says Francis. 'I didn't mean to upset you, Alina.'

Reluctantly, Alina beckons the waiter.

She's cross that Francis thinks she's upset her. Alina doesn't get upset, or emotional. She doesn't deal in feelings.

Well, she didn't *use to*.

What is it that has made her soft like cotton wool? Sofia's near miss? Or the fact that a young woman is being stalked, threatened, and nobody seems to really care about her?

'Order something to eat,' insists Francis.

Alina flips half-heartedly through the menu, finally deciding on an omelette.

'You really like her?' Francis asks, curiously, once they've made their lunch choices.

Alina contemplates her friend's question. It's not that she *really likes* Hannah at all. In fact, in another world, in another time, if they hadn't met under extraordinary circumstances, she wouldn't be interested in Hannah one little bit. The woman sometimes irritates her, with her smoothie culture and strict dietary needs, and exercise, and tailored suits and heels. On the other hand,

149

she sees someone who seems to be exceptional at her chosen career, while appearing to be lost, floundering, but desperately pretending that she's not.

The thought strikes Alina then. Hannah doesn't seem to have anyone apart from her mother and her son. In a world where Alina is surrounded by people who love her, who she could call on day or night, it's a sobering thought.

Alina wants to make Hannah's life better. And she can – she promised to – but so far, she hasn't.

Alina decides to ignore Francis's question.

Their food arrives. Alina picks at it, sullen and unused to the new atmosphere. She orders more drinks. They dine in an uncomfortable silence.

She is about to make her excuses and leave when her phone rings.

She glances at the screen. Willem.

She swipes to answer, a smile in her voice as she greets him.

'Willem!'

'Is Sofia with you?'

Four words that are a knife in Alina's heart.

'What?' The word is barely audible.

'Did you pick Sofia up?' Willem's voice is the opposite to hers. His tone is low, urgent, rough.

'No!' Alina stands up. Her chair scrapes horribly, teetering with the force of her movement.

'I'm at the language school and they say someone picked her up.' Willem's voice is higher than she's ever heard it.

'Who picked her up?' Alina grips the edge of the table. '*Who?*'

'Alina?' Francis is standing too, but Alina doesn't even see her.

'Come down here.' Willem sounds like he's speaking through gritted teeth.

Alina hangs up and is almost at the door when Merle, the owner, stops her.

'Trouble?' he asks.

Merle is a friend. Alina glances back at the table she was sitting at. Francis is still standing, mouth open.

'I have to go. Put it on my tab. Sorry, Merle.'

Lucas is out of the car, on the pavement, his own phone clamped to his ear. He's talking to Willem. She can see the despair on Lucas's face from here.

He spots her coming, opens the passenger-side door and runs back around to the driver's side.

He is pulling away from the kerb before she has fully closed her door.

'What do you know?' she asks.

Her teeth are chattering, she realises belatedly, and she's ice-cold.

'Will went to pick her up, and they said she'd been collected already.' His jaw is set.

Alina clutches the sides of the seat as he abruptly changes gear.

'They've got protocols for that.' She manages to get the words out, but only just. 'Procedures for who is allowed to collect a child.'

'For school, they do. This isn't school. They don't have teachers there on the weekend, it doesn't count.'

Alina brings her hand up and smashes it down on the centre console.

The pain jars through her hand, up her arm.

She unlocks the screen on her phone, stares at it. She itches to call Willem, to have him on the other end of the phone until she can be by his side. But she can't. He will be on the phone, calling the police. He needs to keep his line free.

'She's a kid, though,' she says. 'What sort of adult lets a kid go off on their own or...' Alina puts her hand to her mouth, certain that she's going to vomit. 'Or with someone else.'

She grabs Lucas's arm. The car swerves, the front wheel bumping against the pavement.

'Shit,' Lucas swears.

'Willem said someone picked her up!'

'Yes.' Lucas stares forward, his expression stony.

'What do you think has happened?' Alina's mind kicks into overdrive. 'Who would have taken her? Jesus, is this to do with Sofia's accident? Is someone targeting her?' Her thoughts, panicked and fearful, match her tone: high, spiralling, almost a scream.

What if it wasn't an accident? What if it is Sofia – and, by extension, Willem and Alina – who someone wants to hurt?

She is light-headed, dizzy with the too many thoughts that swirl around her head.

Alina bites the skin around her nails and looks out of the window.

Lucas is battling traffic, trying to cut across the street outside the girls' school. Alina makes a growl of frustration. She was already in the vicinity of Sofia's language school. She could have run there faster than this.

She opens the door just as Lucas forces the car into an opening. He brakes sharply.

Alina tumbles out of the car and dashes across the road without looking.

She can see Willem, pacing up and down by the entrance to the school. A cluster of people are nearby.

She hadn't admitted it on the drive, but she'd prayed hard that when she came here, to this spot, Sofia would be there. She would look chastised, in the funny little tutu she'd chosen to wear today. It had been a misunderstanding. She'd waited by the wrong door. Willem had panicked. But all was good.

But all the people milling around are adults, their faces drawn with anxiety.

Sofia isn't there.

Alina wants to cry and scream.

She reaches Willem, shoving a woman hovering at his side out of the way.

She has no words. She doesn't speak.

He puts his arm around her and slips his phone into his pocket.

'Nobody saw her leave,' he says.

Alina wrenches free from him and whirls around. 'Who was taking the class?' she demands of the onlookers.

A woman, the same one she shoved, takes a deep breath.

Alina studies her. This cool blonde, with her skinny jeans and heels.

Alina brings her arm back and slaps the blonde as hard as she can.

The woman lets out a cry and puts her hand to her cheek.

'You let her leave?' Alina spits. 'She's a little girl, and you just let her leave on her own?'

The woman tries and fails to compose herself. 'Someone collected Sofia,' she explains, her voice wavering with tears that now fall freely down her face.

'Who was it?' Alina asks.

The woman's face goes blank. Alina grabs her shoulders and shakes her. Hard.

'A man!' The teacher gasps. 'A man, I'm sorry, that's all I can remember.'

Alina pushes the woman away. 'That's not all you saw. Describe him: white, Black? Tall, old?'

'W-w-white. Twenties, m-maybe,' the teacher stutters.

'Which way did they go?'

The woman sags again. 'I don't know,' she whispers.

Alina's hand curls into a fist. She will smash this woman in her cool, contoured, stupid face. Over and over again.

A hand closes around hers. She looks down at it. Willem.

'Come now,' he says. 'We'll start the search. Leave her for later.'

Alina nods and allows herself to be dragged away.

They congregate at the bottom of the steps. 'Did you call the police?' she asks.

Her husband gestures to his phone, still clamped to his ear. 'I'm calling them now.'

She looks around at the faces of the people that Willem has gathered. Her father's friend, Jimmy, one of the only links to her previous life. Julia, half a dozen of Willem's Dutch biker friends. Merle has arrived, Francis trailing him.

Their friends.

Aren't they?

She forcibly lowers Willem's hand that holds his phone. 'We'll look first, all of us,' she says.

He hesitates for just a moment before hanging up the call.

Willem was raised differently to Alina. In her youth, there would be no telephone call to 999. She knows that today, when they find her daughter, and the man who has taken her, they will deal with the perpetrator in her way.

But what if you don't find her? The voice is a demon in her ear.

Alina whimpers, but Willem is issuing instructions and does not notice.

'Split up, in pairs.' Willem has his phone out again, but he's not calling the authorities. He is sending all those gathered a photo of Sofia.

Alina looks over his shoulder. It is a photo she hasn't seen before. She scans the outfit that her daughter is wearing. He took the picture today, on these very steps that are behind her now.

She takes the phone from him when he's finished sharing the image and stares at her girl.

The tutu, a high ponytail, her ankle boots that are too small for her but which Sofia refuses to part with. That face, so happy. Even though it's a still shot, Alina can tell Sofia is impatient, eager to get on with the learning that she loves so.

'Alina, you're with Lucas.' Willem's voice – strict, authoritative, so unlike his usual tone – jerks her back to the here and now.

'Okay.' She nods, checks the time.

Almost five o'clock. Saturday rush hour is in full force. People heading home after a day of shopping or working, or on their way out to an early pre-show dinner perhaps. The streets are utterly swarming.

She quickly shares Willem's photo to her own phone and hands his back. He catches her hand and stares into her eyes. 'If there's no sign, we're calling the police.'

Alina wrenches her hand away and marches into the throng of people on the pavement, shoving her phone in their faces.

'Have you seen this girl?'

They are jolted by her aggressive stance, these people who just want to get home or get their evening started. They move around her, an exaggerated sidestep, as if her fury is catching.

She grabs at a man's arm, puts her phone up to his face. 'Have you seen this girl?' she snaps.

Her voice is on the verge of a scream. He looks startled, but glances at the screen. 'No, sorry,' he says, before hastily going on his way.

Alina breaks into a run but is caught by Lucas.

'This way,' he mutters. 'The bikers are checking east, we're going west. All the side streets, parks, doorways.' He jerks her arm, roughly. '*Alina*, listen to me.'

'Yes,' she says. 'Yes, west. Come on, then.'

It's the decent end of the suburb. Alina can't help but feel that if a man has taken Sofia, he would not bring her in this direction. He would go elsewhere, to the neighbourhoods that are less desirable. The thought brings a scalding heat in her chest. She swallows frantically against the vomit that threatens.

She is not a hysterical woman. She never has been. Panic gets nobody anywhere.

But this is her very worst nightmare come to life. Again, only eight days after she'd faced the previous ordeal.

She follows Lucas, tries to get her head in the game. She attempts to look everywhere at once, picking her way over the homeless, stooping to show them Sofia's picture. She keeps her voice clear, but firm, maintaining eye contact, human to human.

In return, they look at the screen, but invariably shake their heads.

She voices her concern, finally.

'We're going the wrong way. She wouldn't have been brought here.'

Lucas throws her a look over his shoulder. 'You think it's just down-and-outs who seek out little girls?'

His reply, his underlying meaning, makes the bile rise in her throat again.

He stops, so sharply that she runs into his large, broad spine.

'What?' she asks, grabbing his arm, looking around.

'That woman lives there.' He gestures down a lane to their left. 'That's the mews place.'

Lucas is right.

Hannah is always out and about. It's one thing that struck Alina after the few conversations she's had with Hannah: the girl never seems to *just be*.

She bypasses Lucas, moving down the lane to the few houses that reside there. 'Which one?' she calls back to him.

He stops outside a gate. Alina pushes it open and strides up to the door.

She puts her finger on the bell and keeps it there until she sees movement inside.

HANNAH, SATURDAY

Marie has made dinner. A meal of the variety she prepares every few weeks. Carbs. Stodgy white food that Marie grew up on. Which she proclaims to be *good for you*.

Tonight, it is a jacket potato, breaded fish, baked beans.

Many times, Hannah has tried to educate her mother on the goodness of grains, pulses, seeds. Greens blended in nut oils and yoghurt sides with berries.

'Bird food,' claims Marie, as she puts another pat of butter in the pan.

Hannah is watching her mother, too tired to fight her tonight. Marie is happy, taking Hannah's silence as approval.

She thinks of that meal she had at Alina's, the one that Lucas made. Those potatoes, that bacon with the big, white stripes of fat. It was fantastic. So were the three courses she had at the fancy bistro. But that's two big strikes against her regime. And now Marie wants to make it a full house.

Marie is taking the plates out of the oven when the bell rings.

It doesn't stop.

'Bloody hell.' Marie puts the plates down and wipes her hands on her apron.

Hannah stares down the hallway.

'Kids?' Marie looks doubtful, and Hannah wonders if she is thinking of Nita, and whoever went to her house and hurt her that night.

Hannah slips off the stool. 'I'll get it.'

The figure on the step almost falls through the door into the house. Hannah puts her hands out, whether to catch or in defence, she isn't sure. There is someone else there: a large, looming presence, dwarfing the woman in front of him.

'Hannah, good evening.'

Lucas.

On her doorstep. He looks pained and troubled. He, too, has his hands out, and is trying to draw the other person back towards him.

Hannah steps back as the woman gathers herself.

'Alina,' she says. 'What are you doing here?'

Alina holds up her phone. The screen is black, but she seems almost delirious as she shows it to Hannah.

'Sofia is missing,' she blurts. 'I… I…' She trails off, her eyes unfocused on Hannah now, looking behind her.

Hannah glances over her shoulder. Oliver is there, on the step that divides the kitchen from the hallway. He watches Alina, his small face alight with curiosity. Marie comes to stand behind him, looking down the hall at the drama unfolding on her doorstep.

'Missing?' Hannah asks. 'From your house?'

Alina shakes her head. Her hands curl into fists and she reverses down the path. 'Someone took her. Jesus, I need to keep looking. I don't know why I came here…'

Hannah looks at Lucas. He has a distressed look on his face, one that previously she could never have imagined him having.

She shoves her feet into her trainers, which are by the door. She doesn't wear them unless she's jogging, but she has a feeling she'll need comfort tonight.

She steps outside and closes the door behind her. 'I'll help,' she calls to Alina, down by the gate now, looking wildly left and right.

'Thank you,' Alina gasps.

Then she's off, heading back towards the high street, Lucas and Hannah following.

'What happened?' Hannah asks Lucas.

'She was at the language school. Do you know it?' he asks.

'The girls' school.' Hannah grips his arm. 'I saw her there today. I was coming back from yours and I stopped near there to buy water.' She lowers her voice. 'There was a man with her—'

Alina is suddenly by her side, her hand gripping Hannah's shoulder.

Her stitches protest. Hannah swallows back the cry of pain and tries to free herself.

'What man?' Alina shouts. She digs her fingers in hard on the tender flesh. '*What man?*'

Hannah groans in pain. Another pair of hands. She watches as Lucas unfurls Alina's fingers, carefully but firmly.

'Alina.' He says her name once, very quietly. It has the desired effect.

'I'm sorry,' Alina cries. 'Jesus, I'm so sorry, but please… You saw a man?'

'I thought it was her father. He was blond, he was wearing a navy suit.'

Alina puts her hands to her face and lets out an anguished cry. 'That's Willem,' she said. 'Was he dropping her off? What time was this?'

'I–I… God. I don't know… maybe three o'clock?'

'We'll keep going, keep looking. Come on.' Lucas gets behind the two women, urges them out onto the busy road. 'I'll keep going down here. You two go back that way, check the doorways, ask the rough sleepers. Look everywhere,' he says.

Alina is looking into the distance, staring at everything but seeing nothing.

She is lost, thinks Hannah.

Lucas appears to have come to the same conclusion. He puts a hand on Hannah's shoulder. His touch is gentle, and he makes sure to keep his fingers away from where she was injured.

'Just keep going east. You'll come across the others, Willem's friends. They're on motorcycles. A few more of our people.' He darts a glance at Alina. 'Just… watch her, okay?'

Hannah nods and gently takes Alina's arm. 'You can count on me. Come on, Alina.'

Alina's walking is stilted and jittery. She comes to a halt every few steps, peering over chest-height fences or down passageways. Some of the fences are six feet. With these ones, Alina grips the top and hauls herself up, grunting with effort.

Hannah watches on, glancing around, waiting for someone to approach Alina, ask her what the hell she thinks she's doing.

Alina drops back down to land on the pavement next to Hannah.

A middle-aged couple pass by, arms entwined, frowning.

'What?' Alina spits at them. 'Fuck off.'

Hannah mouths an apology behind Alina's back and ushers the woman onwards.

Alina breaks free, dashes back to the couple she just swore at and shows them her phone.

'This girl is missing, have you seen her?' she asks. Her voice is hoarse and breathless.

They shake their heads, backing away at speed.

'Alina.' Hannah clears her throat. '*Alina.*'

The other woman jerks her head up and stumbles off the kerb into the gutter.

'Let's go.' Hannah gestures to their route, but Alina remains motionless.

'God. I… can't… if anything has happened…'

Hannah goes to stand by Alina. The woman's face is a mask the like of which Hannah has never seen before.

Pain. Hurt. Misery.

The strangest thought comes to Hannah. If they were to come across Sofia, and anything had happened to the child, Alina would kill herself, there and then.

No. That's not what she'd do at all.

She would find out who was responsible, kill them, and then herself.

The knowledge sends a shiver through Hannah's very soul.

She looks down the road in the direction they are headed. They've passed the girls' school, the place where this all began.

Hannah glances further down the road. Go east, Lucas said. How long are they supposed to walk in that direction?

'Alina,' Hannah says. 'Have you called the police?'

Alina snaps her head up. 'No,' she replies.

Hannah thought as much.

'We'll check the park, but once you walk through it, you're in a whole different area. That's Holland Park. We'll no longer be in Kensington.'

Alina looks at her blankly. 'Do you think I should call them?'

Hannah stares at her, dumbfounded. It's an extraordinary question. Every mother's first reaction would be to dial 999.

Alina resumes walking.

Hannah darts after her. 'Wait! The hostel… Have you checked there?'

Alina seems to stare right through Hannah. 'What hostel?'

'Off the park. It's… Something happened there recently. I remember reading about it. They took a kid, some county lines initiation.' Hannah rubs at her eyes. 'Sofia's not the usual recruit, of course. She's young, they tend to gear themselves more towards impressionable young boys, or so I read in the paper. Kids who don't have anyone looking out for them.' She shakes her head. 'It's a stupid thought… It's just because I read the article the other week. Come on, we'll keep on moving east.'

For the first time, Alina looks a little more focused. 'No,' she says. 'Take me there. Right now.'

'It's a stupid idea. I don't want to waste time. I'm sorry, I'm not being very helpful.' Hannah takes Alina's hand this time, an apologetic gesture.

Alina looks down at it, seemingly surprised to see their fingers entwined. 'Take me there,' she says again. 'Please.'

Hannah nods. 'If you're sure,' she replies. She glances around, getting her bearings. 'It's this way, I think.'

Like a child herself, Alina lets herself be led.

–

'What happened at the hostel?'

They've been walking for about five minutes now.

Alina has been quiet up until now. Hannah still has Alina's hand in hers. It is as though the other woman has reverted to childhood, Hannah her caregiver.

'Sorry?' Hannah asks.

'You said a kid was taken to this hostel.'

'Yes.' Hannah pauses, unsure of whether to speak on. If she does, she needs to choose her words carefully. 'I can't remember where I read it. It was some sort of exposé, I think. I don't know, I barely recall it. Just that it was uncomfortably close to home…'

'I didn't hear about it,' Alina says. 'Why didn't I know about it?' She claps her hands to her face, her mouth a gaping hole. 'What happened to the child?'

'The police got to them. The kid was nothing like Sofia. They were in care. That's where they recruit them from. Because they're easy to get to. That's not Sofia, at all.' Hannah knows she is rambling now, spewing words and phrases that are not going to help Alina's current fragile mental state.

It's not the only reason she can't stop babbling. Walking here, heading to the hostel, it's a risky place to be.

She glances at Alina. Tears are streaming down the other woman's face.

Hannah squeezes her fingers and pulls her across the path.

'Come on,' she says. 'We'll find her.'

The hostel is normally busy, especially on hot summer nights like this one. Students, gap-year travellers, the homeless community who have sourced cash for a room for a night. Tonight, it is eerily deserted.

'Maybe we should call Lucas, or your husband.' Hannah hesitates on the approach to the building.

Her words finally wake Alina. She yanks her hand free, narrows her eyes and looks around.

It's getting dusky now, though still light enough to see.

'I *do* know this place.' Alina frowns. 'The hostel. It's always busy.' She glares at Hannah, as though the sudden solitude is her fault. 'What's going on here?'

'I don't know. We should wait. We should call—'

Before Hannah can even finish her sentence, Alina is off and running towards the building that is shrouded in darkness.

21

ALINA, SATURDAY

Never has she felt this way before. Well, partially, last Friday night when hellfire rained down upon Sofia. Back then, Alina had thought that that was the worst thing that had ever happened – could happen, would ever happen.

How wrong she'd been.

Sofia is missing.

Sofia has been *taken*.

As a result, Alina has been transformed into someone she doesn't even recognise. She is now the creature who looks at herself in the mirror in her wildest, worst nightmares.

The last hour or so is hazy. She remembers being at The Members Club with Francis. A call coming in from Willem. A race to get to Kensington, the subsequent realisation she was practically on the doorstep anyway and had wasted precious time as Lucas fought traffic.

There was fatigue from fury and worry, and some sort of plan with her friends. Her contacts. Willem's bikers. Jimmy. Julia and Lucas. Francis had turned up, Merle hot on her heels. A faint suspicion lingers on the very edges of her mind, a wondering that she tries to swallow down.

Are they really her friends?

Is one of them responsible for this?

She glances over her shoulder at Hannah.

Why is Hannah here, with her?

It doesn't even matter. She admits – or realises – that later she'll be relieved she had a friend beside her.

She eyes the hostel as she reaches it. What she said to Hannah is true. She knows of this place, has passed it many times on her treks up and down the high street. It's bustling, all the time. A mixture of people come here. Most of them are unsavoury. The news about the county lines gang who reside here was unknown to Alina, but she can quite believe it.

It is never this quiet here, though.

Why is it so quiet?

She reaches the entrance and pulls on the door handle. Beside her, Hannah is looking around.

'It's not right, something's not right here,' says Alina. Her teeth are chattering. Her jaw feels funny.

'This area isn't like it used to be. My neighbour was attacked the other night,' says Hannah.

Alina starts. 'Attacked? Here?'

Hannah shakes her head. 'In her house, next to mine.'

'Jesus.' Alina yanks on the door handle again, with even more force.

Hannah is still talking, saying something about her neighbour who lives alone, how she was beaten, but all Alina can focus on is the seemingly empty building in front of her.

She grips the handle with both hands, plants a foot on the frame and pulls with all her might.

The door is locked. There is nobody here.

Sofia is not here.

She sags, her forehead coming to rest on the door. If anything has happened to Sofia, Alina will beat her head

167

on this door until she is so damaged that she can no longer see, or think, or feel, or hurt—

'Alina!' Hannah has her hands pressed to a window. 'She's there!'

She's there.

Does… Does she mean *Sofia*?

Alina abandons the door and for the moment leaves thoughts of wounding herself, and she sprints the few feet to the window. She shoves Hannah roughly aside.

'Sofia!' she shrieks. '*Sofia!*'

It's gloomy inside, she can't see anything. How could Hannah have seen something?

'What did you see?' she screams.

And then, just as Hannah opens her mouth to answer, Alina hears a muffled voice.

'Mama…?'

Alina roars. Her girl is in there. Sofia is inside. She is speaking, sounding… normal. She's not badly injured, then, surely? She's not dead.

That's what Alina mutters to herself as she runs back to the door. She clings on to that thought.

She's not dead. Sofia is not dead.

But the door won't budge. It is locked, or jammed, from the inside. There is no sound, as though nobody else is in the hostel at all.

Alina flies back to the window, draws back her arm and punches at the glass. It wobbles, but it is toughened. Nonetheless, she hits at it again. She sees the blood from her split knuckles, but there is no pain at all.

'Look, try this.' Hannah is there again, holding a piece of metal.

It looks like part of a railing or maybe a bollard, so many of which have been placed around the city.

Alina takes it and smashes it against the window.

On the first swing, the glass cracks.

On the second, it shatters.

A small hole in amongst lines like those of a spider's web. Alina reaches into the gap and pulls at the glass.

An aroma hits her. Mould, dirt, rising damp and the general unkemptness of this awful place.

She is aware of Hannah by her side, her friend's sharp hiss of breath as Alina's blood stains the glass.

Sofia is there now, right behind the jagged pane.

'Sofia.' Alina breathes her name.

'Stand back, Sofia.' This from Hannah, who now has the metal in her hands.

She hits the remaining glass again and again, knocking the sharp parts from the frame.

'Sofia!' Alina is breathless now.

She puts her hand in, and Sofia's fingers touch hers.

Hannah throws the metal down and peers inside. 'Sofia, grab that box, stand on it – we'll pull you through.'

Sofia falters, looks to her mother.

'Do it!' yells Alina.

Sofia clambers atop the box, arms outstretched. For a long, strange moment, to Alina, she looks just like a baby again. She draws her out, holding her so tight that Sofia begins to squirm.

With one hand, Alina takes her phone out of her pocket, unlocks it and passes it to Hannah.

'Call my husband, Willem.' She sinks her face into Sofia's hair.

The silence that surrounds the hostel is broken only by Hannah speaking into the phone. Her voice is calm but clear.

Alina staggers with Sofia in her arms towards the high street.

'I'm fine, Mama,' says Sofia in her ear. 'Can we go home?'

Alina nods and holds on tighter.

Later, there will be questions, investigations, a definite tightening of security.

For now, just to have her girl in her arms – her solid, warm body – is enough.

22

HANNAH, SATURDAY

There is no need for any words, from either of them, but as a cluster of noisy motorcycles makes its way towards them, Alina reaches out and takes a hold of Hannah's hand. Alina's hand is bleeding, oozing blood, but it is as though the other woman doesn't even notice it.

Hannah thinks of her own wounded arm, her ankle, and how fierce the pain was.

Hannah squeezes Alina's fingers, regardless of the bloodied mess, and offers her a smile as the motorbikes come to a halt beside them.

Hannah watches, eyes wide, as half a dozen men climb off their machines and silently surround Alina and her daughter.

Moments later, she sees the big car, Lucas at the wheel, Willem beside him. Willem opens the door before the car has come to a stop. He staggers out, gathers his wife and child in his arms. Alina still has a hold of Hannah's hand. She relaxes her fingers, allowing Alina to shift her hold to her husband, but it is as though Alina can't let go.

'Let's go home,' Willem murmurs.

They stand awkwardly, all four of them.

Hannah is prepared to say her goodbyes, but Alina draws her towards the pavement.

Hannah isn't sure how she ended up in the car as it speeds towards Alina's Richmond home.

She can't protest, as she sits in the back seat, Sofia and Alina next to her. The little girl leans away from Hannah, into her mother's side.

Hannah's house is literally minutes away, but the odd quiet that has fallen stops her from saying anything.

She *wants* to be with Alina, she finds.

As they travel, she hears a rumble behind her. Glancing out of the rear window, she sees the bikers – escorting them – and she allows a small smile. It is as though this family has presidential or royal connections.

Eventually, they turn off up the Arpels' leafy street, pulling into their driveway. The bikers pull up but make no move to get off their machines this time.

Sentry duty now, Hannah sees, as she climbs out of the car.

Inside the house are two more people that Hannah doesn't know. Embarrassed, she throws them a small wave. They look right through her, concentrating their efforts and their hugs on Alina and Sofia.

Hannah wonders if she should say her goodbyes now, or just slip away, unnoticed.

'I'm so glad it all worked out okay,' she says to nobody in particular. 'I should get going now.'

'No, please.' Willem speaks to her for the first time. 'Stay for a moment, if that's okay, if you've nowhere else to be? Have a drink with us.'

'She was just about to have dinner when we dragged her away,' comments Lucas.

'God, I'm so sorry, Hannah.' Alina, still clinging to Sofia, looks over at her. 'Lucas will make you something, won't you, Lucas?'

He nods and starts gathering some ingredients. As he passes her, Hannah catches his arm. 'Please, there's really no need. I'll eat when I get home.'

He hesitates and glances at Sofia. 'She'll be hungry. I'll make some food, there will be plenty if you change your mind.'

She smiles weakly.

Willem nods to the two strangers standing in the kitchen. 'Julia, Jimmy, this is Hannah Barker. Looks like she is our new resident guardian angel. Saving our girl, *again*.'

The man – Jimmy – looks her up and down, tilts his head to one side.

'So, this is the famous Hannah Barker,' Julia says. 'Pleased to make your acquaintance.'

Hannah dips her head. 'I really didn't do anything. Alina was the one who found Sofia.'

It's not true, but Hannah wants to throw the attention someplace else. She shuffles her feet, waits for Alina to correct her, but the woman seems spaced out still, her eyes never leaving her daughter.

'Can I patch you up, *moya lyubov*?' croons Jimmy, gently cradling Alina's hand.

Alina sits obediently on the stool that is pulled up for her, eyes far away as the old man tends to her cuts. She is the child now, sees Hannah.

'Regardless, we're grateful to you, Hannah,' says Willem. He looks at his wife. 'Aren't, we, Alina?'

Alina lets Jimmy tuck in the edges of the neat bandage before turning to Hannah.

She blinks, as if only now realising Hannah is there in her kitchen.

'Come with me,' she says, softly, slipping off the stool.

173

Alina turns and walks back down the hallway, into the lounge where Hannah has been once before.

Hannah hesitates, just for a moment, before following her.

'I owe you, Hannah. And… And I'm really sorry that I failed you before.'

Hannah demurs. 'You didn't—'

'Yeah, I did.' Alina interrupts her. 'I didn't follow through on my promise. I didn't take it as seriously as I should have.' She glares at the wall, behind which her family and friends are gathered. 'I should have. If tonight has taught me anything, it's that life can go from normal to my absolute worst nightmare in a heartbeat.'

Alina slumps into a chair and stares at her feet.

Hannah shrugs awkwardly. 'It's really okay. I'm sure my issue won't be anything near as frightening as tonight was for you.' She is aiming for polite, but it sounds forced and false.

Alina looks up at Hannah. 'I owe you twice over, now.'

Hannah just manages to prevent herself blanching when she notices the look on the other woman's face. Her expression is warmer than Hannah has ever seen it.

'You can trust me. Whatever you want, you've got it. The job, it's as good as yours. The person you want removing from your life is as good as gone.' Alina's eyes pierce through Hannah's soul, all softness from moments ago gone. 'No questions asked. No judgement.'

Hannah nods. 'Thank you,' she whispers.

They look at each other for a moment longer, and Hannah feels herself mellowing.

There is something between them now. Something unbreakable. Alina will do for Hannah whatever needs to be done. She will be cool and calculated.

The game is over. They understand each other completely now.

'Write the information you have. Don't send me any emails, nothing over text. The name, whatever you have. I'll sort it all.' Alina nods to a sideboard lining the opposite wall. Upon it is a notepad, next to an old-fashioned rotary dial telephone.

Hannah takes out her phone and copies the address that she has been sent by text.

After a second's hesitation, Hannah writes down the name of the person that she needs to be gone. She looks at the notepaper, at the information she has shared.

It was so easy, she realises. The accident at the gallery was a high-octane, dramatic incident. One which Alina, in time to come, will retell at dinner parties. This, *tonight*, for Alina, was real fear. Probably the first time in her life she has ever really known pure, abject terror.

She trusts Alina now.

Because now Alina really, truly, does owe Hannah.

She glances at Alina, still in her chair. She is a million miles away, probably still back at the hostel, or before, pounding the streets in a seemingly impossible search for her missing girl.

Hannah vows to give that area a wide berth in the future.

'I'm really glad Sofia is okay,' Hannah says as she replaces the pen in the holder.

She means it.

And she hopes that this family is finished now with drama.

Alina hauls herself out of the chair and leads Hannah back into the hall.

'Lucas will take you home.'

Hannah begins to protest but Alina holds her hand up. 'You don't even stand a chance arguing with me, not tonight.' She smiles and offers up a little shrug. 'Well, not ever, let's face it.'

A little bit of the old Alina is back. Hannah matches her smile while Lucas is summoned.

He was in the middle of cooking, Hannah sees, but the old man called Jimmy slides into his space, takes the spatula from Lucas's hand.

Hannah tries to imagine her house like this, with random people making themselves at home. It is unfathomable.

Sofia is watching her, curiously, and Hannah raises a hand. 'See you, Sofia.'

The little girl turns to her father, buries her face in his chest.

Outside, Lucas walks down to the bikers and confers with them. They roll their machines backwards, creating a path for his car. Hannah steps onto the drive and Alina catches her hand.

Hannah turns, not surprised, because there is something very real between them now, when Alina draws her into a hug.

'Thank you for tonight,' Alina whispers. 'I'll never forget it.'

Hannah nods, pats Alina on the back and steps away.

23

ALINA, SATURDAY

As Hannah hurries down the drive to where Lucas stands, waiting, car door open, Alina turns and heads back inside.

She picks up the notepad that Hannah wrote on, tears the page out and puts it in her pocket before heading back to her daughter.

Sofia is looking no worse for wear as Jimmy passes her food bits from the stove.

'You're okay, my girl?' She takes Sofia's face in her hands.

'Yep.' Sofia shrugs and scoops more food onto her fork. 'I'm sorry, Mama. I… I didn't mean to—'

'Hush.' Alina kisses her head. 'Eat. We'll talk later. You're home, you're safe. You can tell me and Papa what happened when you've finished your dinner.'

She walks away from the kitchen, looks out into the garden. It's dark now. Late. What if the rescue had been delayed? What if Sofia was still out there, now, trapped in that godawful hostel? Alone. Frightened.

What if the undesirables who normally hang out at the hostel had come back to their haunt, found her there? Why had the person who took Sofia left her there in the first place?

Alina's skin crawls. She's itching to question Sofia about the events that made her leave the language school with a stranger and end up in a deserted, locked-up building.

But she can't. She won't, not yet. Later, Willem will lead the questioning of their daughter.

Alina knows herself well enough to know that she absolutely can't. She will become shrill, angry. Perhaps violent. Not towards Willem or Sofia, of course not. But to things in general, whatever might come to hand. Throwing, smashing.

That would do Sofia no good at all.

She beckons Willem over. He leaves their daughter and comes to stand by her side.

'No more language school for her,' she says. 'She is not going anywhere without you, or me, or Lucas or Julia. I want a chaperone with her, *at all times*. In fact, I don't want her leaving this house at all for the foreseeable future.'

'She was targeted, is what you're thinking?' His voice is hoarse, shaky.

For the first time in all their years together, she wonders if he puts the blame on her. Because of her name. Because of who her parents are.

It spikes at her, makes her temper rise, even though he hasn't said anything like that. It was her own thought.

He's wealthy, too, she thinks, churlishly. *The plan might have been a ransom demand that didn't get that far, because of his stupid diamonds.*

They are both high profile. They are both wealthy. As a result of old family ties, Alina has a chequered past. A kidnapping would make sense. The subsequent ransom call. But these – both these occurrences – have not been anything remotely like a hostage situation. Nobody who

178

had money signs in their eyes would take a child and stash her someone like the bustlingly busy hostel.

Except, it wasn't busy, was it?

'Hannah said something happened at the hostel before, recently. County lines gangs, recruiting.'

To her shock, Willem bursts out laughing. She fixes him with an ice-cold stare. To his credit, he stops immediately.

'I'm sorry. But Sofia is the absolute opposite of who gangs like that go after.' He frowns, a deep crease appearing between his brows. 'Is that what made you go there, to the hostel?'

'She read an article, some incident happened there,' Alina answers vaguely.

Regardless, they found Sofia there. That is all that matters to Alina. *That they found her.*

For now, anyway. Later, when Alina has had time to reflect, to ensure that Sofia is okay – mentally, physically – she will look into the hostel. She will find the person who took her little girl. She will find out if it was something to do with the awful county lines, or if it was a hostage situation aimed at her and Willem.

Or if it was something entirely different.

She thinks of Sofia, how utterly beautiful the girl is. She thinks of the kind of men who look at little girls like that.

She claps a hand to her mouth and swallows repeatedly to stop the vomit that threatens. 'Alina?' Willem is there, his arms around her, attempting to comfort but instead providing a stifling, suffocating embrace.

She shoves him off her and reaches into her pocket for the piece of paper where Hannah wrote her persecutor's details. She turns the page over.

Hostel — empty, she writes.

She taps her pen on the piece of paper and shows it to Willem. 'This hostel, where you picked us up, do you know it?'

He shrugs. 'Not really. I've never been there, if that's what you're asking. Why?'

'I do. It's always busy, it's an affordable joint in the middle of the most popular part of the city. It is heaving, all the time.'

Willem crosses his arms, a question on his face.

'It wasn't busy tonight. Willem, it was utterly deserted. The hostel was locked up, there were no residents inside, nobody hanging around outside.' Alina's nostrils flare with a fresh surge of rage. 'Just Sofia, in there, in the dark. Locked up.'

'Not random, then. Planned.' Willem glances into the kitchen where Sofia has almost finished eating her dinner under the watchful eye of Julia. 'By someone who has the power to clear out a place like that.'

'Who?' Alina narrows her eyes. 'Your work – competitors, perhaps? Anything strange going on?'

'No. We're desirable because we're wealthy, you know that. As for enemies, I can't think of any.'

She swallows and asks the question she's been dreading. 'My father... All his... stuff.'

Willem shakes his head decisively. 'Highly unlikely. If it were to do with your family's past, it would be a lot more efficient.' He jerks his head towards the kitchen, where Jimmy is chatting with Julia. 'Can you imagine someone like him using such cack-handed techniques as some sort of retribution?'

Jimmy. Apart from Francis, he is the only one of her friends who knows her parents.

Alina knows Willem is right. If all this had come from her father's history, there would not have been two attempts on Sofia's life. There would have only been one. And Sofia would already be dead.

Alina shivers and wraps her arms around herself. 'Where did Francis go?' she says, suddenly. 'I didn't see her when you all turned up.'

Willem shrugs. His mind isn't on Francis. He is looking ahead, thinking, planning.

Doing the things she would normally be taking care of.

'We'll put Lucas on it,' says Willem, gently. 'Jimmy, too. Julia will do a run-through of everyone at your office, make sure there's no grudge that we're not aware of.'

Alina gazes through the door at the people gathered. 'Jimmy... and Francis...'

Willem squeezes her shoulder. 'They are our friends.'

Are they? Or have they just been pretending all these years? Biding their time.

Alina listens to the sounds of low-key chatter coming from the kitchen. For the first time, it sends a spike of irritation through her. 'Everyone can go home,' she tells him. 'I want to sit with Sofia for a while.'

Julia embraces each of them in turn.

'I love you,' she murmurs in Alina's ear. 'You can call me, anytime, day or night, okay?'

Even Julia's touch, one that Alina normally cherishes, feels off tonight. As gently as she can, she extracts herself. 'I know. Thank you. Goodnight.'

Finally, it is just the three of them: Alina, Willem, Sofia.

They take their daughter upstairs to bed, tucking her in, spending longer than normal holding her.

Sofia eyes her parents warily. 'You're going to ask me what happened, aren't you?'

Willem pats his daughter's hand. 'When you're ready. You can tell us what you remember.'

Sofia reaches over to the shelf above her bed and pulls down a stuffed rabbit. She tucks it into her chest.

Alina's heart cracks down the middle. Sofia's toy collection is purely for show. She hasn't actually held one for years now.

Until tonight.

'A man was waiting for me outside class. He said Jules had sent him… There was a problem here, at home, and he was taking me to Jules.'

Alina stiffens. 'Jules? Did he say Jules, or Julia?'

'Jules,' Sofia says, solemnly, and leans against her dad.

Alina exchanges a look with Willem over her head.

'Julia wouldn't…' Willem trails off.

Alina shakes her head as firmly as she can manage. Julia is family. But she is only referred to as *Jules* by Alina. Nobody else calls her that. And Alina only calls her Jules when they are alone together.

She's a friend, Alina tells herself. She would never…

Would she?

'But, Sofia, you know better than to believe the word of a stranger.' Willem's words are gentle, far more so than Alina's would be if she were to say them.

Sofia's eyes fill with tears.

'I know. I–I remembered when we were walking. I told him I had to go back to the school because I'd forgotten something.' Sofia looks down and the tears fall freely down her face now.

'Then what happened?' whispers Alina.

182

'He picked me up and he put his hand over my face, so I couldn't scream.' Sofia whimpers.

Alina stands up and paces the room, leaving Willem to soothe their girl.

'What did he look like?'

Sofia's face is a mask of misery. 'Thin, tall… He had long, shiny black hair. He had a thing, here.' She strokes the space between her own thumb and finger.

'A tattoo?' asks Willem.

Sofia nods. 'The number 88,' she says.

Willem practically gags.

'What?' asks Alina.

'White supremacist,' he spits. He turns to Sofia. 'How old do you think he might have been?'

'Not old. Not like Uncle Jimmy.'

'As old as me?' Willem prods her.

Sofia shakes her head. 'Not that old.' She gives a tentative smile and Willem laughs.

Alina wants to laugh at her daughter's joke, but her face refuses to comply.

She moves to the doorway and watches the two most precious people in her life.

She clenches her fists behind her back.

Whoever is responsible for this will pay.

They will pay dearly.

24

HANNAH, SATURDAY

It's gone ten p.m. when Lucas drops Hannah off at the mews.

'Nice work tonight,' he says, as he comes round to the passenger side and opens the door for her. 'The Arpels are very grateful. Again.' He smiles at her.

Hannah dips her head as she climbs out of the car. 'It was nothing. It was… pure luck, I suppose.'

Lucas shuts the door. 'You take care, Miss Hannah.'

She nods. 'You too. Thanks for the lift.'

She hurries up the lane, through her gate, and inserts her key into the lock. She pushes on the door, jerking backwards when it only opens a couple of inches.

'Mum!' she calls. 'Mum, the chain is on!'

It seems an age before she hears Marie's footsteps padding down the hall.

'Is that you, Hannah?' she asks.

'Of course,' Hannah replies, impatiently. 'Who else is it going to be?'

She moves from foot to foot while Marie slides the chain.

'Is everything okay?' Marie opens the door just wide enough for Hannah to pass through, then peers out, left and right down the lane.

'Yes, why wouldn't it be?' Hannah slips her trainers off.

'What was all that about, earlier?' Marie asks.

Hannah moves down the hall to the kitchen. 'Alina's daughter was missing. She found her, though.'

'Alina…' Marie follows her. 'The woman from the gallery… The daughter who had the accident?' Her voice is sharp.

'Yes. I helped with the search. She's okay, the girl. They found her, safe and sound.'

'Who found her?'

'We did. At that hostel, near the park.' Hannah leans over to peer into the oven. Her heart sinks as she sees the jacket potato being kept warm in there.

'They found the little girl, in the park?'

'In the hostel. She's fine, though.' Hannah turns the dial on the oven to zero. The light fades to black, the plate of food can no longer be seen.

Marie has slumped in a chair and is looking out into the darkened courtyard.

'Mum.' Hannah goes over to her and crouches by her side. 'Mum, what is it?'

'Everything.' Marie's voice is curiously dull and blunt. 'I don't know if this is the best place for us to be.'

Hannah's heart thuds uncomfortably. 'What do you mean?'

'This girl, the accident, poor Nita next door. Today there is another problem. And it keeps coming to our door, Hannah.'

'This is London. Things like this happen. They almost always end fine.' Hannah looks at Marie blankly. 'Where is all this coming from?'

'I want to take Oliver away, for a little while.' Marie raises her chin, a determined look on her face now. 'For a break. A holiday.'

Hannah opens the fridge and takes out her iced lemon water. 'I don't know if I can take time off from the gallery. Maybe in September, after the summer rush.'

Marie doesn't answer. The only sound in the room is the water being poured.

'I meant… Maybe *I* could take him away for a while,' says Marie after a long pause.

'Without me?' Hannah can't believe what she's hearing. She would never dream of taking a vacation without Marie.

'Just for a while,' says Marie.

Hannah can't even speak. She abandons her water on the counter and heads towards the stairs.

She lingers there, expecting Marie to call her back, tell her she's misunderstood.

But Marie says nothing.

Hannah continues on her way. As she rounds the corner to the stairs, she sees her wedding photo is on display again.

Instead of going to her own room, she slips into Oliver's. His night light is on, the room bathed in a soft orange glow.

She sits beside him, watching him as he sleeps.

She thinks about Marie's words. The strange conversation they just had.

But it wasn't a conversation, was it? Just Marie, telling Hannah that she wants to take Oliver away.

Just the two of them.

There's a pain in Hannah's chest. It feels like grief, like she's suffered a loss.

It's a pain she's felt before. Once before, when Marie withdrew from her.

That time, her mother had disappeared for more than six months, leaving Hannah with her father. It was a long time ago now; Hannah had only been about seven years old. It was the worst time of Hannah's life.

When Marie returned, Hannah had thrown herself at her, clinging to her mother for dear life. For a long time, well into adolescence, Hannah had been petrified that Marie would leave again.

But she didn't.

Instead, her father walked out on them.

He had never returned. More than twenty years without him now, and yet, the loss of him for all that time has been nothing compared to Marie's half-year absence.

Hannah swallows as she watches her son sleeping.

In all the years since that time in childhood, they've been a team: Marie and Hannah.

But in the last few months, everything seems to be falling apart.

'Hannah?' Marie's voice is sharp, her footsteps quick as she flies up the stairs. 'What are you doing?'

Hannah moves out of Oliver's room and meets Marie in the hallway. 'I'm going to bed,' she says, wearily.

She can feel her mother's eyes searing her back as she moves into her own room.

As she closes the door, she sees Marie duck into Oliver's room. She imagines her mum in there, sitting beside the sleeping child. Keeping watch.

She wonders if Alina is doing the same. Does she sit in her daughter's room? Is she watching her sleep? Or is she questioning the girl about tonight's events?

How hard it is to keep everything the way it is, when life is perfect.

A constant battle.

Hannah closes her eyes.

Sleep doesn't come for a long time, and the dawn light is just starting to shine into the bedroom when Hannah finally drifts off into an uneasy slumber.

25

ALINA, SUNDAY

Willem is on the phone on Sunday morning. It's early. Too early, she thinks as she grabs her husband's pillow and puts it over her head.

There is a sharp pain in her hand that makes her wince. She withdraws her arm from under the covers, sees the fat, white bandage. She unfurls it, peers at her palm and her fingers, sliced up, blood still oozing from cuts that look horribly deep.

The night before comes back in a flash. She jumps out of bed and rushes across the hall into Sofia's room.

She's still asleep, her girl.

Alina closes the door and sighs with relief.

She could go back to bed. Would do, normally, but Willem is talking *so loudly*.

She makes her way downstairs, wrapping her kimono around her. Willem is in the kitchen, his laptop in front of him. A video call is in progress.

She walks behind him and drapes herself over him. 'Who is that?' she asks. She squints at the screen. 'Who are you?'

The man on the screen clears his throat. 'Good morning, Ma'am. My name is Richard Bloom, I'm from Cerberus Security.'

Alina nods and rests her chin on Willem's shoulder. 'You're getting security in?'

Willem glances at her. 'Yes. CCTV, foot soldiers. We can't keep the bikers here for ever.'

She laughs but there is no humour in it. 'Foot soldiers? What're you, Russian?'

He doesn't answer and she pulls away from him, strangely hurt.

'Okay, my lovely. I'll leave you to it.'

She goes back upstairs, oddly disconcerted. She hates this. Willem has always been the calm to her storm, the breeze to her hurricane. They have never had security in place, apart from a burglar alarm and a sensor for Willem's diamonds in the basement.

She has loved the freedom of their life. She has never had to worry before, since Willem became her life, about kidnappings or ransoms or attacks. Not like her father.

She has nightmares which *must* come from the old days, of electric fences, and armed guards. Threats which she can't recall in full, a panic room which she can never remember actually being in.

She vowed she would never live like that when she was the adult with her own family.

It's part of why she fell for Willem. He was an archaeology student when they met. He was fun and didn't take life too seriously. He was a million miles away from her stony-faced father. Even when he moved from rock brushing to gem digging, there was no threat. Especially when he chose the path of sustainable diamonds. It was safe. And when her father's company came into her hands and she paid off all the corrupt old boys, and it was finally a legit, legal business, she told herself that she felt safe.

All those times, when the paranoia sprung up – when she lost sight of Sofia for a moment in a shopping centre, or when she heard about an attack on a businessman and Willem wasn't with her – she pushed it down. Told herself that things were different now.

Not any longer. Now, all these years later, she's a target.

Sofia is a target.

The life which she loved is in disarray. She has half a dozen bikers standing sentry in her driveway. Sofia is no longer allowed to go to her beloved language school. Willem is serious and scared enough to surround them with security.

This is exactly how she swore she would *never* have to live.

And it all started with that fucking Tate and his disgusting statue.

She dresses quickly, the rage boiling inside her. Not her normal anger, though. This nestles beside a sadness, and that's even worse.

She looks in on Sofia once more before leaving. The girl is still sleeping. Exhausted from yesterday's drama.

Alina thinks of the man who bodily carried her little girl away, who put his filthy hand over her child's mouth.

Her rage sends red-hot colours in front of her eyes.

Alina slams out of the house and makes her way to the car.

Lucas is with the bikers, chatting amiably. All these people cloistered in front of her home. She loves them all. But this isn't how she wants them, as fucking bodyguards. These men should be inside, sipping at good Russian vodka, playing poker or chess.

Alina feels reckless as she waits by the car. She's smart enough to know why. She's feeling hemmed in, locked up, restricted. She wants to kick back against all this.

She leaves the side of the car and makes her way to the garage. Willem's motorbike is in there. He uses it now and then, on the occasions when he gets on the road with his biker mates.

Alina stares at the bike. It's a sports tourer, gunmetal in colour, cool and fast and dangerous.

Exactly what she needs right now.

She snatches the keys from the safe and climbs on, rolling it down the driveway. The cuts on her hand sting with the motion, but she ignores the pain.

The bikers look at her as she approaches them, before exchanging glances with each other.

'Going somewhere?' asks Lucas, dryly.

'Yes,' she says. 'See you guys later.'

Lucas puts a hand on her arm. 'Alina—'

She shrugs it off and pulls the helmet on. In the mood she's in, she'd love not to wear it, but knows she wouldn't reach the end of the road without being pulled over. And then, again, because of the mood she's in, she'd kick off and end up in a cell overnight.

She knows Lucas wants to prevent her from going on what he no doubt thinks is a death ride. But he also knows better than to stop her.

He watches her, troubled, as she roars off down the road.

She sticks to the speed limit, more or less, because she's not stupid. But at traffic lights she lets the throttle out, enjoying the startled glances of those waiting alongside her.

As she rides alongside the Thames, she screams inside her helmet.

It feels good.

26

HANNAH, SUNDAY

Marie is nowhere to be found when Hannah wakes.

Neither is Oliver.

She goes to the fridge, to the cute little photo of all three of them. Notes are left here, if one of them goes out.

Gone for breakfast – back soon!

Or, *Taken Oliver to the playground, back soon!*

Endless varieties, but always with a reassuring 'back soon'.

Today, there is nothing.

Hannah panics.

Last night, Marie's sudden desire to take Oliver somewhere.

Just the two of them.

Has she done it? Has Marie left her?

Hannah dials Marie's mobile. She hears it vibrating, somewhere close by. It is on the kitchen table, skittering across the top with Hannah's name lit up on the screen.

She races upstairs, into Marie's room. It's neat and tidy, like always. A room in a show home. No mementoes here, apart from a single photo of Marie with Oliver when he was a baby.

Hannah races across to Marie's bedside table and yanks the drawer open.

Her passport, never used but still in date, is there.

Hannah breathes out a sigh of relief.

She tells herself that she's being stupid. Her mother would never go away on a holiday, not without her.

Or is that what she was telling her, in a roundabout way, last night?

She goes back downstairs and tries to calm herself.

Marie has forgotten their note system. That's all that's wrong here. Or maybe she left her a note, and it has fallen.

Hannah lies down flat on the floor and peers underneath the fridge.

That's how Marie finds her, as she lets herself into the house, Oliver trailing behind her.

'Hannah!' Marie drops her shopping bag and comes into the kitchen. 'What's wrong, what're you doing?'

Marie stoops to help her up. Instead, Hannah wraps her arms around her mother.

'Where did you go?' she whispers. She's aghast to hear her own voice catch.

'To the bakery.' Marie gives up trying to pick up Hannah and crouches beside her on the floor. 'Where did you think I was?'

Hannah clears her throat. 'You didn't leave a note.'

Marie glances at the empty magnet. 'You were sleeping. I thought we'd be back before you woke up.'

Oliver comes over and shoves something in Hannah's face. A toy car, electric blue with racing stripes on it.

'Nice. Where'd you get that, the bakery?' She looks up at Marie.

'Bobby gave it to him.'

'Bobby...?'

'We saw Nita,' says Marie as she moves to the kitchen island and unpacks her bag. 'I got fresh bagels; would you like one?'

'No.' Hannah struggles to her feet. 'You saw Nita in the bakery?'

'No. We stopped in on our way home.' Marie meets Hannah's eyes, a challenge of sorts.

'Why didn't you say?' Hannah asks.

'I did!' Marie looks surprised. 'Just now, we told you.'

'You said you'd been to the bakery. You were not going to mention Nita,' Hannah argues.

'I would have if you'd have given me a minute. I come in, you're stretched out on the floor like you were unconscious, or something...'

Hannah barks out a laugh. 'Is that what you thought?'

'No, I was just surprised. I would have told you if you'd given me a chance.'

'Nita's come home, then?' Hannah wanders over to the island and looks at everything Marie has bought. Bread. Bread rolls, bagels, pies.

All those carbs.

'She's feeling better.' Marie fills the kettle from the tap. With her back turned, she says, 'I told her I would have thought it best maybe to stay at her daughter's house for a while longer.'

'Really?' Hannah asks her mother's spine.

'Yes. I'm not sure it's so safe here any longer.' Marie's voice is tremulous as she pushes the words out.

'Here?' Hannah hears her own voice rise a pitch. 'What do you mean, *here*?'

It is a long time before Marie answers her. She sighs, turns around and wipes her hands on a tea towel. 'Here.

This borough. This street.' She lowers her eyes. 'This house.'

'But you're okay leaving me here on my own, in this dangerous place?' Hannah asks.

Marie flushes, her cheeks pink. 'You can take care of yourself. You always have.'

Hannah has no answer to that.

'Are you going to have breakfast with us?' Marie changes the subject.

Hannah looks at all the bread on the island. It smells wickedly good, fresh, and she knows it will still be warm. She thinks of the ingredients for her smoothie, stacked neatly in the fridge, awaiting their preparation.

She raises her chin defiantly. 'Yes, please,' Hannah says. 'I'd love to eat with you.'

Marie's hands still, her body tense. 'Good,' she says.

–

Hannah doesn't have to force down the carb-laden bagels. She smothers them in cream cheese, ignores the cucumber Marie has sliced and eats one after the other. She will feel bad, later, but it doesn't matter, she tells herself.

Because she is going to walk over to Richmond. She will check on Sofia's wellbeing and Alina's too. These carbs will vanish on the long walk.

She ponders upon Alina's behaviour last night when Sofia was missing.

Alina was totally lost in herself. Lost in her own loss. She had no plan, instead going where she was instructed. Lucas, the bodyguard driver man, had seen it too.

She recalls his words.

'Keep an eye on her.'

Hannah would be willing to bet that nobody has ever had to keep an eye on Alina before in her whole life.

She thinks of the moment she peered into that awful hostel and saw the small figure sitting in the corner. Of how Alina had attempted to smash in the window with her bare hands, and then, when the glass was broken, how she'd grabbed those shards and wrenched at them.

She didn't feel the pain. She didn't see her own blood.

That was more like the Alina that Hannah had become accustomed to.

Not the lost, broken, shell of a woman that she'd been before.

And after, later, the bond they both realised had been forged. The promises that Alina made. To clean up Hannah's problem. The dream job that will soon be hers.

Alina will make good on her promises this time. Of that, Hannah has no doubt.

'You enjoyed that breakfast?' Marie breaks into Hannah's thoughts.

Hannah answers coolly, 'It was good, thanks.'

She dresses and returns downstairs, pulls her trainers on by the front door.

'You're staying here today?' she asks Marie as she picks up her key.

'Probably. We haven't got any plans, anyway.' Marie looks up from the sink where she is washing up all the breakfast things.

They have a dishwasher. State of the art. But Marie never uses it.

'I'll be back later,' says Hannah.

She thinks about leaving without kissing Marie goodbye, but it's a heinous thought.

Marie accepts her kiss, but her eyes are faraway, in another time, or place.

Hannah wonders what she is thinking of.

Or who.

–

She passes the gallery and sees Jerry in his usual post outside the entrance. He has his hand protectively on a motorcycle parked on the pavement.

'New wheels, Jerry?' she asks as she reaches him.

He barks out a laugh. 'Just keeping an eye on it.' He looks her up and down, his gaze lingering on the bandage just visible underneath the short sleeve of her T-shirt. 'How are you, Miss Hannah?'

'Fine.' The response is automatic, robotic. 'Thank you for asking.' She pats the seat of the motorbike. 'Should this be parked here?'

Jerry shakes his head ruefully. 'Nope. But the owner doesn't much care for rules and regulations, such as parking areas.'

She remembers the times she's seen Lucas pull up on this very path, and the day he came to collect her from her house. Marie's shock that he'd driven down the pedestrianised lane. The sense of entitlement bestowed upon him by his employer.

She looks at Jerry questioningly. 'The Arpels are here?'

He hesitates before answering. 'Just Ms Arpels.'

Hannah looks inside the gallery. The first floor is relatively empty. She must be down below, in the bowels of the building. Still seeking answers, reasons. Even more so, Hannah supposes, after last night. She is surprised that Alina isn't all over the hostel across the road. Surprised, but also relieved that Alina hasn't returned to the scene of last night's devastating drama.

Hannah pushes open the door, anxious to see what Alina is up to down there. 'Catch you later, Jerry.'

27

ALINA, SUNDAY

Alina has been to the hostel. The building and the surrounding area were just as deserted as they had been last night. Not a soul in sight. The window from which she pulled Sofia out is still broken. It has not been boarded up or repaired by whoever manages the place.

Alina will find out who is in charge there.

In fact, that had been her sole focus: to return home and find a contact for the hostel management. But she'd driven past here, and the very sight of the Momotaro reminded her that she still had no answers as to last week's debacle. And, she hasn't forgotten the promise she made to Hannah last night.

It is a vow she will keep. She knows some of the directors of the board here. Even if she didn't, as Hannah once said, Alina's reputation precedes her. It won't be hard to get shifty Grantham out and Hannah installed in his place. God knows, Hannah deserves whatever she desires.

Having abandoned Willem's motorbike in Jerry's care, she exchanges the briefest of pleasantries with him before going inside.

There, she bypasses everything on the first floor, and stalks down the spiral staircase. Even though the gallery is open, it is quiet so early in the morning.

The door that she had Lucas break down has been replaced, she notices.

Before she rounds the corner, she hears the voice of someone else.

Male. Flirty tones. Young-sounding.

She rounds the corner and sees him: Tate, the creator of the dreadful Lucifer.

The girls are in their element, charming and flirting. He sits on the edge of the counter, eyes downcast, barely listening.

From what she's seen, what she knows of him, this is most un-Tate-like.

'Good morning, Tate,' Alina says.

He glances up, and if she wasn't in such a foul mood she would laugh at the expression on his face. A rabbit caught in the headlights. And she's the monster car that is going to crush him.

He slides off the counter and stands before her, his gaze drifts down to her bandaged hand. 'Good morning, Ms Arpels,' he mumbles. 'How are you? How is your daughter?'

Just the reference to Sofia sends Alina spiralling. He has no right to ask about her. He doesn't *care*. All Tate is concerned about is the wreckage of his horrible project. And the fact that after this, no gallery will want him or his stupid, dangerous works on display.

She resists the urge to tell him to shut up. Instead, she beckons him away from the pricked ears of the cloakroom girls and leads him into the reading room.

'I went through your… thing that collapsed. Were you there when the investigators went through it?'

Tate looks away. 'No. Grantham wouldn't let me stay. He said the investigators had to have space to work.'

Alina snorts. More like, Grantham wanted anything untoward that was found to be kept under wraps.

'So you didn't witness the clean-up?' She sighs.

'Grantham wouldn't let me.' Tate flushes a deep red. 'I'm so sorry, again, I really am.'

She thinks she believes that Tate had nothing to do with it. She could go to that weasel Grantham, insist on having a report of what the investigators found. But if there *was* anything, like that anomaly in the photograph that she still can't quite identify, he wouldn't tell her.

She could take him somewhere quiet, with Lucas's help. But she knows deep down that Grantham is simply protecting his gallery. If someone wanted to hurt Sofia – and, therefore, Alina – Grantham would be so far removed that he wouldn't have a clue.

She lets herself out of the reading room. At the bottom of the stairs, she glances back.

He's still slumped where she left him.

She knows he is devastated but believes that he's more so about the destruction of Lucifer, rather than Sofia's near miss.

Still, there's something… off about him.

She walks around the upper floor, drinking in the special aroma of the gallery. Today, however, it does nothing to calm her. She thinks about going home, but the bikers will still be around; her lovely house will be well on its way to becoming a fortress, and she doesn't want to be there to watch it happen.

'Alina?' A voice, small but meaningful, calls her name, pulling her out of her thoughts.

She looks up and an unexpected smile crosses her face. 'Hannah!'

Hannah visibly relaxes at Alina's friendly tone. 'I was going to take a walk to yours, see how you all are after last night.'

'How kind.' Alina tilts her head. 'You decided to stop off here on the way?'

Hannah shakes her head. 'I wasn't going to, but I got chatting to Jerry outside. He's guarding your bike.'

Alina groans. She had forgotten her mode of travel. Then, a secret smiles creeps over her features. 'Hey, Hannah,' she says, 'do you want to come for a ride?'

Before Hannah can reply, she takes her hand and drags her outside.

There's a spare helmet under the seat and Alina puts it on Hannah's head.

She'd expected her to refuse, politely of course, but something strange had crossed Hannah's face. It had looked oddly like relief. Alina decides that Hannah is excited at the thought of an unplanned trip out on an otherwise boring Sunday.

Alina is under the impression that Hannah doesn't get much adventure in her carefully structured life.

Alina climbs on and rolls the bike onto the road. She pauses while Hannah gets on behind her.

'Put your arms around my waist,' Alina shouts over the roar of the engine. 'And hold on!'

She hurtles down the high street, taking a right turn and going up the walkway that cuts through the park. She fancies she can hear Hannah's gasp at the illegal move; she certainly feels it as Hannah's hands grip her even tighter around her front.

As she races along, she thinks of everything she knows about Hannah. The younger woman's need for control, as shown in what she eats, those terrible smoothies that she calls breakfast. The almost self-flagellation in her walking regime, and the armour she wears as her clothing.

Alina wants to shake it loose from Hannah. For some reason, even though their lives are worlds apart, she is intrigued by this young woman. They share a bond now, she tells herself. One that is now even deeper than the one that had been forged that night at the gallery. On that Friday evening, even though it had been horrifying and traumatic, she'd had Sofia in her sight the whole time. Last night, when her girl was missing, the fear that Alina had felt, the very real need not to even exist any longer if Sofia hadn't been found, was worse than any torture she could even dream of.

Hannah will be in her life for ever, Alina decides. And today, she will show Hannah what it's like to cut loose and have *fun*. The sort of fun that she imagines Hannah has never allowed herself to experience.

She flies through Shepherd's Bush, cuts a right down to Hammersmith, and in no time at all they are crossing the river, making another turn, heading straight towards Battersea.

She slows the bike as she takes it into the park, ignoring the looks from the joggers and the people enjoying an early picnic.

When the bike comes to a full stop, she slides her foot under the kickstand and leans it to standing.

Hannah climbs off. When she takes off her helmet, Alina sees that her hands are shaking.

'Did you enjoy that?' Alina asks.

Hannah shakes out her hair and utters a nervous laugh. 'I-I think so. I'm not sure. Ask me in a little while.'

Alina laughs, loud and long. She points towards the café bar nearby. 'We'll get a drink,' she says.

Hannah nods. 'Wait here, I'll get them. What do you want?'

'Surprise me.'

Alina settles herself on the ground and watches Hannah walk away. The girl looks good today. A bit freer, relaxed in her jeans, shirt and trainers. Those heels and suits are okay on occasion, but this is a much better look.

Hannah needs to cut loose more often. Alina thinks she likes the other woman enough to help her do just that.

As Hannah gets in the line for the café, Alina leans back on her elbows and looks at the sky.

Last night seems like a bad dream, a nightmare that she had and can't quite shake upon waking. But it wasn't a dream. It was real.

She pulls her phone from her bag and calls Willem.

'Where are you?' he asks, instantly, upon answering her call.

Alina's heart sinks. He never asks her that question. He doesn't care where she goes or what she does or who she sees. He is interested and will want all the gossip when she finally returns home, but he never keeps tabs on her.

Suddenly, Willem is her father, worried and panicked and paranoid.

'I'm in the park. I took your bike for a spin.'

'Are you alone?' Willem's voice goes up a notch and it is all Alina can do to keep from screaming.

'No,' she answers shortly. 'I'll see you later.'

She hangs up and switches the phone off.

In a fit of pique, she hurls the phone across the park. It lands near Hannah's feet as she walks back towards Alina, a tray of goodies in her hands.

Hannah stops, goes awkwardly down on one knee, and manages to slide Alina's mobile onto the tray.

'Leave the phone, I don't want it,' says Alina, moodily, as Hannah reaches her.

Hannah puts the mobile into the upturned bike helmet. 'Is everything okay?' she asks.

Alina looks over the tray as she formulates her answer, and the contents cheer her slightly. Hannah has bought coffee, cream cakes and two small bottles of white wine.

'Are you going to have one of those cakes?' she asks Hannah, eyebrow raised.

Hannah meets her gaze. 'Yes.'

'Ha.' Alina smiles and reaches for the wine, glugging it before switching to the black coffee. 'Good. I like your style.'

They drink in silence for a few minutes. Alina watches as Hannah breaks off small pieces of the cake and picks at it like a bird.

'It was Willem on the phone. He's worried, wondering where I am.'

Hannah nods as she takes a sip of her coffee. 'It's understandable. Last night must have been really frightening for you all.'

'It's not understandable!' Alina exclaims.

Hannah pauses, coffee cup halfway to her lips. 'It's… not?'

Alina sighs. What does Hannah know? 'I never wanted to live like this,' she says. 'When I was growing up, my home was surrounded with guards, high fences and patrol dogs. I swore that when I was older, my life would be different.'

Hannah's eyes are wide. 'Why did you have to grow up that way?'

Alina holds her gaze. 'Because that's the way it was. My father chose to do what he did. I had to pay for it.'

Alina looks away across the park, wondering if Hannah is going to press further. Her new friend doesn't disappoint.

'What did he do?'

Alina shrugs, sulky again. 'It's not what he did, it's the way he lived. The deals he made. The way he worked. I chose to get out as soon as I could. I chose to live a normal life, with a normal family. I took over my father's business and made it legitimate.'

'Wow.' Hannah looks impressed. A moment later, she frowns. 'What about your mother?'

Alina feels a pang of sadness. 'She's still with him. A proper wife.' She laughs, but there is no humour in it.

Hannah looks fraught. 'I-I can't imagine it,' she says, 'leaving my mother behind.'

Alina looks at Hannah sharply. 'I didn't leave her behind. She chose to stay.'

'Do you speak to them?'

'Sometimes.' She picks at a daisy in the grass and crushes it between her fingers. 'Rarely.'

She dodges their calls, emails. She can't remember the last time they properly spoke.

Willem doesn't judge her for it. Not out loud, anyway.

'I'm sorry,' whispers Hannah.

'Don't be.' Alina clears her throat. 'It doesn't matter. What matters is that I moved a long way away in order to live a life where I didn't have to be careful. Where my daughter could go to Saturday school and return home unharmed. And now, my husband is arranging for security measures so my home will look like Fort Knox. My name has caught up with me and I'm so mad I could *kill*.'

'Wait, you think that last night wasn't just an accident? You think someone took Sofia, because of *who you are*?'

Alina frowns. Is Hannah stupid? 'Obviously, it wasn't an accident. Sofia was kidnapped.'

Hannah puts her hand to her lips. 'I… I didn't know. I thought she'd wandered off, got lost or something.'

Alina tries to calm herself: Hannah doesn't know the depths that the rot spreads in Alina's maiden name. All she saw last night was a distraught mother. She doesn't know that someone lured Sofia away, using Jules's name as a dangling carrot, as vengeance for some feud that happened generations ago.

She's mad with Sofia, too, Alina realises, and that hurts badly. Stranger danger is the first thing kids learn, all of them, even the ones who have not grown up like Alina.

'Would your son go off with anyone that he didn't know?' Alina asks.

She shrugs. 'I don't think so. I'm sure my mother has told him countless times not to.'

Alina frowns. It's a strange response. In fact, the entire sentence that Hannah has just spoken is off. The fact that she doesn't know if her son would go off with a stranger. The fact that Hannah's mother appears to be the one doing the raising of him. The shrug before she even spoke, like to her it's not a big deal.

She's never experienced it. That's all it is, thinks Alina. If you haven't been there, you can't know.

Alina squeezes her coffee cup so hard that the drink slops over the side. Unhappiness catches at her again.

'I'm just…' She trails off. 'I just don't even recognise myself anymore.'

Hannah nods and they slip back into silence.

It's true, and that's the crux of it, thinks Alina. Two weeks ago, she had everything. No, that's not right. She's still got everything, but a fortnight ago she *feared nothing*.

'My mother is scared of living here now.' Hannah breaks the silence.

Alina stares at her. 'Why?' she asks.

'Our neighbour was attacked in her home.' Hannah's mouth twists. 'I wondered if it was… you know.'

Ah. Hannah's issue that she wants fixing. Guiltily, Alina averts her eyes from Hannah's sudden, piercing gaze. She'd almost forgotten the promises she made last night.

She wonders if that's why Hannah brought up her neighbour, a subtle reminder of what Alina owes her.

'I haven't forgotten,' Alina says, quickly. 'I'm already working on it.' It's a lie, and Alina can't look Hannah in the face.

It doesn't need to be a lie, she tells herself. She can get right on it. Tonight.

Hannah doesn't answer, but simply shrugs.

It only serves to make Alina feel worse, and she reaches for the wine again, downing the remainder of the bottle.

'I *will* deal with it,' Alina promises. 'I *am* dealing with it.'

Hannah smiles. A humouring expression. As though she no longer believes that Alina will deal with anything.

Fury sears at Alina again. In another life, in another time, when she was the person that she was before, Alina would have sorted out Hannah's wishes first thing this morning.

I'm slipping, thinks Alina. She had thought about the curator role earlier, in the Momotaro, about speaking to her contacts on the board. Then, she had been distracted by Tate, and the intention had flown from her head. Her earlier words were true. She doesn't even recognise herself anymore. She's turned into someone she can't stand. Flighty. A woman who provides empty promises and half-baked ideas that never come to fruition.

She feels awful. A failure.

Again.

Hannah drains her coffee and picks up the tray. 'I'll get rid of these. Then I should get home.'

Alina stands up too. 'Do you have to go?' she asks.

Hannah pauses. 'Um, I… I guess not.'

'Spend the day with me.'

It's an impulse move. Something Alina used to do a lot, when she was younger, pre-Willem. Strike up a conversation with a stranger. In the space of an hour, they would become a friend. Another way to kick back against her father's paranoia, and all the rules and regulations forced upon her.

This morning, Alina thought she was hankering after the days when she could live without fear alongside her husband and child. Now, in an instant, she realises she wants to go back into the past. Further back, before Willem, before Sofia. In that glorious time when she came here to this country, and properly rebelled.

Right now, she feels the way she did back then. Itching to get going. It doesn't escape her that she could drop Hannah home and get to work on the promises she has made.

But she doesn't want to go home yet. Not to that fortress.

'What do you want to do?' Hannah asks.

'I know.' Alina grabs Hannah's hand. 'Let's *not* make a plan, we'll get on the motorbike and see where we end up.' Alina's eyes flash dark as she has another idea. 'I'll take you on a sightseeing tour, of all the places we can finish this person of yours.'

It's a shock tactic. In Alina's circle, there's nobody really shockable these days. They know her. And it's a statement to show Hannah that Alina hasn't forgotten, that she will do it.

But it is Hannah who shocks her.

'I'm on board.' Hannah meets Alina's eyes. 'I want to be there. To watch while you do it.'

Alina searches Hannah's face for a sign that she's simply attempting to join her friend in her own special brand of black humour. But Hannah appears deadly serious.

Alina swallows hard. She turns away, but she can still feel Hannah's gaze burning into her.

28

HANNAH, SUNDAY

Back on the motorcycle, heading not over the Thames towards home, but further out. A sign for Brixton catches her eye, a blur at the speed they are travelling.

Hannah relaxes into the ride this time and thinks about the many facets there are to Alina Arpels.

Mother, chancer, risk-taker, avenger, wife, friend, boss. *Killer?*

Hannah feels an electric excitement that she's so rarely experienced in the past.

She doesn't live this way. Her life is controlled in every area possible. When a stumbling block has been in her path, she has always dealt with it herself.

This time, she can't.

Last Friday night was not the first time she'd seen Alina Arpels. Indeed, it was not the first time she'd heard of her, either.

It had been a chance encounter, eavesdropping on a pair of gossiping women at the Momotaro. She had been in there after the job interview that turned out to be anything but. She'd felt defeated, dog-tired, like all those truths she'd just been told had sunk into her bones, turning them liquid, with her body ice-cold. Practically in shock.

She'd gone upstairs, desperately seeking the calming, soothing ambiance that the gallery vibe gave off. Wandering, aimlessly – not seeing, not thinking, not even hearing – until three little words broke through the stupor.

'She's a murderer.'

That was the line that Hannah heard one of the women say. She glanced at them, a few feet away. Gallery-goers, but their eyes were not on the items on display; they were looking at someone across the room.

'Rubbish,' the second woman scoffed. 'Alina Arpels is actually a very good person to have on your side. You need to watch it, talking like that. What is it they used to say? Loose lips sink ships.' She made a mime of a zipper closing across her mouth. 'You don't want her as an enemy; you want her as a friend.'

Unobtrusively, Hannah slid out of sight to stand behind a column.

The other woman snorted. 'I don't want her in my life at all. She's nobody's friend. She just puts people in their place. Or in the hospital.' A dry laugh ensued.

'Her husband is a diamond dealer. Her daughter is only eight, yet she already speaks four languages. She'll have just dropped her kid off at the language school. Imagine, sending your small child there, to learn with the adults, every single Saturday. And, if that isn't enough, her father is in the Russian mafia,' said the first woman, her voice a hushed whisper. 'And even though she doesn't live in this neighbourhood, this is her stomping ground, so shut up and let's get out of here. The walls have ears, you know.'

The paranoia from the second woman was very real. Hannah peered across the room, studying this woman who could conjure up such a reaction from people who didn't seem to know her on a personal level at all.

She *did* look like she was someone, Hannah admitted. Though she couldn't put her finger on it. There was an expensive air about her, even though her clothes and styling did not reek of money. It was something else. The way she moved, perhaps, like she owned the entire gallery, and all of the items and people in it. Or maybe it was how the gallery staff acted towards her: a reverence, stopping just short of a curtsy.

I need someone like that. It had been Hannah's first thought. *I need her.*

Because Hannah's problem, which she didn't even know she had until half an hour before, wasn't going away on its own.

And Hannah needed it to go away.

So had begun her research into Alina Arpels. And the more Hannah found out, the more she knew she had hit her jackpot.

Today, after everything that has happened between them, Hannah knows that they are firm friends. Not only will Alina keep her promises, but she has also opened up to Hannah. Fed her titbits about her past, shared her feelings towards her parents. Most of which, through her own careful analysis and investigation, Hannah already knew. But knowing was one thing. Alina confiding in her, willingly, was something else entirely.

And Alina's feelings about her youth, about her father – that's something Hannah can understand. There is only one difference between them: Hannah would never have left her mother behind.

They come to a stop in the centre of Brixton, a single green strip in a world of grey.

'We'll just chill out for the afternoon,' Alina says as they stash the helmets in the seat. 'I want to get good

215

and loaded with a mate. For one day I want to act like I can live like everybody else.'

Hannah feels her face fall.

'Don't look like that.' Alina shoves Hannah with her shoulder. 'Tonight, I'll make my plan. Tomorrow, I'll deal with it. Today, please Hannah, will you grant me *my* wish?'

Hannah glances around. She can see a few pubs over the road. Not a single one of them looks like the sort of establishment where Alina would normally spend her time.

Hannah feels a pang of anxiety. Alina is impetuous and impulsive. Only half an hour ago, she'd promised to deal with Hannah's problem today. Now, she says tomorrow.

'Hey, I asked if you are up for this?' Alina's voice is rough, distracting Hannah from her thoughts.

The tone of voice brings to mind those two women, the scandalous gossip in the gallery that day. It's a reminder that, though flighty, Alina has balls of steel, and needs to be kept onside.

'Okay,' Hannah says.

Alina whoops and links arms with Hannah, dragging her across the road.

A car swerves, blares its horn, and Hannah holds up a hand in apology.

The pub they go into is as grey as the world outside. It is quiet, no music or chatter. Just a few old men stand in shadowy corners, speaking to nobody. The aroma of fetid beer and stale bodies assaults Hannah's nose.

Alina seems not to even notice the vileness of the interior. She bounces to the bar and orders tequila shots, and separate glasses of vodka doubles.

'Have you got a beer garden, my friend?' Alina asks the bartender.

He looks like a student, long hair flopping over his face. He is thin and twitchy. He nods in the direction of a fire door.

Alina picks up the tray and heads over to it. It is already ajar, and she aims a kick at it and stumbles outside.

'Well, Jesus,' she mutters.

Hannah holds the door open. The sun is bright, at its highest point. Another scorching day.

It could be nice if this beer garden actually resembled anything like a beer garden.

But it's not. The fire door has led to an alleyway linking two streets.

Hannah expects that Alina will turn on her heel and flounce back inside. Instead, she puts the tray down in the middle of the path, sits beside it and picks up the tequila. It slops over the side of the glass, soaking the bandage on Alina's hand. Alina doesn't seem to notice.

'Come on, we've got a party to get started!' Alina calls.

Hannah glances once more into the pub. Nobody has moved. The men are still seated, heads down. The bartender stands motionless, his eyes faraway. She wonders if they know who Alina is.

Hannah lets the door swing closed and walks over to join Alina.

She has seen people who behave like Alina. In the past, when she did her stint at university. There were girls like her there. They didn't care much about the degrees they were doing. It wasn't their money they were spending. They were there on their father's dime, just along for the ride.

When she had a few rare moments of free time, Hannah would watch them with intrigue.

She didn't understand it, how their lives could be so carefree that they could allow themselves such a minimal scope of control.

'Drink,' Alina commands her, passing her a tequila.

Hannah waits until Alina turns back to the tray, and she flicks it into the gutter.

Oh Alina, Alina, how are you going to save me if you're so wasted?

Then, an idea strikes her, out of the blue. She will force Alina's hand. She will take advantage of Alina's drunken state.

She pulls out her phone, scrolls to the last message she received. She hasn't deleted it.

> It doesn't matter if you don't want to see me. I respect your choice. But remember, Hannah, this isn't all about you. There are other people in this equation.

The bold statement, the very entitlement in it, sends Hannah's blood pressure soaring.

There has been no contact since.

She types out a message.

> I'm sorry for before. Are you in London?
> Hannah. X

She holds her breath and waits.

Alina jostles her, passing her a vodka this time.

'You're not being much fun, Hannah.' She pouts.

Alina is prickly again. Soon, that strange fury that Hannah has seen several times before will return. This could be the perfect moment.

Hannah's phone vibrates. She glances at the message on the screen and smiles.

'Hey, Alina.' She holds up her phone so Alina can read what's on the screen, scrolling just far enough for the last text to be seen, and not the one she sent herself.

> I'm in London. I very much need to see you, Hannah. Can we meet?

Alina's face arranges itself into a scowl. For a moment, for the first time, Hannah thinks she looks ugly.

Alina stands up and dusts off her jeans. 'Come on, then,' she demands. 'We'll end this, right now.'

29

ALINA, SUNDAY

She's not blackout drunk, nowhere near it yet, but the tequila and the vodka have given her a buzz.

Everything that came before, all that angst, has hardened to concrete. It seemed like Hannah wasn't going to touch her vodka, so Alina took it back from her and downed it too.

She can see why people turn to alcohol as a crutch. Before now, it's just been something to enjoy: a cosy drink with Willem, a raucous bender with her friends. A civilised beverage with people like Merle or Francis. Alina has never before drunk to feed her rage.

Right now, she can't imagine why not.

'Are you sure you're okay to drive?' Hannah asks as they sweep back through the pub to the motorcycle parked outside.

Alina stares at it, rather astonished to see it is still there, even though she hadn't chained it up.

'Yeah, I'm all good.' She barely considers Hannah's question. Consequences don't even cross her mind.

She swings herself back on the bike with such verve that she almost flies across the other side.

Hannah hesitates before clambering on behind her.

'Where are we headed?' Alina calls over her shoulder.

'Soho,' replies Hannah.

Vaguely, Alina remembers the address that Hannah wrote for her last night.

Guilt spikes at her; she could have gone to Soho last night, or first thing this morning.

Regardless, suddenly she's itching to go, to get there, to do something. It won't be the person who took Sofia yesterday, but it is someone of the same ilk. A bad sort.

Alina clenches her fingers hard around the bike handles. This person will do.

For now.

She'd thought the ride might do her good – wind in her hair, fresh warm breeze. She's not put her helmet on, a fact that Hannah keeps yelling in her ear.

'Shut up!' Alina shouts.

But this ride doesn't feel good. She doesn't feel good. The rage is blazing a trail down her gullet. Who do these people think they are? Stalking Hannah, stealing Sofia?

Another half-thought through the alcohol haze. She wonders vaguely if the person who is harassing Hannah was her lover. A one-night thing that Hannah regrets. The spurned party not getting the message.

She shifts up a gear and her thoughts move to how her day started, with Willem organising all the additional security. The trip to the gallery and seeing Tate. Waste of time that it was.

He had lied to her, this morning.

She's sure of it.

Just another bad person in a city full of them.

And suddenly, she wants to see him again. She wasn't assertive enough this morning. She wants to grab him by his throat and demand he tell her the truth. This morning, he was edgy, cagey. Wanting to speak, but not quite daring to.

They are passing through Kensington; she recognises the high street. She will make a stop at the hostel, see what's going on now. See if she can throw some cash or weight around, and get some more information.

Then they can visit the gallery. Grantham might be there too. She'll introduce him to Hannah, watch his face when she tells him that this woman is his successor. She'll call over Tate, the artist, and she can grab the pair of them and knock their bloody heads toge—

A scream sounds, so close to her ear, so loud, that for a single second Alina loses all sight and focus.

She blinks hard, rapidly, and looks up ahead of her.

She sees Jerry, his usual, gentle face a huge mask of horror. She sees the Momotaro window, coming at her fast. The bump as the motorbike mounts the pavement, thankfully slowing the powerful machine somewhat.

Hannah's face is buried in Alina's spine and her grip around her waist is so tight that she can't breathe.

Brake! She screams it internally, but her hands are slow to follow her own instruction.

Brake!

She feels the skid. Jerry's arm is out now, as though this sixty-year-old man can stop the oncoming bike like some sort of superhero.

At the last second, she swerves so the bike hits the gallery wall side-on. It bounces, almost toppling, before the engine splutters and dies.

Hands are on Alina, on the bike. She's lifted off, set on her feet, where she sways violently. The memory that catches at her is that of Tate's sculpture as it began to move.

A presence looms.

Jerry.

She sees the slight wrinkling of his nose as the smell of the alcohol she has consumed hits him.

'Alina.' He says her name softly. Not Ma'am, or Ms Arpels, this time. But Alina.

Suddenly, he is her father, mild disapproval emanating from him.

'I'm fine,' she snaps.

She's not, though. She is ashamed. And suddenly very, very clear-headed.

She looks around for Hannah. She is standing by the door, staring at the bike which someone has propped up.

'Are you okay?' Alina asks her.

Hannah nods. 'Shall we catch the Tube to Soho?'

Soho? Why on earth would she want to go to Soho?

Hannah is expectant. Alina vaguely recalls the conversation. The harasser. The stalker.

Alina sighs. The fury has gone. Suddenly, she's stone-cold sober and can't believe that she was planning to go to Soho, to deal with Hannah's persecutor in broad daylight. And what was she going to do, anyway? Threaten? Throw some cash to make the problem go away?

Alina looks at the motorbike. The paint is scratched. It means nothing. It is easily fixed, but she's sad and shocked by the sight of it anyway.

'Jerry, can you get Lucas here?' she asks.

She finds that she is trembling.

Jerry nods and pulls his phone out of his pocket.

'Alina?' Hannah comes up beside her.

'Hannah. I'm so sorry.' Alina scrubs at her face with her hands. 'Wait here with me… Lucas is coming. He'll take you home.'

'No, it's… I'm fine. Do you… Do you not want to go to Soho anymore?'

'Maybe another time,' Alina says, weakly.

She drifts away from Hannah, approaching the automatic door of the Momotaro. Once inside, she breathes deeply, doing her best to either calm or kickstart herself back to someone she recognises.

But she can feel eyes on her: Jerry's. He's speaking on his phone, no doubt telling Lucas what a bad girl she has been. Hannah is still outside, looking lost. Looking small and hurt because, once again, Alina has broken her promise and almost caused the still-recovering woman another injury.

She moves past the Japanese tea stand and finds herself at the top of the spiral staircase. She finds she doesn't want to go down there now, where this disaster began.

She walks around the shop, stopping to look at the items.

'Hi, Ms Arpels.'

The voice, the use of her name, makes her jump. She turns around and sees Tate slumped in one of the armchairs.

Strangely, the fury doesn't come, not like it did on the ride over here.

She is simply weary now. And those armchairs look damn good.

She takes a seat next to him.

'Why are you always here, Tate?' she asks him, curiously.

He shrugs.

Alina raises her eyebrows. He seems a bit salty this afternoon. A bit… edgy, maybe.

She swivels in her chair. 'What?' she asks. 'What aren't you saying?'

He lowers his eyes. 'I don't trust them,' he says. 'Look, I found something. I showed it to them, to that manager, and the investigators. I'm hanging around until I know they're going to act.'

'What do you mean, "you found something"?'

He looks at her sideways on. His lip is curled in a sulky scowl. 'In the pile of Lucifer. I found something.'

Alina breathes deeply. 'What was it?'

He sighs. 'A black square thing. I don't know, like, maybe a really small battery pack? It wasn't supposed to be in Lucifer. Obvs, I mean, it was a metal sculpture.'

'Where is it now?' Alina asks him. She is energised, invigorated.

She'd *known* there was something off about the accident!

'I don't know. That guy took it, put it in a bag and last I saw, it was in his office.'

Alina stands up. 'When was this?'

'This morning. Just after you were here.'

Alina feels a prickle of excitement. She knew, right from the time she took the photos of the crumpled form, that there was something in the debris that shouldn't have been there.

She stands up, reaches over and hauls Tate up from his chair.

'Come with me,' she commands.

Down the spiral staircase again. She glances outside, sees Willem's bike still on the pavement. Jerry is there, one hand on the seat. What a guy. No sign of Hannah.

For a moment, Alina feels a spike of guilt.

She will deal with it, she promises again. But right now, the cause of her daughter's accident is her priority. And who knows, whatever Tate found might be the link to everything that's been happening.

'He's not here,' says Tate when they get to the lower floor. 'He went out earlier.'

Alina grins and turns to the cloakroom girls. 'Ladies, do you remember what happened the last time I wanted to get in one of your rooms and it was locked?'

They nod, nervously, in unison.

She points to Grantham's office. 'I want to get in there. My man Lucas will be here any second. Today I am prepared for you to unlock it for me.'

The first cloakroom girl, the one Tate was flirting with this morning, jumps up from her chair. She hands over a bunch of keys.

'It's the red-labelled one,' she says.

Alina smiles. 'Good girl. Come on, Tate.'

She stands by the open doorway, watching as Tate scours the room for the bag he saw. It was a Momotaro-branded bag, which doesn't help, as Grantham's office is filled with them.

Should she be targeting him, Grantham? Or rather, is he the one targeting *her*?

She had dismissed him, because he is soft and stupid, and nothing at all to do with the world she comes from. But soft and stupid also equals pliable. Has someone approached Grantham?

But *why*?

Alina shakes her head. The thoughts, the worries – the same ones – are going around her head, over and over. No wonder she doesn't feel like herself.

'Got it!' Tate holds up a bag. It's a small one, from the gift shop. Alina snatches it from him and looks inside.

It has one item in it. Small, square, black.

She tips it out into the palm of her hand.

Tate peers at it. 'Do you know what it is?'

Alina frowns and closes her fingers around it. 'Yes,' she says. 'I do.'

30

HANNAH, SUNDAY

Now, as she walks away from the gallery – from Jerry, the bike and Alina – Hannah feels deflated.

She had been on the cusp of having her problems sorted.

So, so close. Within touching distance.

And now Alina, flighty one that she is, has crashed her bike and moved on.

Hannah wants to scream.

Her phone buzzes, vibrating against her in her back pocket. She pulls it out, hopeful that it is Alina, back on form and ready to go.

Hannah freezes, mid-step.

An enquiry as to her whereabouts. Polite, yet Hannah knows that's just a front.

Damn it.

She shouldn't have let Alina get distracted and walk away. She should have nudged Alina again and again until the woman did what she promised she would do.

Hannah turns around, looking back at the gallery. It's not too late. Alina is still in there. Hannah can go back, appeal to her, remind her of what she has done for her.

A large, black car rolls smoothly past Hannah. Lucas!

Hannah breaks into a run, sprinting back over the road. She reaches Lucas just as he steps out of the vehicle.

'Lucas!'

He frowns at her, taking in the bike, the scrapes on it, the helmet – the one Hannah was wearing – still on the pavement.

'What happened today?' he asks. 'Where is Alina?'

'I'm right here!' Alina sweeps out of the automatic door, Tate scuttling along behind her. 'What's going on? Why is everyone looking so worried?'

Hannah's breath catches in her throat. This is the Alina she knows. This… haughty woman, the one who takes no crap, but who freely dishes it out.

'Alina!' Hannah steps in front of her. She's determined now to lock this thing down before another day, before another hour, even has passed. 'I need to speak to you, straight away.'

'Hannah?' Alina frowns at her. 'I thought you'd gone. I said we'd give you a lift home, didn't I?'

Hannah takes a deep breath and puts a hand on Alina's arm. 'I can't wait any longer,' she says. 'I've helped you, more than once. You have promised me you would assist me. I need your help. *Now.*'

She expects Alina to bluster, to make false promises, to placate her the same way she does Lucas or the many men in her life. Instead, Alina looks faintly impressed at Hannah's forceful tone.

'Yes. I should have acted earlier. I… I wasn't myself before.' Alina leans in and puts her hands on Hannah's shoulders. 'I'm back. And I'll deal with this. *Tonight.*'

'Really?' Hannah takes Alina's hand and looks into her eyes. 'Are you sure you can?'

Alina nods, once, firmly. 'Tonight. I swear to you.'

Alina leans in and hugs Hannah before stepping back. She holds up a gift bag from the gallery. Her eyes are gleaming.

'Trust me, Hannah. I'm dealing with everything tonight.'

She winks, walks jauntily to the passenger side of the car and slides in.

–

Hannah watches her drive away. She wonders what Alina's parting words mean.

I'm dealing with everything tonight.

Tate comes to stand beside her. 'Friend of yours?' he asks.

She frowns at him, wondering if he has a clue who she is. Does he even remember that his rotten sculpture sliced her open just the previous weekend? She turns to face him.

'I'm Hannah,' she says, by way of introduction. She waits for recognition to cross his features.

Instead, he barely looks at her.

'I was at your opening night,' she says, pointedly. 'When the accident happened.'

Now, he reacts. He glances at her, fear and distress in his eyes. 'Turns out it might not have been an accident after all.'

Hannah's heart pounds. 'What?' she asks.

Moodily, he kicks at the kerb.

'I don't know,' he says. He stares after Alina's departed car. 'But if she's on the case, I suspect we're all in for it.'

Hannah walks home after saying goodbye to Jerry. She moves past the motorbike. It's been left where it crashed, propped up outside the gallery. The helmet is still on the pavement.

She thinks about the sense of entitlement there, the fact that a motorbike, stylish and expensive, can be so easily discarded by Alina.

Jerry will keep an eye on it. She imagines that if nobody has been sent by the Arpels when it comes to his knocking-off time, he will wheel it inside.

That's the sort of man that Jerry is.

Hannah's phone buzzes again. She looks at it.

Belatedly, Hannah remembers she never replied. She wavers, unsure of how to play it now. Should she continue with her current theme, apologetic and promising to meet up? Or simply ignore it and let Alina deal with it tonight. As long as Alina *does* deal with it tonight.

Hannah thinks back to moments ago. *That* was the Alina she has been counting on. Focused, ready for action.

She feels uncomfortably hot as she treks the short walk home.

Something else to think about now. What did Alina find in that gallery that has reignited her fire?

31

ALINA, SUNDAY

Willem is shouting. Sofia is staring open-mouthed at her father. Rarely does Willem raise his voice.

'I will pay for your stupid bike,' Alina says, rolling her eyes.

He grabs her shoulders. 'Christ, woman. You think it's my bike I'm concerned about? You think I wouldn't smash up ten motorcycles just to keep you safe?'

She pouts.

'Don't do that.' He lets go of her and walks over to the window.

Alina's heart drops. Willem never does that. Never acts that way towards her. Her personality amuses him. It never irritates him.

What has her life become?

She goes over to Sofia and wraps her arms around her girl.

She had a bath last night, Sofia did, before she went to bed. Alina inhales. She's sure she can still smell that rotten, damp scent from the hostel.

She sniffs harder and realises it is coming from the light jacket she has on.

She tears it off and slings it in the washing machine.

'Lucas is taking Gerard to get the bike,' Willem announces as he taps away on his phone.

'Look, I'm sorry about the bike. I'm sorry for going off this morning—'

'Alone. When you know that we are being targeted,' cuts in Willem, pointedly. 'Drinking, too, and getting on the bike.' He gives her a look that he's never aimed in her direction before. 'Reckless. Stupid.'

She swallows back the tears that threaten. 'Jesus. Anyway, I wasn't alone. Hannah was with me.'

'Hannah…?'

Alina lets out a dramatic screech. 'The woman who has saved your daughter's life, *twice*!' she shouts.

Willem passes a hand over his eyes. *God, he looks tired*, thinks Alina. Willem never looks this way. He has the energy of ten men, and the humour of a hundred. What has happened to him?

What has happened to us?

'Look. I went to the gallery, saw that Tate, spoke to him again. Something fishy is going on. They found something in the wreckage of his sculpture, and they were not going to tell anybody. I can't help but think it's too much of a coincidence. The sculpture collapsing, the… The hostel.' As she speaks the words aloud, she realises they are true. It's been needling her…

For the first time, Willem perks up. 'What did they find?' he asks.

She puts the Momotaro gift bag on the counter and takes out the black item. Willem looks at it curiously.

'It's a pager,' he says.

Alina nods. 'Yep. Willem, who even has a pager anymore? And why was it in the installation?'

'What did Tate say about it?'

233

She tells him how Tate saw the investigators with it, how it was passed to Grantham and he had locked it in his office. 'Tate's so young, he didn't even know what it was.'

She thinks back to Tate handing it over to her. His words that he thought it looked like a battery pack or similar device. Was he being truthful, or acting dumb?

Truthful, her gut tells her. He honestly has never seen a pager before in his life.

'You think this Grantham has something against you?' He puts his arm around Sofia. 'Against us?'

'No. Not him.'

'Someone approached him?' Willem frowns. 'Alina, think hard, who have you pissed off recently?'

'Nobody!' She is affronted, but immediately chastised.

Okay, she's annoyed plenty of people, but certainly not in the recent past. There were all those men, all the old ones that she laid off from her father's company. But that was years ago.

She scowls at her husband and his insinuations. 'Why are we so sure this is aimed at me? What about you?'

He shakes his head. 'In my business? Come on, who the heck is offended by lab-created diamonds?'

'Diamond traders?' she shouts back. 'You're changing the lie of the land. People are intrigued by your creations. You're putting the others out of business.'

Willem scoffs. 'Not a chance. The old-school people will stick to what they know. It's the younger generation who want my goods. There's no fight over my gems.'

Alina sighs.

'I don't like it. I don't like what's happening. And I don't like what our life has suddenly become.' She gets off the stool. 'I'll be in the office; I've got work to do.'

'Julia has been in all day; she's got it all in hand.'

She grimaces. 'Not that kind of work,' she says.

She is gone before he can ask any more questions.

Tonight's work is for Hannah.

She has promised her. And Hannah delivered. *Twice*.

As she settles herself behind the large, oak desk, she takes out the piece of paper where Hannah wrote the details of the person harassing her.

Alina runs her fingers over the indentation made by the ink.

Who is this person?

She shakes her head. No. No questions. Just delivering. It doesn't matter who this person is; they just need to be dealt with.

Upstairs, she hears a commotion in the hallway. Lucas, she imagines. Back with Gerald and Willem's motorbike.

She doesn't want to see them. She must get this job done; then, once it is over, she can start to focus on whoever is targeting her own family.

Willem's scratched-up bike is very low on her list of priorities.

She is just switching on her computer, when there is a small tap at the office door.

'Hello, Alina?'

Alina stands up. 'Francis?'

Francis ducks inside, swishing over to Alina and kissing her on both cheeks. 'I had to come.' Francis lowers her voice. 'I heard Sofia was taken! I came to help, but you had a lot of people there, looking out for you.'

Alina hugs her friend, trying to ignore the uncomfortable feeling that has crept over her.

Yesterday, one minute Francis was there, then she was gone.

'I apologise, I didn't even think to call you. It was a stressful day.' The words Francis just spoke make her narrow her eyes. She pulls away and regards her oldest friend. 'What makes you say she was taken?'

Francis flaps her hand. 'That's what I heard. Is it true? Someone *kidnapped* her?'

How did Francis hear that? Alina certainly didn't tell her. She studies Francis intently.

Her friend, Francis. Her oldest friend.

One who knew Alina's father, way back when.

'What did the police say?' Francis asks.

Alina laughs, dryly. Francis has the grace to blush.

'Sorry, darling girl, I know you don't work that way. But how long was she missing?'

'Hours.' Alina sits back down in her chair. She's being melodramatic, as is her way. Suddenly, though, because it's Sofia she's talking about, it doesn't seem right to exaggerate. 'More than an hour, anyway,' she concedes.

Suddenly, she remembers Francis's words at lunch the day before. How she was almost scathing about her employee, Hannah. 'In fact, your employee came to the rescue again.'

'My employee?'

'Hannah Barker.'

Francis frowns. 'How on earth did she help?'

Alina waves her hand in the air. 'She lives nearby, she helped with the search. There were a lot of us looking. We split up, Hannah and I found her.'

'Where?' Francis breathes.

'Do you know that hostel off the high street? Sofia was in there.' Alina recalls the place, the smashing of the window, the stench of the building, the thought that her girl was *locked inside*. She presses her fingers to her lips, feeling as though she might throw up.

Francis shakes her head. 'Alina, I'm so sorry for you. I take it Sofia is okay, physically?'

'Yes.' Alina utters a shaky laugh. 'She's doing better than me, anyway.'

She shivers. Her words are an echo; she spoke that very sentence to Hannah the day after the sculpture collapsed.

'The accident last week, now this.' Francis shakes her head. 'Why is all this raining down on you, all of a sudden?'

Alina regards Francis. She's known the woman a long time. Francis is her art-world contact. Francis is the one Alina goes to if she is redecorating, or if there is an opening or an event. She knew her folks, long before she knew Alina, so what?

She stands up, certain that she's right in her thinking, her decision made. 'Wait here, will you?'

She jogs out of the office, through the hallway and into the kitchen.

Willem is still there; Lucas has joined him now. Sofia and Lucas are at the stove. They are cooking borscht, a sour soup, with meatballs that Sofia is rolling out.

'All right, Alina?' Lucas asks.

She takes in the scene. Lucas, friend and bodyguard, wearing his ridiculous chef's apron. Willem, husband, love of her life, giving a running commentary on Lucas's food.

And Sofia. Daughter. The best thing that Alina has ever done.

She wants to cry that someone would hurt her family.

She snatches up the pager. 'Save some food for me.'

She heads back to her office, moving along the marbled hallway. She wishes more than anything that, for tonight, she could forget what has been happening. She would take Francis and drag her upstairs, make her eat with them. They would crack open the drinks, carry on until the early hours.

She takes a deep breath and swings back into her office. Francis is up, looking at the photographs that adorn Alina's wall.

'I love looking at these. Those people. Some of my favourites. Some of them gone too soon.'

The photographs are mostly black and white, or sepia. Alina glances at them, the family wall. She's unsure why she keeps them on display.

She shakes her head, dark hair whipping around her face as she pulls herself back to the business at hand. She puts the pager on the desk.

'What's this?' Francis props her glasses on her nose and peers at it.

'This is what caused Tate's sculpture to collapse,' says Alina.

Francis frowns. 'It's a bloody pager. Why would Tate have a *pager* in his installation?'

'He didn't.' Alina throws herself back into her chair and regards the wicked thing lying on her desk. 'It shouldn't have been in it, but it was.'

'Hot damn.' Francis shakes her head in dismay. 'This thing, if it works, if it went off, it could be the reason why it fell. They work by vibration, you know.'

Alina slams her palm down on the desk. She feels the sting and relishes it.

'I know what a pager is! I'm old enough. Tate isn't – he didn't know what it was. But who even has a pager these days, Francis? I mean, when was the last time you even saw one of these?'

Francis picks it up gingerly. 'Funnily enough, not that long ago.'

Alina sits bolt upright. 'What do you mean?'

'I mean, we had an event at the gallery, at my gallery. We got the idea from this thing they did in Brooklyn.'

'Brooklyn?'

Francis nods, a small smile on her face. 'Over in the USA, they had all these pagers intercepting messages which were then printed out as part of the display. It got political, as such things often do.'

'Political? What do you mean?'

'Invasion of privacy, or something like that. We did it over here, in the Harman Gallery. But we put a different spin on it: we let people send their own messages, which we then printed out.' Francis looks off to the distance, a smile playing around her lips. 'It was fun. Just a limited-time thing, but successful. There were marriage proposals, pregnancy announcements. Something a bit different to draw the crowds in.'

Alina nods. Something different. That's the thought she had that night at Tate's opening. That to succeed, everything must be different. A twist, or a reveal, is paramount.

Hell, even fashion shows need to be shocking these days.

Francis is still talking, reminiscing, but Alina isn't paying attention.

Something is niggling at her, like a worm in her mind. She can't quite put her finger on it.

Francis falls silent, apparently noticing that Alina's mind is elsewhere. 'Anyway, I just wanted to stop by, make sure you and your darling girl are okay.'

Alina stops her. 'Stay for dinner?'

It's a peace offering. A way of apologising for her attitude towards Francis yesterday, the near row they had over Hannah. And for the doubt she had towards her oldest friend, which Francis isn't even aware of.

A split moment of hesitation and Alina grabs on to it. 'Please,' she says. 'It's been such a stressful time. I really want my people around me.'

Francis looks flattered to be referred to as one of Alina's 'people'.

'Is Lucas cooking?' she asks as they make their way upstairs.

'I think all three of them are,' Alina replies as they reach the kitchen. 'Hey, gang. Set another place at the table!'

32

HANNAH, SUNDAY

The bedsit makes Hannah's skin crawl.

She had to show up for the meet. Must try and at least keep things as normal as possible until Alina can deliver on her promise of… what?

Hannah's intention is to try to find out if this person harassing her by text is also the same one who has been watching her, observing from a distance. The one who scared her in the park. The one who touched her. Who pushed her…

She wonders now if she should have left it until Alina arrived and dealt with it.

Dealt with it.

It is the phrasing they have been using. All very British. Alina's chosen words could be interpreted in a manner of ways.

End this.

Hannah closes her eyes briefly and wonders how her life has come to this.

'Now, what was all that about?'

She opens her eyes at the sound of Grace Perry's voice. She takes a moment to study the young woman in front of her.

Blonde hair, the coloured streak that had been blue at their first meeting, red on the second, is now a startling pink. Another ring in her nose. Bangles that sound like an orchestra as she hands over Hannah's coffee, which she hasn't asked for.

There is something different in Grace's stance, too. Before, both times, she had been open, hopeful, filled with a joy that Hannah found rather nauseating.

Today she is steely, cooler. Those horribly familiar green eyes are like lasers.

'What was what about?' Hannah feigns innocence.

'Your text. You said you didn't want to see me again.' Grace sits down on the sofa next to Hannah.

Hannah leans forward to put the strong-smelling coffee on the table. When she sits back down, she manages to put some space between them.

'You're worried,' Grace says, in a soft tone. 'Please, don't be. I'm not here to cause trouble for anyone.'

But you have. You are.

'It's not that.' Hannah shifts uncomfortably. 'Well, I suppose it kind of is.' She forces out a laugh. 'I panicked, which sounds really silly…' She trails off, unsure where to go from here.

After all, she is simply stalling.

'Is?'

'Huh?' Hannah says, blankly.

'You said "is", present tense. I assumed you had a change of heart when you messaged me.'

'I did. I have.' Hannah feels the back of her neck prickle with unease. 'I'm sorry for what I said.'

She expects Grace to smile, in that lovely, innocent way she does. She imagines the joy to return, expects this woman to be easily placated.

But Grace does none of those things.

Her prickling neck turns into a full-on sweat. Jesus, where is Alina? When is she intending to *deal with this*, as she's promised?

Another thought strikes Hannah in the uncomfortable silence that ensues. One that she should have considered a lot earlier than this.

'Have you... told anybody about us?' she ventures.

She steels herself. If Grace has confided in someone else, she might not be so easy to dismiss.

'No.' Grace's reply is short.

Hannah wonders if Grace is lying.

She glances at her phone, lying next to her on the horribly sagging sofa. She picks up the coffee and forces herself to sip at it.

She tries not to blanch. Coffee is the devil. All that artificial stimulation makes her quake.

'Do you want something with that?' Grace asks.

Hannah nods gratefully. It is an opening, a sure sign that Grace is forgiving her, or that she is at least heading in that direction.

Keep her onside. She's dangerous, after all.

'Thanks,' she says as Grace heads towards the tiny kitchenette area.

She imagines the girl will return with cream. At the very least, milk. Anything that she can dump in the brew to tone it down a little.

As Grace busies herself opposite, Hannah picks up her phone and taps out a text to Alina.

As an afterthought, she types the address of the bedsit at
the end of the message.

She hits send and flicks the volume to silent, just as
Grace returns.

Grace sets down a tray. Upon it are two sad-looking
cakes. Cream cakes. The cream looks watery. The crys-
tallised sugar that coats them makes Hannah's intestines
tighten in protest.

'They've got a bakery in the little corner shop down-
stairs,' says Grace as she moves the tray a little closer to
Hannah.

Hannah has seen the little corner shop downstairs. If
she was desperate, she wouldn't even buy a bottle of water
from it.

She smiles politely and looks around. This one room is
where Grace is living. The sofa on which they are seated
looks a hundred years old. The carpet is threadbare and
moves under her feet when she stands on it. The kitchen
area is a stovetop with two rings, a travel-size kettle, and
cupboards which were once probably white but are now
yellowed with age and lack of ventilation.

Hannah notices that there is no fridge. These cakes
have been sweltering in the summer heat since Grace
purchased them. She sits back and lowers her gaze to her
black coffee. No wonder she wasn't offered any milk.

'This place is…' She slowly trails off.

Shit, is what she wanted to say. Hannah rarely swears.
She's no Alina. But this time, she was about to make an
exception.

244

It would be wrong. If she commented on how putrid this bedsit is, Grace might nudge Hannah for an invitation to stay at her house.

She closes her eyes again. She imagines Grace's face if she saw her mews house. It would seem like a palace to this uneducated individual.

No, that's wrong. Grace isn't uneducated. She's got a degree, the same as Hannah, even in the same area. But while Hannah chose the business route of the art world, Grace seems content with being a struggling artist.

She glances at the girl next to her. She's frowning again, a little indentation between her brows.

Internally, Hannah screams at herself. *Play nice!*

She blurts out the first question that comes to mind, 'What's it like where you come from?'

Grace smiles. That annoying, self-satisfied smugness is back on her face.

'It's awesome. We live in the countryside, lots of walks on our doorstep. We're on the coast. Cork is the nearest big city, within easy reach. Dad works there, and Mum does the accounts in the village. She works only a couple of days a week, always has, so she had plenty of time for us kids.' Grace leans her head back on the filthy sofa. 'It was a perfect way to grow up. It still is.'

'You don't want to leave there, then?' Hannah jumps on her last statement.

'My heart will always be in the auld country, wherever I am.' Grace emphasises her Irish brogue and collapses with laughter, all previous coolness towards Hannah apparently gone. 'But it's not going anywhere, my home. No matter where I go in the world, I can always visit my folks.'

'You said "kids", before. How many of you are there?'

'Nine. Four brothers, four sisters.' Grace grins. 'We're real close.'

Hannah imagines it. Eight other siblings. That would be eight brothers and sisters too many for Hannah.

'And you haven't... mentioned me?'

Grace's face falls a little. 'They're brilliant, but... they wouldn't understand.' She gives a rueful laugh. 'They don't understand a lot about my life.'

Hannah is intrigued. 'How so?' she asks.

Grace places her hands in her lap. 'They're really cool, but a little... conservative. Very old school. Women should be married by the time they turn twenty-five. Men need to do a certain kind of job. My brothers are carpenters, one is a mechanic. My sisters are all engaged or married, and some of them are already mothers.' She gives Hannah a conspiratorial wink. 'I'm the black sheep.'

Hannah's phone vibrates on the seat beside her. She snatches it up and exhales with relief.

It is Alina.

I'm ready. I'll do it tonight.

Hannah shoves her phone in her pocket and stands up.

'You're leaving?' Grace is crestfallen.

'It's work,' Hannah lies. 'I'm so sorry.'

Grace stands up too. 'You didn't even touch your cake!'

Thank God.

Hannah smiles tightly. 'Next time.'

'There will be a next time? You're not going to get all weird again?'

Hannah shakes her head vigorously.

Grace nods uncertainly and walks her the couple of feet to the door.

'See you soon.' Hannah steps out into the hall, the pungent aroma of stale piss hitting her hard.

'Hannah?'

Hannah turns. Grace stands on the threshold of her bedsit, her face very serious.

'I'm not letting go of us. What we have.' Grace smiles. 'What we *could* have.'

Hannah nods and feels her face flush. 'I know. Me too. I'll see you very soon, Grace.'

Sooner than you think.

33

ALINA, SUNDAY

The impromptu dinner party is a huge success. And it is exactly what Alina needed.

Friends, family, good food and even better drinks. Francis is charmed by Lucas, a man a good fifteen years her junior, as she is every time they meet. He flirts shamelessly, and Alina is in fits of laughter at this often-unseen side to him. Willem seems to have forgiven her for her recklessness.

Her paranoia fades away to almost nothing.

Almost nothing, but not entirely. Alina isn't stupid. She will remain on her guard against everyone. The acknowledgement of this causes a hard stone of misery in her stomach, but she does her best to ignore it.

At eight o'clock, Willem takes Sofia up to bed.

Francis and Alina move into the lounge, Lucas trailing them with a tray filled with ingredients to make cocktails.

'It's a Sunday night,' Francis protests, her words slurring ever so slightly.

'Fuck it, I've had a tough week,' replies Alina as she gestures for Lucas to start using his mixing skills.

'In that case, as your friend, I absolutely must support you,' says Francis, seriously.

They laugh, long and loud.

'Sofia seems fine. No damage done,' comments Francis.

Alina nods and ponders upon her friend's words.

Seems fine.

Seems...

And there was the danger.

She's well-rounded, Sofia is. They raised her that way, intentionally. Fame, on her father's part, infamy on her mother's – it can do strange things to offspring. Their combined wealth means that Sofia would never have to do a day's work in her life. Neither did Alina and nor, to a slightly lesser extent, Willem. But what are you without a challenge, tasks, a career, something that takes hard work and brings sometimes rewards, sometimes pitfalls.

Alina has seen the next generation, in all its forms.

The girls, the daughters of her father's colleagues and enemies. They wouldn't know how to cook a meal to save their lives. Alina rarely cooks, but it doesn't mean she can't. If she had to, she could knock up a decent-tasting borscht with the best of them.

She knows the other generation, too. The ones who imagine that breeding is the way to an easy life.

Settling, as Alina sees it.

She will never settle. Neither will Sofia.

As much as she groans about Sofia's addiction to her language school, she's always been proud of her girl's persistence in her pursuits.

And now the language school is over. It makes her sad.

She could get a tutor. But she had some years of home-schooling in her youth. It's no way to live. It's no way to learn.

It's no way to raise a child, shielding them from the world and all its horrors.

She thinks of the CCTV, all those cameras that are in the process of being arranged to surround her home.

She hates it.

She will find out who is doing this to them. Her life *will* return to normal.

'Ah, we've lost you.' Francis pouts. 'You're at that awful in-between stage.'

Alina looks up, startled. 'What?'

'You're maudlin. You've had just enough alcohol to fall into a hole. You need to keep it going, climb out the other side into merriment,' urges Francis.

Alina laughs and clasps her friend's hand across the couch. 'I'm fine, I was just thinking about Sofia, how I don't want to stifle her. We never have, Willem and me. We want her to grow up experiencing everything in life and choosing her own path.' Alina smiles but it is a little bitter. 'Because she doesn't have to. She could live her life out never having to work for anything.'

Francis nods, sagely. 'We all could. Even me, darling. I could retire tomorrow. But I shan't. It's so terribly important to have something to work for, to cherish, to get lost in.'

'Yes.' Alina squeezes Francis's hand. 'That's why I enjoy Hannah's company. She's conscientious in her work, controlled in her whole life.' She wrinkles her nose. 'Too controlled, actually, but maybe, in time, I can make her relax a little more.' She laughs. 'A happy medium is what we all strive for.'

Francis frowns. 'You're… friends, then, you and Hannah?'

There is something about Francis's tone that strikes Alina as… odd.

'You really don't like her?' she comments.

Before Francis can answer, Alina's phone vibrates. Talk of the devil.

> Please tell me when we can get this situation dealt with. It's becoming urgent.

She should have dealt with this before now. First thing this morning. *Yesterday*, for goodness' sake.

She types out a quick reply.

> I'm ready. I'll do it tonight.

'I have to go out, Francis,' says Alina.

Francis takes her arm. 'I should go, anyway. I have to pop into the gallery.' Then she is suddenly miles away.

Alina squeezes her arm. 'You okay?'

Francis smiles, but it doesn't quite reach her eyes. 'Fine, just something I need to check.'

The frivolity of earlier has gone. Alina helps Francis up.

Francis was right: they didn't have anywhere near enough alcohol. Apparently, they are both on a downer now.

'Come on, then. Lovely Lucas will give you a lift with me.'

As she lets Francis out at her gallery, Alina feels a certain sense of wistfulness. How she would love to forget her own plans, go inside with Francis, spend the evening on her own personal tour while her friend catches up on whatever work she needs to do.

But she can't.

She has work of her own. She has a promise to keep.

After waving goodbye to Francis, Alina directs Lucas to the address in Soho.

He frowns at her. 'And why are we visiting a place like that tonight?'

'This is the person who is stalking Hannah. Grace Perry.' She leans between the seats. 'What do you mean, "a place like that"?'

'It's a shithole, a real baaaad area,' he drawls.

Good, thinks Alina. The very fact that it is an undesirable location makes it far easier for her to get in and out without anyone watching.

'Don't pull up too close,' she tells Lucas as he swings the car around. 'Drop me off at least five blocks away.'

He turns to look at her. 'You don't want me in there?'

She shakes her head. 'I'll do this on my own.' Her reply is a mere whisper. She feels her mouth turn down. Alina rarely whispers.

He gives her another glance. This one she ignores.

They drive the rest of the way in silence.

As they pull up streets away, Lucas looks out of the window. 'I don't like this,' he says.

'Don't do that,' Alina replies, sharply.

He looks at her in the rear-view mirror. 'Do what?'

'Treat me like that. You've never done it before. Don't start now.'

He turns around in his seat and reaches for her hand. 'I know. It's just what's been happening lately. The gallery fiasco, Sofia going missing, you and the bike...'

She can feel herself hardening as he speaks. As though he is her father. Why do people keep talking to her this way lately?

But she's also glad. She needs this anger that Lucas has stirred up in her. She won't diffuse it. She will *use* it.

She gets out of the car and begins to walk in the direction of Grace Perry's place.

Lucas was right, she thinks as she approaches the address. This area is awful. Worse than, or at least on a par with, the hostel last night.

What sort of woman lives here? And how would this stalker think she even has a chance to get in Hannah's life? Because Hannah, though tightly wound and edgy, is class personified.

Alina checks her watch. It's a little after ten p.m. The street is not deserted, but the people passing by are not potential witnesses. These guys have somewhere to be, deals to strike, drops to deliver, money to collect. They will not get involved in Alina's business.

And what is her business?

She is not sure. She has told Hannah she will *deal with it*. Until she gets inside, Alina doesn't know exactly what that means.

She vaguely recalls what she said earlier, in her alcohol-ridden angst. That she would *end* this girl. She reddens. Booze-fuelled words.

She will leave – this woman will leave when Alina instructs her to.

Alina pushes herself off the wall she has been leaning on and jogs across the road to the building where Hannah's persecutor is residing.

Not a house, she sees when she reaches the door. Judging by the numbers on the mailboxes, it's not even flats.

Bedsits.

Alina curls her lip.

She braces herself on the frame of the door and raises her leg to aim a kick, when she realises it is ajar.

She lowers her foot and pushes it open.

The hallway is rank. Bare lightbulbs, only one of which is working, cast a dull, yellow glow which shows the stained walls and the depressing, threadbare doormat.

There are five rooms on this level. Four numbered apartments, and an additional one which Alina reckons is a closet. The room at the furthest end of the hall is Grace's.

Alina heads towards it but pauses by each of the other three doors and puts her ear up against them. The first two are empty – no light coming from underneath the doors, and no sound from within.

The third one has a thumping bass coming from it and the sharp, pungent smell of weed.

Alina allows herself a small smile. There will be no problem there.

She concentrates on Grace's door. She could knock on it, give the woman a chance to answer.

But she doesn't want to.

With a sneer on her face, Alina aims and kicks.

It takes three goes, panicked screaming inside all the while. The frame splinters and the lock buckles. Next door, the music continues blasting.

Alina shoulders the door open and barges her way inside.

She takes in the room, for that's all it is: one room. She recalls the fifth door that she'd thought might be a closet and realises it must be a shared bathroom. She swallows against her disgust.

In the middle of the room stands a woman who can only be Grace Perry.

Alina looks her up and down. She is not what she expected. Grace Perry does not look like she belongs in this dive.

She looks young, and a strange mixture of vulnerable but a little tough with it.

'You're not looking for me.' Grace speaks and Alina frowns.

'Huh?'

'I imagine you're looking for whoever was here before me,' Grace says. 'I only got here yesterday, so I can assure you that you're not seeking me.'

Alina kicks the door closed behind her.

'Grace Perry.' Alina says her name and notes the confusion on Grace's face.

'Yeah…'

'You've been making a bit of a nuisance of yourself, haven't you?' Alina says.

Grace's face crumples. Suddenly, she looks as young as Sofia. Alina throws this thought from her mind.

'I can't believe this. Hannah sent you… Are you kidding me?'

'Nope.' Alina tilts her head to one side. 'No joke. So, we've got a few options. Let's start with this one: are you going to back off from Hannah and leave her the hell alone?'

Inexplicably, Grace's eyes fill with tears. 'If that's what she wants. I already told her that. She was the one who messaged me today.'

Alina narrows her eyes. 'So why are you still here, then? Why are you still hanging around if you're prepared to let her go?'

'Because it's not all about her!' The sudden volume from this petite woman startles Alina.

Alina takes a step forward, closing the distance between them. 'What are you talking about?'

'It's none of your business!' Grace is suddenly ferocious, furious. A pocket-sized ball of indignation.

Involuntarily, Alina takes a step back.

No questions asked. That was the deal.

'Who else is this about?' Alina asks, despite herself. Her voice is quiet now, but assertive.

'Marie,' Grace says.

'Marie…?' Alina searches her mind, comes up blank.

'She's Hannah's mother.' Grace stares at Alina defiantly. 'And she's my mother too.'

34

HANNAH, SUNDAY

Hannah knows she won't sleep when she gets home. She clutches her phone in her hand, wondering if Alina will contact her to say that it is done.

And… *what* will be done? That is the question.

She shivers, part fear, part anticipation.

As she turns into the lane, she sees a light on in Nita's window. She's returned for good, then. Hannah imagines her in there, unable to sleep, listening out for any noise to suggest someone is breaking in again.

Hannah lets herself into her own house. Marie is still up, watching a reality television programme in the lounge.

Hannah pauses in the doorway and watches her mother for a moment.

She tries not to look at her differently now. It's not Marie's fault; clearly, she didn't want the child who would grow up to become Grace, or she wouldn't have given her away.

How much she has wanted to grab her so-called sister by her thin shoulders and shake her until her teeth fall out.

She doesn't want you! She would scream. *She gave you away!*

'Hannah, you're home.'

Marie had been dozing, Hannah sees now. She slips into the room and bends to kiss her mother's cheek.

'What have you been doing all day?' Marie looks wary as she asks the question.

For a moment, Hannah wonders if Grace has already got to their mother.

She studies Marie's face but she looks like she always does.

'I went to Battersea.' Hannah thinks of Grace's location and is satisfied with her answer. That awful bedsit is nowhere near Battersea.

'On your own?'

'No, with a friend.' Hannah smiles tightly. 'Do you want a cup of tea, Mum?'

'Which friend?' Marie ignores Hannah's question.

Hannah dodges Marie's third degree and skips lightly to the kitchen. 'I'll put the kettle on,' she calls over her shoulder.

She starts to sweat as she idles in the kitchen. Something is off, and it has been for a while now. If she's truthful, it has been for as long as she can remember.

It's not Grace. It can't be. Marie is oblivious to her sudden arrival. Has no idea that the woman wants to insert herself into their lives.

But it's something.

It's not *her*, Hannah. She's a model daughter. Got her mother out of Edgware, brought her here, to live in luxury.

No, she reassures herself, it's something else.

Not her.

She flicks the kettle on and stares out of the window. It's late, the streetlights are on, casting their dull yellow glow that Hannah used to find comforting.

As she stares, her breath catches in her throat.

A shadowy figure is there.

Again. Right outside her home, in the area behind the courtyard, the narrow strip of land that borders the play area.

It's not uncommon for pedestrians to walk along the tiny alleyway. But it is unusual for anyone to stop there, just… standing.

Waiting.

Watching?

She was sweating a moment ago. Now, Hannah turns cold as ice. She leaps forward and snaps the blind down.

It must be Grace. Alina has not visited her. Or if she did, she was too late. Grace must have slipped out, come here.

How long will it be before the girl gets up the nerve to knock on their door and introduce herself to Marie?

'I'll make the tea.' Marie comes through to the kitchen.

Hannah jumps and spins around.

'Jesus, Hannah, what's wrong?' Marie stares at her.

'Nothing.' Hannah fumbles in her pocket for her phone. She scrolls frantically to Alina's number, presses call. At the same time, she composes a message:

> Someone is here right now. Outside my house.

Hannah paces the kitchen.

'Hannah.' Marie's voice is sharp.

She is wrenched from her internal fears as Marie steps in front of her. She stabs at the button to end the call and looks over Marie's shoulder.

'I'm fine,' Hannah mutters, before her mother can ask her what's wrong again.

'No, you're not.' Marie puts a hand on Hannah's wrist.

It is like an electric shock. Marie rarely touches her voluntarily.

Hannah wraps her own fingers around Marie's wrist to keep it in place. It is calming, soothing, loving. Hannah dips her head until her cheek rests against Marie's hand.

She feels the tension as Marie tries to free her arm. 'Don't, Mum. Just let me...' She doesn't finish her sentence.

'Tell me what's wrong.'

Hannah shakes her head.

Her world, the one she has worked so hard for, is hanging by a thread.

'Promise me you won't leave me, Mum.' Hannah's voice is small, like it used to be when she said these very same words to Marie, all those years ago. 'Promise me it'll just be us, for ever.'

Hannah expects – *hopes* – that Marie will gather her in her arms and hold her tight.

Instead, Marie manages to pull her arm away. She moves to the other side of the kitchen and turns away.

Hannah stares after her. She wants to cry. She wants to scream. She wants Marie to say that she gave Grace away because she only ever wanted Hannah. That if Grace came here, Marie would slam the door in her face.

'Hannah.' Marie slumps into a chair by the window. 'What happened?' Marie's voice grows wary. 'What... What did you do?'

Ice is creeping over Hannah's skin. Marie has never asked her that.

She snaps her head up sharply. 'Nothing. Why would you ask me that?'

Marie lowers her head. 'You know why.'

There is a pain in Hannah's chest, like her breastbone is cracking in two. 'I-I don't know why.'

She does. She knows exactly why.

But she never thought Marie knew.

'Because of…'

Don't say his name. Don't say his name.

Marie draws in a breath and meets Hannah's eyes. 'I know what happened with Nita.'

Nita!

Hannah exhales shakily. '*Nita?*'

'I talked to her… She didn't want to tell me—'

Hannah stands up, effectively cutting Marie's words off. She doesn't want to hear them, doesn't want to know what lies that troublemaker Nita has been whispering in Marie's ear.

She walks fast towards the door, expecting Marie to call after her, chase her, but when she glances back, Marie is still seated in the chair, head bent, a single tear tracking its way down her cheek.

The vision stills Hannah. Marie doesn't cry. She used all her tears up a long time ago.

On him.

She closes the door on both her mother and memories of the past, and hurries away from the house. She moves down the lane, breathing hard.

'Hannah.'

The voice that speaks her name is gentle, soft, and she looks up at the figure that stands before her.

She feels a vice squeeze her chest.

And Marie is mere feet away, just a small distance separating them from this madman who is intent on following her.

She glances at her phone, the unsent message still on the screen. She was wrong. It's not Grace stalking her outside her home.

The man takes one step forward and the tightness in her chest flutters.

One more step, until he is standing underneath the streetlight.

She doesn't know if it is his stance, the defeated posture, the sadness in his expression, but suddenly everything becomes horribly, terribly clear.

She knows exactly who this man is.

35

ALINA, SUNDAY

Alina is in a struggle with herself. She shouldn't have asked any questions. Shouldn't have listened when Grace started to talk.

Grace and Hannah's relationship is irrelevant. Does the fact that they are bound by blood matter? Suddenly, it makes all the sense in the world. Why Hannah was so reluctant to disclose the name of the person she wanted out of her life.

Alina's phone buzzes in her pocket but she ignores it and focuses on Grace, who is standing in front of her, that defiant look on her face.

'You've warned me off. You've done what she paid you to do,' Grace spits. 'Fine, I've got the message. I won't go near Hannah again.'

'And Hannah's mother?' Alina asks.

Grace juts out her jaw. 'My mother, you mean?'

Alina stumbles. 'Yes, I… guess.'

'Look, she left her name for me, in a file that was sealed until I was twenty-one. If she didn't ever want to meet me, she wouldn't have done that.' Grace's voice is cold. Her meaning is very, very clear. 'I will introduce myself to my mother. If *she* tells me to get lost, then I shall.'

Alina is a little impressed. Five minutes ago, she kicked this girl's door in. Still, Grace is standing up for herself.

'So, are we done?' Grace asks.

Alina isn't sure. She lifts a finger and points it at Grace. 'You stay away from Hannah Barker. You understand?'

'Yes.' Grace's voice wobbles ever so slightly.

Alina steps around the splintered frame, into the hallway. She looks at the mess, the shards of wood that litter the space. Across the way, the bass is still thumping.

Alina sweeps out into the street and makes her way back to Lucas. She passes a cashpoint, just across from where he is sitting in the car. She puts her fingers in her mouth and whistles to him.

'How much cash have you got on you?' she asks, as he ambles over.

'There's an envelope in the car. You left it there when we went to the bank.'

Bank? Alina frowns. They went to the bank months ago, withdrew a large sum for some job somebody wanted cash payment for. Bodywork on one of the cars, she recalls dimly – not of her doing, that time. But Willem had also withdrawn the cash and paid, and she'd not been back to the bank since.

'Show me.' She follows him back to the car, gets in the front seat and rifles through the envelope.

There's at least three grand in there. She counts the notes, peeling off two thousand, and shoves the rest in her pocket. Then she takes a pen out of the cup holder and scribbles an address on the back. On the front she writes a note.

Pay for the door damage. Use the rest to go home.
There's nothing for you here.

She hands the envelope to Lucas.

'Deliver this to that Grace woman.' She takes in his outfit. A turquoise checked shirt that makes him look like he's on his way to a barn dance.

Leaning over the back seat, she picks up his leather jacket. 'And put this on when you see her, for God's sake.'

Affronted, he takes the coat from her and watches as she gets out of the car and slams the door. Lucas rolls the window down. 'Where are you going?' he asks.

'I need air,' she tells him.

It's not a lie. That bedsit was awful; she's sure that the stench of weed and general filth is clinging to her. It reminded her of the hostel. The stale, filthy air.

He gives her a nod but doesn't pull away from the kerb. Instead, he looks out of the rear window.

Alina thumps the roof of the car. 'Get going. I'll see you at home later.'

'Wait.' He opens the centre console in the car and passes something to her.

She stares down at the object. Metal knuckledusters. The old Alina would have laughed, but suddenly, this item seems like something maybe she should be carrying.

Her eyes blur, unexpectedly.

'Just keep it in your pocket, yes?' Lucas says, gently.

She nods, offers him a small smile as he drives slowly off, towards the bedsit.

She wanders down the road, thoughts of Hannah and Grace swirling through her head. So, the interloper, Hannah's stalker, is her very own sister. Idly, she wonders what happened. Adoption? Separated parents? After all, Hannah's father is out of the picture. Maybe he took Grace, while the seemingly revered and worshipped one, Marie, kept Hannah.

Maybe Grace was a problem child, out of control, and was sectioned or something.

Alina chuckles to herself, thinking of the way Grace refused to back down.

She hopes she's warned her off. She has a feeling Hannah might not be satisfied with her giving the younger girl a simple warning. But Hannah never specified her wish.

Deal with her.

I want her out of my life.

They had been Hannah's words.

And now, Alina has dealt with it.

'Miss, spare any change?'

Alina glances up at the voice. She's in a side street, and every few feet there is a person, sitting amongst their few possessions. Blanket. Bag. Dog. Cup of coins.

It's a hot night, but what do these guys do in the winter months?

She thinks of the hostel, of the addicts who use it as their base.

She looks into the face of the man who called to her.

'I don't have any change,' she tells him.

He nods and even gives her a smile. 'No worries, thank you.'

He's young. She thinks of Sofia and knows that no matter what happens to her and Willem, their child will never live on a street. How did this man get here? What's his story?

And that, right there, is her downfall. Wanting to know everyone's stories.

She remembers the wad of cash; some of it still sits in her pocket. She peels off two twenties. He stares at it as though it is a winning lottery ticket.

'Have a good night,' she says.

As she puts her hand back in her pocket, she remembers her phone vibrating, earlier, when she was with Grace. She looks at the screen and sees a missed call from Hannah.

Alina thinks about calling her back, but decides that she wouldn't actually mind seeing the other woman in the flesh. Perhaps she will confide in her about Grace. Perhaps, this time, she'll actually admit that they're sisters!

Alina swears to herself at the valuable nugget of information that Hannah failed to disclose.

As she walks back down the alley to the main road, she slows her step.

Was it a valuable piece of information? Didn't Alina reassure Hannah that this whole process would be on a no-questions-asked basis?

A stream of taxis drive towards her, all with their lights on. The third one stops for her, and she directs him to Hannah's mews home.

She pays him in cash, throwing too much onto the front seat, and is out of the car before he can ask if she wants her change.

She hesitates near the entrance.

Somewhere close by, she hears the sound of glass shattering. Alina's throat constricts.

From the shadows, somewhere, comes a peal of laughter, swearing.

Just a broken bottle. Nothing to do with her. Not aimed *at* her. Nobody is in danger tonight.

She peers down the mews lane. Two people are there. Alina instantly recognises Hannah's silhouette.

She knows the man too, she realises. Despite the hood he wears, she recognises his stooped posture, small build, and restless demeanour. The man from the park. The one she thought was a reporter.

Unseen, she gapes at them. Him? He's the one who has been spying on Hannah? Has been following her?

She is perplexed. Is he with Grace? Has she recruited him to keep an eye on Hannah?

Her face darkens as she remembers the night Hannah got attacked, in the park, after she left Alina's.

She pulls out her phone, taps out a quick message to Lucas, telling him where she is, and to get there now.

She puts her hands in her pockets, feels something cold and hard against her fingers.

The knuckleduster that Lucas gave her.

Her fingers, still bandaged, itch for her to slide the cool metal onto them.

Rage.

It is much better than fear. She welcomes it, allows it to grow like a flame, hot and red and fierce.

She turns into the lane, darting a look at Hannah as she passes her.

Hannah is hemmed in by the man, distress written all over her face.

She looks at him.

'Now, look—' he starts, hands up, palms towards her, a promise that he is no threat, simply because she has caught him.

She draws her right hand from her pocket.

He is right in thinking that tonight, he is not the threat. Alina is.

She draws her hand back, like her father showed her. A small jab to his face.

He is short in his stooped position and her fist catches him on the side of his head. In the glow of the streetlight, she sees the flecks of blood leap from his scalp.

He staggers back into the shadows.

She can still hear him, breathing heavily.

Hannah is suddenly there, right by Alina's side. 'Do it! End him, please.' Her words are high-pitched with intent.

Hannah's words stop Alina in her tracks, just for a moment.

End him?

She doesn't mean to physically *end him*, Alina thinks.

End *this*, is what Hannah means.

End this situation where Grace and this man are hassling her, *tormenting* her.

She meets Hannah's eyes and sees her pupils, dark and huge.

'Go inside. Stay there,' she instructs Hannah.

Alina turns back into the darkness, seeking the man who will feel the full wrath of her fury.

—

She remembers Hannah's story about the neighbour who was attacked. She would bet her life that this man is responsible for that, as he sought Hannah but got the wrong house.

She flexes her fingers again and stomps off down the lane.

He is nearing the other end now; she sees him as he passes underneath the only other streetlight down there. He is staggering, one hand to his head, and he is easy to reach because he is unable to walk in a straight line.

She approaches him as he nears the end of the alley. With no more walls to cushion his unsteady run, he staggers to the right, finally falling in the grassy area of a deserted playground.

Alina bends over him, her face inches from his.

'What do you want with her, the pair of you?' she rasps at him, her voice almost gone as though she has been screaming.

He wheezes in her face. She takes pleasure in seeing the blood that runs down his forehead. He has his hands up, his eyes closed. She can feel him trembling beneath her.

'I only need to talk to her,' he manages.

She shakes him. The back of his head hits the ground, and he groans.

The sound is guttural.

He shields his face again with his hands. 'I just came to talk to Hannah. I'm worried about her, she's… Something is wrong—'

With a grunt, he rolls to the side on the ground and sits up. He is breathing hard.

He holds one hand up, the other supporting him. 'Please,' he whispers. 'I don't know you. I'm just worried about Hannah. About her son, and about her mother too. She's not well…'

A shiver of apprehension runs through Alina. He knows Hannah's family members. He knows she has a son.

'Please,' he says. 'Just warn Marie. Just tell Marie that it's happening again.'

Marie.

Hannah's mother.

It's the second time her name has been mentioned tonight.

Alina pauses.

He sees it, seizes upon it. He reaches up and grabs Alina's wrist. She yanks her arm, but he holds on tight.

'Who is she to you?' she whispers.

He gasps, revitalised as though sensing he is finally being given a chance to speak. 'Marie is my wife.' He chokes the words out. A froth of blood, foaming and bubbling, stains his lips. 'Hannah is my daughter.'

36

HANNAH, SUNDAY

Hannah shuts the door, locks it and slides the chain across. She leans her head against the wood, imagining what is happening outside.

Alina is in a fury. The way she looked at Hannah, a silent message had passed between them. Alina will deal with it tonight, and Hannah is sure she will go all the way.

She shivers and lowers her head. Her chin drops to her chest.

She can't believe it was him. All this time he has been following her. She never even recognised him until tonight. It's no wonder; she barely looked at him back then, when he lived with her, when he called himself her father.

He looks older. More than twenty years older. She has hardly thought of him since he walked out the door that very last time.

'Who is out there?'

Marie comes up behind her. Hannah jumps and spins around.

'Mum, you scared me.' She puts a hand to her chest.

'Hannah. We need to talk.'

'No, we don't.' God, why is Marie suddenly so... confrontational?

She moves around her mother, telling herself that she feels soothed, finally, as though what Alina is doing out there has put a balm over her very heart.

She can't believe it, though. Can't believe that her father is the shadow man. A thought strikes her: could he be working alongside Grace? The pair of them together, colluding to get back in Marie's life, using Hannah as a road map.

She attempts to reassure her own internal struggle.

The threat – both of them – has diminished. In minutes, thanks to Alina, it will cease to exist at all.

Hannah smiles and throws her arms around Marie. 'We're fine,' she says softly in her mother's ear. 'We're fine, and nothing is going to hurt us ever again.'

She can feel Marie's shoulders shaking. Is her mother aware that outside these walls, someone from their past has been spying on them?

Worse than that: have the echoes of their past already reached out to Marie?

No.

Marie gave Grace away, sent her father away too.

If they had approached Marie, either of them, or both, her mother would have sent them packing. Hannah has no doubt about that. But at least this way, she's saved her mum the trauma of revisiting those painful times.

'Everything is going to be okay now.' Hannah holds Marie tightly and buries her face in her mother's neck.

Marie wriggles herself gently out of Hannah's grip. 'It's not going to be okay now.' Marie's voice is trembling. 'I… I don't know what to do any longer. I'm so close to giving up. If it wasn't for Oliver…'

It is like a knife in Hannah's heart. An ache forms in her very marrow.

Belatedly, she remembers Marie's stilted words earlier, about Nita, and what ill their neighbour has been speaking about Hannah.

Now this: Marie, pulling away, wanting to run away, just like she did all those years ago.

'You're talking nonsense,' Hannah manages.

If only Marie knew how hard Hannah has been working to protect her.

Marie sinks to sit on the bottom stair and puts her head in her hands. 'I need some time. I need some space.'

Marie has her shoes on. Hannah has only now noticed, and a light jacket too.

Hannah positions herself in front of the door. Marie can't walk out there. Can't be exposed to what Alina is doing to her husband at the end of the lane.

Marie won't care because she doesn't love him. She only loves Hannah. But still, to Marie, the scene will be shocking, and Hannah does not want her to have to witness that.

A headache has started now. Hannah rubs her temple. Marie needs time. Maybe her idea of a holiday was a good one. Just them. Somewhere private and exclusive, where there is nobody else around.

'It will be okay, Mum,' says Hannah.

Marie looks down at the floor. 'Will it?' she asks.

Her voice is dull, flat. At her tone, hopeless, Hannah's chest aches a little more.

Marie grips the banister and hauls herself up. 'I just need a little breathing space.' She glances at her daughter. 'I'm going for a walk, just around the block.'

'No. You stay here.' Hannah takes the chain off the door. 'I don't want you out there after dark. Not with everything that's been going on lately.'

Marie stares at her. She looks almost incredulous. 'Hannah...' she begins.

But Hannah shakes her head. She doesn't want to hear any more of Marie's fears.

'I'll make it better, Mum,' she says as she unlocks the door. 'You go to bed. Everything will be better in the morning.'

Gently, she assists Marie to standing and watches as she heads slowly up the stairs.

She's covered her own panic well, she thinks, all things considered.

Marie just needs time. Time to relax and realise there's nothing to worry about, not while Hannah is here.

She opens the door and steps outside. Locking the door behind her, she puts the key in her pocket.

She pads silently down to the bottom of the path. Taking care to stay in the shadows, she peers out into the lane.

It is empty.

He is not there.

Neither is Alina.

She can't hear anyone, either.

She walks down the lane, past Nita's house. Out of the corner of her eye she sees the flick of a curtain. She snaps her head towards it.

Nita's face is there. Their eyes meet, just for one second, before the curtain falls back into place.

Hannah continues to the very end of the lane. She pauses at each gate, looking down. She fully expects to see his crumpled form propped in a doorway. The life fading from his eyes as he bleeds out.

But there is nobody.

He has gone.

She scuffs around at the end of the lane, using her phone's torch to light up the ground.

There! Blood spatter, on the edge of the play area.

Hannah wraps her arms around herself.

Alina wouldn't have left him to be found. She would have called Lucas or, more likely, he was already lying in wait somewhere nearby. The clean-up crew.

She sinks to her knees and touches the still-wet blood with her finger.

Finally, all her problems have gone.

Hannah tilts her head up to the moon and closes her eyes.

37

ALINA, SUNDAY

Family. All Hannah's family. Grace; her sister. This man; her father. Marie, seemingly at the centre of it all.

It doesn't matter! she tells herself silently. The identity of who Hannah wants out of her life does not matter. *Why* Hannah wants to destroy her family isn't relevant.

She owes Hannah.

And none of the information she's gleaned tonight should detract from that.

Should it?

'Get up.' She puts a hand under his arm and shoves until he manages to stand.

He staggers dizzily.

From down the lane, she hears the click of a door.

It will be Hannah. For reasons she can't yet explain, Alina doesn't want her here right now.

She gets behind Hannah's father and nudges him hard with her shoulder. 'Move,' she hisses.

They cover a few metres, down to the next pathway. Alina grabs his coat and pulls him out of sight.

'Please...' he moans.

'Shut up.' Alina digs her phone out and calls Lucas.

He answers immediately. 'I'm nearly there, where are you?'

She does not know the name of this alley. She glances to the right and groans, unable to believe the landmark that is in her sight.

'Alina?'

'At the hostel. Meet us at the hostel, okay?'

She hangs up and turns to Hannah's father. 'What's your name?' she asks.

'Ray.' He coughs, red-flecked spittle spotting his lips.

Alina blanches in disgust. 'Were you here last night?'

He raises his head and peers around him, before looking back at her, confused.

He opens his mouth to speak, but coughs again. This time, she feels it land on her face, surprisingly warm.

She surveys him: the damage that has been caused, by her, by Hannah's request.

Suddenly, it is hard to look at him.

She gets behind him and propels him past the hostel. And how different it looks today: every window is lit up; people are milling around outside.

She must go there. She must question all these people. She wants to parade this small, beaten man around the place and ask if Sofia's disappearance was because of him.

She knows it's not wise, though. Nobody would own up to anything.

No, she needs to be cleverer than that.

'Sit here.' She lowers Ray down onto a low wall, far enough away that none of the hostel-goers see anything other than the silhouette of a young woman assisting a seemingly older gent.

'Look…' He coughs again and wipes his mouth with the back of his hand. 'Listen, I don't know what you think—'

'Hush. We wait here.'

Lucas rolls up minutes later. He pulls the car onto the kerb, slams his way out of the vehicle and stomps across towards them. He is an imposing figure, Alina realises.

Ray bleats and hoists himself off the wall. He tries to run, but only manages to wrap his feet around each other. He tumbles to the floor.

Lucas stands over him and raises his eyebrows at Alina.

'Take him to a hotel, check him in.' Alina locks eyes with Lucas. 'Get him some medical attention.'

Lucas shrugs and lifts the man up.

All three of them walk towards the car. Lucas opens the rear passenger door and puts Ray inside.

'What are you going to do?' Lucas asks.

'I'll be home soon,' she replies. It's not an answer, but it's all she's prepared to give him.

She watches Lucas shift the car into gear; Ray's face at the window, a mixture of fear and resignation.

When the car is out of sight, Alina pulls her hoodie up over her head and walks across the grass towards the hostel.

She feels a slight sneer tug at her lips. Now she is the hooded figure. Now *she* is the threat.

She stops next to a couple sitting on the lawn. 'Hey,' she says. 'What was going on here last night?'

They stare at her, blank faces, mouths slightly open.

Alina smiles tightly. 'Never mind.' She moves on, seeking someone more lucid.

Soon she reaches the hostel building. There are more people here. Nobody really notices her. She looks down at her black jeans and hoodie. She fits right in.

There is a piece of chipboard over the window she smashed. She flexes her hand. The cuts on her fingers stretch painfully.

'What was going on here last night?' she asks. 'The place was deserted. I mean, literally, there was nobody here *at all.*'

'Trouble, innit,' says one youth.

She gives him a once-over. God, he is so young.

'What sort of trouble?' she asks him.

A man who has been sitting on the steps stands up and makes his way over to them.

'Why'd you want to know for?' he asks.

His voice is nasally, a whine in it. His face is thin and ferret-like; his eyes tiny blue slits, the iris almost totally hidden by huge pupils.

She shrugs. 'I came by, and the lights were out. I was supposed to be meeting a mate here, hanging, you know?'

'No. I don't know. I wasn't here last night.' He kicks out at the younger lad, catching his shin with a heavy boot. 'None of us were here last night.'

The boy opens his mouth and then, at a single look from his friend, he clamps it shut.

'Yeah, not here last night.'

Alina walks back to the main road. She dials Lucas's number. 'Can you collect me when you're done?' she asks when he answers. 'Same place as before.'

He won't be long, she knows. She kicks around the hostel site, walking the perimeter, searching for... anything. Answers, clues, leads.

But there is nothing here.

There is nobody who will talk to her here.

Headlights blink twice on the road. Lucas. She makes her way across the grass, down to the street.

'Where did you take him?' she asks as she slides into the passenger seat.

'The Barbican,' he answers. 'They've got a doctor on site.'

She nods her approval. The Barbican is a very expensive hotel, with a twenty-four-hour concierge and a doctor in residence.

Lucas glances at her, sideways on. 'Do you want to tell me who he is?'

She doesn't answer his question. Instead, she asks, 'Did you see the girl, Grace?'

'Yes. She's a feisty one, isn't she?'

'Yep.' Alina leans her head against the seat rest. Suddenly, she is very, very tired. 'She's also Hannah's sister.'

He flicks a glance her way.

'And,' Alina continues, 'that man you dropped off is Hannah's father.'

'No shit?' He turns to face her. 'Did you just find this out?'

'Yep.' She feels her lips curl into a grin.

Lucas frowns at her. 'Something funny?' he asks.

She shakes her head and grins widely. 'They're all related. The father, the sisters. Whatever happened to Sofia wasn't anything to do with them. Wasn't anything to do with me, or my past.' She breathes out, and the sound is shaky with relief. 'None of it was anything to do with me.'

Someone else's family drama.

She still doesn't know if Ray and Grace are working together to intimidate Hannah. Can't understand why they'd *want* to be part of a family that clearly doesn't welcome them.

She reminds herself, harshly, that it doesn't matter.

Sofia is up when Alina gets in, despite Willem putting her to bed before cocktail hour earlier. She skips over to her daughter, puts her arms around her. 'I missed you,' Alina whispers.

'You've been gone a lot, Mama,' says Sofia, seriously.

Yes, she has. Too much time spent on sorting out everyone else's lives.

'Where's your dad?' Alina asks.

'In there.' Sofia points towards the lounge. 'We're going to watch a film. Will you watch with us, Mama?'

Alina grips her girl even tighter. She can think of nothing she would rather do, and she tells her that.

Sofia beams. 'We're having drinks and snacks,' she explains, as she steps on the high stool to reach the cupboard.

The motion is triggering. Alina sees Sofia slipping, falling, smashing her head.

But Sofia has done this a hundred times before. Alina closes her eyes briefly. When she opens them next, Sofia is holding an armful of snacks.

'Pass them to me,' Alina says, holding out her arms and allowing Sofia to stack them up.

Alina feels her insides tightening in protest as she watches Sofia close the cupboard door and climb back down from the stool.

Her smiles only come freely once Sofia is back standing safely upon the floor.

38

HANNAH, MONDAY

Her phone is no longer a clanging symbol of doom.

Hannah realises this as she snatches it up and sees Alina's name on her screen.

'Alina!'

'We need to talk.'

There are no niceties and Hannah's heart sinks a little.

'When?' Hannah asks.

'Now. Meet me at the gallery.'

'Momotaro?'

'No. The Harman Gallery.' There is a brief pause. 'You'll be on your way to work soon, right?'

Hannah whispers her agreement and hangs up.

Alina must want to update her on her father and Grace. Will she tell Hannah what has become of them? Or will she use delicate language today?

They have been dealt with.

Hannah wonders if she will want to know how.

Another thought strikes her. Were they working together, her father and Grace?

More importantly, are they truly in her past now? Is there absolutely no chance that they will come back?

Hannah picks up her bag. There's only one way to find out.

The Harman Gallery is empty when Hannah arrives. Locked up. It doesn't open until ten o'clock, but Francis is normally around.

Not today.

Hannah has the keys, though; Francis begrudgingly handed them over, entrusting her as a keyholder. She doesn't like Hannah, but she trusts her professionally.

She's just turned off the alarm in the lobby when she hears footsteps clattering up the stone stairs.

'Alina, hi,' Hannah greets her.

Alina surprises her by swooping in for a hug.

'How are you?' Alina asks as she pulls off her jacket. 'Don't suppose you've got some coffee on?'

Hannah closes the front door and locks it.

'I will in a moment. Come on through,' she says.

She's relieved, she realises, as she leads Alina down the hallway to the kitchen area.

She had been concerned that Alina might act differently around her. She doesn't know why. After all, Alina was repaying a debt. No questions asked. Besides, she thinks Alina is the least judgemental person she's ever met.

In the kitchen, Alina is perusing the stack of coffee pods.

'This one,' she announces, pulling it out and passing it to Hannah.

Hannah glances at it. Caramel. Sickeningly sweet. She rearranges her face in case Alina sees her distaste, and flicks on the machine.

'Did you… deal with everything, last night?' Hannah asks, aiming for casual as she busies herself with cups and saucers.

'Yes.' Alina nods. 'The girl won't bother you again.'

Hannah swallows down the relief that courses through her. 'Thank you,' she says softly.

'She was your sister.'

It's not that statement in its entirety that Hannah notices, but rather the tense that Alina uses.

Was.

She *was* your sister.

Not *is.*

How to answer?

She will front it out.

'That's right.'

She dares to glance at Alina. The other woman has a strange half-smile on her face.

'You didn't want a sister?' Alina's tone is one of amusement.

Hannah finds herself relaxing even further. This woman understands. Never before has Hannah encountered anyone who might appreciate the way she feels about an attempted infiltration of her family.

But Alina isn't like anyone else.

She's an anomaly. She has issues with her own father.

Just like Hannah.

There's a long moment of silence.

And then Hannah does something she's never done before.

She tells her new friend *everything.*

Marie, her mother, is special.

But… special doesn't cut it. It's not the right word.

There are no words to describe how important Marie is.

The word *important* isn't even correct.

Marie is everything.

From the outside, they were a perfect family of three. A normal family.

Hannah's dad went to work all day. He played football on a Sunday. Marie would bundle Hannah up and take her along. They would stand on the sidelines. Marie would cheer when her husband scored a goal, or when he set one up for a teammate.

Hannah wouldn't see any of the game, though.

She would stare up at Marie, never take her eyes off her.

Marie didn't work. She was at home, morning until night. On the odd occasion, Marie would go out with her friends, for a drink, for a meal, perhaps down the local bingo hall.

When she returned, Ray, Hannah's dad, would sag with relief.

'She won't settle without you,' he would say, his voice barely audible over the sound of Hannah's screams.

Eventually, it became easier for Marie to stay in.

A companion was needed for Hannah, her parents decided when she was seven years old. A brother or sister.

She wasn't happy in school, clinging to Marie at the morning drop-off.

'She'll be fine once she's inside, with her friends,' said one of the other mothers at the gate.

Hannah's teachers told a different story.

'She's too isolated. She needs to get used to other people, other children,' Marie told Ray.

Ray smiled at his wife and ran his fingers in a lazy circle on Marie's stomach. 'A boy, this time,' he said.

Marie grinned back. 'You can't order the sex of the baby,' she teased him back.

Hannah, listening silently from the doorway, came into the room.

She wrapped her fingers around her father's. At his daughter's touch, never normally instigated by her, he grinned with pleasure.

Hannah raised Ray's hand to her mouth and bit the tender, fleshy part of his palm, hard enough to draw blood.

–

Another baby didn't come easily. For three years her head had been filled with a cloud of despair at the thought of sharing Marie but finally, it looked like it wasn't going to happen.

Until just after the Easter holidays, when Marie sat Hannah down and explained about the new, imminent arrival.

'A festive baby,' said Ray. He chucked Hannah under her chin. 'What a Christmas present that will be.'

Hannah moved out of his reach and fixed her eyes on Marie's stomach. Still flat. Nothing to say or show that a baby was in there.

She turned away.

–

Not a Christmas baby, but a Boxing Day one.

They had nobody to come and sit with Hannah – all the babysitters and childminders only came once and never again – so the three of them, soon to be four, went to the hospital together.

Hannah sat rigidly on the waiting room chair. She ignored the kindly nurses, and anyone who offered her drinks and snacks. She ignored her father when he came out of the delivery suite to check on her.

As it got later, and the hours wore on, sometimes she heard Marie's screams.

'It's okay, all part of nature,' said a young orderly as he wheeled a trolley past her.

Hannah looked away from him. Her hands clenched into fists.

The baby came eventually. Hannah's father was overjoyed. Hannah's mother was fatigued and sore, and she shifted uncomfortably on the bed.

Visitors came. Only a few, because their friendship group had shrunk over the years.

'They had to cut her,' Ray told a woman who Hannah vaguely remembered from the past.

She glared at the baby in her mother's arms. The child had hurt Marie, was still hurting her, she saw, as Marie winced in pain from trying to feed.

The baby didn't cry much. Not like Hannah. She cried silently as Marie slipped away from her.

–

It was an August bank holiday. Hot and sunny, and Hannah's father had a barbeque going in the garden. Marie was in the kitchen, humming as she prepared the meats that would be cooked in the garden. Hannah looked at the steaks. The white, marbled fat that ran through them. The excess blood that sat in the bottom of the discarded polystyrene trays. They smelled like metal and Hannah felt the vomit rising dangerously in her throat.

She moved to the bowl of salad. Looked at the crisp, fresh green leaves and inhaled the scent of the cucumber.

A squawking noise sounded in the corner.

'I'm going to take the baby up for a nap!' Marie called to Ray through the open window.

He gave her a nod. 'Can you pass the steaks, please, love?' he said back.

Hannah stepped away from the salad. 'I'll take them out, Mum,' she said.

Marie couldn't hide her surprise.

She stroked Hannah's cheek. 'That would be really helpful, thank you.'

Her father was equally shocked when Hannah came to him with the tray of bloody, fat-streaked meats.

He took the tray from her and paused.

Had she been Marie, he would have thanked her, gripped her around her waist and planted a kiss on her cheek. Or he'd have wobbled the tray, painted a mask of panic on his face as he pretended to be at risk of dropping it.

To Hannah, he simply said, 'Thank you.'

Hannah moved off down the garden and let herself out of the gate into the street. She felt her father's eyes on her, but he didn't call after her.

Striding down to the corner, she turned left and considered the years to come.

The baby would grow into a child, would insert itself even further into her mother's life. Would demand more and more of Marie's time. Would take all her energy, all her attention.

All her love.

Hannah let out a small gasp as she turned the next corner. Back on her own street now, approaching the front door.

She let herself in, paused in the hallway and glanced up the stairs.

She heard the faint notes of the baby's mobile. Ahead, in the kitchen, Marie's shape moved around the room. Plates selected gently, so as not to wake the child in the room above her head.

Hannah slid her shoes off and moved soundlessly up the stairs.

The baby wasn't asleep. It stared up at Hannah, gums bared, bright emerald eyes wide.

The crib was by the window. The window was ajar, allowing a stale, hot breeze to enter the room. Hannah glanced outside.

Her father was down there. Smoke billowed around him. A thin, tall orange spire of flame reached up towards the sky. He waved a cloth ineffectually at it.

'Ray!' Marie's voice floated up from the kitchen. She wasn't panicked, though; she was laughing.

Slowly, silently, Hannah pulled down the shade at the window and turned to the crib.

The baby smiled.

Hannah reached into the crib.

The baby laughed.

–

She stood outside the room on the landing for ages. The scent of cooked meat clung heavy in the air. Footsteps came down the hall, rounded the corner to take the stairs two at a time. Her father's shadow loomed large on the wall.

'Hannah!' He came to a stop at the sight of her. 'Where did you go? I've been looking for you.'

He hadn't.

He was coming up here to check on the baby.

'Nowhere,' she said.

She slipped past him and moved down the stairs.

At the bottom, she paused. Waited a beat.

The distress call that rang out from the nursery above her was like nothing she'd ever heard.

39

ALINA, MONDAY

Alina crosses her arms and rubs at her shoulders, as she surveys Hannah and thinks of the story the other woman has just told her.

Thank heavens for the father's arrival. The baby was saved with, it seems, seconds to spare.

Alina wonders what happened next. The baby – Grace – was adopted out? Hannah remained in the family home until her father, unable to deal with his life, left them? How did that even all work? Did he ever tell Marie that Hannah had attempted to kill their baby?

She regards Hannah intently. Sibling jealousy. It's not unheard of. In fact, though she's got no siblings, and neither has Sofia, it's rather common, or so she's led to believe.

But how can it get to this? To one child leaving, the other staying.

Alina draws in a breath as realisation hits. The father left with Grace. Hannah remained with Marie.

Hannah interrupts Alina's thoughts. 'You understand, don't you?' Her voice is low and urgent.

Alina is pretty sure that the other woman has never told anyone this story. How could she, apart from maybe a doctor or a therapist?

For the first time ever, Alina doesn't even know what to say.

Instead of speaking, she busies herself with the coffee, so she doesn't have to look at Hannah. She's sure her face would betray her.

'It all came together after that,' says Hannah.

Her tone is one of pure normalcy.

Alina swallows. Hannah's words don't even make sense. 'What do you mean?'

'*They* fell apart. *We* came together, me and Marie.'

'Your parents fell apart?'

Hannah nods sagely.

Alina leans forward. 'Hannah, what did your father do to you?'

Hannah frowns. 'What do you mean?'

'I mean, what sort of abuse are we talking about here, for you to want him out of your life?'

Hannah's frown deepens. 'There was no abuse. My mother wouldn't have stood for that, not in a million years.'

Alina scrubs at her face. 'So... why?'

'Because I didn't want him there. Or that baby. It was always supposed to be me and my mother.' Hannah shakes her head. 'Don't you understand that?'

The silence grows and stretches until it covers them both.

–

Footsteps sound in the hallway. Heels on marble.

The door is pushed open. Francis stands there, a pile of papers in her arms. She looks from Alina to Hannah.

'Oh. Morning, ladies.' Her voice is uncertain, her smile tremulous.

'Francis.' Alina forces a smile in her friend's direction.

Hannah's eyes are wide. 'You… You know each other?'

Francis approaches Alina and lands a kiss on her cheek. 'Only for ever.'

Alina clears her throat. Her coffee is in her hands, still untouched. She walks a couple of strides to the sink and places the cup in there.

'I've got to go,' she says.

Her voice sounds distant and unfamiliar. Her eyes feel filmy, as though she's drunk too much, or needs to sleep for a week.

Francis stands back to allow her to pass.

'See you soon?' There's a question in Hannah's tone.

Alina pauses. How strange that the question should come not from one of her oldest friends, but from Hannah, the girl she's known only a couple of weeks, and their relationship was only ever supposed to be a business one.

'Yep. See you… soon.' Alina puts her head down and flees the gallery.

She heads home, back to a house that is empty. Maybe not empty. Willem is probably in the basement. Sofia is at school. Her office door is closed, but she can hear the clicking noise of a computer. Julia is in there, working away.

Alina heads to the den and picks up her iPad. She hits the FaceTime icon, scrolls the list of dialled numbers to get her parents'. She reaches the bottom before she sees their names, so long it has been since she called them.

She swallows and hits the call button.

The tone hums for a long time before a face appears on the screen. Her mother.

'Lina!' Only her mother calls her that.

Alina squints at the screen. Her mother looks happy, a wide smile on her face. She sounds slightly out of breath.

'Mama?' The word almost breaks Alina. She coughs. 'Where were you?'

'Watching the festival preparations!' Anya says.

'Festival…?'

Anya flips a hand impatiently. 'The carnival! It goes right past us.'

Alina calculates the date. It's the White Nights festival, celebrating that unique season over there where the sun never fully sets. If they're watching the preparations, it means Alina's parents have moved house.

'You… You've moved?'

Anya lets off peals of laughter. 'You know this. I told you this, Alina. Four years since!'

'Where's Papa?' Alina demands.

Anya rolls her eyes. 'Outside, trying to direct the workers.'

Alina falls back to sit upon the comfortable sofa. 'It's… It isn't dangerous, you being there? So close to the… festival?'

Anya scoffs. 'Such drama. Always, from you, the theatrics.' Anya is speaking in English, and she pronounces it '*teatrics*'.

'I worry about you both,' Alina says in a low voice.

She doesn't. She hasn't done for years, or at least has told herself this. It is easier to pretend not to care.

'One would not think that is the case.' Anya sniffs. 'You don't call, you don't write. How is my girl, my princess granddaughter?'

Without waiting for an answer, Anya carries on talking. Something about street vendors in the festival, a ballet performance, their vegetable plot that Alina's father has constructed.

All this time, all her adult life, since Alina escaped with Willem to a land that was free and safe, her childhood memories have grown darker and darker. Yet, here is her mother, talking about the local goings-on just like any other normal parent might.

'Mama,' Alina interrupts. 'How dangerous was it, when I was growing up?'

Anya sighs. 'Not so different as to how it is now. Always, where there is money, there is threat. You know this, darling.'

'Was that why we had guards, dogs, electric fences?' Alina presses her mother. 'Because we were wealthy?'

'Dogs?' Anya's eyes are wide. 'Electric fences? My goodness, your imagination, all these years on, still running wild.'

Alina leans closer to the screen. 'We didn't have those?'

Anya flaps a hand. 'We had a cook. We had a driver. You remember him, he used to take you to school.'

School. The place where all the girls told Alina what she presumed was the truth about her father's business. The shipping line a front for his true, criminal connections.

Could it all be untrue? Could it be, as Anya pointed out, simply Alina's 'theatrics' at work, and rumours spread by people who were envious?

'How is your husband?' Anya's tone changes, becomes slightly cooler.

Always Willem is her husband, never referred to by name.

'He's fine,' says Alina, weakly.

Her mother's screen spins, and Alina feels a pang. Anya, even with her excellent English and love of technology, hasn't grasped the notion of flipping the cameras instead of turning the whole device around.

'We keep your cards up, all year round.' Anya's voice is faint as she ducks out of shot to show a view of the mantlepiece, the ten cards that stand proudly upon it.

Alina blinks. She knows these Christmas cards. They are the ones she and Willem send to their friends each festive season. But she's never sent any to her folks.

Willem must have done this.

Anya's sudden cry, her face out of view, frightens Alina. 'Mama, what is it?'

She hears panic in her voice, hates the vision that has sprung to her mind. Men, entering her mother's house, armed with batons, guns, all sorts of weapons.

'Here, look, here he is! Had his fill of silly old festival interference. Look, Lina, your papa is joining us.'

Alina wipes her forehead with the back of her hand.

His face comes to the screen. He is wearing half-moon glasses that are new. Or maybe they are not new, Alina thinks – he could have had them for a decade now.

'Papa,' she says. 'How are you?'

He peers over his lenses and waves without speaking, before he is shoved violently to one side.

'It's a *video*,' Anya hisses in angry Russian. 'You can speak. She can hear.'

Lev lets off a stream of Russian questions. He talks about what was his business, how he enjoys seeing it mentioned in the newspapers and on the exchange. Alina doesn't know what to say.

'You don't do anything, now?' she asks, finally, when her father pauses for breath. 'You don't... do any other work?'

'No work. It's leisurely now,' Anya answers for him. 'Fun times, relaxing. Papa, he is in the garden, in the greenhouse. I have my friends, my *Durak* games. I take their money.' Anya laughs.

Alina tries to picture it: her mother with her cronies, playing cards. Her father, pottering around his garden, tending to his blooms and his vegetables, avoiding the women who have taken over his home for the afternoon.

The vision won't materialise, no matter how hard she tries.

She screws her eyes shut. 'When I was little, we lived behind fences, there were guards.' She swallows hard. 'You were threatened.'

Anya frowns. 'Why do you speak of guards, of silly fences? You should have written books, my girl, your imagination is superior.'

'I remember it differently.'

'We insisted on driving you everywhere. We wanted to know where you were at all times. You didn't like it, but we had money, we had to be careful.' Anya clucks crossly. 'Lina, you know this. You are the same with your daughter, no?'

Alina's gaze drifts to the window, where she can just see the edge of one of the security cameras that Willem had installed.

'Because you should have a driver,' chastises Anya. 'With the company that you own. You have money, people you care about, you need the precautions.'

'That's... That's all it was? A precaution?'

'Of course.' Anya's voice is sharp now.

Just a precaution.

What about the nightmares? What about the memories I have?

She sits in deep thought as Anya and Lev exchange a rapid-fire conversation.

Are they one and the same, she wonders. These memories that she suffers from, is it possible that they are not recollections, but simply nightmares?

She sits up straight. 'I have to go now,' she says. 'I'm glad you're both well.'

'Lina, don't leave it long again, do you understand?' Anya shouts through the screen.

Alina nods. 'I won't, I promise.' Her voice breaks, but the signal is fuzzy now, so maybe they don't notice.

She closes the lid of the iPad and goes in search of her husband.

40

HANNAH, MONDAY

Hannah busies herself with her work. There's an exhibition coming up at her gallery. Not one like Tate's, not all grandeur and shock value.

No, this one is a standard showing, but impressive, nonetheless. *Icons* is the name of it.

And what is an icon?

That was what Francis asked her staff when she came up with the idea. The responses naturally differed through the age groups, from old Hollywood stars to modern-day celebrities. Francis was of the opinion that she'd like to see the portraits of the unsung heroes, from Bletchley Park lesser-known legends to smaller-category Nobel prize winners.

It was an interesting debate.

Not that Hannah was very involved.

After all, what did Hannah care for icons? Her own hero was beside her in the form of Marie, and always would be.

There had always only been one legend that Hannah cared about.

But now… Now there is Alina.

Hannah shivers as she thinks of the other woman.

Hannah had been meticulous in her research of Alina Arpels, since that first time she'd heard her name and seen her at the Momotaro.

She is shocked that Francis knows her. Alina never mentioned it, despite knowing that Hannah works here. Her boss has never mentioned Alina, either. But why would she? Francis avoids small talk, especially with Hannah.

And perhaps they are not close friends, merely acquaintances? Maybe Alina doesn't even like Francis that much. After all, she left as soon as Francis came into the room.

Alina… The only other person in the world who Hannah has ever met that seems to be on her own wavelength.

Never before has she told anybody the story of the baby.

She's barely even thought of it since it happened.

Now, since her confession, *that day* goes round and round in her mind.

Barbeque weather, just like it is today and has been for weeks.

As clear as if it were yesterday, she can see her father standing at the bottom of the stairs. The tentative smile he gave her. The change in his expression as he flicked his gaze from her to the baby's nursery. The way his feet sounded like thunder as he took the stairs two at a time.

The moment of silence, when it seemed the whole world had stopped, before a scream reverberated around the house.

She'd never thought a man could sound that way.

Hannah's mother didn't say much. Didn't speak, either. Hannah's father was much the same, though sometimes Hannah caught him looking at her.

He never said a word, though.

They muddled along, through the remainder of the summer, into winter. Christmas came, and on the baby's birthday, on Boxing Day, Marie vanished.

'She needs a break,' explained Ray, Hannah's screams drowning out his words. 'She'll be back, she just needs a rest.'

Marie did return, eventually. Hannah sobbed in her mother's limp arms.

'I knew you'd come back,' she cried. 'I knew you'd never leave me.'

Ray watched on but said nothing. Sometimes, he would shake his head, as though contemplating something unsurmountable.

Hannah eavesdropped on their whispered conversations. The only time they spoke was late at night.

The arguments were urgent and rushed, so quiet that Hannah couldn't make out what the crux of it was, though on occasion she heard her own name mentioned.

Before Christmas came around again, Ray was gone, and the baby was gone.

It was just the two of them left.

As it always should have been.

And life had been pretty much perfect in the twenty years since.

Up until recently.

Up until Clark.

Up until… Oliver?

These days, Marie is out of sorts. Quiet, smiling less. Just like she was before, all those years ago.

Is that why Marie has been off lately? The memory of that long, hot summer when there were four people in their family?

At least this time, they are really gone. Grace, Ray.

Clark too.

Although they might be gone, there seems to be an endless supply of people ready and willing to fill the space they've left.

Nita… and even Oliver, demanding more and more of Marie's time and attention.

But the main ones, the urgent ones, have been dealt with.

Ray and Grace.

She needs to ask Alina what she's done with them. Well, not what she's done – Hannah doesn't need to know that. All she requires is the knowledge that they will not return, neither of them.

As Hannah does a walk-through of the gallery, she thinks about the way Alina lives.

There are three of them. The diamond-dealing husband, the daughter. But Alina's home is pretty much like this gallery: an open-door policy, people coming in and out all the time. Her own staff making themselves at home, cooking in her kitchen, for goodness' sake!

Does Alina get fed up with the constant stream of people in her space? Does she ever just want to shut and bolt the door, and be alone with the one she loves best?

And who would that be, she wonders?

The husband, or the child?

Because there can only be one. Hannah knows that from experience.

Perhaps, she debates, it is neither of them. What of Alina's own mother? She was left in a land far away when the husband lured Alina overseas with his glittering wares. Is Alina even now plotting how she can get her own mother back?

She looks at the gallery wall, and the nuclear family in a particular painting, all with smiles on their faces.

Lies. All lies.

Love doesn't grow and spread the more people there are.

It gets squashed down, divided.

She thinks of her own son, of how she goes out to work, and by the time she comes home in the evening, it is Marie who has fed him, clothed him, loved him.

It seems exhausting. And there is no more love left for Marie to bestow upon Hannah.

The pregnancy, when Hannah found out about it, was a shock. Clark, of course, was thrilled. Marie, when Hannah imparted the news, seemed stunned.

And suddenly, things changed for the better. Marie wasn't always back home in her own house. She was at Hannah and Clark's home, fussing over Hannah, keeping a close eye on how her pregnancy was doing. And the distance that had existed between mother and daughter since Hannah's childhood had gone.

Marie was back, more nurturing than ever. Clark was suddenly nothing more than a distraction.

More than that; Clark was what Ray had once been.

An annoyance. In the way. Always there, talking to Marie, hugging her, creating a distance between Hannah and her mother.

After Clark was no longer around, it made all the sense in the world for Marie to move in with Hannah and the baby.

Life had been good. It had been almost perfect.

Then, Oliver started toddling, started demanding. He reached for Marie always, seeing as she had been his main caregiver.

Then had come the interloper, seeking out their mother. How could she? Wasn't it as clear as day that Marie had given the baby away? Shouldn't that very fact be all that Grace needed to know to realise she was unwanted?

Hannah had disposed of her – via Alina, of course – and of the father that wouldn't stay in the shadows. That should be the end of it.

Finally.

'Is it over?' Hannah whispers to herself in the quiet of the gallery room. 'Is it done now?'

41

ALINA, MONDAY

He's pleased to see Alina when she keys in the code for the basement door in search of him.

Always, he is pleased to see her.

He takes off the strange contraption that he wears on his face to check for inclusions in his gems. Underneath it, he has on another mask. He holds up a hand to stop her in her tracks, points to the coatrack beside her.

'Put the respirator on if you're coming in.'

Obediently, she does as he tells her. Even though she likes to think she's a risk-taker, she knows the importance of wearing the protective equipment when he's heating up certain stones. The mercury and poisonous vapours released by some of these gems can kill in minutes.

'I spoke to my parents,' she blurts out when she's got the correct gear on. Her voice is muffled under the mask.

'Oh, how are they?'

'You send them Christmas cards?' Her voice goes up an octave.

He shrugs. 'It is polite. I took their only daughter to another country and you… Well…' He pulls a face.

Alina pounces on it. 'What?' she demands. 'I… what?'

'You don't seem to miss them very much or update them on our life. They like my cards. They like to hear our news.'

Alina's heart melts a little. This man. This lovely, kind, thoughtful man. How did she get so lucky?

'You had a nice chat?' he asks. 'It's unlike you to call them.' He looks pleased at this new development.

'Do you think they're dangerous?' she asks him now.

He frowns at her. 'Dangerous?'

'You know how it was when I was growing up. All this with Sofia…' She sighs and sits down on the stool opposite him.

He matches her sigh. 'Everything has some element of danger. Anybody who is well known, who has money, has to be careful.'

They are almost the same words that her mother used.

'They were talking to me about the old days,' she says. 'Putting me straight on some things that happened.'

She hangs her head. *Some things that* didn't *happen*, she thinks to herself.

Willem frowns. 'What do you mean?'

Theatrics! She hears in her head. *Drama queen!*

Could what she believed were memories really be that wrong?

Alina turns away from him. 'Oh, nothing. Listen, I'm going out. Are you here for dinner? We'll eat together, all three of us, yes?'

He turns back to his gems. 'You mean, will I cook?'

She laughs. 'Yes.'

'It will be my absolute pleasure, my darling. See you later.'

She watches him for a while, bent over his work desk.

–

Outside, in the glaring sunshine, the uncomfortable respirator off her face, she finds the street is peaceful. Bar the occasional humming noise. It sounds like a fly, or a hornet or something.

Alina frowns, looks up at the pitched roof of the porch. The CCTV is turning, capturing her in its red eye.

She sticks her middle finger up at it and stalks to the garage.

Lucas is there, polishing Willem's motorbike. The damage has gone; it looks good as new.

Lucas stands up. 'We're going out?'

Alina shakes her head. 'Nah, you're fine. I'm just running some errands.'

She takes the keys to the Mercedes. Not the one that Lucas drives her around in, but the smaller one that rarely gets used. She slips into the cool interior and blasts the air con, waving to Lucas as she edges out of the garage.

She passes the other car, the big one, and takes a moment to survey the tinted windows. She'd wanted bulletproof ones, she recalls, when they went car shopping. The salesman's eyes had popped out of his head then, and he'd laughed uncertainly.

Alina had been serious.

Misconceptions from her youth?

Drama that she has forged within herself as part of her personality.

Theatrics, Anya calls it.

Willem says the same about her.

Alina drives to the Barbican and heads up to Hannah's father's room.

He opens the door but keeps the chain on. An eye with fresh bruises peers out at her.

There is a long moment of hesitation, on both sides of the door.

Finally, as if he's convinced himself she's not there to hurt him further, he slides the chain off and opens the door to her.

Alina goes into the room and looks around.

It's a good room, an expensive one. A lounge area, a polished dining table, and a floor-to-ceiling window overlooking the lush grounds. In the distance, she can just spot Marble Arch.

'Why are you concerned about Hannah?' she asks, after politely declining his offer of coffee.

He stands in bare feet on the cool tile of the kitchen area.

'She's not well,' he says. 'She's never been well.'

'In what way?' she asks.

Ray sighs and reaches for the coffee pot. He pours two cups, even though she's said she doesn't want one.

'She never spoke to me. Never liked spending time with me.' He meets her eye, but only for a split second. 'I never did anything to her.'

Alina nods. 'Go on.'

'She just wanted her mother. Not like a clingy child, you understand. It was… It was so much more than that. Almost an aggressive need.'

'An obsession,' states Alina.

'Yes!' Ray thumps his fist on the counter. 'That's it, exactly.'

'You had another child?'

Ray, only moments before animated, folds into himself. He abandons his coffee cup and shuffles across to the lounge area, where he sinks onto an armchair.

'Yes,' he whispers.

'Grace,' Alina says.

He frowns. 'I'm sorry, I don't understand?'

A cold chill travels the length of Alina's body. 'The baby…'

'Peter.' Ray's face is ashen. 'Our little boy was called Peter.'

Her horror is written on her face, plain for him to see. He darts little glances at her, brow furrowed, confusion mixed in the absolute lethargy that seemingly covers his body and mind.

Alina moves to the counter. Picking up the coffee he has poured for her, she downs it in one.

'Do you have anything stronger?' Her voice is strangled.

'It's the one supplied by the hotel. It's the only brand they do, I think.'

She wasn't talking about coffee.

'What happened to Peter?' She's relieved when her voice comes out a little more normal.

'An ill-fitting mattress, they said. He got caught up in it. Turned himself the wrong way round, they said.' Ray stares at the wall.

'But you don't think…'

'No.' He stares at her. 'No, I know it didn't happen like that.'

It was the same story that Hannah had confided in her. Minus the tragic ending.

It is on the tip of her tongue to ask why he didn't report what had really happened. Before the question leaves her mouth, she thinks about it. If it were Sofia, and there had been another baby after her. A baby that Sofia didn't want in her home. Her little daughter, not really getting the implications of her actions if she were to decide to rid the home of that baby.

She has no answer to her own question, which remains unasked.

'And so you left?' she asks Ray.

Ray shakes his head. 'Marie was the one who left.'

This is unexpected. Alina picks up Ray's abandoned coffee and downs it too. '*Marie* left?'

'For a while.'

Alina comes to join him. She sits on the armchair opposite. 'What happened?'

Ray stares into the middle distance. 'Marie needed a break after... After Peter. I looked after Hannah. She screamed all day, all night. When her voice went, she smashed things. I don't understand how the police were never called. I never understood why nobody came...'

To help me.

The words he didn't say are the ones Alina knows he was thinking.

'But Marie came home?'

'Eventually.'

'You... never had any more children?'

'No.'

But you did. You just don't know about her.

'And you walked out on them.'

'Yes.'

'But you kept an eye on them.'

It is suddenly so clear. She understands this now. A life lived in the background, on the periphery. Like her own father, checking on the business that once belonged to him. Like Willem and his Christmas cards to Russia. Those were nice things, though. Ray has simply been waiting all these years for another nightmare to come.

'You've been watching for a long time, unseen. She knows about you, now. She's *seen* you.'

He nods, thoughtfully.

'Why?' she presses him. 'Why allow yourself to be seen now?'

'Since Clark.' His tone is dull, dead. 'Then, when she left the gallery covered in blood, I knew something was happening.' He stares at Alina, his expression almost pleading. 'Hannah plans very carefully; there is a reason for every single action she makes. Do you understand?'

He seems to know an awful lot about a woman he hasn't had contact with for decades.

She doesn't answer his question. Instead, she asks another of her own. 'Hannah's husband?'

Ray shrugs. 'I was there the day they took him away in a body bag.'

'You were *there*?'

'Watching,' he says. 'From a distance. I blend in.' He catches sight of himself, of his ruined face, in the mirror on the wall. 'I used to blend in.'

She ignores the slight accusatory tone. 'What happened to her husband?'

'I don't know.' Ray meets her eye for just a second. 'But a week later, Marie had moved in with her and the baby.'

'You and Marie...?'

Ray looks at Alina, away from his reflection. 'I haven't spoken to her in more than twenty years.'

'But you watch her. You watch them both.' A thought strikes her. 'You keep an eye on the baby. Hannah's son...?'

Ray nods. 'As much as I can.'

Alina thinks of herself, of how much she mentions Sofia in conversation, of the hundreds of times a day she thinks of her girl. Hannah rarely mentions her own child. All she talks about is her mother.

Marie.

The child, her own baby, is a mere shadow in her life.

But what about when he grows? What happens when his voice is louder, his presence more pronounced, like his father before him?

Alina stands. 'You can stay here as long as you need.'

He peers at her, his mouth working. Alina waits.

'What's she like now, in person, up close?' he asks.

Curiosity fills his tone. It seems he has only ever clashed with Hannah.

Alina thinks about the woman who saved her daughter's life.

Uptight had been her first thought. Grudging admiration for what seemed like a strong, independent woman. Affection, in most recent days.

'I haven't known her long,' Alina replies.

Ray leans his head back in the chair. His eyes, dead as anything again, land on her. 'Okay.'

She sweeps her gaze over him. 'I'll be in touch.'

He doesn't get up when she lets herself out. He's exhausted. He has the appearance of a man who won't live much longer. She's pretty sure there's nothing wrong with him, nothing of a terminal nature. He's just worn down.

Worn out.

–

Revved up now, she finds herself back at the hostel, and this time she has come prepared.

The two same youths are there, eyeing her as she approaches.

She pulls out an envelope full of cash. 'I want to know why this place was deserted the other night.'

The younger one is practically salivating. Alina focuses her attention on him. The other one has longing in his eyes, mixed with fear. He backs away. Head down, he strides off past the trees, fading into the crowds on the high street.

'Someone paid the *padre* to clear the place.' The remaining youth licks his lips.

Alina passes him some neatly folded notes. 'Where is he?'

He grabs the money and grips it tightly in his fist. 'Inside.'

The *padre* is a weaselly looking man with long, greasy hair and a thin pointed face. He can be no more than twenty years old. And though their physical similarities are nothing alike, he reminds her of Grantham from the Momotaro.

Alina narrows her eyes as she contemplates how to play this.

With the truth, she decides.

'You brought a girl here, the other night,' she says, as casually as she can manage.

There is a beat before he replies, 'Nah, no girls here.'

His eyes travel lazily over her body. He is not afraid. He does not know who she is.

'You can tell me.'

He stares at her. 'I have no idea what you're talking about.'

She fingers the wad of cash in her pocket and slides a few notes out.

He looks torn, his mouth twisting, his eyes hungry. Eventually, he holds his hand out. She sees the blurred ink: the number 88.

The tattoo was one of the answers she was seeking. Alina is burning. She wants to take the stack of money and push the notes one by one down his throat until he chokes on them. She wants to watch him turn red, then blue. She wants to hear his last breath.

Instead, she drops the money on the dirty floor where Sofia had to sit only a few nights ago.

As she walks away, she hears his heavy breathing as he drops to his knees to collect his riches.

42

HANNAH, WEDNESDAY

It's been a couple of days since Hannah heard from anyone.

No texts from Grace.

No visits from Alina.

Nothing of the man who has followed her since the day she chased him out of his home.

They're gone. Her sister, the one she never wanted, is gone. Her father, the one she never needed, is gone.

But so is Alina.

It's a disturbing thought, the realisation that she might actually miss having Alina in her life.

Hannah has never missed anybody before, other than Marie.

They are in the kitchen, Hannah and her mother. Marie is scrubbing the post-breakfast worktop. Hannah has tried to please her mother this morning, by eating poached eggs without any coaxing.

Although, Marie still doesn't seem very happy. She's been darting strange little looks at Hannah. Not just today, but for a while now.

Hannah glances at her watch. She's got no work today. She will spend the whole day here with Marie.

'We'll spend the day together today, Mum,' she says.

Marie's cleaning cloth stills.

She begins to say something, but Hannah's opened up her iPad and is scrolling down the local news feed.

It's there. The news she's been waiting for, *searching* for.

A body has been discovered in the park. The park with the hostel in it.

How fitting for a location, she thinks.

Grace.

Or Ray?

She reads on, but the article, as brief as it is, makes no reference to whether it is a male or female.

It must be one of them. Though it really should have been both. It will be both, eventually, she tells herself. Because Alina owes her.

'Hannah. Hannah?'

'Huh?'

Marie is standing behind her. Hannah jumps guiltily and slams the iPad closed.

'What is it?'

Marie is staring strangely at her. 'Someone is at the door. Are you expecting anyone?'

Hannah swallows. 'Stay here,' she says.

She thinks of every imagined possibility of what is behind the door. Ray, beaten and bloodied. Grace, pale and furious. Or someone else who has discovered what she has done.

She takes a deep breath and pulls open the door.

It's Alina! And she's smiling. Hannah knows her own expression is one of unguarded joy to find her new friend on her doorstep.

'Hi!' she greets her enthusiastically.

Alina reaches up for a hug. Hannah welcomes it.

Hannah… *enjoys it*.

Is this what it's like to have a friend, she wonders?

'Are you busy?' Alina lounges against the doorframe. 'Want to hang for the day?'

She hasn't scared Alina off. The strange wiring inside her own brain, the part of her that she's never before shown to anyone, has not made this woman flee.

Because Alina understands.

'I'd love to spend the day with you,' Hannah blurts. She feels her face reddening. She steps outside and pulls the door to behind her.

What would Marie think if she heard Hannah speaking that way to someone other than her? And hasn't she just promised to spend the day with her mother?

Then, she thinks of Marie's friendship with Nita, of her wistful looks when she gets to thinking about the past, and her heart tightens and cracks in her chest.

'Let me get my shoes on,' she says. 'Wait here.' She ducks back inside, reaches for her shoes by the door.

'Are you off out?' Marie calls from the kitchen, where she's still cleaning.

Hannah hurries down the hallway. 'Yes.' She narrows her eyes at the bottle of wine and two glasses on the table. They weren't there just a moment ago. 'Are you expecting company?'

'I thought I'd invite Nita over, if you're going out.'

Hannah lets the sigh escape.

Marie raises her chin. 'Is that a problem?'

'I just… don't like—'

'Nita? Say it, Hannah, you don't like Nita.'

Hannah straightens her spine. 'I was going to say I don't like how much you drink alcohol around her.'

Marie lets out a laugh. Hannah stills at the noise. Never has Marie laughed at her before.

'What else have I got, Hannah?' Marie gestures to the bottle and Hannah sees now that it is only half-full.

Hannah's lip trembles. 'Me,' she says. 'You've got me.'

'But not Nita, is that right, or any other friends?'

Hannah forgets that Alina is waiting outside. She sinks down on a chair and reaches for her mother. Marie withdraws her hand, wrapping it around the wine glass.

The rejection stings.

'You were at her house that night, Hannah.' Marie takes a long sip of wine and averts her eyes.

'What night?' Hannah watches in horror as Marie drains her glass before replying. It's morning, only just past breakfast. What is Marie *doing*? More to the point, what is Marie *saying*?

'The night Nita got attacked. You offered to take Bobby home after he'd had tea here. What did you do? Did you jam her door, so you could sneak back later? Because you were still up when it happened, weren't you?'

Hannah remembers all too well that night. The crying that Marie heard, how she practically forced Hannah to investigate alongside her. How, at every turn, she shepherded Hannah ahead of her, making her open Nita's door, move the chair, shift the offending toy from the jammed frame, while she, Marie, simply issued directions.

Hannah's prints are all over Nita's place. Marie made sure of that.

Why? Why would Marie *do that*?

Hannah stands up fast. Her chair screeches on the tiled floor. 'How can you *think* that it was anything to do with me?' she cries.

Marie doesn't answer.

Tears sting Hannah's eyes as she rushes away from Marie. Out of the kitchen, down the hall. A blurry shape sits on the periphery of her vision. She wipes the backs of her hands across her eyes.

Oliver. Standing in the hallway. He stares dolefully up at her.

Hannah crouches down in front of him.

Her small son flinches backwards.

A memory, unbidden, of another child, in a time before. One that never grew old enough to learn to flinch away from her.

'You ready?'

Hannah looks up. Alina is on the doorstep, peering through into the house. Hannah burns with embarrassment. How much has she heard?

But it doesn't matter, Hannah reminds herself. *Alina understands.*

–

'Is your neighbour okay now?'

Hannah gives her a quizzical look. Neighbour…?

'You said she was attacked. In her home, the other night.'

Hannah averts her eyes. She'd told Alina that when they were searching for Sofia. The other woman had been in such a mess, almost a disassociated state, that surely she can't remember that detail.

Maybe she doesn't. Maybe she was eavesdropping and heard Marie's terrible accusation.

'She's fine,' she says, as airily as she can manage.

'Oh, I see.' Alina stops and gives a little secret smile to Hannah. 'You don't like this neighbour?'

Hannah suppresses a shiver. It's like Alina can see into her very soul.

And that's okay, she tells herself.

'She's…' She trails off, unsure how to explain her feelings about Nita. 'She's intrusive. Always round our house. Always doing stuff with Mum.'

Alina nods thoughtfully and starts to walk again.

Hannah studies the other woman's profile.

You really do get it, she thinks.

She feels lighter as she strolls down the road beside Alina. Lighter than she can ever recall feeling.

Suddenly, Marie and all the things that her mother wants to get off her chest but doesn't say are a mere distant cloud inside her mind.

Hannah reaches out and takes Alina's hand in hers.

'Thank you,' she says, shyly.

Alina glances down at their joined hands. She squeezes Hannah's fingers and then relaxes her grip.

Hannah, though, remains steadfast in holding Alina's hand.

43

ALINA, WEDNESDAY

'What happened to your son's dad?'

They are in the park. The same one where Hannah's father first approached Alina.

That day seems so long ago now. Alina was reeling with indignation and a simmering rage about the gallery's failings, the artist's inadequacy.

Back then, Hannah was just a person whom Alina needed to thank in the most profuse way possible.

She thinks of her own actions, her own words. The way she sent the letter to Hannah, on their embossed stationery, the grandiose gesture of sending her driver to Hannah's door. The way she'd shown off Willem's diamonds to her; the way she'd sat in her big house, waving a virtual wand as she'd offered Hannah anything her heart desired.

She thinks of Willem's suggestion that she should have sent Hannah a fruit basket or a hamper.

Alina has been lying on her back, staring at the cloudless sky. The sun is blazing down. She relishes the burn on her face.

Now, she props herself up on one elbow.

'Your husband?' she asks again, as a half-thought makes itself known in her hazy brain. 'Was he… Was it like your… Like the baby, when you were a little girl?'

She expects – *hopes* – for a sharp glare from Hannah. Outrage. A denial.

Instead, Hannah meets her eye for the briefest moment before dropping her head to her chest.

Alina knows that look. She's seen that expression, many times. From Sofia, her eight-year-old daughter. The reaction after an untruth told, or bad behaviour.

It strikes her then: how very childlike Hannah is, in spite of the classy looks, the professional front, the serious nature.

'He was a good man,' says Hannah, eventually, her voice a mere whisper. 'A perfect father. A decent human. But Marie really liked him. She loved him.'

At this, a shadow crosses Hannah's face.

Alina bites her lip.

'How did you…?'

Hannah shrugs. 'He took all his pills – every single last one.'

But he didn't. You fed them to him… Alina doesn't vocalise her thoughts.

She thinks of her own husband, of how Willem does his best to mend the distance, both physical and emotional, between Alina and her own folks. Of how he does it in his own, quiet way. Keeping the peace in a way that's acceptable to both sides.

Lev and Anya have never loved Willem the way Alina has. In fact, at the beginning, they despised him for taking their daughter overseas to a new life.

She imagines if she were Hannah, if she had arranged for her own parents to simply cease to exist in order to make her own life…

Her own life what? Easier? Less complicated? Just so she, Willem and Sofia could exist in a perfect little bubble.

She thinks of Hannah's confusion at the Arpels' close-ness with Lucas and Julia, her narrowed eyes when they're invited into Alina's home, to cook in her kitchen and break bread together.

'I couldn't do it again. To Grace, I mean,' says Hannah suddenly. 'Not after… Not after the baby. Not after Clark.'

Alina sits up fully. Does Hannah regret it, then? Both deaths, brother and husband? She asks her this.

Hannah shakes her head vigorously. 'No, not for a second. But someone would have found out who she was, her link to me. They'd start thinking it was strange. These deaths, with me, the common denominator. Or worse, Marie. What if they'd started looking at Marie?' Hannah shudders, though to Alina, she seems fully unaware of it.

'And when I made you the offer, it seemed like the perfect answer.' Alina folds her arm behind her and lays back to rest her head on it.

'Yes,' says Hannah, simply.

Alina closes her eyes against the glare from the sun.

Silence ensues between them.

–

There were never any strings attached to Alina's offer.

This is what she's thinking when she leaves Hannah at the entrance to the mews lane and walks on down the high street.

'I'll see you again, right?' Hannah calls after her, some-thing almost like panic in her voice.

Alina nods and waves.

She passes the Momotaro Gallery on her left, but the place where she has spent so many happy days goes past in little more than a blur.

She resumes her train of thought. No conditions to her offer. Anything Hannah wanted, in return for saving Sofia's life.

Hannah wanted somebody out of her life. Alina had the balls and the means to do it.

What does it matter that it wasn't some errant ex-boyfriend or some dangerous, stalker type? It matters not a jot.

Alina had promised Hannah anything.

This was what Hannah wanted.

She believes that Alina has answered her prayers. She does not know that Grace has simply been paid money to go away, or that Ray is living in the lap of luxury in a hotel nearby.

Alina picks up her pace as her thoughts turn to Sofia. She will be home now, safely ensconced in the now security-ridden home that Willem and Alina have built for her.

The home is safe. Sofia is safe. Thanks to Hannah.

Who has saved her, not just once, but *twice*.

Alina walks briskly past the hostel. A single, thin strip of police tape flaps gently in the breeze. She allows herself a smile. It looks more like a grimace as she recalls being here two nights ago. The police tape is now the only reminder that the tattooed man who took her daughter is no longer here at all.

44

HANNAH, THURSDAY

She's never had a friend before. Sure, there are acquaint-
ances, mostly within her professional world, people like
Jerry. He took care of her the night of the accident, but
that's just the sort of man he is. He's not a friend.

Francis is not a friend.

The other girls who work within the gallery and the
industry are not her friends.

For all those years, she didn't need a friend. She had
Marie. But Marie has changed. She's got her own friends.
And Marie's time is always taken up with Oliver.

Oliver…

The bigger he gets, the more he seems to want Marie.
The more Marie seems to cling to *him*.

She ponders the possibility that Oliver might have been
a mistake.

She could ask Alina. She wants to see Alina again. She's
never had a friend she can bare her soul to.

'Hannah!'

Francis's shrill voice jerks Hannah back to the present.

She scowls, automatically, before hurriedly rearranging
her face into an expression of work professionalism.

'Francis, how are you?' she asks, politely. 'Did you need
me?'

'It's ten past ten,' Francis says.

Hannah stares at her blankly.

'Ten past the time we open up!' Her manager's voice goes even higher.

Hannah blinks in disbelief. Can't Francis unlock the gallery door?

'Right,' Hannah says. She pushes on the desk and stands up. 'I'll open up, then.'

She edges past Francis, who is still standing in the doorway.

'I shouldn't have to tell you, Hannah,' calls Francis, as Hannah makes her way down the hallway towards the main door.

Hannah ignores her as she gets the ring of keys out of her pocket and glances through the partially glazed door.

Nobody is waiting. No tourists, eager to get in and see the wares that the Harman Gallery has to offer. No coachloads of schoolkids. No pensioners or eager youths.

This place is hardly on a par with the Momotaro, where crowds start queuing up half an hour before opening.

Francis is a joke.

This place is a joke.

Now that all the family business is dealt with, maybe Hannah can broach the subject of getting a new curator on board at the Momotaro with her powerful new friend Alina.

She pauses in the hallway, imagining her dream job.

A shadow falls across the glass as Hannah turns the key in the lock.

Okay, so there's one person waiting.

She pulls open the door and comes face to face with her own mother.

'What are you doing here?' Before Marie can answer, Hannah feels a strange little kick of something akin to excitement in her chest. 'Is it Oliver? Has something happened to him?'

'Oliver's fine.' Marie grips the strap of her handbag and takes a deep breath. 'We need to talk, Hannah.'

She doesn't ask who is looking after the boy.

'I'm at work.' Hannah's voice is stilted and cold. Never before has she spoken to Marie that way, though the need to has been building for a while now.

Since I met Alina.

'It won't take long.' Marie walks up the remaining steps and into the gallery. 'I need to talk to you about what you did to Nita.'

The excited feeling of a moment before turns to anxiety. 'I'm at *work*!' she exclaims.

Marie pulls a ten-pound note out of her bag and lays it on the reception desk. 'And I'm a paying customer.'

'Goooooood morning!' Francis's voice has changed from shrill to fake, Hannah notes, as her boss rounds the corner and beams at Marie. 'And how are you this fine morning?'

Before Marie can answer, Francis scoops up a leaflet advertising the upcoming *Icons* show.

Marie takes it, even appears to be listening as Francis launches into her spiel.

But her eyes never leave Hannah.

Hannah backs up a step.

The strange feeling has changed now, moved from irritation to downright panic.

Marie never confronts Hannah. And today, that's the only way to describe Marie's stance.

Combative.

Confrontational.

Hannah averts her eyes, turns on her heel and marches swiftly back to her office.

Hannah closes the door and sits back down at her desk. After a while, she can hear other visitors, walking the rooms, exclaiming as they view what the gallery has to offer.

She wonders what became of Marie. Has Francis still got her hemmed in in the reception area? Is her boss taking her mother on a personalised tour? Does Francis know who Marie is? Has Marie told her?

She imagines them together, Marie spilling all Hannah's secrets to her boss.

Her chest tightens, an iron grip, before softening a little.

Marie doesn't know all her secrets, Hannah reminds herself.

She may suspect, but she doesn't *know*.

She hears her own breathing coming fast, shallow inhalations, like she can't get enough air into her lungs.

Alina, she thinks. *I need her…*

She scrabbles around in her bag and pulls out her phone. She is halfway through scrolling to Alina's number when her office door opens.

She looks up, fully expecting to see Marie filling the doorway. But it's just Francis again.

Suddenly, breathing is a little easier.

'Hannah.' Francis's face is white and pinched. 'I need some help from you, please don't sit in here all day. We've got a show coming up, and I need you to do what I pay you to do.'

Hannah swallows down the vitriol that she wants to spit in Francis's face and stands up.

'Certainly, Francis.' Hannah fixes a smile onto her face. 'Tell me what you need.'

Francis leads her up to the third floor, to the large walk-in cupboard where they keep their props and supplies from past exhibits.

'All this needs an inventory doing. It's… Everything is just dumped in here and we need some order.'

Hannah agrees but doesn't mention that it's *Francis* who shoves everything inside after a showcase ends. If it were Hannah's job, everything would be listed and cross-referenced and stored correctly.

She thinks of her home, of how sparse it is; how whenever she needs anything, she can put her hands straight on it. How she's encouraged Marie to have only what possessions she really needs.

A tidy home is a tidy mind.

And Hannah acknowledges that her own mind needs to be kept as neat as possible.

'You're good at stuff like this.' Hannah blinks in surprise at the sudden softness of Francis's tone, so different to how the older woman normally speaks. 'Maybe we can work together?'

There is no glow felt from the praise. Hannah knows Francis is right. Hannah's organisational skills are epic.

She nods and surveys the boxes and bags. 'Of course,' she says. 'I'll make a start now.'

She reaches for a large, plastic container and flinches as Francis's fingers close around her wrist. Francis smiles, kindly. 'We'll do it together,' she says.

Hannah stills.

Francis narrows her eyes and produces a clipboard with a list attached. 'I've got the file of everything that should be in here,' she says. 'We'll do it properly, and we'll know exactly what we're missing.'

There is a strange little smile on Francis's lips, cold and hard and… mean?

Hannah's own face feels as cold and stiff as marble.

'Okay,' she mumbles.

As they get to work in the otherwise silent room, Hannah is sure that Francis can hear the beating of her heart, which sounds as loud as a thunderstorm inside her head.

45

ALINA, FRIDAY

'I need to see you.' Francis pauses. 'It's a matter of complete and utter urgency.'

Normally, Alina would be thrilled to hear from a friend. And Francis's statement promises gossip and scandal. Usually, an irresistible temptation.

It's Friday, however. Later today, Willem is off on another business trip. A couple of weeks ago, she was in this very same position. Willem was getting ready to fly out, Alina had decided to spend the evening at the Momotaro with Sofia. A treat to mark the start of a weekend on their own.

But everything has changed since that Friday, and the Saturday just gone.

Now, Alina wants to be at home. Or, more accurately, wherever Sofia is.

Twice, Sofia has almost been lost to her. Twice in the space of as many weeks. And don't they say things come in threes?

'What is it, Francis?' Alina says. 'Can you come over here?'

'No. I need you to see this with your own eyes.'

Alina glances at the clock. It's two forty-five. School will be out in fifteen minutes. Before, Alina would have called Julia or Lucas, asked them to collect her girl and stay at the house with her until she returned. It's not that she doesn't trust them, far from it. But she trusts nobody more than herself now.

'Willem!' Alina moves to the top of the basement stairs and shouts down to him.

'It's safe,' he calls back. 'Come on down.'

She clatters down the stairs. Her husband is bent over his desk, poring over a piece of paper. 'What time are you leaving?'

'Six o'clock,' he replies.

Alina puts the phone back to her ear. 'I'll come now. I have to be home by five, though.'

'That will be plenty of time.' Francis's voice is crisp and businesslike. 'Come to the gallery.'

She hangs up and turns to Willem. 'Can you pick up Sofia from school?' she asks. 'I'll be back in a couple of hours at the most.'

Willem has been packing his briefcase. Alina glances at the jewels he has selected for his latest sales venture. Not just diamonds, but pieces he's created here, in this very basement. She touches a cinnabar gem and closes her fingers over it.

'Of course I'll pick her up,' Willem says without looking up from his list.

Alina looks at her watch. It's now two fifty. School is out in ten minutes. It can take that long just to navigate the traffic on the main road. Sofia will be waiting to be picked up. She'll be alone on the school steps, just like she was the last time.

'*Willem!*' The panic that rose without warning bursts from her.

He turns to her, eyes wide. 'What?' he asks. 'What's wrong?'

She presses the back of her hand to her mouth. He was the one who put these rules into place, who added all the security cameras and extra measures. Has he already forgotten the night Sofia went missing? Alina is sure the way she felt then will be branded on her like a burn for the rest of her life.

'Don't worry. I'll pick up Sofia,' she says, tightly.

Willem stands up and looks at his watch. 'Sorry, I didn't realise that was the time. I'm going now. I'll call her on the way, tell her to wait inside until I get there.'

Alina's exhalation is shaky. Willem's face is a portrait of concern. She forces a smile. Her husband has never seen her this way before.

Sure, she's always been dramatic. Theatrical, as her mother would say. A princess, spoiled and demanding. But that persona has always been a front. Something to play at, something which always amused Willem.

It's no longer a costume she wears.

Her paranoia has proved itself to be real.

She walks back up the stairs, stopping when Willem catches her hand.

'Alina,' he says quietly.

Her shades are propped on her head. She flips them down to cover her eyes before turning to face him, not wanting him to see the panic on her face.

Their fingers interlink and he puts his face close to hers.

'I hate to see you like this.'

For the first time, his voice – his presence – doesn't quell her trepidation.

It will take time, she tells herself. Two horrible incidents, in such a short space of time.

She reminds herself that the threat has gone. The man with the 88 tattoo. The man who snatched Sofia.

He is gone now.

So low down on the food chain was he, that his murder reflected his life, deserving of only a short article in the local press.

She acted hastily, too quickly, though. She should have questioned him under duress, found out *why* he took Sofia. Because it made no sense, the county lines theory. Those kinds of people they recruit. They have a type. Sofia – delicate, small, female – made no sense whatsoever.

Alina thought that perhaps the man took Sofia for nefarious reasons. That he saw the little girl and in some corner of his terrible mind he imagined himself doing things that Alina can't even stand to think about.

But it made no sense. To kidnap her, yes, but to somehow use his influence as the *padre* to clear the hostel, to stash Sofia in it while he left the premises… That made Alina think that he was acting upon orders, rather than his own wants and needs.

The tattoo he sported, the neo-Nazi badge of honour, and the way his eyes shined when she flashed the cash, spoke volumes. He had no morals, no scruples, would do anything requested of him if payment was promised.

But who made the request? That's the question.

It's too late to ask now. The *padre* is gone, dead, and despite Alina's bravado and hard exterior, it had been her first time.

And it had been so very easy.

She'd thought later that maybe she is her father's daughter after all.

Then she remembered: that was all untrue, anyway.

Her past, the man her father was… Well that was all in Alina's mind, apparently. Willem has no idea. And he never will. No police have come knocking on her door. Why would they? Alina and Willem are an upper-class family living miles away from the scene of the crime. The authorities do not know that this man took Alina's daughter and hid her. And the remaining ones, the ones who were told to keep away that night, will never tell.

But Alina is still so tightly wound, even now, after it's finished. She needs to chill, as Sofia would say.

So why does she feel like the nightmare isn't over yet?

Because it's not. Because there is more work to be done. But Alina has to be very, very certain of her suspicions before performing her final act.

She apologises for shouting at Willem a moment ago. He tells her he understands why she reacted the way she did, as he overtakes her on the stairs and grabs his keys.

'I'll see you before you go?' she calls after him.

But he's in a hurry, because of the way she acted, and he doesn't hear her question.

–

Francis is at her gallery, anxiously looking out of the window. Alina gives her a small wave and waits patiently as her friend comes to the entrance door.

'Come in,' Francis gestures her inside, poking her head out and looking left and right down the street.

Something is off. Francis is normally rather laid-back, in social company, anyway. This afternoon, she seems edgy.

The gallery is still open, and Alina glances around, wondering if Hannah is working today.

'Is Hannah in?' Alina asks as she stands in the lobby of the gallery.

'No, she was on earlies, so she's gone home.' Francis pauses meaningfully. 'Which is why I didn't call you until now.'

Alina puts her head on one side and regards her friend. 'What's up, Francis?'

'I got to thinking when I left yours after dinner the other night. Before that, actually. Talking about those technological things, the installation we did.'

'Technological things?' Alina is confused.

Francis waves her hand impatiently. 'Those pagers. I told you: we learned of that event in New York, we decided to do something similar here, at this very gallery. Anyway, I was still thinking about it, couldn't get it off my mind. Guess what I found?'

'What?'

Francis draws in a deep breath and crooks a finger at Alina. 'Follow me.'

Alina follows her friend down the corridor, down the steps and into the office portion of the gallery.

'In here,' says Francis, leading Alina into what appears to be a storeroom.

'What's all this?' Alina looks around the room, lined with shelving units on all four walls, all holding large boxes and items covered with sheets. It's surprisingly tidy for Francis.

'This is where we keep items from past events, installations, etc. Some things, like the lighting rigs, we use a lot. Some things we will probably never use again, but you know me... Hoarder.'

Alina utters a small laugh. 'So, what did you want to show me?'

Francis's face turns very serious. 'This.' She points to a box on the table in the centre.

Alina walks over to it, lifts the flaps and peers inside.

She gasps.

It is a box of pagers.

She picks one up and studies it. It appears identical to the one that was found in Tate's wreckage of Lucifer.

'So, they are more common than I thought,' Alina muses as she turns it over in her hands.

'No, they're not,' Francis says, sharply.

Alina looks up at her sudden change in tone. 'What do you mean? You've got about a hundred of them, right here!'

'Nope.' Francis's nostrils flare. 'There are fifty in that box. Correction, there *should* be fifty.'

Alina rolls her eyes. 'What are you saying?'

'I'm saying that one is missing.'

Alina drops the pager back in the box. Her eyes glint dangerously, but she says nothing.

'I got Hannah in here this morning. I demanded that she take an inventory with me.' Francis steps closer to Alina and puts a hand on her shoulder. 'I've never seen her break so much as a sweat before. She's an ice queen. Cool, calm and collected. Today, when I asked her to do this task, I swear I thought she was going to pass out.'

Everything that has not been said is all that Alina can hear.

'She saved my girl. She saved her twice.' Alina scowls at Francis. 'I don't know what your beef is with Hannah, but leave me out of it.'

'Alina! I'm talking to you as your friend—'

Alina stalks out of the room. 'I have to go. Willem is going away tonight.'

'Alina, wait!'

But Alina is gone, down the stairs, out into the hot London afternoon.

She's breathing hard, practically panting, when she becomes aware of her phone ringing.

An unknown number.

She hesitates, just for a moment, before answering the call.

'Ms Arpels?' The voice on the other end falters.

Alina has never spoken to this person before – indeed, she's never even heard *them* speak. But she knows exactly who it is.

'Yes, this is she,' Alina answers, willing her voice not to quiver.

'I-I need to speak to you, in confidence…' The woman's voice fades away to nothing.

'It's okay,' says Alina, forcefully. 'I'll come to you.' She pauses, thinks ahead. 'Expect me tomorrow.'

'But—'

'Don't worry,' Alina interrupts. 'I'll sort everything.'

46

HANNAH, SATURDAY

Hannah replays the stocktake with Francis over and over in her head.

It had taken all day yesterday. They worked mostly in silence, only speaking to mark up the total number of every item.

Her boss had saved the pagers until last. Forty-nine pagers. One missing.

It doesn't mean anything, Hannah tells herself. They've been through the whole room, and barely any box had the full quota of items that it should have had.

It doesn't mean anything.

Certainly not to Francis, anyway.

Hannah is back at the gallery today. It's her day off, but she wants to have a look around, without her boss breathing down her neck.

But Francis is here too, before Hannah, which is unheard of.

Their paths cross in the reception area.

'Hannah, are you due in today?' Francis frowns.

'No, just… I left some papers here last night, flyers for the exhibition. I meant to look at them over the weekend.' She circles Francis warily.

'Fine.' Francis retreats down the hall to her office.

There are no flyers. Well, there are, but Hannah has approved the mock-ups ages ago. Instead, she sits in her own office until she can stand it no longer.

As Hannah prepares to leave, she passes Francis's closed door. She listens hard, wondering if she can hear Francis's hushed phone conversation, or if it is simply in her own head.

There is so much inside her head.

Too much. It's beginning to hurt.

No, that's not right. It's been painful inside her own mind since she can remember.

Sometimes, like now, she wonders how it would feel if someone switched it off.

Switched *her* off.

She attempts to right herself. At least one of her problems has gone. She thinks of the article she read, the body that was found in the park. Hannah walked past it, saw the police tape herself. But she's heard nothing more and she needs to know who it was.

Ray, or Grace?

A red film slides seamlessly over Hannah's vision.

Why not both of them?

It should be both.

She takes out her phone and is about to start checking the local news sites again when Francis's door swings open.

'Hannah, you're still here?' Francis asks, her voice clipped.

'Yeah, just leaving.' Hannah tucks her phone in her pocket. 'Francis, did you hear about the body found in the park, the one near the hostel?'

Francis looks her up and down before retreating into her office and opening up a filing cabinet to peer inside. 'Couple of days ago? Yes, why?'

Hannah breathes deeply before taking a punt. 'I heard it was a young girl, isn't that tragic?'

Francis frowns. 'Where did you hear that?'

'Someone said it. That place is quite near to my home, you see.'

Francis piles everything she has removed back in the drawer and slams it shut. 'What are you talking about?'

Hannah watches her boss. She's the untidiest person Hannah knows. Her filing is haphazard and messy. It's no wonder she can never find anything. It is also slightly comforting. She's still looking for all the items they couldn't locate for the inventory.

Francis moves on to the large corner cupboard and stares inside, her glasses propped atop her head.

'It wasn't a girl,' Francis says as she starts shoving items aside. 'It was a man's body they found in the park.'

Hannah's heart suddenly beats very fast. It was Ray.

It's good, but what of Grace?

'One of those worthless residents,' comes Francis's muffled voice as she moves deeper into the cupboard.

'What?' Hannah is distracted now.

'A resident of that awful hostel, that's who was found dead,' calls Francis. 'Only twenty years old, apparently.'

Hannah blinks very rapidly. The red is back, clouding her vision, filling her ears with dead noise.

It's *not* Ray.

She turns on her heel and marches down the hallway, away from Francis, and out of the door without saying goodbye.

She's walking home, a blanket of misery covering her. She reminds herself that she's heading towards Marie, but for the first time ever, the thought doesn't help.

It adds to the anxiety.

She stops on the pavement, allowing herself to be shoved and exclaimed at by the pedestrians who shunt into her back.

What has happened to her life?

She hears the sound of her phone ringing in her bag. Alina's ringtone! She claws it out, almost dropping it in her haste to answer the call.

'Alina!' Her voice is breathless, high-pitched with excitement.

'Hannah, how're you doing?'

At the friendly tone of Alina's voice, all the worries dissipate.

'I'm okay.' Hannah can hear the smile in her own voice. 'What are you doing?'

'I'm on my own. Sofia's at a sleepover. Willem's away on business.' Alina's voice turns cajoling. 'I don't suppose you're free?'

'Yes!' It's practically a shout from Hannah. 'Where are we going?'

'Come over. I'm in Willem's basement workshop. While the cat's away...' Alina giggles. 'I'm just running an errand. I'll be back soon, let yourself in.'

'Okay. See you soon.'

Hannah slips her phone back in her bag, steps to the kerb and sticks her hand in the air.

A taxi screeches to a halt. Hannah clambers in and gives the driver Alina's Richmond address.

'Fast as you can,' she says.

She smiles the whole way there. Basks in the glow that Alina still wants her in her life; she's opened her door to Hannah, trusts her to be in her glorious home alone, while Alina finishes up whatever chore she's out doing.

Hannah decides not to let Marie know she'll be late.

In fact, she thinks – hopes – that tonight, if Alina's family are away, she might not send Hannah home at all.

47

ALINA, SATURDAY

Alina scans the area carefully – circling, watching – much like Ray had done in recent times.

Ensuring that the occupant of the mews house is home alone.

She looks to her companion. 'Wait down there, give me ten minutes, then I'll meet you out here.'

She watches as the figure obediently vanishes down the lane.

She forces her hand to rap smartly on the front door.

The woman who opens the door does so cautiously.

'Marie?' Alina asks.

Marie opens the door a little wider and scrutinises Alina.

'Thank you for coming,' she says. 'I know you're Hannah's friend, but I really wanted to speak to you.'

'Friends' is not how Alina would describe their relationship, but she doesn't correct the older woman. 'Can I come in?'

'Of course. Hannah's not here,' replies Marie. 'Actually, have you seen her?'

'Not recently.' It's not really a lie. There is no need for Marie to know that at this very minute, Hannah is waiting over in Richmond, for Alina to return.

Marie hesitates. 'I'm sorry for calling you.' She looks down at the ground between them. 'I don't know why I did.'

Alina smiles gently. 'Yes, you do.'

Finally, Marie pulls open the door fully and stands back. 'Please, come in.'

Oliver is in the living room. Hannah's boy. A wisp of a thing. He sits on the edge of the sofa, sneaking glances at the adults in the hallway.

Marie reaches behind her and pulls closed the living room door.

'Would you like a drink, perhaps?' Marie's voice is uncertain.

'Yes.' Alina nods. 'Yes, I would, very much.'

They move through to the kitchen. As they pass the bottom of the stairs, Alina pauses to look at the photo on a small table.

Hannah, on her wedding day. The groom, dead now, is beaming at his bride, like he can't understand how he ended up with this woman who is on his arm.

'What happened to Hannah's husband?' Alina asks as she sits down at the kitchen table.

Marie is at the sink, filling the kettle. At Alina's question, her back stiffens.

'He passed away.'

'I know.' Alina narrows her eyes as she stares at Marie's spine. 'How?'

'He took his own life.' There is no emotion in Marie's voice, as though she used it all up a long time ago. Now, it's just stating bare facts.

Bare *lies*.

She reminds Alina a lot of Ray.

Marie clicks the kettle on. There is no more talk while it is boiling. The silence stretches on as Marie spoons coffee into two cups and gets the milk out of the fridge.

'No milk for me, thanks,' Alina says. 'Black is fine.'

Marie carries the cups over and sits down in a chair opposite Alina.

Alina takes the time to study the older woman. Outwardly, Marie looks fine: she's dressed casual but smart, and she looks good for her age.

Alina scrutinises her closer.

She *doesn't* look fine. She's got on a full face of make-up. Beneath it, the foundation is sinking into the deep lines around her eyes and mouth. Her eyes, which Alina had thought rather blank, are not at all. Every so often, there is a flash in them. The windows open briefly. There, in that split second, Alina can see fear and fatigue in equal measure.

She not only sounds like Ray, but she looks like him too, the exhausted husband who left them so long ago. He escaped, but he's still haunted, because he's still watching.

Alina thinks of her own persona. Her overconfidence, how very loud and boisterous she is. Underneath, through the tiny cracks, she's petrified.

So scared that the past she thought she remembered so clearly is going to catch up with her.

A past she manufactured. So intensely that it was real to her.

Just like Hannah.

'I really don't know why I called you,' Marie repeats her earlier statement. 'I got the impression from Hannah that you're... influential.'

'You're worried.' It's not a question, rather a statement, from Alina.

347

Marie almost gasps on an inward breath. 'Yes.'

'You want me to help you.'

Marie nods, the motion almost frantic.

Alina is reminded of a woman at the end of her rope. On her last nerve. If it were not for Oliver, Alina imagines that Marie would no longer be here.

Alina decides to help this woman who is essentially a stranger.

'Hannah knows that things are not right with herself.' Alina injects a casual, almost breezy tone into her voice. 'She's talking about going away.'

Marie's entire body jerks. She raises her eyes to meet Alina's. 'Going away? Going where? And when did she tell you this?'

'It doesn't matter, any of that. How would you feel about it, Marie, if Hannah… wasn't here any longer?'

Marie doesn't answer, but her whole body seems to relax. Even the lines around her eyes seem to diminish somewhat. It is all the answer that Alina needs.

'Oliver?' Marie is like a jack-in-the-box, springing upright at the thought of her grandson.

'Oliver stays here, with you.' Alina takes another deep breath; baby steps, she cautions herself. Saying the truth without speaking the actual words. 'You understand that it's better that Oliver stays with you, away from Hannah, don't you?'

Marie meets Alina's gaze. 'I understand.' Her tone, like the expression in her eyes, is grave, quiet, serious, as if she gets exactly what Alina is saying.

Emboldened by whatever it is that passes between them, Alina speaks again. 'She won't come back, Marie.'

There is a sob from Marie. It comes from so deep inside her that it is like part of her soul has splintered.

But there is no protest. Alina takes Marie's silence for what it is.

Her blessing.

There really is no need to spell it out to the woman. It is best to leave it this way, with Marie thinking that, perhaps, her daughter is somewhere else. A new place, where there are not many people. Where Hannah can live freely, her obsession gone, finally happy.

It's a farce. Marie will be aware of that, deep down. But they both know all too well: it is so easy to pretend.

Alina leaves her coffee untouched when she gets up to leave.

She exits the kitchen, passing the closed living-room door on her way out. She turns back to look at Marie.

The older woman has remained at the kitchen table. Her mouth is a gaping hole; her face is soaked with tears that, even now, continue streaming down her cheeks and neck, wetting her shirt, dripping to sit upon the tabletop.

The pain she emits shoots through Alina.

'I don't know how it came to this,' Marie sobs. 'I thought if I kept her close, gave her what she needed, she would be well again.'

'It wasn't you. It was never you.' Alina clears her throat. 'Five minutes more, then clean yourself up.' She jerks her head in the direction of the living room. 'He's so little, he'll be fine. Soon, he'll forget.'

Marie gasps and scrubs at her face with the back of her wrists. 'Yes,' she says, brokenly.

Alina stops at the front door. 'Someone wants to meet you,' she says.

Marie stares at her. 'Who?' she asks.

Her voice is high-pitched with fright. It will take so very long for that fear to fade. Marie has been on tenterhooks for more than twenty years.

'Her name is Grace. She's been searching for her birth family.' Alina watches Marie's reaction carefully.

The older woman's face is still a world of pain, but there's something else in there too. A light, the smallest glow, a tiny thread of hope.

Alina opens the door.

On the other side, hovering in the front garden, stands Grace.

Alina gestures at her to go inside and leaves.

Before she reaches home, Alina shifts her own persona. She leaves behind in Hannah's home what she was, turns into the woman that Hannah knows her to be.

It works. Like Marie, like Ray, Alina can put on a front with the best of them.

48

HANNAH, SATURDAY

She hears Alina as she bustles through the door, calling out for Hannah as she sweeps through the house.

'In the kitchen!' replies Hannah.

It's where she waited, not wanting to roam around the house alone. Not wanting to do anything to break the trust that her new friend has in her.

She has been able to smell Alina in here. A curious mix of fruity fragrance and sharp alcohol. It's not soothing, not like walking into the Momotaro. This aroma hints of danger, of excitement, of never knowing what's coming next.

A wholly unfamiliar concept to Hannah, but one that has hooked her, nonetheless.

'Come down to the basement!' Alina yells in reply.

Before Hannah has even crossed the large foyer, she hears the music blaring from downstairs.

A thumping bass, nothing like Hannah's taste in music, but hearing it here, now, it promises an exciting evening with her best friend.

The front door is closed and bolted, she sees, and through the side window, in the light breeze that blows, she sees the dangling wires flapping against the front door.

She had noticed it when she arrived, the messy entrails of the camaras, now nothing but a short wire, crudely hacked off.

Hannah moves to the open basement door and hurries downstairs.

Alina stands in the centre of the sparse room, in a strange get-up of orange boiler suit and a mask covering her face. The furnace is going full blast: so much heat in a room that was ice-cold the only other time she'd been down here.

'Hi, how are you?' Hannah says. 'Your CCTV has been vandalised; do you know about it? Have you seen it?'

Alina pushes the mask backwards, so it sits atop her head. She laughs. 'Of course I know. I did it. I told you, Hannah, I hate having to live like that, so I decided not to.'

Hannah puts her handbag on a workstation that is cluttered with tools and instruments.

'I thought you were concerned about security, about Sofia?'

Alina crosses to the side of the room and turns down the volume on the music. 'Life's too short to worry.'

Hannah wishes she could agree. All she's done these last few weeks is worry. About Grace, about Marie finding out that Grace is looking for her. About her father and how he's suddenly spying on her *all the time*. How long has he been doing it? What might he have witnessed her do in the last twenty years?

Thinking of it all reminds her of her short conversation with Francis. The body in the park, who was not one of the people she'd imagined it to be.

She sidles up closer to Alina.

'My father, and Grace...' Hannah swallows. 'Did you... Did you have an update for me?'

Alina turns to face her. 'I do,' she says. Her voice is grave and serious. 'I've dealt with them. Both of them. They won't bother you again.'

The relief is dizzying. Hannah reaches out a hand to steady herself against the wall. It's cold underneath her palm, in spite of the furnace that blasts out. It, along with Alina's words, soothes Hannah.

Alina slams the mask back down over her face. Through the Perspex, Hannah just about makes out her smile.

'Want to have a go?'

Hannah glances at the tabletop. 'At what?'

Carefully, Alina picks up a tiny stone with her gloved hand. 'Creating your own piece.'

There's a clear box in the middle of the table. Inside it is a stone, reddish in colour, about the size of a man's fist.

'You can make a gem out of that rock?' Hannah asks. 'What is it?'

'A mineral.' Behind her mask, Alina's eyes crinkle as she smiles. She walks over to the safe that Hannah has seen before.

'That,' says Alina, pointing to the box, 'becomes *this*.' She reaches into the safe and picks something up.

It's a standard gift box, one seen in jewellers all over. Nestled on a white cushion is a blood-red gem.

It's stunning. Hannah hears her own breath catch in her throat. It looks like it belongs at the gallery. She envisages it on display, and a hitch of excitement catches at her throat.

That's what she could take to her new, dream job. Beauty, hidden inside a plain-looking rock. Concealed, for years and years. Exposed, by talent and wanting.

She will suggest it, she decides. If Alina can get Hannah into Grantham's role at the Momotaro, they could work together.

It would be a hit, and it would be something new.

It would be something beautiful.

She turns to Alina.

'You made that?'

Alina tosses her head and affects a modest stance. 'My husband isn't the only one with the creative gifts.'

'Wow.'

Alina yawns as though she's bored now. 'Actually, it's easy. Do you want to try?'

Hannah can see it now. Her own work, on display alongside her best friend's.

She smiles so wide, it hurts her cheeks.

'Yes. I'd love to.'

49

ALINA, SATURDAY

She talks Hannah through the heating of the cinnabar stone, holding the one she swiped from Willem's travel case as an incentive.

Hannah seems entranced by it. Alina wonders what makes her want this stone so much, rather than the glittering diamonds she'd shown her one time.

Is it the gem, the blood-red colour, or the poison inside it that somehow calls to her?

She stands back as Hannah gets to work.

Any second she expects the other woman to ask why Alina is wearing all the protective gear, while she, Hannah, is exposed.

But Hannah says nothing. Instead, she works as directed, stopping every few moments to look up at Alina.

She wants praise, Alina thinks.

And with that adoring look, just for a second, Alina wavers.

Live bravely. She reminds herself of the Japanese directive.

Behind her mask, she closes her eyes and thinks of Sofia, and what almost became of her, twice.

It works.

'Good job,' she manages to say. 'You're a natural.'

If Hannah notices the break in Alina's voice, she doesn't comment upon it.

Alina waits for the change to come, for the realisation to hit Hannah. When it does, she speaks again.

'I know what you did,' Alina says to the back of Hannah's head as the other woman bends over her work.

Hannah is clearing her throat, repeatedly, as the vapour from the mercury is released around her.

Hannah drops the stone, puts her hand to her mouth and turns to Alina.

Alina stifles a gasp. Hannah's eyes weep blood. It's the single most horrifying thing Alina has ever witnessed.

Even worse than the pools of claret on the gallery floor that Friday night. More terrible, even, than Sofia being kidnapped.

Hannah opens her mouth, perhaps to protest, perhaps to ask what Alina means. No words emerge. Instead, a thin trail of red-coloured drool tracks its way down Hannah's chin.

'You used my girl to get to me, to get me to do what you wanted. *Twice*,' she emphasises.

Hannah's lips are moving, but Alina can hear nothing. Alina moves as close to her as she dares. Is Hannah saying that she's sorry?

She can't tell. She wishes she knew.

It's over so quickly.

Alina doesn't know if she's relieved, or if she'd wanted it to take longer.

It should have been slower, she concludes.

It should have been far more drawn-out and painful.

But it's done, regardless.

Alina gets to work. Normally, when she's cleaning up after being down here, she blasts out music. Today, there is silence. She doesn't want to hear a song in the days or years to come and be reminded of this time down here.

Alina checks her watch as she finishes the deep clean of the basement.

Nearly dinnertime. Sofia will be home soon. Julia has been despatched from the shipping office to collect her. Lucas has been given an impromptu weekend off. There is nobody at Alina's home today.

Alina pulls off her mask and suit, and sniffs the air experimentally.

It smells like it normally does down here. A slight aroma of burning dust, that's all. The bleach and other agents Alina has used are not overpowering.

She walks to the furnace and peers in the glass window. The temperature is as high as it can go.

There will be telltale signs inside the furnace. From here, she can see a piece of jagged, burned metal. But nobody will ever know it used to be the zipper on a handbag.

Nobody else will ever see it.

When she sifts through the ash, she will find white fragments. She knows that. She tells herself she is prepared for that.

She pats the pile of industrial bags that sit ready and waiting for the remains.

When they are cool, she will dispose of them accordingly.

The job is done.

Almost…

50

EPILOGUE

It's been a week since Hannah met her end in Alina's basement.

Alina has listened to Francis's phone calls, complaining that *Alina's friend* hasn't turned up for any of her shifts.

'How odd,' Alina comments to her friend. 'I haven't heard from her, either.'

Francis is the only person who has mentioned Hannah Barker.

It was Francis who set the cogs in motion, unknowingly verifying the suspicions that Alina hadn't even yet admitted she had, with the tale of that missing pager. God, that had been hard, being so cool and blasé to her oldest friend. But she'd had no choice. Because when Hannah didn't go into work at the Harman Gallery for her next shift, she knew Francis would contact her.

It had all clicked into place – it had started to ever since Hannah's own admission of how she ousted her baby brother from her life. It was all because Hannah needed a job doing.

The planning that had gone into Hannah's scheme was nothing short of breathtaking. Had this happened to someone else, Alina would have been full of admiration.

But there was nobody else. It had been aimed at Alina, constructed to look like saving Sofia was an act of epic bravery on Hannah's part.

The final nail in Hannah's coffin was what had happened at the hostel.

It made sense, all of it. It was not someone from Alina's past – or, rather, from her parents'. It was nothing to do with someone that Willem had upset, or their combined wealth.

Hannah needed to get her unwanted sister out of her life. That was the crux. But Grace was feisty and tough, and she wouldn't go quietly. By her own admission, Hannah couldn't do away with her, like she had with Peter, with Clark. Like she might someday need to with Oliver. Grace may well have told someone about her family. The one she had found. The one she was determined to get to know.

Somehow, at some point, Hannah had come across the name Alina Arpels, had heard the rumours about the Russian woman for whom nothing was off limits.

How to approach Alina – that must have been Hannah's question. She had come up with the idea to sabotage Lucifer, to make herself a hero in saving Sofia from certain death.

She had the knowledge of the structure. She had the tools, too.

But the plan was… flimsy. There were fifty people in the gallery that night. How on earth could Hannah ensure that Sofia was in the firing line?

The question had roamed around in Alina's mind, and finally, the answer had revealed itself, as she searched her memories, travelling all the way back to the very first time she had invited Hannah into her home, the day after the accident, to thank her. Now, she remembers Hannah's words, verbatim.

'I… *She was standing there, and she was just the cutest little thing.*' Hannah had dropped her gaze to the floor. '*Our eyes met, I waved at her… What if she thought I was calling her over for some reason? She walked straight into the path of that awful pile of metal.*' Hannah had put a hand to her lips; Alina remembers the tear that had tracked its way down her cheek.

Hannah could have been on stage at the West End, with those acting skills.

And Alina had fallen for it, hook, line and sinker, attempting to reassure Hannah that Sofia's near miss wasn't her fault. She placated the other woman, told her – boasted, really – that Sofia was overconfident, sociable, too much sometimes. *She'd placed blame on her own girl for wandering off.*

Hannah had indeed covered her own back at that very first meeting. In case Sofia mentioned it, in case the little girl told her mother that the only reason she walked in Lucifer's path was because Hannah had called her over.

Hannah's plan wasn't flimsy, at all. It was meticulous, *genius*. An admission after the crime, told in such a way that Alina never saw it as the confession it was.

Now that she has got to know Hannah, none of it rings true. Hannah is not maternal, nor a guardian angel. Alina now knows that the only person Hannah would throw herself in the path of falling blades for is Marie, her mother.

Not a child. Not even her own son, Oliver. Certainly not Sofia, a stranger's daughter.

She had orchestrated the whole incident, banking on Alina, with her reputation and riches, to offer Hannah anything she wanted in return for saving Sofia's life.

And Alina had walked right into it. Fairy godmother, at Hannah's service.

Only, she hadn't come through, had she? Alina had been distracted, had not taken Hannah seriously enough. Had stalled her for one reason or another, so much so that Hannah had had to strike again. Had to become Sofia's saviour again.

And once more, on the night that Sofia went missing, Hannah had told Alina that she'd seen Sofia, just before the start of the lesson, on the steps of the language school. Had disclosed this information to Alina's face, as they joined in the search for the missing girl.

Hiding in plain sight, just like the first time.

The story that Hannah had told, about the article she'd read, somewhere – about an arrest being made at the hostel because of county lines gangs – was seemingly untrue. Alina had scoured the papers. Had found nothing.

When had Hannah decided to pay the unsavoury, awful man to lead Sofia away and stash her in the hostel? If what Hannah had said was true – that she'd seen Sofia there as Willem dropped her off – she'd have had only a couple of hours to locate someone who would do anything for money. Hannah was good, but not that good.

No, Alina was certain that it had been a back-up plan all along, the *padre* on standby.

What if her plan had gone wrong? What if the neo-Nazi had taken both the money and Sofia, using her for his own heinous intentions?

Hannah hadn't counted on Alina having brains as well as brawn. Hadn't realised that her own boss, Francis, was one of Alina's oldest, most trusted friends. Hannah also hadn't realised that her own mother, the revered Marie, would be a key part in orchestrating the end of Hannah.

No, Hannah wasn't so clever, after all.

–

She didn't stay once she'd ushered Grace into what was now Marie's house, one week ago. She didn't wait to witness their reunion. Alina is not their chaperone, or mediator, or go-between.

She is not their friend. Not even an acquaintance. Not anymore.

Now, she is back there, for one last time. Lingering in the small entrance to the mews lane where Hannah Barker and her neurosis and paranoia used to live.

In the green area beyond Hannah's former home, a familiar figure is in sight, waiting where she has instructed him to.

He looks better, she sees, as she moves swiftly down the lane towards him. More his age, rather than the old, old man he so recently appeared to be. His injuries are beginning to heal, both inside and out.

Alina purposefully does not look at the house where Hannah used to live. She strides on, greeting him at the bottom of the lane.

He averts his eyes, still wary.

'It's time to actually knock on that door, now,' she tells him.

His eyes dart here and there, his face dragged down with sudden anxiety.

'It'll be okay,' she says. 'Marie will be pleased to see you.'

Ray swallows hard.

Alina moves around him and carries on her way.

–

Now her job is done, she realises that it isn't wise to stay here. London is a big city with a population of over nine million people. But the neighbourhoods are close, and the faces are familiar. She doesn't want to run the risk of bumping into any member of this family unprepared.

She thinks of where she can go, with her own family, and those who love her.

Anywhere, she concludes, and she's filled with a raw excitement, unfamiliar and new.

Maybe Alina and her family will make a trip to see her own parents. Maybe lessons can be learned here, on how to repair, or regenerate. On how to see things as they actually are, instead of letting nightmares fester and grow. Maybe she'll see for herself whether her memories are false or not.

She'll be far away from the Barker family, which will be a good thing. She's spent a little time with Grace over this last week, and she's come to realise that the younger girl harbours ideas of being Alina's friend…

She shudders. Grace is nice enough, dedicated to her passion for the arts. From the outside, she seems just fine.

But so did Hannah.

Which reminds her…

She pulls out her phone and dials Francis's number. The very last item on her to-do list.

'Hi, you,' she says, when her friend answers. 'Listen, I have a young woman in mind for the manager's position at your gallery. She's rather brilliant, and she knows the art world inside out.'

There's a brief pause at the other end before Francis lets out a nervous laugh. 'Hannah's not coming back, then?'

'I told her to call you – Grace Perry is her name,' Alina answers, sidestepping Francis's question. 'Anyway, I must dash. Catch up soon, okay?'

She deletes Francis's number. And that of Grace, and Hannah's and Ray's too.

It's the only way. Alina is too naturally curious to stay out of their lives.

And she knows what curiosity did.

As she walks towards a new future, she finds herself hoping that none of that uniquely bad blood has somehow found its way into another of the Barker family's DNA.

Perhaps she will watch them from afar, she concedes, like Ray did.

A nice compromise.

Just to make sure.

Acknowledgements

As always, I am so thankful for my family; my parents, Janet and Keith Hewitt, brother Darren, Cat, Joan, and much love to the newest arrival, Isla!

To Marley, my constant writing companion.

Thank you to my agent, Laetitia Rutherford, and everyone at Watson, Little. The whole team at Canelo publishing; Siân Heap and Alicia Pountney, thank you for your support and enthusiasm, and your incredible eye for detail. Kate Shepherd and Thanhmai Bui-Van who work incredibly hard to get the books out into the world.

Copy editor Daniela, who did a wonderful job picking up those things that slip through the net and require clarification or attention, and Vicki Vrint, who did a great job on the proofread.

The writing community – those wonderful storytellers of all genres. I am so thankful to call you my friends.

Big thanks to Claire Armstrong, my unofficial publicist!

The bloggers, publishers and book clubs; everything you do is appreciated.

My crime-writing support system, Marion Todd, Sarah Ward, Sheila Bugler and Rachel Lynch, our daily chats are everything!

Finally, a huge thanks to you, the reader, and as always, as long as you keep on enjoying my books, I'll keep on writing them.

Pitfalls and Possibilities in Family History Research

Pauline M. Litton

Published by
Swansong Publications
c/o 2 Florence Road,
Harrogate HG2 0LD

ISBN: 978-0-9553450-1-2

First published 2010

Acknowledgements:

*My grateful thanks to the Borthwick Institute for Archives, University of York, and to the West Yorkshire Archive Service for permission to reproduce the documents marked in the list of Illustrations with * and ** respectively. I am also especially grateful to the Borthwick Institute and its staff for the help and assistance they have given me throughout this project.*

Thank you to my kith and kin (friends and family) for allowing me to use a number of their personal documents and for offering help and advice with this book. It would be iniquitous to name any of them individually, as I would be sure to overlook some, but I feel I must mention 'the old guard' with whom I have, during the past 35 years, shared an as yet unfinished journey through family history, with all its pitfalls and possibilities, disappointments and delights.

Following the publication of the original articles I received many letters offering further examples to reinforce points I had made, and many of these have been incorporated into the text, so I extend my thanks to all these correspondents.

Pauline M. Litton
Harrogate
February 2010

Printed and bound by
Winstonmead Print, Loughborough

CONTENTS

ILLUSTRATIONS

INTRODUCTION

Always read the introduction to any book, CD or website.

This book is based on a series of articles which appeared in *Family Tree Magazine* between 1998 and 2001, which have all been expanded and updated. It is intended for those family historians who would like further inspiration on how to pursue this fascinating hobby of ours. It is not a book on how to undertake your family history research: there are many excellent texts which will provide such guidance for beginners. Some subjects, for example military matters and using newspapers, have not been covered in depth because, again, there are specialist books/websites available but see Chapter 24 (*Miscellany*) for a few pointers on various topics.

The book contains many references to internet sites but, with the exception of ScotlandsPeople, does not name any commercial websites. For details of these, *Peter Christian*'s book *The Genealogist's Internet* (published by TNA) is highly recommended.

In an endeavour to ensure that, as far as possible, each chapter can be treated as a complete unit a certain amount of repetition will be evident (see below). Instead of an index the text contains numerous sub-headings and cross-references in the hope that this will better aid the reader in following up particular areas of interest and will cater for those readers who wish to 'dip into' selected topics.

Where a topic is thought to be of sufficient interest, a chapter (in particular, Chapters 12 and 13) has been devoted to the subject to enable the interested reader to pursue it in more depth. A summary of the relevant information in a more general chapter will, of necessity, cause some duplication.

As much of my own research has taken place in the north of England it follows that many of the examples quoted come from this area. Where a place-name is not followed by the name of a county, it can be assumed that the place is in Yorkshire.

Where appropriate, the book attempts to point out any significant differences both in terminology and between records in the north and south of England, together with references to records in other regions of the British Isles. However, it must be emphasized that, even where the 'rules' differ, the principles are equally relevant to research anywhere in the country.

A few books are mentioned in the text but I have not included a bibliography as there is a plethora of books available on the subject of family history research; additionally, some websites have informative introductions which you should read. The *Gibson Guides for local and family historians*, the *My Ancestor was ... series* and *Chapman's Records Cameos* are most useful; details can be found on the websites of *Family Tree Magazine* or *The Family History Partnership*.

ABBREVIATIONS

A2A	Access to Archives (see TNA website)
ARCHON	(see TNA website)
BDM	Births, deaths, marriages
BMD	Births, marriages, deaths
BT	Bishop's Transcript
CMB	Christenings, Marriages, Burials
CRO	County Record Office
CWGC	Commonwealth War Graves Commission
DNB	Dictionary of National Biography
FAQ	Frequently asked questions
FFHS	Federation of Family History Societies
FHC	Family History Centre
FHS	Family History Society
GENUKI	Genealogy UK & Ireland
GRO	General Register Office
HMC	Historical Manuscripts Commission
HMSO	Her Majesty's Stationery Office
IGI	International Genealogical Index
IHGS	Institute of Heraldic and Genealogical Studies
IPS	Identity and Passport Service
LDS	Church of Jesus Christ of Latter-day Saints
LMA	London Metropolitan Archives
OED	Oxford English Dictionary
ONS	Office for National Statistics
OPCS	Office of Population Censuses and Surveys
PR	Parish Register
PRO	Public Record Office
RC	Roman Catholic
RD	Registration District
RO	Record Office
SOG	Society of Genealogists
TNA	The National Archives
WYAS	West Yorkshire Archive Service

CHAPTER 1

PITFALLS

IF YOU AGREE WITH ANY OF THE STATEMENTS BELOW, PLEASE READ THIS BOOK.

♦ *That can't be my ancestor; we've always spelt the surname with two t's, not one (or with an i and not a y, or beginning with H and not A or E, or W and not R, or with e on the end ...).*

♦ *I am a direct descendant of Captain Cook/Lord Nelson/ Shakespeare.*

♦ *She was born in 1801 because she says she's 40 in the 1841 census.*

♦ *She must be registered, she was born in 1839.*

♦ *He was born on 20th September. His birth will be registered in the September quarter.*

♦ *Grandfather was born in September so his parents can't have married during that year, I'll look the year before and earlier.*

♦ *Of course they were married ... .*

♦ *He was 80 when he died so he was born in... .*

♦ *He was always known as Tom so he must be registered as Thomas.*

♦ *I knew her as Auntie Gladys; she must be my mother's or father's sister.*

♦ *She was called little Cis so she must have been Cicely or Cecilia.*

♦ *She's described as his mother-in-law in the 1851 census so she must be his wife's mother.*

♦ *They're baptised on the same day so they must be twins.*

♦ *His 1841 birth certificate gives a time of birth, he must have a twin.*

♦ *He's baptised as Jacobus in 1710 but there's no burial for him, only a James in 1763 who isn't baptised in that parish.*

♦ *All these parishes are in Oxfordshire, the (modern) road atlas says so.*

♦ *My family has always lived in West Hartlepool, why can't I find the 1851 census returns?*

♦ *Great-grandad came from Newcastle so he must have been a Geordie.*

♦ *Harrogate was in the West Riding so all the records will be in a West Yorkshire record office.*

♦ *He was a blacksmith so he can't have been working down the pit.*

♦ *His wife was called Ann in three successive censuses so she must have been the mother of all his children.*

♦ *They both said they were 21 on their marriage certificate so they were both born in... .*

♦ *The 1861 census says he was born in Mellor but I can't find his baptism. No, I haven't checked the 1851 or 1871 census returns to confirm this.*

♦ *The name is Blomiley in the 1700s. Blummelie, Brimiley and Bromley are nothing to do with my family.*

♦ *The minister wrote my ancestor's name as Amery in the marriage register and he must be correct. What if he did sign as Emery?*

1

- *Of course she could read and write; she signed the marriage register in 1786.*
- *There's no entry in the index to this printed Parish Register for Joe Bloggs.*
- *There's no entry in the Bishop's Transcript for my ancestor. Why should I check the Parish Register as well, they're identical copies?*
- *Of course she married in this county; my ancestors didn't move about.*
- *He wasn't born in that county as there's no entry for his baptism in the IGI.*
- *They married in the Parish Church in 1775 so they were Anglicans.*
- *They were Anglicans so they must be buried in the churchyard.*
- *I've checked every William Smith in the microfiche version of the IGI and he isn't there.*
- *My great grandfather left his son only one shilling in his Will. They must have fallen out.*
- *My ancestor was a farmer. He must have left a Will.*
- *My ancestor was an agricultural labourer. He won't have left a Will.*
- *My ancestors lived on the Isle of Man (or the Channel Islands); of course they are part of the United Kingdom.*

WHAT IS A PITFALL?

Look it up in a dictionary and you will find it defined as *a concealed pit as trap for man or animal, an unsuspected difficulty or danger* or *an error into which it is easy to fall*. If you prefer, call it a problem. Somewhere there may be a family historian who claims never to have encountered a pitfall in their research but most of us, if we are honest, will admit to being bruised all over by the number of falls we have taken whilst our family trees have been growing. I hope this book will make you aware of many of the pitfalls to be found in sources ranging from the internet to printed books and geographical features (via oral information, census returns, civil registration, parish registers, Wills and more), how to avoid them and how to turn at least some of them to your advantage.

Many years ago, when lecturing on *Pitfalls and Possibilities*, I was accused of putting the entire audience off because I came up with so many possible problems that everyone was convinced they were barking up the wrong trees and I made the mistake of not stressing that it is almost always possible to climb out of a pitfall and move on. Once you realise that there could be one ahead, in any situation, you learn to tread warily, be prepared, and more often than not you do not fall into the trap. By being more positive, a knowledge of which dangers you might encounter can help you to overcome or by-pass what you thought was a dead-end.

Ask any gathering of family historians to relate one pitfall into which each has fallen and you will gain some idea of the number and diversity of possible problems. The most experienced will often admit to making the most elementary errors because, in the 1970s, when family history as we know it was in its infancy, the majority of researchers worked in isolation and there was no one to tell us of the mistakes we might be making.

FAMILY HISTORY COMES FULL CIRCLE

The rise of family history societies, holding regular meetings and producing journals; the popularity of family history conferences; the growth of courses on how to trace your family history; and the co-operation and exchange of knowledge and ideas consequent on these developments changed the face of family history beyond recognition. The increasing involvement of the Church of Jesus Christ of Latter-day Saints (LDS) in the transcription of records, particularly parish registers and bishops' transcripts; their production of the Computer File Index (later the International Genealogical Index), made freely available to family historians via microfiche and now on the internet; and the development of their remarkable library in Salt Lake City together with their establishment of Family History Centres (see p.51) throughout the world enabled researchers to expand their horizons and made it much easier for those living outside the British Isles to participate fully in the search for their ancestors. 'Reciprocal research' became the name of the game, with family historians everywhere prepared to help each other by looking up items in record offices and libraries within their home areas and explaining the good things or the problems encountered in the research. Pitfalls were as plentiful as ever but the common ones became more widely publicised and there was usually someone prepared to help you climb out of whatever hole you had dug yourself into. Thirty years on, things appear to have come full circle. Computers and the internet have almost hi-jacked family history and, while the amount of information available online is incredible (and increasing daily), the number of pitfalls is increasing exponentially, largely because people click a button, enter an internet site and expect instant gratification.

The most dangerous pitfall, spelled out in almost every chapter in this book, is the belief that it is not necessary to read the introduction or instructions which come with any book, microfiche, index or internet site.

Pitfalls come in all shapes and sizes, and in all sources. It is rather like playing *Snakes and Ladders* - one mistake uncovered may mean you slither down a small snake to the line below (with one generation 'lost'), another may send you careering down a huge serpent from near the end of the game back almost to the beginning (and mean climbing all the way back up a different tree). Never despair; there may be a ladder in the next square which helps you to climb rapidly upwards again.

RESOLUTION: **I will always adopt a positive attitude when reading about pitfalls.** It is usually possible to climb out of pitfalls and move on; being aware of possible dangers can help you to avoid traps.

CHAPTER 2

GEOGRAPHY, BOUNDARIES, TRANSPORT AND TIME

THE UNITED KINGDOM

A very common pitfall for family historians is to assume facts about the past from present circumstances. Look at a current 'British' passport and on the cover is stamped 'United Kingdom of Great Britain and Northern Ireland'. For most people this is all they need to know; for family historians it is a different matter. They need to **be aware that the United Kingdom and the British Isles are not the same.** The British Isles (geographically) includes Great Britain (England, Wales and Scotland); the whole of Ireland; the Isle of Man; the Channel Islands, consisting of the Bailiwick of Jersey and the Bailiwick of Guernsey (which includes the smaller islands), and any other off-shore islands. The Isle of Man and the Channel Islands are British Crown Dependencies and are considered as part of the UK for purposes of defence and census taking; otherwise, they have their own parliaments, laws, civil registration systems (see p.91), systems of land holding (similar to the manorial system) and while their parish registers are similar to those of England and Wales they are not identical (see p.93). **When checking any set of records, particularly online, make sure that they refer to the British Isles and not just to the U.K.**

GEOGRAPHY

Never take anything for granted:
I was born in one Yorkshire pit village, brought up in another, and began researching my family history in the firm belief that all my ancestors were Yorkshire born and bred and had always been connected with coal-mining. In fact, my four paternal great-grandparents were born in Derbyshire, Warwickshire, Suffolk and Yorkshire - the other three families had all migrated to Yorkshire in the late 1800s as coal-mining expanded in the north-east of England while ironstone mining declined in the midlands and agricultural depression hit East Anglia.

How did they travel north in the 1870s and 1880s? Probably by rail, which at that time was the easiest and cheapest form of transport. Fifty years earlier they would have travelled by canal or struggled for days on foot or by cart. Today, their journeys would be accomplished by car, on trunk roads or motorways (or even by air), in a couple of hours and with the aid of a road atlas. At least three pitfalls in one sentence: it is surprising how easy it is to forget that two hundred years ago, people did not have their own transport, 'public' transport was non-existent in most areas, a lot of roads were muddy tracks, travelling was usually a slow process (even the stagecoach - one of the faster forms of transport - took four or five days from *York* to *London*), and maps were produced in plenty but not for the 'average person' who had no need for them and probably could not read them anyway.

MAPS, ROAD ATLASES AND GAZETTEERS

One of the most dangerous mistakes a family historian can make is to use a modern map, road atlas, internet site or satellite navigation system and assume that it reflects a landscape which would have been familiar to their ancestors. County boundaries have changed; railways and canals have come and gone; motorways have been carved out; and place-names have appeared, disappeared or changed. This may seem a very obvious statement to make but people do still fall into this trap. A road atlas is precisely what it says - it shows various categories of roads but it does not generally distinguish many of the natural features which controlled your forebears' lives. For this you need to study an Ordnance Survey (OS) map - preferably the one inch to the mile series; I recommend the reprints of the first edition (1840s - black and white; magnifying glass essential) and the seventh edition (1960s - before motorways distorted the situation).

Always try to use a map which dates from before 1974 and shows the historic counties of the British Isles, not the modern administrative ones. Similarly, if looking up place-names in a gazetteer, make sure it was published before 1974. Some years ago, whilst checking forms for the British Isles Genealogical Register (BIG R), which listed surnames being researched in each county, it became clear that a lot of contributors, particularly from overseas, were relying on modern maps. One gentleman had entered 16 place-names as being in Oxfordshire, whereas before 1974 they were all in Berkshire (we wondered which family history society he had joined); Peterborough occurred many times as being in Cambridgeshire but before 1965 it was in Northamptonshire (where most of the records remain) and between 1965 and 1974 in Huntingdonshire (which was 'abolished' in 1974 and merged into Cambridgeshire). Examples of such county 'adjustments' are numerous - always check which pre-1974 county you should be dealing with and which Record Office holds the records you need to study.

Recommended gazetteers:

Bartholomew's Survey Gazetteer of the British Isles (9th edition, reprinted in the 1950s is a good one to aim for) which lists place-names for the whole of the British Isles, with their pre-1974 counties and often additional information.

Lewis's Topographical Dictionaries for England, Wales, Ireland and Scotland, several of which are available on CD, are an invaluable source of information.

England was first published in four volumes (plus an atlas of county maps) in 1831 and went through another six editions by the end of the 1840s. Information on places includes county; hundred/wapentake; parish, archdeaconry and diocese;

population and much more. The first edition is perhaps the most useful for family historians as it pre-dates the major re-organisation of dioceses which began in 1836. Later editions include the poor law union (established 1834) in which a place was situated.

Wales was first published in two volumes in 1833, with later editions in 1844, 1845 and 1849. County maps were included in the volumes.

Ireland was first published in two volumes, with a separate atlas of county maps, in 1837, with a second edition in 1842.

Scotland was published in two volumes, with a separate atlas of county maps, in 1846.

'LOST VILLAGES'

According to archaeologists, up to 3000 villages and towns in England and Wales have disappeared since the middle ages. Most had vanished before the mid-16th century (when PRs begin) but some are much more recent departures. Landlords in the 18th century forced tenants out of their homes and razed villages to clear the land for sheep grazing; villages and towns, particularly along the east coast, have been 'lost to the sea' (*Dunwich*, in Suffolk, being an oft-quoted example); a few were 'commandeered' for military purposes; others, especially in the 20th century, were drowned when reservoirs were built. In Scotland, many settlements were lost during the 'highland clearances'; in Ireland many were abandoned in the mid-19th century. If you fail to locate a place in a modern gazetteer, try the ones suggested above. You may well find it listed and, from the information given, be able to pinpoint its location and so work out what has happened to it.

HOW MANY PLACE-NAMES ARE UNIQUE?

While reading the BIG R forms it also became clear that many people knew the name of a place with which their ancestors had been connected but not the county it was in. Some had obviously made what they hoped was an intelligent guess; others had left the county blank. Making an assumption about the county in which a place-name is situated is not just a pitfall, it can be the edge of a minefield. Some place-names are unique - I know of only one *London Apprentice* (in Cornwall, and now well-known because of its proximity to the *Eden Project*) and one *Ryme Intrinsica* (in Dorset) - but Bartholomew's *Gazetteer* lists almost 100 places with *Norton* as part of their name and well over 100 with *Sutton*.

With common names like these it is not just a case of identifying the correct county or even the correct country. Yorkshire has at least 11 *Sutton*s. Of these, four are parishes and nine have a qualifying name, ranging from *Sutton Bank* to *Sutton under Whitestone Cliffe*. The latter is one of the four parishes but in many records it is entered simply as *Sutton* - the inhabitants knew which *Sutton* they meant so why write out the full name? The parish of *Sutton upon Derwent* is some 15 miles south of this and villagers from both parishes would use the same market towns and might marry there or in nearby parishes - again, *Sutton* would be enough identification for many incumbents and most census enumerators. If you try one *Sutton* and the entry you want is not there, do not be discouraged - look in a gazetteer and check out the rest.

A variation on this theme comes when there are two well-known villages, towns or cities bearing the same name. There are at least 25 places called *Newcastle* in the British Isles, mostly in Ireland, but say the name to a majority of people and they will automatically think of *Newcastle upon Tyne* in Northumberland (since 1974 in Tyne & Wear) - unless, of course, they live in the midlands where *Newcastle* means *Newcastle-under-Lyme* in Staffordshire. A census enumerator faced with the one word might well add a county which he thought was the correct one. If you cannot find an entry in one *Newcastle,* try the other one - and if both fail, try the villages with that name (or see the next paragraph). The same applies to *Richmond* (Surrey or Yorkshire - and in the latter county, the town near *Darlington* or the village near *Sheffield*); *Kingston* (*upon Thames* in Surrey or *upon Hull* in Yorkshire); *Thorpe Underwood* (Northamptonshire or Yorkshire); *Water End* (Bedfordshire, Essex or Hertfordshire); and to countless other places. Be especially careful in the London area – *Brixton, Euston, Islington, Kensington, Kilburn, Marylebone, Paddington, Piccadilly* and *Soho* are all names associated with the capital and 99% of people who told the census enumerator they were born there would mean in the *London* one but there are (or were) villages or locations with these names in other English counties – *Brixton* in Devon and Wiltshire, *Euston* in Suffolk; *Islington* in Yorkshire and Norfolk; *Kensington* in Liverpool; *Kilburn* in Yorkshire and Derbyshire; *Marylebone* near *Wigan* [Greater Manchester]; *Paddington* in Cheshire; *Piccadilly* in Manchester, Warwickshire and Yorkshire; and *Soho* in Birmingham. **Look at any gazetteer and see just how many place-names are at least duplicated.**

PLACE- NAMES AT HOME AND OVERSEAS

Remember that the early colonists gave many of their settlements familiar place-names. There is the *City of London*, Ontario in Canada (and, from experience, people writing from there to someone in England often give their address as 'London', only the envelope/stamp revealing that the letter is from *London*, Canada, not London, England); *Halifax* in Nova Scotia, Australia & the USA; and *Newcastle* and *Richmond* in Australia, South Africa and the USA. In the West Indies, Jamaica (captured by the British in 1655) is divided into three counties - Cornwall, Middlesex and Surrey - and the capital of Surrey is *Kingston.* Soldiers, settlers including planters and indentured servants, convicts, buccaneers and slaves, all produced descendants and the earliest Anglican Parish Registers on the island date from the 1660s. Again, most people telling an incumbent or census enumerator that they were born in *Kingston* would mean one of the many in England but occasional ones would not (and *Kingston-on-Thames* and *Kingston*, Jamaica are both in counties called Surrey). Someone listed as being born in *Manchester*, Middlesex could be an error on the enumerator's part or could have been born in Jamaica in the parish of *Manchester* in the county of Middlesex.

Even more confusingly, there are localities in England called, for example, *Gibraltar, Londonderry, Moscow, New England, New York*, and *Washington* and several towns have *New Zealand* areas within them. If you have military ancestors it is at least possible that they may have had children born on the 'Rock' of *Gibraltar* or in *Washington* DC, as opposed to in *Durham*, but the one born in *New Zealand* could have been born in *Buckinghamshire, Cheshire, Derbyshire* or *Wiltshire* and not thousands of miles away. There are also at least six places called *Scotland* (all in different counties) and two called *Wales* in *England* – it only needs an illegible county name on the census form or an enumerator who merely entered *Scotland* into his book to send you on a long and time-consuming wild goose chase.

There are no places called *Sydney* in the British Isles but you may remember the item on television where a couple who thought they had booked, via the internet, tickets to *Sydney*, Australia were surprised to land at *Sydney*, Nova Scotia. Canadian airport officials said that they often receive luggage destined for Australia but not usually people. When doing an internet search we were once very excited to find some cheap airfares from *Manchester* to *San Francisco*; fortunately, before we booked, we discovered that the fares were from *Manchester Boston* Regional Airport in New Hampshire, USA (their website is flymanchester.com). **When googling a place-name on the internet do not accept the first one you find - make sure you have the correct country and county.**

HAS THE NAME CHANGED?

What do you do when you can find no mention at all of the place you are looking for? Remember that the name may have changed. 'My family has always lived in *West Hartlepool* [Co. Durham], why can't I find them in the 1851 census returns?' The simple answer is that in 1851 *West Hartlepool* did not exist. There was the historic town of *Hartlepool* and, five miles away, the township of *Stranton* - within 20 years, as the area became the centre of an industrial boom, this township was swallowed up by the newly-named *West Hartlepool* but in 1851 the census returns are under *Stranton*. We do not always realise just how much the rise of a local industry - in this case, shipbuilding - can affect an area. Ten miles from *West Hartlepool* is *Middlesbrough* - in 1829 it was in the parish of *Acklam* and its population was 40. In 1830 the Stockton and Darlington railway was extended to *Middlesbrough*; by 1841 the population was 7,631; by 1881, 55,288. Your ancestor may have been born in *Middlesbrough* in 1820 but is far more likely to have moved into the area to find work.

The rise of a particular industry in a locality can also affect the name. The introduction of the saffron industry to East Anglia led, in the 16th century, to the village of *Chipping Walden* in Essex changing its name to *Saffron Walden* (that piece of information was originally gleaned from **The Antiques Road Show** - you never know where you will find useful snippets of information; the possibilities are endless). The development of glass-making and the presence of limestone and sand necessary for the process in the *Castleford* area in the West Riding of Yorkshire in the 18th century led to the neighbouring manor of *Houghton* changing its name by 1793 (the first reference quoted in the **English Place-Name Society** volume for the area – these volumes are another source of endless possibilities) to *Glass Houghton*. There will be other places whose names have been amended due to local industries.

Farther afield, in *Chicago* in the USA the population in 1833 was 350. In the late 1840s, the arrival of the *Chicago Union Railroad* and the *Illinois and Michigan Canal* saw *Chicago* become a major transportation hub and by 1880 the population had risen to 500,000.

In Cheshire, the same thing happened to *Crewe*, which was originally a hamlet in the parish of *Barthomley*. *Crewe* became one of the country's major railway junctions. Close by was the parish of *Coppenhall*, consisting of two villages, *Church Coppenhall* and *Monks Coppenhall*. Look at most modern maps and the only *Coppenhall* reference you will find is for *Coppenhall Moss*, in the northern part of the *Crewe* conurbation. The *Coppenhalls*, like *Stranton*, were absorbed into a 'new town'. The railway, according to some sources, was responsible for another name change which has confused many family historians. Travel on the M6 motorway in Cheshire today and you will see a sign to *Sandbach* and *Holmes Chapel*. Look for Parish Registers or early census returns for *Holmes Chapel* and you will not find any references - keep looking and you will find records for *Church Hulme*. *Church Hulme* was also called *Hulmes (Holmes) Chapel*; today the village is *Holmes Chapel* but the ecclesiastical district remains as *Church Hulme*. *Church Hulme* and *Cheadle Hulme* were both stations on the railway line from *Crewe* to *Manchester* (opened in 1842) and the similarity of the names was apparently causing confusion so it was decided that *Church Hulme* should use its alternative name of *Holmes Chapel*.

COUNTY AND PARISH BOUNDARIES

Did it matter to our ancestors where county or parish boundaries were? They needed to know in which parish or township they lived - and where its boundaries were - because that unit controlled their lives (payment of tithes; payment of poor rates or poor relief; settlement laws) but county boundaries mattered little. We need to know both boundaries because a place's precise

9

location often determines in which record repository documents relating to it have been deposited and therefore where you are likely to find the records relating to your ancestors.

Boundaries often followed natural features, like rivers or valleys, or man-made ones like roads, and it was these which most concerned people. There used to be a common belief that our ancestors did not move about, that they were born, married and died in one small area. This may have been true for some communities - I knew people in Wensleydale in the 1960s who had never been out of the Dale - but there was far more movement than early researchers realised and much of it was controlled by geographical features.

Assuming that you have found records for a family in one parish but not all the events you hoped to find are in the parish register, what do you need to consider when deciding where to look next (apart from Nonconformity)? Did your ancestors live in a village, a hamlet or an isolated farm house? Was the village on a coaching route or what passed for a 'main' road? Did this road lead to a market town? Most people would visit these at some point and the nearest market town is always a good place to check if you cannot find a marriage. Market towns tended to develop where roads met, bridges crossed rivers, or valleys intersected and such places were commonly close to county boundaries which followed these features. **Never consider a place in isolation; always look at its geographical position**.

In the 21st century one can travel from *Leeds* in Yorkshire to *Manchester* in Lancashire in an hour along the M62 motorway which crosses the Pennines, the range of hills often described as 'the backbone of England'. On one of the higher and more remote stretches, close to the Yorkshire/ Lancashire county boundary, you pass an 18th century farmhouse standing defiantly between the motorway's two carriageways which, as you whizz past it, appears to be surrounded by moors. The farmhouse is in Yorkshire in the township of *Rishworth* which was in the parish of *Halifax*. Its nearest chapel was *Deanhead* in the parish of *Huddersfield*, while the parish of *Rochdale*, in Lancashire, came to within three miles of the farm. Records relating to these parishes are spread between at least five record offices.

County maps such as those published by the *Institute of Heraldic and Genealogical Studies*, by many record offices, and others available on the internet, generally showing early 19th century parish boundaries within the counties, are very useful but can drop you into a plethora of pitfalls if you are not careful. It is all too easy to look at a county map (which often has thick lines round the edges of the county to show ecclesiastical jurisdictions), to think of it as a distinct unit and to search registers or other sources for that county alone. I admit to having searched at least 50 parishes in Derbyshire for earlier generations of a family before I realised that the village where they lived was less than a quarter of a mile from the Nottinghamshire boundary - and there they were, in the first parish across the county 'line' but on a different map and with registers in another record office.

It is also tempting to look at parishes as shown on these maps and to see them as clearly delineated areas. In fact, many parishes have incredibly convoluted boundaries and some consist of several villages some distance apart, with other parishes coming between them, but it is not possible to show this within the constraints of the maps. A similar pitfall occurs with county boundaries - a parish map of Worcestershire shows that 'detached' parts of the county exist, situated several miles inside the counties of Gloucestershire, Herefordshire, Staffordshire or Warwickshire; *Dudley*, for instance, is surrounded by Staffordshire. *Birmingham* is in Warwickshire but many of its present-day suburbs were in Staffordshire.

The Phillimore Atlas and Index of Parish Registers, which includes all the IHGS county maps, prints alongside each one an 1834 map of the county, showing geographical features and the main roads running into (and out of) the county. As with introductions (the importance of reading which cannot be overstressed) many people ignore these maps whereas studying them would show just how 'flexible' many parish boundaries were and how many market towns are close to county boundaries. In some cases, only a bridge separates one town or county from another; in others the county boundary runs down the main street; in a few instances the boundary runs through the middle of a house (see p.227).

Rivers and hills played their part in influencing which church a family attended. At first glance, there may appear to be a parish church or chapel very close to where your forebears were living but you may find them patronising a church which is some distance away. Is there a river between their home and the nearest church and, if so, is there a bridge close by? Or did they have to walk a mile to a crossing point, another mile to church, then reverse the process, whereas another church is farther away but easier to reach on foot? Is there a steep hill between home and church, with a longer but more level walk to a neighbouring one?

If your ancestors lived in a large and widely spread parish then the position of the parish church could determine both where they worshipped and where you might find elusive entries. The parish of *Prestbury* in Cheshire included one market town (*Macclesfield*), 10 chapelries and 23 townships and stretched for 15 miles from north to south. The parish church was in the north of the area and parishioners living in the south, on the edge of the Peak District, were far closer to parish churches and market towns in Derbyshire and Staffordshire, as well as to several other Cheshire parishes, than they were to their own church and market town. Whatever the law said about using the church of the parish in which one lived and had a settlement, there were always those who found it more convenient to use the nearest church and plenty of clergymen who were happy to bend the rules (which technically prohibited them from poaching another church's parishioners) provided it was made worth their while.

TRANSPORT: TRAVEL ON LAND AND BY WATER

People have always moved, whether voluntarily or under duress, but how they travelled around the country depends very much on when and where they lived. In an age when travel within Great Britain tends to revolve around motorways and airports, it is easy to overlook the fact that, in the 17th, 18th and part of the 19th centuries at least as many people travelled by water as by road. ***The Book of Common Prayer*** (1662 edition) contains the supplication *That it may please thee to preserve all that travel by land or by water ... we beseech thee ... Good Lord*. This reminds us that travelling was often a dangerous business (many people made their Wills before embarking on a journey), and makes the point that travel by water ranked equally with that by land.

I keep stressing the dangers of relying on a modern road atlas when trying to work out how our ancestors might have moved around the country and I make no apology for returning to the pitfalls inherent in assuming that a modern map reflects a countryside which would have been familiar to our forebears. Do not assume that they relied principally on a network of roads, as we tend to do. **Between the 16th and 19th centuries they were at least as likely to travel by sea, river, canal or railroad as by road**, and even then many of the 'roads' they used would not appear on any map. Failure to understand the changing pattern of the communications network, and the importance of travel by water, can lead to an elusive ancestor being 'sunk without trace'.

Ideally, you should look at a road map (until the 19th century, often published in book form rather than as a map in its modern sense – see p.14) and read diaries or accounts relevant to the century in which your ancestor lived to gain an idea of how people were moving around. *John Ogilby*'s ***Britannia***, published in 1675, describes *the Principal Roads of England and Wales ... distinguisht ... into Direct Roads and Cross Roads, calling such Direct as proceed Directly from ... London, to the less Central Cities, Capital Towns or other Eminent Places of the Kingdom; and calling such Cross [roads] as lead from some of the said Lesser Centers to another like Capital Town or Place of Eminency.* Of his 85 itineraries, at least 50 either begin or end at what was then a seaport. Many rivers, which later silted up, were still navigable and towns which we today regard as being inland ones - like *Arundel, Chester, Exeter* and *York* - were ports.

SCOTTISH ROADS

Ogilby can be excused his omission of Scotland (also known as North Britain) because, when he was writing, there were few roads there worthy of the name. Before the 19th century, English cartographers at least tended to show only those to *Edinburgh, Glasgow* and *Portpatrick* (the closest crossing point for

Ireland). *Daniel Defoe*, describing the North of Scotland in his *A Tour Through The Whole Island of Great Britain* (1724-1726), concentrates on the coast, seaports and rivers. The 1742 edition of *The Present State of Great Britain and Ireland* does not mention roads in Scotland but says *there is scarce any Part of it above 40 miles Distant from some Bay, Creek or Arm of the Ocean* and makes it clear that, with the exception of the movement of cattle, both goods and passengers usually travelled by water.

The famous tag

Had you seen these roads before they were made,
You would lift up your hands and bless General Wade

refers to the military road building programme embarked upon in the 1720s by this English general, which led to the gradual development of a road system in the Highlands. *Wade*'s roadbuilding extended as far north as *Inverness* (but no further) and linked the town, via the Great Glen, to *Fort Augustus* (built 1729 at the southern end of *Loch Ness*) and on to *Fort William*. His brief when he was sent to Scotland in 1724 included instructions to build a galley with oars and sails *for the swift movement of troops* and supplies on *Loch Ness* – travel by water would remain the favoured means of transport in Scotland for a long time yet.

ENGLISH AND WELSH ROADS

Until well into the 18th century (and the introduction of turnpike trusts and toll roads), the majority of roads in England and Wales were little better than rutted tracks, dustbowls in summer and quagmires in winter, and many people found it easier to travel by water. A Yorkshireman wanting to travel north to *Newcastle* or Scotland, or south to *Norwich, London* or *Dover*, or a Welshman heading for *London, Bristol* or *Liverpool*, was as likely to do so by boat as by coach, cart, or on horseback or foot. On many rivers, which could not cope with large ships, both goods and passengers were moved considerable distances by shallow draught boats (in Cheshire, 'flats' transported salt from the 'wiches', *Middlewich, Nantwich* and *Northwich,* to the Mersey; in Norfolk, keels and wherries moved coal, timber and grain from the coast at *Yarmouth* to *Norwich*). In *London*, the Thames was regarded as a major highway. Dip into *Samuel Pepys' Diary* and note how often he travelled by river: in three days in March 1669 he went 'by water' to *the Temple, White Hall*, his home (in *Seething Lane*), *Greenwich*, and to see *Mr Wren*. Market towns are often suggested as likely places to find a 'missing' marriage; ports and coastal or riverside villages may prove equally fruitful.

Daniel Paterson's *The Road Book: a New and Accurate Description of all the Direct and Principal Cross Roads in Great Britain*, first published in 1771, ran to 17 editions in his lifetime (with *Edward Mogg* taking over the 18th edition in 1826). *Paterson* concentrated on 'mapping' roads but his accompanying text, and the increasing number of references to bridges over canals in each succeeding edition, gives some idea of the dramatic changes which occurred in Great Britain and Ireland during the Canal Era, from around 1760 to 1840 (see below).

PART OF PAGE 254 IN *MOGG'S* 18ᵀᴴ EDITION OF *PATERSON'S ROADS* (1826)
Note the two Turnpikes (toll gates); the bridges over the river Derwent and the Cromford Canal; and the named country seats of the local gentry.

MEASURED from HICKS'S HALL.	From Chesterf.	LONDON TO CHESTER-FIELD.	From London
		From	
ALLESTREE. Allestree Hall, *Wm. Evans*, Esq.	150¼	Hicks's Hall *to*	
	24¼	* *DERBY, Derb., p.* 218	126
		Through Derby,	
		To Nottingham 16 *m.*	
DUFFIELD. *J. Balguy*, Esq.		*to Ashbourn* 13¼ *m.*	
HEAGE TURNPIKE. Wingfield Manor, Col. *Halton.*	22	Allestree, *Church*	128¼
	19¾	Duffield, *Church*	130½
		½ *m. farther,*	
		to Wirksworth 9 *m.*	
PEACOCK INN, opposite, Alfreton Hall, Rev. *H. C. More-wood.*		Cross the 🚣 river Derwent	
	17¼	Bargate	133
		1 *m. farther,*	
ALFRETON contains a rude, ancient church, having an embattled tower with pinnacles: its inhabitants are chiefly employed in the manufacture of stockings, brown earthenware, and in the neighbouring collieries. The weekly market is held on Friday. It is said that at a place called Greenhill Lane, some distance from the town, an urn, containing about 700 Roman coins, was found by a labouring man while repairing a fence.		*to Ashbourn* 12¼ *m.*	
		To Nottingham 17 *m.*	
	14	Heage 🚩 Turnpike	136¼
		Cross the 🚣 Cromford canal	
	10¼	* Peacock Inn	140
		to Wingfield 1 *m.*	
		To Alfreton 2 *m.*	
		London to * *ALFRETON*	
		142 *m.*	
HIGHAM. Ford House, Mrs. *Holland*; and Oyston Hall, *William Turbutt*, Esq.	8¼	Higham	142
	7	Stretton, *entrance of*	143¼
		To Mansfield 9½ *m.*	
TUPSTON, beyond, Wingerworth Hall, the property of Sir *Henry Hunloke*, Bart. at present a minor; and Stubbing House, *Charles Gladwin*, Esq.		*to Matlock* 6½ *m.*	
	5½	Clay Cross 🚩 Turnpike	144¾
	4½	Tupston, *end of*	145¾
		to Bakewell 13 *m.*	
CHESTERFIELD, before, at Walton, Walton Lodge, *Joshua Jebb*, Esq.		*To Mansfield* 12 *m.*	
		* *CHESTERFIELD,*	
		Church	150¼

14

CANALS

Thousands of miles of canals were built, starting with local ones constructed to enable particular products to be moved around more easily and forming eventually a national network. New towns were created - *Stourport* in Worcestershire grew up where a major canal and two rivers met; others expanded - *Stoke on Trent*, not meriting a mention in *Paterson* in 1778, by 1826, with a population of 30,000, ranked with *Uttoxeter* and *Burslem*, largely thanks to *Josiah Wedgwood* and the construction of the *Trent and Mersey*

Canal. Factories, wharves and warehouses were built close to the canals and people gravitated to these areas. Many families, owning or working on barges to transport goods, lived on them and travelled extensively along the canals. In some places, the network of inland waterways was used by the populace as an alternative to the highways.

Tracing ancestors who lived, worked, or travelled on the canals is like tracking coachmen, ostlers and grooms who, particularly during the great coaching era (1780s-1840) moved up and down the principal coach roads, often being employed at inns. You may find that they returned regularly to one church to record family details but often they baptised children at various points along the canals or the roads. A canal worker could be born in Staffordshire, married in Cheshire, and baptise children in Worcestershire, Lancashire and Yorkshire; an ostler working on the Great North Road (later the A1) could be born in Yorkshire, married in Hertfordshire, and baptise children in Leicestershire, Lincolnshire, Nottinghamshire or London.

ROADS

Contrast an old map with a modern road atlas, and note how many villages which were originally on the old coaching route are several miles away from the modern motorway and can easily be overlooked if you are trying to follow a mobile family's progress. *Retford*, in Nottinghamshire, was by-passed in 1961 and is now some three miles from the A1. *Ferrybridge*, a hamlet in the parish of *Ferry Fryston* in Yorkshire, was described in *Langdale*'s 1822 ***Topographical Dictionary of Yorkshire*** as a *post town* because the Great North Road ran through it and there were at least three Inns (The Angel, The Greyhound and The Swan) where post horses and coach horses could be obtained. The A1 in this area has changed its route several times and, travelling on the road today, you will see the power station but not the village. *Tadcaster*, described by *Lewis* as *a great thoroughfare* and by *Langdale* as being *on the high-road to London* is today almost five miles from the A1.

Inns abound on the major roads but the majority of innkeepers and publicans will be found on minor roads and tracks, catering for villagers, pedlars, carriers, drovers and travellers who travelled mostly by horse or on foot. Away from the principal roads, people used tracks between villages; drove roads (for moving sheep and cattle from Scotland, northern England and Wales to London and other major centres of population); packhorse routes (with packhorse bridges which were too narrow to be used by vehicular traffic) which criss-crossed the country and included, amongst many others, stannary ways bringing tin from Cornwall and saltways leading from the Cheshire and Worcestershire brine pits. These roads, often known today as 'green roads' or bridleways, are what *Shirley Toulson*, in her 1983 Shire Album, called **Lost Trade Routes**. If an ancestor suddenly appears in a village, often marrying a local girl, it is a good idea to study an old map and see if a 'green road' passes through the area.

RAILWAYS

The coming of the railways in the 1820s marked the beginning of the end of the supremacy of canals and coach roads. In 1822 at least 40 mail or stage coaches and 32 commercial wagons a day passed through *Leeds* and 18 companies moved goods and passengers by water. By 1853, the number of coaches and water conveyance companies had halved; the only wagons listed were those belonging to the railway companies; and at least 30 passenger trains a day left from the town's four railway stations.

Thousands worked for the railway companies and following their careers and their families can present you with the same problems as tracking the whereabouts of coachmen and canal workers. Tracing one family, of which three successive generations were railwaymen, shows how much movement there could be. Within 50 years members of the family had moved from west Lincolnshire to *Whitechapel* in London; from London to Yorkshire; back to Lincolnshire (on the east coast) and then to Leicestershire. The first generation railwayman married a girl from a neighbouring village in Lincolnshire at *Whitechapel* in London; the second generation, born in *Whitechapel*, married an east Lincolnshire girl in *Bolton* (near *Bradford*, Yorkshire) in 1897; the third generation moved from Lincolnshire to *Birstall* in Leicestershire.

Both *Bolton* and *Birstall* are mentioned elsewhere in this book but the former is the well-known one in Lancashire and the latter the one in Yorkshire - do not assume that a place-name is unique because few of them are (see p.6).

If you have ancestors who worked on the railways it could pay you to track down a copy of *Alan Jowett*'s **Railway Atlas of Great Britain and Ireland** (Guild Publishing, London: 1989) which includes maps of all the railway lines built and all the stations on them (with an index to the stations).

TIME

Living in the 21st century, when many holidays involve crossing a number of time zones, everything is timed to the minute and one hundredth of a second can be vitally important, it is difficult to realise and understand that, before the mid-19th century, time as we know it was largely irrelevant to our ancestors. The day's work began soon after dawn and ended at dusk, often with a meal-break when the sun (if visible) was overhead. The church bell would ring to tell people it was time to go to church, in the 19th century the factory hooter or whistle would tell workers when their shift was about to begin (and paid 'knockers-up' would have tapped on bedroom windows to ensure that factory workers did not arrive late and risk having their pay docked); their lives were controlled more by the human body clock than by mechanical means.

Until the arrival first of stage coaches and later of the railway network few people were aware that 'noon' or 'mid-day' did not occur at the same time in all parts of the country (never mind the world). *Greenwich Mean Time* had been established in 1675, as an aid to help mariners determine longtitude at sea, but *local mean time* was used elsewhere so that when it was noon in *London* it was 11.40 am at *Lands End*, 11.50am in *Bristol* and 11.54am in *Leeds*; noon in *Aberystwyth* would be 12.22pm in *Norwich*. Look at the website for Christ Church Cathedral in *Oxford* and read that *The advertised time for Cathedral services is five minutes later than 'normal time' (GMT or BST depending upon the season) because the Cathedral still keeps the old Oxford time which is five minutes west of Greenwich. Thus, 6.00pm Oxford time is 6.05pm GMT/BST.*

Exact time mattered little until the need for national timetables arose. Guards on stage coaches carried timepieces set to gain around 15 minutes in 24 hours when travelling east to west (and to lose 15 minutes when going west to east) but 'timetables' were more flexible – of the 40 coaches leaving Leeds daily in 1822 all but one was advertised to leave 'on the hour' but many would leave a few minutes late.

Railway timetables needed to be more accurate and railway companies began to adopt '*London* time' for their trains, especially after 1852 when the development of the telegraph made it possible to transmit time signals from *Greenwich* to any station in the country. Some stations introduced clocks with two minute hands, one showing local time and the other GMT. It was not until August 1880 that the **Statutes (Definition of Time) Act** received the Royal Assent and a standard time was established for Great Britain. *Ireland* continued to use *Dublin Mean Time*, which was 25 minutes (and 21 seconds) behind GMT until 1916; *the Isle of Man* adopted GMT in 1883, *Jersey* in 1898 and *Guernsey* in 1913.

CHAPTER 3

NAMES

What's in a Name? must rank as the most used title for family history articles (and I do admit to having used it myself back in the 1970s). The answer, for family historians, is 'not a lot'. This may seem a strange statement to make about a hobby which is based almost entirely on names of one sort or another but it is true. Placenames, surnames, Christian names (and there's a pitfall for a start because nowadays, to be politically correct, they should be called forenames) have always been fluid, their spelling often dependent on chance.

One of the original pitfalls started *That can't be my ancestor; we've always spelt the surname with two t's, not one.* This stems from a friend in the early 1970s who was 'stuck' for a long time as she could not accept that *Josiah Whitaker* could be her ancestor because as she said ... (and the Christian name was a relatively uncommon one). Nowadays we know that *Whitaker/Whittaker/ Witiker/Whiteacre* and other variants can all be the same surname. **Remember that phonetic spelling is nothing new.**

ACCENTS, PRONUNCIATION, SPELLING AND HANDWRITING

Pronunciation has always played a major part in how names are spelt. The gradual development of so-called 'Queen's English' tends to make us forget that regional accents in the past were far stronger and far more common than they are today. Most people will admit to some difficulty understanding 'broad Scots' or 'broad Yorkshire' (both phrases are quoted in the OED). Bear in mind that two hundred years ago (when there was much movement of population between the pairs of counties mentioned) a Yorkshire tyke would have had as much difficulty interpreting a Norfolk dumpling's speech as a Cockney would have had with a Scouser (London and Liverpool for the uninitiated). If the 'in-comer' was the local vicar or the census enumerator, who was expected to write down names and places which he could barely make sense of and which his informants could not spell, the problem was compounded.

Be aware of possible problems when dealing with any surname beginning with a vowel or with 'H' or 'Y'. The surname *Eunax* (*Unax, Eunuch* and three other variants) clearly caused problems for the incumbents of a West Yorkshire parish when the family arrived in the mid-17th century (and disappeared again fifty years later). Did incumbents of other parishes through which the family passed have similar difficulties and might they have spelt the name as *Ewnacks, Younax* or even *Iunacks*?

Lessons learnt from compiling a (Cheshire) marriage index include *Allatt/Hallett; Amery/Emery/Hemery; Ankers/Hankers; Eardley/Y[e]ardley; Earlam/Irlam; Edge/Hedge; Ikin/Hickin; Olding/Holding; Umpleby/ Humpleby;*

Utley/Hutley; Whatmough/Watmore/Whotmoff and many, many more.   One particularly tricky problem comes when a surname beginning with a vowel or certain consonants meets a Christian name ending with an 's' sound - notably *Alice, James* and *Thomas*.   Thus, in parish registers, *James Pierpoint* married as *James Spearpoint*, *Thomas Anderson* as *Thomas Sanderson* and *Alice Peak* as *Alice Speak*.   It is also worth thinking about the newsreaders' favourite, *Laura Norder*.

Certain consonants can lead you towards another range of pitfalls. *G* and *J* can be interchangeable - *Garrard, Gerrard* and *Jerrard*. The pronunciation of *D* and *J* can be almost indistinguishable, as in *Dewsbury* and *Jewsbury* or *Jewison* and *Dewison*. *W* and *K*, like *H*, tended to be added or subtracted at the whim of the writer: *Ray* and *Wray*; *Roe, Rowe* and *Wroe*; *Right* and *Wright* (see p.273); *Neeshaw* and *Kneeshaw* (see p.256); *Nibbs* and *Knibbs*; *Nott* and *Knott*; *Nutsford* and *Knutsford*.

Most of the examples given above relate to the initial letters rather than to the middle sections or the ends of the names. Do you say *bath* or *barth*, *grass* or *grarss*, *pass* or *parss*? You would never spell the words with an *r* in them but what would you have done in the 18th century if you had been a northern vicar, told that a bridegroom from outside the area was called *Charles Pa(r)ss*? Several of them did include an *r* and one re-invented the name as *Charles Sparse*. My Yorkshire birthplace of *Castleford* is delivered as *Carstleford* by the BBC but said locally as *Casselfud*.

Do you say the surname *Cilgram* as *Silgram* or *Kilgram* (or even *Gilgram* or *Gilgrass)*, and *Ceel* as *Seel* or *Keele*? As most of the sources to come are either indexes, or are at least partially indexed in some form, it is a point which you need to bear in mind. Speak a few names out loud, listen to what you say, think how you would spell it phonetically (which many registrars, enumerators and parish clerks were obliged to do), and you may be in for quite a shock.

A few years ago, a Yorkshire friend's grand-daughter was learning to read, using the Letterland Storybooks, based on child friendly phonics. Hearing her mother say *Airy atman's owse* (instead of *Hairy Hatman's House* - it does exist, honestly; look on the internet) brought home forcibly both the problems faced by 'incomers' to a strange county and the difficulties facing teachers trying to teach by this method in a county where *h* is commonly dropped.

Say *chair* with a Birmingham accent and it comes out as *chur*, say *church* and it sounds like *cherch*; *lorry* in parts of Lancashire is pronounced *lurry*; *hutch* will often sound like *hatch* if said with a 'southern' accent and *Monday* like *Munday* with a northern one. One of my earliest family history memories is of an encounter with a man searching unsuccessfully in the GRO indexes for his Irish ancestors called *Moynes*. It was years later, reading the words of an Irish song, that I realised that *fine* rhymes with *Boyne* and the name was, in fact, *Mines*. Spelling permutations for the middle sections of names are limitless and, if you can't find the person you are looking for, you usually

19

have to sit, muttering the name over and over in different accents and hoping for inspiration, or look at the IGI for other possible spellings. It was interesting to realise, when updating the late *George Pelling*'s **Beginning your Family History** in 1998, that to him (with Sussex ancestry) his mother's maiden name of *Passifull* was a standard spelling, with *Percival* as a variant, whereas to me, from the north of England, *Percival* is the norm and *Passifull* the variant. Readers will not be surprised to learn that, in many indexes, *Percival* and *Passifull* are indexed separately and, in addition, *Passifull* comes under *Pasifull* but *Parsifull* under *Percival* - the letter *r* is again the determining factor and, as you can see from previous references, it is a letter which can creep into a name quite unexpectedly.

There is another technique you can try, recommended many years ago by a local historian from a village high up in the Pennines. Hold your nose, say the name, and write down what you hear. The common cold has been around for a very long time, as have problems with sinuses and adenoids, decongestants are a relatively modern discovery, and many of our ancestors would have talked as if they had a permanent heavy cold. Try it - it produces interesting possibilities.

Think how many people would have had some form of speech impediment (I was teased when young because my middle name of *Mercer* always came out as *Mertha* and I still have great difficulty pronouncing names such as *Thistlethwaite*). Common problems are pronouncing *r* as *w* (with, for instance, *Railton* becoming *Wailton*) and *ll* as *w* (so *Bellamy* might become *Bewamy*). Also consider how many people lost most (or all) of their teeth in centuries before dentures became common. Speaking with no teeth in can make a tremendous difference to what the listener hears.

Do you always pronounce the ends of your words clearly or are you guilty of running them together (like *Charles Pass*) or of clipping them so that *Culling* comes out as *Cullen*, *Holding* as *Holden* (or *Olding*), *Parkinson* as *Parkins* or *Hollingshead* as *Hollinshed*? *Baskerville* and *Somerville* are, in some areas, written as *Baskerfield* and *Somerfield* and the same no doubt applies to other names with one of these endings. It might sound unlikely but it is always worth checking for names ending in, or including, double *ff*. I have come across *Daintith* spelt as *Dentiff*; *Hough* and *Brough* will often appear as *Huff* and *Bruff, Coughin* as *Coffin*, and *Bough* as *Boff*. The confusion which can be caused by *ough* does not end there - for *Loughton* try *Lawton*, for *Broughton* try *Brereton*, and for *Houghton* (or *Haughton*) try *Horton*. I am sure many of you will have similar examples of names not being what they seem.

The way a name can be pronounced in one way and, for no apparent reason (although there is usually an etymological explanation if you dig deeply enough), spelt in another was brought home to me when someone in Canada researching the name *Hudson* in the East Riding of Yorkshire said 'but of course in the parish register it's spelt *Hodgson*'. Soon after that I received a request from someone else to locate a marriage in Cheshire of *James Hudson* and *Martha Walker*. I failed to find it under *Hudson* but I found it under *Hodgson*. Other unexpected surname pairings of spellings and pronunciation include *Featherstonehaugh* and *Fanshaw* (and in some cases *Fewston*); *Mountford* and *Mumford*; *Cholmondeley* and *Chumley*; *Menzies* and *Mingis*. The Radio 4 presenter James *Naughtie* pronounces his surname as *Nockty*.

Having listened to yourself repeating a surname in a variety of ways, write the name down and look at your handwriting. Bad penmanship - whether by a 17th century cleric, a 19th century enumerator or in your own scribbled notes - causes as many pitfalls for family historians (and postmen) as do erratic spelling and apparently inconsistent pronunciation. The envelope below reached us eventually in Harrogate, Yorkshire - via Kent.

The subject will occur again in connection with all the major sources but it can be a salutary experience to note the weaknesses in your own handwriting. I know that in mine the letters *m, n, r* and *u* are badly formed when I write quickly and whilst I know what I have written, other people may not. I am obviously not alone in writing these four letters badly. For twenty years I have believed that the vicar of *Feltham* in Middlesex was Dr *Kilgom* (see p.97) because two people who gave me information on him spelt it thus; double-checking for this book I discover that he was, in fact, Dr *Kilgour* and that he also appears on the internet as Dr *Kilgorn*.

I do not condemn the vicar whose handwriting on our own copy marriage certificate sent to the GRO in 1968 led to our appearing as *Littar* in the index (see p.74) - *on* and *ar* are very easily confused and handwriting tends to tail off just as spoken names do. Whilst lecturing over the years, I have shown the certificate to hundreds of family historians and not one has yet managed to translate the vicar's own signature.

21

REVERSED LETTERS SYNDROME

Keep in mind what is sometimes referred to as 'reversed letters syndrome' (a form of word blindness) where two letters in a name are reversed. This is extremely easy to do, either when writing or typing (how many times in a newspaper do you see *form* and *from* used in a context where it is clear the wrong word has been typed) and it can affect searching for a name in an index. I have a tendency, when typing, to mistype *Joseph* as *Jospeh* and many early clergymen wrote *Jhon* for *John*. Look in the IGI and you will currently find 1136 instances of the surname *Jhonson* (the vast majority dating from the 16th and early 17th centuries). The 1881 census index has 33 *Jhonson* entries, most of which are obvious mistranscriptions (either by the original enumerator or by the 20th century transcriber), confirmed by the appearance of *Jhon* as a forename on the same page. A baptism entry in a 16th century parish register for *John Smacome son of William Samcome baptised* demonstrates just how easy it is for such errors to be made (and the correct surname was *Smallcombe*).

PLACE-NAMES AND SURNAMES

Place-names seem to be even more prone to serious spelling/pronunciation pitfalls than do surnames - perhaps because many of them are shortened forms of long names - and, in some cases, asking advice from someone born in the county where the name originates may be the best way of translating it. How else would you work out that *Hazeboro'* in Norfolk is spelt *Happisburgh* and *Horsfield* in Staffordshire is spelt *Alstonfield*; or that *Appletreewick* in Yorkshire can be pronounced *Aptrick* and *Belvoir* Castle, seat of the Duke of Rutland, is pronounced *Beaver*? *Mildenhall* in Wiltshire (not to be confused with the better-known village in Suffolk) is pronounced *Minal* (its online community website is called Minal); *Launceston* in Cornwall is often *Lanson* (and this version appeared on the side of several stage coaches) and *Cleobury Mortimer* in Shropshire is apparently *Clibbrey* to the locals.

Klaus Forster's *A Pronouncing Dictionary of English Place-Names* (published 1981 by *Routledge & Kegan Paul*; currently out of print) will tell you how a place might be pronounced if you know the correct spelling but I do not know of any book which operates the system in reverse.

Remember that place-names can be changed – *Bugsworth* in Derbyshire became *Buxworth* in 1935 and, in Yorkshire, the villages of *Middle, Nether* and *Over Shitlington* (between *Dewsbury* and *Wakefield*) became *Middlestown, Netherton and Overton* in the early 20th century. None of the villages were parishes (*Bugsworth* was part of *Glossop* parish and the others came under *Thornhill* parish) but other records, such as Hearth Tax Returns and Land Tax Assessments, will usually be filed under their original names.

Never assume that your surname derives from a placename and, if it does, make sure you link it to the correct place. There are villages called *Litton* (deriving from the Anglo-Saxon for graveyard) in Derbyshire, Dorset, Somerset and Yorkshire, and families totally unrelated to each other can be found in all four counties and elsewhere. My husband's line stems from Derbyshire but a surprising number of people assume that, because we live in Yorkshire, he originates from the Yorkshire family and also that, as it is a relatively uncommon surname, all the families must somehow be connected.

Litton as a place name and surname goes back a long way. *Fleetwood* is an old-established surname but the town of *Fleetwood* in Lancashire was built and named in the late 1830s by *Sir Peter Hesketh Fleetwood*. *Saltaire* in Yorkshire (now a World Heritage Site) was a model village built in 1853 by *Sir Titus Salt* on the banks of the river *Aire* for workers in his mills. *Telford* in Shropshire, named after *Sir Thomas* of canal and bridge fame, only acquired that name when designated a New Town in 1963.

Placenames can influence surnames: *Etchells* occurs as a surname in north-east Cheshire because of the villages of *Stockport Etchells* and *Northen(den) Etchells*. When members of the *Etches* family from Derbyshire and the *Ethell* family from Yorkshire moved into *Stockport* both were recorded in the Parish Registers as *Etchells* because that was a surname (and spelling) which was familiar to the parish clerk. Similarly, the nearby Derbyshire village of *Mellor* presumably accounts for the *Miller* families in the same area who periodically appear as *Mellor*.

SURNAMES: LOCAL OR NATIONAL?

Try not to fall into the trap of assuming that a surname is common - or uncommon - because you live in an area where this is the case. Always check to ascertain if the surname you are interested in is common everywhere, is concentrated in a few areas, or is rare. *Bann* is a surname from south-east Cheshire. Until the 19th century and the coming of the railway it was relatively common within twenty miles of *Prestbury* (the Cheshire one; not the Gloucestershire one where *Cheltenham* racecourse is situated) but very uncommon elsewhere. Almost any *Bann* will prove to originate from this small area; however, there is one big pitfall - they can be confused with *Bain, Bane, Band* and *Banner* which are all more common and easily misread as Bann if the handwriting is not well-formed and clear or if the accent is strong or the pronunciation unclear.

Similarly, until the mid-19th century, *Arnfield* was almost exclusively a Derbyshire surname, concentrated in the north-west corner of the county. Between July 1837 and December 1850, of the 178 instances of the name listed in the GRO indexes, 115 were in the registration district of *Hayfield*, 11 in *Manchester* and 9 in *Stockport* (the nearest large market towns). Only five were registered outside Derbyshire, Lancashire and north-east Cheshire. Little wonder that some *Arnfield* researchers, living in the *Hayfield* area, were convinced that the name was common everywhere and failed to realize how rare it was elsewhere. *Armfield*, on the other hand, easily confused with *Arnfield*, does occur nationwide (although it is at its strongest in *Arnfield* territory).

VARIANTS

Another of the 'original pitfalls' encapsulates the problem of surname variants. *Blomiley, Blummelie, Brimilow and Bromley* (plus many other versions) are all spellings used in the 1700s in Parish Registers in north-east Cheshire for members of one family, most commonly spelt *Blomiley*. In the IGI almost all the variants appear under either *Blomiley* or *Bromley*; in the GRO Indexes very many pages separate them. Nine of the variant spellings can still be found in the *Manchester South* telephone directory. How many bearers of these names today - unless, of course, they are dedicated family historians - would recognise the possibility that they might all be distantly related?

NAME CHANGES

Entertainers often take new names at some stage in their careers - *Marion Morrison* became *John Wayne*; *Harry Webb, Cliff Richard*; *Peggy Hookham, Margot Fonteyn*; *John Eric Bartholomew* and *Ernest Wiseman, Morecambe and Wise* - and most people will forget (or never know) what their original names were. Authors often use pen-names or pseudonymns: the *Bronte* sisters used the names *Acton, Currer* and *Ellis Bell; Mary Ann Evans* wrote as *George Eliot; Douglas Reeman* writes about 20th century naval action under his own name but uses the pseudonymn *Alexander Kent* when dealing with the same subject during the Napoleonic period; writers of horror novels, *Stephen King* and *Dean Koontz,* have both published novels under pseudonyms.

Some of our ancestors did exactly the same, but, lacking the publicity given to entertainers and authors today, it can be extremely difficult to spot the changes and very easy to fall into the trap of trying to trace the forebears of what is, in effect, a non-existent person.

DOUBLE-BARRELLED SURNAMES

The increasing tendency towards the modern use of double-barrelled surnames by couples who wish to retain both their surnames tends to mask the fact that such names were adopted by our ancestors for a variety of reasons and they can cause all sorts of pitfalls for family historians.

Some people inherited property conditional on taking a new surname, usually to keep alive a surname about to become extinct in the male line as evidenced by an entry in the **London Gazette** (see p.269): *Whitehall, March 7, 1837. The King has been pleased to give and grant unto Henry Worsley, of Newton-Villa, near Swansea, in the county of Glamorgan, Gent., eldest son of Nathaniel Worsley, of the same place, Gent., by Margaret his wife, deceased, which Margaret was the only surviving daughter of Thomas Benison, sometime of Greenwich, in the county of Kent, and afterwards of Kentish Town, in the county of Middlesex, Gent., and sister of John Benison, Esq., also deceased, His Royal licence and authority that he, the said Henry Worsley, and his issue may (in compliance with a direction in the last will and testament of his late maternal grandfather, the said Thomas Benison) henceforth assume, take and use the surname of Benison, in addition to and after his present surname of Worsley.*

Many people in this position hyphenated their original and their new surnames, often with the original surname first; some later 'dropped' their old name but others retained the 'double-barrelled' name. *The Dukes of Marlborough* and their family have borne the surname *Spencer-Churchill* since 1807 (and still do) but *Winston Churchill* rarely used the double-barrelled name and is universally known by a single surname. Some double-barrelled names were not hyphenated; *David Lloyd George* (his mother was a *Lloyd*) is always known as *Lloyd George* but look in the GRO indexes for his marriage and you will find it registered as *George: David Lloyd*.

Illegitimate children were sometimes given their father's surname as a middle or final name, the mother hoping that he would marry her and enable her surname to be dropped to make the child appear legitimate (see p.119). Step-children often bore two surnames (see Copyhold Tenure p.29).

Donald John Rallison-Sadler was born and married with that name. In the GRO indexes his marriage is entered twice, as *Rallison-Sadler, Donald J*; and as *Sadler, Donald J.R.* By the time his children were registered, the *Rallison* had been dropped, and when he died his death was registered as *Jack Sadler* (see p.30).

When checking any index of names, it is advisable to check both elements of a double-barrelled name.

People bearing common surnames sometimes changed their surname or added an additional surname to distinguish themselves. *An Index to Changes of Name 1760-1901* by Phillimore and Fry (1905) includes almost 200 entries involving the name *Smith* and well over 100 for *Jones*.

NATURALISATION

Watch for immigrants who either Anglicised their surname with, for example, *Schmidt* becoming *Smith* and *Schneider* becoming *Taylor*.

Some people adopted a new name because no-one could pronounce their original one. Others changed their surname on or after naturalisation. The actress *Helen Mirren*, according to her autobiography, was born as *Ilyena*

Vasilievna Mironov but is registered in the GRO indexes as *Helen L. (Lydia) Mironoff.* Websites referring to her give varying details - some accurate, some not. Her Russian father, *Basil (Vasiliy) Mironoff* was naturalised in 1949 and in 1951 changed his name by deed poll to *Basil Mirren* (**London Gazette** see p.269).

A recent obituary for *Roy King* stated that he was born as *Marian Piekarski* in 1944 but started school as *Roy King.* The **London Gazette** reveals that his father (also called *Marian*) was naturalised in 1949 and changed his name to *Michael King* by deed poll in 1961.

BLACKAMOORS AND EGYPTIANS

From the time of the Roman Empire, *negroes, blackamoors* (a term also used to describe Asians) and *Ethiopians* (used to describe any black person) found their way to Britain in larger numbers than is usually realised. An entry in *Calne,* Wiltshire parish register in 1586 records the burial of *Maria Mandula advena et aethiops* (stranger/foreigner and Ethiopian) and a letter written by Elizabeth I in 1596 to the mayors of leading cities stated *of late divers blackmoores brought into this realm, of which kind of people there are already here to manie* [too many] ... *should be sente forth of the land.*

In the 18th and 19th centuries in particular, the number of both Africans and Asians in the country increased markedly. They were generally to be found as servants (there are many portraits of society ladies with the almost obligatory little black boy by their side), sometimes as coffee-house keepers or as boxers (*Bill Richmond* and *Tom Molineaux* 'the Black' being the best known). A few, like *Olaudah Equiano* (who wrote a famous autobiography), became well-known. When they marry most, but not all, parish registers will specify their foreign origins. Phrases such as *two Asian blacks* or *both negroes* occur and when *Olaudah Equiano* (renamed and baptised as *Gustavus Vassa*) married *Susanah Cullen* in Cambridgeshire in 1792 he was described as *an African.* Many, especially when they were baptised as Christians, bore surnames chosen by their employers, like the baptism at *Sheffield* in 1773 of *Anthony Williams a Sambo age about 23,* or were named after their employer's residence/estate as at *Kilnwick* where in 1746 *Beswick: a black aged about 30 years servant to the late William Draper of Beswick Esq. was baptised and his name called John.* Others were referred to as *the blackamoor/blackmore* or *the more/moor;* in some cases the definite article was dropped and the description became a surname.

Some bore the name of the estate overseas on which they had worked (usually as slaves) and you can hit a brick wall here. Also do not make the mistake of trying to link them into the (legitimate) family of the plantation owner. Others were given the name of the island from which they came to Britain, like *Tom Granada a negro,* baptised at *Birstall* in Yorkshire in 1769, or of the parish where they were baptised. It is worth checking whether documentation survives for estates, particularly in the West Indies, owned by well-known families which may include genealogical details of some of their slaves.

Egyptians, otherwise known as *gipsies* or *romanies*, were also in England in the middle ages. An Act was passed in 1530 ordering their expulsion from the country, followed by further legislation in 1554 imposing the death penalty if they did not either settle down or leave (similar laws were passed in Scotland). As with the *blackamoors*, however, the *gipsies* remained and their numbers increased. At *Leeds* in June 1572 *Elizabeth child of Anthony Smawleye, the egypsion* was baptised; at *Masham* in 1664 *Matthewe son of John Grainge, a trouper neare Barwick as they report, his wife goeinge amongst a people caulled Jipsyes was baptised;* and in 1668 *Samuel Pepys* recorded in his diary that his wife and friends *went to see the gypsies at Lambeth and have their fortunes told.* In 1797 in Cambridgeshire, *Selah daughter of Edward and Rose Hern* was baptised, with her parents described as *Egyptians* but as the 19th century advanced this description became less common. Particularly in census returns, gipsies are often referred to as travellers, tinmen, peg-makers and pedlars.

If you suspect that you may have gipsy ancestry the surnames favoured by leading gipsy families include *Boswell, Cooper, Grey, Herne, Lee, Lovel* and *Smith*. It could be worth your while to contact **The Romany and Traveller Family History Society**.

FOUNDLINGS

The Foundling Hospital and its children are dealt with in more detail in Chapter 21 but foundlings do appear in parish registers. The surnames they receive can often provide a clue as to their origins as abandoned children but be wary as many of the names also occur as ordinary surnames. A few were given surnames such as *Found* or *Foundling*, including one christened as *John Foundhere* with the incumbent's comment *because he was.* In 1726 *Frances Chance (a child found by chance)* was baptised. Many were named after the feature where they were found as in 1838 when *Joseph Step of the workhouse, a child found on Mr Blugden's step* was baptised. There is no birth registration for this *Joseph* (see p.85) but his death is registered in the following year. Other surnames bestowed on such children include *Church, Porch, Pew, Door, Lane, Street, Field* and *Garden*. One poor child was baptised and buried in 1753 as *Christian Unnamed, a foundling of unknown parents.* Many of these children died soon after they were found but some survived and, if you cannot locate parents for your ancestor, this is one possibility which you could consider.

ALIAS

The appearance of **alias** (which translates as: *otherwise known as*; in modern terminology *aka*) in a record indicates the use of two names and the possible reasons for this are many and various.. *Vel* which translates as *take your choice* or *if you like* is also sometimes used in the same context. The most important thing to remember is that people could, in general, call themselves by whatever surname they chose. If you cannot find any trace of the person you are seeking, and there is no reference to an *alias*, do bear in mind that there could have been a complete name change - deserters from the army and navy, runaway apprentices, criminals on the run, wives or husbands leaving their partners, might all change their names.

Alias is often used to signify that a name may be spelt in a variety of ways - for example (see p.24) *Blomiley alias Blummelie alias Brimilow* - and, where the incumbent or parish clerk is obliging enough to provide this information, you are fortunate. It may also be used when a surname metamorphoses into a more commonly-used form. I wondered why the surname *Strongitharm* (strong in the arm), which occurs fairly frequently in Cheshire until the mid-18th century, suddenly virtually disappeared. It was only when I came across a single entry for *Armstrong alias Strongitharm* that I realised where it had gone. In the 1881 census *Strongitharm* survives in Lancashire but there is only an occasional entry in Cheshire. It is, however, more likely that you will find yourself, as I have, trying desperately to work out which, of at least six possibilities, is the 'correct' surname for your ancestor. My 4 x great grand-father surfaced in Yorkshire in 1792 when he married (and made his mark) as *George Marsh*. At the baptism of his first child he was recorded as *Marsah alias Chapel*, by the fourth as *Chappel alias Marsah*, by the eighth as *Mercer*. Thirty five years after *George*'s first appearance, his grandchildren were being baptised as *Marsay alias Chapel*, *Mercer alias Marsay* and *Marsa*. The name crystallised as *Mercer* (my middle name) but, 40 years after finding *George*'s marriage, I am no nearer to knowing his real name or from whence he came.

A statement by Churchwardens at *Middlewich* in Cheshire in 1826 makes clear another situation in which *alias* was often used: *John Williamson being described as 'Williamson alias Lamb' does not proceed from him having assumed a false name, but from his father when a child having been brought up with a family of that name and on that account being generally called by it among his neighbours and associates* (see p.67).

Catholic Priests, returning from Europe, where they had attended seminaries, to preach secretly and illegally in England (particularly in the 16th and 17th centuries) often used an alias to guard against being recognised as a member of a recusant family.

The situation regarding copyhold tenure (land held by virtue of an entry written into a Manorial Court Roll) was responsible for many *aliases*. On the death of a tenant the land reverted to the Lord of the Manor, who would normally transfer it to the copyholder's heir; if the heir was a minor and his mother re-married, the child might well use his step-father's name but also retain his father's name as an alias to maintain his claim to the copyhold land.

PLACE-NAMES

Many place-names also come with an alias. The practice is relatively widespread in Wales, where names can be either in Welsh or anglicised (*Ynys Mon alias Anglesey*, for example). Yorkshire has a number of examples including the parishes of *Long Marston alias Hutton Wandesley, Whitkirk alias Whitechurch* and *Woodkirk or Woodchurch alias West Ardsley* (with *West Ardsley* having its own alias as *West Ardsley alias Westerton*). The Lincolnshire parish of *Lutton alias Sutton St Nicholas* is not another example of a *Lutton/Sutton* mix-up (see p.82) the two names have different derivations. The church is *Sutton St Nicholas* but most records will be found filed under *Lutton*. In 1836 *Bullock Smithy* in Cheshire changed its name to *Hazel Grove*; look in the TNA catalogue and you will find references to *Bullock Smithy alias Hazel Grove* because all pre-1837 records are under the original name. As with *Holmes Chapel* (see p.9), **bear in mind that records will commonly be found under the less familiar original name**.

SCOTLAND

In Scotland, where some clan names were, at various times, proscribed (forbidden) aliases are often found when the ban was lifted and the original name could again be used. An example often quoted is the *Clan McGregor* which was proscribed for much of the 17th and 18th centuries and whose members in the meantime adopted a number of other surnames including *Drummond, Graham, Grant, Murray* and *Stewart*. *Rob Roy* (*McGregor*) at times used his mother's surname of *Campbell*. In the aftermath of the 1745 Jacobite rebellion (after which highland dress and bagpipes were proscribed), many clansmen also thought it prudent to adopt a different surname for a time, and could later use either name, with the other as an alias.

CHRISTIAN NAMES

Surnames could be altered by a stroke of the pen; Christian names could be changed almost at will. *He was always known as Tom so he must be registered as Thomas* is a very dangerous assumption to make. In the first place, despite what many people believe, it was, and is, perfectly possible to register or christen a child as *Tom, Dick* or *Harry* rather than *Thomas, Richard,* and *Henry* or *Harold* - and *Dick* and *Richard*, if the surname is a common one, will be separated by a good many pages in the GRO indexes so if you look under *Richard* there is not going to be a *Dick* on the same page to catch your eye. In one Yorkshire parish in the 1760s children were christened as *Franky, Lenny, Sam(m)y* and *Tom(m)y*, at least a century before such abbreviations came into common usage.

Whatever someone was commonly called, are you sure that this was their first name? How many people do you know who have two or more forenames and use one of the later ones? Two girls I was at school with had *Evelyn* as a first name but were always known as *Carol* and *Doreen*. A recent item on television showed a bewildered old lady ignoring hospital staff who were saying her name, and accusing her of being deaf for not answering, because they were calling out a forename which she had not used for 70 years but which was on her paperwork. Then again, how many of us have several forenames but answer to something completely different? For forty years I knew a neighbour as *Jack*; it was only when I saw his marriage certificate (to confirm his wife's Christian name - see p.83) that I discovered he was actually *Donald John*. The cricket umpire *Harold Dennis Bird* is known all over the world as *Dickie;* the cricketer *Andrew Flintoff* is widely known as *Freddie*; the jockey *Rupert Walsh* as *Ruby*; the golfer *Eldrick Tont Woods* as *Tiger*. A school friend named *Michael* went through his secondary schooldays as *Charlie* (or Charles) because during his first week there one of the masters said '*You're a right Charlie*' and the name stuck. Over a ten day period in the obituaries of a national newspaper the following were to be found*: Lawrence Arthur Stafford (Tom); Herbert (Jack); Leslie George (Bill); Sidney Keith (Jerry); Gladys (Joye); Josephine Cecilia Agnes (Joan); Muriel (Frances); John Charles (Mike).* Recent entries have included *Kenneth Charles (Jack/Ken/Bill)* and *James Frederick Thomas George* (always known as *Sam*).

If you think that this paints a pessimistic picture, do not despair. Many people who rejected their given names retained part of them in the names they chose to use so a little thought and imagination may solve your problem. I have a distant cousin *Eric* whose birth I tried, and failed, to find in the GRO indexes. Years later, talking to another cousin, I discovered that he was registered as Fred**eric**k but disliked the name so called himself *Eric* (but retained the initial *F.* above his shop door). On similar lines, the late archivist and family historian *F.G.Emmison* signed himself *Derick* - the spelling gives a clue here. It is possible to play an almost never-ending word game on these lines: *Fred* may come from *Frederick* or from *Alfred*; *Al* could be *Alfred* or *Albert*; *Bert* could be *Albert* or *Bertram* or *Cuthbert* or *Robert* and so on.

Of girls' names, *Elizabeth* possibly has more permutations than any other, including *Elizabeth, Eliza, Beth, Betty, Betsy, Bessie, Libby, Lily, Lisa, Lizzie,* and *Tibby* all of which can also be given as names in their own right. It took me a long time to discover that my great-aunt *Lily* was registered as *Mary Elizabeth*, because no one in the family remembered her by that name. Occasionally you will find entries such as *Betty alias Elizabeth* but the use of the word *alias* is less common with forenames than with surnames.

Margaret runs it a close second, with, among others, *Madge, Maggie, Maisie, Margery, Margot, May, Meg, Megan, Daisy, Greta, Peggy and Rita.* Common diminutives from *Mary* include *Mally, Molly and Polly*. Where documents are written in Latin, as parish registers often were until 1733, and Roman Catholic registers until the late 20th century, *Mary* was translated as *Maria*. Most people transcribing and translating such documents automatically change *Maria* to *Mary* but, as with *Jacobus* (usually 'translated' as *James*), there have always been children baptised as *Maria* (often in Catholic families) and *Jacob* (particularly in families which used Old Testament names for their children).

Some Christian names were popular in the late 19th century but are used infrequently today. My mother and several friends of her generation were named *Winifred*; some retained the name, others used *Winnie*, one was always *Wyn* and the only current bearer of the name that I know is *Freda*. Of three ladies I have known called *Bertha* one did use the name; the second called (and signed) herself *Bea* (and most of her friends assumed this was short for *Beatrice*); and the third was known to family and friends as *Betty*.

Christian names can be very deceptive.

As a further pitfall, remember that Christian names in the past were not always specific to the gender you might expect. Today names like *Carol, Evelyn, Hilary and Lesley* can be used for either sex; and *Pat, Chris* and *Sam* might be given as 'proper' names or as shortened forms of *Patrick* or *Patricia, Christopher* or *Christine, Samuel* or *Samantha*. In the past, names like *Anne, Florence, Lucy, Marie, Shirley* (think of the wrestler *Big Daddy*, whose real name was *Shirley Crabtree*) and *Wendy* were used - particularly among the aristocracy - for men. *Florence Nightingale, Charlotte Bronte*'s **Shirley** and *J.M.Barrie*'s *Wendy* are widely regarded as being the first use of these names for women. On the other hand, *Christian, Douglas, Julian, Matthew and Philip* were used as girls' names, as occasionally was *Montague*. I have seen *Matthew* alias *Martha* specified on occasion but most of the others have to be worked out from other evidence and, if the entry is pre-1733 and in Latin, and the child is described as *fil*, which can mean son or daughter, it may be extremely difficult to decide the sex. Remembering the fluidity of spelling, *Francis* and *Frances* are incredibly easy to confuse and need careful attention when you come across them (see pp.98 & 102).

Names such as *Major, Squire, Parson, Duke, Prince* and *Earl* long used as Christian names (see p.56) can cause confusion - and lead to family historians assuming that their ancestors were of higher social status than they in fact were (which may be what some parents intended). No-one has satisfactorily explained why these names were so used. Were they straightforward surnames used as Christian names or an attempt to 'upgrade' a child's social status? An exception is *Duke*, short for *Marmaduke*, which was widely used in the East Riding of Yorkshire, and less commonly in the North Riding. According to most authorities on names, *Marmaduke/Duke* was rare outside Yorkshire but in some parishes in the county, particularly in the 17th and 18th centuries, it ranked among the most popular boys' names.

Surnames were often given as Christian names. Illegitimate children (see p.119.) were frequently given part of the father's surname - pity the girl baptised at *Catton* in 1691 as *Balderston Teale daughter of Dorothy Teale and John Balderston senior of Low Catton* - and many families used the mother's maiden name for a child. In some families this name would continue to be used for generations but, with the fluidity of spelling, it often metamorphosed into something quite different from the original name. The *Tipper* family of Staffordshire, and later of Lancashire, baptised a son (usually the eldest) in each generation as *Loton* until well into the 19th century but none of the descendants knew why. Tracing back through PRs, the first baptism of a *Loton* was located in 1702, the son of *Daniel and Ann Tipper*. In 1698 a marriage took place between *Daniel Tipper* and *Ann Loaton*, and the marriage allegation was for *Daniel Tipper* to marry *Ann Lawton*. Similarly, in 1740 *Thomas Lee* married *Dorothy Bernard*. A son was baptised as *Barnet Lee* in 1749; two generations later, in the same family, *Barnard Lea* was baptised and *Barnard* was still being used in the 1950s.

Children 'of indeterminate gender' (the modern phrase) have always been born. In 1750 in Cheshire *Sarah Richardson commonly called Peter and Maria Sproston* were married (and their first child was baptised a year later with the same wording for the father). If they, or any couple with a similar problem, had left the parish where their situation was known would they have dropped the *Sarah commonly called*, leaving anyone researching the family looking for a non-existent baptism for *Peter Richardson*?

RESOLUTIONS:

I will remember that there are no hard and fast rules governing the spelling of names of whatever sort but there are guidelines which may help me to avoid some of the pitfalls connected with them.

I will bear in mind that many of my ancestors were illiterate and that many of the ministers, registrars or enumerators who listened to their voices, and then filled in the entries, spoke with very different accents. They were quite capable of writing either what they thought was said or what they thought should have been said.

CHAPTER 4

RELATIONSHIPS

Was *little Cis* christened as *Cecily* or *Cecilia*? Was *Auntie Gladys* really the speaker's true aunt? Was the *uncle*, who 'lived in a big house with lots of furniture, ornaments and clothes' and whom the elderly gentleman remembered visiting regularly with his mother, truly his uncle? Can anyone correctly claim descent in the male line from *Captain Cook, Horatio Nelson* or *William Shakespeare*? The answer to all these questions is no. **Relationships may not always be what they seem** and pitfalls abound.

ORAL HISTORY AND RELATIONSHIPS

One of the first steps recommended to anyone setting out to trace their ancestors is to talk to all their relatives and find out what they know or remember about the family. Sound advice, but bear in mind that memories (at any age) can be fallible, deliberately suppressed or falsified. People remember what they want to, and forget the unpleasant episodes. Your great-aunt may tell you scandalous tales about her sisters and their lives but will do all she can to prevent you finding out that her parents married only three months before (or six months after) she was born; she will go into minute details about her respectable brothers and their descendants but 'blank out' the one who did not conform and his existence will only come to light when you find his name on a census and ask who he was. Be careful here - touching a raw nerve may cause a previously rich vein of information to dry up completely. Illegitimacy, suicide and mental illness are among subjects which many older people still find it difficult to cope with and some of them resent the fact that we can now find out, via official records, facts which they have spent a lifetime concealing.

Do not make the mistake of talking to one loquacious relative and assuming that you have learnt everything about the family. Question other relatives and you may well end up with additional information and a completely different 'take' on a family situation. Remember that, particularly from the 18th to early 20th centuries, many children left home at an early age (particularly girls who went 'into service') so the eldest daughter, to whom you have spoken, may know less about family affairs than her younger siblings. If you find new information, always be prepared to revisit a relative (provided they are willing - do not expect everyone to be as interested in family details as you are). It is surprising what can suddenly be dug out from what you thought was an exhausted mine of information. I believed my mother and my aunt (her sister) had told me all they knew about one couple until a chance remark, years later, made my aunt exclaim *but they were second cousins* and that opened up a whole new field of research. My mother (the elder daughter) maintained she had never known this fact.

When visiting relatives you will almost certainly be shown photographs, possibly dating as far back as the 1860s, many of them with no indication as to whom they represent. Do not fall into the trap of assuming that because several relatives have shown you the same unlabelled photograph this will be true of the next one you see and omit to turn it over. I have six copies of a photograph of what was an unidentified couple - until I found the answer scribbled on the back of photograph number six. **If your family has a 'maiden aunt', often the unmarried daughter who remained at home to look after her parents, she is often the most fruitful source of labelled photographs and family stories.**

'ARTIFICIAL' RELATIONSHIPS

The instances in the first paragraph serve to remind us that anything we are told (verbally or in writing, because many people can only make contact with far-flung relations by correspondence or e-mail) should never be accepted as true before it has been confirmed from other sources.

Little Cis proved to be the youngest child in a large family, known so consistently to all her siblings as *little sis[ter]* that they had great difficulty recalling her proper name. A memorial card sent to me, following the publication of the original article, for *Jane Hannah (Cissy) aged 21* is another example of the same situation.

Auntie Gladys was not the sister of one of the parents of her 'niece'. It seems to be the custom nowadays to call almost anyone by their Christian name from the first contact but well within living memory it was unthinkable for a child to use the given name of an adult. Close friends and neighbours of the child's parents would become known as *Auntie Gladys* or *Uncle Tom* and an elderly person, recalling events of half a century earlier, may well not think to explain that these were not blood relatives.

The *uncle*, with no name but thought of for more than fifty years as 'my rich relative up north' turned out to have been the local pawnbroker - a classic case of 'false memory' with a grain of truth in the story but the details twisted out of all recognition. (For anyone too young to know, the weekly visit which many people made to the pawnshop was known as *going to see uncle.*)

Until recently there was a tendency, particularly in rural areas, for a man to refer to his wife as *mother* in conversation and, particularly in American films, you will often hear someone referred to as *son* when what is meant is *young man*.

Many people start researching their family history because they are told that they are related to royalty or to a famous person. In some cases the story may be true but, more commonly, someone in the family has made an assumption on the basis of a shared surname and, as time passes, what was originally *We might be connected to ...* becomes *We are related to ... .* Three groups of my *Chamberlain* relatives in Australasia, all originating in Warwickshire but with no communication between them for almost a century, claim (imaginary) descent from the 19th century statesman and *Birmingham* social reformer, *Joseph Chamberlain*. Many of England's heroes - like *Cook* and *Nelson* - have no legitimate descendants; *Cook*'s progeny all died childless; *Nelson*'s line was continued via his illegitimate daughter, *Horatia*; both have descendants through collateral lines but there are still those who claim direct descent because they bear the surname of *Cook* or *Nelson*. In the case of *Nelson*, his titles passed first to his brother and then to his nephew, *Thomas Bolton*, who assumed the surname of *Nelson*. It was not uncommon, in cases like this or when a daughter's husband inherited his father-in- law's estates, for a change of surname to take place (see p.24).

BLOOD RELATIONSHIPS

Understanding relationships is something which many people find difficult. Most of them have no idea of the difference between a first cousin twice removed and third cousins - and do not care. However, the difference can be crucial to the family historian and there is no substitute for learning the differences from one of the many charts and diagrams which endeavour to clarify, in particular, the various degrees of cousinship. I make no attempt to explain the situation - merely **warn readers not to fall into the very big pitfall of trying to construct a family tree based on perceived relationships after talking to friends and relatives**. I had one true aunt (my mother's sister) and no first cousins; apart from this my nearest relatives are second cousins (the grandchildren of my grandparents' brothers and sisters). Their parents and my parents were first cousins but referring to anyone as *cousin so-and-so* went out of fashion long ago so any adult within the family circle was referred to as *uncle* or *aunt* and, to this day, the children of my second cousins refer to my late mother (their first cousin twice removed) and myself (their second cousin once removed) as *aunt*. I doubt if either they or my daughter (their third cousin) could explain the various relationships. Second and 'once removed' cousins may sometimes be called half-cousins.

Conversely, my husband has a nephew, the son of a much older brother and so only three years his junior, who refused to call a boy so near his own age *uncle* and therefore insisted that they were cousins; **be aware that people of similar age may not be of the same generation**. On the same lines, my aunt was, correctly, my daughter's great-aunt but how many people do you know who like to be called *great-aunt* (or the alternative *grand-aunt*); she didn't. I always called my aunt's husband *uncle* although he was not a blood relative but a relative by marriage or *in law*.

When this uncle registered my maternal grandfather's death in 1969, he described himself as *nephew* of the deceased, rather than *nephew by marriage* or *in law* and I suspect most people would do the same. My paternal great-grandfather wrote his Will in 1916 (twenty years before he died) naming as executors his eldest son and *my nephew*. I wasted a great deal of time trying to tie this nephew into his family tree before discovering that he was, in fact, *his wife's nephew*.

IN-LAW AND STEP RELATIONSHIPS AND INCEST

The in-laws is a phrase which is generally used to describe the close relatives of one's spouse (father/mother/brother/sister) but very few people understand the significance of the term for family historians searching pre-20th century records. Today it appears possible in this country to marry almost anybody except your parents and siblings but look in any but the most modern prayer book and you will find the table below (taken from a 1731 edition) which remained unaltered from 1563 until 1907 and contains 30 forbidden relationships for men and the equivalent 30 for women).

A TABLE of Kindred and Affinity, wherein whosoever are Related, are forbidden in Scripture, and our Laws, to Marry together.

A Man may not marry his	A Woman may not marry her
1 Grandmother,	1 Grandfather,
2 Grandfathers Wife,	2 Grandmothers Husband,
3 Wifes Grandmother.	3 Husbands Grandfather.
4 Fathers Sister,	4 Fathers Brother,
5 Mothers Sister,	5 Mothers Brother,
6 Fathers brothers Wife,	6 Fathers Sisters Husband.
7 Mothers Brothers Wife,	7 Mothers Sisters Husband,
8 Wifes Fathers Sister,	8 Husbands Fathers Brother,
9 Wifes Mothers Sister.	9 Husbands Mothers Brother.
10 Mother,	10 Father,
11 Step mother,	11 Step Father,
12 Wifes Mother.	12 Husbands Father.
13 Daughter.	13 Son,
14 Wifes Daughter,	14 Husbands Son,
15 Sons Wife.	15 Daughters Husband.
16 Sister,	16 Brother,
17 Wifes Sister,	17 Husbands Brother,
18 Brothers Wife.	18 Sisters Husband.
19 Sons Daughter,	19 Sons Son,
20 Daughters Daughter,	20 Daughters Son,
21 Sons Sons Wife.	21 Sons Daughters Husband.
22 Daughters Sons Wife,	22 Daughters Daughters Husband
23 Wifes Sons Daughter,	23 Husbands Sons Son,
24 Wifes Daughters Daughter.	24 Husbands Daughters Son.
25 Brothers Daughter,	25 Brothers Son,
26 Sisters Daughter,	26 Sisters Son,
27 Brothers Sons Wife,	27 Brothers Daughters Husband,
28 Sisters Sons Wife,	28 Sisters Daughters Husband,
29 Wifes Brothers Daughter,	29 Husbands Brothers Son,
30 Wifes Sisters Daughter.	30 Husbands Sisters Son.

Kin(dred) are blood relatives, *Affinity* is relationship by marriage and the list of forbidden partners included, among others, *all the in-laws and step-relatives, regarded as blood relatives because when a couple married they became one flesh.* **Do not forget that this table related only to men and women whose spouses had died. Divorce was not an option** (until 1857 it required a private Act of Parliament). Some denominations (including the Roman Catholic Church) included godparents and their children within the forbidden degrees of affinity.

No clergyman would knowingly unite a couple who were within the forbidden degrees so many people contracting such an alliance would marry far from home, often in a city, abroad or in Scotland. The child of any such marriage could technically be classed as incestuous. If you come across an ancestor, before the 20th century, accused of incest, or an infant baptised as a *child of incest*, it does not necessarily mean, as it usually would today, a relationship between father and daughter or brother and sister; it is more likely to signify one between a man and his deceased wife's sister (legal from 1907) or a man and his deceased brother's widow (legal from 1921). Relationships between a man and his sister-in-law were particularly prevalent in an age when many women died in childbirth and an unmarried sister was often drafted in to care for the husband and children. Between 1837 and 1907 you may find that such couples risked marrying in a Register Office. It is worth remembering that, **until 1908, incest (whether by blood or affinity) was a sin in the eyes of the church (and could be dealt with by an ecclesiastical court) but was not a crime in civil law** (see p.270).

If you find yourself dealing with Jewish ancestors remember that the Jewish laws regarding forbidden degrees of marriage differed in some respects from those of the Anglican church and English law. A widower was permitted to marry his deceased wife's sister; a widow might marry her deceased husband's brother if she had no-one to support her; a man could marry his niece and a woman her nephew. Before the 20th century many of these marriages took place abroad, to avoid possible conflict with local customs.

TERMINOLOGY

The definition of some relationships has changed over time and attaching the modern meaning to references found in records, particularly those dating from the 16th to mid-19th centuries, can cause you serious difficulties.

ADOPTION officially began as a legal process on 1st January 1927. Almost anyone 'adopted' before this was fostered or 'taken into' a family and it is unlikely that any documentary evidence will survive.

COUSIN can be very widely interpreted and can cover almost any degree of relationship either by blood or by marriage. Historically it was frequently used for nephew or niece and sometimes for next of kin.

GODPARENTS OR SPONSORS played a more prominent role in the past than they do in many families today. Their purpose was to take on special responsibilities for the Christian upbringing of their godchildren. Note that the Roman Catholic Church required one godparent of each sex but the Anglican Book of Common Prayer required *at least three godparents, of which two are to be of its own sex*. You will occasionally find them named, but with no further details, in Anglican registers in the 16th and 17th centuries. Roman Catholic registers (where these survive) may be much more revealing as they sometimes provide more information about godparents or sponsors.

HALF-BROTHER (OR SISTER) share one biological parent.

KINSMAN is defined as the nearest relative by blood but is sometimes loosely used to describe a relative by marriage.

KITH AND KIN means friends (kith) and blood relatives (kin).

NEPHEW, cited earlier, can mean nephew or nephew-by-marriage. It was also used historically for grandson and for the illegitimate son of a cleric (this primarily from the period when England was a Roman Catholic country and clerics could not marry; sometimes found in early Wills).

NEXT OF KIN historically meant the nearest blood relative. A wife, in the eyes of the law, was not her husband's next of kin. In this century, when (particularly in hospitals) it is possible to name a person of choice as your next-of-kin it can be difficult to understand the complications which could arise, for example, if a husband died intestate or if the son or daughter of a first marriage (the next-of-kin) disliked their stepmother.

NURSE CHILD (see p.239 for a legal definition and p.67): before adoption became legal in 1927 this usually refers to a child being fostered by a relative or by another family.

ORPHAN is defined as *one deprived by death of a parent*. It is usually taken to mean the loss of both parents but do not make this assumption without proof. Many an heiress who had lost her father was treated as an 'orphan' and 'adopted' by a family with eyes on her inheritance.

STEP relationships resulted from the re-marriage of a widowed parent (and originally came within the degrees of affinity of those forbidden to marry) but did not involve a blood relationship. Particularly in the 1851 and 1861 census returns, family members whom we should today describe as *step* relatives were most commonly listed as *in law*; see Chapter 8 for more details.

STEPCHILD also meant *orphan* (and the OED gives this as the first meaning of the word, ahead of the above).

RESOLUTION:

I will remember that not all relationship are *blood* relationships. They may be relationships *in law*, *step* relationships or *unofficial* relationships.

CHAPTER 5

INDEXES AND INDEXING

Indexes dominate family history research, especially for those just beginning to trace their ancestors. Whether you read a book; surf online, via free or commercial websites; use CDs; look at microfilm or microfiche at your local library, archives repository (record office) or family history society, you will find that much of the material you first encounter is in the form of an index.

They come in all shapes and sizes, ranging from the International Genealogical Index (IGI) with around 100 million entries for the British Isles to specialist ones dealing with, for example, coastguards, entertainers and gamekeepers. Always ask, when visiting a record repository or library or joining a family history society, whether they hold any indexes which might help you, or whether they are aware of any held elsewhere. Many societies and individuals do make a charge for consulting their indexes. It is advisable to ascertain if a fee applies before asking them to undertake a search - and, unless you are using e-mail (and even then if you need something to be posted to you), do not forget to enclose a stamped addressed envelope or International Reply Coupon(s) with your enquiry.

Indexes can be incredibly useful, and may help you to locate an ancestor in minutes, rather than days, of searching, but they can also send you scurrying along false trails and plunging into pitfalls from which you may find it difficult to escape. **It always pays to read any introductory matter provided before using them.** I recently looked at a booklet of a parish register covering, according to the cover, *Marriages and Burials 1813-1837* and, forgetting my own insistence on always reading the introduction, looked at the index at the back of the booklet, found no reference to a marriage for the surname required and put the booklet aside. If I had read the introduction before starting the search I would have read that the booklet contains an:

> *Alphabetical Index of Bridegrooms (plus information from the marriage entry)*
> *Alphabetical Index of Brides (cross-referenced to the bridegroom)*
> *Transcript of Burial Register*
> *Alphabetical Index of Burials*

Rather obviously, alphabetical lists do not require an index, so the index at the back covers only the burials transcript and, if I had not then read the introduction, I would have missed the marriage (which was there). The same pitfall applies to census indexes, particularly those with several villages included in one booklet (see below).

The IGI, the General Register Office (GRO) indexes, indexes to census returns, parish registers, Wills and numerous other records, are all secondary (if not tertiary) sources. As soon as you start making an index from a primary source mistakes and omissions will creep in (and that is

not counting the errors and omissions in any primary source, as demonstrated throughout this book). Having spent more than 25 years compiling a county marriage index, 40 years dealing with parish registers, and as long carrying out family history research, I can honestly say that I have never come across a totally accurate index, whether compiled by hand or by computer.

When the original articles were written, beginners were most often advised to consult the indexes to the IGI and the 1881 census (on fiche or CD as the internet, ten years ago, was in its infancy). Since then both have become integral parts of the Church of Jesus Christ of Latter-day Saints (LDS) familysearch.org website but most of the pitfalls and possibilities regarding the different systems used to index names in the two projects remain the same - and are sometimes compounded on being put onto the internet. To summarise briefly, the IGI groups similar surnames together under one 'chosen' variant (using a 'soundex' system: see p.57); the microfiche version of the 1881 census index is strictly alphabetical so you have to search every possible spelling individually as a difference of one letter can place a name several frames away from its expected spot (more on these two indexes below).

Most other indexes, whichever source they deal with, fall somewhere between the two and it is always worth checking which format has been adopted before using an index. Check to see whether an index is *Alphabetical*; *Alphabetical, some phonetic insertions* (for example:*Goff/Gough* or *Earlam/ Irlam* filed together); *Surname Index*; *Full names*; *Full transcript* and so on. At the risk of generalising, many family history societies have concentrated on the compilation of baptism, marriage, burial and census indexes, with specialist indexes more often being the result of an individual's specific interest (see above). Guidelines for indexing have been published from time to time but no standard format has been adopted and it is all too easy to fall into the trap of assuming that a format familiar to you is the one in general use.

This may appear to be stating the obvious but remember to check whether the Christian/forename or surname comes first in an online index. Many online indexes have the names in that order but some put the surname first and, where forename and surname are reversible - as in, for instance, *George Michael, Bradley James, Keith Allen* - you may, almost without thinking, type in the names in the order you expect and find yourself faced with an unexpected list of results. **Always ascertain which indexing system has been used for the source you are looking at** and do not settle for a 'quick look' for a name without bearing in mind that it may be listed under something very different.

Remember that nothing should be taken on trust. If you find an index reference for a name on page/folio *271* but when checking the original document you cannot find it, look at *217* and *127*: typographical errors are depressingly easy to make. Similarly, if the village where you hope to find your ancestor is covered by folios *153-174*, do not limit your surname index search to just

40

those numbers in numerical sequence. In the days when indexes were typed and prepared manually, if a slip of paper was found later it was easier to add the omitted number at the end of the sequence so that a *Booth* (see below) on folio *161* might be indexed after one on folio *735*.

When looking in an index to any source, do not forget to allow for spelling variations caused by the original writer's own preference (for *Brookshaw* check *Bruckshaw*, for *Phythian* look under *Fythian*) or the accent of the person giving him the information (for *Hainsworth* try *Ainsworth*). Bear in mind that Gothic capital letters at the beginning of a surname or a placename can easily be misread (*Warhurst/Marhurst*; *Kilburn/Hilburn;Parley/Varley*); ends of names are notorious for tailing off and being very difficult to read (see p.21); and, on microfilm especially, it can be impossible to tell whether a name is *Nevill* or *Nevitt*. It is recommended that any index being compiled is checked by at least two people, and does not depend on one person's interpretation of the original handwriting, but in many cases this has not been done.

If you think an entry *should* be there, in any kind of index, and it is not, it is always worth searching the original record. Those compiling transcripts and indexes are only human and they can make mistakes, misread names or omit entries.

The **IGI** merits a chapter to itself (see Chapter 7) and the **National Burial Index** is explained in Chapter 16 but comments on census and marriage indexes are included here, with further references in later chapters.

CENSUS INDEXES

Census Indexes, principally to the 1851 and 1861 censuses, compiled mostly by family history societies from the late 1970s onwards (some are still being worked on today) are much less used since census returns from 1841 to 1911 have become available on various commercial websites (the 1881 is free to view) but it is still worth including details on their compilation both for those people who do not use a computer and to help you avoid pitfalls encountered online.

Broadly speaking, census indexes fall into two main categories: those which give the surname, piece number and folio number and those which go into greater detail and may include Christian name, age, relationship and place of birth (very few include occupation). The former involves you in more work, because you have to check the census returns for all references to that surname in the location to find the individual you want (and in the case of a common surname in an urban area this can run into the hundreds: there are 220 *Booth* references and 379 for *Smith* in the four piece numbers covering *Stockport* Registration District in 1851). The latter enables you to construct 'instant families' but can be as dangerous as building pedigrees from the IGI (see Chapter 7).

Pitfalls in census indexes also fall into two principal categories, those generated during their compilation and publication and those caused because you misinterpret the entry in the index; never assume that a middle-aged couple and a clutch of children sharing a folio number are a married couple and their offspring (see pp. 65 & 255). Be very sure precisely which piece number(s), or parts of one, are included in an index - read the introduction or the title page and note which folios (or enumeration districts) are covered. Some will embrace a whole piece number including several hundred folios and possibly dealing with an entire Registration District; others will contain only a few folios covering a single village. Several villages may have been included in one publication but indexed separately so you have to be very careful that you peruse the relevant section; a city and its suburbs, on the other hand, may be split between several publications.

Do not fall into the trap of looking at a family history society's list of publications and assuming that, because they do not list an index for the place you want and it is within their sphere of influence, one does not exist. *Dukinfield, Mottram in Longdendale* and *Stalybridge*, for example, are historically and ecclesiastically in Cheshire but administratively in Lancashire, and you will find 1851 indexes for this area published by *Manchester and Lancashire FHS* and not, as you might expect, by a Cheshire society. 1851 census indexes for *Dent, Garsdale* and *Sedbergh*, (transferred from the West Riding of Yorkshire to Cumbria in 1974 and with records now held in *Kendal CRO*), were published by *Cumbria FHS*; those for *Bentham* and *Thornton in Lonsdale,* parishes immediately to the south of *Dent* but now in North Yorkshire (with records at Northallerton), were published by the *Lancashire Family History and Heraldry Society.*

Indexes to the 1881 census are available principally on microfiche, CD, and on FamilySearch. The three types of index differ in format: those on microfiche are in strict alphabetical order so, for any given county, entries for the surname *Bann* will be together and any variants of the name will be listed separately. A difference of one letter, *Ban, Band* or *Bain* instead of *Bann*, can mean that entries may be several fiche apart. Every possible variant spelling of a surname will need to be checked individually and it is easy to overlook the unexpected variant which occurs once because the enumerator failed to form one letter properly or misread one letter on the original census form.

On the CD set and on familysearch.org if you are certain of the spelling of the surname, tick the box for *exact spelling only* and you will receive all the entries for that specifically spelt surname. If you are uncertain of the exact spelling, or cannot find the entry you require, do not tick the *exact spelling* box and enter into the world of variant spellings. In the CD version, all *Bann* entries are listed under *Bann* but *Bain(e)/Baines/Bane/Baynes* are listed separately. On FamilySearch all five names are listed together which entails careful searching. In both indexes *Band* is listed as a separate surname. Similarly with *Litton* (see p.57), in the CD version *Litton* and *Lytton* are indexed together; on FamilySearch *Litton* is indexed under itself but *Lytton* is under *Layton/Leighton*. **You need to keep your wits about you when searching these indexes.**

Looking at the 1881 census online is easy but many researchers (including some who work full-time with computers) prefer to use the CDs because it is possible to 'dig deeper' in this version and locate entries which are extremely difficult, or impossible, to find online.

Mary Ann Shaw stated in the 1851 census that she was born *in a stage coach between Nottingham and Derby*. I noted this entry in passing about 40 years ago, when one could still look at the original census enumerators' books at Portugal Street in London, but did not note down any details. When the 1881 census became available on CDs in the late 1990s I looked to see if I could find her to ascertain whether she had 'rationalised' her birthplace in the intervening 30 years. I found her without too much difficulty, on the CD containing census returns for **Midlands East Counties** (which included Derbyshire and Nottinghamshire), and she repeated her 1851 entry word for word. In the National Index (of names) on CD, I then located her by putting in her name, approximate year of birth and place of residence from the census entry (she was a widow aged 64 and living in Alfreton in Derbyshire). This index lists, in columns, both county of birth and county of residence when the census was taken and, in her case, the first column for county of birth was left blank. Nobody (and plenty of experienced people have tried) has yet succeeded in finding an entry for her, under her own name, in the 1881 census index online. She was eventually traced online by putting in the name of a son who was living with her in 1881 and that brought up the full household census entry. The program used for the online version does not appear to cope with entries which differ from the norm (in this case, where the place of birth column was left blank). There are many entries in the census where either the county column or the place of birth column is left blank (or N[ot] K[nown] is written). How many other people, like *Mary Ann*, have 'slipped through the net' and cannot be located in the online index?

MARRIAGE INDEXES

Marriage indexes are beginning to appear online but many of them are digitised images of indexes which were previously available in book form, microform or on CD. Such marriage indexes, which normally cover the period prior to 1837 when civil registration begins, vary greatly in size and composition. Some, like **Boyd's Marriage Index**, give only the year of the event, not the exact date. Others are indexed by the name of the bridegroom only, so a list of females bearing a surname cannot be provided. Most compilers will be able to provide you with a list of parishes and dates covered by their index so, if you draw a blank with a particular event, you should know which parishes you do not need to search. Do not assume that all indexes are held on computer - many still consist of slips of paper in shoeboxes and what can be extracted from a computerized index at the click of a mouse may take many hours to put together manually. Before consulting a marriage index, bear in mind the pitfalls given earlier in this chapter - is it compiled strictly alphabetically; are there phonetic insertions; could the initial letter have been misread; could the ending have 'tailed off' and been impossible to determine - and read the chapters dealing with marriages in parish registers.

INDEXES ARE NOT PERFECT

Some researchers place far too much reliance on indexes, without taking their faults into account. **Never forget that any index is only as good as its source material and its compilers**. If the incumbent lost the scrap of paper on which he had written details of your ancestor's baptism before he found time to enter it into the parish register then there will be no entry in the IGI (and probably no surviving entry anywhere); if your family lived in a 'no-go' area, where the census enumerator dared not deliver and collect forms, there will be no entry in the census or its index. If either gentleman misheard or misunderstood what was said to him, often in an unfamiliar accent, the name written down may bear little or no resemblance to your family surname. In Cheshire, John *Ardern* and Samuel *Hordern* would have been surprised to know that the rector recorded them both as being called *Haldern* and Mary *Hordern* might not have recognized herself as Mary *Hawthorn*. Be aware that surname variants may not be grouped in the IGI as you expect. You might justifiably expect that *Park(e), Parkes* and *Parks* would be listed together whereas you will find the first one under *Park*, the second under *Parco* and the third under *Perkes*.

Index compilers often have to battle with poor handwriting, fading ink or poor microfilm and, however many checks are made, some errors are inevitable. Capital letters are particularly prone to misreading - *Higinbotham* as *Wiginbotham*; *Kenworthy* as *Fenworthy, Henworthy* and *Renworthy*; *Lutton* as *Sutton*; *Tidmas* as *Fidmas* and *Jidmas*; *Trubshaw* as *Frubshaw* - and watch for the stroke across the letter *t* which can often be invisible, especially on microfilm, so that *Bennett* is read as *Bennell*, *Kett* as *Kell*, *Chatten* as *Challen* and *Martin* as *Marlin*.

CALENDARS (OF DOCUMENTS NOT DATES)

A calendar, in this sense, is a list of documents arranged chronologically, usually with summaries attached. State Papers, Estate Papers, Deeds and Probate Documents are often calendared. Particularly with pre-20th century listings, before you start searching **make sure whether you are dealing with an index**

or a calendar. An index will usually be in alphabetical order, a calendar will be sorted only by the first letter of the word (occasionally by the first two or three letters). In the *West Riding Registry of Deeds* (see p.266) for example, surnames are calendared from 1704 to 1794 and are alphabetical thereafter. It is all too easy to overlook the change and, having used the post-1794 indexes, to see *Hickson/Higgins/Higson* following each other in an earlier section, and fail to realise that *Hutchinson* appears before and *Harrison* after them (because they are calendared by the first letter only). Similarly with the Wills Indexes at The Borthwick Institute for Archives in York, which cover the majority of Yorkshire Wills, those to 1731 are indexed alphabetically; those from 1732 to 1858 are calendared by the initial letter. (There is now an online index on a commercial website which makes searching much easier.)

RESOLUTION:

I will remember that the International Genealogical Index, the 1881 Census Index, and any other available indexes, are very useful but they all contain errors, omissions and pitfalls.

TWO EXTRACTS FROM THE BORTHWICK INSTITUTE'S CALENDARS OF WILLS FOR AUGUST 1761 AND MARCH 1792

These extracts are for less common letters. When dealing with common letters (especially B, H, S and W) there can, especially in the 19th century, be pages of calendared entries for one letter for any given month.

CHAPTER 6

RECORDS AND REPOSITORIES

NATIONAL ARCHIVES REPOSITORIES IN THE U.K.

THE NATIONAL ARCHIVES (TNA)

TNA, created in 2003, is the official archive for England, Wales and the central UK government. It includes what were four separate organisations – the Public Record Office (PRO) [see p.52], the Historical Manuscripts Commission (HMC), the Office of Public Sector Information (OPSI) and Her Majesty's Stationery Office (HMSO). Many books and online sites will include references to these organisations, and to the Family Records Centre (FRC) which closed in 2008; inputting any of them into a search engine should transfer you to the TNA site.

TNA is situated at: Ruskin Avenue, Kew, Richmond, Surrey TW9 4DU. Before planning a visit you should contact them by letter or phone (tel. 0208 392 5200) or check their website at www.nationalarchives.gov.uk

An increasing number of the more popular classes of documents held by TNA are being digitised, in partnership with commercial firms, and made available online.

SCOTLANDSPEOPLE (sic) CENTRE

This is a partnership between the General Register Office for Scotland, the National Archives of Scotland and the Court of the Lord Lyon.

It is situated in General Register House, 2 Princes Street, Edinburgh EH1 3YY (tel. 0131 314 4300). There is a daily charge for researching and a seat can be booked by phone (from 2010 it will be possible to book online and pay in advance).

Their website www.scotlandspeople.gov.uk is the official government source of genealogical data for Scotland and contains the records of civil registration, census returns, parish registers, Wills and much more.

SCOTTISH ARCHIVE NETWORK (SCAN)

This project, whose partners are the National Archives of Scotland, the Heritage Lottery Fund, and the Genealogical Society of Utah, aims to provide a single electronic catalogue to the holdings of more than 50 Scottish archives. Details of these archives can be found in the SCAN directory on www.scan.org.uk

PUBLIC RECORD OFFICE OF NORTHERN IRELAND (PRONI)

PRONI is the official archive for Northern Ireland. It holds public records, mainly covering the period 1921 to the present day, and many privately deposited archives.

Its current address is 66 Balmoral Avenue, Belfast BT9 6NY (tel. 028 9025 5905) but it will be closing its search rooms in September 2010 in preparation for a move to a new record office in the Titanic quarter of Belfast in mid-2011. Further details can be found on www.proni.gov.uk

THE NATIONAL LIBRARY OF WALES
THE NATIONAL LIBRARY OF WALES
The National Library of Wales is a national repository and holds many of the records of interest to family historians including parish registers, BTs, marriage allegations and bonds, probate records (see p.195) and much more.

Its address is The National Library of Wales, Aberystwyth, Ceredigion, Wales SY23 3BU (tel. 01970 632 800) and website www.llgc.org.uk

The bulk of this chapter relates to record repositories in England and Wales but most of the points made are equally relevant to repositories elsewhere.

RECORD OFFICES IN ENGLAND AND WALES

County Record Offices, Record Offices (both generally with 'Record' in the singular), Archive(s) Offices or Services, and some History Centres, Libraries and Local Studies Sections all contain original documents and will, in general, be referred to in this book as 'record offices'. Many of the original County Record Offices, established in the early 20th century, have changed their names (and their areas of coverage) over the years so make sure you know which one covers your area of interest. One of my favourite family history maxims is 'never take anything for granted'. **One of the deepest pitfalls you can fall into is to assume that, because you know the records and record offices of one county or one country, those of another will follow the same pattern**.

UNITS OF LOCAL GOVERNMENT

According to many books dealing with family and local history in England and Wales, the *Hundred* and the *Parish* are the units of local government with which you will need to be familiar to locate certain records - the Hearth and Land Taxes, for instance, in the *Hundred*; bastardy, settlement and poor relief papers in the *Parish*. In many areas this is true but counties did vary in the names and units they used. In Yorkshire and Lincolnshire, instead of the *Hundred* you will need to know the *Wapentake*, in Sussex the *Rape*, in Kent the *Lathe*, and in Yorkshire and Lancashire, at least, often the *Township* as opposed to the *Parish*.

A parish originally consisted of a township, or several townships, in which was built a (parish) church. Most parishes were of a size capable of handling their own affairs, both ecclesiastical and civil. Over time the government delegated more and more duties (including levying and administering poor relief and maintaining the highways) to them. Some parishes were too large for this to be practicable and, principally in these cases, a township was a

47

division of a parish which could levy its own poor rate and appoint its own local, as opposed to parish, officials such as overseers of the poor and constables.

Do not make the mistake of equating parish and township; in certain counties the whole poor relief system was administered by township and not by parish. The (large) historic parish of *Halifax* in Yorkshire was made up of 23 townships, almost all of which had their own overseers of the poor and their own records. References to *Halifax* in the Local Government section of **Guide to Calderdale District Archives** generally refer to *Halifax* township only and not to the parish but it is easy for those accustomed to thinking in terms of parish administration to make the wrong assumption and not to check for separate township records. Administrative names can cause another pitfall for anyone unfamiliar with local government re-organisation as explained below. Look in a guide to find record repositories in *Halifax* and *Huddersfield* in Yorkshire and you may well draw a blank; you will locate them under *Calderdale* and *Kirklees* respectively.

WHERE WILL YOU FIND THE RECORDS?

The 1974 changes, coupled with the 1962 Act which empowered local authorities to collect historical manuscripts, meant the creation of many more record (or archive) offices and, in some counties, involved a re-shuffle of records. You may find a county which still has just one record repository holding original documents (see below) but Yorkshire and Lancashire, for instance, have at least 10 each, Kent has 5, Essex and Suffolk 3 each. **It is also always worth checking whether a parish 'moved' from one county to another and then ascertaining which records are where**. You will often find that records which could be moved *en bloc*, like parish registers, are with the 'new' county but documents which would be difficult to separate out remain with the 'old' one.

In some counties the simplistic answer 'in the County Record Office' will still be true. Bedfordshire Record Office (currently known as *Bedfordshire & Luton Archives & Records Service*), for example, holds almost all the original records for Bedfordshire, as does Cheshire Record Office (now *Cheshire & Chester Archive & Local Studies Service*) for Cheshire. The latter incorporates many of the records from the former *Chester City Record Office*. It is always worth checking whether a county retains a separate city record office - as, for instance, does the *City of York*. In Yorkshire, to view records for the parish of *Halifax* you would need to visit four separate repositories; for *Harrogate* the number rises to six (see below).

There are no rigid rules as to which records are held where and changes in the law since 1962, when the Local Government (Records) Act was passed, particularly those in 1974, 1996, and 2008 when local government re-organisation took place, mean that records may well not be where you expect them to be and, in some cases, may no longer be where they were when you looked at them twenty years ago. Among the original pitfalls was *Harrogate was in the West Riding, so all the records will be in a West Yorkshire record office*. In 1974 *Harrogate* was transferred from the West Riding into the county of North Yorkshire; some of the parish registers are held in *Leeds* (West Yorkshire) with others in *Northallerton* (North Yorkshire); the BTs are similarly divided, as are Wills and marriage 'licences'; the parish chest (including poor law records) is in *Northallerton* (North Yorkshire); land tax, quarter sessions records and deeds are in *Wakefield* (West Yorkshire); census returns are principally in the local library or in *Leeds* library, which has a complete set for the historic county. (Other records are at TNA in *London*, making up the six repositories mentioned.) *Harrogate* is by no means unique in having widely scattered records but, to those accustomed to compact sets in a single repository, such dispersion can come as a shock.

RECORD OFFICES: DETAILS TO NOTE BEFORE VISITING

It is an exaggeration to say, concerning records and record repositories, that no two counties are alike but it can seem like that. There are books dealing specifically with record offices and their holdings. You are recommended to read, in advance of a sortie into unknown territory, both a general book and, if possible, one relating to the particular repository you intend to visit. On the TNA website, consult the *Archon Directory* (gives details of U.K. record repositories and their holdings) and *A2A* (Access to Archives) which lists catalogues describing archives held locally in England and Wales.

Doing this should enable you to avoid the frustration of arriving on the doorstep at 9am to find that the repository is: always closed on that day of the week; shut that week for its annual stocktaking; not open till 10am but stays open until 7pm that night; open but you did not book a microfilm reader, they are all full and everything you want to look at is on film; open but the records you require are in another office fifty miles away. Many offices do not produce documents during the lunch period (commonly 12 noon to 2pm) and a number close for a period at lunchtime. Where the office is open on a Saturday (note that many are closed on Saturdays with others open one or two Saturdays a month only), documents usually have to be ordered in advance of the day. **Be aware that in most offices you will view the documents you need to look at in microform and not the original documents**. Microfilm viewers vary greatly between those which you have to wind manually, frame by frame, and more modern ones which enable you to whizz the film backwards or forwards at the press of a button. Many people find that three hours is as long as they can work at a reader before the text begins to blur or they develop a headache. It pays to take a short break from film-reading at regular intervals or your concentration will lapse and you will start to miss things. Record Offices are increasingly putting some of their records online; check whether this is the case before your visit - it could save you time and allow you to concentrate on material which can be viewed only in the record office.

It is also worth ascertaining in advance: whether there are disabled facilities; if the office is on the ground floor or upstairs (and whether there is a lift); where the nearest car parking is (on-site, in a nearby street, or in a public car park - make sure you have coins in your purse or pocket!). Do not assume that because 'your' repository will photocopy records on the day or possesses a microform print-out machine that they all will. In some offices, photocopying is still done on a weekly basis. Make sure you are carrying pencils as almost all record offices forbid the use of pens of any sort; many record offices will lend, or sell, you a pencil but you may encounter one which does not, on the day when all your fellow researchers are using propelling pencils so you cannot borrow one. Be aware that some record offices will not permit pencils which incorporate an eraser. It is also a good idea to carry a magnifying glass as some records are in minute handwriting and not all machines have magnification facilities.

If you wish to work on your laptop for a long period, make sure that the office has electric sockets available and whether you need to book one in advance. Some modern offices have ample sockets but some older ones struggle to provide one. An increasing number of offices are allowing the use of digital cameras to copy documents; check in advance whether this is permitted.

Be prepared to deposit your handbag and other accoutrements, including large files and laptop cases, in a locker. An increasing number of repositories are introducing this rule, partly to make sure you do not absentmindedly put a document into your file and partly because of the increasing number of thefts. It is all too easy to leave your handbag under your seat, wander off to change a reel of film or look at an index, and come back to find the bag has vanished or been rifled. One major library, which does not provide lockers, has notices affixed to every microfilm reader saying 'theft is an everyday occurrence in this library'.

LIBRARIES

The library mentioned above is much used because it holds the census returns on microform for a large area. This is another trap for the unwary. If your local record office holds copies of census returns you tend to think this is the norm. In fact, you will find that libraries are the more likely place to find census returns; copies of the GRO indexes; in some cases, full sets of the IGI and possibly access to some commercial websites (see below). In most record offices you need to book a seat in advance. This is not common in libraries but some will permit you to reserve a microform reader if you are travelling a long distance - it is worth checking.

READERS' TICKETS

Many offices require researchers to obtain a Reader's Ticket on their first visit. The one used by an increasing number of record offices is that of the *County Archives Research Network (CARN)* which is free and, once obtained, is valid for four years and allows access to all other offices in the network. Even here there are pitfalls. Application must be made in person, bringing official proof of identity validating your name with your permanent address and signature. The only document which appears to fulfil all the criteria is a driver's licence. Failing this, a passport or credit card provides name and signature but needs to be accompanied by a document with your name and address on it, such as a bank statement or a utilities bill. A few record offices, especially those with university connections, ask for a passport photograph and sometimes a letter of introduction; they may charge for issuing a reader's ticket. **Always check in advance what is required**.

DIOCESAN RECORD OFFICES

Ecclesiastical records (on which more later - see Chapters 10-19) will usually be found in record offices but do not make the mistake of thinking that, because your local one holds both parish registers and bishop's transcripts for their area, the same will be true elsewhere. **In many counties the record office also serves as the diocesan record office but this is not always the case**. *Lichfield Record Office*, for instance, holds the BTs (and Marriage 'Licences' and Wills) for the historic diocese of Lichfield, which included Staffordshire and Derbyshire, together with parts of Shropshire and Warwickshire. Always ascertain before your visit which records they hold, either as original documents or on microform. It is also worth asking what they have in printed form and what indexes are available to help researchers.

LDS FAMILY HISTORY CENTRES

These are small genealogical libraries attached to some LDS churches (currently there are about 75 FHCs in England and Wales); click on 'Library' on the FamilySearch website for details of whereabouts, opening hours and a contact number. They are open to anyone, not just church members. They generally either hold (on microform or via computer), or can obtain from the main library in Salt Lake City, much of the information detailed on the FamilySearch website. Some centres additionally hold much local information covering their area. The FHCs are manned by volunteers and are open only on certain days and at certain times, which vary from centre to centre. Always make an appointment in advance. Note that they are unable to respond to mail enquiries.

Some libraries and record offices provide free access to certain commercial websites (often for a restricted period of time). A number of FHSs have also purchased subscriptions to these sites and make them available for their members to search.

RESOLUTIONS:

I will always ascertain before visiting a record office whether I need to book a seat/microform viewer/electric socket in advance.

I will check that the record office holds the records I wish to view, in what format they are available and whether I need to order them in advance.

I will make sure that the office is open when I wish to visit.

I will not arrive with a friend and assume that they can be 'fitted in' without notice.

I will observe the Quiet Please notices and leave the search room if I wish to talk at length to someone.

FROM THE 1849 ROYAL KALENDAR AND COURT & CITY REGISTER

PUBLIC RECORD OFFICE.

Established by the Act 1 *and* 2 *Victoria, c.* 94.

HEAD OFFICE, *Rolls House, Chancery-lane.*

BRANCH OFFICES, *Rolls Chapel—Tower—Chapter House, Poet's Corner —and Carlton Ride.*

Office Hours, 10 *till* 4.

Keeper & Custos of the Records, The Master of the Rolls.
Deputy Keeper, Sir Frs. Palgrave.
Secretary, F. S. Thomas, esq.
  Assistant Keepers, 1st *Class.*
Thos. Palmer, esq. *Rolls Chapel.*
T. D. Hardy, esq. *Tower.*
Henry Cole, esq. ⎱ *Carlton Ride.*
Jos. Hunter, esq. ⎰
  Assistant Keepers, 2nd *Class.*
H. G. Holden, esq. *Rolls Chapel.*
Chas. Roberts, esq. *Tower.*
Fred. Devon, esq. *Chapter House.*
W. H. Black, esq. *Rolls House.*
Clerks, H. J. Sharpe, *Tower.*
J. Burtt, *Chapter House.*
Walter Nelson, *Carlton Ride.*
W. Lascelles, *Rolls House.*

J. P. Redington, ⎱ *Carlton Ride.*
T. M. Green, ⎰
John Edwards, *Rolls House.*
J. T. Kentish, *Rolls Chapel.*
C. A. Cole, ⎱ *Carlton Ride.*
J. J. Bond, ⎰
W. B. Sanders, *Tower.*
M. Fenwick, *Rolls Chapel.*
P. S. L. Hunt, ⎱
P. Turner, ⎬ *Carlton Ride.*
J. E. Gibson, ⎰
A. Kingston ⎱ *Tower.*
W. P. Glover, ⎰
G. Knight, *Rolls House.*
A. May, *Chapter House.*
J. Gairdner, ⎱ *Tower.*
F. S. Haydon, ⎰

CHAPTER 7

INTERNATIONAL GENEALOGICAL INDEX

HISTORY OF THE IGI

Remember that the IGI is an index, not necessarily including all the information from the original record. Having found a likely entry on the fiche or online, always check the primary source before claiming an ancestor. There may be helpful information in the full entry which can either confirm your 'missing link' or dash your hopes.

The IGI, whether you use the microfiche version (still preferred by many experienced researchers) or the online version, contains perhaps more pitfalls and possibilities for the family historian than any other source. There cannot be many readers who are unaware of its value to family historians but how many really understand it? Since its original appearance in 1972, as the Computer File Index, it has revolutionised family history research but each microfiche edition (1972, 1981, 1984, 1988 and 1992) had its own characteristics and produced its own problems. The 1992 version was the last to be produced on microfiche.

In 1994 it became available as part of the FamilySearch program, initially on CD and now online, and a whole new raft of possible pitfalls has been created. Before beginning your search online, click onto and read the *Tips on how to search the IGI* which appears at the top of the screen when you first enter the Advanced Search section and you should be able to avoid some of them. In the original articles I stressed the importance and significance of using the *Parish and Vital Records List* fiche, supplied with sets of purchased fiche, and the *Instructions for using the IGI* fiche, also supplied. How many present day researchers have access to these fiche, or take the trouble to search them out? Knowing that the answer is 'very few' in both cases, and that all the information they contain is not available with the online version, however hard you search, I make no apology for describing in some detail both what can be learnt from the *P&VRL* fiche and from the *Instructions* fiche about the information contained in the IGI. Lacking at least some knowledge is rather like trying to drive without knowing the Highway Code.

Much of the information contained in this chapter relates to the microfiche versions, which are still commonly used, together with comparisons to the online version. The microfiche editions commonly held by organisations and individuals are 1988 and 1992 (the last one to be issued). Sets of the earlier versions are still in use; treat them with caution. In the early 1980s versions a few parishes were given incorrect codes so that their entries appeared in the wrong counties. These errors were corrected in later editions but if your library or family history society still uses an old edition you could be caught out.

Parish & Vital Records List fiche

These fiche list, by county, the parishes and Nonconformist places of worship microfilmed for eventual inclusion in the IGI, together with the dates and events (christenings and marriages) covered and the source used for the information. **Not all the parish records listed as having been microfilmed are currently included in the IGI.** Records marked with a double asterisk have been microfilmed but are not necessarily included in the IGI edition you are searching. If you do not actively look for those **s you may think you have searched the records of a parish when in fact you have not. The list of microfilmed parishes used for the 1988 edition was repeated almost verbatim in 1992 (asterisks and all), so it can be very difficult to tell which parishes have been added to the IGI since 1988. For recent developments see details of the *British Isles Vital Records Index* later in this chapter.

The *P&VRL* fiche tell you the source from which the information was abstracted and the dates covered and this should always be checked. The 1988/1992 fiche tells you that baptisms for *Macclesfield St Michael* in Cheshire are in the IGI (from the parish registers) from 1712 to 1760 and from 1771 to 1812. The intervening 11 years are not missing; they were, for some reason, simply not included at the time of extraction. I know of two people, one of whom abandoned the research, the other who wasted time and money searching neighbouring parishes, because they did not check the *P&VRL* to spot the gaps in coverage. For many counties the source is Bishops' Transcripts rather than Parish Registers. All sets of BTs are incomplete but the *P&VRL* does not indicate gaps in these records - you may fail to locate an entry in the IGI, hunt far and wide, and then discover, on consulting the parish register, that your ancestor is there all the time but that, as the relevant BT is missing, there is no mention of him in the IGI.

IGI COVERAGE

The potential for locating birth/christening and marriage (but not normally death/burial) information on your ancestors within the IGI is immense (the above problems notwithstanding) but so is the likelihood of barking up completely the wrong tree. Remember that it is not the answer to all your family history problems. **The IGI is far from complete**. For some counties coverage is as high as 90%, for others (where there was resistance to the LDS microfilming programme) it may barely reach double figures. The author of one article I read adopted an ancestor *because this is the only possible entry on the IGI* - and that in a county with less than 20% coverage. Always check that both baptism and marriage entries for a parish are included; in some cases only one type of entry has as yet reached the IGI itself. It is not totally accurate: it contains errors and omissions, some stemming from mistakes in the original documents, others from mistakes in the transcription and inputting of these records. It is compiled from a variety of sources, some more reliable than others; some more complete than others. Also **be aware that, for many parishes, IGI coverage begins only in the early 18th century** whereas the parish registers may go back to the mid-16th century.

Until 1988 the majority of entries were taken from parish records, as part of the controlled extraction programme, and those put in by individual LDS members from their research were complete, including definite dates and specific churches. (Some experienced researchers still prefer to use this version.) From 1992, incomplete entries from individuals have been included so you may find '*John Smith*. Relative *Thomas Brown*. Male. Birth. About 1797 of *Stockport*'. Such dates and places can be extremely unreliable. As a rough guide, if a name in the online version is in capital letters it denotes an entry from the controlled extraction programme (with the batch number commonly beginning with C, J, M or P) or a complete entry from an LDS member. Note that P means the entry was extracted from a printed source, rather than the original record (see Chapter 17).

Lower case entries are generally submitted by LDS members but have not been verified and many, especially if the entry says *submitted after 1991*, are both incomplete and based more on assumption than known fact. If you look at a 1992 fiche you may see that people have, for instance, made the dangerous assumption that a birth/christening date is twenty one years before the marriage date they know; claimed a marriage date about a year before the known baptism of a child; and supposed that the person was born in the place where they later married. All these are pitfalls described elsewhere in this book. **The IGI is not something which can safely be tackled 'cold', without some knowledge of its strengths and weaknesses.**

THE INSTRUCTIONS FOR USING THE IGI FICHE

If you do have access to these fiche, it will pay you to look through them.

You can construct an entire family tree of many generations by sitting in front of a microfiche reader or computer, then uproot it when you check the entries with the original records and discover that the patriarch at the head of your tree died aged six months. **The *Instructions for using the IGI* fiche tell you that the use of the word 'Infant' or 'Child' in columns B & E on the fiche means the person died before the age of eight. Unfortunately there does not appear to be access to these columns in the online version.**

How many of you have puzzled over apparent duplicate entries, wondering whether your ancestor is the *Mary Smith* married in *Aldborough* [West Riding of Yorkshire] or the one married in *Aldbrough* [East Riding] on the same day, without realising that the two entries refer to the same person but are taken from two different sources (perhaps a PR and an individual's research) and a difference of one letter can create two different entries. Similarly, have you skimmed the list looking unsuccessfully for a *Frances,* but ignoring *Francis_,* who married *John Smith*: the line after the name indicating that the sex is different to what you would expect from the name? Both situations are explained in the **Instructions** fiche.

In 1992 an article in **Family Tree Magazine** concerning the occurrence of double-barrelled Christian names like *Major-Major* and *Squire-Squire* in the IGI sparked off a flurry of correspondence. If any of us had bothered to read the **Instructions** fiche, which clearly states that the appearance of such hyphenated names is a method used by the LDS church to denote uncertainty over the meaning of an entry (was Major being used as a rank or a Christian name?) and that they are not direct entries from parish registers, much time and speculation could have been saved. Almost 20 years on, the question as to their meaning still crops up regularly in family history publications. Other names which received the same treatment include *Prince, Doctor, Admiral, General* and *Parson.* The reason for the use of such names has never been agreed but it was probably an early form of 'social climbing' (see p.31).

The online version has not continued the hyphenation but, checking the first 50 instances of *Major Smith* and *Squire Smith* to confirm this, produced interesting results. There were 18 *Major Smiths* from the controlled extraction programme, with the other 32 all being entered by individual LDS members, and 21 *Squire Smiths* from the extraction programme, with 29 from individuals. The first five *Squire Smith* references were to the same baptism, with one entry from the extraction programme and four from individuals. The first two entries (including the extraction programme) gave the father's name as *John*, the other three gave the parents as *Timothy* and *Amy*. Whom do you believe?

Another trap into which you can fall: enter *Major Smith* into an **All Resources** search and the entries will appear in no apparent order, enter it into an **IGI only** search and they will be in chronological order.

TRANSCRIPTION ERRORS

Although computer generated, the IGI is compiled by humans from records created by humans so it will always contain errors and omissions. In the parish records, which provide the basis for the majority of entries in the IGI, incumbents and parish clerks made mistakes. Transcribers created new or incorrect names when they had difficulty reading the original documents or when faced with unfamiliar names. Search the IGI for *Eliph Robinson* and you will not find a trace of him under that name. You will find him born and christened in 1806 as *Elijah* (two separate entries created from the same PR entry which gave both date of birth and of baptism) and married in 1835 as *Cliff*; the original entries are clearly *Eliph/Eliff* but you can see why the transcribers had problems. Put *Eliph Robinson* into the IGI online and you will be referred to *Olive/Olivia*. *Mr Robinson*, incidentally, ended his life as *Eli* - another pitfall as *Eli* was a much more common name than *Eliph* - and, finding him as *Eli Robinson* in census returns and on his death certificate, you would have failed to find a baptism or marriage for him.

If you cannot locate an entry under the name you expect, write it out several times in varying handwriting styles and think how it might appear to someone unfamiliar with it. When checking entries for *Mottram-in-Longdendale* in Cheshire in the 1988 edition of the IGI against the original Registers it was apparent that many names had been misread. A poor quality private microfilm had been used for the extraction because the LDS Church had not been permitted to film in the county. Filming has since taken place and, in the 1992 edition, most of the errors have been corrected but quoting a few examples from 1988 will illustrate some of the pitfalls into which the transcribers fell, and may suggest ideas of where else you might look for missing entries. *Uright Halme* in the 1988 edition proved, in 1992, to be *Wright Hulme*. *Jonn Wilson Masmesley & Mary Ann Falkner* in 1988 are *John Wilson Walmesley* and *Mary Falkner Birchinough* in the PR (and 1992 IGI). Look at the original entries and, again, it is very easy to see how the mistakes were made. The writer of the PR had a distinctive style which, even with knowledge of the local surnames, can be extremely difficult to interpret. In particular, capitals *H & K*; *M & W*; *F & T, I & J* are very easily confused - not just in this parish but anywhere. The ***Instructions*** fiche warns of the pitfall of initial capital letters and quotes *Kerfoot* being misinterpreted as *Herfoot*. In *Mottram*, *Warhurst* emerged as: *Warhurst, Harhurst, Marchart, Marhurst* and *Narhurst*. **It is always worth checking surnames beginning with a range of letters - you may spot something vital**.

INDEXING PROBLEMS

Most LDS records are indexed using a 'soundex' system (devised in the USA in the 1930s; people whose names, although spelled differently, were grouped together because they 'sounded alike'). As you will see, this has advantages and disadvantages. In the IGI, both on fiche and online, a surname and its variants are usually said to be listed together so under *Leigh* (a common Cheshire surname) you will also find *Lea, Leah, Lee* and *Lees(e)* - although the variant *Legh* is indexed under *Legg* and *Lear* under itself. The exception is the 1981 edition in which, due to a computer error, all surnames were listed strictly alphabetically. However, the system is not as simple as it might seem at first glance and you should check each possible variant individually to make sure you have covered them all. All *Litton* entries in a county are grouped together. *Lytton* is an alternative spelling common in early parish registers when *i* and *y* were interchangeable - but it was some time before I realised that there were no *Lytton* entries mixed with the *Littons*. Look up *Lytton* and you will be referred to *Layton* under which it is indexed, along with *Leighton*. *Haywood* or *Hayward* (often interchangeable) is a common surname; under *Haywood* you will find *Heawood, Hewood* and *Heywood* but

Hayward, Heaward, Heaworth and *Heyward* will all be found under *Howard* (the presence or absence of the letter *r* determining where the variant is indexed). On the fiche there is no cross-reference with *Haywood* suggesting that you check *Hayward* (or *Howard*). There are 25 'see also' possibilities with *Howard* but *Haywood* is not one of them. **You need to keep your wits about you to make certain you cover every contingency**.

Another big pitfall - again described on the *Instructions* fiche - comes when an occupation and a surname become confused. Many of our ancestors did not use commas but were overfond of capital letters and it can be almost impossible to tell in a parish register whether *John Smith Cooper*, *Thomas Brown Chapman* or *Mary Jones Weaver* are people with two surnames or one surname and an occupation. The problem cuts both ways - in the IGI *John Smith, cooper* may be indexed under *Cooper* and *Thomas Brown Chapman* under *Brown*. If you fail to find an entry you are looking for but you know the person's occupation it is always worth looking under that.

APOSTROPHES AND PREFIXES

Apostrophes in the IGI can cause problems. The surname *I'Anson* spelt thus is indexed under *Ianson* in the fiche version; if originally spelt *Ianson* it is under *Anson*. *Frances I'Anson*, the *sweet lass of Richmond Hill* (in Yorkshire, not Surrey) was baptised at *Wensley* in 1766 but any search for her in the IGI under either variant given above will fail - the transcriber read the name as *Janson* so she is indexed under *Johnson* of which *Janson* is taken to be a variant. (However, you will find reference to her in the *Pedigree Resource File* section on FamilySearch.) In the fiche version, names beginning with *O* (like *O'Brien*) are easily located once you realise that they are all grouped together at the very beginning of the *O*s, immediately after the *N*s and before *Oades*. Similarly all the *Mac* entries are listed under *Mc* and positioned immediately after *Maz*, not where you might expect to find them after *Mab*. A word of warning: do not make the mistake of believing that because a surname includes *O* (or, to a lesser extent, *M[a]c*) in one generation it will do so in the next. It is always advisable to look for the name without the prefix (and to be prepared for variant spellings) - many an *O'Reilly* mutated to *Riley*. Conversely, one *Duffy* family from Ireland became *MacDuff* when they moved to Scotland so, if a family vanishes, it might be worth adding a prefix and searching again.

CHRISTIAN NAMES

Christian names is one area where the IGI online can simplify searching. Look at the online version and you may well find the *William Smith* you could not locate in the microfiche version (one of the original pitfalls). The online version will provide you in one search with entries for *William* and all possible variants. On the microfiche version you will have to check all possible spellings, set out in strict alphabetical and punctuation sequence, which include *Will, Will., William, Willm, Willm., Wm* and *Wm.* (I found 24 variations in Yorkshire) and do not forget that before 1733 the name may well be entered under *Gulielmus* (which can have almost as many variations as *William*). This is one instance where a full stop matters! Most names have alternative spellings - *Ann* and *Anne*, for example, are listed separately in the microfiche version with *Anna* between them. *Elizabeth* can rival *William* in its variety of spellings and abbreviations. *Elis.* and *Elizth.* may be many columns apart on the fiche, with *Elisabeth, Eliza, Elizabeth, Elizabetha* (before 1733) and many others - including unrelated Christian names like *Elisha* - between them. Again, in the microfiche version this is another case where a full stop matters, with a long list of *Eliz* entries in chronological order followed by an equally long list of *Eliz. .* Do not forget that a girl christened as *Betsy* or *Betty* may call herself *Elizabeth* when she marries, or vice versa. Also bear in mind that children with two Christian names will be found at the end of the list on the microfiche - girls called *Mary* will be named in chronological order, followed by *Mary Ann, Mary Anne, Mary Ellen, Mary Jane* and so on. In the online version they are all mixed together, with the addition of *Maria* and *Marie*.

Keep an eye on the guide names in large letters at the top of each frame of a fiche which enables you to keep track of the alphabetical ordering of surnames. Run your eye down the surnames on a frame, without checking the guide name, and it is easy to become disorientated, especially if variants outnumber the surname under which they are indexed. Years ago I had problems finding *Jessop* on the Yorkshire fiche because I found frames of *Jewison* and was convinced *Jessop* should be before these. Eventually, looking at the guide name, I discovered that *Jewison* is under *Jesson* (and so precedes *Jessop*). This problem does not occur online as entering *Jewison* will bring up the entries for both names (and other variants). Ticking *use exact spelling* will provide you with the *Jewison* entries only but be careful – there are currently 29 entries with the name spelt *Jewisson* which will not appear in the *Jewison* list.

BRITISH ISLES VITAL RECORDS INDEX

The second edition of this was produced on CD in 2002. It contains approximately 10½ million birth/christening records and almost two million marriage records. The records include many of the parish registers etc. marked with double **, and earlier entries for some parishes previously covered only after about 1720, both as described earlier in this chapter. **These records are not included in the IGI. They are currently included on the Record Search pilot available via FamilySearch;** this also contains information from a variety of other sources and individuals and is well worth consulting.

CHAPTER 8

CENSUS RETURNS 1801-1911

1801-1831

The first decennial census took place in the British Isles in 1801 (apart from Ireland, where the first census was 1821). The early censuses between 1801 and 1831 were concerned mainly with statistics and did not require personal information to be given. However, many of those responsible for gathering the statistics did so by recording details of the people in their areas and an increasing number of such 'returns' are being found in parish registers, parish chests, ROs, museums and libraries. It is always worth asking if a local repository has any such early census returns; you may find that they contain as much, if not more, information than the 1841 returns. *Colin Chapman's Pre-1841 Census & Population Listings in the British Isles* lists most known pre-1841 censuses, together with suggestions for many other lists of names which were compiled by church or state from the Domesday Book onwards and which just may have survived for the parish or village in which you are interested.

1841 ONWARDS

The possibilities of finding vital information about your ancestors in census returns are endless; the pitfalls are legion. The returns most used by family historians are those for 1841-1911 for England, Wales, Scotland, the Channel Islands and the Isle of Man, to which the general points made in these articles relate. What you learn, however, and how accurate or complete the information is, can be governed by which 'source' you use to search the returns.

Almost all the returns for Ireland in these years were destroyed either in the 1922 conflagration in Dublin (1821-1851) or by government order (1861-1891). However, the 1901 and 1911 returns for Ireland survive and are available to search.

CENSUS RETURNS: AVAILABLE IN SEVERAL FORMATS

Many people who are just beginning their research will head straight to online sites. The 1881 census can be searched for free online; almost all sites offering the other returns are commercially orientated. On some you can consult the indexes for free but you will usually have to pay (either by subscription or via pay-per-view) to read a transcription or view the original census page. **Be aware that the quality of the transcription on the major commercial sites is not uniform**. Everything can depend on how good the transcribers were, whether they could read 19th century handwriting, and how well they knew the place-names in the areas they were working on (see the chapters on *The IGI* and *Indexes & Indexing* for some of the problems encountered). If you fail to find an ancestor where you expect, it will pay you to check at least one other site where you may find another (correct) interpretation of a name or place. One site has *Unthank* transcribed as *Nuthank* (see *Reversed Letters Syndrome* p.22) and *Vessey* on one site appears as *Nefsey* on another (see p.102).When downloading a census page, which you are paying for, it can be fatal to economise and to print out just the single page. If the family you want is the last one on a folio and ends with, say, a two year old child, do not make the mistake of assuming that this is the complete family. On the next page you may find other family members, from grandparents to grandchildren. Similarly, if your complete-looking family is at the top of a folio, look at the previous page to make sure that the head of the household is not living in the same building as, or the one next door to, his parents or siblings.

Census returns are also available on CD, in microform, or in book form and many libraries, record offices, family history societies and individuals hold copies in these formats, particularly for their own areas. Those on CD or microform can often provide more information more easily than can be found on online sites. The 1881 census is available both on CDs and on microfiche and it is possible to 'dig deeper' into the returns with less effort and knowledge than is required to find an answer online (see *Mary Ann Shaw* p.43). Most transcriptions and indexes were produced by individuals and family history societies before the arrival of the internet and these can still be very valuable. In addition to commonly knowing the names in their area, and therefore often being more accurate in that sense, they will tell you which piece numbers they cover and will often give, in full, the details of the individual enumerators' routes, which are included at the beginning of the returns for each Registration District but are not included 'on the surface' of the online sites. In most cases, the information is there but, unless you are an experienced computer user, it can take a considerable amount of time (and frustration) to dig deep enough to find it. The value of these enumerators' routes is described later in the chapter (see p.63 and p.72).

BACKGROUND

As with almost all new legislation, the first attempts to implement the census showed up flaws in the system. Most of these were dealt with as succeeding censuses were ordered but some were never fully rectified and the human element (what individual enumerators were prepared to do or undergo to carry out their instructions) should always be borne in mind. Remember that the purpose of the censuses was to enable the government to collect various sets of statistics relating to the population - its growth or decline, age, movement, occupations and so on. The fact that the method chosen to do this - listing almost everyone in the British Isles by name and in families or households - happened to produce information of value to family historians is an incidental bonus.

Pitfalls in census returns are plentiful but many can be avoided by doing some homework first. Books on tracing your ancestors should all deal with how to use the census returns, and some of the problems encountered, but if you read *Making Sense of the Census: Census Records for England and Wales 1801-1901 Revisited* by *Edward Higgs* (2005) and *Making Use of the Census* by *Susan Lumas*, both published by TNA, you will be in a much better position to find your way round the returns. It will also pay you to read the chapter on *Indexes and Indexing* (p.39).

ANCESTORS WHO MAY NOT BE RECORDED

The early census returns listed only those resident in the British Isles. If, during the 19th century, your ancestor was a soldier in barracks (or under canvas) on home soil he should be recorded by name in the census in the usual manner; if serving overseas he will appear only as a statistic because the military authorities provided the government with a head-count of officers, other ranks, and dependents of those stationed abroad but did not list their names until 1911. Similarly, in 1841 and 1851 those serving in the Royal Navy who were on shore on census night were recorded by name but those on board ship or at sea survive only as statistics; from 1861 their names and details were recorded.

The 1841 census contained less detail than later ones and no provision was made for recording the names of several groups. As well as those off-shore in the armed services, if your ancestor was in the merchant marine, at sea on a fishing boat, on a barge, tramping the country looking for work and sleeping in a barn or under a hedge, or even a nightworker on shift, you are unlikely to find him listed by name because he did not form part of a standard household at midnight on census night. Provision was made for some of these groups to be named in later censuses but several are still unrecorded (except as statistics) in 1851 and some, itinerants and travellers in particular, evaded the enumerators throughout the 19th century. There were always some who made a 'protest vote' by avoiding being enumerated, including a number of suffragettes in 1911.

THE CENSUS 'RETURNS'

Do not forget that, with the exception of the 1911 census, the 'census returns' which we view today in microform or online are not the original household schedules which your ancestors filled in, and which do not survive. Our 'returns' are the enumerators' books, into which they copied information from the forms. The books were then forwarded to London for clerks to extract the required statistical information. As soon as you realise this you should be prepared for the returns to contain unforced errors.

Did your ancestors fill in the form by themselves (often with help from one of their children who could read and write where their parents could not) or with assistance from the enumerator or a neighbour. The form may have been filled in by the householder in an almost illegible scrawl. The enumerator may have filled it in while standing on the doorstep as a harassed mother tried to remember exactly where her twelve children were born. He may have discovered when transcribing a form into his book that half the questions were unanswered or entered into the wrong columns, or even that he had collected forms from some houses which were not in his district. Pitfalls galore for the contemporary enumerator, from which he had to extricate himself by using his initiative and hoping no-one in authority would notice a few discrepancies. For the 1911 census, it is the original household schedules which have survived, not the enumerators' books.

There are other reasons why an individual or a family may not be recorded in a particular census. In rural areas (and certainly in the Pennines) there are instances where a remote house is missing from one set of returns. Perhaps the form was not delivered because the enumerator was unaware the house was there; or it was not collected either because the family had gone to market and there was no one at home, or it was several miles away and pouring with rain and the enumerator's horse had gone lame. Plot the route taken by the enumerator for the previous and succeeding censuses, compare it with the Ordnance Survey map, and it can become obvious which farm was missed and why. In such rural areas, successive schedules entered in the enumerator's book were not necessarily next door neighbours; the two households could be an hour's walk apart.

In poorer parts of industrial cities it must have been very difficult at times to ascertain how many people were actually living in a crowded cellar - especially when beds were occupied on a shift system. The enumerator was given his area but he was responsible for working out how many buildings were occupied and by how many families (or households) and the accuracy of his survey would depend to some extent on how conscientious he was. There were buildings into which individual enumerators were not prepared to venture because of the likelihood of receiving physical abuse from the occupants and how many faced (and tackled) the problem encountered by this London enumerator in 1841:

The Houses in Jane Place are occupied principal[ly] by Prostitutes who denied ...that any male had slept therein on Sunday night ... However upon careful enquiry among neighbours, he [the enumerator] ascertained that not less than 12 or 14 males (whose ages varied from 20 to 50 years) had abided in the said Jane Place on the night of the 6th inst.

The enumerator (male until 1891, in which year women could first be enumerators) was given a certain area to cover - usually around 200 houses in an urban area or 15 miles in the countryside, both of which it was considered could be walked in a day - but how he achieved this was left largely to his discretion. In towns or cities you may find that a long street is split between several enumeration districts - read the description of the area covered which is given at the beginning of each district to see if it is stated that only part of, or one side of (see p.72), the street is being covered (or was built at the time). Work out whether he walked straight along a main road, then went back and covered all the side roads, courts and cellars, or whether he turned off every few yards to deal with a 'side issue'; if the latter, it was all too easy to miss the occasional house on the main road. Check the schedule numbers in the first column on the left of the page (not to be confused with the house numbers in the next column) to make sure the run is complete. Most enumerators, but not all, apparently put their schedules in order before making up their books but if a form was collected at a later date, or if two sheets stuck together and this was not noticed at the time, you may find the details entered, out of order, at the end of the book. Also at the end of the district you may find separate returns for larger institutions - prisons, hospitals, workhouses, barracks, schools - and for ships or boats which were moored in the area on census night.

MISSING ENTRIES

Once the statistical data had been extracted the returns were stored in unsatisfactory conditions and some were damaged. If you fail to find the family, or the address, you want, this may be the reason. Damaged pages were not always microfilmed but they may survive and be readable under ultra-violet light and a few folios were also accidentally omitted during micro-filming so it is always worth checking with TNA to see if this could be the case. Some piece numbers (which each contain returns from several enumeration districts) are permanently lost. For example, for the 1861 census 16 piece numbers do not survive at all and sections of another 81 are missing; details of these (and missing sections from other censuses) are being noted and can be found on a number of websites. In other cases, the first or last pages of a book may be missing. The folio numbers (top right hand corner of odd-numbered pages), which are the numbers commonly used when indexing the census, were stamped on by the Public Record Office when the enumerators' books came into their hands. They started foliating from the first surviving page and do not take account of any pages which were missing by that stage. Look at the printed page number (at the top of the page in the centre) and if folio 1 is stamped on, say, page 10 you will know that some pages are missing. At the end of the book, if you find a prison or workhouse with very few entries, and more staff than inmates, you can be fairly sure that pages are lost.

RELATIONSHIPS IN THE CENSUS

Were the households which the enumerator recorded in his book always what they appear to be or did your ancestors lay traps (deliberately or otherwise) for him and for you?

The following, from the 1841 census, looks like a standard family of parents and children, all born in Cheshire:

James Bann   *(40)*
Ann Bann   *(30)*
Samuel Bann   *(15)*
George Bann   *(13)*
Mary Bann   *(10)*
James Bann   *(7)*
Ellen Bann   *(5)*
Ann Bann   *(4)*
Alice Bann   *(3)*

Bear in mind that the 1841 census gave less information than later ones, with only one Christian name recorded, no relationship stated between members of the household, ages of those aged 15 and over supposedly 'rounded down' to the nearest 5 years below, and the question about places of birth asking only if people were born in the county or country in which they were then living.

All the above 'family' was born in Cheshire and the ages of *James* (41), *Ann* (33) and *Samuel* (17) were correctly 'lowered' but little else is as it seems. *James* and *Ann* were living together but did not marry until 1844. The first four children belonged to *James'* first marriage (his first wife died in 1833); the next two were *Ellen* and *Ann Beard*, actually aged 10 and 8, children of Ann's first marriage; *Alice* was the child of *James* and *Ann*, registered in 1838 as their legitimate child. As if that is not enough pitfalls, *James* had two older sons, aged 23 and 20, who had already left home. If you fall into the trap of assuming that *James* and *Ann* are husband and wife and parents of the seven children, you would not consider that there could be older children. We shall never know whether *James* or *Ann* gave false names and ages for the two young *Beards* or whether the enumerator when filling in his book thought a mistake had been made and 'rationalised' them into what appeared a normal sequence.

The couple I took to be *James'* parents were living in the next village - *Thomas Bann* (58) and *Mary Bann* (61) (this enumerator ignored the 'round down' recommendation) - until I looked them up in the 1851 census to find them described as *Thomas Bann*, head of family, unmarried, aged 69, and *Mary*, sister, unmarried, aged 73. **It is never safe to assume relationships in the 1841 census.**

From 1851 onwards, relationships were stated but were linked specifically to the *Head of the Family* (generally the person to whom the schedule for the house was delivered) and can easily be misinterpreted. If the head was a man, all his children should be described as his sons and daughters but do not assume that his present wife was necessarily their mother. Family members whom we should today describe as *step* relatives were most commonly listed as *in laws*. [see p.36] Be wary of accepting any relationship at its face value in modern terms. If a married man of 50 describes a woman of 80 as *mother-in-law* she may be his wife's mother (as we would normally expect) but equally she may be his *step-mother*.

In 1881 *John* and *Anna Baker*, aged 46 and 36, were living in Yorkshire with seven children ranging from 20 years to 6 months - again, what looks like a normal family is an illusion. *Anna* (actually *Hannah*) is *John*'s third wife; the first two had both been called *Ann* and three of the children were born to the second wife (*John*'s children, *Anna*'s step-children but this is impossible to detect from the census return). According to the enumerator's book all the children were born in Staffordshire; true except for the youngest who was born in Yorkshire in 1880 (see p.87). Again, whose mistake - the informant or the enumerator?

When the wife has children from a previous marriage this can often be detected - but watch for unexpected pitfalls. In 1861 *William* and *Sarah Chamberlain*, aged 26 and 36, were living in Warwickshire, with children *Rebecca* (12), *Samuel* (8) and *Martha* (4) all bearing the surname *Cater* and described as *daughters-in-law* and *son-in-law* to *William*, and a baby, *Sarah Chamberlain*, described as their daughter. Their mother, *Sarah*, had previously been married to *Samuel Cater* and it appears from the return that the three older children all belong to her first husband and are *William*'s step-children. Appearances can be deceptive. *Martha* was not *Samuel*'s child; she was almost certainly *William*'s. As I later discovered, she was born on 11th January 1857, three and a half years after *Samuel* was killed in a mining accident (see p.90), and registered on the 29th as the illegitimate daughter of *Sarah Cater*. Four days later *William Chamberlain* and *Sarah Cater* married and on 7th March *Martha* was baptised as *Martha Chamberlain*. When it came to filling in the census form, however, they used *Martha*'s registered name and I fell headlong into the trap of assuming she was *Samuel Cater*'s daughter.

Thomas Chamberlain, *William*'s father, married *Martha Randle* in 1831 but was not at home in the 1851 census, when *Martha* was described as head of the household and married, with *William* aged 14 and five other siblings living with her. Twenty five years ago, I did not see anything unusual in the fact that *Thomas* was not at home on 30 March 1851 or that *Martha*, a married woman, was described as the family's head. (Female heads of households are generally widows or spinsters.) Incidentally, on the *1851 British Census CD* (covering Devon, Norfolk and Warwickshire only; published by the LDS in 1997) *Martha* is wrongly described as a widow - at the risk of labouring the point, **always check the original return; transcriptions, like indexes, are fallible**.

Many years later I learnt that *Thomas* was transported to Australia for 10 years in 1844 for the theft of a wether teg (two year old castrated ram), made his way back to England probably in 1853, found his wife had died of TB, and discovered that, in addition to the five children he had left behind, there was another one born in 1848 (and listed in the 1851 census as *Martha*'s daughter). It was discovering the late baptism of this child which provided the vital clue to *Thomas*'s story. *Martha* died in March 1852 and her daughter was baptised on 2 January 1853 as:

Susanna bastard child of Martha Chamberlain of Bedworth, weaver.
NB The mother of this child is dead. Her husband is a Transport. He was not the father of their child.

By 1861 *Thomas* had remarried and was living with his second wife and their child, with no-one else in the household.

James Bann and his son *Samuel, Hannah Baker, Samuel Cater, Sarah Chamberlain* (late *Cater* formerly *Randle*) and *Thomas Chamberlain* all married twice; *John Baker* and *Ann Bann* both married three times. **Remember that second and third marriages were commonplace**, as many women died in childbirth and men in work-related accidents or from occupational diseases. **Do not fall into the trap of believing that a man's wife in the census is necessarily the mother of all his children**.

Watch for the situation where a son and his family are living in the same house as his father; the son's children will usually be described as grandchildren to the head of the house but some enumerators treated each family unit separately when assessing relationships so you may apparently find a 75 year old head, with sons apparently ranging from 50 years down to two - possible but unlikely. You may find that the words *in law* are omitted from spouses of sons and daughters living in the parental house so that they appear as children of the head. Also be aware of the situation where a married daughter (possibly with her children) is living with her parents but without her husband. Enumerators, who were encouraged to put ditto marks for repeat surnames in a household, sometimes 'lost' the daughter's married surname in this way; it is always worth keeping an eye on the 'Condition' column and, if a daughter is described as married, being suspicious if she still appears to bear her maiden surname.

The term *nurse child* (see p.38) is often the equivalent of *foster child*. In 19th century census returns the term usually applies to a young child living in a separate household from its parent(s). An infant might be temporarily 'boarded out' with neighbours or relatives if a new sibling had been born and the mother could not cope (look at nearby schedules to see if this could be the case). It is worth checking later census returns to see if the child is still living with the same family - and whether it retains its original surname or has 'adopted' the surname of its 'new' family (see p.28).

In the census returns of 1841 and 1861 each house was marked by // and each family within that house by / (from 1871 \\ and \ were used) so, in theory, it should be possible to work out separate groups living in the same house but it was all too easy for the enumerator to put a / against the wrong line or to leave it out. In 1851 the enumerator was instructed instead to draw a line under the first four columns to separate each house and from half way across column 2 and under columns 3 and 4 to show different groups within that house. This obviously involved more effort, so probably less accuracy, and was not repeated.

BOARDERS AND LODGERS

The position of boarders and lodgers within houses is a vexed one which appears never to have been properly understood by enumerators. It was intended (certainly from 1861 onwards) that a distinction should be drawn between *boarders*, who ate with the family, and *lodgers*, who just rented a room, or part of one, and should be separated from the main household by /, but it is obvious that in many cases neither enumerator nor householder appreciated the difference. In some boarding houses, lodgers were listed as either weekly or nightly lodgers. All that can safely be said is that it always pays to note any boarders, lodgers or servants within a house as they may well turn out (particularly the boarders) to be relatives of the family they are living with, especially if they are born in the same area as someone in the family. The 'extended family' was the norm and if one family group made a success of life in a new area, relatives tended to follow and stay with them until they could establish themselves independently.

COULD YOUR ANCESTORS ANSWER THE QUESTIONS TRUTHFULLY?

Where did your parents meet? In what year did you pass your driving test? How many brothers and sisters did your mother have? If you do not have instant recall of all the answers, spare a thought for your ancestors. They were asked questions on the census form, and by the enumerator, which they found just as difficult (if not impossible) to answer correctly. Many also thought the questions were intrusive - why did the government want to know how old they were and where they were born? - so they were 'economical with the truth'. **Where possible, check as many sets of census returns as you can for your ancestors. They may have given incorrect information in one census but revealed the true facts in others**. In 1861, *Daniel Wild* and his wife, *Esther*, living in *Mellor* in Derbyshire, both said that they were born there but in 1851 and 1871 they said (correctly) that they were born respectively in *Biggin* and in *Edale* in Derbyshire. Relying on the one inaccurate return would have made it extremely difficult to locate *Daniel's* baptism which took place at *Hartington*, two miles from *Biggin* but 20 miles away from *Mellor*.

Much depends on who answered the questions - a husband might not know where his wife was born, a wife might be unaware of her husband's exact age, a child could be ignorant of information about its parents or grandparents, and a 'guesstimate' would have to serve for the elderly relative with a failing memory who lived with them. Until I needed a birth certificate in my teens, I believed that I was born in the village where I was brought up whereas I was actually born in the town, 26 miles away, where my mother's parents were living (and, in times past, it was very common for a young wife to return to her mother's home for the birth of her first child). Similarly, until I researched my family history and discovered that they were born in the same year, I believed that my grandmother was three years older than my grandfather. If a 19th century enumerator had relied on my answers to those questions, both would have been unintentionally wrong.

PLACES OF BIRTH

Incorrect information was often given to the enumerators because people genuinely did not know the right answers to the questions and had no means of finding them but there were many instances where they could have told the truth but chose not to. The information given was supposed to be confidential but, then as now, many mistrusted the government's intentions. Some, particularly the elderly, apparently thought it prudent to say that they were born where they were then living to avoid any possibility of being 'removed', under the laws of settlement, to their place of birth which could be hundreds of miles away. Others found it easier to say that all their children were born in one place, rather than trying to remember the precise village for each one. People sometimes did not know their place of birth but did know their place of baptism and gave this instead.

Some found it simpler to 'rationalise' their birthplace to the parish or the nearest town or city. If you cannot easily locate an entry for an ancestor in the parish registers for a place of birth given in the census, it is always worth checking whether it was an 'umbrella' which sheltered other places. In 1831 the **parish** of *Halifax* in Yorkshire had a population of 109,899 living in 23 townships and chapelries but only 15,382 of these were living in the **township** of *Halifax*. However, for people born in the parish but living far away, it was easier to say, or write, *Halifax* than *Hipperholme-cum-Brighouse* or *Rastrick* (names familiar to lovers of brass band music). How often, if you are asked in conversation today, 'where do you come from', do you start with the country (if on holiday abroad), followed by the county, then by the nearest town/city, and only then by the village if it appears that the questioner knows the area you are talking about?

A few people doubtless amended their places of birth as they grew up. *On a ship at sea*, *in a barn* and *not known* were not birth locations which many would choose to carry through life. *Mrs Mary Ann Shaw* (see p.43) maintained that she was *born in a stage coach between Nottingham and Derby* - a truthful answer but one of little use to anyone trying to find her baptism or where her

69

family lived and it begs the question of whether she could honestly answer the 1841 question which required a precise county of birth. Many told the truth but, being illiterate, had no means of verifying what was written down phonetically. The effect which pronunciation can have on placenames has been dealt with previously. The Kent enumerator who interpreted *Scampston*, said by a Yorkshireman, as *Skamtea*; the Yorkshire man who 'heard' two Shropshire places as *Arcale [Ercall]* and *Asifolk*; the Devon migrant who said his birthplace of *Woolfardisworthy* as *Woolsery* and the Londoner who translated *Hendrebiffa* in Flint as *Nendrebisa* were all doing their best but inadvertently creating pitfalls for future family historians.

AGES

Relying on data from one census return for your ancestor's place of birth is risky; accepting the ages given in census returns as accurate is even more so. As *Edward Higgs* says, in his book (see p.62) ... *the ages reported in the census must be regarded as only rough approximations of fact.*

John Hinchliffe was baptised on 28 May 1798. In 1841 he was *42* and correctly given as *40* on the census return (see p.65), in 1851 his age was given as *48*, in 1861 as *66*, in 1871 as *76*. Were the inconsistencies deliberate or not?

Do not fall into the trap of approaching the question from a modern standpoint, where your age is well documented and hard to conceal. Many of our ancestors, especially those born before 1837, could not remember in which year they were born and, with no pension or 'age concessions' to look forward to as they grew older, they generally did not need to know. Many others 'adjusted' their ages to fit their circumstances. A woman marrying a man younger than herself could knock years off her age and her husband need never find out; a 17 year old youth wanting to marry could say he was 'of full age' and retain that four year discrepancy for the rest of his life; a young man seeking employment might add years to make himself appear more experienced; an older man looking for work might take years off to appeal to a prospective employer and these 'white lies' would appear in the census returns to be accepted as true ages by their descendants.

It was also common practice to refer to someone as being, for example, *in their fortieth year*; this meant they were aged 39 but it was often interpreted by enumerators and clergymen as 40. Similarly, when someone said they were *'about 50'*, this tended to be written down as *50* - ages ending in 0 and, to a lesser extent, in 5 are often suspect (on certificates and in parish registers as well as on census returns). Ages were often estimated and the older a person was, the wider the gap between belief and reality tended to be. Many records contain references to centenarians, who often turn out to have been 'only' in their eighties or nineties. The son of *John Hinchliffe*, mentioned above, when registering his father's death in April 1877, gave his age as *85* whereas in fact he was *78* (two years older than he had claimed to be in

1871). Is it coincidence that there had been an older brother *John*, who died as an infant but would have been 85 in 1877?

OCCUPATIONS

Occupations in the census, like ages, can be misleading. Words change their meanings: a *clerk* may mean a man in Holy Orders and not an office worker. A man described today as a *printer* will commonly work with paper and books but, in the census, is more likely to have been printing patterns onto material in a mill. A *mechanic* in the 19th century would usually be working in a factory or mill and operating a machine of some sort. Similarly an *engine man* would not be working on the railways but operating a machine, and a *millman* would not have ground corn but would have been a factory worker. A *blacksmith* may have been operating the village smithy but could equally be working down the mines, maintaining the pit ponies and equipment. In many cases a word could have two distinct meanings, often dependent on whether it is found in a rural or urban census return. A *crofter* could be either a tenant farmer or a textile worker who bleached cloth; a *cropper* could be a tenant farmer (paid with a share of the crop) or a textile worker who sheared the nap from cloth. *Prostitutes, pickpockets* and *pensioners* were as likely to describe themselves as (financially) 'Independent' as to name their professions.

Scholar did not mean, as it would today, that a child was 'enjoying' full-time education. As with ages, *Edward Higgs* says *the definition of the term 'scholar' in the census instructions* [1851] *was vague and became vaguer over time*. A child (over the age of five) might be attending school regularly; working in a factory and (supposedly) attending school for a limited number of hours per week as required by the Factory Acts; learning a trade like lace-making (instruction in this could be taken to mean 'learning' and equated with school); or attending Sunday school. The term was very much open to interpretation.

Pitfalls and possibilities galore: anyone who has filled in a market research questionnaire will know just how difficult it can be to remember what you bought where and when, and how much it cost. Remember that our ancestors had just the same problems answering the enumerator's questions and (even if they could read) they did not have to hand all the paper records which we take for granted.

A CAUTIONARY TALE

In the 1841 census *Thomas Dews*, a *mechanic*, was living with *Rachel* (whom I knew to be his second wife; I had no idea of his first wife's name) and children (from his first marriage) *Edwin* and *Sarah* aged 11 and 8. I knew from the 1851 census that *Edwin* had been born in *Ossett* so the next move was clearly to check the PRs where I found *Edwin* (baptised 29 March 1830) and *Sarah* (baptised 17 June 1832), children of *Thomas and Ellen Dews, clothier*. Their ages fitted perfectly for a census taken on 6 June 1841 so I had no hesitation in accepting them, looking next for the marriage of *Thomas* and *Ellen*, then their baptisms. Much later, looking at earlier years in the same PR, I spotted baptisms for *Edwin* (13 September 1829) and *Sarah Ann* (31 July 1831) children of *Thomas and Ann Dews, machine maker*, and this proved to be 'my' *Edwin*. With the benefit of hindsight and experience, I now know that I fell into at least five traps by accepting, without further thought, the first likely entries I found. No prizes for deciding what they are but, if you can figure them out, you should be able to avoid the same pitfalls in your own researches.

RESOLUTIONS:

I will remember that the quality of both CDs and online sites is variable. Some provide extremely good images of the original documents, some are of poor quality (especially of the 1841 census, which was written in pencil). Transcriptions are equally variable. I will always, if possible, check census returns for more than one year to verify whether consistent information is given.

I will accept that my ancestors often could not, or would not, provide truthful answers to the questions on the census form.

I will read the cautionary tale above and see just how easy it is to make mistakes.

AN ENUMERATOR'S ROUTE IN HARROGATE IN 1851

Piece number HO 107 2282: Folios 357-372:
All that part of the Ecclesiastical District of Bilton with Harrogate comprised in Central Harrogate including Beulah Place, Queen's Place, Chapel Court, Prospect View, Prospect Villa, Prospect Hill, the whole of the East side of Parliament Street, Chapel Street (both sides) including all Courts and Yards not named behind the last mentioned Street, Strawberry dale and Cheltenham Place.

Note: *Prospect Place and all cottages behind the same* are on the next enumerator's route (folios 373-386); *the **West** side of Parliament Street* is four routes further on, on folios 434-443 (see p.64).

CHAPTER 9

CIVIL REGISTRATION IN ENGLAND & WALES

Most standard written works, and many websites, on researching your family history explain the history and development of the system of civil registration and its records. They describe the main differences between the national General Register Office and local Register Offices (based on Registration Districts), and their respective indexes. Online access to the national and local indexes to the records of civil registration (which are principally birth, marriage and death certificates) changes almost weekly, as more go online via both free and commercial websites (see p.77), so make sure that you are looking at a current site.

THE GENERAL REGISTER OFFICE

The origins of both the GRO and local register offices can be found in the 1836 Acts of Parliament which established the registration service; in 1970 the GRO became part of the Office of Population Censuses and Surveys (OPCS); in 1996, following another merger, this became part of the Office for National Statistics (ONS); and, since April 2008, the GRO is now part of the Identity and Passport Service (IPS), which is an executive agency of the Home Office. This series of name changes is not really a pitfall but you do need to be aware of the various acronyms as they will crop up in books and on websites and could confuse you. Official government websites will direct you to the IPS site but many other sites have not been updated. It is well worth looking through the answers to FAQ on the IPS site. Note that the GRO's postal address (Smedley Hydro, Trafalgar Road, Birkdale, Southport PR8 2HH) is unchanged.

GRO (NATIONAL) INDEXES

From the beginning of civil registration on 1st July 1837 quarterly indexes (three months in arrears, so the first index volumes cover July to September 1837) to Births, Deaths and Marriages have been maintained; handwritten volumes from 1837-1865, typescript ones thereafter. The indexes were compiled from details submitted by local register offices (see below). From the March quarter of 1866 age at death is included in the deaths indexes. From the September quarter of 1911 onwards, the mother's maiden surname is included in the births indexes; and from the March quarter of 1912 a wife's maiden surname is given alongside her husband's name (and his surname against her entry) in the marriage indexes. In 1984 the system of indexing by Quarter was dropped, since when volumes have covered a year's events.

A point worth noting: until 1851 the forms provided for the clergy to make their copy certificates for the GRO included four marriages on one page (in 1852 this was reduced to two although some clergy continued to use the old forms until their supplies ran out). This can cause problems when searching the indexes for a marriage between a couple who both bear common (for the relevant area) surnames. With eight surnames on the page it is possible to find an apparent match in the index which, on ordering the certificate and receiving a negative response, turns out to be the groom from one marriage on the page and the bride from another.

Years ago, if a family historian wanted to consult these indexes in person there was no alternative to a visit to London as the only available set of indexes was the one kept originally at Somerset House, later (from 1973) at St Catherine's House and finally (1997-2007) at the Family Records Centre. Many books and websites still refer to them as the *St Catherine's House Indexes* but they are generally known today as the *GRO Indexes*. Today, the volumes can no longer be seen by researchers but their contents can be seen on microfilm or microfiche in many repositories throughout the world and online on many websites. This increased availability makes it possible for many more people to have access to the indexes but it also creates a new range of pitfalls and problems which need to be borne in mind.

There are some differences between the original set of bound indexes and the various available sets of microform (film or fiche) and online indexes. Without going into too much detail, the LDS church microfilmed the indexes more than 30 years ago, using the manuscript indexes to 1865 and the typed ones from 1866 onwards; all their Family History Centres should hold copies of at least some sections of this filming. **Microfilms** supplied by the GRO in the 1980s also used the early manuscript indexes. However, a typed copy of the pre-1866 indexes was prepared, presumably during their re-typing programme in the 1970s; this contained less information, for example giving initials only for second names, and was used when the **microfiche** version was made.

The set of bound indexes was manually amended when incorrect or omitted entries were reported, verified and accepted by the GRO (and errors and omissions are still being found) but the microform copies, taken from masters made years ago, will obviously not include recent alterations. Also, on checking two incorrect entries, both reported to the GRO and amended in the bound indexes (see pp.21 & 83), on both **FreeBMD** (see p.77) and assorted commercial sites it is clear that these amendments have not been picked up and most online indexes still show only the incorrect names. Amendments and insertions were made in the indexes by putting a mark or a cross against either the incorrect entry or where a name had been omitted and hand-writing the correct version at the bottom of the page (some pages have several such entries); only by using a site which takes you straight to an image of the complete page of the GRO index volume, rather than routing you through a digital index, will you find the corrected entries. Even then, your problems may not be over. The *Cyril/Sybil* confusion (see p.83) is amended but the RD and number (*Pontefract* 9c) has become *Kennington* 9c, and trying to order a certificate with this reference would result in a rejection of the application.

A few repositories hold complete sets of the microform indexes but most (including LDS Family History Centres, record offices, libraries and a few family history societies) hold only partial sets. It is always advisable to check covering dates in advance of a visit, and to remember that at many repositories it is essential to book a microform reader in advance and that your time on it may be limited to an hour or two per day. If searching online you are advised to ascertain which 'set' of indexes has been used on any particular site.

Since the withdrawal from circulation of the index volumes, complete sets of the indexes to 2007 are available on microfiche at *TNA Kew, City of Westminster Archives Centre, Birmingham Central Library, Bridgend Reference and Information Library, Greater Manchester CRO* and *Plymouth Central Library.* Also available at these repositories are indexes to Overseas BMD 1761-2007 (see **Miscellaneous Returns** p.90) and Adoptions 1927-2007. These locations receive updates to the indexes for you to view in person. This system is expected to continue until free online access (long promised but frequently delayed) can be provided.

THE 'UNKNOWNS' SECTIONS IN THE GRO INDEXES

Many, perhaps most, researchers are not aware that, in many quarterly births and all quarterly deaths volumes, there is another section, following the A-Z names sections, covering *Unknowns*, people whose details were unknown to the person registering the event. Most of the births are concerned with abandoned babies and foundlings (and many of them feature in the *unknown deaths* in the same quarter) but *unknown deaths* are registered on a far larger scale than is generally realized. It becomes apparent that, particularly in the 19th century, some people just 'disappeared' and their deaths will never be explained so do not make the mistake of assuming that your ancestor's death must be registered by name in the RD you expect. In 1865, for example, there are 26 pages, of 40 entries each, of *Unknown* people's deaths being registered. This means that over 1000 bodies were found in that year alone and not identified. As communications and means of identification increased, the number of *Unknowns* decreased - in 1984 there were 48, in 2006 there were 3 (2 male, 1 female). Deaths were predominantly of males (and before 1866 no ages were given; after that some ages were guessed at but many left blank) and around half of the deaths were registered in coastal regions. If you cannot find a death for an ancestor it could be worth a look at this section in case, even with the sparse information provided, you can make a connection. Journeymen, travellers, pedlars, soldiers, sailors, fishermen - men who left home to work or find work and were never heard from again - could well end up dying, through illness or by accident, a long way from home and never be identified. Remember particularly that men who worked at sea were often far from home and a look at local newspapers or local history websites for a coastal RD with several deaths in one quarter may reveal the names of ships which sank off the coast and which you just may recognize as coming from your missing ancestor's home port.

LOCAL REGISTER OFFICE INDEXES

From 1837, local registrars (registrars of sub-districts) had to send hand-written copies of all certificates they had issued in the previous three months to their superintendent registrars, for checking and onward transmission to the Registrar General, whose office then compiled a quarterly national index (see above). When their register books (births and deaths), from which these copies had been made, were full the books had to be delivered to the superintendent registrar, *who shall cause Indexes of the Register Books in his Office to be made* (and these local indexes are increasingly becoming available online). See below for more on local register offices.

Some websites class these local indexes as 'primary sources', because they were usually compiled from the original register books, and the GRO indexes as 'secondary sources', pointing out that errors inevitably creep in each time records are copied. It is worth noting that the regulations issued for registrars state *It is not absolutely necessary that the Registrar should himself make out the Copies. He may employ a Copyist, if he see fit.* This covers the copies of birth and death certificates to be sent quarterly to the GRO. How many superintendent registrars used a copyist to compile the indexes *he shall cause ... to be made* and how many indexes were compiled months, if not years, later? In both cases, bear in mind the handwriting problems described elsewhere in this chapter. Local indexes can be more accurate than the national ones but some of them are at least one stage removed from being 'primary' sources.

You also need to remember that it was the registrar's duty (not always fulfilled) to obtain from the Anglican clergy and others permitted to perform marriages (Quakers and Jews) copy certificates of all marriages which had taken place during the preceding quarter and to forward them to the superintendent registrar en route to the GRO. These were not indexed or copied before being forwarded so local register offices did not have indexes to marriages in their districts. Marriage Registers are deposited only when the volume is full (see p.83). What you should find in the superintendent registrar's office is Marriage Notice Books, containing notices of intended marriages which were to take place in the Register Office; prior to 1898 in Nonconformist (including Roman Catholic) places of worship as until this date a registrar had to be present at all these marriages; or involving Quakers or Jews. Many local authorities are gradually transferring their indexes to computer, compiling indexes for marriages (see **UKBMD** below) and improving the services they can offer.

SEARCHING THE INDEXES ONLINE

The national indexes are available online via a number of commercial websites. These tend to have different terms and conditions for searching them; some use copies of the original indexes, others offer first a transcript of the indexes and then a separate tier of payment to view the original index entry. **A word of warning - having found the index entry you require, be wary of instantly pressing the button to order a certificate via that website. Some commercial websites charge more than the standard price to supply certificates. Also be aware that any certificates ordered by post or by phone from the GRO incur an extra charge.**

Free BMD is probably the most widely used of the 'free' websites. This is an ongoing project, by volunteers, to transcribe the national GRO indexes. **It is not yet close to completion** and it is sponsored by several commercial websites. Do not make the mistake of pressing the 'search' button to look for an entry before reading the 'Home Page'; doing this is likely to drop you into a series of pitfalls. If, on the 'Information Page', you read the *General Information and Statistics* sections (the latter including coverage charts and details of Registration Districts) you will be better equipped to use the site successfully. If you do 'search' immediately and cannot find an expected entry, check out the coverage charts (which provide a breakdown by event and year of the percentage coverage). If the coverage for a particular quarter is less than 100%, the district you need could be one of those not yet covered. Be aware that the 'soundex' system (see p.57) has been used for this site (and for several others). When looking at an entry on this site, there is no significance as to whether a surname is in upper or lower case. Where the entry has been transcribed twice, by two separate transcribers whose transcriptions match exactly, there is one entry in bold; where the entry has been transcribed only once the entry will be in regular text. Where an entry has been transcribed twice but the transcriptions do not match exactly (because one transcriber has misread a word or made a typing error - see below), the two entries are printed one under the other, in regular text (not in bold). Click on the Registration District name and you will be connected to the **GENUKI** site mentioned below for a full list of all places in the RD. However, if the RD name is in italics, clicking on this will tell you that there appears to be an error in the entry. Quoting two examples from the *Ethell* family demonstrates the types of errors made by transcribers - *Betham Ethell*, married in 1843, is listed as being registered in *Maldon* [Essex] whereas he was married in *Malton* [Yorkshire] RD (and this error is repeated for other *Malton* entries). *Rachel Ethell*, born in 1849 in *Pontefract* is entered twice with two different page numbers, *329* and *529*, of which the latter is correct. It will normally be apparent which the correct entry is but check carefully before ordering the certificate. Click on the spectacles beside either entry to view the scan of the GRO index page from which the transcription was made and (as is emphasised throughout this book) it will be very clear just how easy it is to make mistakes when transcribing.

UKBMD is a hub which provides links to around 1500 websites (both free and commercial) which offer online transcriptions of (among other things) UK BMD indexes and census returns. You are advised, as usual, to read the introductory information given on both the *Local BMD* and *GRO BMD* tabs; **GENUKI** (see Registration Districts p.80) can be accessed from here. Many local authorities, responsible for registration districts, are (often in conjunction with local FHSs), putting their indexes online. Some are checking the indexes against the original entries to improve accuracy and are also indexing marriages from 1837 onwards. In an increasing number of areas, it is possible to order certificates direct via their websites.

HOW ACCURATE ARE THE INDEXES?

This is a vexed question; both local and national indexes do contain mistakes. Some entries or partial entries have been omitted accidentally from the national indexes (often the name of one party to a marriage), but, in many cases where searchers assume the indexes are faulty, the answers are there but not in quite the expected form. Previous chapters have mentioned regional accents and the fact that many local registrars had to make their best guess as to what name was being said to them in a possibly unfamiliar accent. With handwriting, which could vary from copperplate to barely decipherable, figures which could be badly formed, unfamiliar surnames and placenames, and indexes which had to be compiled manually, it is not surprising that errors occurred. The nature and extent of these errors is gradually being revealed as comparisons are being made between records held by local register offices, the quarterly returns submitted to the GRO and the GRO indexes. **Slapdash recording, copying and failure to meet deadlines was common and 'lost in the post' is clearly not a new phenomenon**.

Local indexes should contain fewer errors as the copyist/clerk should have had the opportunity to become familiar with local registrars' handwriting and would often be able to query unclear entries face to face. By contrast, the clerks at the GRO had to cope with handwriting from every registrar and most of the clergy in the country. If, in the GRO indexes, you find several names with a similar, but not identical, spelling, sharing the same volume and page reference, do not rush into ordering copy certificates of all of them (as some people admit that they have done). Stop and think! It is often the case that the clerk felt impelled to list several possible variants because the writing was impossible to decipher accurately. If, in the marriage indexes, you find entries for, say, *John Smith* and *John Henry Smith* sharing a reference, the same proviso applies. This will almost certainly be for the same entry but if both names appeared on the marriage certificate (one in the names column, the other as the signature) the clerk indexed both.

Having already confessed to the main weaknesses in my own handwriting (see p.21) spare a thought for the clerks who, whilst indexing, misread *Sant* as *Saut*, *Swarbrick* as *Swanbrick* and *Terrington* as *Ternington*. Remember that the GRO indexes are compiled in a strict alphabetical sequence - unlike the IGI which often groups variant spellings together - so a difference of only one letter can be enough to throw you completely when searching for a surname. It is very easy, when looking in a hurry (and most family historians will admit to trying to 'beat the clock' and searching as many years as possible in one visit to a library or to a website), to forget everything except the one spelling you expect to find. Bear in mind both the possibility of mis-indexing (as above) and that the name may not be spelt as you expect; *Clark* and *Clarke* are often interchangeable (as are *Whitaker* and *Whittaker* - never mind *Whitakers*, *Whiteacre* and *Witticar*). I well remember, in my early days as a family historian, searching the bound volumes 1837-1865 (that was 114 volumes, each weighing - or so it seemed - about half a ton) for the surname *Ethell* and later having to heave them all out again to check for *Ethall, Ettal, Hethall* and *Ithell*.

It is a good idea to keep a written list of which names (and variant spellings) you intend to check - and look at it regularly to make sure you have done what you intended; there are few things more infuriating than looking at pages of scribbled references whether you are a hundred miles away from the indexes or online, and being unsure whether you checked a particular variant in a certain quarter. It always pays to keep a strict account of which quarterly volumes you have searched. Check lists are available in various 'family history packs', which enable you to cross off each volume as you search it, or it is easy enough to prepare one yourself. You may think, when the rhythm of your searching is broken because a particular microform is not immediately available - whether it is being used by someone else, mis-filed, or being repaired – or a certain quarter is not yet on the website you are using that you will remember which one was missing and go back for it later but, as any practised family historian will tell you (usually from bitter experience), you will not. **Never rely on your memory - always write down what you need to follow up later.**

At least two new forms of error crept into some of the early national indexes in the 1970s, when the GRO undertook a retyping programme, and some of the handwritten volumes were replaced by typed ones. Inevitably, there were typing errors and omissions.

The Roman numerals (see p.101) used from 1837 to 1851 (see Registration Districts below) were replaced with Arabic numerals. It is easy to make a mistake when converting these numbers. *XXVI (26)* covers part of Wales; reverse two figures - *XXIV (24)* - and you can find yourself wondering why your Welsh ancestor is registered in Durham, and experience difficulty if trying to order a certificate; omit one figure - *XVI (16)* - and the same Welsh ancestor will apparently have moved to the Midlands.

Several people researching unusual surnames, who had previously extracted all the references to their names from the handwritten indexes, found that these surnames, often amounting to only a single entry per quarter, had sometimes disappeared from the microfiche version. The entries were still there, tacked onto the end of the previous surname, noticeable only because the researchers knew what should be there and the Christian names were out of alphabetical sequence with, say, *Alice* following *Zillah* (from the previous surname). If you suspect this might have happened to a name you are searching for, track down a copy of the handwritten volumes and you may find a vital entry.

A point worth bearing in mind is that registrars and clergy were paid a fee both for entries in their registers and for the certified copies they made. There were several cases, particularly in the early days of the registration service, of registrars being prosecuted for making up entries to boost their income. Where such offences went undiscovered it is possible that there are still a few phantom entries lurking in the records. You would be most unfortunate to latch onto one of these entries but it is as well to be aware of the possibility. Registrars were also known to 'poach' births from neighbouring districts, if they knew about them and arrived on the scene first, so if you cannot find a birth where you expect it is worth checking adjoining districts.

REGISTRATION DISTRICTS

By 1838 619 Registration Districts (each with a superintendent registrar) had been created, based on the Poor Law Unions; a few of these had no sub-districts but most had between one and nine, each with its own registrar, of whom 2193 had been appointed. There were three RDs with 10 sub-districts (*Bolton* and *Manchester* in Lancashire and *Huddersfield* in Yorkshire) and one (*Bradford* in Yorkshire) with 11; *London* and *Leeds* each contained more than one RD. By 1891 there were 633 RDs and 2110 sub-districts.

RDs in urban districts would usually cover a small area with a large population, those in rural districts would have a large area with a small population; certainly before 1875 events in the latter were more likely to escape registration.

Be aware that RD boundaries have always been fluid and some places have, at various times, been in several different districts. Local government re-organisation, particularly in 1974 and 1996, saw major changes. Some districts disappeared altogether and their records were dispersed; this will not affect you if you order certificates online or by post from the GRO but it may cause problems if you want to order from a local register office/local authority website. **GENUKI**, a very good and detailed site to consult, provides a complete list of local register offices and their histories.

Registration District names, as given in the indexes, can cause many pitfalls for the unwary. Some are misleading: the 'classic' is *West Derby* which, as most experienced researchers will know, is part of *Liverpool* and has no connection with Derbyshire; another problem-causer is *Richmond*, with one RD bearing that name in North Yorkshire and another one in Surrey. Others are difficult to track down because the names refer to the old administrative districts and not to any recognizable town: how many people know that *Bucklow* RD (identifiable today from the sign for the village of *Bucklow Hill* near *Knutsford,* Cheshire) originally included *Altrincham, Knutsford, Lymm and Wilmslow* or that *Thingoe* RD covered a large area round *Bury St Edmunds* in Suffolk? The simplest way of resolving the whereabouts of an unfamiliar RD and its sub-districts is to consult the Codes employed in the GRO Indexes, given in full in many family history publications and on online sites.

Note that the system of numbering for RDs has changed several times. In 1852 it changed from Roman to Arabic numerals (plus a letter); from 1852, *West Derby* is followed by the Lancashire reference 8b (Derbyshire is 7b); Cheshire is 8a and Suffolk is 4a. As a rough rule of thumb, from 1852 to 1946, the farther north a RD is, the higher its number so the London area is covered by 1, 2 and 3a and Yorkshire by 9 (Wales is 11). In 1946 the axis was changed: the four northern counties and parts of Yorkshire became 1a-b and the regions were then numbered clockwise around England and Wales so that Suffolk, coincidentally, remained as 4, London (previously 1) became 5, Wales 8 and Cheshire and Lancashire 10. The system changed again in 1974, when almost 200 historic registration districts were abolished.

LOCAL REGISTER OFFICES

Local register offices are now administered by local authorities. The address of any one should be found in the relevant telephone directory (usually under *Registration of BDM*) but please make sure that you are aware what facilities these can offer before you contact them. North Yorkshire, for example, has re-structured the registration service in the county, amalgamating its ten Registration Districts (including *Richmond*) into a single North Yorkshire Registration District with a central repository in *Harrogate* for all the County's BDM records back to 1837 and reading room facilities for family historians. At least one other county introduced a similar system but has just had to dismantle it, following local government re-organisation and the establishment of unitary authorities.

The biggest pitfall you may encounter at local Register Offices is that (unless they are already computerised) they cannot necessarily provide you with a marriage certificate without knowing the exact date and the precise church or chapel where the ceremony took place; a GRO reference is of no relevance or use to them. This is because they may have register books from 50 different churches and chapels which have been filled and deposited. The entries in these books will probably not be indexed (but see p.78 /**UKBMD**) and to find a particular entry could necessitate searching many books.

The strongest possibility is that you will find a local registrar who is prepared to be more flexible than GRO staff are normally allowed to be. A classic case was a postal application for a birth certificate for *Emily Bessie Frosdick* in a particular area and quarter. The GRO said that there was no such birth. The local Register Office, when approached, replied that they had a very similar entry; would this be acceptable? She proved to have been registered as *Emily Betsy Frosdick*. Similarly, the GRO has been known to reject an application because the occupation given on the form differs from that on the certificate even if other details agree; local offices will sometimes ask if an alternative occupation could be correct.

The local Register Office can also come into its own if details of an event cannot be found in the GRO indexes or if a certificate issued by the GRO appears to be incorrect. If you are convinced that an entry should be in a particular Registration District but there is no trace of it in the central indexes, or that the placename on a handwritten or typed GRO certificate does not exist, it may be worth asking the local Register Office to look either in their indexes or at the original registration entry to see if the name has been 'lost' or misread at some stage in the indexing process.

In some cases, local knowledge will enable registrars to suggest how a surname may have been spelt in their area, depending on the local accent or (in the early days of registration) on the whim of the registrar. They may also know which neighbouring districts could contain the entry required, given that Registration District boundaries have varied considerably over the years.

CERTIFICATES IN GENERAL

Until recently, certificates supplied by the GRO were usually handwritten or typed onto a pro forma blank certificate rather than scanned or photocopied (many from local offices still are) and clerks were not necessarily practised at reading old or bad handwriting. From my own certificates I have an *Edwin* whose certificate called him *Edward* and a *Maria* who appears as *Mary* and I spent months, when living in London, searching for a place in Yorkshire called *West Sutton* which turned out to be *West Lutton* (one letter was misread by the clerk writing out the copy certificate in 1968 and, having since seen the 'original' in photocopied form, most people would have made the same mistake).

Original certificate is a very misleading phrase to use. Many family historians use it to refer to copy certificates found among family papers, as opposed to copies purchased from the GRO. In fact, original certificates (i.e. the registration of a birth or death) should be found only in local Register

Offices. In the case of post-1837 marriage certificates, two registers had to be filled in at the ceremony; one was retained at the church (and will commonly now be found in the local record office), the other was held at the church until full and was then forwarded to the local register office. Everything else, including the copy you receive when you marry, or register a birth or death, is almost invariably a copy. I stress this because, since the scanning of certificates has become more common, several people have been heard to say that they must purchase a certain one because they want a specimen of their ancestor's signature. With very few exceptions this is the one thing which you will not obtain. As almost all their information is copied, very few certificates issued by the GRO will include original signatures, although some local register offices were apparently submitting their copies to the GRO as Xeroxes from the 1960s. The 'twin' marriage registers (see above) are the only documents from which you may be able to obtain a photocopy/photograph of an original signature on a marriage certificate; remember that, in some rural parishes, marriage registers begun in 1837 are still in use so the church will be your only option. After a Quaker marriage the couple normally retained the original document, and copies were made for the local Monthly Meeting and for the GRO, so it is always worth endeavouring to ascertain if anyone in the family still holds the certificate.

Both the original registration entry and copy certificates may contain errors, ranging from the wrong date for an event to an incorrect name or age. When *Martha Cater Chamberlain* (see p.66) married, the minister entered her name on the certificate as *Martha Kate Chamberlain* - the substitution of a familiar Christian name for an unknown surname (used as a middle name) and, as neither Martha nor her husband could read or write, this was a mistake which was never corrected. If the error on a copy certificate can be shown to be a modern clerical one, the GRO will usually exchange the faulty certificate for a correct one.

Having an original registration amended, however, is not a simple procedure. It can involve a considerable amount of paperwork and many people who discover an error and intend to put it right decide, when they realise what it entails, to leave it as it is. If a registration is altered, both the original and amended details will normally be shown on a copy certificate and the index should be updated but be aware that there is no guarantee of this.

Years ago I helped a lady named *Sybil*, born around 1900 in Yorkshire, to find her 'missing' birth entry. She came in the middle of a family of 11 and it was only after abstracting births for all her siblings and combing the years between the eldest and the youngest for any other births in her uncommon surname that we found her registered as *Cyril* and one year older than she had always believed. The evidence required before the GRO would accept her existence included statements from her (elderly) surviving siblings that *Cyril* had never existed and she had; if the birth certificate had not been necessary before she could obtain her pension she might well have remained 'in hiding' for ever.

A common assumption is that the copy certificate which emerges from the GRO will always show identical information to that which appears on the original registration. This is usually the case but bear in mind that, in the case of marriages, it can be worth checking the church register in addition. The 'condensed' certificate below, from an Anglican church register, shows four alterations, initialled by the incumbent, including the insertion of a non-existent middle name for one of the parties and an alteration to the groom's signature. The version sent to the Superintendent Registrar presumably contained these alterations as 'fact' and the abstract from the GRO copy certificate below includes them all, with no indication that they were not part of the original marriage entry; the church register was an eye-opener! The groom, incidentally, was registered at both birth and death as *Joe* but married as *Joseph* - another pitfall.

:— 1	2	3	4	7
When married	Name and surname	Age	Condition	Father's name and surname
Dec 26th	Joseph Senior Foster	19	Bachelor	William Senior Foster
1 887	Margaret Ann Atkinson	17	Spinster	Alexander Atkinson

ried in the Parish Church according to the rites and ceremonies _____ by after Bann

marriage olemnized :een us, { Joseph Senior Foster / Margaret Ann Atkinson } in the presence of us, { Jos / Sus dgar H Rand _____ Vicar }

Clerks and relatives could both make mistakes. *Eli Mercer* registered his granddaughter's death on 25 March 1885. The certificate originally said *Mary Elizabeth son of* but this has been altered to *daughter* and a note on the certificate says *clerical error in Col. 5 corrected 8 April 1885 by the Registrar in the presence of Eli Mercer, grandfather.* How many worse errors went un-noticed if the relatives were illiterate or did not bother to look at the piece of paper brought back from the Register Office?

So if you find an entry which you are fairly confident is yours but are concerned that the person died three days before the date given on his tombstone, was six weeks younger than you thought he was (see p.86), and is called *Edward* not *Edwin*, do not give up hope. Your instinct could well be right and the informants wrong.

The format used for certificates remained unchanged from 1837 to 1969 but, from 1 April 1969, changes (see below) were made to birth and death certificates.

BIRTH CERTIFICATES

When civil registration was introduced in 1837, parents were not obliged to provide information about a birth unless requested to do so by the registrar. Penalties were put in place for refusal to register one if the registrar knew about it, but until the Registration Act of 1874 (effective 1875) made it compulsory to register events, registering a birth was, in a sense, voluntary (and some people believed that a baptism certificate was all the documentation they needed) so *She must be registered; she was born in 1839* is not a true statement. In the first 37 years of the system a number of births (some estimates are as high as 10%) were never recorded. This applied particularly to illegitimate children and was especially prevalent in the 1830s and 1840s. One possibility, if you cannot find the birth of a female ancestor in these years, is to hunt for one of her brothers. Some families registered the births of boys but not girls. Until 1874 a mother registering an illegitimate birth could name the putative father; after this date he could only be named on the birth certificate if he was present at the registration and gave his consent. There are currently proposals to revert, under certain circumstances, to the original situation. The Legitimacy Act of 1926 (effective 1927) allowed children to be legitimised by the subsequent marriage of their parents, provided that neither had been married to a third party at the time of the birth. The original entry was annotated to refer to the new entry and the legitimised birth was re-entered in the indexes, sometimes many years after the birth (see below).

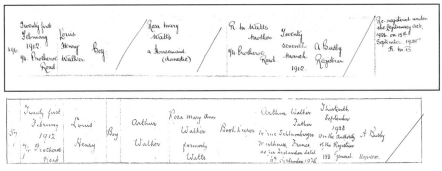

From 1837 parents were given six weeks (42 days) to register a birth; after six weeks and up to six months, the event could be registered on payment of a fine; after six months no registration was allowed. Look at the certificates you hold and you will see that many couples delayed registering until the sixth week. It was fairly common for a parent, arriving to register a child a few days late, to 'adjust' the birth date to come within the 42 days. If you find that your ancestor's birth date in the family bible differs from that on his birth certificate, or if he appears to have been baptised before he was born, this is the most likely explanation. Always remember to look for a birth in the quarter you expect and in at least the following quarter - a child born in a remote area in late December and registered in early April (when the snows melted) as being born in mid-February (to avoid a fine) will be two quarters beyond where you would expect.

Do not forget that, **if the parents had not agreed on a name for the child when they registered the birth, it may be found in the GRO Indexes at the end of the entries for the surname in question, listed under** *Male* **or** *Female* (see p. 272). They then had twelve months to register a Christian name which could be added to the certificate but, as a payment had to be made to add the name to the certificate, many did not bother. Production of a baptism certificate was necessary to register the name so it may be easier to search for this event.

On later certificates if the time of birth is given it usually signifies a multiple birth but be aware that in the early years of registration, in some districts, the time of birth was included as standard.

Many birth certificates are purchased by family historians with the sole purpose of determining the mother's maiden name so that they can search for a marriage. **When ordering a birth certificate, make sure you apply for a full certificate, not a 'short' certificate**, introduced in 1947, which is sometimes adequate for official purposes but includes only name, sex, date of birth and RD (no details of parents). Determining a maiden name can be fraught with difficulties as our ancestors were sometimes economical with the truth and at other times genuinely may not have known which name to give. *Alice Bann* (see p.65) was born in 1838 and registered as the legitimate daughter of *James Bann* and *Ann*, late *Beard* formerly *Sykes* (a form of words which reveals that *Ann* was a widow). In fact *Alice*'s parents did not marry until 1844. Bear in mind that *Ann* will appear in the GRO index at her marriage as *Ann Beard* (her first husband's name) and not as *Ann Sykes* (her maiden name) but her father's name (revealing her maiden name) should appear on the certificate.

On the birth certificates of three of the children of *John and Hannah Baker* (see p.66), *Hannah*'s maiden name is given successively as *Duffield, Dingley* and *Tingley*. Her father was *Samuel Dingley*, her mother *Nancy Duffield* (both dead before *Hannah* married). Theirs had been a common law marriage; *Hannah*'s birth was not registered (her brother's was, and as a legitimate child) and she was clearly unsure which name to give. *Dingley* seems to have won because *Tingley* is presumably a Yorkshire registrar's attempt to interpret a Staffordshire accent, helped by the fact that there is a hamlet called *Tingley* about five miles from where the registration took place. Note that the youngest child was born in Yorkshire but, according to the 1881 census (see p.66) she was born in Staffordshire like her siblings.

No.	When and where born	Name, if any	Sex	Name, and surname of father	Name, surname, and maiden surname of mother	Occupation of father	Signature, description, and residence of informant
51	Eleventh March 1877 2 Stewpony Yard Darlaston	Hannah	Girl	John Baker	Hannah Baker formerly Duffield	Coal Miner	X The Mark of Hannah Baker mother 2 Stewpony Yard Darlaston

Columns:→	1	2	3	4	5	6	7
No.	When and where born	Name, if any	Sex	Name, and surname of father	Name, surname, and maiden surname of mother	Occupation of father	Signature, description, and residence of informant
51.	Twenty-Seventh September 1878. 6. Pinfold Street. Darlaston	George	Boy	John Baker	Hannah Baker formerly Dingley	Coal Miner	X The Mark of Hannah Baker mother. 6. Pinfold Street. Darlaston.
273	Twentyfirst August 1880 3 Park Row, Normanton	Jane	Girl	John Baker	Hannah Baker formerly Tingley	Coal Miner	X The Mark of Hannah Baker, Mother, 3 Park Row, Normanton

The effect local place-names can have on surnames - with, for example, *Ethell* and *Etches* both becoming *Etchells* in the area surrounding villages of that name - has been dealt with on page 23.

During the 19th and early 20th centuries thousands of children were registered as being born *in the workhouse*. In 1904 the Registrar General instructed local registrars that, to safeguard the future interests of such children, their birth certificates should disguise this fact by using a fictitious address or a non-committal street number. Many such certificates use the name of the street on which the workhouse was situated and add a non-existent 'house' number. As this institution was often the only available infirmary or hospital 'difficult' births might well take place in the workhouse. If you find an ancestral birth registered here, particularly in the late 19th century, do not jump to the conclusion that your ancestor was necessarily a long-term resident of the workhouse.

From 1 April 1969 the format, and shape, of birth certificates was altered. They now include the usual address of the mother and the places of birth of the father and the mother. From 1986 the mother's occupation has also been included.

MARRIAGE CERTIFICATES

Of course they were married... and *Grandfather was born in September so his parents can't have married during that year, I'll look the year before and earlier* are two statements guaranteed to send many family historians headlong into some very dangerous pitfalls. *Common law* marriages - with no religious or civil ceremony (so no documentary evidence) but the couple living together, and being accepted, as man and wife - have always been popular. When a marriage did take place it is never safe to assume that it took place nine months or more before the birth of the first child. A high percentage of brides (possibly as many as 40% in some years) were pregnant when they married and a surprising number of couples did not marry until after the birth of their first (or even their last) child. In the days before divorce was common, many couples 'changed partners' but could not marry until their first husband/wife died and this might not be for many years. Until 1858, when the ***Matrimonial Causes Act of 1857*** made divorce easier for men, at least, to obtain, the only method of obtaining one was by a private Act of Parliament. The ease with which a divorce can be obtained today misleads many researchers, who cannot understand how impossible it was for their ancestors to obtain one until well into the 20th century.

They both said they were 21 on their marriage certificate so they were both born in ... is a misconception which causes innumerable headaches for family historians. *21* and *of full age* should both mean that the couple were aged 21 or over (and so did not need parental permission to marry) but all too often they do not. Two of the daughters of *John & Hannah Baker* (*Hannah and Jane*: see p.87) gave their ages as *21* when marrying aged *17 years 1 month* and *17 years 6 months* respectively. Brides often tended to knock a few years off their ages, especially if marrying a younger man, and bridegrooms might add a few years, particularly if marrying an older woman.

The column asking for the fathers' names could cause much heartache to bride or groom, particularly if they were illegitimate and even more so if other people at the wedding were not aware of this fact. Which was worse - to give a plausible name (often that of a grandfather or stepfather) to the minister or registrar to ensure 'respectability' or to say nothing and risk the word 'Unknown' being entered in the column for all to see? There were also many, born illegitimate but whose mother had married when they were very young, who were unaware that in naming their stepfather as their father they were not telling the truth. In fact, there was no legal obligation for this column to be filled in - it could either be left blank or have a line drawn through it - but few, particularly in the 19th century, were aware of this. Many researchers have jumped to the incorrect conclusion that a blank column automatically means illegitimacy whereas it can simply mean that the person declined, for whatever reason, to name their father. In the father's column on the marriage certificate of *Christiana Kneeshaw* (see p.254) the words *Natural Child* are given. Illegitimacy or the involvement of a stepfather might wrongly be assumed from the 1897 certificate for Charlotte *Grimoldby*, whose father was named as *John Henry Thomas*. His name was *John Henry Thomas Grimoldby* but his three Christian names filled the column and the vicar omitted to add his surname.

The same column was also supposed to state if the father was deceased. **Do not fall into the trap of assuming that if a marriage certificate does not say that the father of bride or groom was deceased then he was alive.** I have known people search indexes for fifty years after a marriage for the father's death only to discover that he died the year before the event. Some ministers would forget to ask the question, some people would not know the answer, and others probably thought there was an ulterior motive behind the question and refused to answer.

'Accommodation addresses' were as common in the past as they are now. If bride and groom give the same address do not assume that they were living together, or that the address was the family home of one of them; it is equally likely to be a lodging house where they were establishing a residence qualification to marry in the church of their choice. In the early 20th century it was common for large stores, in London and other cities, to provide 'living-in' accommodation for their workers. Apprentices might also lodge with their masters and many servants would live at their employer's address.

Occupations on marriage certificates can be very suspect - many a tradesman became a 'gentleman' for the day, farm laboureres often promoted themselves to farmers and a solicitor's clerk might well omit the clerk.

DEATH CERTIFICATES

Until 1875 the onus was on the registrar to find out about, and register, a death. From 1875 the responsibility for registering a death was transferred to the nearest relative of the deceased (or other suitable person if no relatives were known).

Ages at death can be notoriously unreliable - after all, the only person who should have known the true facts was not there to give them. As a rough rule of thumb, be wary of ages on death certificates which end in '0'. Many such ages are estimates, rather than true ages. Ask anyone to tell you how old his grandfather was when he died (without checking documentary evidence) and you may be surprised how few can answer correctly. *Thomas Ethell* on his 1842 death certificate was given as *90*; at his burial three days later he was *88*; he was correctly *83*. See also the example of *John Hinchliffe* on page 70.

Names at death can cause problems, particularly when a woman has married for a second (or even third) time. Her family maintained that *Hannah Baker* (see p.66) had died the week before Easter in 1921 but there was no trace of a death. They also said that the surnames *Dingley* and *Gibbons* 'rang bells' but no-one could remember why. *Dingley* turned out to be one of her maiden names (see p.86). It was a long time before it occurred to me to search for her death under *Gibbons* – and there it was, correct date and registered by one of her *Baker* sons. It transpired that she had married a second time but that Mr *Gibbons* had died soon after and she had reverted to being *Grandma Baker* for more than 20 years. When asking a relative who, as

89

a child, had lived with *Hannah* for several years how she could not have known this – surely post would have been addressed to Mrs *Gibbons* - I was met by a blank look and 'but we didn't get post in those days'.

As with birth certificates, changes were made to the shape and format of death certificates in 1969. Instead of the age at death they now include the date and place of birth of the deceased. This can provide family historians with vital additional information but equally may drop them into an unexpected pitfall. If age at death is often a 'guesstimate' how often is date and place of birth the same? Ask several people where they were born and then ask them to check their birth certificates; it is surprising how many people believe, incorrectly, that they were born where they were brought up (for many years I was, myself, in this category - see p.69). If someone, without access to a birth certificate, registers the death of a neighbour, friend or care home resident who has always said *I've lived here all my life* the information they give could well be wrong. Check who the informant is - relatives are more likely (although by no means certain) to be correct.

In 1919, local registrars were told to adopt the same tactic for deaths as had been introduced in 1904 for births to disguise the fact that the event had taken place in the workhouse (see p.87).

Remember that, with very few exceptions, a death cannot be registered until a positive identification of the body has been made so, if a ship goes down at sea with no survivors, generally speaking the deaths of those on board cannot be registered. If a body from, for example, a shipwreck or a mining accident is recovered several years later and is identified, the death will be registered as at the date of recovery but the age given will be that which applied when the person actually died. If an inquest is held, the death will be registered in the quarter when the inquest was completed, which may be some time after the death, or discovery of the body, (especially if there was an adjournment).

1853: DEATH IN A MINING ACCIDENT; REGISTERED BY CORONER 3 MONTHS LATER.

1853. DEATH in the Sub-district of Foleshill in the County of Warwick							
When and where died	Name and surname	Sex	Age	Occupation	Cause of death	Signature, description, and residence of informant	When registered
Third July 1853 Foleshill	Samuel Calor	male	24 years	Iron Stone Miner	Accidental Fire Stink	W.H Seymour Coroner Coventry	Thirtieth September 1853

MISCELLANEOUS RETURNS (OVERSEAS REGISTERS)

Finally, do not overlook one of the deepest pitfalls of all - your ancestor may not be in the 'main' GRO indexes at all (even as an *Unknown* - see p.75). He or she may have been born, married or died in one of the colonies; elsewhere overseas; or even on board ship. Was your ancestor employed by the East India Company; serving in the army or navy; on a 'work exchange' to America (surprisingly common in the 19th century); emigrating; abroad on business; or doing missionary work? Details of many of these events may be found in the GRO's *Miscellaneous Returns*, which include births, marriages and deaths recorded by British Consuls and High Commissioners (from 1849); births, marriages and deaths at sea; returns from the Armed Services and deaths in the Boer War and both World Wars These returns are widely available on microfiche, and are online on a commercial website. **To order a certificate for an Overseas Event, either online or by post, requires a different form to that used to order certificates from the main indexes.**

BRITISH ISLES, OTHER THAN ENGLAND AND WALES

Do not forget that the family may have lived for a time in Scotland or Ireland, the Channel Islands or the Isle of Man which all have their own systems of civil registration, with varying starting dates.

SCOTLAND: civil (statutory) registration began on 1 January 1855; indexes and extracts (an officially certified copy of an entry) are available on the ScotlandsPeople website.

IRELAND: a registration system for marriages where one or both parties was Protestant began on 1 April 1845. Full civil registration began on 1 January 1864. From 1922 copies of civil registration records for Northern Ireland have been forwarded to the GRO in Belfast; for the Republic of Ireland to GRONI in Belfast. **Civil Registration Indexes for all of Ireland 1845-1958 can be found on the Record Search pilot on FamilySearch.**

ISLE OF MAN: civil registration of births and deaths was introduced in 1849 but was not made compulsory until 1878. Civil marriage registration for Dissenters was made available from 1849; civil registration of all marriages was compulsory from 1884.

CHANNEL ISLANDS: Jersey: civil registration was introduced in August 1842. **Guernsey** and the other Channel Islands: civil registration of births and deaths began in October 1840 and of non-Anglican marriages in January 1841. Anglican marriages were not registered with the civil authorities until 1919. From 1925 onwards, records for all the islands (except Jersey) are held by the Registrar General on Guernsey.

RESOLUTION:

I will endeavour to read Michael Foster's *A Comedy of Errors or The Marriage Records of England and Wales 1837-1899* (1998: New Zealand) to gain an idea of just how many errors and omissions and how much mis-indexing occur in the GRO marriage records and indexes in this period. I will remember that births and deaths records and indexes will be similarly affected.

CHAPTER 10

Parish Registers (General)

and Bishops' Transcripts

Parish registers are dealt with, to some extent, in any book or online site on how to trace your ancestors but compressing almost 500 years of legislation concerning them into a few pages inevitably leads to dangerous generalisations and mistaken assumptions being made because, until the 19th century, they tended to be very individual documents, which frequently did not conform to a set pattern.

Coverage of parish registers on the internet has lagged far behind that of civil registration and census returns but now that these are mostly online attention is turning to church registers and these are increasingly becoming available on both free and commercial websites. Many so far online for England and Wales have been taken from printed volumes and from booklets prepared by family history societies and reading *Chapter 17: Published Parish Registers and Transcripts* will give you an idea as to why these should be treated with caution. Some ROs are gradually digitizing their registers and putting them online but, again, these become, in a sense, secondary sources and errors and omissions can creep in. Some counties are putting original images of their registers online. You are advised to read the introductory pages to any site before beginning to search it, principally to ascertain how complete the coverage is. If you have problems finding an expected, or hoped for, entry online try to ascertain what source has been used for the entries. Searching the original register books or BTs may well be the answer. Scotland's OPRs (old PRs) to 1854 are online on ScotlandsPeople.

The term *parish register* is commonly interpreted as applying to the records of the established church in a country (the Anglican church in England and Wales, the Presbyterian Church of Scotland, the Church of Ireland) but the Episcopal Church of Scotland and the Roman Catholic Church also have parishes and registers, many Nonconformist registers (particularly from the late 18th century) follow very similar formats and some institutions including workhouses, the Foundling Hospital, and London lying-in hospitals maintained their own baptism registers. This book concentrates on Anglican registers but references to other denominations and institutions are included and many of the pitfalls mentioned apply to all types.

Bear in mind that the commencement dates and survival rate of parish registers varies widely within the British Isles. In *England*, hundreds of registers survive from various dates in the 16th century (but see p.94 for how many are *original* ones); in *Wales* only four registers pre-date 1550, with another 65 beginning between 1550 and 1600; in *Scotland* (where the keeping of registers for baptisms and marriages began in 1551) less than 20 registers pre-date 1600; in *Ireland* there are no pre-1600 registers (the first requirement to keep them was in 1634); the first PR in the *Isle of Man* dates from 1598; a few registers in the *Channel Islands* begin in the 16th century but more than half date from the 17th century. Never assume, if your research moves from one country into another, that a similar situation will exist where parish registers are concerned. Those in Scotland and Ireland generally begin later, survive less often, and contain less information, than those in England and Wales.

FORMAT OF ANGLICAN PARISH REGISTERS TO 1812

One of the deepest pitfalls into which many people fall is to believe that because the Sovereign or the government said that something should happen, it did so (and in a uniform manner). Nothing could be further from the truth. From *Thomas Cromwell*'s *1538 ordinance* ordering the keeping of parish registers in England and Wales onwards, officialdom has specialised in 'laying down the law' but failing to create the machinery to make sure that the law is enforced. The quality of parish registers, and the information they contain, can vary from year to year, parish to parish, diocese to diocese, country to country, and depends far more on the inclinations of archbishops, bishops, individual incumbents and their parish clerks than on what the government decreed should happen. There are certain periods when you may find more information than you expect, others when you will find less and some when you will find none at all.

SIXTEENTH CENTURY PARISH REGISTERS

Cromwell's *1538 ordinance* specified that each parish should maintain *one boke or re[g]istre* into which, each Sunday, the day and year of all christenings, marriages or burials, together with the name of any person involved in such an event, taking place in the previous week, should be entered. There was no mention of what material the books should be made from so most parishes used paper books, few of which have survived, and no suggestion as to what format should be used in the register. It did not specify that the names of the parents of a baptised child should be given (only the Christian and surname of the child was required until Canon 70 of 1603) but so many incumbents added at least the father's name in 16th century baptisms that plenty of family historians incorrectly assume it to be standard practice. The use, in an Anglican register, of *born* and *died*, as opposed to *baptised* and *buried*, often - but not always - points to the person concerned being a Nonconformist (see p.96); some ministers made a distinction between *baptised* and *christened* (see p.114) or *buried* and *interred* (see p.172); and you can tell a lot about an incumbent's attitude to his congregation from the way he describes events concerning suicides and illegitimate children.

ORIGINAL PARISH REGISTERS?

How many 'original' parish registers are exactly that? If you have read anything on the subject you will know that many (if not most) registers with entries from 1538 or 1558 are copies made about 1598, when it was ordered that the paper books be replaced with ones made of parchment. This is frequently apparent when entries for the whole period to 1598 are tidily written in the same handwriting - most original registers are in widely differing scripts, with additions, amendments and crossings out. The same criterion applies to later books. Be suspicious of any which present a uniform appearance over a long period. Many registers were copied from the originals by dedicated clerics or church officials, often because the original register was in poor condition (in which case always check for missing years if a page went astray, or for years out of sequence if the register fell apart and was haphazardly put back together). Sometimes the fact that it is a copy is stated but often it is not. Now that most registers are viewed on microfilm or microfiche it can be extremely hard to realise that you are dealing with a copy and not the original. There is an almost contemporary copy of the parish register of *Topcliffe* (near *Thirsk*) in Yorkshire for the period 1695-1769. The copy comes first on the film as PR/TOP/1/2, with no indication that it *is* a copy, and the original follows as PR/TOP/1/3. Very few researchers would even think to look at the second reference. Copies are generally easier to read than the originals but often less accurate.

INFORMATION IN PRE-1813 PARISH REGISTERS

How much information should you expect to find in a pre-1813 parish register? An experienced researcher will tell you that this is as unanswerable a question as 'how long is a piece of string'? Those with less experience often fall into the trap of assuming that far more information should have been included in registers than is the case. Between 1634 and 1637 *Archbishop Laud* of Canterbury visited 20 dioceses in the southern province and in his Visitation Articles asked the clergy of the Archdiocese whether at baptism ... *is the mother's Christian name therein registered as well as the father's* ... . An entry in the parish register of *Gwaenysgor* in Flintshire in 1636 stated that *Laud* required that after a baptism the mother's name should be recorded as well as that of the father, implying that this had not been the practice before that date. The incumbent of *St George the Martyr* in *Canterbury* took matters even further by beginning, in 1634, to include the mother's maiden name as well as her Christian name but it seems likely that he misinterpreted the requirement as other incumbents (unfortunately for us) did not follow his lead. By the late 18th century it was common for baptism registers to include the mother's Christian name but this was not compulsory until 1813 and some parishes - including very large ones like Leeds - named only the father until

1812. This complicates matters if there are several men bearing the same Christian name and surname in the parish or if you try to do a 'parent search' on FamilySearch. Also, despite centuries of effort, neither parliamentary statutes nor church decrees ever succeeded in the long run in forcing people to go to a church either to worship or to be baptised, married or buried. Attempts to make clergymen keep rigidly standardised registers met the same fate. To assume that there *must* be an entry for your ancestor in a register somewhere is to risk plunging into a pitfall out of which you will never be able to climb – you may have to rely on evidence from other sources.

Between 1538 and 1754 some PRs include separate records of baptisms, marriages and burials in columns on the same page; others use different parts of the same book (often putting marriages in the middle); many run all three types of event together in a chronological sequence. These early registers can be very difficult to read in microform. After 1754, from which date marriages were supposedly kept separately, most parishes used the front of the book for baptisms and the back (with the book turned upside down) for burials.

LEGISLATION AFFECTING THE FORMAT OF PARISH REGISTERS

1643-1660

The period from 1643 to 1660, covering the civil war, the Commonwealth (1649-1653) and the Protectorate (1653-1660) - the latter two commonly referred to as the *Interregnum* - during which period many PRs were maintained poorly, if at all, can cause problems. In 1645, confirming a declaration of 1643, *The Directory of Public Worship* replaced the **Book of Common Prayer**, and birth, marriage and death were declared to be secular matters. *A fair Register Book of vel[l]um* was to be purchased by the parish and kept by the minister and entries made therein. Some parishes continued to use their existing PR, others purchased a new book as required but few of these appear to have survived. Based on the example from *Diss*, Norfolk, below, if the PRs contain no entries for much of this period it may be worth asking whether there are other parish papers which could contain entries for these years.

The 1653 *Act touching Marriages and the Registering thereof; and also touching Births and Burials* (see p.142 for more details) decreed that a Parish Register (registrar) be appointed. At *Diss* the appointment process is described: *Whereas by a late Acte of Parliament bearing date the xxiiij th day of August in this present yeare 1653 it is ordained that in every Parish there should choyse be made of a fitt person for to keep a register of all marriages, Births and Burialls according to the sd Acte, We the Inhabitants of Diss aforesd doe make choyse of Edward Wiseman of this towne to be Register for our Towne in Wittness whereof we have hereunto sett our hand.* The declaration is signed by the Minister and 22 inhabitants and *Mr Wiseman* took the oath on 4th

January 1653/4. However, this register is accompanied by the note: *Bound June 1820. Having been discovered accidentally amongst some old Parchments in a box.* How many other registers, begun in 1645 or 1653 and abandoned in 1660 when PRs were brought back into use, suffered the same fate?

A number of registers begin in September 1653 and continue in use after 1660. There is a chance that you may be lucky and find that marriage entries to 1660 include the names of the couple's fathers and possibly of other relatives (see pp.143 & 154). Also during this period *born* and *died* are used regularly, rather than *baptised* and *buried*.

STAMP ACTS

The government sometimes tried to use the registers as tax ledgers. *The 1694 Stamp Act* (taxing vellum, parchment and paper) failed to raise the expected revenue so another Act, effective from May 1695, introduced a tax on births (not baptisms), marriages and burials (and bachelors and widowers) and this was reinforced by a further Act, effective from 24 June 1696. In general, incumbents adapted their existing PRs to meet the needs of the tax assessors.

Some parishes did purchase new books, that for *Askham Bryan* beginning
A Register for Births, Burials & Weddings
At Askham Bryan From
may day the same Begins 1695.
This is the earliest PR to survive for the parish although the BTs survive intermittently from 1604 (see p.112).

The Acts also referred to children who were not christened *according to the Rites and Ceremonies of the Church of England* (principally Quakers) whose parents were nevertheless liable to pay the taxes; births of such children were to be reported to the incumbent or parish clerk within five days or a fine of 40s[hillings] was payable. Marriages not conforming to Church of England regulations were also taxable. Some incumbents began to enter *born...* [instead of baptised] *Quaker; Quakers married according to their custom; Quakers married after their manner at the Meeting House* and *Quaker buried in their place.* This practice generally continued for a short period only but can be very helpful in locating Quaker ancestors in a parish.

From 1698 to 1699 (a new register began 25 March 1700) the incumbent of *Hodnet* in Shropshire often annotated the register with who was to pay the tax and the amount to be paid:

> *Allice dau. to Thomas Charleton and Sarah baptized. The father living in Marchamley to pay the taxe 2s [hillings]*
> *Thomas Parton and Anne Browne married. The man, living in Peplow, to pay the taxe 2s 6d.*
> *Elizabeth dau. to John Bury and Anne Jenks buried. The grandfather, Richard Bury of Weston, to pay the taxe 4s.*

The 1783 Stamp Act (see p.116 for details) also produced a flurry of new registers. Read the following comments entered in *Diss* PRs and it becomes clear that some parishes maintained two parallel registers. Always check whether this is the case, particularly if there is no reference in the PR you are looking at to either payment of the tax or pauper status.

At this period an Act of Parliament took place, which requires a Stamp Duty of Three-pence upon the Entry of Burials, Births or Christenings. And accordingly a Stamped Vellum Register Book was procured by the Churchwardens, for the Entry of Burials, Births or Christenings paying Tax.

But Entry continues to be made in this Book of the Burials, Births or Christenings of Paupers; they being exempted by the above mentioned Act of Parliament from the tax.

August 1786: The Stamped Register Books being filled up, and the expense of them being found very great; a Licence was taken out; and Entry of Burials, Births and baptisms of Persons taxed and also of Paupers will be made in this Book promiscuously. Entries from this date until March 4 1794 *when the tax was repealed and ceased at this time* state whether the person was a pauper or was taxed.

HOW WELL WERE PARISH REGISTERS MAINTAINED?

Even if your ancestor was baptised (as an infant, child or adult) or buried the event may well not have been entered in the parish register. Do not assume that parish registers are necessarily a complete record of events within the parish. The law might say that the register should be removed from the parish chest every Sunday, and the week's events be entered, but it did not always happen. Many entries were scribbled on scraps of paper, or the incumbent or parish clerk relied on his memory until he had access to the register, and most researchers will come across notes in registers relating to entries *omitted at the proper time* because memory failed or the piece of paper disappeared. How many others were forgotten and never recorded? (See Baptisms: Chapter 11.) The PR for *Sherburn in Elmet* contains no entries for 1745 and 1746 but there are entries in the BTs (for which the churchwardens were responsible).

Marriages could be equally problematic. The PR for *Church Minshull*, Cheshire, in 1651 records *Thomas Dutton brought two strangers to be married* but gives no details. At *Church Hulme* in Cheshire, in 1807, there are two blank entries in the Marriage Register and a note in one of the spaces: *When the above marriage took place this Register book was locked up and could not be got at, in order to enter it therein* and, as there are no entries for marriages in the Bishop's Transcript (see p.110), there appears to be no record.

At *Feltham* in Middlesex, according to a note added into the marriage register, no registers were kept between November 1753 and July 1771. The marriage register during much of the incumbency of *Dr Alexander Kilgour* (1798-1818) (see also p.114) is a travesty with pages of signatures or of the marks (but no names) of people being married and the signatures or marks (but no names) of the witnesses, and with nothing else filled in - no names of parties, no places, no dates. Well into the 1800s the register contains many complaints referring to events which the by now deceased *Dr Kilgour* had failed to record.

This is one of the worst examples of a badly kept register but, to a lesser degree, its faults are repeated time and again throughout the country. There can be very few parishes which have maintained their books perfectly during the course of several hundred years and a thorough examination of most registers will reveal at least occasional blips.

In some parishes there is clear evidence that events were recorded during the year (possibly in a notebook) but that the parish register was written up once a year. At *Stockport* in Cheshire, between January 1801 and December 1812, the baptisms (and burials) for each year are separated into male and female entries and entered as separate annual lists (with females following males). As has been said before, every time an entry is copied out it increases the likelihood of an error creeping in - did the scribe copy accurately from his original source or did he omit the occasional entry or mistranscribe the odd letter, perhaps converting *Frances* to *Francis* - and would you have realized, when flicking through the microfilm, that there are two separate lists?

If you find yourself researching in a parish where the registers include the minimum of information it is often worth searching neighbouring parishes which may have more detailed registers. Even if you do not find a direct ancestor there you may discover collateral lines. *Dade* and *Barrington Registers* (see Chapter 12) may supply you with details of grandparents for baptisms, and of parents for adult burials. A few hundred yards away in a neighbouring parish you may be given only the name of a child's father or *John Smith buried*.

FORMAT OF PARISH REGISTERS FROM 1813

The first parish register format which most family historians encounter (as they begin to work backwards from civil registration certificates and census returns) is the one which came into existence in England and Wales on 1 January 1813, following *George Rose's Act of 1812*. From this date separate printed registers for baptisms, marriages and burials had to be maintained, in books supplied by the King's printer but at the expense of the parish. The format for baptisms and burials remains unchanged to this day; that for marriages was altered in 1837 but has remained the same since then. Despite centuries of endeavour, this was the first (largely) successful attempt to impose a standard form of registration within the Anglican Church and searching 19th and 20th century PRs is, in general, much easier than looking through earlier ones.

Even after 1813, when a printed format first became standard, what was actually entered in the register could vary considerably from parish to parish. The first column on the burial page is headed *Name* so all the clergyman was bound to enter there was the name of the person being buried. The fact that some included marital status (for men as well as women) and often, particularly for women, named the spouse while others included the parents' names at children's burials is a bonus, although nowhere near equal to the entries in *Dade* registers (see Chapter 12). Similarly with baptisms, the first column reads simply *When baptised* so the incumbent was under no obligation to add the date of birth but many did so, especially when dealing with a multiple baptism of several children from one family on the same day.

You might expect registers of rural parishes (where the incumbent would probably know most of his parishioners and where the year's entries for all three types of event might fit onto one page) to include more details than those in large industrial cities (some of which had by the 19th century several thousand entries for each type of event in one year and a constantly changing population) but it does not always follow. Some rural parishes were administered for absentee incumbents (pluralists: see p.192) by poorly paid (and sometimes almost illiterate) curates, who took little interest in their parishioners and less in keeping their registers accurately, whereas some industrial parishes were in the hands of dedicated men who kept immaculate registers and tried to make sure that members of their flock were, at the very least, baptised. The number of baptisms (often with ages or dates of birth) which took place when such men launched a determined campaign - like *Henry Bellairs* at *Bedworth* in Warwickshire in the early 19th century - emphasizes a major pitfall: **it is never safe to assume that your ancestor was baptised soon after birth**. (See also p.116-7.)

DATES IN PARISH REGISTERS

Be very careful when dealing with dates in parish registers. Much of Europe (the Catholic countries) adopted the new style Gregorian calendar (with the New Year beginning on 1st January and adjusted by omitting 10 days) in 1582; Scotland began the year with 1st January from 1600; England and Wales did not follow suit until 1752 and to that date retained the old style Julian calendar where the year officially began on 25th March with January, February and most of March coming in the previous year. Unless the system of *double-dating* (writing the date as, say, 25 January 1727/8) is adopted when copying out register entries your family tree can become very confused. A couple marrying in May 1723 and christening their child in February 1723 have been married for nine months but without *double-dating* the child can appear to have been born three months before the marriage. The IGI, and some other sites, do not use *double-dating* but transfer events in the affected period into the succeeding year so that February 1723 will appear not as

February 1723/4 but as February 1724. This clarifies the above situation but do not fall into the trap of looking for the full entry in the parish register in 1724 and failing to locate it - you will find it among the 1723 entries. *Double-dating* is frequently used when registers are transcribed and/or published.

Stay alert! Some incumbents used the New Style (NS) and began the year in their registers from 1st January before it became law, others did not adjust immediately and continued to use the Old Style (OS) for years after 1752 (in a few cases until as late as 1812) . In most registers it is 1751 which contains nine months (25th March to 31st December) but a few incumbents, realising years later that, to adjust to the NS calendar, one year had to have only nine months, began the next year of their register on 1st January (in *Topcliffe* parish registers - see p.94 - 1763 is the nine months year). If you are working backwards through the register, it is easy not to realize that this has happened and to think that three months of entries are missing. 1752 should have no entries between 3rd and 13th September (2nd September was followed by 14th September; the necessary adjustment having by now increased to 11 days).

Pre-1752, incumbents who abbreviated dates in their registers can lead you astray. If you encounter one who wrote *8th of 8th* 1732 (or, more commonly, *8th 8ber*) do not make the mistake of interpreting this as 8th August 1732 when it is actually 8th October. September to December (based on the Latin numbers) are the seventh to the tenth months in the Julian calendar but the ninth to the twelfth in the Gregorian. **Despite modern computer practice, you are advised always to write dates using letters for the months**: **2.10.1789 is 2nd October 1789 to most Britons but 10th February 1789 to Americans**.

REGNAL YEARS

The regnal year starts with the date of the accession of each monarch and runs for twelve months (the first regnal year of Elizabeth II ran from 6 February 1952 to 5 February 1953). Acts of Parliament used this dating system until 1963, from which date *Acts of Parliament shall be numbered according to the order in which they are enacted in the calendar year, so that the first Act of 1963 will be known as '1963 c[hapter].1' instead of bearing title such as it would at present '11 & 12 Eliz.2, c.11'.* Statutes relevant to parish registers, civil registration, Wills and other legal documents are often cited by regnal year - do not panic, there are plenty of books and websites which translate regnal years into calendar years. The system is sometimes found in early parish registers, particularly during the reign of *Elizabeth I*, but usually both calendar and regnal year are given, as can be seen in *Leeds* PR ... *every person's name wedded ...from the fourth day of Aprill, In the yeare of o[u]r lorde God 1589, in the xxxj yeare of the reigne of o[u]r soveraigne lady queen Elizabeth.*

ROMAN AND ARABIC NUMERALS

The example on page 100 from *Leeds* PR includes both an *Arabic* (1589) and a *Roman (xxxj)* numeral. Today, Arabic numbers are almost universally used and Roman ones occur infrequently - on some clocks and watches, for the year a television programme was made, and in the preface/introductory section of books are instances which spring to mind. The GRO used Roman numerals from 1837-1851 and Arabic ones thereafter (see p.79 for possible pitfalls). In PRs the year is usually given in Arabic numbers but dates are often in Roman ones until the late 16th century in England or the 18th century in Scotland (and the same applies to sums of money in Wills and inventories). The sight of these numbers, in old handwriting, in original documents can come as a nasty shock but there are plenty of books and websites which explain them. Some published PRs stick rigidly to the original format (*Luke darwyne of Holbeck had a childe Christeynide the Sayme xxvjth Daye of maye Anno dni 1572, namede Elizabethe)* but, in most, dates in Roman numerals are converted to Arabic ones and the entries are put into a standard (shorter) format. This normally consists of the date, name of the child and name of the father but watch for the few parishes which follow the above format and give the name of the father, the date, and then the name of the child.

QUAKERS (SOCIETY OF FRIENDS)

Quakers have always objected to the names of the days of the week and of the months because of their pagan connotations so they use numbers instead. Until 1752 the 'first month' was March (with much debate as to whether the year began on 1st or 25th March) and the 'twelfth month' was February. From 1752 January became the 'first month' and December the 'twelfth month'. Again, *double-dating* is recommended when transcribing pre-1752 entries and (as above: p.100) it is recommended that, for any period, you substitute letters for numbers as the practice of putting the month before the day was often used. Gravestones in the Friends' Burial Ground at *Carperby* in Wensleydale, Yorkshire as late as 1970 are still using this format – (JAW) *born 27th of 9th month 1882 died 7th of 1st month 1970*. (For more details about Quaker gravestones see p.173.)

LATIN IN PARISH REGISTERS

Before 1733 Latin (of a sort) was often used in parish registers in England and Wales, and there are plenty of Latin word lists available in book form and online with translations of commonly-used words, numbers and Christian names. There are also good online courses in Latin and in palaeography (old handwriting). One phrase to be wary of is *eodem die* (often found in pre-1733 date columns) – it is easy to write this in your notes and think that you can work out the meaning later but it is no help to discover, when you are back in Australia or have logged off a commercial website, that *eodem die* means *the same day* and that you should have looked at previous entries to find the one giving the actual date. Remember that Latin was used in Roman Catholic Registers until the mid-20th century.

Most Christian names are similar in Latin and English but, among others, be wary of *Anna* which can mean *Ann(e), Hannah* or *Nancy*; *Jacobus* which may be *Jacob* or *James*; *Maria* which is commonly *Mary* but sometimes *Maria*; *Radulphus* which is usually *Ralph* but may remain as *Radulph*; and *Gulielmus* which is *William*. If in doubt, look at the Bishop's Transcript for the same year (if it survives), which may well be in English. Bear in mind that *filius* and *filia* (son and daughter) were often abbreviated to *fil:* or simply *f.* Coupled with the tendency to abbreviate Christian names, this can cause major problems. *Fran: fil. Jo: Smith* could be *Francis son*, or *Frances daughter*, of *John, Jonathan* or *Joseph Smith* and, if the BT fails you, there is no easy answer.

Latin word endings change depending on whether the subject is masculine or feminine, singular or plural. In general, words relating to masculine subjects in PRs and Wills end in *-us* (singular) and *-i* (plural) and those with feminine subjects in *-a* (s) and *-ae* (pl.)

THE (OLD ENGLISH) ALPHABET

Researchers often experience difficulty in reading documents from the 16th to the early 18th centuries as the style of handwriting and the formation of some letters are very different from that to which they are accustomed. The old form of *th* looks like a modern *y* so *ye* is actually *the* and *yt* is *that*. One tip, if you are struggling, is to extract entries from a later period, which you can read, and then gradually work backwards through the PR, looking for names with a similar structure.

The use of capital letters at the beginning of words was customary by the mid-16th century but the 'rule' was not always applied (and looking at PRs you can usually find words which you think should have a capital letter beginning with a lower case one and vice versa). Watch out for double *ff* particularly at the beginning of a name. Before the introduction of capital letters, the use of such double letters commonly served the same purpose; *ffrancis* and *ffrances* (and *ffiennes* and *ffaulkner* as surnames) can be found to this day although most people replaced the *ff* with *F* by the end of the 18th century.

THE LONG OR LEADING S

The letter which is responsible for more misunderstanding than any other is *s*. Until at least the 18th century *s* was commonly written as a *long s* (see pp.103 and 243 for examples); for a double *ss* the first letter was sometimes written as a *long s* and the second as an 'ordinary' *s* (hence the term *leading s.)* Look at the example from *Pocklington* PR on page 169 to see just how easy it could be to confuse *two long ss* with double *ff*; as late as the mid-19th century census returns, some enumerators were still using the *long s* and a website bemoans that *Crossland* and *Crossley* have been mis-indexed as *Crofsland* and *Crofsley*. It was the invention of printing which created the worst confusion. Italics could cope with the *long s* (as on pp.243, 271 and below) but 'ordinary' type could not, so the letter was usually printed as an *f* but with a nub on the left side only and not 'crossing' the letter (or with a nub on the right) as in a genuine *f*. In early printed documents and books it can be impossible to distinguish between the two and transcribers and indexers, right down to the present day, have misread the situation and inserted *f* instead of *s* so 'creating' surnames which have never actually existed.

EXTRACT FROM GREY'S ECCLESIASTICAL LAW 1735

(note in particular *refuse* and *himself)*

> *A.* It ſeems in theſe Caſes, that the Biſhop, (inaſmuch as he hath done his Duty) may *re-ſuſe both*, without ſubjecting himſelf to any of the ſaid Inconveniencies: Tho' it is affirmed by ſome, that in ſuch Caſes he may award a ſecond *Jure Patronatus.*

BRIEFS, PEW LISTS, LEGACIES AND THE WEATHER

As well as details of baptisms, marriages and burials PRs may contain all sorts of miscellaneous information. Some parish clerks and churchwardens used the registers as a 'parish note book' and entered notes on terriers (see p.192), briefs, pew rents, legacies left to the parish, taxes paid and even the state of the weather and the harvest. There is always the possibility that you may pick up an interesting snippet of information relating occasionally to your ancestor or, more often, to the place where they lived.

BRIEFS

Briefs were the equivalent of a modern 'flag day'. A letter (usually called either a *Church Brief* or a *King's Letter*, because it was issued by the sovereign as head of the church) was distributed to churches throughout England licensing a collection to be taken for a specified object of charity. The collection was often taken in church (with a box being passed from pew to pew) but some parishes undertook a house to house collection and official collectors were appointed to receive the contributions and see them safely delivered to the 'object of charity', be it people held for ransom by barbary pirates, 'distressed Protestants' in Europe, churches which needed rebuilding (often after a fire) or individuals who had suffered through fire or flood.

Wragby parishioners donated 6s 2d for *Edward Christian of Grantham* in 1664; 4s 0d for *George Williams of Rampton in the county of Cambridge* in 1670; 5s 6d for *Stephen Harrison of the City of Durham* in 1671.

In 1711, *Beverley St Mary* collected £1-0s-5d for the relief of *Charles Empson, late of Booth in the parish of Howden who suffered by fire and water to the loss of £2000 and upwards.*

The *Beverley* register (printed by the YPRS in 2008) contains more than 100 pages of briefs for the period 1700-1766, giving the amount of loss suffered by the supplicants and the sum collected in the parish, and many naming individuals from most of the counties of England, Wales and further afield. This is an exceptional PR but some briefs are noted in many PRs and it could be worth your while to browse through any you come across.

In this age of 'climate change' and flooding, it is interesting to read in *Thornton-in-Lonsdale* PR that in 1736, 1s 5½d was collected for *Storm of Hail at Mobberley &c in Com. Chester*, followed by another 11d the following month; that at *Clapham* 3s 7¼d was collected for the people of *Mobberley*; and in *Beverley* that *William Yarwood and others* lost £1905 in the hailstorm. Other briefs reveal *an inundation of the sea* at *Brighthelmstone [Brighton]* in 1723; a flood at *Halifax* in 1724; a hurricane at *Hornsea* in 1733; a hailstorm at *Standon* in Hertfordshire in 1739 (*Joseph Ives & sufferers*); a flood at *Foulness* in Essex in 1741 (*Daniel Jackson and others*); and a hailstorm at *Bermondsey, Newington, Lambeth* and *Camberwell* in 1751 (affecting *John Atfield & 42 others*).

In March 1715 a brief was received in Beverley *For relief of the Cowkeepers in the Counties of Middlesex, Surr[e]y and Essex, the loss of whose Cows (in number 5,418) and Calves (in number 439) amounts to the sum of £24,539-14s and upwards, at the rate of £6 per Cow, including loss therein by milk and rent* and £3 18s 9d was collected from house to house in the following week. There had been major outbreaks of cattle plague (now called rinderpest) in England in 1348 and 1480, and the 1714/15 outbreak was followed by another in 1745. In the days before insurance, and when no compensation was payable, entries like this bring home how hard life could be for our ancestors, deprived of their livelihood by such disasters.

Briefs were abolished in 1828.

PEW LISTS

Fixed pews (an enclosed seat in a church, also called stalls or seats) were uncommon before the 16th century but became increasingly common as the century advanced. In 1701 *Humphrey Prideaux* published **Directions to Church-Wardens for the Faithful Discharge of their Office** (by 1895 it was in its 16th edition: the duties of church-wardens were many and various and the position was no sinecure). He wrote *As the Church-wardens have the care of the Church, so also have they of all the Seats therein, and not only to repair them, but also to see that good Order be preserved in them ... that every Man regularly take that Seat and that Place in it which he hath a right to...* (repeated verbatim in the 1895 edition). There were rules relating to the positioning of pews, and who should sit in them, but, as in so many other cases, what happened was very much down to individual churchwardens and their interpretation of the regulations. *Richard Gough*'s **History of Myddle**, written at the beginning of the 18th century (and of which several editions have been published) is based on the families who, at that time, occupied pews, or parts of a pew, in a Shropshire parish and provides a fascinating account of village life and characters. In some PRs, plans of pews within a church survive. In others there are lists of pewholders and, if you are fortunate, these may be amended as people died or moved house (many pews were annexed to specific properties). In the 1570s, when seats were being installed in *Leeds* Parish Church, many names of parishioners are given (together with the names of the churchwardens, of whom there were usually about 10 at a time - see p.190). In 1577, for instance, *Mem: that William Clyffe haithe bulded one stalle in the little Allay, upon the sou[th]e syde of the Churche, and haithe geven for the rome of the same stalle unto the churchwardens for the Churche workes, ij shillings.* In 1582, *... it is agreed ... that Alice Walker, wyff of Thomas Walker, laite wyff of James Cowper, shall quyetlie have and enjoye, a sufficient place or rowme for hir selfe in one Stalle which was laite hir said husbands, James Cowper, for and during hir Lyffe.*

LEGACIES LEFT TO THE PARISH

Many parishioners, in their Wills, left sums of money to the parish, to be invested and the interest to be paid out annually, usually for the relief of the poor of the parish or township or to enable children to be put out as apprentices. Many churches contain *Charity Boards* detailing such donations and it is worth trying to locate such a board for the parish where your ancestors lived; they may be named as having given money or you may be able to visualise them receiving a handout, either of money or of loaves of bread, particularly at Christmas and Easter.

WEATHER

As well as meteorological events (hail, rain, snow and wind) mentioned in Briefs, some incumbents and parish clerks also made notes of outstanding events. *Aurora Borealis* (the Northern Lights) were seen *with great brilliancy* in England in early March 1715/16 and *Francis Lupton* (see p.113) wrote in his personal notebook: *3 March, upon the night before did appear the greatest* light in the air, north west at 9 in the evening, the like not known in the memory of man, upon the 6th in the evening the strongest.

John Cock noted in *Thornton in Lonsdale* PR: *March 16th 1719 is Memorable for a prodigious Quantity of Snow falling which being driven by a violent Wind Drifted the ways and roads to that degree they were not to be travelled on for many days nay the Storme went so high that [next] door Neighbours... cou'd not visit one another without difficulty ... [until] the wind abating with boots on their legs and spades in their hands, they made a Communicacion from one house to another.*

Thomas Stubbings, the parish clerk of *Seaton Ross* noted interesting details on a blank page in the burial register:

> Ine the yeare 1783 was verey drye and followed by a hardwinter it be gan December 24th 1783 and continued with some Intermillion till april 4th Hay got from 3^d pr Stone to 8^d 1784
>
> In the year 1826 was averrey dry Summorer Oats and Spring grain Ingeneral averrey bad crop and Wheate In general verrey good Water was Sold in this town by Thos Whitcliff he fetched it from Bielby River at 1^d pr Buckot the winter following hay was Sold at 1^s pr Stone and upwards Harvest Commenced this year on Everingham Feast Monday all in general the Same week Thomas Stubbings Parish Clerk
>
> A High Wind Blowed down Houses and Barns the Evening of the Las day of the year 1778 A High Wind that Blowed down Houses and Barns and a great Deal of Plantations and Timber trees on the 7th day of January 1839

106

BISHOPS' TRANSCRIPTS (BTS)

WHAT ARE BISHOPS' TRANSCRIPTS?

Bishops' Transcripts are contemporary 'copies' of parish registers in England and Wales. (Similar transcripts exist from 1733 in the Isle of Man; there are no other BTs of this type elsewhere in the British Isles).

The first mandate ordering their compilation was issued by the Convocation of Canterbury in 1597, and confirmed in 1603, saying that *the churchwardens shall once every year, within one month after the five and twentieth day of March, transmit unto the Bishop of the diocese, or his Chancellor, a true copy of the names of all persons christened, married or buried in their parish, in the year before (ended the said five and twentieth day of March), and the certain days and months in which every such christening, marriage, and burial was had.* The transcript was to be on parchment, signed by the minister and the churchwardens (if your ancestor was a minister or churchwarden you may well be able to see his genuine signature here) and forwarded to the relevant diocesan registry where it was to be *faithfully preserved*. It was intended that the BTs would be used if the PR was damaged or destroyed and would be available for purposes of comparison if it appeared that the PR had been subject to *alteration, erasure or forgery*. How effective the mandate was will be seen elsewhere in this chapter. As with much government legislation, what the mandate said and how well it was enforced depended very much on individual incumbents and churchwardens. Some bishops made strenuous efforts to ensure that its terms were complied with, others did not. BTs continued generally until the mid-19th century (in some areas until the end of that century).

LOCATION OF BISHOPS' TRANSCRIPTS

Usually they are to be found in a county or diocesan record office. Do not make the mistake of assuming that PRs and BTs are kept in the same repository. They often are but it pays to check with the likely record repository, before setting out on a journey. In Cheshire, for example, both types of record are at the record office in *Chester* but, for *Durham*, the PRs are largely in *Durham CRO* whilst the BTs are in *Durham University Library* Archives and Special Collections. BTs for the five counties included in the original Diocese of *Lincoln* (Lincoln, Bedford, Buckingham, Huntingdon, Leicester) have been sorted and dispersed to the relevant county repositories but those for the four counties in *Lichfield Diocese* (see p.51) are all still held at *Lichfield Record Office*. Yorkshire has one principal repository for each historic Riding, between them holding a large proportion of the county's original PRs, but none of these holds any BTs, the bulk of which are at the Borthwick Institute for Archives at the *University of York*, with most of the remainder (principally for parishes in the *Archdeaconry of Richmond*) at the West Yorkshire Archive Service office in *Leeds*. Those for Wales are all at the National Library of Wales in *Aberystwyth* with the exception of a few border parishes whose records are in *Chester* and *Hereford*.

If you need to consult BTs for a parish both before and after the mid-1830s (where they survive) bear in mind that you may have to visit two repositories. A major re-structuring of dioceses began in 1836 and this resulted, in some cases, in a division of the records. Berkshire, for example, previously an Archdeaconry in the diocese of Salisbury, was transferred in 1836 to the Diocese of Oxford but its BTs were not, so its pre-1836 BTs are in Wiltshire & Swindon Archives (in *Chippenham*); post 1836 BTs are in *Oxford* (as are those for Buckinghamshire after about 1845). The Diocese of *Ripon* (now the Diocese of *Ripon and Leeds*) was created in 1836 and covered a large part of the West and North Ridings of Yorkshire so many parishes, with BTs in *York* until the mid-1840s, have later ones in *Leeds*.

The LDS church has microfilmed BTs for many counties and a substantial number of entries in the IGI are taken from this source (see p.54).

SURVIVAL RATE OF BTS

The survival rate for BTs varies greatly between dioceses. Do not expect to find BTs for every parish from 1597. In some counties a number do survive from this date (even earlier in a few counties; Kent has BTs from 1558, Lincolnshire from 1567) but Essex, London and Middlesex have virtually no BTs before 1800; Hampshire and Surrey very few; Durham and Northumberland few before 1760. BTs for several dioceses begin after 1660; others survive from various dates in the 18th century. Cathedral churches often did not keep them and many Peculiars (see p.185), because they were outside the normal jurisdiction of the bishop, submitted them sporadically if at all. Equally, do not expect them all to be called BTs; at the Borthwick Institute they are listed as *Parish Register Transcripts*; in East Anglia (and sometimes in Lincolnshire and Kent) they are often known as *Archdeacon's Transcripts* or *Register Bills*. Be aware that, for many dioceses, the documents have been sorted and micro-filmed by parish, so that you can search a straight run almost like a PR, whereas in others the BTs for whole deaneries, archdeaconries or even a diocese for each year are stored, and have been filmed, together.

WHAT INFORMATION MIGHT A BT CONTAIN?

The standard definition of a BT hides a host of pitfalls and possibilities. BTs are most useful when you do not have access to the PRs because they do not survive, are still at the church, in a different record office to the one you are visiting, or are damaged (and in some cases BTs are in much better condition and easier to read than the PR). However, to rely on them to the exclusion of the PR is a very risky procedure. While, in the majority of cases, the PR will contain more entries and more information than the BT, in a substantial minority of cases the reverse is true.

Ideally, you should consult both PR and BT for any entry relevant to your family tree. Do not fall into the trap of believing that the entries in the two sources will be precisely the same. **BTs pre-1733 will often be in English when the equivalent entry in the PR is in Latin**. You will find instances of entries in one source but not the other and often, when there is a pair of entries, there may be considerable differences between them. Where names vary significantly it can be very difficult to know which is correct and you may need a third source (census, Will or family bible) to help you decide.

At *Alne*, in Yorkshire, in 1750 the PR (correctly) has *George son of John Forster* baptised but the BT gives *John son of John Forster*. At *Acomb* in 1793 the PR (and the printed PR) have *Thomas son of Thomas Holmes* baptised whereas the BT (correctly) has *Thomas son of John Holmes* baptised. Such errors are not common enough to concern most people but, if you are having difficulty locating a particular baptism, where all his (and in such cases it usually is 'his') siblings can be traced in a parish, it may be worth double-checking entries where father and son apparently bear the same Christian name - and, if you find two *John son of John* entries (and no infant burial) cross-checking with the other source just in case the writer's thoughts were temporarily elsewhere.

REMEMBER THAT THE BT IS A COPY

There is another pitfall, more common to BTs than PRs, connected to the fact that parishes were responsible for providing (and paying for) their own parish register books and parchment for the BTs. Watch out for the parsimonious scribe who saved space, particularly with baptisms, by running entries on from each other, rather than starting each entry on a new line. Many people, when searching for a baptism for a child whose Christian name they already know, will run their eye down the left hand side of the page or parchment, where the Christian name is usually to be found. Looking at:

> *John son of Thomas Smith and Peter son of*
> *James Brown chr. 23 July Nathan son of*

would you have spotted *Peter Brown* or *Nathan*?

Do not forget that the BT is a copy, whether of the PR or of the scraps of paper used to compile it, and all copies are prone to errors. The choice of wording for the pitfall *There's no entry in the BT for my ancestor. Why should I check the Parish Register as well, they're identical copies?* was very deliberate. Many years ago, when searching for my 4 x great grandfather, *William Pickering*, in *Greasley* in Nottinghamshire, I looked at the BT (in the CRO) but failed to check the PR (at that time still held at the church), and did not find him. Study the entries overleaf and see why - it is a very easy mistake for a copier to make (and hopefully no-one needs reminding that spelling was fluid):

PR: *16 Mar 1800*   *William son John & Ann Bealey bapt.*
         16 Mar 1800   *William son Robert & **Mary Pickerell** bapt.*
         23 Mar 1800   *George son of Robert & Sarah Shaw bapt.*

BT: *16 Mar 1800*   *William son John & Ann Bealey bapt.*
         16 Mar 1800   *William son Robert & **Sarah Shaw** bapt.*

Three children in the PR became two in the BT, with the second child acquiring the parents of the third. *William Pickerell* and *George Shaw* both had fathers called *Robert* and it would take only a momentary lapse of concentration for the writer, on resuming, to see the word *Robert* and continue writing from where he thought he had left off.

WHO COMPILED THE BTS?

Once again, much depended on the individuals involved. When the system of PRs and BTs was established at the end of the 16th century, the minister was largely responsible for writing up the PR but the churchwardens (see p.107) were given charge of the BT. Some churchwardens took their responsibilities seriously and produced immaculate documents; others scribbled out the minimum amount of information required (note that the original instructions required only the dates and *the names of all persons christened, married or buried,* nothing was said about including parents' names for baptisms; relationships or ages for burials; and anything except the names of the couple for marriages); a few added pithy comments to individual entries. Watch out for a tendency for BTs sometimes to omit marriages: at *Rillington* in Yorkshire (see p.181), they are not recorded from 1802-1812; at *Church Hulme* in Cheshire (see p.132) from 1754-1812 (and, as this was a chapelry to *Sandbach*, it is easy to assume that there were no marriages after 1754 and to search unsuccessfully in the PR of the mother church); at *Wattisham* and *Preston* in Suffolk from 1755 to the mid-1760s (and the PRs are missing for these years). After 1837 it is rare to find marriages recorded in BTs. At the next level, some bishops (or their staff) kept an eye on the returns (and chased up late or missing ones) while others appear to have filed them unread - often in poor conditions so that many have been damaged or not survived.

I do not know of a single parish which has a complete run of BTs from 1597 to 1837 (excluding the mid-1640s to 1660 when none were kept) and it is essential, as you work through a set of BTs, to note the dates - not just the years - covered by each document. This can be difficult because the heading at the top of the parchment has often faded or is difficult to locate on microfilm but it can be vital.

LADY DAY COMPLICATIONS

The 1597 mandate (see p.107), said that BTs were to cover the period from Lady Day (25 March: prior to 1752 the start of the New Year) to the following Lady Day. However, it became customary for the BT to be handed in when the Bishop, or his representative, made his annual visitation to an area and this can cause a major pitfall for the unwary searcher. Some churchwardens ended a BT on Lady Day, put it ready for the visitation (which might be several months later) and did not start the new one until after that event so that entries for weeks or even months (particularly in April and May) may not be recorded in the BT; others appear to have used arbitrary dates. At *Taxal* in Cheshire, one BT covers the period 20 April 1758 to 10 May 1759 and the next goes from 10 June 1759 to 4 June 1760 so the entries for 11 May to 9 June 1759 (including two marriages) appear only in the PR.

Often the year written on the outside of a BT (and this is commonly the year listed in a record office's calendar) is not the main year of that document. One covering 25 March 1740 to 25 March 1741 will often be titled 1741 - the year it was filed in the registry - and it is easy not to realise that you are actually looking at the BT for 1740. This problem is compounded after 1752. As mentioned above, some parishes continued the Lady Day tradition right through to 1812, others dated their BTs from 1 January to 31 December (making the change at varying times between 1752 and 1812) but the date on the outside will frequently be the year following that to which the entries relate. It is also very easy to overlook the fact that, where the Lady Day tradition persists, the first three months of the calendar year after 1752 will appear on the BT for the previous year. **Searcher beware!**

SEARCHING LARGE BTS

The size of pre-1813 BTs can vary from a piece of parchment three inches square to one almost as big as a double-bed sheet. The former tended to go missing because they were so small and easy to lose, the latter can be incredibly difficult to search accurately on microfilm. Some larger ones, when being filmed, required ten or more frames to cover one year with parts of frames overlapping and often no indication of month or year on a frame. There is sometimes the added complication of entries from chapelries being listed independently but included on the same BT as the mother church. It is very easy to think you have searched all the columns on the sheet when, in fact, you have missed one, or part of one. Anyone who has battled with BTs for parishes like *Leeds* or *Halifax*, each with several chapelries, will understand the problem.

SEARCHING BTS AFTER 1813

Rose's *Act of 1812* amended the rules regarding BTs. From 1813, copies of the events of the previous year were to be made on duplicate copies of the baptism, marriage and burial forms provided for the PRs. The copies were to be made by the end of February, signed and verified, and transmitted *by the Post* to the registrar of the Diocese by 1st June. From this date (barring a few errors, omissions, spelling mistakes and the odd one which went astray) the BTs, become what many people mistakenly assume they have always been- contemporary copies of the PRs. After 1837 marriages are rarely included in BTs; the introduction of civil registration (see p.83) required the keeping of two marriage register books and it was generally thought that a third copy was unnecessary.

BISHOPS' TRANSCRIPTS MAY PRE-DATE PARISH REGISTERS

Finally, it is worth noting that in many areas, particularly in the first half of the 17th century, BTs (although never a continuous run) can pre-date PRs, often by fifty years or more. Of more than twenty parishes in the Diocese of York whose earliest surviving PRs begin between 1653 and 1655 all but three have at least some earlier BTs. It is always worth asking the record office if there are earlier BTs for the parish you are interested in.

BT ([REGISTER] BILL) FOR HARPHAM 1694
(note that the two marriages include only the wife's Christian name)

RESOLUTION:

I will remember that pre-1813 Parish Registers do not have a set format and what is included at any given time may differ from parish to parish. I will remember that PRs and BTs may contain different information and will always try to look at both if they are available.

CHAPTER 11

BAPTISMS

Making the assumption that your ancestor was baptised in an Anglican church soon after birth can cause you all sorts of problems. If you fail to find a baptism in the expected register, particularly if other siblings are baptised there, it may pay you to look further afield – in the BTs if they survive (see Chapter 10) or try Nonconformist registers - but it may equally well be that the entry never existed. This shows up most clearly when some change in the law suddenly persuades large numbers of people that they, and their children, ought to be baptised for purely practical reasons (to obtain written evidence of their existence) or when incumbents or parish clerks feel the need to protect themselves against accusations of not keeping proper registers.

Francis Lupton, parish clerk at *Leeds St Peter* in Yorkshire from July 1694 (and also responsible for several churches and chapels most of which did not at this date keep separate registers) was obviously covering his back when he wrote on 31 January 1694/5 *Wanting Room to Ingross the Rest of the Baptisms which were in the year 1694, I am forced to place them upon the second Leaf ... where you may find the names of such children as were Baptised at the Old Church. Mr Mawde, curate at the old Church, hath Baptized Children in many men's houses, and neither he nor the parents acquainted me therewith, and Likewise many children at the several Chapels, and as for Presbyterian Children* [whose births should have been entered in the PR following the 1694 Stamp Act] *not one Ingrossed because of their obstinacy, and Let them and others blame them that are blameworthy* [spelling modernised]. How many events were never officially recorded can only be estimated from researching local families and noting 'missing' baptisms of children named in Wills.

Do not forget that many pitfalls mentioned in previous chapters still apply. Surnames are infinitely variable and similar spellings are always worth investigating: *Bracegirdle* in north-east Cheshire in the 17th century is also recorded as *Brassgirdle, Brasskettle, Bratchgirdle, Brescudel* and *Bretchgyrdell* and *William Milner*'s children in Yorkshire in the mid-18th century were baptised variously as *Milner, Miller* and *Milnes*. Handwriting can be hard to interpret, especially if dealing with an unfamiliar name. Remember *Eliph Robinson* who appears in the IGI as *Elijah* and *Cliff* (see p.56). Entries may be missing because the incumbent lost the scrap of paper on which he wrote the details or they may be hard to find because the scrap of paper surfaced months, or even years, later and the entry was recorded in the register, often wherever a space could be found. Not all incumbents were as helpful as the one who wrote *for remainder of baptisms for this year see 15 pages back.* Baptists, Quakers and the Salvation Army did not baptise infants (the latter two principally because they objected to the use of water) and by no means all Anglican or Nonconformist baptisms are of infants (see p.115).

BAPTISM & CHRISTENING: PUBLIC & PRIVATE BAPTISM

Baptism and *Christening* are not strictly synonymous - the former indicates acceptance into the Christian church (and permits burial in consecrated ground); the latter involves the giving of Christian name(s) - but they are used interchangeably by most incumbents and legislators. Sometimes *double baptisms* occur when entries for both a *private* baptism (usually performed at home soon after the birth and often when the child was not expected to survive) and a *public* baptism or christening (when the child was *received into the Congregation of the Church*) find their way into parish registers, possibly several months apart, and mislead researchers into thinking they are dealing with two children. A Suffolk incumbent explained the system clearly in his registers: *Robert son of Joseph Pettit and Sarah his wife (late Sarah Last) was born March 19 1796, was baptised privately March 28 1796 and was received in the Church April 10 1796.* Similarly at *Hemsworth* in 1808 *Catharine daughter of Mich[ae]l Woodcock, Surgeon was born Feb: 20th 1807, baptized 2 days after, but not christened until April 26th 1808.* A Cheshire incumbent demonstrated where problems could arise when he noted against an 1813 baptism *entered on July 4 when privately baptised and entered again on September 26 by mistake when christened.* At *Sherburn in Elmet* a note at the bottom of page 137, covering late 1826 baptisms reads *12 December William son Edward and Jane Lewis, surgeon born 4 December. More legally entered when it (sic) was formerly (sic) christened in church, see page 149.* On page 149 appears: *7 April 1828 William Hunter son of (details as above) baptised. Half-baptised* is sometimes used instead of *privately baptised* as in the example from *Feltham*, Middlesex (see p.97): *1 Mar 1821 George William son of George and Elizabeth Turner bapt. ... said by his parents to have been half-baptised by Dr Kilgour the day after its birth - born 30 September 1817.*

DOUBLE BAPTISMS

As well as the above examples, there are numerous reasons for baptisms apparently occurring twice (sometimes in different parishes). Children born away from home would often be baptised soon after birth and then recorded later in their 'home' parish register. On 9 February 1777, at *Sutton on the Forest*, *John Hill*'s son *Richard* was baptised. On the same day *Richard*'s elder brother, *William*, was *received in the Church; child was born and baptised 29 July 1775 in Province of Nova Scotia, North America.* The IGI lists both *Richard* and *William* as being baptised on 9 February - without looking at the full entry in the PR it would be easy to assume they were twins.

114

If the family classed as gentry, children might be baptised where they were born but later entered, as a record, in the PR of the church connected with their family. Remember that PRs were accepted as legal documents and succession to an estate could depend on a verifiable baptism entry. It was also common for girls, of whatever social standing, to return 'home' to their mother for the birth of their first child and for the child to be baptised there.

Children baptised into one religious persuasion but who later converted to another may well have two baptisms. *John Kirk* (born 1800) and *Mary Kirk* (born 1805) were baptised as adults in a Methodist chapel in *Macclesfield*, Cheshire in 1824. In 1837 (see p.116) *Mary* was baptised in *Prestbury* parish church and in 1864 *John* was baptised in *Pott Shrigley* parish church (both in Cheshire). In all three registers the dates of birth were given: without these it would be difficult to accept that *John* was baptised for a second time aged 63. Anyone finding either Anglican baptism would learn the standard post-1812 details; finding the Nonconformist entry reveals that *John* was the first son, and *Mary* the second daughter, *of Thomas Kirk, collier of Adlington by Ellen Maddocks daughter of George Maddocks husbandman of Poynton*. Bear in mind that some Nonconformist registers include more detail than Anglican ones and may approach the amount of detail given in *Dade* and *Barrington* Registers (see Chapter 12). Many provide at least the mother's maiden name.

ADULT BAPTISMS

If you find an adult baptism in an Anglican church it is always worth casting round to see if you can locate an infant baptism or registration in a Nonconformist record which may provide more detail. *Richard Savile a Quaker aged 17* baptised at *Sutton on the Forest* in 1779 might be found in Quaker records. Many converts to the Roman Catholic faith, particularly in the 19th century, will prove to have earlier Anglican baptism entries. This can cause problems if the Catholic baptism does not indicate that the person being baptised is an adult, or if both entries are included in the IGI; again, you can be misled into believing there are two people instead of one.

If you find a marriage but cannot find a baptism for one of the couple, look in the days immediately preceding the marriage, on the marriage day itself or even later. Many incumbents would not marry couples without evidence that they were baptised Anglicans. On 6 August 1764, in Yorkshire, *Elizabeth Jackson* was baptised as *an adult* and, on the same day, married *William Barchard*; and in 1825 the baptism took place of *Rebecca daughter of Thomas and Elizabeth Harrison, quaker, born 11 July 1791 and wife of William Whytehead.*

Many registers will give no details of non-infant baptisms but some do. In 1712 *Rebecca* daughter of *Sara Carr* alias *Redmaine* [*Sara Carr* had married *John Redmayne* in 1709] was baptised at *Thornton in Lonsdale* receiving *the ministration of publick baptism of those of riper years* and in 1808 *Benjamin Whiley a Blackmoor at riper years* was baptised there.

Watch out for: children born in rural areas in winter, or during haymaking or harvest, who were frequently baptised with the next sibling to be born; those with peripatetic parents - in the armed forces, Nonconformist ministers, gentry, coachmen, pedlars, canal or railway workers among others - who may have children baptised in unexpected places; and those who may have saved the whole batch to baptise when they finally settled down (often many miles and several counties away from the birthplaces of both parents and children).

Remember that parishes would go to great lengths to avoid becoming responsible for a child which might become a charge on the parish and would enter as much information as possible in the register. Does anyone claim *William Nightingale* who was baptised at *Kirk Smeaton, in 1778 son of Thomas Nightingale (dead some months ago) and Ann delivered at Wentbridge being conveyed thither by the vagrant cart on her road to her settlement* or *Robert, son of John and Betty Robson,* privately baptised at *Bilbrough,* in 1769 with a note *NB The father died in the Garrison at Hull and served 14 Months Apprenticeship at Leeds.* These two mothers were permitted to baptise their children in Yorkshire, then sent on to their places of settlement which could be many miles away.

At least these baptism entries provide clues for researchers to follow, unlike the entry in *Almondbury* (*Huddersfield*) PR in 1826, *Sarah daughter of ... baptised. The Parents left and never gave in their Names.*

THE EFFECTS OF GOVERNMENT LEGISLATION ON BAPTISMS

1694-6 STAMP ACTS
See p.96 for details.

1783 STAMP ACT
The best known tax on entries in parish registers is the 3d stamp duty in force from 2 October 1783 to early March 1794 in England, Wales and Scotland: predictably, in many parishes there was a noticeable rise in baptisms in September 1783, often of children rather than infants, followed by a decline in October 1783, and with another sharp rise in mid-1794 as parents brought entire families for baptism when the tax was lifted. Some people avoided the tax by claiming to be paupers, who were exempt from payment. Many clergymen were sympathetic to those trying to escape paying the tax and, particularly in Scotland, they might help their parishioners by baptizing a child but not entering it in the register.

CIVIL REGISTRATION
In May and June 1837 in England and Wales and in late 1854 in Scotland (because many people misunderstood the purpose of civil registration which

116

began on 1 July in the former and on 1 January 1855 in the latter) churches in some areas were deluged with requests for baptisms, both from those who had never been baptised and from those who had been but thought they needed a piece of paper to prove it. In England during the last week in June, for example, *Sheffield* Parish Church saw 605 baptisms (out of the annual total of 3653); 900 people (mostly adolescents and adults) were baptised in *Macclesfield*, Cheshire and 650 in *Heanor* and *Ilkeston* in Derbyshire. **It is always worth further investigation of an IGI baptism reference from June 1837.**

Naming Patterns (Christian names)

In Scotland, the eldest son was commonly named for the paternal grandfather, the second for the maternal grandfather and the third for the father; the eldest daughter was usually named for the maternal grandmother, the second for the paternal grandmother and the third for the mother. In England and Wales there was no set naming pattern, although the eldest son was often named after his father and the eldest daughter after her mother.

Particularly in the 16th and early 17th centuries, when infant mortality was common, some families were so determined to keep a certain Christian name alive in the family that they baptised several living children with the same name in the hopes that at least one would survive into adulthood. *John the Elder, John the Middle and John the Younger* were named in one Will; whether the three brothers were known by nicknames and how future generations ascertained from which brother they descended are two possible pitfalls from this situation. In the late 18th century *James Spilling* in Suffolk baptised his sons as *James Robert, James William* and *James Michael*, presumably on the same principle but providing them with an alternative name – **never assume that a child is known by its first Christian name.**

Naming a child after one of its godparents was also common practice (see p.118). *Ninian Gale* had two daughters baptised as *Alice* in 1579 and 1585, and named in his Will as *Alice the elder and Alice the younger*, and this seems likely to have been due to different godmothers with the same Christian name. Unfortunately, godparents are very rarely named in Anglican parish registers.

The rise and fall in the popularity of Christian names could fill a book on its own. Many statistical surveys from parish registers, census returns and other sources, principally covering the 17th to 19th centuries, give *John, Thomas* and *William* as the three most popular names for boys and *Mary, Elizabeth* and *Ann* for girls. Broadly speaking, names tended to be biblical, classical or arrived (like *William*) with the Norman Conquest. Old Testament names were originally much used by the Anglican Church but later tended to be more popular with Nonconformist families. Roman Catholics were obliged to bear a saint's name (and remember that those converting to Roman Catholicism were usually baptised with a saint's name or a spiritual name, such as *Faith*, if their original Christian name was not considered suitable). It

117

is often the case that families would use either Old Testament or New Testament names for their children but not mix them; this can sometimes help to distinguish between two families with parents bearing the same Christian and surnames in the same parish and baptizing children within weeks of each other (something which often happened). Certain names can sometimes provide a clue to help locate other children in the family. If you find a daughter baptised as *Kerenhappuch*, look for older siblings called *Jemima* and *Kezia(h)* - these were the three daughters of Job and were usually given in sequence - and locating a *Jacob* after 1733 could well lead you to elder brothers *Abraham* and *Isaac*.

Individual names tended to be popular (almost common) in certain areas (see *Marmaduke* p.32) or particular parishes. An uncommon name originally used by one or two families would often spread as bearers moved (particularly girls when they married) or as the local landowner or lord of the manor became godparent to many of his tenants. *Ferdinando* was being used from the mid-16th century in Cheshire by the *Stanley family, Earls of Derby*, and in Yorkshire by the *Fairfax* family and the name occurs frequently during the 17th century in these counties in families at all levels of society. *Cassandra Swynnerton*, making her Will in Staffordshire in 1564, left to *all my godchildren that demand it within one year of my decease, 12d each*. To her four godchildren bearing the name *Cassandra*, however, she bequeathed sums of money ranging from ten to forty shillings and, in two cases, a cow. It would appear that naming a child after a godparent could prove to be a wise move, as well as hopefully preserving and spreading the uncommon name.

Just how useful an uncommon Christian name 'adopted' by a family can be is demonstrated by the use of the name *Gervase* (also spelt *Jervis/Jarvis*) by the *Litton* family from Derbyshire. The first known reference to the name is in 1702 in *Ashbourne*. Over time branches of this family moved into Staffordshire, Cheshire, Lancashire and Yorkshire. The name was used in all branches until at least the 19th century (one branch living in Yorkshire still uses it today) and to find an ancestor bearing this name should enable you to connect to the Derbyshire family, rather than to the unrelated families mentioned on page 23.

TWINS

There was no obligation for incumbents to state that children were *twins*. Some did but many simply described two (or more) children born to the same parents and baptised on the same day as *children of ...* To assume that such an entry necessarily refers to twins is dangerous. Be very careful if using anything other than the parish register itself – a depressing number of transcribers, whose work has either been included in published parish registers (see Chapter 17), put onto CD, or is available online or in ROs, inserted *twins* into their transcripts when there is no indication that the children in the entry were such.

Twins originally referred to a multiple birth of any number of children. A baptism in *Tickhill* in 1696 refers to *Gartrude dau. of Benjamin Wrights, one of the three twins, the other two were stillborne.* On 2 May 1702, at *Sherburn in Elmet, Hannah dau. Elkanah Nicholson (being one of three twins and born on 1 May)* was baptised. This was followed on 4 May by the baptisms of the other two twins, *Elkanah* and *Mary*, born on 4 May. It is a little known fact that 'delayed interval delivery' means that twins can be born several days apart. Still at *Sherburn*, in 1768, *Mark, Luke and John, twin children of Stephen Gill, cowper*, were baptised. A son *Matthew* had been born almost exactly a year earlier. Note that none of the entries names the mother, only the father. According to the OED, the first reference to triplet and quadruplet, referring to three/four children at one birth, is as late as 1787. A common combination of names for three girls at one birth is *Faith, Hope* and *Charity*.

ILLEGITIMATE CHILDREN

There can be very few family trees which do not contain illegitimate children. Some were a 'one off' mistake (following celebrations at haymaking, harvest or Christmas); others were the result of rape, coercion or incest (see p.37); many were born to couples in a stable relationship who could not marry, usually because one of the couple already had a spouse but the marriage had broken down and divorce was impossible (see p.88).

There are many words used in parish registers to describe a child born out of wedlock. They range from *illegitimate, bastard* or *base born* (the ones most commonly used) to *chance begotten, misbegotten, natural* and *spurious*, with a wide range of insulting variants dreamt up by incumbents. Before 1733, when Latin was used in PRs, *ignotus* (father unknown), *filius/filia populi* (son/daughter of the people) and *filius/filia nullius* (son/daughter of none) were used. The fathers, if named, could be described variously as *imputed father, reputed father* or *putative* father. The former is sometimes taken to mean that the man did not accept responsibility for the child, whereas the other two usually mean that they did accept it but there are no hard and fast rules.

Look carefully at the names given to illegitimate children as the mother often gave a clear indication of the child's paternity - *Richardson spurious son of Anne Hague* is a giveaway, as is *William Smith, bastard child of Elizabeth Cheetham*. Nothing could be clearer than the 1766 entry in Birstall's baptism register: *Joseph Charlesworth bastard son of Mary Armitage of Bierley; Joseph Charlesworth of the same putative father*. Some were baptised after the mother had married (like *Rebecca Carr* p.115); others when the mother married, as (in 1779) *baptised James illegitimate son of Barn[a]bas Brown and Mary Wilson both of Burton who were married this day*; or when a more tolerant minister arrived in the parish who would baptise the child without adding words of stricture on the mother in the register. Do not assume that the mother's husband is the father of her illegitimate child

119

unless the entry, as above, specifically says that he is. In Suffolk, *Elizabeth Smith* gave birth to an illegitimate daughter in 1765 and married *Thomas Christmas* two years later - but a bastardy bond makes it clear that *Isaac Christopherson* was the father of the child. In many areas, one illegitimate child was not considered a lasting disgrace as it proved that the mother could bear healthy children.

How much information you may find about an illegitimate child in a PR depends very much on the individual incumbent, the practice in the parish and whether the mother could, or would, name the father of her child. Parish officials would go to great lengths to determine the father of an illegitimate child, so that he could be forced to take financial responsibility for it. Some mothers, particularly if they had a choice of possible fathers, would name the one whom they thought would best be able to support them and the child so do not automatically assume that the man named is the father - look for bastardy bonds and other documentation for confirmation. Many incumbents named only the mother in an illegitimate baptism entry (sometimes adding words like whore and strumpet and often stating if she had borne more than one such child over the years) but others made it a policy, if possible, to name the father. At various times in the 18th century, attempts were made to persuade incumbents to keep a record of illegitimate children and, if you are lucky, you may find a page or two in the baptism register with such a list (see p. 121 for an example from *Sherburn-in-Elmet*) but, like so much church and state legislation, it was ignored more often than it was obeyed.

Some entries provide a telling glimpse of social history. A baptism entry on 11 Aug 1782, at *York St Olave* records the birth on 15 July, in the Poor House, of *John Heels son of Sarah Heels, wretched idiot both deaf and dumb; father some wicked unprincipled Villain in the poorhouse, whose name cannot be found out, for reason very obvious.* A very different entry appears in the register of *Haslington* in Cheshire: *Baptized 18 February 1763, Hannah Greenacres alias Wright a Bastard of Elizabeth Greenacres, who was the Bastard of Martha Greenacres by Tho: Bloor of Crew-gate, who was the Bastard of Mary Greenacres by one Patrick Strong.* To this entry the incumbent added, possibly tongue-in-cheek, *A goodly breed.*

A burial entry at *Tickhill* in November 1640 of *Another of Edward Pagdens soe supposed begotten on the body of his wives sister and fathered on two souldiers,* with the entry in the BT saying simply *another of Jane Herrings,* appears to refer to an ongoing incestuous relationship (see pp.36-37), demonstrates how easy it could be to foist an illegitimate child onto someone passing through the parish, and serves as a reminder that it pays to check both PR and BT.

A 'correction' by a 19th century Cheshire clergyman to a baptism entry reveals a practice which probably occurred widely but has not been proven. Under what appears to be a normal baptism entry for the youngest child in a large family he writes *their grandson, not their son; illegitimate child of their daughter.* Concealing a daughter's indiscretion as her younger sibling would be one way of avoiding the 'disgrace' and, in some areas, was probably easily achieved. Census entries, where the last child in a large family is recorded as being 10 or more years younger than his nearest sibling, suggests that the practice may have been an established one.

A Register of Illegitimate Children.
Baptised.

20. Nov. 15 Thomas Son of Mary Settle of Sherburn, born the 6th Instant.

71. Ap. 9 Thomas Son of Mary Nordin of Sherburn born the 23. of March last.

June 25 Nancy Daughter of Mary Ellinson of Barkston.

July 4 Thomas Son of Grace Summers of Sherburn Widow.

72 Apr. 16 William Son of Isabel Nicholson of Milford.

June 1 John Son of Eleanor Smith of Sherburn.

Mar. 4 Sarah Daughter of Hannah Alat of Lumby.
773

Sep. 26 Richard Dent Son of Ann Dent Petergate
1772 York, born at York On Sunday 26th Sep: and baptized at Sherburn On Saturday 26th September by me John Rogers Curate.

Joseph Fountayne bastard Son of Margaret Fountayne of Milford Widow Born Sep. 12th 1782. and baptized Sep. 29th

Joseph Fountayne the above bastard Son of Margaret died Oct: 28th and was buried in the Church yard Oct: 29th 1782. being 46 days old.

Robert Second Bastard Child of Ann Fordyce of Sherburn born 26th January baptized Feb: 5. 1783.

See Illegitimate Children continued about the middle of this book.

121

CHAPTER 12

'DADE' REGISTERS

EARLY ATTEMPTS TO INCREASE INFORMATION IN PARISH REGISTERS

So-called *Dade Registers* (1770-1812), have been known to family historians, particularly those researching in Yorkshire, for many years. The term has come to be used almost generically to cover any baptism or burial (and a few marriage) registers which include information additional to that required by law. However, *William Dade* was only one in a long line of antiquarians who felt that parish registers should contain more detail than they did. In the early 18th century several of them attempted, by writing articles and publishing suggested formats in learned journals and in *The Gentleman's Magazine*, to encourage Anglican clergymen to expand the content of their registers and you may be fortunate and find an incumbent who adopted one of these formats, if only for a short period.

The Yorkshire antiquarian *Ralph Thoresby* had addressed the problem in 1715 in *Ducatus Leodiensis* [History of *Leeds*] when he praised, and gave examples of, a system of Register keeping developed by his friend *Thomas Kirke* of *Adel* near *Leeds* which, between 1685 and 1705, included much more detail than the average Parish Register. Baptism entries included date of baptism (together with the day of the week); child's name and surname; father's Christian name, profession and place of residence. For 1691 and 1692 date of birth and mother's Christian name were also included. Marriages included the date and day of the week; the names, ages, places of residence of the couple; and whether the marriage was by Banns or Licence (see p.143 for examples). Burials included date and day of week; name; age; place of residence; relationship (wife/son etc.); profession (for males); and cause of death (see p.169). It is not known whether the system was *Kirke*'s own idea or whether he saw something similar being used elsewhere - there may be other parishes in England or Wales with similarly informative registers.

Thoresby's *Ducatus Leodiensis*, and the rising tide of complaints about the inadequate state of parish registers in the mid-18th century, influenced a number of other clergymen in Yorkshire, and further afield. In 1744 *Timothy Lee* introduced a system similar to *Kirke*'s in *Ackworth* (see p.169); in *West Rounton* causes of death were included from 1754 and there will be other examples. *T.D.Whitaker*, another well-known northern antiquarian whose wife had been a *Thoresby* from the same family as Ralph, was using the 1715 format in *Whalley* and *Heysham* in Lancashire from the 1790s (and was most annoyed when 'Parliamentary Authority' forced him to abandon it after 1812).

In 1764 the antiquarian and herald *Ralph Bigland* published ***Observations on Marriages, Baptisms and Burials, as preserved in Parochial Registers. With sundry specimens (etc.)*** An example of the baptism format read:

*Nov. 17 1708 John Bannister 3rd son of John Banister of Woodbridge, in com.
Suffolk, mercer, and Mary his wife (2nd daughter of William Jones of
Penzance, in com. Cornwal (sic), merchant) was born on the 20th day of
October, and baptized the 17th day of the next month following.*

The question of adopting this format, the one used by *Kirke*, or an even
more extensive one was clearly under discussion in the late 1760s. *Colyton* in
Devon (Diocese of Exeter) included the mother's father's name from 1765 (to
1777). *Husthwaite* Parish Register, after the entries for 1769, includes a note
*The form of keeping this parish Register from the end of the year 1769 is some
improvement of that plan recommended by Mr Thoresby in his* **Ducatus
Leodiensis**, *as promising to afford much clearer Intelligence to the researches
of Posterity, and now first adopted by Robert Peirson, Curate of Husthwaite AD
1770.* The Register from January 1770 included the same information as do
Dade Registers (see below) **except** that the names of grandparents were not
included in baptism entries. The incumbent of the neighbouring parish of
Coxwold adopted the same system in May 1770, making it retrospective to
January. Neither parish ever adopted the complete *Dade* format.

WILLIAM DADE AND HIS REGISTERS

William Dade was born in 1740, the son and grandson of Yorkshire
clergymen. He attended *St John's College Cambridge* (as did a high
proportion of Yorkshire clergymen), graduating in 1762. He was ordained
deacon in 1763 and priest in 1765, both in *York* by the Archbishop, and
between 1763 and his death in 1790 he was variously curate, perpetual curate
or rector of five parishes in York and two in the East Riding. Whilst the
Dictionary of National Biography remembers him almost solely as an
antiquarian, family historians owe him a tremendous debt of gratitude for
developing a format for the keeping of Parish Registers which, in the areas
where it was adopted, can prove invaluable.

When he was appointed Curate of *St Helen* and of *St Olave* in *York* (two
separate parishes but often held by one cleric) *Dade* decided that *Thoresby*'s
suggestions did not go far enough. He wrote in the Parish Register of *St
Helen, The following method of ascertaining the births and baptisms, deaths
and burials in this parish of St Helens, York, was introduced in 1770 by
William Dade (the third and youngest son of the Rev. Thomas Dade, Vicar of
Burton Agnes and Rector of Barmston, in the East Riding) Curate of this
Church. This scheme if properly put in execution will afford much clearer
intelligence to the researches of posterity* [note the identical wording to *Robert
Peirson*, above], *than the imperfect method, hitherto generally pursued.* He
introduced the same system simultaneously at *St Olave*; in 1773 at *St Mary
Castlegate* and *St Michael Spurriergate* when he acquired these livings; and
in 1776 at *Barmston* and *Ulrome* when he succeeded his father there.

BAPTISM REGISTERS

Infant's Christian Name and Seniority.	Infant's Surname.	Father's Name, Profession and Abode.	Mother's Name and Descent.	Born.
Matthew 1st Son & 2d child.	Browne	Matthew Browne, Upholsterer in high ousegate, youngest Son of Matthew Brown in michlegate gardiner, by Elenor, relict of Brian Fairfax of wetherby apoth, & daught of Tomas Sidgley of cheshunt in Hertfordshire, Fruiterer.	Mary the daughter of Samuel Roe of Bakewell in the County of Derby, turner by Dorothy his wife, the daughter of Robert Slach of Hayfield	on monday the 18th of April
Thomas posthumous	Bennet	Thomas Bennet, Panthirer deceased, Son of John Bennet near Liverpool in Lancashire, Farmer	Elisabeth, daul of Richard Addy late of Bohemy in the parish of Sutton Farmer by Ann his Wife daul of John Dalton of Kendal Strel Brewer.	on Sunday the 3d of April

The 1774 baptism entry, above, for *Matthew Browne*, on 1st May (Baptism column to the right of Born column omitted), at *St Michael Spurriergate*, one of the first printed Registers to use the *Dade* format, demonstrates both the information which *Dade* intended should be included and how valuable entries in such Registers can be - who would expect an 18th century child in York to have a mother from Derbyshire and a paternal grandmother from Hertfordshire and where else could you hope to find such details?

The following entry for *Thomas Bennet* reveals the limitations of the system which was dependent on someone present at the baptism knowing the required details. *Thomas*'s mother, assuming that she was the informant, obviously knew the details of her late husband's father but not of his mother. Many entries provide the parents' names, with *descent unknown* stated for one or both of them.

BURIAL REGISTERS

These contained columns for *Christian Name; Surname; Descent, Profession and Abode; When Died and Where Buried; Age and Distemper [cause of death]*. If the deceased was a local person the Register could well contain information covering several generations, as well as a potted biography. The entries below, the first two from *York St Olave*, the third from *York St Mary Castlegate*, demonstrate just what could be learnt from a burial entry:

Thomas Phillipson; widower, in early life gardiner, then keeper for 18 years of Long Room at Scarborough; eldest son of late Thomas Phillipson, governour of Scarborough Castle; abode at son-in-law Simpsons Coffee House, Petergate; died 28th buried 30th October 1770; buried in churchyard near grand-daughter Simpson's grave; aged 77 years; dropped from chair upon chamber floor and expired immediately.

Elizabeth Kendal; widow of Thomas Kendal, gardiner of this parish; dau. of Thomas Carter, farmer of Dunnington by his wife Ann Hall; abode at her son-in-law's, Duke Green's, cobbler of Bootham; died 1ˢᵗ and buried 3ʳᵈ June 1771; buried in churchyard; aged 88 years; ast[h]ma.

Ann Wiggins wife of Mr Wiggins of the Frier Walls; Relict of Mr William Lee of Leeds; daughter of Mr John Lee by Alice his wife daughter of Alderman Corney of this City; died 21ˢᵗ and buried 23ʳᵈ November 1774 and buried in the Chancel; age 66 years; nervous.

The entry from *York St Sampson* speaks for itself:

| Ann Groves | 2ⁿᵈ Born of Samuel Groves of Bromsgrove in Worcester-shire Farmer by Mary Hornby his Wife | Died on Wednesday ye 29 October at Clifford's Tower on Peasholm green were she had come for the Inspection of the curious & was buried in ye Church Yard on Friday ye 31 October; was in Height four Feet; round the Breast 4 Feet 2 Inches; round the Hip 4 Feet 6 Inches; round each Leg 18 In⁵; weighs 2 Cwt | 5 years | Dropsy |

MARRIAGE REGISTERS

Both *Dade* and *Archbishop Markham* (see below) were concerned principally with baptism and burial registers. However, *Markham*'s instructions provided for a marriage register to be kept which was to include columns as illustrated below:

When married.	Names of Persons Married.	The Man's Profession.	Title.	Age.	Banns or Licence.	By whom Married.	In whose Presence Married.
February 1784 166	*Robert Tate of Manchester & Elizabeth Hill of this Parish* *This Marriage was solemnized between us Robert Tate Elizabeth Hill*	*Confectioner*	*Batchel Spinster*	*22 19*	*Licence*	*P Marsh Rector*	*Betty Braithwaite Ann Markham*

MARRIAGES at St. Martin's, Micklegate, for the Year *1784*.

Hardwicke's *Marriage Act* (see Chapter 13) had been in force since 1754 and most of the clergy appear to have thought that the marriage registers they were currently using were adequate and proceeded to ignore *Markham*'s instructions. Some marriage registers, using the recommended columns, were printed but most of those known are hand-ruled and hand-written. A few incumbents went further than required and included the names of the fathers of bride and groom. *Sherburn in Elmet*, from 1783-1799, commonly included the names of all four parents, where these were known (see p.150), and also stated where a bride or groom was born illegitimate, often including the name of the mother.

WILLIAM MARKHAM AND DADE REGISTERS

Early in 1777 *William Markham*, Bishop of Chester since 1771, was translated to York as Archbishop. There is some evidence to suggest that *Markham* and *Dade* had met previously, possibly in *Manchester*. *Markham* wasted no time in deciding that the *Dade* system of keeping baptism and burial registers should be adopted more widely. In April 1777 he began his primary Visitation of his Archdiocese. It took him several months, in stages, to complete this as he visited deaneries across Yorkshire and Nottinghamshire. Little documentation survives for this Visitation but it is clear that he 'required' the adoption of *Dade*'s system (excluding only the seniority of the child in the family), to be implemented immediately following his meeting with the clergy of each deanery. The vicar of *Bilbrough* wrote in his Parish Register in April 1777 *It is required that for the future the following Forms be pursued and adhered to ... See Directions to the Clergy and Churchwardens given at the Primary Visitation of the most Reverend Father in God William by Divine Providence, Lord Archbishop of York, in the year 1777.* The vicar of *Alne* went further, including in his Register the reason given by *Archbishop Markham* for his decision: *As great Complaints have arisen of the Registers of Marriages, Births and Burials belonging to several Parishes being inaccurately kept and drawn out, so as not to identifie and ascertain the Persons &c whereby they have not their due Weight in Point of Evidence: it is required ... etc..* Both men then (as did many other incumbents) adapted their existing Registers to coincide with the format already being used by *Dade* in 'his' churches and added examples of baptisms and burials from earlier months.

It would seem that the system was recommended and not made compulsory as there does not appear to be any evidence of attempts being made to force recalcitrant clergy to comply with the requirement. It was adopted most widely in *York* and the surrounding area (more than 100 parishes in the *Archdeaconry of York* maintained *Dade* registers for at least part of the period 1777-1812), and in market towns like *Selby, Sherburn in Elmet* and *Skipton*, but was ignored by many of the growing industrial towns and cities (until 1812 *Leeds* Parish Register did not include even the mother's Christian name in baptism entries). The *Dean and Chapter of York* endorsed it for parishes within their jurisdiction during a Visitation in 1778. It was also adopted by parishes in the *Archdeaconry of Richmond*, which formed part of the Bishopric of Chester (see p.127). Elsewhere, it appears that the willingness of individual incumbents or parish clerks to put in the extra time needed to compile *Dade* Registers determined whether the system was adopted or not.

Some parishes enthusiastically began to gather information for the new format but very soon discovered that they could not keep up the impetus and reverted to less informative entries (*Dade*'s own parishes of *Barmston* and *Ulrome* both lapsed soon after his death in 1790). The number of parishes which included all the recommended details is limited, and the number who maintained the system from its inception to its demise when *Rose*'s *Act* took effect in 1813 is even smaller, but many parishes included *some* additional details. **It is worth bearing in mind that not all parishes felt obliged to enter the extra details in the Bishop's Transcripts so it is essential to check the original Registers to know if a parish was a Dade one.**

To begin with, most incumbents were obliged to take up pen, ink and ruler and draw their own columns and insert headings and some parishes continued this through to 1812. It was not long, however, before enterprising printers began to produce books already ruled and headed. The earliest known of these were printed to order in *York* by 1773, when that for *St Mary Castlegate* begins, but the printing profession presumably speculated that many more would be required and made sure that stock was to hand when parishes needed to purchase a new Register book. The availability of such volumes had a considerable effect on the number of *Dade* Registers. Many parishes which had ignored the Archbishop's Directions in 1777 suddenly conformed when they were obliged to purchase a new Parish Register book and obtained a printed one. Some ignored many of the columns but others started to keep full *Dade* Registers at varying dates - *Pocklington*, for example, from 1779, *Askham Bryan* from 1783, *Arksey* from 1795, *Rylstone* from 1803, *Osbaldwick* from 1808, *Bowes* from 1810. Visitations by Archdeacons to their Deaneries also had an effect - *Robert Markham*, 5th son of the Archbishop, was appointed Archdeacon of *York* in 1795 and, following his primary visitation (and probably reminding the clergy of his father's Directions), a number of incumbents suddenly began to keep *Dade* registers. **It is always worth searching the whole period 1777-1812 in a Parish Register as it needs only one Dade entry (possibly of a much older or younger sibling of your ancestor) to strike gold.** In the IGI, *Dade* baptism entries can often be identified by one of the symbols indicating 'relatives named in source'.

BARRINGTON REGISTERS: SPREAD OF MORE DETAILED PRS

Markham was succeeded as Bishop of **Chester** by *Bielby Porteus* who, during his Primary Visitation in 1778, attempted to introduce a similar system for parish registers in his diocese (which included Cheshire, Lancashire, Cumberland, Westmorland, part of Yorkshire and part of North Wales) but with even less success than *Markham*. A number of parishes in Cheshire complied for a time (*Alsager, Davenham* and *Macclesfield* among them). The Chapelry of *Witton* (*Northwich*) introduced the system in 1779 and continued it until at least the 1860s, maintaining after 1813 an auxiliary baptism register in addition to the one required by law. Parts of the *Archdeaconry of Richmond* also maintained 'extended' registers, many from 1783 (see below). It is worth enquiring at record offices for any of the counties named above as to whether they hold any '*Dade*-style' registers.

Meanwhile the brothers *Daines* and *Shute Barrington* (the former an antiquarian and naturalist, the latter a bishop) became involved. In 1781 *Daines Barrington* published details of a *proposed form for improved registers* (see below) and forms incorporating his proposals were printed by *J. Nichols* of London and *Mr Collins* at Salisbury (and probably other printers).

[8]			
B A P T I S M S.			
Date.	Aged.	Name of the Child.	Names of the Father and Mother.
1781. May the 4th	— Days.	John Smith, Son of	John Smith, Labourer, and Mary his Wife, formerly Mary Evans.

That same year *Shute Barrington*, Bishop of *Llandaff* since 1769, undertook his fourth triennial Visitation of his Diocese, during which he recommended the adoption of a *New Method of Registering* which for baptisms was identical to his brother's form except that it also included date of birth. For burials he included: *the date; name of the deceased; names of father and mother; age; supposed cause of death; where buried (in what part of the church or churchyard)*. His success rate was not high, and his translation to *Salisbury* in 1782 meant that many parishes soon abandoned the system, but a few parishes did continue to use it. *Shute Barrington* introduced the system into his new Diocese (but including the age at baptism, rather than the date of birth) and some parishes in Berkshire and Wiltshire (both within the Diocese of Salisbury) started keeping these registers by 1783.

The year 1783 saw the introduction of a tax on births, baptisms, marriages and burials (see p.116), and of a sudden surge of interest in other Dioceses in increasing the amount of detail in parish registers, principally so that they could keep an accurate record of tax to be paid. Printed register books *conformable to the Act* were produced and some Bishops clearly issued instructions to their clergy to improve their registers. *Lewis Bagot* became *Bishop of Norwich* in 1783 and many registers in Norfolk and Suffolk began to include the mother's maiden name in baptisms, and also in burials (of their children). See page 114 for an example of the format commonly used for baptisms in this Diocese. A baptism from *Yelverton* in Norfolk in 1791 will take some beating: *Thomas son of Thomas Sherwood and Mary his wife (late Mary Wate before that Mary Cooper and before that Mary Custing spinster) was received into the body of the church.*

Shute Barrington moved from *Salisbury* to become Bishop of *Durham* in 1791. In 1798 he issued instructions to the clergy of his Diocese to 'upgrade' their Registers to include information similar to, but not as extensive as, *Dade* registers. He required only *the place of nativity of the parents* in baptism registers and not full details of the grandparents. Like *Markham*, he appears to have had less than total success in gaining his clergy's co-operation. An example from the baptism Register of *Alnwick*, Northumberland demonstrates what should have been included: *Isabella Henderson, 1st daughter of John Henderson, husbandman of Faceyspack, native of Long Horsley Northumberland, by his wife Sarah Simpson, native of Ospeth, Yorkshire, born 17 June, baptised 19 July 1807* (later baptisms give the mother as being of *Leeds*). Another from *Tynemouth*, Northumberland, where two children were baptised on 11 March 1804, reminds us not to assume, from an index, that such children are twins and always to try to ascertain whether a common place name should have a suffix (see p.6) - if both parents had given their parishes of birth as *Middleton* and not specified the county or included the suffix, how easy would it have been to think they came from the same one: *Mary Ann 3rd daughter of Ralph Nesham of Monkseaton, weaver, native of Middleton Tyres [Tyas], Yorkshire and his wife Sarah Murton of Middleton in Teesdale, Co. Durham, born 1 September 1800* and *John 1st son of same born 22 November 1802*. Entries from these parishes and from *Berwick on Tweed* show clearly just how mobile the coastal population was in the 18th and early 19th centuries.

As well as the counties mentioned above as using either the *Dade* or the *Barrington* format, there are a few examples known in other counties, accounted for by the purchase of new Registers (*Chertsey* in Surrey; *Barrington* format 1809+) or by the arrival of an incumbent who had previously lived in Yorkshire and brought the system with him (*Moreton*, Essex; 'true' *Dade*). Some of the Welsh Nonconformist Registers, especially those of the Wesleyan and Calvinistic Methodists in the early 19th century, used a printed format very similar to that of a Dade Register.

RESOLUTION:

When I find a baptism or burial entry between 1770 and 1812 which includes minimum details I shall consider looking for entries for baptisms and burials of older and younger siblings in case the PRs at other times give expanded details.

CHAPTER 13

LORD HARDWICKE'S MARRIAGE ACT 1753

Ask almost any family historian what they know about this Act and they will probably say 'it introduced printed forms for marriages, which had provision for the names of the parties, their marital status, their parish of residence, the groom's occupation, signatures (or marks) of bride and groom and of two witnesses ...' The Act did not require all the above information to be recorded - if you are fortunate enough to find so much detail you must thank someone different.

THE ACT

Lord Hardwicke's *Act for the better preventing of Clandestine Marriages* reached the statute book in the summer of 1753 and came into effect on 25 March 1754 in England and Wales (the Act never applied in Scotland, Ireland or the Channel Islands, to marriages overseas or to Quakers or Jews *where both the parties to any such Marriage shall be of the People called Quakers or Persons professing the Jewish Religion respectively*; the Isle of Man passed a similar Marriage Act in 1757). Everybody had to be made aware of the new rules governing marriage but a large proportion of the population could neither read nor write; thus the Act was to be read out in all Parish Churches and Public Chapels on one Sunday a month in September, October, November and December 1753 and on the Sundays preceding the Quarter Days of 25 March, 24 June, 29 September and 25 December in 1754 and 1755. How much of the Act, couched in legal jargon, was comprehensible to most of the congregations who were subjected to its reading, presumably in addition to a lengthy sermon, is a different matter.

Prior to the Act, all that was required for a valid marriage in the British Isles was a declaration of mutual consent by the couple - a situation which persisted in Scotland until well into the 20th century. The Church maintained that marriages should take place by banns or licence, in church, with a clergyman officiating, between the hours of 8 a.m. and noon, during divine service; marriage was also not permitted at certain times of the year, notably during Lent and Advent. The majority of couples conformed out of tradition and because they thought it might become necessary to prove that the ceremony had taken place; an entry in the Parish Register was regarded as proof positive, and accepted in a court of law. However, there was nothing to stop a couple being married elsewhere and it will never be known just how many unrecorded marriages took place before 1754; there are some entries in Parish Registers of couples *lately married by a couple beggar* (see p.145) or *with a hedge-priest* (clergymen without a benefice who wandered the country and would marry couples cheaply with no questions asked and often no written record) but these references are likely to be the exception rather than the rule and most such marriages were not recorded. One of the pressing reasons for *Hardwicke*'s *Act* was to curb the increasing number of clandestine (secret) marriages taking place in certain areas, notably around the Fleet Prison and in the Mayfair Chapel, in *London* - reckoned to account for well over half the annual number of marriages taking place in the Capital.

Hardwicke's original Bill had a stormy passage through the Lords, the Commons and its Committee Stage, the version eventually reaching the statute book creating almost as many problems as it solved. Nevertheless it remained substantially in force until the 19th century, despite frequent attempts to have it repealed. Its main provisions concerned the Publication of Banns, Marriages by Licence, the position of those marrying under the age of 21, and the type of Marriage Register in which the events were to be recorded. Unfortunately, amidst the controversy and argument which surrounded the Bill's passage to an Act in the first half of 1753, no-one seems to have remembered to incorporate any mention of responsibility for implementing whatever measures were finally agreed upon. When the Act came into effect in 1754 it proved to be so loosely-worded in parts that possible interpretations were legion; decisions as to what action was to be taken seems to have been left to the clergy, although whether at diocesan, archdeaconry or deanery level is unclear as very little supporting documentation is known to survive.

As the Act was intended to prevent clandestine marriages, it gave prominence to the publicity available through the Publication of Banns. Couples were to be obliged to give seven days' written notice to the minister of their intention to marry, stating their true names, their addresses and how long they had lived there; the Banns (as had long been customary - see p.153) had then to be published on three successive Sundays during Morning Service, immediately after the Second Lesson (it was estimated that the largest number of people would be present at this time, latecomers having wandered in and no-one having left before the sermon).

The Act stated that *All Banns of Matrimony shall be published in an audible manner in the Parish Church, or in some publick Chapel,* **in which publick Chapel Banns of Matrimony have been usually published ...** (emphasis added). In addition to the Parish Church, many parishes had several Anglican chapels, in which marriages had long been performed. It had been the custom for such chapel marriages to take place either after the granting of a Licence or after the calling of Banns in the Parish Church. In the latter case a certificate (stating that Banns had been called and where) was handed to the minister at the chapel. If taken literally, the emphasised section effectively prevented not only many chapels from continuing to perform marriages as the Banns had not *been usually published* there but also called into question whether buildings such as *Westminster Abbey* and *St Paul's Cathedral*, neither being a parish church and neither having been accustomed to publishing banns, could continue to marry couples. In *York Minster* banns had been published in the 17th (see p.142) and early 18th centuries but, from 1730 onwards, all marriages had been by Licence. Marriages in the Minster ceased on 20th October 1753 and a single entry in 1762, for a marriage by Special Licence, is annotated *the last Marriage in York Minster* (later marriages took place in the nearby church of *St Michael-le-Belfrey*).

There does not appear to be rhyme nor reason in the way the clause was interpreted but its effect, in certain areas at least, was to restrict marriages to the Parish Church alone. In the north of England, particularly in the growing industrial towns, this created some very difficult situations - *Manchester* had eight 'marrying' chapels before 1754 but after the Act only the Parish Church was licensed and marriages there in any one year soon ran into four figures; *Leeds*, with 10 chapels, was in the same situation; *Halifax* had two chapelries in which marriages ceased after 1754 and two in which they continued. On the other hand, *Stoke-on-Trent*, the largest parish in Staffordshire, had five chapels, which all continued to perform marriages, and it was common practice for couples to marry in any one of the chapels within the parish boundaries so a couple from *Whitmore* might marry at *Norton le Moors*, about 10 miles away, and merely be described as being *of the parish of Stoke*. In rural areas the situation was even more chaotic - marriages ceased in some chapels (*Prestbury* in Cheshire 'lost' eight chapels), in others they continued for a few years but then stopped abruptly, in yet others they ceased in 1754 then started again a few years later.

There were clearly disputes between incumbents and curates of chapels within their parishes as to whether the curate could continue to perform marriages (and thus deprive the incumbent of the parish church of the fees involved) and this may well account for the cessation of marriages in some chapels, when the parish incumbent realised that marriages were still being performed there, and the resumption in other chapels when the curate appealed to higher authority. *Barnsley*, in Yorkshire, was a chapelry to *Silkstone*. The curate continued to perform marriages at *Barnsley* but the vicar of *Silkstone* objected and in 1782 the curate applied to the Archbishop of *York* whose representative responded, *I am directed by the Arch Bishop to say in answer to your letter, that if as you represent Marriages were usually solemnized in Barnsley Chapel before the passing of the Marriage Act His Grace thinks it most regular that all marriages of Persons residing within the Chapelry should be solemniz'd in that Chapel and not elsewhere.* Some curates kept a Marriage Register but failed to enter any marriages into the Bishops' Transcripts after 1754 (as at *Church Hulme*). The advice to family historians searching for an elusive marriage after 1754 is to check very carefully in just which chapels within a parish marriages continued (or re-started) and where they might be recorded; never assume that all, or even neighbouring, parishes in an area followed the same pattern.

The conditions for the granting of Marriage Licences were also tightened up by *Hardwicke's Act*. Licences could be issued by *any Archbishop, Bishop or other Ordinary or Person having Authority to grant such Licences* but the marriage had to take place in *a Parish Church or Publick Chapel* belonging to a Parish or Chapelry in which one of the couple had resided for at least four weeks preceding the granting of the Licence. This put an end to the practice of going to the nearest episcopal court (in practice an official appointed by the church court, commonly located at the Cathedral) to obtain the Licence and promptly being married in a side chapel there or in a completely different church to that named on the document. People living in places *having no church or chapel wherein Banns have been usually published* (extra-parochial places) could have their Banns called, or obtain a Licence, for the marriage to take place in an adjoining Parish but only the one named on the document. The *Archbishop of Canterbury* retained his right to issue Special Licences *to marry at any convenient Time or Place* but these were very sparingly issued - almost all Licences which family historians will encounter are Common (Ordinary) Licences (see p.159).

The legal age at which a marriage could take place was 12 for girls and 14 for boys, with parental consent being necessary for anyone under 21. Canon 62 of 1603 stated that *No minister,* **upon pain of suspension for 3 years** (emphasis added)*, shall celebrate matrimony between any persons when banns are thrice asked, ... before the parents ... of the parties to be married, being under 21, shall either personally, or by sufficient testimony, signify to him their consents given to the said marriage. Hardwicke's Act* was intended to place stricter controls on the marriage of minors but the wording of the Act could be interpreted as laying down different rules for those marrying by Banns and by Licence. Many of the clandestine marriages the Act was intended to prevent involved at least one under-age partner and usually took place well away from the couple's home parish(es); thus the Act clearly stated that, for marriage by Licence, if either of the parties was under 21, not a widower or widow, and parental or guardians' consent had not been obtained for the minor, then the marriage *shall be absolutely null and void to all Intents and Purposes whatsoever.*

In the case of Banns, provided that they were properly published three times, and no objection was raised by parents or guardians, the Minister performing the marriage ceremony could not be punished by the church (i.e. suspended) for marrying an under-age couple and the marriage was not said to be void. At *Braithwell* in 1786, *Jonathon Miles, Esq. & bachelour aged 16, and Betty Harrison, spinster aged 15, both of this parish*, were married by Banns (and both signed their names). In other words, for marriage by Banns there must be no parental objection whereas for marriage by Licence (written) parental consent must be obtained. Debate as to whether *Hardwicke's* civil law concerning Banns over-ruled existing canon law regarding parental consent continued into the 19th century.

If an objection **was** raised, as was the case at *Scampston*, Yorkshire in 1757 when *Hannah Coats'* father forbade the Banns after their first calling *she being only 19 years of age, and he* [her father] *not thinking it a proper match* then the Publication of Banns was to be void. His objection was recorded in the Marriage Register but a year later he relented and another entry in the Register reads *I do approve entirely of the said marriage and heartily join [with the couple] in desiring the Minister to publish and Marry them*. The Minister was obviously covering himself against any possible charge of permitting a minor to marry without parental consent.

Marriages were also to be void if solemnised other than in a Church or Chapel *where Banns have been usually published* (unless by Special Licence), and if Banns had not been properly called or a Licence not obtained from a competent authority. Any clergyman breaking these rules could be tried and convicted of felony and *transported to... His Majesty's Plantations in America for the Space of fourteen Years*. The threat of this may well account for the cessation of marriages in many chapels.

References throughout the Act were to events taking place in the *Parish Church or a Publick Chapel*. This had the effect, intentional or otherwise, of making marriages in Nonconformist places of worship illegal. These had taken place before 1754, being valid though irregular marriages after a declaration of consent, but they were 'outlawed' in England and Wales by the Act. Jews and Quakers, as already stated, were exempted from its provisions and some Roman Catholics continued to marry in their own churches (often with a parallel ceremony in an Anglican church to meet legal requirements) but Baptists, Presbyterians and Independents mostly complied with the Act and married in an Anglican place of worship.

A considerable part of the Act is devoted to the proper recording of Marriages taking place after 25 March 1754; it is the resulting documentation, the so-called *Hardwicke*'s *Marriage Registers*, which has led to most of the misunderstandings concerning the Act.

THE REGISTERS

THE REQUIREMENTS

The general belief among family historians today, and possibly among many of the 18th century clergy, was that the Act ordered the keeping of printed forms to record details of marriages performed. It did not. The wording of the Act reads *And for preventing undue Entries and Abuses in Registers of Marriages ... the Churchwardens ... shall provide proper Books of Vellum, or good and durable Paper, in which all Marriages and Banns of Marriages respectively, there published or solemnized, shall be registered, and every Page thereof shall be marked at the top, with the Figure of the Number of every such Page, beginning at the second Leaf with Number One; and every*

Leaf or Page so numbered, shall be ruled with Lines at proper and equal Distances from each other, or as near as may be; and all Banns and Marriages ... shall be respectively entered, registered, printed or written upon or as near as conveniently may be to such ruled Lines, and shall be signed by the Parson and such entries shall be made on or near such Lines in successive Order.

The Act then goes on to say that *all Marriages shall be solemnized in the Presence of two or more credible Witnesses, besides the Minister...* and an Entry, containing certain facts regarding the marriage, shall immediately be written into the Register *in the Form Or to the Effect following.*

THE IMPLEMENTATION

Nowhere does it state that the Register is to be printed as opposed to hand-drawn and there is no suggestion as to whether it should be the responsibility of Church or State to make sure that the Registers are introduced and maintained as laid down in the Act. It is abundantly clear that in many parishes the churchwardens and others did not comply precisely with this part of the Act. **The number of hand-drawn registers is proving to be greater than was previously thought**. These range from perfectly lined and written volumes, virtual copies of the printed ones described below, through ones which continued to be written in columns or mixed with baptisms and burials as many early Parish Registers were, to small notebooks with un-numbered, un-lined pages. Some parishes started with good intentions but within a few years had ceased drawing lines and numbering entries or pages. A few parishes maintained both their old Register and a new printed one and it is worth noting that in a contemporary circular letter to the clergy from *Dr Sharpe*, at that time Archdeacon of Northumberland, he wrote: *Besides this entry in the new Register it may be proper to continue the Entry of Marriages in the old Register in the common way. Partly for making the common searches (in cases not respecting the Validity of Marriages) more easy, and partly in Guard against the danger of the new Register being by accident destroyed.*

Many of the handwritten registers are of vellum (made from the skin of young animals) or of parchment (made from adult animal skin which, incidentally, was not an option within the Act). Printed registers are generally on paper and the prices quoted by *Thomas Lownds* speak for themselves: *Twenty-five Sheets of Demy contain 400 compleat Registers [entries], and are sold at 4s, Medium 6s, and Royal 8s. Those on Parchment, Demy Size at 6d, Medium 9d and Royal 1s per leaf. The Vellum, Demy Size at 1s 3d, Medium 1s 10d and the Royal 2s 6d per leaf some of which are bound up in proper Sizes for large or small Parishes.* Few Churchwardens, made responsible by the Act for providing the Registers, would have been prepared to pay for vellum or parchment leaves.

THE PRINTERS

The vast majority of the printed Registers used in 1754 are produced by two London firms, *Thomas Lownds*, and *Joseph Fox & Benjamin Dod*. These two appear to have had a virtual monopoly of the production of printed forms for much of the 18th century although from 1754 a few local printers were also producing printed marriage registers. By the end of the 18th century, the names of many more local printers were beginning to appear on Registers and a wider variety of formats was being used. Some parishes were maintaining two separate Marriage Registers, one for marriages by Banns and a separate one for those by Licence - watch out for this practice; the second book is easily overlooked, especially if viewing the Registers in microform (see p.155-156).

Lownds and *Fox & Dod* used very different formats and a letter in the **Gentleman's Magazine** for March 1754, proposing a method for registering banns and marriages pursuant to the late act, *which appears to me less liable to objections than any that have yet been recommended by repeated advertisements* implies that a sales drive had been taking place. Neither firm appears to have been a clear winner with, for example, the Dioceses and Archdeaconries covering Yorkshire and Suffolk favouring *Lownds*; those in Bedfordshire and Northamptonshire tending towards *Fox & Dod*; and Cheshire and Wiltshire being fairly evenly divided. Adjoining parishes often used different printers so the decision as to which form to use would seem to have been taken at parish level rather than imposed by a bishop, archdeacon, or other ecclesiastical authority.

MISCONCEPTIONS ABOUT THE ACT'S REQUIREMENTS

The example of the *Form of Register* given in the Act (and reproduced on p.135), on which all subsequent registers were based, does not contain many of the features which most family historians associate with *Hardwicke's Act*. The parish of residence of both parties should have been, and in most cases was, given but the omission of the word *of*, following *parish*, from the Act (and from both printers' forms) meant that some incumbents (like *Cheadle* in Cheshire) got away with putting *of the Parish* to mean anyone not *of this Parish* without bothering to specify from which parish they actually came. There is no mention in the Act's example of marital status of the couple or of occupation for the groom, so legally there was no requirement to enter this information, and the section relating to *with consent of Parents/Guardians* only needed to be completed *if both or either of the Parties married **by Licence** be under Age* . The entry was to be signed by the couple, the minister and two credible witnesses. No mention was made of legal penalties if these directions were not followed - in some parishes only one witness signed the entries and this was clearly someone connected with the local church (perhaps the Parish Clerk or Sexton) who signed several pages of entries in advance. In the marriage register of *Feltham* in Middlesex there are signatures (or marks with no names attached) and witnesses (if they could write) but the rest of the entry, including the names of the couple, is completely blank. No evidence has been found that the validity of these marriages was ever challenged.

THE PRINTERS' FORMS

The printed forms produced all followed the format given in the Act but spaced out the details more. The two principal printers were at variance on how Banns should be recorded; the Act said they should be registered but gave no example. In addition, each printer provided a page of examples of what information they suggested should be included in the Register. It is these pages which generally determine what details will be found in a Marriage Register as many clerks/incumbents followed the printed examples to the letter; those who used hand-drawn registers often hand-wrote a similar set of examples in the front of the register book.

Fox & Dod produced separate forms for Banns and for Marriages, often bound together, most commonly with marriages in the first half of the book and banns in the second. They provided a title page with details from the Act

---

Forms of MARRIAGE-REGISTERS filled up.

I. A Form when th. Marriage is folemnized by Banns and the Parties of Age. N° I.

Benjamin Matthew on   -   -   -   -   of [this] Parifh, Widower, - - - - - -

- - - - - - - - - - *and* Anna Maria Blachford Widow, - -   *of* [the]

Parifh of St Martin in the Fields in the Liberty of Weftminfter, and County of Middlefex, *were*

Married in this [Church] *by* [Banns]   - - - - - - - - - - - - -

this fourteenth   - - - - *Day of* September *in the Year One Thoufand Seven Hundred*

and Fifty four   - - - - - *by me* Jeremiah Speedwell [Vicar].

This Marriage was { Benjamin Matthewfon,

folemnized betweenUs { Anna Maria Blachford,

In the   { Thomas Southern.

Prefence of { William Knox.

II. A Minor by Licence with Confent of Parents or Guardians.   N°. 2.

(including the statutory example) and another page with four examples, which covered: *Marriage by Banns with Parties of Age* (see p.137); of *a Minor by Licence with Consent of Parents or Guardians*; *by Banns when one lives in an extra-parochial place*; and *by Licence and by Order from the High Court of Chancery*. All their examples included the names of the couple and their parishes of residence, two included marital status but none included occupations. The bottom section was arranged so that the signatures of the couple were on the right hand side of the page and of the witnesses on a lower line on the left hand side of the page. Their Registers included blank sheets and a comment *the writing Paper at the End is designed for an Index of the Names of the Parties, and Numbers for the several Registers [entries]* although very few parishes appear to have made more than a token attempt at an index.

Lownds followed the Act's format and adjusted the signatures in the same way as *Fox & Dod*. He combined Banns and Marriage into one form (as below).

DIRECTIONS HOW TO USE THIS REGISTER-BOOK.

Page your Book, and put Numbers to the *Regifters*; and when Banns are publifhed, and the Marriage immediately follows, regifter them in the following Form.

Banns of Marriage between *Thomas Crookfhanks* and *Mary Wilkinfon* were *publifhed on the* 7th, *the* 14th, *and the* 21ft *Days of April*, 1754, *by me John Jamefon, Rector.*

N° 1. *The faid Thomas Crookfhanks* ———— of *the* Parifh *of Saint Andrews, Holborn, in the City of London, Bookfeller,* —— —— *and the faid Mary Wilkinfon,* —— —— —— *of this* Parifh *Spinfter* — —— —— —— —— —— —— *were*

A Form by Banns. Married in this *Church* —— —— by *Banns* — —— —— —— —— this *Fourteenth* —— —— Day of *April* —— —— . in the Year One Thoufand Seven Hundred and *Fifty-Four* —— by me *John Jamefon, Rector* —— —— ——

This Marriage was folemnized between Us { *Thomas Crookfhanks* —— —— —— —— { *Mary Wilkinfon* —— —— —— ——

In the Prefence of *George Finchley*
Edward Holland

His instructions and examples were included on one page, clearly provided as a loose sheet, intended to be cut to size as required (with various sections which could be cut off for smaller registers) and pasted in the front of the book. Only two examples were given, one *by Banns* (see above) and one *by Licence where the woman resides in a different Parish.* Both examples gave parishes of residence, occupation (but not marital status) for the male and marital status for the female. However, it was *Lownds'* note which followed the examples which has caused most problems for family historians. *Lownds* wrote, *You may suspend Registering the Publication of Banns till the Parties attend to solemnize the Marriage, or ask a Certificate of the Publication, and if a Certficate is delivered* [which meant that the marriage would be taking place in another parish], *enter the Publication of Banns, and the Remainder of the Register will answer for a Marriage by Licence, or may be filled up with a*

Stroke of your Pen ... . Many incumbents or clerks preferred to enter the Banns and leave the rest of the entry blank (or crossed through as suggested) but some economically-minded ones took advantage of *Lownds'* suggestion, as at *Coxwold*:

Some researchers and indexers today have found the banns the easiest part of the entry to read and failed to check the entries themselves or the signatures so have missed some marriages completely and have included others as marriages when they were merely the banns.

WHAT YOU MIGHT FIND

What you find in a Marriage Register depends very much on the clergyman or on which printed Register his churchwardens bought or copied. While the majority of incumbents were content to include in their Registers either as little information as was legally permissible or, at most, the amount of detail suggested by their preferred printer, a few chose to add additional facts. Occasionally you may find *Catholic* or *Dissenter* added to a name in the Marriage Register, or the ages of the couple included. The Act did not specify that a name should be given in the register for any parent consenting to the marriage of a minor by licence. However, in some parishes the father's (or mother's, if she was a widow) name is included, although neither printer allowed much space for this, and the Act's example was ambiguous enough for some clergymen to record that parental consent had been given for the marriage of a minor by banns. Potter's **Bill to take an annual Account or Register of the People &c**, which criticised the format of Parish Registers as being inadequate, had been defeated in Parliament in 1753 but discussion concerning its suggestions rumbled on, particularly in various learned societies much favoured by clergymen. A few of them began to include extra details even before *Hardwicke's Act* came into effect and they were among the ones who, after 1754, tended to include all the details which people have incorrectly associated with the Act. (See also Chapter 12: *Dade Registers.*)

CONCLUSION

Lord Hardwicke's *Marriage Act* was an attempt by the State to eradicate clandestine (secret) marriages and to ensure that, after 25 March 1754, all marriages either by banns or by licence were carefully documented with certain conditions being complied with. However, the Act, as it reached the statute book, was worded so loosely that its requirements could be (and were) interpreted in any number of ways by those putting them into effect. The blame for this cannot altogether be laid at *Hardwicke*'s door. Interference by one House of Parliament with the legislation of the other is nothing new and, as *Dr Sharpe* wrote, *the first two clauses relating to Register Books were added in the House of Commons, and for want of time, and for other Reasons, could not be altered or rejected by the Lords without losing the Bill ...* (which was passed on the day before parliament rose for the summer recess).

The legal implications of non-compliance are not stated in the Act, although *Death as a Felon, without Benefit of Clergy* is the penalty for *falsely making, altering, forging or counterfeiting* an entry or a marriage licence or for destroying any part of a Register. It is unclear, from the evidence found to date, if partial or total non-compliance rendered a marriage void or voidable and hence any off-spring illegitimate. Entries in marriage and banns registers from 1754 must be examined far more carefully than has generally been done in the past. You may find your missing marriage forming part of the marriage entry for a totally different couple, or in a 'second' marriage register.

Registers were standardised by *Rose*'s *Act of 1812*. This required the use of printed *Books of Parchment, or of good and durable Paper **to be provided by His Majesty's Printer** as Occasion may require, at the Expence of the respective Parishes or Chapelries ...* . A printed copy of the Act, together with one book of each sort (baptisms/marriages/burials) was to be sent to each Parish or Chapelry - the government had learnt its lesson and tightened its procedures.

RESOLUTION:

I will remember that Marriage Registers between 1754 and 1812 could consist of printed forms or be handwritten books and that the amount of information included (over and above the statutory minimum: see p. 135) can vary considerably from parish to parish.

CHAPTER 14

MARRIAGES

Before beginning to search for a marriage you need to remember that all the pitfalls regarding spelling, handwriting and missing entries mentioned previously also apply here. Bear in mind that 'common law' relationships occurred frequently (see p.88); divorces or annulments were virtually impossible (see p.88); marriage to a wide range of kith and kin was forbidden (see p.36); apprentices could not marry; many men went (voluntarily or otherwise) into the army or navy and could be away for years at a time - after seven years with no news their wives often felt free to re-marry. Re-marriage was common; it is estimated that at least 25% of marriages involved a widow or widower (although marital status is often not stated). While the majority of marriages (particularly after 1754) took place in the bride's parish, a substantial minority took place in either the bridegroom's parish or in a parish convenient to both of them, with one of the couple establishing the necessary four weeks' residential requirement.

TIME OF MARRIAGE

Until 1886 marriages could only take place between *8am and 12 noon*; the time was then extended to *3pm* and, in 1936, to *6pm*. **Marriage was also forbidden at certain times of the year**, principally during *the 40 days of Lent* (Ash Wednesday to Easter Saturday) and *the 24 days of Advent* (preceding Christmas Day).

MARRIAGES BEFORE 1754

Trying to locate marriage entries before *Hardwicke*'s *Marriage Act* came into effect in 1754 can be very difficult and frustrating. Some pre-civil war registers have been lost and others were not well-kept. With perseverance, however, details of many marriages can be tracked down. Check to see if there is a BT (see p.107); many marriage bonds or allegations (see p.159) survive where the marriage entry does not; and you will often find a record of a marriage in one parish when the ceremony took place in another (whose registers may be lost). A few Nonconformist and Roman Catholic marriage registers survive for this period; most are in class RG4 (Non-Parochial Registers & Records deposited in 1840) at TNA and entries can be found on FamilySearch.

Do not expect to find the same amount of detail in early registers as you should find after 1754. The amount of detail included in a marriage register before 1754 depended largely on individual clergymen and, particularly in the 16th century, was often minimal; in one Yorkshire parish it developed from *Robert Middlebrook and his wife were marryed* (1544) via *Edward Watkinson and Margaret his wife* (1569) to *William Bauldwin & Isabel Emmot* (1598). The latter format, giving the names of the couple but little or no additional information, was one commonly used countrywide between 1538 and 1754. There are no signatures or names of witnesses to help you.

If the PR contains 'unhelpful' entries, like those at *Sherburn in Elmet* in 1743 where *Dame Halliley's servant and (blank) were married* and *Jno. Nettleton and Mr Parson's maid were married*, check whether the BT survives; there is no entry to match the first couple but in the BT *John Nettleton and Mary Hodgson were married*.

Remember that couples were not obliged to be resident in the parish where they married. A couple (especially if they obtained a marriage licence) could marry almost anywhere: in 1703 *Benjamin Pool* of *St Michael's Cornhill, London* married *Ann White* of *Longford*, Shropshire in *Lichfield Cathedral* in Staffordshire; in 1723 *Captain Robert Brown* of *Beverley* in Yorkshire married *Mistress Jennet Haliburton* of *Kelsey* in Teviotdale, Scotland in *York*; and in 1736 *Thomas Berkley* of the *Isle of Man* married *Barbara Gartside* of *Manchester* in *Wigan*, Lancashire.

1653-1660: MARRIAGES DURING THE PROTECTORATE

The period 1653-1660, when marriage was by law a civil and not a religious ceremony, is an exception to the general rule. Registers in these years may contain either no marriage entries at all or, if you are lucky, may provide more detail than at any time before 1837. Marriages, performed by a Justice of the Peace, could take place in church or elsewhere (see below). Where there was a good relationship between the local JPs and the incumbent, the register may look as if it continues as normal; where there was not, no records may survive. As described on page 94, be wary of neatly written lists of marriages covering the period (and possibly parts of the previous decade); many incumbents whose registers had not been maintained wrote them up from memory, scraps of paper or information from couples who had married. Entries may be missing, dates (if given) may be inaccurate and names can be miswritten or misspelt. Banns entries, often surviving where details of the marriage itself do not, can be invaluable for this period (see p.154).

The parish of *St Michael le Belfrey* in *York* (very close to the Minster) began a new register in October 1653, giving details of Banns and where they were published. Most were called in the *Minster* (for which the earliest surviving marriage register begins in 1681) and others in *Thursday Market* (the principal site for the selling of foodstuffs, now St Sampson's Square). Where details are given of who performed the marriage, it sometimes says where it took place - *by Alderman Taylor ... at his owne house; by... Lord maior Sr. Thomas Dickinson, at his owne house; by Mr Mace, in Bellffraies Church.*

The Register of Civil Marriages 1653-1660 belonging to Richmondshire (published by the YPRS in 1930) includes banns and marriages covering a wide area of the North Riding, stretching from Wensleydale in the south to the river Tees in the north. The following entry (abbreviated format) demonstrates that if there was an objection to the marriage, much additional information may be forthcoming:

Married on 2 May 1657 by Henry Bartlett, Edward Welbancke aged 30 and Ann Myles aged 20 both of the parish of South Cowton. Banns published on 20, 27 September, 4 October 1656 at the Market Cross [in Richmond]. Consents: on 29 September Robert Welbancke uncle to him and Sith Welbancke mother to him objected but on 2 May they consented. Witnesses [to marriage] Arthur Murthwaite, Dorothie Crawe, Issabell Myles mother to her, Henry Jackson, Register.

Take care: Pitfalls ahead

It is only when you read entries like this, or one written by a clergyman who kept detailed registers, that you realise just how many pitfalls can be created by the minimal entries which many incumbents made.

Look at two Yorkshire marriages:

1698 at *Adel: 3 Nov. John Waite, aged 72, & Margaritt Constantine, aged 50, both of this parish married by Banns. The 6th wife*

1733/4 at *Thornton in Lonsdale 3 Jan. Christopher Thornbeck of Ingleton, practitioner in Physick & Surgery widower & Sarah Harling of Leck in the parish of Tunstal widow married by Licence*

and see how many incorrect assumptions could have been made if the names alone had been given. *John and Margaret* were not young and single; he was five times a widower, she was probably a widow, and they almost certainly could not become parents. If looking for a marriage for *John Waite*, who was baptising children in the area in 1700, with no idea of his wife's name and without knowing their ages (for example if using the IGI), it would be all too easy to claim this couple. In the second example, neither *Christopher* nor *Sarah* lived in the parish where they married; both had been married before; and *Sarah* would not have been baptised as *Sarah Harling*. Pre-1754 marriage entries do not commonly include marital status. **Always bear in mind that the bride might be a widow, therefore baptised under a different surname, and that the groom could be a widower with children born to an earlier wife.**

As Parish Registers were legal documents, and could be produced as evidence in legitimacy and inheritance cases, many families made sure that a record of baptisms and marriages was kept in their 'home' parish register, whether or not the event had taken place there (see the Banns entry for *Thomas Browne* p.154). The entries in *Macclesfield* PR for the daughters of *Captain Anthony Booth*, Alderman of that town, show clearly that things were not always what they seemed. In 1661 the register records that *Jasper Howley son of John Howley of Ra[i]now in this parish & Rebecka Booth daughter of*

Captain Anthony Booth of Macclesfield were married at Pott [Shrigley] Chapel. The earliest surviving marriages in *Pott Shrigley* register are 1685 and there is no BT so this *Macclesfield* entry is the only record of the event.

His daughter *Sarah* is recorded in 1668 as having married *Mr Richard Piggert, Parson of North wytch [Northwich] at Stopford [Stockport]* - there is no entry in the *Stockport* register. The comma between *Piggert* and *Parson* is my insertion (following further research). When *Macclesfield* marriages were printed in the parish magazine the groom appeared as *Mr Richard Piggert Parson of Northwytch.* Both before and after 1754 watch carefully for occupation names, like *parson, clark/clerk, chapman, cooper, farmer, shepherd, tanner, taylor, turner* which are also surnames; capital letters proliferated in early registers but punctuation was uncommon and it is an easy mistake to make, especially for transcribers and indexers.

On 21 November 1671 *Mr Thomas Rhoad* married *Mrs* (short for Mistress, here used for a spinster of some social standing rather than signifying a married woman) *Hanna Booth, daughter of Captain Anthony Booth late of Macclesfield.* That is all that is written in the *Macclesfield* register. However, a marriage bond survives, issued on 11th November, which states that *Mr Thomas Rode* was a gentleman from *Takeley* in Essex and that the marriage could take place at *Manchester, Prestbury* or *Stockport.*

Marriages generally took place by banns or by licence but, until the late 17th or early 18th centuries, parish registers frequently did not state by which - it is always worth checking for marriage 'licences' which will often provide information to supplement the marriage entry. 'Licences' frequently gave a choice of churches for the marriage. Where three churches are given they were often the home parishes of the couple and a neutral church (frequently a local market town), with no guarantee that any of them would be the church where the marriage actually took place. The event may be recorded in all or (as in the case of *Hanna Booth*) none of them. If more than one register records the marriage, and nothing apart from the names of the couple are given, it can be impossible to know in which parish, or county, the marriage was actually solemnized.

Before 1754 it was usual but not essential to marry in a church. The fact that thousands of clandestine marriages took place in the area round the Fleet prison and elsewhere in *London*, in Peculiars and Liberties (see Chapter 18) and over the Scottish border is well known and documented. What is often overlooked is the number of marriages celebrated countrywide by *couple beggars* or *hedge priests* (itinerant clergymen with no parish), who would perform the ceremony almost anywhere in return for cash. It will never be known how many couples were united by this method because the events usually went unrecorded. Some details may appear in registers when a family decides it would be prudent to have a written record of the event. An entry in *Over Peover*, Cheshire, PR states in 1701 that *Philip Antrobus and Rebecca Heyes marryed in or near to Macclesfield.*

In 1677, no doubt following the Bishop of Chester's Order of 1676 (see p.155) and his Visitation in 1677, *Thomas Tatton* and *Ellin Lingard* are said at *Northenden* in Cheshire to have married *without licence or publication [of Banns] according to Law* and at *Mobberley* in Cheshire, also in 1677, *John Whitticors and Ellen Booth* were *married by Robert Leigh* and *Thomas Jackson and Margaret Barrow* were *married by Richard Kingston,* both entries stating *neither by Licence nor by publication.* Other parishes in the diocese may well have similar entries in that and following years and a similar situation may be found in parishes in other dioceses, particularly following a visitation by the bishop.

Entries may also surface when a clergyman questions his parishioners. The following, transcribed line by line from *Wilmslow* in Cheshire, and with no years or dates mentioned (1703/4 is the best guess), is, I trust, self-explanatory:

> *Mr Usherwood Rector of Wilmslow and Madam*
> *Eudoria Belgrave of Kilworth in Leicestershire*
> *were married Peter Bent of Eccles Parish in*
> *Lancashire and Esther Finney of Chorley*
> *were lately married by a Couple beggar Selby Warren*
> *of Bollen Fee and Mary [blank] of Pottshrigley*
> *were lately married by a Couple beggar William*
> *Furnival and Mary Willms both of Pownall Fee*
> *Samuel Clarke of Bollen Fee and [blank] Wood*
> *of Newton Couple Beggar.*

Another example of the same situation occurs at *Bowes* in 1725 where the curate noted in the register that two couples, *John Laidman & Elizabeth Railton* and *Richard Bidham & Elizabeth Watson*, all four from *Bowes*, *illegally married as appears from Certificates they shewed to the Curate and Churchwardens of Bowes.*

From 1754 onwards, a situation like the above should not arise; some pitfalls were removed but others were created.

MARRIAGES AFTER 1754

Hardwicke's *Marriage Act* of 1753 is considered by most family historians to mark a watershed in family history research in England and Wales. It applied only to England and Wales (and excepted Jews and Quakers); Scotland and Ireland continued until the 19th century to use a marriage entry format similar to that used in England before 1754 (and note that *Rose*'s *Act* of 1812 did not apply to Scotland and Ireland). The changes made to the content of Anglican marriage registers by the terms of the Act were less far-reaching than many people believe but numerous pitfalls - many of them unintentional - were created by the wording of those terms. This section summarises some of the traps you may fall into, and some of the possibilities for finding extra information; for further details see Chapter 13.

Many books will tell you that, after 1754, marriages had to take place in the parish church. Be wary of this statement. The Act effectively stopped marriages in Nonconformist chapels and Roman Catholic churches, and in many Anglican ones, but at *Halifax*, in Yorkshire, for example, where two chapels ceased to perform marriages, another two, as well as the parish church, continued and maintained separate registers. After 1754 marriages in the parishes of *Manchester* in Lancashire and *Prestbury* in Cheshire were performed only in the parish church but before this date each had eight 'marrying' chapels. *Stoke-on-Trent*, until 1807 the largest parish in Staffordshire, had five chapels which all continued to perform marriages until well into the 19th century (see p.132). Of these, *Norton-le-Moors* has been described as the 'Gretna Green of the Potteries' and *Whitmore* chapel, in 1795, saw more marriages performed (105) than there were people living in the village. **Always check the records of any chapelries within a parish to see if there are pre- or post-1754 marriages.**

Perhaps the biggest mistake you can make when looking at marriage registers between 1754 and 1812 is to assume that there was a standard format for these (*Rose*'s *Act* did introduce one in 1813). The amount of detail recorded on printed forms or in handwritten books (both were permissible) after March 1754 was down to individuals, be they clergymen, parish clerks or the printers who produced the Marriage Register Books which many parishes purchased. See pages 150, 152 and 248 for examples of handwritten registers, two of which include much extra information, including ages of the parties. **Marital status, occupation of the groom, and place of residence within a parish** - all of which many people assume will be included in a marriage entry - **were not required by law until 1837.**

Printers (see p.136) provided a sheet of examples of how to fill in the 'marriage register', issued with their printed registers or sold separately to parishes which chose to continue to write their entries in blank books, and these were generally glued into the front of the register begun in 1754. One popular printer, in his examples, included the marital status of both parties but no occupation whereas another gave occupation but no marital status for the groom but included this for the bride. Many incumbents stuck rigidly to the format of these examples so the information you find varies with which printer's sheet was used.

Never assume that a man was a bachelor because his marital status is not given. Remember that a high proportion of marriages involved one or both of the partners marrying for at least the second time. In June 1781 *Parson Barret* cooper married *Sarah Burgess* with no mention of marital status for either. Sarah died and in July 1783 the same man married *Mary Holland*; she was given as a widow but he was not described as a widower. With this example it is worth repeating the previous warning about possible confusion between surnames and occupations - misread or misindex his name and he could end up as *Parson Barret Cooper*, or as *Barret Cooper, Parson*, rather than as *Parson Barret* who was a cooper [barrel maker].

Always compare the name in the marriage entry with the signature. Apart from eliminating possible surname/occupation confusion, it is noticeable that incumbents often wrote a surname as they thought it should be spelt, only for the bride or groom to sign as something very different. One incumbent wrote out a marriage entry for *John Haldern*, who signed his name as *Ardern*, and another one for *Samuel Haldern*, who signed as *Hordern*. The following names, with their 'matching' signatures in brackets, come from a five year period in one Cheshire parish: *Amery (Emery), Badiley (Batley), Cawley (Corley), Chessus (Chesworth), Halcock (Alcock), Hatchett (Adshead)* and *Hayes (Eyers)*. At *Sherburn* in 1835 *Joseph Eyres* married but signed as *Joseph Hares*; at *Huttons Ambo* in 1801 *Richard Ethell* married and signed as *Richard Hithall* (so the mistakes were not always made by the incumbent).

In other cases it is fortunate that the couple could write, though the marriage entries were not corrected. *Sandbach*, Cheshire, marriage register records in 1775 that *William Cotton* married *Sarah Cotton* by Banns - but she signed as *Sarah Bostock* - and in 1795, at *Mottram in Longdendale*, *James Mellor* supposedly married *Martha Mellor* by Banns but he signed as *James Hall*. How many 'clerical errors' were perpetuated in entries where the person could not read or write and made their mark against an incorrect name?

On the subject of signatures, **do not assume that your ancestor could or could not write on the basis of one marriage entry**. Girls who could write, marrying men who could not, sometimes thought it politic to make their marks; others learnt to write their name so that they could sign their marriage entry. Unfortunately, some were taught to write their new married name, were caught out when told to sign their maiden name for the last time, and ended up making their mark after all. I can only assume that the Cheshire schoolmaster who made his mark in 1826 was suffering from a broken wrist.

Watch out for those parishes which maintained what amounted to two marriage registers after 1754. Some continued to enter marriages (usually with minimum detail), along with baptisms and burials, in a single register exactly as they had before, whilst maintaining a separate volume which complied with the terms of *Hardwicke*'s *Act* (see p.135). It is easy, when working through a register, to fail to realise that you have passed 1754 and should be looking for the separate volume which will contain more information.

The extra information should include the names of the witnesses. These may be relatives of the bride or groom but do not jump to this conclusion until you have looked at some previous and succeeding entries. Where more than one couple married on the same day you will often find that they acted as witnesses for each other. In some parishes one or both witnesses are almost always parish officials, frequently the parish clerk, the churchwardens, or the sexton, and they sign almost every entry for page after page (often well in advance of the event).

Rose's Act of 1812 introduced a slightly different format for marriage registers, asking for the names and parishes of the couple, whether the marriage was with the consent of parents or guardians, the date and celebrant of the event, signatures or marks and witnesses. Compulsory printed registers were published by the King's Printer and a volume was distributed to every relevant church/chapel. No mention was made of marital status or occupation; some incumbents continued to include them; others reverted to the legal minimum required. The phrase *with the consent of {parents/ guardians}* seems to have perplexed many incumbents - despite the fact that it had also been included in the 1753 Marriage Act - and care needs to be taken when looking at these registers to see how they interpreted it. The phrase was intended to apply when one or both of the couple was under 21 and needed parental permission to marry but, as with so much government legislation concerning parish registers, this was not made clear. Some incumbents interpreted it correctly, using the phrase only when required and often leaving that part of the entry blank when it did not apply, and *with the consent of parents* usually means (and sometimes says) that a minor was involved; others filled in the phrase routinely for every entry; yet more, obviously unsure what to write, entered *with the consent of those whose consent/permission is required by law.* Only by studying previous and subsequent entries can you, hopefully, ascertain whether a minor is involved in the entry you are looking at.

Aberford in Yorkshire, used two parallel Anglican marriage registers for much of the 19th century. The first one follows the format introduced by *Rose*'s *Act* and contains marriages 1813-1880, fully signed and witnessed as required by that Act. The second is in a standard 1837+ format, fully filled in, signed and witnessed. Again, searching the first one, would you realize that, after 1837, you should be looking for a different register with more information? **Keep your wits about you.**

If you are looking for a marriage for a man with a common surname, even if you know his wife's Christian name, do not accept the first entry you find without trying to corroborate that you have the right person. Eight *John Smiths* married in east Cheshire in 1823 including, on January 9 by Licence at *Bowdon, John Smith bachelor of Ashton under Lyne, Lancashire and Esther*

Heyes spinster of Bowdon. On January 16 by Licence at *Warrington* (then in Lancashire*) John Smith of that parish married Esther Poole of Wilmslow in Cheshire* - remember that, whatever books or internet sites may say to the contrary, many marriages did take place in the bridegroom's parish. If you were looking for *John Smith and Esther*, baptising children in *Wilmslow*, would you immediately have latched onto the first marriage or would you have checked over the county boundary for a marriage in Lancashire?

Do not be surprised if you come across a marriage which appears to have taken place twice. The penalties which could be imposed on the clergy if they infringed the terms of *Hardwicke*'s *Marriage Act* were severe, and there were a number of circumstances under which, if a couple broke the rules, the marriage could be declared null and void. Where any irregularity, or possible problem, came to light it was often considered advisable to repeat the ceremony. When *John Hollingworth* and *Mary Ann Hollingworth or Sidebottom* married by licence in Cheshire in 1831 a note in the register stated that the couple *were originally married in the parish church of Doncaster on 8 January 1826 but as they were then and still are generally resident in this parish it has been deemed expedient to repeat the ceremony*. How many other couples who married away from home did the same but without the incumbent bothering to note the fact of the first ceremony?

Couples who eloped and married (legally) in Scotland might similarly later marry in their home parish. On 11 November 1775 *Ralph Audley*, gentleman, and *Joan Penlington*, daughter of *William Penlington* Esq. of *Nantwich* were married at *Nantwich*, with the comment *Joan Audley late Joan Penlington being married in August last to the said Ralph Audley in North Briton commonly called Scotland*. In 1820 *William Ward*, who had married *Emma Jones* in Scotland, applied for a licence stating that *in order to obviate any Doubt that may hereafter arise touching the Validity of the said Marriage he ... is desirous of being married again to the said Emma Ward formerly Jones ... in the parish Church of St Oswald in Chester*.

Marriages where one of the parties had been under age and parental consent had not been obtained might marry again when both reached 21. In April 1771 *John Meek*, widowman and farmer, married *Sarah Hilditch*, spinster, both of the parish, by Licence at *Astbury* in Cheshire. The entry is annotated *This marriage declared null and void by the 11th section of the marriage act* (the one dealing with marriage of a minor by licence - see p.133) and the couple married again by licence at *Astbury* in October 1773, presumably when Sarah reached 21. On the second occasion *John Meek* was described as a butcher and no mention was made in the entry of his marital status. Some couples married claiming that both were resident in the parish where the banns were called, and were obliged to marry again when it came to light that one of them was not. In 1787 *Ralph Dale*, bachelor aged 24, and *Mary Frost*, spinster aged 22, both of the parish, were married at *Witton* in

Cheshire with the incumbent adding *this couple was married at Manchester before illegally* (20 May 1787 at *Manchester* Collegiate Church).

There are very few *Dade marriage registers* (see p.125-126) but those that there are can contain a wealth of information, as two examples from *Sherburn in Elmet* demonstrate.

Firstly, on *19 February 1784 Ingram Varley butcher of Sherburn aged 22, son of Ingram Varley of Sherburn farmer & innkeeper by Ellenor his wife daughter of John Tate of Berwick in Elmet farmer married Ann Forster of Sherburn aged 62 by Licence.* No details of Ann's parents are given but the marriage allegation describes her as a spinster.

The forty year difference in their ages is not an error - *Ann* died in January 1785 *aged 62 of fever* (and *Ingram* remarried in 1787 to a girl of his own age). The marriage allegation (see p.162) gives his age as *22* and hers as *30 years and upwards* (see also marriage bond on p.194).

Marriage between a much older man and a young girl was not common but it happened - probably when he needed a housekeeper and she needed a protector or when the overseers of the poor decided that two could live as cheaply as one and 'persuaded' two people on parish relief to marry. In such cases, ages of the couple were often given as in 1778 at *Over*, Cheshire when *Peter Proudlove widower and salt officer aged 76 married Martha Barker spinster aged 15 by Licence.* The converse (young man, older woman as with *Ingram Varley*) appears to have been rarer and an entry at *Mottram in Longdendale*, Cheshire in 1780, when *Daniel Broadbent aged 23 married Martha Cheetham aged 83 by Licence* impelled the incumbent to add *N.B. A peculiar marriage.*

Secondly, on *13 July 1787 Nathaniel Haines of Sherburn husbandman aged 28 came to Sherburn when a boy out of Ackworth Hospital an apprentice to Mr William Barber of Sherburn married by Banns Phillis Morris of the same parish spinster aged 35 daughter of Matthew Morris of Kippax cloth drawer by Mary his wife daughter of Henry Atkinson of the same parish farmer.*

Between 1757 and 1772 *Ackworth Hospital* (about eight miles from *Sherburn*) was an outpost of the *London Foundling Hospital* (see Chapter 21) and, during these years, several thousand children were apprenticed out, mainly to farmers or mill-owners, all over the country. To find their origin and their employer named is very uncommon; if you hit a brick wall with an ancestor who appears from nowhere in the late 18th century it could be worth your while to investigate Foundling Hospital records.

AGE AT MARRIAGE

Until 1929, in general the legal age for marriage in England, Wales, Scotland and Ireland was *14* for a groom and *12* for a bride. From 1754 in England and Wales consent of parents or guardian was required if either party was under *21* (*18* from 1970); parental consent was often stated before this date, particularly on marriage allegations. Before 1929 in Scotland parental consent was not required for a valid marriage under the age of *21*, which accounts for many of the 'Gretna Green' type marriages involving couples from England which occurred until a 21 day residence qualification in Scotland was introduced in 1857.

From 1929 the legal age was raised to *16* for both male and female (except in the Republic of Ireland where it was not raised until 1975).

Marriages under 16 have never been common; those at 12, 13 and 14 are very rare and many supposed examples involve a mistaken identification or refer to a betrothal; a number of 15 year olds (particularly girls) did marry (see examples on pp.133 and 150). If a post-1813 marriage register states that the event takes place *with the consent of parents/guardians* this should (but see p.148) mean that one or both parties were under 21.

ROMAN CATHOLIC MARRIAGE REGISTERS

After 1754 Roman Catholics (particularly if they required a record of the marriage for legal or inheritance purposes) were obliged to marry in an Anglican church but often had a second Catholic ceremony. Some priests maintained their own records, from varying dates in the 18th century, and these may contain additional information to that in the PR, although, as in the Anglican Church, much depended on individual priests. In 1835 *Stephen Talbott and Margaret Swinnerton* both of this parish married by Banns at *Adbaston*, Staffordshire; on the same day an entry in *Swynnerton Roman Catholic Register* records simply that *Stephen Talbott* and *Margaret Swinnerton* married. *Valentine Barker and Sarah Barnes* were married by Banns in the parish church of *Holme-on-Spalding-Moor* in January 1779 (he of the parish, she of *Cliff*, parish of *North Cave*). The register for *Holme Hall (RC) Chapel* in the East Riding of Yorkshire records that *On 28th day of January An. 1779 Valentine Barker, Son of the late Valentine Barker and his Wife Ann, whose maiden name was Winter of Weighton, took to Wife Sarah Barnes, born at Kellenhaugh in the County of Lincoln, and received the nuptial Benediction in the Chappel at Holme in presence of Jourdan Brisby, his Uncle, Peter Brisby, his Cousin, Winefride Kidder, Ann Carlisle and others assembled on the occasion.*

Baptisms and Marriages at *Holme Hall Chapel* had been recorded in a paper book since 1744 (and copied into a vellum one used from 1766) and the note entered by *Dom. John Fisher*, OSB throws some light on the recording of marriages of Roman Catholics from 1754: *1754 The Act of Parliament taking place att this Time whereby Catholicks were put under an Obligation of being marryed at Church and registered there, otherwise the Marriage declared null and to no effect as to all Intents and purposes: It was judg[e]d useless to continue the Register any longer, as their Marriages are to be found in the Church Register. However as it seems now the Desire of the Apost[oli]c Vic[ar] that a Marriage Register should be accurately kept by Cath. Pr[iests]: so will resume it from* [August 1764 but it petered out from 1780 onwards]. Not many priests appear to have followed his example, most presumably agreeing with the first part of his statement.

RESOLUTION:

I will not expect to find as much detail in pre-1754 marriage entries as I hope to find in post-1754 ones.
For post-1754 marriages I will be aware that occupation, marital status and age were not compulsory before 1837 and very few parishes included all these details.

MARRIAGE REGISTER FOR THE PARISH OF ACKWORTH 1761/1762
(another variation on a handwritten register; note the use of signatures/ marks as the only instance of the couple's names and that occupation, marital status for both parties and their ages are all given.)

CHAPTER 15

BANNS AND MARRIAGE LICENCES, ALLEGATIONS AND BONDS

Did your ancestors marry after the publication of banns or the purchase of a marriage licence? The odds are that they did - because one or other was a prerequisite of marriage in a Christian church - but do not assume that, because you find evidence of banns or a licence, the marriage necessarily took place. **Each document was valid for three months** so, if you cannot locate the marriage entry within that time, prepare yourself for the possibility that there was no wedding. Banns, or the documentation relating to a licence, are evidence of an expressed intention to marry, not proof that the intention was carried through. Some people have always changed their minds at the last minute; parents have prevented minors from marrying; previous spouses have come forward to prevent a bigamous marriage; employers have forbidden their apprentices to marry; the law has stepped in and imprisoned (or even transported) one of the couple for some offence. **Never** (except during the Interregnum - see p.95) **accept that a marriage occurred until you have seen the entry in the marriage register or BT.**

BANNS

In many early registers you will find the words *by publication* or (particularly in Scotland) *by proclamation* used to describe marriages by banns. You may also find marriages described as taking place *by certificate*. This commonly refers to a marriage by banns where one of the parties came from another parish and had to provide written evidence, in the form of a certificate handed to the minister conducting the ceremony, that the banns had also been called in the other parish and no objection made. After 1837 *by certificate* may refer to a superintendent registrar's certificate issued, after notice of the marriage had been posted for the requisite three weeks at the register office, to permit the marriage to take place in church.

1653-1660: THE PROTECTORATE

Details of banns will rarely be found in registers before the middle of the 18th century - they were read out in church but there was no obligation to keep a written record of them. The exception to this was the period 1653-1660, when a system of record keeping similar to civil registration was in force: banns could be called in church or market place, and the marriage performed by a Justice of the Peace either in church or at his office or home. Unfortunately, many of the records from this period have not survived (see p.142) but more banns than marriages appear to be extant and these can provide a genealogical goldmine as shown in these two 1655 examples from Cheshire:

On the 8th, 15th and 22nd April 1655 Banns were called at *Cheadle*, Cheshire for *Thomas Browne, taylor of this parish, son of James Browne of Cheadle, deceased, and Ellen Berch of Didsbury, parish of Manchester, daughter of John Berch of Didsbury, deceased.* Where they married is debateable but the Banns details are recorded in all three of the churches connected with the two families. On 23rd April there is an apparent marriage entry, repeating the above information, in *Manchester* PR; followed on 1 May by a similar entry in *Didsbury* PR - saying that the marriage took place at *Stockport* (where there is no trace of it).

Alderley, Cheshire PR records that on *3 October 1655 The intention of marriage betwixt John Daniell, son of Elizabeth Daniell, widow of Alderley, and Rebecca Gandie, of Prestbury, daughter of James Gandie of Millton, having been published in the Towne of Macclesfield, in the Markett Place, three several Market dayes, betwixt the houres of Eleven and Twoo of the Clock ... the twentieth day of August, and no exception lodged to the contrary they were married before the Right Worshipfull Thomas Breareton of Ashley esq., Justice of the Peace.*

BANNS BEFORE 1754

From the late 17th century onwards, PRs often indicate whether a marriage was by Banns or by Licence; some include the dates when the banns were called, others do not. When this practice begins differs from diocese to diocese.

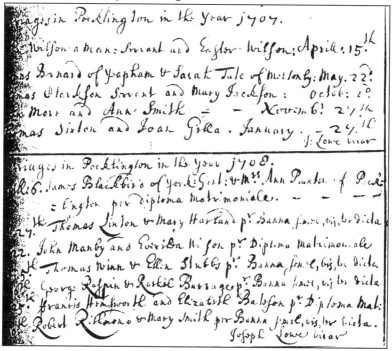

154

The Bishop of *Chester* issued an order for *a strict registring (sic) of Weddings* in 1676; the Archbishop of *York* ordered *that in the weddings it should be noted wether (sic) with Banns or Licence* in 1692. In both dioceses the orders were generally obeyed but not with alacrity - it took years before the practice became well-established (*Pocklington* adopted the practice in 1708. Before 1733, where the PRs were in Latin, you may find, as in *Pocklington, Banna semel bis ter dicta* - Banns called once/the first time, twice, three [times]. Some incumbents noted only when a marriage was by licence (*Diploma Matrimoniale* in *Pocklington*), leaving one with the assumption that all other entries were by Banns. It is always worth checking for details of a licence even when this is not stated - incumbents did make mistakes.

BANNS AFTER 1754

The *1753 Marriage Act* (see Chapter 13) ordered that banns be recorded and from this point, in England and Wales, you will often find a Banns Register either combined with, or kept separately from, the Marriage Register. There was no standard format laid down for marriage registers, with content depending on individual printers, and the same applied to banns registers. Some printers combined the banns and the marriage entry into one unit; others bound the marriage register at one end of the book and the banns register at the other; yet others produced two separate books.

The 'combined' entry can produce a deep pitfall. One of the most popular printers devised a format which included a (relatively small) designated space for the banns to be written out, with the marriage entry below. He then (see p.138-139) added a rider to his sheet of examples suggesting that if the banns were called but the marriage did not take place in that parish, then a marriage by licence (of another couple) could be used to fill the marriage space. A number of parishes adopted this economical suggestion for saving paper (see example on p.139) but, fortunately for us, most used it for only a few years after 1754 because it is easy, when looking at a register, to read the names from the banns section and to forget to check the signatures or marks in the marriage section, so totally missing the different marriage by licence.

Watch out for another printer who had the same idea of combining the two elements but who gave more prominence to the banns than to the marriage entry. His books can sometimes be found in record offices classified as banns registers (only). If you come across a parish whose marriage register is not listed as surviving but which has a banns register it is always worth checking that the record office has not misclassified the register in this way. Also beware of the printer who produced separate formats for marriages by banns and by licence. The two may occupy separate books or be bound together with the two sections (one headed **Publications**, the other **Marriages)** in one book. If you are looking at the register in microform it is all too easy to run through one section, think you have reached the end of the register, and not realise that you have missed 'half' the entries. *Pocklington* (see below) separates out its marriages like this (between 1785 and 1812) as does *St Andrews, Holborn*.

Publications.

Banns of Marriage between _Edward Hodshinson Bachelor_
No. 2 _____ of this Parish _____
and _Ann Shadder Spinster_ _____ of this Parish
of _____ were publiſhed
on Sunday the _first_ of _May_
on Sunday the _second eight_ of _July_
on Sunday the _fifteenth_ of _July_
and were Married in this _Church_ this _Twenty fourth_
Day of _May_ in the Year One Thouſand ~~Seven~~
eight Hundred and _three_ by me _Richard Wadsworth A. M. Curate_
This Marriage was ſolemnized between Us {_David Hodshinson X Mark_
Ann Hadders
In the Preſence of _Wm Ireland Robert_

Banns of Marriage between _Daniel Smith, Bachelor_
No. 3 _____ of this Parish _____
and _Elizabeth Anderson single Woman_ of this Parish
of _____ were publiſhed
on Sunday the _twentieth_ of _November_
on Sunday the _twenty seventh_ of _November_
on Sunday the _fourth_ of _December_
and were Married in this _Church_ this _fifth_
Day of _December_ in the Year One Thouſand ~~seven~~
eight Hundred and _three_ by me _Rich. Wadsworth A. M. Curate_
This Marriage was ſolemnized between Us {_Daniel Smith's X Mark_
John Todd {_Elizabeth Anderson_
In the Preſence of _Mary Nylton's X Mark_

Banns of Marriage between _Joseph Cheetham, Bachelor_
No. 4 _____ of this Parish _____
and _Sarah Haines, Spinster,_ _____ of this Parish
of _____ were publiſhed
on Sunday the _twenty seventh_ of _November_
on Sunday the _fourth_ of _December_
on Sunday the _eleventh_ of _December_
and were Married in this _Church_ this _twelfth_
Day of _December_ in the Year One Thouſand ~~Seven~~
eight Hundred and _three_ by me _Rich. Wadsworth A. M. Curate_
This Marriage was ſolemnized between Us {_Joseph Cheetham_
Sarah Haines X Mark
In the Preſence of _John Matton_
Richard Haues

Marriages

No. 1 *Josiah Bodwell* of the Parifh *of Hull* ____ and *Ann Baskett* of
this Parifh *Spinster* ____ were ____
Married in this *Church* by *Licence* ____
this *seventh* Day of *August* in the Year One Thoufand Seven
Hundred and *ninety eight* by me *F. Baskett (minister)*
This Marriage was folemnized between Us { *Josiah Bodwell* { *Ann Baskett*
In the Prefence of *Kingsman Baskett, sen.*
Elizabeth Baskett

No. 2 *Nicholas Chicken* of the Parifh *of St Michael*
York ____ and *Elizabeth Puddleston* of
this Parifh *Spinster* ____ were
Married in this *Church* by *Licence*
this *twenty one* Day of *October* in the Year One Thoufand Seven
Hundred and *ninety eight* by me *Wm Williamson, curate*
This Marriage was folemnized between Us { *Nich. Chicken* { *Elizabeth Puddleston*
In the Prefence of *John Williamson*
Robt Cotton

No. *John Beck* of this Parifh *Singleman*
____ and *Mary Howe Spinster* of
this Parifh ____ were
Married in this ____ *Banns*
this *29th* ____ Day of *November* in the Year One Thoufand Seven
Hundred and *ninety eight* by me ____
This Marriage was folemnized between Us {
In the Prefence of ____

No. 3 *William Marshall* ____ of the Parifh ____
____ and *Ann Hall Spinster both* of
this Parifh ____ were
Married in this *Church* by *Licence*
this *sixth* Day of *December* in the Year One Thoufand Seven
Hundred and *Ninety Eight* by me *A.C. Plummer officiating Min*
This Marriage was folemnized between Us { *William Marshall* { *Ann Hall*
In the Prefence of *Ann West*
Geo Horsley

157

Banns registers have long been a neglected source of information. They are not included in the IGI or in some marriage indexes (because they are not records of marriages). Banns-only entries in combined registers are also often omitted from these sources. Some printed parish registers (see Chapter 17) do not even mention the existence of banns books for their parish; others do not transcribe them and dismiss them cursorily with, for example, *Volume III is a Banns Register.*

It is always worth checking the banns register, if one survives. Often there will be no additional details to those included in the marriage entry but sometimes there will and one extra word, giving marital status or occupation, could be all you need. At *Alderley*, Cheshire in 1754 the marriage register records that *Richard Wych* married *Margaret Atkinson*; the banns register says that *Richard* was a *cordwainer, son of Wm: Wych of Sossmoss* and *Margaret* was *a housemaid at Alderley Hall*. If you are seeking someone who has disappeared from his or her home parish and cannot be found in neighbouring ones, look in the banns register and you could find an entry for them to marry someone from a completely unexpected parish, maybe hundreds of miles away, where they then settled. Many such couples married by licence but at *St Mary Bishophill Junior* in York, in 1814 *Jonathan Stansfield*, stonemason of *Newark upon Trent*, Nottinghamshire and in 1815 *James Lamb*, slater of *Alnwick*, Northumberland both married local girls after banns. The 1759 banns entry for *John Hill* and *Mary Brailey*, married at *Alderley*, whilst being of no help in locating where the couple originated, demonstrates clearly why some marriages are so hard to find; *both strangers and peddlers without any place of constant abode but who have resided a month last past at Samuell Cashe's, in Nether Alderley* [presumably to establish a residence qualification].

In most churches, marriage by banns was much more common than marriage by licence. When the marriage register for *Leeds* parish church, begun on 27th March 1754, was completed on 6th May 1760 a note was added: *Number of Marriages in this Volume 1495.*
In all 1299 by Banns and 196 by Licence in this Volume.

Putting up the banns, obtaining a licence and getting married all had to be paid for and this could prove expensive, especially if two sets of banns were involved. Some couples, particularly in urban areas where the incumbent was unlikely to know them personally, claimed that they both resided in the same parish and generally got away with it (but see p.149-150). By contrast, others decided that a licence, while being a little more expensive than paying two banns charges and obtaining a certificate, was less trouble.

Banns books will usually be kept in the same record repository as the parish registers, most commonly in a county, local authority or diocesan record office (see Chapter 6).

Marriage Licences, Bonds & Allegations

Marriage 'licences' are normally to be found in diocesan record offices (see Chapter 6). In many counties, the CRO is also the DRO but in some areas to view a marriage 'licence' you will need to visit a different record office, sometimes even in a different county (see, for example, *Lichfield* p.51).

Many CROs and DROs have indexed their bonds and allegations and some are available online. *The National Library of Wales* has an online index to marriage bonds in Welsh Dioceses.

Marriage licences in England and Wales could be issued by Archbishops or their officials, Bishops, some Archdeacons or their surrogates (deputies), incumbents of some Peculiars and, after 1837, by Superintendent Registrars. Marriage by licence was virtually unknown in Scotland.

Contrary to popular belief, **marriage by licence was not the prerogative of the middle and upper classes.** Many of them married by banns, just as many labourers married by licence. A licence was often favoured if: the couple came from different parishes; the girl was heavily pregnant; the man was in the armed forces; the couple were Roman Catholic or Nonconformist and did not want to attend the parish church to call the banns; or to avoid gossip or speculation in the neighbourhood.

Most family historians will have ancestors who married by licence, rather than by banns, but very few will have seen a marriage licence. This was given to the groom, to hand to the minister at the church, and very few survive. What you may well have seen, having tracked down the relevant documentation in a county or diocesan record office, is a *marriage allegation* (the couple stating their intention to marry, alleging that there is no reason why they should not marry, and naming a church for the marriage to take place) and/or *a bond* (surety for the truth of the allegation, usually entered into by the groom and one other, often a relative of bride or groom, a neighbour or an employer). These are commonly, but inaccurately, referred to in books and on websites as marriage 'licences'. Registers of marriage licences issued survive for some dioceses but generally contain less information than allegations and bonds.

The survival rate of allegations, bonds and registers of licences varies between dioceses. Some have good coverage from the late 16th century, others only from the late 18th century. Do not assume that the pattern in one diocese will be repeated in another. Many series of allegations and bonds begin in the 1660s when marriage licences, abolished during the Interregnum, were restored. From this date many dioceses used printed forms, particularly for bonds with the allegation sometimes being handwritten on the form. Until 1732 Latin was often used but names, ages, places and occupations (where given) can usually be picked out; look for scribbled notes saying, for example, *aet[atis]* [age] *ille 32, sua 27* [his 32, hers 27], *caelibes* [both single]; *vid[ua or*

159

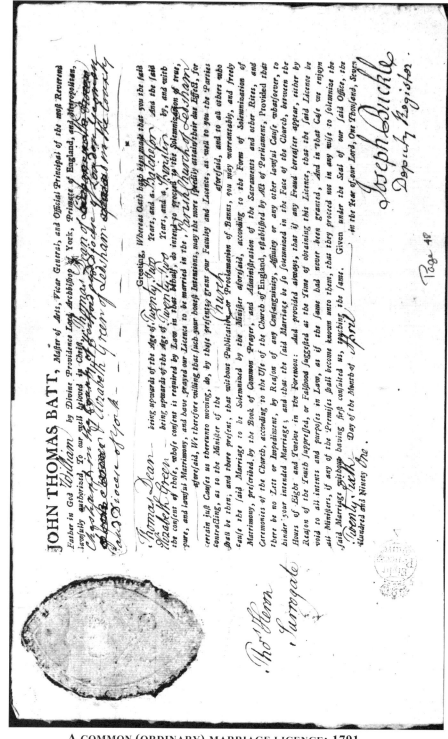

A COMMON (ORDINARY) MARRIAGE LICENCE: 1791

uus] [widow, widower] and *opp[idum]* [of this town]. Remember to look on the back of a printed bond as in some dioceses it was common practice to write the allegation here. If the PR is in Latin, you may find a marriage by licence described there as *per Diploma Matrimoniale* (see p.154).

From 1733 separate printed forms were often used for bond and allegation so check for both - and for any additional paperwork generated when a minor was involved. Parental consent for the marriage of a minor was required, and often noted on any documentation, from 1603; following *Hardwicke's Marriage Act* of 1753 this was essential to ensure the validity of a marriage and a statement of consent should accompany (or be written on) the allegation.

Bear in mind that, before the rules were tightened in 1754, a marriage allegation (or a marriage) may be found a long way from where the couple lived. To many couples and clerics, possession of a licence mattered more than what it said. The Diocese of Lichfield covered the counties of Derbyshire and Staffordshire and parts of Shropshire and Warwickshire. The bishop or his officers issued marriage licences from the cathedral to couples from all four counties and, even if the licence named a 'home' church for the marriage to take place, many couples ignored this and married in the Cathedral immediately after obtaining the licence. Before 1754 couples from *Birmingham* [Warwickshire] seem to have been particularly fond of marrying in the Cathedral and the following examples give an idea of the wide area covered by those who did the same: *1701 Henry Stringfellow of Chesterfield [Derbyshire] & Lydia Marrall of Abbots Bromley [Staffordshire]; 1701/2 Richard Holland of Whitchurch & Mary Jones of Newport [both Shropshire]; 1707 Ralph Tompson of Wytherly [Leicestershire] & Abigail Ward of Mancetter [Warwickshire]; 1708 William Jones of Kilsfield [Montgomeryshire] & Susan Sansom of Salop [Shropshire].* Archbishops could grant licences to marry anywhere in their archdioceses (and Canterbury anywhere in the country). If a couple came from different archdioceses, the licence should have been granted by Canterbury but some, particularly involving people from Lincolnshire and Derbyshire (which were in the southern archdiocese; Nottinghamshire was in the northern), will be found in the records in York. If a pre-1754 marriage is said to be by licence, and you cannot locate the documentation, it may be lost but it is worth casting round a wide area - and, if you have the allegation but not the marriage, check the cathedral and the churches occupied by archdeacons or surrogates who were issuing licences in that diocese.

From 1754 onwards the wording of allegations, bonds and licences was to a large extent defined by law but, as with marriage registers, the exact format used depended on bishops and their printers and some included more detail than others. *Allegations* begin with the date followed by *On which Day appeared personally* (see examples on pp.162 & 163); *bonds* with *Know all Men by these Presents That we ...* (see p.194 for an example). Post 1754 allegations and licences normally named only one church for the marriage to take place, and that where one of the couple had been resident for at least four weeks. The bond may also name the church - those in the Diocese of Norwich, for example, usually do but those in Chester and York do not. After 1823 bonds were no longer required but a few dioceses did continue to use them.

The ages of the couple were included in allegations from 1754 - often, but not always, being given before this - but the phrasing *he/she is of the age of ... and upwards* created a loophole of which many took advantage. *21 and upwards* may mean that the person is truly 21, younger than 21 but marrying without parental consent, or much older. The best recommendation is to treat *21 and upwards* with suspicion and search for other evidence to confirm the age. If a specific age is given (and it does not end in 0; see p.70) it is likely to be accurate to within five years but remember that many people before the late 19th century did not know their exact ages.

Just how misleading some ages on allegations are can be seen from the allegation for *Ingram Varley* below (see p.150 for *Ann Forster's* true age).

The *Nineteenth* Day of *February* in the Year of our LORD One Thousand Seven Hundred and Eighty *four*

ON which Day appeared personally *Ingram Varley of Sherburn & within the Jurisdiction of the Dean & Chapter of York Butcher*

and, being Sworn on the Holy Evangelists, alledged and made Oath as follows, That he is of the Age of *twenty two* Years and upwards and a *Bachelor* and intends to marry *Ann Forster of the same place*
Aged *thirty* Years, and upwards, and a *Spinster*

not knowing or believing any lawful Let or impediment by Reason of Consanguinity, Affinity, or any other Cause whatsoever, to hinder the said intended Marriage: And he prayed a Licence to Solemnize the said Marriage in the *Parish Church of Sherburn* aforesaid, In which said *Parish* the said *Ingram Varley* ———— further made Oath, That *the* said *Ann Forster* ———————— hath had *her* usual Abode for the Space of Four Weeks last past.

On the same Day the said
Ingram Varley
Was Sworn before Me

John Rogers. Surrogate,

Ingram Varley

During the period September 1822 to about April 1823 a short-lived law required those applying for a marriage licence to provide details of their baptisms. In December 1822 *Lawrence Peel* of *Ardwick* in Lancashire and *Elizabeth Radcliffe* of *Ecclesall Bierlow* in Yorkshire applied for a licence.

The allegation said both were widowed and *of the full age of twenty one years and upwards*. The baptism certificates below reveal that *Lawrence was 65* and *Elizabeth was 47*.

If you locate an ancestral marriage by licence in these months, do seek out the documentation. As well as their true ages, the baptism certificates give the names of *Lawrence's* parents, and that he was baptised at *Blackburn*, and of *Elizabeth's* father and that he was a silver cutler of *Sheffield*.

SPECIAL LICENCES

The documentation described above relates to *ordinary* or *common* marriage licences. Do not fall into the trap of thinking that, because your ancestor married by licence, it was a *special* licence. Before the 20th century, less than 1% of the licences issued were *special* licences, issued by the Archbishop of Canterbury in England or the Archbishop of Armagh in Ireland (and, apparently, by the Bishop of Sodor and Man) which enabled a couple to marry at any convenient time or place - commonly in a church not licensed for marriages or in a private house and often outside the permitted hours of 8am to 12 noon (extended to 3pm in 1886 and later to 6pm). The word *special* does not appear on the licence but may be mentioned in accompanying paperwork (see p.166). In England and Wales in 1747 only 11 special licences were granted; in 1757 there were 50 and the Archbishop of Canterbury issued guidelines trying to restrict such licences to the aristocracy, Privy Councillors and members of parliament.

The RC register of *Holme Hall Chapel* in Yorkshire contains the following note: *The Hon[oura]ble Apollonia Langdale* [the *Langdales* were the leading RC family in the area] *was married at Bath to the Hon[oura]ble Hugh Clifford, eldest Son and Heir to Hugh Lord Clifford of Ugbrook in Devonshire on the 2nd day of May 1780 by special Licence at her Mother's House; the two others* [her sisters *Mary* and *Elizabeth* who had married in 1778 and 1779 respectively] *were also favoured with the same special Licence, to which the Peerage entitled them*. The marriages of the three sisters demonstrate just how widely the aristocracy, and perhaps particularly Catholic families, sought for spouses for their children. *Mary*'s husband was from *Essex*, *Elizabeth*'s from *Ireland* and *Apollonia*'s from *Devon*. *Mary* married at Lord *Langdale*'s seat (*Holme Hall*), *Elizabeth* in *London* and *Apollonia* in *Bath*.

In 1880 there were 43 special licences issued. Out of 300,000 marriages in my North and East Cheshire marriage index (1538-1837), only one (in 1812) is specified as being by special licence. The original documentation for special licences issued before 1754 should be found in the records of the Vicar General of the Archbishop of Canterbury, from 1754 onwards they should be in the records of the Faculty Office of the Archbishop of Canterbury. Both officials also issued common licences on behalf of the Archbishop. The Vicar General could issue licences to marry in any parish within the Archdiocese of Canterbury, the Faculty Office could issue a licence for a couple to marry in any parish in England or Wales where one of them lived so, if you cannot find an expected marriage in the Archdiocese of York or in Wales, it is well worth checking these records. The records relating to these officials are held in *Lambeth Palace Library* but they have been filmed and are available in microform in several places. *The Society of Genealogists* holds microfilm of the calendars for both offices, together with indexes to many of them, (see their website for more details) and these are also available on a commercial website.

SPECIAL LICENCE (1963) AND ACCOMPANYING LETTER

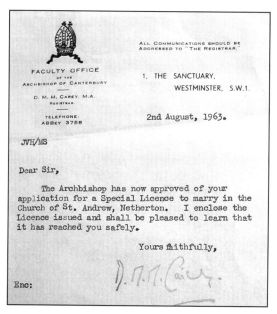

Arthur Michael by Divine Providence *Archbishop of Canterbury* Primate of all England and Metropolitan by Authority of Parliament lawfully empowered for the Purposes herein written To our Beloved in Christ _____ *of the Parish of Same* *Mrs. Horbury in the county of York Bachelor and* _____ *of the Parish of Middlestown with Nettleton in the same county Spinster* _____

Health **Whereas** as it is alleged *Ye* have purposed to proceed to the Solemnization of a true pure and lawful Marriage

earnestly desiring the same to be Solemnized with all the speed that may be *That* such your reasonable desires may more readily take due effect *We* for certain causes Us hereunto especially moving do so far as in Us lies and the Laws of this Realm allow by these Presents Graciously give and grant Our **Licence and Faculty** as well to you the Parties contracting as to all Christian People willing to be present at the Solemnization of the said Marriage to celebrate and solemnize such Marriage between you said contracting Parties *between the hours of eight in the forenoon and six in the afternoon in the church of Saint Andrew Netherton Wakefield in the said county of York* by any Bishop of this Realm or by any Minister in Holy Orders of the Church of England *Provided* there be no lawful let or impediment to hinder the said Marriage and provided also that the Solemnization thereof takes place within three calendar months of the date hereof **Given** under the Seal of Our **Office of Faculties** at Westminster this ____ *Thirtyfirst* ____ day of ____ *July* ____ in the year of our Lord One thousand nine hundred and sixty-*three* ____ and in the ____ *third* ____ year of Our Translation

J.A.A. Carey

Registrar

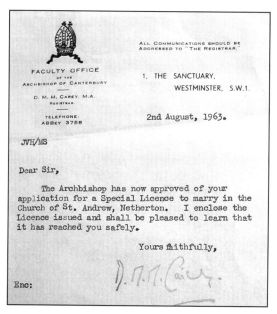

FACULTY OFFICE
OF THE
ARCHBISHOP OF CANTERBURY

D. M. M. CAREY, M.A.
REGISTRAR

TELEPHONE:
ABBEY 3758

ALL COMMUNICATIONS SHOULD BE ADDRESSED TO "THE REGISTRAR."

1, THE SANCTUARY,
WESTMINSTER, S.W.1.

2nd August, 1963.

JVH/MS

Dear Sir,

    The Archbishop has now approved of your application for a Special Licence to marry in the Church of St. Andrew, Netherton. I enclose the Licence issued and shall be pleased to learn that it has reached you safely.

Yours faithfully,

D. M. M. Carey.

Enc:

166

CHAPTER 16

BURIALS & MONUMENTAL INSCRIPTIONS

CREMATION

Land on which to build the first crematorium in England was purchased at Woking in Surrey in 1878 and **the first cremation took place there in March 1885**. By 1940, about 4% of deaths were followed by cremation; today the figure is approaching 75%. Cremation is now accepted almost as the norm and it is very easy to forget that, until well into the 20th century, almost everyone had to be buried. So why can we not find entries for some of our ancestors in parish registers or in cemetery records?

DIFFICULTIES IN LOCATING BURIALS

In Scotland and Ireland it may be because parish registers in general, and burial registers in particular, were not widely kept until the 18th century. Throughout the British Isles it may be because they were buried elsewhere - in a *Nonconformist, Roman Catholic* or *Quaker* burial ground (any or all of which could be found in some areas by the 18th century); from the 19th century in a *private, municipal* or *workhouse* cemetery; from the 20th century in *'green' burial grounds*; *overseas*; *at sea*; *on their own property*, a practice permitted since the 17th century (when Quakers won the right to be buried in unconsecrated ground) and which continues to this day. Puritans, particularly in the 16th century, asked to be buried not in the churchyard but in *a barn, outhouse or field*. There are instances of atheists being buried in the middle of a field (see p.173.) and of people being buried in their own gardens (*Johnny Morris* of **Animal Magic** fame and the novelist *Barbara Cartland* are among the better known names to have taken this option - both had large gardens). When this practice occurs today, it is usually considered newsworthy enough to merit a paragraph in the local paper.

Bear in mind that many churchyards, particularly in urban areas, were full by the mid-19th century and your ancestors are most likely to be buried in a municipal cemetery (unless a space remained in a family grave in a churchyard). **Remember that many cemeteries are divided into denominational sections**, often including ones, among others, for *Anglicans, Roman Catholics, Nonconformists* of all persuasions, *Jews* and *Muslims*. Make sure that you check the records for all Sections as people may not be buried in the one you expect. Some cemetery and crematoria records have been indexed; others have been put online by local authorities; many cemeteries are included in the **National Burial Index** (see p.168).

Do not assume that all burials took place within a few days of death. Some bodies were never recovered - from shipwrecks in deep water or mining accidents, for example - and without a body there could be no burial. Remains might come to light months, or years, later; those lost on the moors in winter were unlikely to be recovered before spring; bodies washed up on the seashore could have been in the water for months. (See also page 90 which explains how late recovery of a body in such circumstances can affect the date of registration of a death under civil registration; for wartime deaths and burials see *Miscellaneous Returns* on p.91 and *The Army* on p.260.)

The National Burial Index (3rd edition: 2010) is a collection of burial records transcribed and indexed from local parish records, Nonconformist records, cemeteries and crematoria in England and Wales by member societies of the *Federation of Family History Societies* and individuals (more details can be found at www.ffhs.org.uk). While the new edition contains 18 million entries this is only a small proportion of burials which have taken place. It will reveal some elusive burials but many will continue to evade detection, perhaps because: they did not take place where you expect; they were not recorded in the parish, or any other, register; or they cannot be identified. Who, for instance, could claim *The ragged inkman commonly called 'there he goes' his real name unknown* buried in *Hull* in 1805. Sometimes when plague or other epidemics struck an area, mass graves were dug well away from inhabited houses and the dead were buried, with no record being kept of who went into the grave.

Remember that people have always travelled far more than we give them credit for, whether for business, pleasure or health reasons, and, if they died unexpectedly far from home, their burial will probably be recorded where they died. In general, only wealthy families could afford the cost of transporting a corpse back to its home parish for burial.

BURIAL REGISTERS

As with baptism and marriage registers, the amount of information you will find recorded in parish burial registers depends on individual clergymen and bishops. Until *Rose's Act* came into effect in 1813 (see p.98-99) the only details legally required were the date of burial and name of the deceased. This is all you will find in some registers until 1812. Female names may be limited to entries such as *Old Arthur's wife, Old Mother Brown, Mrs Smith, John Smith's wife, Widow Smith*, or *John Swallow's mother*.

BURIALS IN WOOLLEN

Several Acts of Parliament were passed, the principal ones in 1666 and 1677, ordering that, to boost the English woollen industry, bodies (excluding plague victims) should be buried in a woollen shroud and not in any garment made of *flax, hemp, silk, hair, gold or silver* (or in a coffin lined with any of these), with a penalty of £5 (half to the informant, half to the poor of the parish) if this was not done. It became common practice for a relative - if there was one - to be the informant, thus halving the fine.

A good example occurs in the printed PR of *Norton-in-the-Moors* in Staffordshire: *18 June 1680 Henericus Ford sepult* [buried] *et non Lanatus* [literally: not woolly] *soe that there was a warrant from Sr. John Bow[y]er granted for distress and 50s payd to Thomas Ball, for the poore, and 50s to Jeven Maire the informant.* When *Elenor filia Gulielmi Bancks de Keasden* was buried at *Clapham* (Yorkshire) in 1678 she was described as *non lanata.* At Bugthorpe in 1756, *Mrs Mary Payler* of the parish of *St James, Westminster she not being buried in woollen 50s was paid to the use of the Poor of the parish of Bugthorpe by the Undertaker of her Funeral.*

POCKLINGTON BURIAL REGISTER SHOWING TWO BURIALS NOT IN WOOLLEN

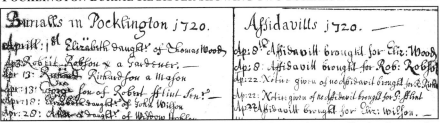

An affidavit (written statement, confirmed by oath, usually in front of a Justice of the Peace) that the burial had been carried out as required was to be handed to the incumbent within eight days of the burial and [he] *shall keep a Register in a Book* of such affidavits. This wording was open to interpretation; some incumbents did keep a separate book (which may survive in the parish chest, as may some original affidavits); others adapted their existing registers and either added *Affidavit/Affdt/Aff* after the burial entry or divided the page into two columns, one for names and the other for affidavits. Where some form of the word is added to almost all entries, it can often be assumed that, if it is omitted, the burial did not take place in woollen and the fine was paid.

The Act remained in force until 1814 but was generally ignored after 1770.

INFORMATION IN PARISH REGISTERS

By the late 17th century some ministers and clerks began to include more information. In Yorkshire, in 1692, *Thomas Kirke* at *Adel* recorded that *Ellen Willson aged 65 wife to Cudbert of Addle died of old age and was buried on Saturday June 18.* Similar detailed entries continued for 20 years. In 1745/6 *Timothy Lee* at *Ackworth* recorded the burial of *Jeremiah Waring of Low Ackworth aged 54, son of Jeremiah & Margret, died of Feaver.* Of the 33 burials recorded at *Ackworth* between December 1744 and December 1746, 11 died of *feaver,* five of *consumption,* four each of *old age* and as *infant,* two from *smallpox,* two in *childbed,* one of *dropsy,* one *drowned,* one of *lunacy* and for two no cause of death was given. He continued to include cause of

169

death and age for the next 30 years and in 1767, at the end of the burials for the year, involving eight male and seven female inhabitants, and one male and five female Foundlings (see Chapter 21), *Rev.Dr.Lee* listed the causes of death for that year:

After 1783 (see Chapter 12) additional details, particularly ages, were commonly given in PRs and if you are fortunate enough to find a burial entry in a *Dade* register you may find information taking you back three generations. As with death certificates it always pays to be suspicious about ages, particularly for the elderly, ending in *0* or *5*. In a period when few people knew their exact age, it was common practice to estimate to the nearest five years. Some incumbents did include interesting snippets of information in their registers, as at *Ashton under Lyne* in Lancashire in 1791 when *buried Isaac Hall of Staley Bridge who ran naked from the Bridge to Stailey Mill on 19th November and died on his return through the Inclemency and extreme Coldness of the Night* and at *Rillington* in 1817 when it was recorded that *Richard Holtby of Scampston, aged 63, died whilst eating his dinner.*

MISSING BURIALS

A 1691 entry at *Adel, buried a woman, a Stranger, died in child-bed at Brearey,* illustrates why some ancestors, who died away from home, can never be identified. A person travelling alone, carrying no identification, could easily turn into an anonymous statistic. If you find such an entry in a bishop's transcript, it pays to check the parish register. You may find that a name has been added later, when friends or relatives came searching for the person and identified personal effects. No-one appears to have claimed *An old woman (name unknown) a wandering pauper - died thro' disease, inattention to herself and the inclemency of the weather - from Coroner's verdict* who was buried at *Thirkleby by Thirsk* in January 1817 or *A man name unknown died on the York road in the Township of Tollerton. [Coroner's] Verdict, died of effusion on the brain caused by fatigue and the heat of the weather* buried at *Alne* in September 1865.

Robert Rigg, on the other hand, buried at *Thornton in Lonsdale* in 1695, was either travelling with a companion, carrying paperwork, or had talked to someone before dying as his burial entry describes him as *a poor man of Wiandermeer in the Countye of Westmerland being upon his Journey for the*

170

Spa at Kna[re]sborough [near *Harrogate*] *in Yorkshire for the recovery of his health ... dyed at Thomas Nicholsons house in Masongill.* More detail was often given about named non-parishioners than about parishioners, in the hope that the burial fees could be recovered from the family or the deceased's home parish.

If you cannot find an ancestor's burial in his home parish, or, from the 19th century, in the local cemetery, try: the nearest spa (people from Scotland, Ireland and about half the counties of England are buried in *Harrogate* and almost every county is represented on plaques on the walls of *Bath Abbey*); *London*; towns and villages on the coast or close to coach roads, drovers roads and pack-horse roads. Consider whether the person might have been in the army or navy; emigrated; found work far from home (particularly in the late 18th/19th centuries when many towns quadrupled in size and drew in workers from a wide area either to build manufactories and houses for the workers or to work in the mills, factories and mines); or worked as navvies (see p.233) building either canals or railways. Fatal accidents were common in all these trades.

Do not fall into the trap of thinking that because a family lives in a parish, and uses its church for baptisms and marriages, they will necessarily be buried there. The *St Quintin* family lived at *Scampston Hall*, near *Rillington* from the 17th century but, wherever they died, they were taken back for burial in the family vault at *Harpham* near *Bridlington*. The incumbent at *Rillington* tended to note ... *St Quintin buried at Harpham* in his register but many ministers would not bother and, without this, you could be left wondering if some families had discovered the secret of eternal life.

Bear in mind that a widow or widower would often move away after their partner died (perhaps to live with one of their children) but might well be taken back 'home' to be buried, especially if a double grave had been purchased. In some families, it was customary for a married daughter to be buried with her parents, rather than with her husband. Equally, if an Anglican parent died whilst living with a Nonconformist child they might well be buried in a Nonconformist burial ground.

Undertakers are first noted in the mid-17th century. By Victorian times undertaking was a well-established profession. There are firms still operating today which were founded in the 19th and early 20th centuries. Some of them have retained their records, others may have deposited them with a local record office which might also hold records from firms which no longer exist. If you are fortunate enough to locate such records you could find details - particularly in Appointments Diaries - of where bodies were to be collected from or delivered to which might enable you to locate a 'missing' burial.

WHAT THE LAW SAID

By both ecclesiastical and common law an incumbent had to permit a body to be buried in his churchyard, *except the Party deceased were denounced Excommunicate ... or were unbaptized or had laid violent Hands upon himself* (*Richard Grey*: **English Ecclesiastical Law** 1735) or was an executed criminal, but he was not obliged to read the burial service for anyone who was not a baptised member of the established church.

How strictly this was observed depended on the personal preferences and prejudices of individual ministers. Many incumbents were prepared to allow burials of such people (particularly of unbaptised babies and of suicides who were judged insane), often in the (unpopular) northern section of the churchyard. Some would allow a burial service; others would not. Some entered these events in their registers; others did not bother. The register at *Tickhill*, in 1658, records *William Scaley of Tickhill a servant to Mr Hansbye layed violent hands upon himself buried in the highway.* Suicides, excommunicates, highwaymen, witches and some criminals were all at various times *buried in the highway*, sometimes at cross-roads, but such burials are often not recorded. After the *1752 Murder Act* the bodies of those executed for murder (and there were plenty) were either to be hung in chains or given to anatomists for dissection; the **Capital Punishment Within Prisons Act of 1868** (which followed the cessation of public executions in May that year) said that they were to be buried within the prison where they were executed. This remained in force until death by hanging was abolished in 1965; records of these burials should be contained within prison records.

Dissenters (Roman Catholics and other Nonconformists) were entitled to a Christian burial. Again, incumbents varied in how they dealt with this situation. Some treated dissenters as ordinary parishioners and gave no indication of religious persuasion in the burial register; others would add *papist/catholick/recusant* or *dissenter* after the name, or might write *tossed (or tumbled or thrown) into the ground at night* (as in 1625 at *Tickhill* when *Jane Jacksonne [was] buried in the night); buried with no service* or *interred without any office or ceremony of the Church.* Entries which read *interred* or *died* rather than *buried* are often an indication of a dissenter's burial. Others permitted non-Anglican burials to take place outside the canonical hours of 8am to 3pm, and, certainly by the late 18th century, a few allowed Catholics to be buried inside the church, like *Catherine Stourton* who, in 1784, was interred (Anglican register) /buried (Catholic register) in *Holme on Spalding Moor* Church *in the evening*, and at *Burghwallis* where, in 1802, *George Ann Esq., a Papist*, was *buried in the Chancel* and there is a memorial nearby to *George* and his (Catholic) father.

MONUMENTAL OR MEMORIAL INSCRIPTIONS

Standing in a churchyard, watching a sheep (often used as the parish lawn-mower) scratching itself on a gravestone and seeing the surface of the stone disintegrate into dust before one's eyes brings it home that monumental inscriptions may not be as permanent as our ancestors hoped.

Some counties have an almost complete record of MIs for their county; others have many churchyards or cemeteries still to be transcribed. Ask your local record office, library or family history society, or look online, whether MIs for a particular burial ground have been recorded. This is especially relevant for Scotland and Ireland where burial registers are often deficient and an MI may be the only source of information about a death.

Remember that many Nonconformist, Roman Catholic, Quaker and Jewish congregations had their own burial grounds, as did some landed families (possibly including servants as well as family members) and that it is permissible to be buried in non-consecrated ground so stones may be found in fields, gardens or orchards ('green burials' do not have gravestones). Enquire locally whether there are any small graveyards or individual stones; they may be overgrown and forgotten by all but the oldest inhabitants but could contain the clue you seek.

On the road from *Hawes* to *Appersett* in 1975 a single stone (said to belong to an atheist) stood in a field. Local information said that it used to have a stone archway as an entrance and iron railing surrounds, which were taken away during the war and the field was used to plant potatoes. The stone (which could not be located in 2009) read:

Erected in memory of James Jackson of High Shaw Paddock in Lunds who departed this life 28th July 1836 aged 66 years
Also of Fanny his wife who departed this life on 15th March 1835 aged 69 years
Also of Jane their grand-child daughter of James and Mary Jackson of Appersett who departed this life on 16th June 1834 aged 7 years.

QUAKER GRAVESTONES

Quaker gravestones (see p.101) differ from other inscribed gravestones in that, until recently, they contain much simpler inscriptions. Few early stones survive because, throughout the 18th century, Quakers were exhorted to stop *the vain custom of erecting monuments over the dead bodies of friends by stones, inscriptions &c* and to remove existing stones.

It was not until 1850 that the *London* yearly meeting said that graves might be marked by *a plain stone, the inscription on which is confined to a simple record of the name, age, and date of the decease, of the individual interred* and, with one exception (see p.174) the earliest surviving inscriptions in any of the three Quaker burial grounds in Wensleydale date from the mid-1860s. Many of the 19th century inscriptions match the limited criteria listed above but there was a tendency (which is to be welcomed by family historians) for date of birth to be given instead of, or as well as, age at, or date of, death. Some families retained this simple format until at least the 1970s; others, from the late 19th century, added relationships, phrases such as *In remembrance of* or *In (loving) memory of* and even, for one elderly couple in 1893, *They will be long remembered for their usefulness* so that the stones differ very little from 'ordinary' gravestones.

QUAKER GRAVESTONE FROM HAWES, WENSLEYDALE

TRANSCRIPTIONS OF MONUMENTAL INSCRIPTIONS

Recording MIs has long been a popular occupation so you may find that there are several versions of the inscriptions for a churchyard. Do not make the mistake of relying on any one of them because you think the information they contain will be the same whether they were made in 1900 or 2000; **always check all available transcriptions because no two will be identical**.

A modern transcript may be easier to use, often being typed and indexed, than a handwritten Victorian one but it may be less accurate because the stones have worn and (unless the dates and ages have been checked against the burial register) it is easy to misread certain figures - *1* and *4*, *0* and *9*, and *3*, *5*, *6*, *8* and *9* being perhaps the most obvious. (When I transcribed the stone above in a Quaker burial ground in 1975 I read a date as *1820*; looking at it again in 2009 and in a better light it is clearly *1829*.)

The earlier transcript will almost certainly contain MIs which no longer survive. Perhaps the stone has fallen face downwards or its surface has worn or fallen away; flat stones have become buried under grass; some stones may have been moved and piled against a wall or broken up to make paths or walls around the churchyard. It may, however, omit entries which will be found in a later transcript because further interments took place after the first recording was made, and additional inscriptions have been added to the stone.

One noted antiquarian recorded many graveyards in Cheshire. When some of his transcripts were checked against modern ones for the same burial grounds a number of stones in each had been omitted and, when these were plotted on the graveyard plans, it became obvious that he had seated himself on a stone, recorded all the MIs he could see around him, then stood up and moved on but forgotten the stone on which he had been sitting. Other early transcribers recorded only inscriptions inside the church, or stones relating to notable local families or particular surnames; some omitted those which were buried in brambles or covered in ivy; many did not peel back the turf to reveal buried stones. Do not fall into the trap of assuming that a recording covers all the stones in a burial ground; always check to see if the transcriber states exactly what has been included or omitted.

Where there is a churchyard or cemetery plan to accompany a recording, study it in conjunction with any MIs for the names in which you are interested. You may think that number *27*, which you know to be a family grave, is a long way from *117* so the two are unlikely to be connected but they may prove to be adjoining plots, depending on which way the transcriber was walking round. Remember that family graves may be grouped together but not in the same row - always look at the row behind and in front. Bear in mind that many people were buried in common graves, on which no stones could be placed, or could not afford the cost of a monument. 'Guinea graves' usually have stones, giving name, age, and date of death of those (unrelated people) interred below. Consider yourself fortunate if you find MIs for your 'working class' ancestors (particularly in urban areas) before the late 19th century or for any ancestors, in a churchyard, before 1700.

If you fail to locate an MI for an ancestor, but find one for other members of the family, do not assume that the missing person is buried elsewhere, although this may be the case. Often the last member of a family to die is in the grave but not listed on the stone because there was no one left to arrange for the inscription to be added. On the other hand, if you do find an MI, do not automatically believe that the person commemorated is buried in the grave.

MEMORIAL INSCRIPTIONS

Many inscriptions include memorials to family members buried elsewhere and the stone may, or may not, make this clear. A *Webster* family stone in *Hawes* (North Yorkshire) churchyard names 10 people, including two who were *interred at the Necropolis, Liverpool*: always follow up such entries - there may be more information in the burial registers there.

A stone, also in *Hawes*, commemorates 14 people (parents and 12 children), spanning a hundred years from 1803 to 1903. The names, not surprisingly, are engraved on both sides of the stone.

On the first side:

> *In loving remembrance of William Chapman who died at Borwins June 17 1845 aged 72*
>
> *Also his affectionate wife Elizabeth who died October 18 1839 aged 58*
>
> *Also Abraham their youngest son who died May 30 1899 aged 77 years*

On the reverse:

> *Also of their children*
> *Two died in infancy 1803-1807*
> *Esther died at Burtersett 1825 aged 21*
> *Elizabeth died at Beckbits 1857 aged 33*
> *Christopher died at Hawes 1862 aged 50*
> *Alexander died at Borwins 1866 aged 56*
> *Isabella died at Hawes 1877 aged 71*
> *William died at Liverpool 1880 aged 80*
> *Mary died at Rossendale 1882 aged 65*
> *George died at Borwins 1886 aged 70*
> *Abraham died at Weymouth 1899 aged 77*
> *John died at Liverpool 1903 aged 84*

The list of children was clearly engraved after *John*'s death as they are all listed in chronological order of their dying - this is clearly a memorial inscription. *Abraham* appears both on the front of the stone with his parents and on the back with his siblings; *George* has his own stone elsewhere in the churchyard; there is no indication whether any of the daughters was married.

Always look on the reverse of an upright inscribed stone to check whether there are additional entries there (this applies particularly to 'Guinea Graves') and, if you find an apparently blank stone, look on the back, because it may turn out to be the inscribed side. In many churchyards (like *Hawes*), the inscribed side of the stone usually faces east so, walking up the path to the church, you will often find that the stones on one side of the path appear to be blank.

Do not forget that kerbs round graves, sometimes almost buried in soil or grass, often contain inscriptions and that upright gravestones may have sunk several inches into the ground, so that at least the last entry is buried and invisible; these (together with 'hidden' flat stones) may need to be carefully 'dug out' (with permission from the incumbent or cemetery superintendent). Kerbs and stones may have been removed when the burial ground was landscaped or to make it easier to manoeuvre a lawnmower up and down the rows; if this has happened since 1906 there should be a brief record of any inscriptions involved held by the local council. If you have difficulty locating which department deals with cemeteries, try Leisure and Amenity Services.

War Memorials, whether in church, churchyard or elsewhere, give names which can usually be followed up to provide more information, whether via service records, Commonwealth War Graves Commission headstones or via their website at www.cwgc.org

MIs inside churches pose their own problems. They should be better preserved, not having been exposed to the weathering suffered by external memorials, but may be just as difficult to locate or read. In larger churches, with hundreds of plaques or monuments, they may be positioned so high that you need a ladder or binoculars to read them. In a church which has undergone alterations and additions they may be in the vestry, concealed behind the organ, or hidden under a carpet in the aisle. Some churches contain crypts and family vaults but these are often not accessible; check for an old history of the church, or for the notebooks of a local antiquarian who may have been permitted in the past to see the coffins and record their inscriptions and ask the incumbent if he has a copy. **Do not forget that not all MIs are stone monuments or plaques** - check the windows, bells, and all church furniture and plate, any of which may contain a memorial inscription. Seats in churchyards or cemeteries and local parks or beauty spots may also bear dedications.

If the name of the monumental mason is carved on the stone or plaque, look in a modern Directory to see if the firm is still in business. Many such firms are long-established and may retain their records; if the firm has ceased to exist, records may be deposited with the local record office.

GRAVESTONE IN THE CEMETERY: PILGRIM'S REST, SOUTH AFRICA.

The area was officially declared a 'gold field' in 1873 and thousands flocked there, including many from Wales.

(Note the spelling of Glanmorgan. Did the stone mason make an error or did he misinterpret the Welsh accent?)

CHAPTER 17

PUBLISHED PARISH REGISTERS
AND TRANSCRIPTS

As explained in Chapter 10, much of the parish register material currently available online, particularly on commercial websites, is taken from volumes of published parish registers, most published by county Parish Register Societies or by individuals. This chapter highlights the usefulness of these published volumes but also points out their drawbacks.

PARISH REGISTER SOCIETIES AND THEIR VOLUMES

The Parish Register Society was founded in the mid-1890s and several counties and individuals followed suit. Yorkshire, Lancashire, and Staffordshire, among others, established Parish Register Societies which are still publishing today. Some parish register societies also hold large numbers of, as yet, unpublished transcripts which may be available for consultation - always worth enquiring although you may find that the transcriber's handwriting is almost as difficult to interpret as the original register. Some societies are gradually inputting these transcripts onto computer and making them available on CD or online but, as one Society's caveat says, *Please bear in mind that these transcripts have been handwritten by volunteers, some more than a century ago ... they have been entered onto computer by more volunteers, using a variety of computer programs ... They should not be taken as a definitive copy of the original parish register which should always be consulted to verify details. W.P.W. Phillimore* is probably the best known of the individuals responsible for publishing parish (mainly marriage) registers but estimates of the error rate in many of his volumes vary between 5% and 10%. The volumes published by these societies and by individuals are of immense value to family historians but both the published registers and their indexes contain pitfalls galore for the unwary.

Be aware that, with *The Parish Register Society* volumes, the title on a bound book can be misleading. The Society rapidly published volumes from several counties - at least 50 in the decade after 1896. Libraries subscribing to the series often bound a number of volumes into one book, with just the place-names on the cover. I have Volumes 5-7 in one book - parishes from Yorkshire, Warwickshire and Suffolk but with no indication of the counties on the spine. Volumes 56 and 57 for *Hazlemere* and *Farnham* are also combined - easy to assume that these are the two parishes in Surrey whereas the *Farnham* referred to is the one in Yorkshire.

The Yorkshire Parish Register Society published its first volume in 1899, and I use mostly Yorkshire volumes and indexes as examples in this chapter because I know the series well, but the same principles apply to all published registers. Until the mid-20th century, a published parish register meant just that: little attempt was made to compare the register with the Bishop's Transcripts, which were often not available for public scrutiny. As time went on, the BTs were consulted where there were gaps in the PRs but the comparison of PR and BT, and the incorporation into the text of all variations and additions, is a relatively recent development.

Beware of applying today's standards to volumes published nearly a hundred years ago when transcribing and indexing registers was carried out by dedicated individuals without the aid of modern technology and often with little experience of reading old handwriting (one transcriber recorded every instance of *Lemuel* in a volume as *Samuel*). Transcriptions were handwritten copies of handwritten registers (and all readers should by now be aware of the pitfalls that can create). Ultra-violet light was not available to enhance faded ink so early published volumes will contain some entries marked 'illegible', which today can easily be read in the original register, and others which are 'best guesses' for names which turn out to be something completely different. At least one transcriber wet the pages of a register in an attempt to 'bring up' the writing - it may have helped him at the time but now no-one can properly check his interpretation. Copy was often typeset by printers unfamiliar with the names involved (again, readers should know from experience with the IGI and census indexes the problems that can cause) and proof-reading was often cursory. Indexing was, to many, a chore - they were transcribing registers to preserve the documents from damage, not with the intention of making life easier for family historians a century on - and the quality and extent of their indexes varied enormously.

ALWAYS READ THE INTRODUCTION OR PREFACE

Published parish registers can be a godsend to family historians but, repeating myself *ad nauseam,* if you do not read the Foreword/Preface or introductory pages you can waste a great deal of time, effort and possibly money. Some commercial websites have put the text of published registers online without including the introductory pages or, in some cases, footnotes or comments which they regard as extraneous information. The first entry in the published register for *Hodnet* in Shropshire dates from 1540 (with a note above that the register begins in 1539); the first surviving register dates from the late 1650s. The register covering 1539 to the mid-1650s was, according to the introduction, *lost prior to 1830* but a few entries from this volume, mostly relating to the *Vernon* family, had been extracted by a local antiquarian before its disappearance and these are included at the beginning of the published register (three and a half pages covering more than 100 years). This fact is made clear in the published volume but looking at references to *Hodnet* registers online it is clear that several researchers assume that they have searched the complete registers when they have not. It is tempting to take a book from the shelf, glance at the title, look in the index, find no mention of the name you are seeking, and mentally cross that parish off your search list. Do not! Experienced researchers, professional and amateur (myself included), have fallen into this trap. *There's no entry in the index to this published Parish Register for Joe Bloggs* (one of the original pitfalls) may be true but looking at the preface could well tell you that, while Joe is not in the index, he could still be in the text, or in the PR or BT, and you could save yourself months, if not years, of fruitless searching in other parishes.

Never believe that the dates given on the cover are an accurate record of what is inside. They are almost invariably the years covering the first and last entries in the volume but there is no guarantee that baptisms, marriages and burials are covered for the entire period. To give a few Yorkshire examples: the *Askham Richard* volume says it covers 1579-1812 but it does not include marriages 1754-1812; *Cowthorpe* is listed as 1568-1812 but baptisms and burials end in 1797; *Harewood* does say on its cover Baptisms 1614-1812 and Marriages 1621-1812 but most available lists of published registers merely give 1614-1812 with no mention that burials are not included in the volume; *Howden* (in four volumes - undated on the covers) from 1543-1770s does not include the baptism register from 1659-1702 (which has since been published by the YPRS) but this only becomes obvious after careful study of the Prefaces to all four volumes; *Huggate* supposedly covers 1539-1812 but the preface makes clear that the register covering 1627-1707 is lost and not included in the published volume. The volume covering 1633-1703 has since been found but it is clear from online references that some researchers are not aware of this.

RILLINGTON AND SCAMPSTON: AN OBJECT LESSON

Rillington (published by the YPRS in 1946) points the way to a different set of problems. The dates on the cover are 1638-1812 (marriages are, in fact, included only to April 1803). There is no mention in the text that the register covering 1689-1769 is badly damaged, the BTs were not consulted, and there are hundreds of partial entries, many not containing a surname, which do not appear in the index (see p.181). Almost all the entries - at least for baptisms and burials - are complete in the BTs (and are indexed in the IGI as the BTs were the principal source used) but the published register does not tell you this. Even the preface is misleading. From the statement that the volume includes baptisms for the chapelry of *Scampston* from 1783 *in which year separate Registers were instituted* one would infer that *Scampston* baptisms are included from 1783 to 1812; however, only the years 1783-1786 appear in the published volume but entries for most later years appear in the IGI as *Scampston* entries are included in *Rillington* BTs.

The above statement about separate baptism registers for *Scampston* implies that there are no earlier registers of any sort for *Scampston*, which was a chapelry to *Rillington*. There is, in fact, a marriage register beginning in 1756 and most of its entries are included in the IGI - except for the period 1803 to 1812 when marriages are omitted from the BTs. Look back to the previous paragraph and note that this is also the period when marriages at *Rillington* are not included in the published volume. Recourse to the original registers is currently the only option.

ENTRIES FROM RILLINGTON PRINTED PR; EXTRA INFORMATION FROM BTS

```
  ✳                              ⸾1751⸾
       (entries illegible).
4 Aug . . . ipson of Scampston. Tabitha d. John PHILLIPSON, serv. bp.
8 Aug. . Widow.  Mary CURDOXE a poor widow bur.
18 Aug . Clark Labourer.  Mary dau. Wm C. bp.
16 Oct. . of Hannah Firey.+ Wm JOHNSON by Banns
1 Dec. . Oxendale Thos BAXTER + Jane O. by Banns
8 Dec. of Robt Warton of Scampston Labourer. Eliz dau. of. bp.
8 Dec. Wm Wilson Labourer. Lydia dau. bp.
12 Dec. Mowarin Labourer.  Thomas son Thomas bp.
19 Jan. Thomas Medd Labourer. Thomas son bp.
22 Jan. Thompson Labourer. Joseph son William bp.
26 Jan. of Thos Simpkin Husbandman. Mary dau. bp.
18 Feb. Daughter of Francis Willison of Scampston Labourer. Isabel bur.
18 Feb. Milner Yeoman. Thomas bur.
                 Lady Day 1752.
12 Apr. of John Petch. "ab. David son. bp.
30 May of Isabel Petch. John PETCH yeo. bur.
11 May Spencer Yeoman. Richard bur.
11 Jun . Humble a poor Widow. Eliz. bur.
14 Jun . Daughter of (blank) Collison.  Mathelia. (blank also in BT)
2 Jul . Francis Lepington & Jane Harwood. by Banns
11 Jul . Daughter of Peter Hodgson Labourer. Catherine bp.
Jun . 28th Bap: Richard Son of William Johnson.
Aug . 18th Buryed Elizabeth Wife of George Lowson Husbandman.

✳ 5 Apr Ann dau. Wm HODGSON lab. bp.
12 May Esther dau. Nichol RUSTON husbman bp.
16 Jun Mary dau. John MILNER lab, bp.
```

LOCATING SIX ETHELL ENTRIES: A SALUTARY EXPERIENCE

Thomas and Deborah Ethell/Ithell married at *Scampston* in 1782 (see p.248) and baptised two of their three children there; their daughter baptised an illegitimate child there and married at *Rillington* the following year. Where, apart from the original registers, can you locate the six entries?

The marriage of *Thomas and Deborah* appears in the IGI as taking place at *Rillington-cum-Scampston* - giving the impression that it took place at *Rillington*. The baptism of their elder son *John* in 1782 appears twice in the IGI, once on 13th October with a 'P' reference, meaning it has been extracted from a published PR, and then on 24th October with a 'C' reference, meaning it comes from the controlled extraction program (*Rillington* BTs) - this baptism did take place at *Rillington*. Their younger son, *Richard*, baptised on 17th March 1784 at *Scampston*, appears only once in the IGI, with a 'P' reference as he appears in the four years of *Scampston* baptisms included in the published *Rillington register* - he is included in the BT but the entry is omitted from the IGI. Daughter *Hannah*, baptised at *Scampston* on 7th January 1790, also appears once in the IGI with a 'C' reference.

In 1809 *Hannah* had an illegitimate daughter, *Mary*, baptised at *Scampston* but not appearing in the IGI. On checking the *Rillington* BTs, entries for *Rillington* church and *Scampston* chapel are generally listed separately but for 1809 and 1810 *Scampston* entries were not included so *Mary* is recorded only in the *Scampston* register. In 1810 *Hannah* married *James Hudson* at *Rillington*. Marriages from April 1803 (when a new register began) to the end of 1812 are not included in the published register for *Rillington*, and for the decade before 1813 they are not included in the BTs so, in this case, the only record is in the *Rillington* marriage register.

Four out of six entries do appear in the IGI; the other two (being omitted from the BTs) can be found only in the original registers. One further pitfall, until 1812 *Rillington* BTs run from Lady Day (25th March) to Lady Day (see p.111) so *Richard*'s baptism (17th March *1784)* appears in the *1783* BT and *Hannah*'s (7th January *1790*) in the *1789* one.

INDEXES

None of the above problems and omissions would be apparent if merely glancing through the indexes to a parish register and many other possible pitfalls would be in your path. Until recently there was no standard format for the compilation of such indexes and you are always advised to check the characteristics of any index to a published register before searching it.

Some indexes are of surnames only; others include Christian names. Watch for those indexers who, with pre-1733 entries, translated Latin into English so that *Radulphus Thornenely (sic)*, marrying in *Emley* in 1668, is indexed as *Ralph Thorneley*. Also remember (another of the original pitfalls) that a man baptised as *Jacobus* in 1710, and indexed as *Jac.*, may die in 1763 and be buried and indexed as *James* (for which *Jacobus* is the Latin).

Be aware that some, but not all, indexers used asterisks or numbers or letters to indicate that a name occurs more than once on a page. Always make very sure that you check the whole page and do not stop at the first reference to a name. A small *5* or a letter *e* in the index should tell you that there are five mentions of the name on the page; an asterisk is less revealing and if you stop at *Samuel son of Samuel Jackson*, you may miss more entries further down. If you find an unindexed volume, look to see if it is one of several published for that parish with page numbers running continuously. Then check the most recent one where you may well find an index for all the volumes. *Rothwell* to 1812 is in 3 volumes with 1109 pages. The index to all volumes is in Volume 3 on pages 1022-1109 but no multiple occurrences of names on a page are shown. Volume 1 of *Howden* has no index; Volumes 2 and 3 are numbered consecutively and the index for both volumes is at the end of volume 3. The two volumes for *Arksey* (published in 2001 and 2003) are also numbered consecutively with the index in Volume 2.

If, after listing all the references to a name from an index, and referring to the published text, you find yourself with plenty of possible baptisms for the required name but no adult burials for a century thereafter, it is worth checking the original register. Particularly with 'mixed' registers (with baptisms and burials combined) it is easy to put *bap* when you mean *bur* - incumbents and transcribers ancient and modern fall into that trap - and not all published registers were double-checked for accuracy.

Most indexers will group variants of a surname together under the principal spelling (listing the variants alongside) but it is always as well to make sure that all the ones you know of are under one heading - what is an obvious variant to you may not have occurred to the indexer. In the published *Leeds* Registers, *Iles* and *Isles* are indexed together, sometimes with *Illis* included, but *Hiles* is listed separately: in the IGI all four come under *Hill*.

RESOLUTIONS:

When consulting any published parish register:
- **I will <u>always</u> read the introduction to the volume.**
- **I will never rely solely on the volume's index.**
- **I will use it only as a finding aid and never treat it as definitive.**
- **When using a website involving parish registers I will ascertain what sources have been used to compile it**, whether primary or secondary; if published volumes or transcripts have been used, I will remember that they are rarely 100% accurate.

CHAPTER 18

PARISHES, PECULIARS, LIBERTIES, EXTRA-PAROCHIAL AREAS AND GLOSSARY OF ECCLESIASTICAL TERMS

You have found an entry for your ancestor in a parish register. Do you know whether that parish was an 'ordinary' parish, a peculiar, or a liberty or whether your ancestor lived in an extra-parochial area adjacent to the parish - and do you need to know?

Church-controlled documentation features prominently in this book but, so far, mostly from the angle of the records themselves and what you might (or might not) find in them. Before moving on to Probate (Wills and Administrations) records - which until 1858 were also church controlled - a basic understanding of the types of jurisdiction in the title should help you to avoid some of the more obvious traps you can fall into, and find records which are easily overlooked but might be vital to your research.

PARISHES

The first pitfall to avoid is the belief that the organisation and administration of the Church of England has always been simple and straightforward. Its structure developed in the 16th century from a system which had been operating throughout the British Isles for more than half a millennium, during which time Roman Catholicism had been the accepted form of worship. This system consisted of five tiers - *parishes, rural deaneries, archdeaconries, dioceses* (controlled by a bishop) and *provinces* (with authority vested in an archbishop) - and is described, in general terms, in most books and online sites which deal with tracing ancestors. There are certain aspects which merit explanation, given that many areas (like *peculiars, liberties* and *extra-parochial* areas) did not fit neatly into this system.

A *parish* was originally an ecclesiastical area which had its own church and clergyman (civil parishes were a later development; closely linked to 19th century poor law administration). At the risk of over-simplification (because, inevitably, there are exceptions) there was a north/south divide in the way the parochial system operated, controlled more by geographical conditions than by whether an area came within the province of Canterbury or York. In the southern province (with the exception of cities and large towns - *London* had more than 100 parish churches, *Norwich* 35, *Oxford* 15, *Cambridge* 14, *Chichester* 12) a parish tended to be a compact unit, with one set of registers and records. In the north and north midlands, a *parish* could spread over a vast area (*Halifax* parish in 1831 covered 75,740 acres and served a population of 109,899) and include several *chapelries* (with their own curates, some licensed, particularly before 1754, to perform marriages) and many *townships* (a place for which a constable was appointed and which was

184

responsible for its own poor). In such parishes the incumbent often had to delegate some responsibility for both religious and practical matters to subordinates, who frequently kept their own registers and records. These were sometimes, but by no means always, deposited in the main parish chest. **Always check to see if documents for a particular chapelry or township are filed separately from the main parish records**; sometimes even in a different record office.

In the southern archdiocese *rural deans* did not have a prominent role, with *archdeacons* exercising much more authority. In the Diocese of York, which included three archdeaconries, 13 deaneries and 600 parishes and where a deanery might contain more than 30 parishes spread over a wide area (that of *Pontefract*, for example, stretched from the *Lancashire border* to the *Leeds* boundary and included *Bradford, Halifax, Huddersfield* and *Wakefield*), *rural deans* played a far larger part (more so than the *archdeacons*) in the running of the church and its affairs, particularly with regard to probate (see Chapter 19).

The size and extent of dioceses varied greatly. Until the major re-organisation beginning in 1836, when new dioceses were created and the boundaries of ancient ones were re-drawn, there were some 25 dioceses in England, and four in Wales. **Never assume that an ancient diocese can be equated with a county**; Sussex and the Diocese of Chichester coincided but Bedfordshire and Berkshire, for instance, each formed 'only' an Archdeaconry (the former in the Diocese of Lincoln, transferred to Ely in 1837; the latter in that of Salisbury until 1836, thereafter in the Diocese of Oxford - so pre-1836 BTs are held in Wiltshire, post-1836 ones in Oxford). In 1822, the diocese of *Rochester*, with 91 parishes in Kent, was the smallest diocese; that of *Lincoln*, with 1,380 parishes and extending as far south as Bedfordshire and part of Hertfordshire, was one of the largest. Most records of interest to family historians, which can be separated out (bear in mind that not all can), have by now found their way into appropriate county record offices but always check what diocesan record offices hold: *Lichfield*, for example, still holds the BTs, Wills, and Marriage Allegations & Bonds for much of four midlands counties (see p.51).

PECULIARS

These were areas - ranging in size from a single parish to substantial areas (the Peculiar of the Dean and Chapter of York included at least 38 parishes and townships in four counties; the Dean of Salisbury had jurisdiction over some 43 parishes in three counties) - which until the mid-19th century stood apart from the five-tier system and were not subject to normal ecclesiastical jurisdiction. Some dioceses in England (like York and Salisbury) had large numbers of peculiars; others, like Chester and Durham, had none; Wales had one and Ireland, two. Royal Peculiars, *a Place of Worship [which] belongs directly to the monarch and not to any diocese or province*, also existed and included areas as diverse as *Westminster Abbey; St George's Chapel, Windsor;* the *Deanery of St Buryan* in Cornwall; *Wimborne Minster* in Dorset; the *Deanery of Bridgnorth*, and *Shrewsbury* in Shropshire; *Penkridge, Tettenhall* and *Wolverhampton* in Staffordshire; and *Middleham* in Yorkshire.

Almost all of them kept parish registers, and these are usually deposited in county or diocesan record offices, but researchers need to be aware that, where Bishops' Transcripts, Marriage Bonds/Allegations and Wills/Administrations are concerned, the situation is much more complicated.

BTs should have been returned annually to the relevant bishop, archdeacon or peculiar authority but many peculiars, being outside the bishop's jurisdiction, were lax about making or submitting them. Peculiars which came under the control of an ecclesiastic (be he bishop or archdeacon) or ecclesiastical body (like a dean and chapter) were likely to make returns but those under secular control did not always do so. Some peculiars have an almost complete run of BTs; some (like *Middleham*: see above) have none at all; many fall between the two (with coverage generally at its weakest before 1813). When using FamilySearch or the IGI it is advisable to ascertain whether a parish was a peculiar because the BTs, rather than the PRs, were used for many counties; *Selby Abbey* (see p.126), with PRs dating from 1580, is listed in various sources as being included in the IGI but, before 1785, BTs survive only for *1746, 1760, 1780* and *1782* - it would be all too easy to find a relevant entry in one of these years and to assume that, because no earlier references to the surname appear in the IGI, the family did not enter the parish until the mid-18th century.

These BTs will not always be kept where you might expect. Do not assume that, because the parish registers are held in the 'home' county, the same will apply to the BTs. These may well remain among the records of whichever authority or individual controlled the peculiar (although there may be microfilm copies in the 'home' county). In Yorkshire, the district of Allerton and Allertonshire, including 14 parishes (among them *Northallerton* which houses the North Yorkshire County Record Office) was a peculiar jurisdiction partly of the Bishop of Durham and partly of the Dean and Chapter of Durham so the classes of records mentioned above will all be found in the University of Durham (BTs after 1813 are at the Borthwick Institute for Archives in York).

Many peculiars had the right to issue marriage licences for marriages to take place within their jurisdiction and the accompanying bonds and allegations may survive independently of the main series in a diocese. For example, those issued by the *Dean of Salisbury* are held at the Wiltshire and Swindon History Centre in *Chippenham*, those by the *Dean and Chapter of York* are at the Borthwick Institute. An Index to the latter (also including licences issued by many of the smaller peculiars in Yorkshire) has been published and is available online. It includes in excess of 11,000 marriages and names more than 200 churches where a ceremony could take place. There are at least eight other separate marriage indexes for peculiars at the Borthwick. Records of a few Yorkshire peculiars are held at WYAS Leeds. Always ask whether there are other indexes apart from the main series of bonds and allegations for a county. Also bear in mind that, before 1754, a few peculiars (like *Peak Forest* in Derbyshire, sometimes called the *Gretna Green of the Peak*, which was extra-parochial, extra-episcopal and a liberty) could issue marriage licences to any couple who applied, regardless of where they lived, and could perform marriages at any time of day. Marriages covering the period 1727-1754 at Peak Forest have been transcribed (and are available online, with an index, on the Derbyshire section of **GENUKI**); from 1747-1754 the parishes of residence of the couple are given and they range through Derbyshire, Cheshire, Lancashire, Nottinghamshire, Staffordshire, Yorkshire and as far afield as Cumberland so it could pay you to search here for a missing marriage. (The Chapel was founded in 1657 but earlier records have been lost; marriages continue after 1754 but only between couples of whom one or both lived in the liberty.)

Most peculiars had their own probate courts (see Chapter 19 for more details).

LIBERTIES

Liberties, in essence, were areas which were exempt from the normal judicial system and often had the right to hold their own courts (in some cases including quarter sessions). They were part of the secular (civil) system of government but at times impinged, directly or indirectly, on the ecclesiastical system. The liberties (or rules) of the *Fleet* and *Marshalsea* prisons in London - areas outside the prisons in which prisoners were sometimes permitted to reside and notorious for clandestine marriages - are probably the best-known instance where liberties and the church 'collided'. Where, as often happened, the person holding the right of jurisdiction in a liberty was an archbishop or other senior cleric it can be difficult to distinguish between a peculiar and a liberty. All that most readers need to be aware of is that there may be extensive records for a liberty, which may need to be sought elsewhere than in the expected record office.

EXTRA-PAROCHIAL AREAS

When the parochial system was established in England substantial areas of countryside were excluded and many of these remained as *extra-parochial areas* until well into the 19th century. Look at any of the English county maps produced by the IHGS and on the majority you will find such areas marked; for example, the *New Forest* in Hampshire; *Deeping Fen* in Lincolnshire;

Haverah Park in Yorkshire; *Skiddaw Forest* in Cumberland; *Delamere Forest* in Cheshire (see below).

Do not fall into the trap of thinking that a forest was a heavily wooded area like a modern conifer plantation. Many of them were royal hunting grounds and included heathland, moorland, arable land and lakes as well as trees, together with houses and lodges where the foresters (responsible for maintaining the game to be hunted) lived. Originally they were sparsely populated areas and their few inhabitants were normally exempt from paying tithes and poor rates to the church (although they were supposed to pay their tithes to the crown instead). This meant that they were outside the 'social security' system operated by parishes.

By 1538, when the keeping of parish registers became required by law, many of these extra-parochial areas were quite heavily populated so provision had to be made for the inhabitants to have access to a church to be baptised, married or buried. *Peak Forest* Chapel (see above) was built in 1657 by the Countess of Devonshire for the use of the foresters of the royal forest. As a general rule those who dwelt in such areas were permitted to use *the Parish Church or Chapel belonging to some Parish or Chapelry adjoining to such Extra-parochial Place.* If the extra-parochial area was a small one, it may be obvious which church they could use but *Delamere Forest*, stretching across a wide area of central Cheshire, was bordered by 22 townships from five parishes so its inhabitants had a choice of several venues - providing they paid the usual fees to the relevant minister.

BABES IN THE WOOD

Where do 'Babes in the Wood' fit in? Look at the Parish Registers for the parishes bordering *Delamere Forest* in Cheshire, *Whitegate* and *Tarvin* in particular, and you will find, in the 18th and early 19th centuries, a large number of baptism entries for illegitimate children born to mothers described as *a stranger from the Forest* or *from the Forest House.*

The term *a stranger* meant that the mother did not have a settlement in the relevant parish. *The Settlement Act of 1697* laid down that every person must have a *home parish* or *parish of settlement.* This was usually where they had been born, where they had served a full term of apprenticeship, where they had been employed with wages for at least a full year or where they paid a certain sum in rent. Before they could move to another Parish they had to provide a Settlement Certificate stating that their 'home parish' would be responsible for them if they should need poor relief. Illegitimate children often became a charge on the Parish where they were born, especially if the mother died or abandoned the infant, so the Vicars of *Whitegate* and *Tarvin*, although prepared to baptise the children, made it clear by their descriptions that neither mother nor infant had any claim on the parish. If the mother should try to obtain help from the parish the Overseers of the Poor could repudiate the claim.

It was noticeable that none of the entries at Whitegate named the mother's Parish of Settlement although in other cases, when an illegitimate child was baptised, the incumbent would specify *... son of ... a stranger from Manchester bapt.* Obviously *the forest* was a 'convenience address', well away from prying eyes and officialdom. Delving into the *Arderne Collection* in *Chester*, as members of this family had been *chief forester, bow bearer and bailiff* for *Delamere* throughout the 18th century, it soon became obvious that the practice of sending unmarried girls sometimes quite long distances to the foresters' houses to give birth had been a long standing one. It was also clear that the foresters, whose running of unofficial 'maternity homes' presumably provided them with useful additional income, had encountered problems.

Samuel Hornby housed a pregnant *Katherine Harrison* and, as a result, nearly found himself with an unwanted child to bring up. Papers in the *Arderne Collection* illustrate the lengths to which a Parish was prepared to go to escape responsibility for a bastard child. According to a Removal Order dated 12 March 1711/12 from the Overseers of the Poor of *Winwick and Hulme* in Lancashire, *on or about the Twentyth day of January last past in the Morning of the same day there was a young Male Child in the Parish Church Porch of Winwick which hath ever since been Chargeable to the said Township.* Investigation had shown that *the Child's name is William and it is a Bastard and was Born in the House of Samuel Hornby upon [sic] the Forest of Delamere in the County of Chester upon the Body of one Katherine Harrison Singlewoman.* The Overseers sought an order from the Magistrates to remove the child from *Winwick* and return it to *Samuel Hornby* as being his responsibility and the magistrates *declare and ajudge the said House of the sd. Samuel Hornby ... to be the place of the Birth and Legal Settlement of the sd. William the sd. Bastard Child of the sd. Katherine Harrison* and ordered the Overseers to convey the child to *Samuel* who was to *receive and provide for the sd. Child according to Law.*

Samuel appealed and eventually managed to escape responsibility for the child but the case must have given him, and his fellow foresters, a nasty shock and before long they had developed a system of indemnity bonds, very similar to the standard bastardy bond, to cover themselves. The bonds indemnify a Forester as opposed to a Parish but they do state the mother's home parish. In most cases the bond has been entered into by a man bearing the same surname as the expectant mother, making it look as if it was generally her father, as opposed to the child's father, who was accepting responsibility for payment.

The wording of the bond concerning *Phoebe Pownall* makes it clear that her presence in the Forest had been arranged by her family. An indemnity bond for £100 (the usual sum) was given on 20th January 1753 by *Peter Pownall of Over Whitley in the County of Chester, Yeoman and James Pownall of the same place, Yeoman ... unto Robert Brock of the Forest of*

189

Delamere ... that Whereas a certain woman called Phebe Pownall singlewoman is now with child of a Bastard Child or Children and at the instance and request and by the prouvements of the above bounden Peter Pownall and James Pownall is entertained by the above named Robert Brock at his dwelling house in the said Forest of Delamere and is intended to be there delivered of such Child or Children which may become chargeable to the said Robert Brock and the Keepers and inhabitants of the said Forest the *Pownalls* would *well and sufficiently free, acquit, discharge, save and keep harmless and absolutely indemnify the said Robert Brock ...* against any expenses incurred *concerning the Birth, Maintenance, bringing up, Education, Settlement or nourishment of the said Child ... and concerning the said Phebe Pownall.*

Parallel situations existed elsewhere. At *Cotgrave* in Nottinghamshire, between 1785 and 1811, 73 illegitimate children were baptised and recorded as being *from the Lodge in the Wolds*, an extra-parochial area comprising one farmhouse and 25 acres on the fringes of *Cotgrave* Parish. An 1832 county directory states, *It is said the house here was once a noted Lying-in Asylum for pregnant ladies who wished to secrete their illegitimate offspring* ... (***Journal of Local Population Studies,*** Number 15; Autumn 1975). *Brigadier Goadby*, in ***An Early Maternity Home at Stonelands*** detailed a very similar scenario in an extra-parochial area near *Asthall* in west Oxfordshire and there are doubtless many more.

So if you find a likely baptism in an unlikely place; look at a map, see if there is an extra-parochial area nearby, ascertain if there are surviving papers left by the owner or occupier of the area, and you might find that your ancestor was a true 'babe in the woods'.

GLOSSARY OF ECCLESIASTICAL TERMS USED IN THIS BOOK

ARCHDEACON: a senior clergyman, one stage below a bishop. His role was mostly administrative; his responsibilities included keeping an eye on the clergy of his archdiaconate (see **VISITATIONS**) and his Court commonly dealt with a wide range of matters, including probate and matrimonial causes (mainly adultery and fornication).

ADVOWSON: the right of the **PATRON** (see below) to present a person to a living; became a marketable commodity.

BENEFICE: position usually as vicar or rector of a parish with income and/or property.

CHURCHWARDENS: commonly two for each parish, one appointed by the incumbent, the other by the parishioners, but in parishes with several chapelries, there may be a warden for each chapelry. Their primary responsibility was to keep the church or chapel in good repair, make sure that services were properly conducted, and report any 'misbehaviour' to the archdeacon at his visitation. They were also charged (see p.107) with the preparation of the Bishops' Transcripts.

They had duties under civil law, including dealing with the payment of poor relief and keeping vermin under control. Churchwardens' Accounts, where they survive, can be an invaluable source of information on parish life (see p.251).

CLERK/CLERK IN HOLY ORDERS: an ordained clergyman in the Anglican Church. Until the 19th century most Anglican clergymen attended either Oxford or Cambridge University and details of their parentage/careers (not always complete or accurate) can be found in *Venn*'s ***Alumni Cantabrigienses*** or *Foster*'s ***Alumni Oxonienses***, available in various formats including book form (in libraries), on CD and online on a commercial website. A useful website if looking for a clergyman ancestor is www.theclergydatabase.org.uk (incomplete but ongoing).

CONSISTORY COURT: the bishop's court for the administration of ecclesiastical law within his own diocese.

CURATE: an assistant to the Rector, Vicar or Perpetual Curate.

EXCHEQUER COURT: existed only in the province of York; dealt with the majority of grants of probate including those for PCY.

IMPROPRIATOR: see Lay Rector.

INCUMBENT: in England may be a rector, vicar or curate-in-charge of a parish. (This is the term commonly used in this book to cover all such clergymen.)

LITERATE [MAN]: a cleric admitted to Holy Orders (ordained) without a university degree. In the Diocese of York between 1750 and 1799 almost half of those ordained were literate men rather than graduates; between 1820 and 1825 the percentage rose to just over half. The practice occurred in other dioceses but not to the same extent.

LIVING: see Benefice.

MINISTER: clergyman (especially in Nonconformist & Presbyterian Churches).

NONCONFORMIST: person not conforming to the beliefs and practices of the Church of England. Generally refers to Baptists, Quakers, Methodists, Congregationalists, Presbyterians; also sometimes used of Roman Catholics.

OFFICIATING MINISTER: clergyman taking services and performing marriages in a church where he was not the appointed incumbent.

PARSON: properly refers to a Rector but since the 18th century is often used to refer to any clergyman.

PATRON: historically the person on whose land the church was built. The Patron reserves the right to appoint the incumbent, subject to the approval of the bishop. The right of patronage could be bought and sold. Patrons include the Crown, Bishops, Cathedrals, University Colleges and individuals.

PERPETUAL CURATE: priest nominated by lay rector (impropriator) to serve parish which had no vicarage. Once licensed by the bishop could not be removed without revocation of the licence (hence the name). Income not derived from tithes. Often referred to as vicar.

PLURALISM: the holding of more than one benefice at a time. This was a very common practice until the Pluralities Act of 1838. Of just over 100 parishes and chapelries in Yorkshire beginning with the letters A or B, listed in the replies to *Archbishop Drummond's* 1764 Visitation questions, 48 were served by pluralist clergy. The bishop's permission was needed for plurality if the benefices were more than 30 miles apart; many cases of pluralism involved adjoining parishes. (See p.123 for parishes held by *William Dade* and p.257 for those held by *Thomas Nelson*.)

PRIEST: ordained minister. In Anglican Church has authority to administer sacraments.

RECTOR: clergyman originally entitled to the *Great & Small Tithes*.

  LAY RECTOR: Following the dissolution of the Monasteries in the 1530s, their confiscated property (often including the right to tithes) was disposed of by the king. Those taking over the property, known as Lay Rectors or Impropriators, inherited the right to the tithes. See **PERPETUAL CURATE**.

In modern 'Team Ministries', the senior member of the clergy team is often called the Rector, even if from a parish which previously had a Vicar.

RECUSANT: person refusing to attend Church of England services. Commonly used to refer to Roman Catholics but can be applied to any Nonconformist.

RURAL DEAN: appointed by the bishop as head of a group of parishes in a given area. In the Diocese of York, rural deans undertook duties usually performed by archdeacons in other areas.

TERRIER: a terrier (commonly called a glebe terrier) was a written survey or inventory of land and other property held by the incumbent for the support of himself and his church. It was often very detailed and, as well as naming the fields, may include information about the rectory/vicarage, the church and church plate. The terrier often includes names of tenants of church land and also names of the holders of adjoining lands (see *Clapham* terrier on p.193).

TITHES: originally one-tenth of the yearly produce of land payable by parishioners to the parish church to support it and its clergymen. In the early days much was payment in kind - hence the building of tithe barns. Tithes in kind were gradually replaced by money payments and the 1836 *Tithe Commutation Act* (see p.267) hastened the process.

  GREAT TITHES: also known as rectorial tithes. These consisted mainly of crops including grain, hay and wood.

  SMALL (LESSER) TITHES: also known as vicarial tithes. These included livestock and their produce (milk, eggs, etc.), vegetables and fruit.

VESTRY:

  OPEN VESTRY: a meeting of the parish ratepayers who were responsible for electing the parish officers - churchwardens, overseers of the poor, overseers of the highways, parish constable. They set the parish rate which raised money for the church, the poor, the upkeep of roads and bridges and much more.

SELECT VESTRY: in large and heavily populated parishes, a number of ratepayers (not more than 20 or less than five) elected annually to deal with parish matters.

Where Vestry Minutes survive they may provide detailed information on the running of the parish.

VICAR: clergyman entitled to the *Small Tithes*.

VISITATION: official visit of inspection to check on temporal and spiritual affairs carried out principally by archbishops, bishops, archdeacons and, in some areas, rural deans. Often preceded by the sending out of a questionnaire, requiring a written response from individual clergymen.

1778 TERRIER FOR CLAPHAM

A true and perfect terrier of all the Glebe lands Gardens and Tithes and other Ecclesiastical Dues belonging to the Parish Church of Clapham

A Vicarage House twenty yards long and six yards broad, within the Walls, which consists in the Ground Floor of three Rooms, two of which are papered, one boarded with Deal and the other floored with Stone, with a Pantry floored with clay, a cellar, and two small offices, one floored with Stone, and the other paved, a Staircase and Gallery which lead to six Chambers, two of which are papered and floored with Deal, one papered and floored with Ash, one other floored with Deal and the remaining two with Ash, a Barn eleven yards long and five broad, a Brewhouse four yards square, all which are built with Stone and covered with Slate, one Good Garden fenced with Stone, one Croft called Goods[?]Croft, adjoining to the Church Yard containing about Thirty Perches of Land in which are five trees, value ten shillings the rent of both which is worth ten shillings and six pence yearly. The Churchyard Fence is made by the Parish[i]oners. One Croft called Pighill, thirteen Perches, Rent five shillings yearly bounded on the East, West and North by Lands belonging to Mr Harrison and on the South by Lands belonging to Robert Shuttleworth Esquire. The Moiety of the Tithe Corn in the Hamlet called Feizar let at the yearly Rent of two Pounds twelve shillings and six pence, and five shillings and one Penny a Modus for Hay and some small Tithes throughout all the Parish, value about four Guineas yearly. Easter Dues value about fourteen Pounds, Surplice Dues value six Pounds yearly half of the Mortuaries.

Also four Closes in this Parish called Yowbers about thirteen acres, adjoining together were lately purchased by Benefaction from Queen Anne's Bounty in the year one thousand seven hundred and sixty six, bounded on the East by Lands belonging to the late Mr Lupton, on the West and South by Mr Waddington's Lands and on the North by the Turnpike, all exceedingly well fenced with Stone and are now let at the clear yearly Rent of fifteen Pounds and ten shillings.

Also George Battersby of Newby left to the Parish Church of Clapham the sum of twelve shillings yearly, for preaching two annual Sermons, one on the 21st day of January and the other the 23rd day of April yearly forever which is duly paid.

The furniture of the Church, a very good brass Candlestick with sixteen branches, one other for the Pulpit with two branches, three Bells, one Clock, a good Communion Table with a very Handsome Cover, and proper Linen, two pewter Flagons, two pewter Dishes and two silver cups, no inscription or weight marked, Surplices, Bible and Common Prayer Books very good.

MARRIAGE BOND FOR INGRAM VARLEY: 1784
PARISH OF SHERBURN IN THE PECULIAR OF FENTON
(see p.162 for Allegation)

CHAPTER 19

PROBATE (WILLS, ADMINISTRATIONS ETC.)

The subject of probate and its associated records - Wills, Letters of Administration, Inventories, Bonds, Death Duty Registers (from 1796) - is a complex one. There are plenty of books and websites which deal specifically with Wills and all guides to tracing your family history will include sections on the subject. This chapter aims to suggest potential pitfalls within probate laws and records. Be aware that many books relate only to England and Wales, and of these some deal entirely with the period after 1858 when *England, Wales and Ireland* switched probate from ecclesiastical to civil control (see p.196). The *Channel Islands* and the *Isle of Man* have largely retained control of their own probate matters. *Scotland* has always had a very different system with commissary courts controlling probate until 1823 and sheriff courts thereafter (see p.196).

WILLS AND WILLS INDEXES ONLINE

The number of Wills Indexes online on national, local authority, free and commercial websites is increasing almost weekly. Almost all of these cover Wills proved before 1858 (the two known exceptions are emboldened below). There is currently no online index to English and Welsh Wills proved after 1858; First Avenue House (home of the Probate Service which presently forms part of the Family Division of the High Court) and TNA have *microfiche* indexes to these Wills. Copies of the annual indexes should be held by District Probate Registries; some have been deposited in local record offices. *The National Library of Wales* has an online index, and free access to digital images, of Wills proved in Welsh Ecclesiastical Courts from the 16th century to 1858. Most Irish Wills were destroyed in 1822 (some abstracts and indexes survive); *an Index of Irish Wills 1484-1858*, where documentation (other than just an index entry) is available is online on a commercial website. *ScotlandsPeople* has free access to the indexes of Scottish Wills from 1513-**1901** and facsimiles of the original documents can be ordered and paid for online. (Note that the original Wills are no longer available to view in Edinburgh.) Cheshire is the first English county to match Scotland, with a free online alphabetical index of Wills proved in the county between 1492 and **1940** and copies of the original documents can be ordered online. The quality and coverage of indexes to Wills proved in ecclesiastical courts in England before 1858 (including the PCC and PCY - see later in this chapter) varies widely. Always read any introductory material. Ascertain whether an index covers **all** pre-1858 Wills proved in a county or diocese, including those proved in Peculiars (see p.185); those from a particular archdeaconry or deanery; those from a restricted area; or those abstracted by an individual and relating only to certain surnames. It is possible to order copies of some Wills online at rates ranging from £3 to £10 and upwards, others have to be ordered direct from the relevant record office. It pays to check exactly which source has been used for the images you purchase - some sites provide facsimiles of the original documents, others of the entry from the volume of registered copy Wills (see p.206).

WILLS AFTER 1858

When the second edition of *Burn*'s ***Ecclesiastical Law*** was published in four volumes in 1767, Wills accounted for almost an entire volume - over 300 pages ranging from who could make a Will through to the final accounting when probate had been granted and the effects distributed. When the first edition of *Sir Robert Phillimore*'s ***Ecclesiastical Law of the Church of England*** appeared in the 1870s neither Will nor Probate even appears in the index, so completely had responsibility for Wills been removed from the church courts. The ***Court of Probate Act*** of 1857 (with a separate Act for Ireland), which came into effect on 11 January 1858, transferred the power to prove Wills and grant Letters of Administration from the church courts to civil jurisdiction and established Principal Probate Registries in London and Dublin (and District Probate Registries throughout England, Wales and Ireland). Locating Wills after this date is generally far easier than finding earlier ones, but remember that many Irish Wills were destroyed in 1922.

If your ancestor died late in 1857 and you cannot find a Will in the indexes at First Avenue House it is worth checking the relevant ecclesiastical court - it is surprising how many Wills were proved in the first 10 days of January 1858. Similarly, if you know that your ancestor died on an off-shore island after 1858 but you cannot find a Will there, look at the Principal Registry indexes; many people moved to the islands but owned property on the mainland and, if this was the case, the Will should be recorded in the Principal Probate Registry.

A great many more Wills were (and are) made than ever go to probate. Proving a Will costs money so, if the only items concerned are household goods, clothes, and cash in hand (which is all that many people leave), and there is agreement among the beneficiaries to abide by the document's terms, it has always been common practice to sort out the legacies privately and not to go to the expense of registering or proving the Will. In these cases you may find a copy of the Will among papers at home or with the family solicitor but many will have been destroyed once their terms have been carried out.

It is also worth looking among family papers in case someone did not make a formal Will but left written instructions as to how they would like their effects distributing. My great-grandmother, dying in 1933, with a daughter and daughter-in-law who were not the best of friends, listed everything (pictures, china, linen and bedclothes) and said who should receive what, with the injunction (below) *and don't mind if one gets a bit more than the other.* The second extract reveals what she considered to be important items at the time: *wireless and speakers, washing machine, bed warmers, radiator and marmalade machine.*

(Clarice to have the downstair Colored Curtains)(Bertha to have the upstairs Colored ones)
(Clarice to have my Label cloths with border on)
Clarice to have (my Clothes & to the best she thinks with)
Share all the Rugs Cushions covers etc
And don't mind if one gets a bit more than the other
Bertha to have my summer Fur.

(Clarice to have my
Wooden Bedsteads And the Bed
Linen that she prefers. also
Pillows if she needs any.
(Ben to have. my Wireless set
+ Speakers also the Washing Machine
(Eli to have the Bed Warmers)
(Eli (Ben to have the Radiator)
Jean to have the Plant + Pot
(Also the (marmalade Machine)

197

*Whitaker's **Almanack*** has, annually, provided a useful summary of current probate practice in England & Wales, and also in Scotland, over the last hundred years. The changing attitude to the making of Wills can be seen from its statements. From the 1880s it says (for England) that *Every man having a wife and family should make his Will*; by 1939 this has become *Every person should make a Will*; by the 1970s *Every person over the age of 18 should make a Will*. From 1837 to 1969, Wills could only be made by those aged 21 and over; before 1837 girls of 12 and boys of 14 could make Wills (in Scotland any person over the age of 12 and of sound mind still can). Wills could not be made by idiots (defined in *Burn* as one who *cannot number to twenty, nor can tell what age he is of, nor knoweth who is his father or mother, nor is able to answer any such easy question)*, lunatics (whilst insane; in a lucid period they could) and convicted traitors or felons (whose goods and lands were forfeit to the crown).

A common, but inaccurate, belief is that a married woman could not make a Will until the Married Women's Property Act came into effect in 1883 as, until this date, all that she owned became her husband's property on marriage. **A married woman could, under certain circumstances, make a Will before this date *with her husband's consent*** (which is why you will often see entries in pre-1858 calendars of Wills like *Mary Brooke (wife of John Brooke).* Spinsters and widows have always been permitted to make Wills. Do not forget that, in England, a marriage subsequent to the making of a Will revokes the Will (unless it was specifically made *in contemplation of the marriage)*; in Scotland a marriage does not affect the Will but the later birth of a child not named or provided for may do so.

A Scotsman has always been obliged to leave part of his estate to his widow and children (assuming he has any); in England this applied until the 17th century (when it lapsed), and from 1976 (since when close dependents can claim *reasonable provision* from an estate). In between, a man could dispose of his goods, if not his lands, as he chose.

WILL & TESTAMENT

Have you ever wondered why a *Last Will and Testament* is almost always referred to simply as a Will, but the person who made it is called a Testator (Testatrix if female) and dies testate (intestate if no Will has been made or found)? Until the **Statute of Wills of 1540** the two were usually separate documents - *a Will related to land (realty) and a Testament to personal or moveable property (personalty)*; there were many more of the latter than the former as few people had any rights over the land they lived on so could not pass control to their descendants. After 1540, when the statute made it lawful to bequeath land, it became common practice to combine the two as the *Last Will and Testament*. The document became known colloquially as the Will but testator and (in)testate - derived from the Latin for witness - survived.

In *Scotland* the distinction between *heritable property* (land, buildings and minerals in the ground) and *moveable property* (everything else) was maintained until the 20th century and each has its own set of records. Confusingly, a Testament here relates to moveable property and refers to the records of the confirmation of executors (named in the Will if there is one, appointed by the relevant court if not), rather than to the Will itself (although, if one exists, it will be included in the Testament).

Do not fall into the trap of believing that, because your ancestor did not own any land or property, he (or she) will not have left a Will or, conversely, that because he did there has to be a surviving Will. Today, when one is bombarded from all sides with advice to make a Will, to avoid the complications which can ensue if a person dies intestate, it can be difficult to conceive the attitude to making a Will which prevailed in past centuries. Many people regarded it as tempting fate to make a Will whilst they were fit and healthy and made no move to record their wishes until they were (or thought they were) about to breathe their last. Some left it too late; others (who sign earlier documents in a firm hand) could manage only a shaky mark; a few made Nuncupative Wills (an oral statement, written down and its authenticity sworn to by witnesses but not signed by the testator) or Holograph Wills (in the deceased's own handwriting but not witnessed: see p.200-201). Sudden death, from accident or disease, was a common occurrence and lack of a Will could cause major complications for the family left behind.

'CUT OFF WITH A SHILLING'

Missing heirs, entailed estates, sons *cut off with a shilling* and daughters disowned for running off with a groom have kept generations of novelists in business. Researchers today, finding ancestors left the proverbial shilling or omitted altogether from a family Will, tend to envisage a dramatic or romantic story but things are not always what they seem.

Leaving someone a shilling, in earlier Wills often written as *xijd* (i.e. *twelve pence* - see p.212) does not necessarily mean that there is a rift in the family. It is much more likely that the person so treated has already received their share of the family lands, money or goods, perhaps on setting up in business, emigrating or marrying. The testator is making sure that they cannot make a claim that they have been 'forgotten' and sue for a share of the estate. If someone is *cut off with a shilling*, or left absolutely nothing, because of a family quarrel this is often stated, in no uncertain terms, in the Will. *James Spilling* (see p.117), making his Will in Suffolk in 1819, left his estate to his housekeeper, his sons and his late brother's heirs, *rejecting for ever my two undutiful Daughters Rhoda and Mary and their heirs in succession.*

Note that the money from his estate is to be equally divided between his children Ellen and John (except for £10) because provision has already been made for daughter Ann.

STATEMENT BY THE REVEREND THOMAS ROWBOTTAM AND THE REVEREND RICHARD INMAN THAT JAMES CRABTREE'S WILL AND SIGNATURE ARE IN HIS HANDWRITING.

Appeared personally the Reverend Thomas Rowbottam of Anston in the County of York Clerk and the Reverend Richard Inman of Todwick in the same County Clerk and being sworn on the Holy Evangelists alleged and made oath that they knew and were well acquainted with the Reverend James Crabtree late of Laughton in le Morthen in the County of York Clerk deceased for some years before and to the time of his death and during such their knowledge and acquaintance with the said deceased have several times seen him write and also write and subscribe his name whereby they have become acquainted with his manner and character of handwriting and subscription and having carefully viewed the Paper Writing hereunto annexed purporting to be the last Will and Testament of the said deceased beginning thus "In the name of God Amen I do make this my last Will & Testament in the Form manner following" ending thus "and thereby appointing my two above said Children Ellen & John Crabtree Executors of this my last Will Testament" and thus subscribed "Jas Crabtree" they these Deponents do verily and in their consciences believe that as well the name or words "Jas Crabtree" so set and subscribed as aforesaid at the end of the said Paper Writing as the whole series and contents thereof were and are of the proper Handwriting and subscription of the said James Crabtree deceased.

On the Seventh day of August one thousand eight hundred and thirty five the said Thomas Rowbottam and Richard Inman were duly sworn to the truth of this Affidavit before me

Thomas Rowbottam

Rich Inman

Thomas Sutton

Surrogate

201

The fact that a known relative is not mentioned in a Will should not be taken as evidence that they are either dead or alienated from their family. It often means that previous provision has been made for them. If a wife (particularly from the middle or upper classes) is not mentioned in her husband's Will, but there is no evidence of her death, it may well be that a marriage settlement was drawn up making provision for her should she be left a widow. This will come into effect when she becomes one so there is no need to mention her.

The son who is to take over the estate (be it freehold or leasehold) may be doing so under established inheritance laws (commonly involving an entail) so, again, there is no question as to his right to inherit and no point in paying a solicitor to state the obvious. Generally land would pass to the eldest son (or the nearest male relative if it was entailed) but in some areas, where the custom of Borough English prevailed, the youngest son (or youngest brother if the deceased had no son) would inherit and in some cases the estate would be shared equally between all the sons. Daughters will often have received their share as a dowry on marriage. If grandchildren are mentioned but not their father or mother, do not assume that the parent is dead unless there is specific reference to *my late son/daughter*.

Conversely, the fact that someone is named in a Will should not lead to the assumption that they are still alive. Wills were often made when the testator was ill or about to go on a long journey, put in a drawer and then forgotten about until the testator eventually died. *Moses Longden* lived for three years after making his Will (see p.203). Always check the date the Will was written and the date it went to probate - there may be many years difference; most of those named in the Will may be dead, other children or grandchildren have been born who are not included, and the testator's circumstances may have changed.

RELATIONSHIPS

Relationships stated in Wills may also not be as they seem. *In laws* were, in the eyes of the church at least, treated as blood relatives (see Chapter 4) and many a testator omitted the *in law* so making, say, his wife's brother or his sister's husband appear to be his own brother. Remember also that, until the middle of the 19th century, *step-children* were commonly described as *in laws* so *daughter-in law* is as likely to mean *step-daughter* as son's wife.

Nephew and niece equally need to be treated with care (see the examples cited on pp.35-36). *Cousin* and *kinsman* can similarly be very widely interpreted and can cover almost any degree of relationship either to testator or spouse.

Do not fall into the trap of assuming that the wife of a testator named in his Will is necessarily the mother of his children, named in the same document. Second (and third) marriages were common and, whilst a man will often specify if his wife has children by a previous marriage, he will not state if his children belong to his present wife. The phrase *my now wife*, commonly used by testators, is generally assumed to mean that he had had a previous wife (or wives) and she is his present one. This is often - but not always - the case; do not make such an assumption without looking for corroborative evidence.

WILL OF MOSES LONGDEN MADE 1764

Wills can also provide surprises when a testator refers to the lady whom parish register entries or civil registration certificates have identified as his wife as ... *who lives with me as my wife.* Remember that, until relatively recently, divorce was not an option for most people. There were many couples who, whether because one of them had a spouse still living or because they were forbidden to marry under church law (see Chapter 4), lived together with no-one being aware that they were not married. Any children by the relationship would be regarded as illegitimate so the father would have to spell out the situation, name his 'wife' and any children, and acknowledge them, or they would run the risk of receiving nothing from his estate.

***Natural child* is a phrase sometimes used in parish registers to denote an illegitimate child but do not make the mistake of thinking that it necessarily means this in a Will.** It can equally refer to a man's legitimate off-spring *begotten [by him] and especially in lawful wedlock.* Unhelpfully, the phrase can have these two completely contradictory meanings and careful study of the wording of the document is advisable to ascertain in which sense it is being used.

IDENTIFYING WILLS OF NONCONFORMISTS

Particular attention should be paid to the wording of the Will if you think you may be dealing with a non-Anglican family. Especially in the 18th century in England and Wales (until the Catholic Relief Act of 1778) Roman Catholics were discriminated against to the extent that they could not legally buy or inherit land and they could not officially be executors, administrators or guardians (of children). Various ways of circumventing the prohibition on land ownership were found, often by putting it in the name of a Protestant friend or relative who may, partly for this reason, be named as an executor and the use of such sentences as *to the disposal of my executors whatsoever is not mentioned in my Will* is often a pointer to a Catholic connection.

Wills of Anglicans and Roman Catholics usually contained a religious preamble beginning *In the name of God, Amen...* . The omission of this preamble may well indicate some form of Nonconformity, as may the striking out of certain phrases from probate or administration bonds. Before 1858, such bonds were required by the church courts which controlled probate matters and were usually written in language which was not acceptable to certain denominations. ***The Minutes and Advices of the Yearly Meeting of Friends*** [Quakers], for example, said in 1773 *which bond contains several titles ... which it is inconsistent with our religious principles to acknowledge, such as 'The most' or 'right reverend father in God'... 'by divine providence' &c ...* and recommended that friends *should endeavour to obtain consent to strike out such parts ...* . An example of an acceptable form of bond was also given, so if you find such a one, lacking the customary religious terminology, be aware that you could be dealing with Nonconformity.

WHERE TO FIND A WILL BEFORE 1858

Before starting to search, make sure you understand the basic structure by which the Church of England was administered (*parish/rural deanery /archdeaconry /diocese/ province*) and the areas (*peculiars, liberties* and so on) which in part stood outside this system because this is very relevant to which probate court may have been used to prove your ancestor's Will. (See Chapter 18.)

It also helps to know the composition of the archdioceses. Until 1836, the dioceses of *York, Chester, Carlisle, Durham and Sodor & Man constituted the Archdiocese of York (northern province)* whose highest probate court was the Prerogative Court of York (PCY). *All other dioceses in England and Wales were part of the Archdiocese of Canterbury (southern province)* whose highest court, the Prerogative Court of Canterbury (PCC), theoretically took precedence over the PCY. However, there are Wills in the PCY records which one would expect to find in the PCC - it is always worth checking both courts.

Just as there was, to some extent, a north-south divide in the way the parochial system operated (see pp.47-48) so there was with probate. **Do not make the mistake of assuming that the provinces of Canterbury and York** (the southern and northern provinces) **followed the same rules**.

ARCHDIOCESE OF CANTERBURY

In the archdiocese of Canterbury the majority of Wills of 'ordinary' people were proved in an *archdeacon's court*, reaching the *consistory (bishop's) court* if possessions were held in more than one archdeaconry in the diocese and the *PCC* if in more than one diocese in the province, so archdeaconry court, consistory court and PCC indexes and records will normally need to be searched (as well as any Peculiar courts in the area). Indexes and Wills for some dioceses and archdeaconries are available to search online (see p.195); others are still dependent on card or microform indexes and print-outs of Wills. Suffolk, for instance, was part of the diocese of Norwich in the archdiocese of Canterbury. Wills for the *archdeaconry of Suffolk* (covering East Suffolk) are held in the record office at *Ipswich* (with microfilm copies in *Lowestoft* record office), together with a card index. Those for the *archdeaconry of Sudbury* (covering west Suffolk) are in *Bury St Edmunds* together with a part manuscript (on microfilm)/part card index. If probate was granted in the *consistory* court the records are in *Norwich* (with indexes published by the Norfolk Record Society); and any proved in the *PCC* will be in *London* (or online – see p.206).

ARCHDIOCESE OF YORK

In the ***diocese*** of York, straightforward Wills were dealt with at *deanery*, as opposed to *archdeaconry*, level and then registered in the *Exchequer Court* (equivalent to a *consistory* court). In three other dioceses within the archdiocese of York - Carlisle, Durham and Chester - the relevant *consistory* *court* dealt with probate for the whole diocese; in the diocese of Sodor and Man (until 1847) probate was dealt with by either the *consistory court of Sodor and Man* or by the *archdeaconry court of the Isle of Man*. If goods were held in more than one jurisdiction in the diocese of York, or in more than one diocese in the northern province, jurisdiction passed to the *PCY* (whose probate matters were also dealt with in the *Exchequer Court*). If goods were held in both provinces, probate was normally granted by the *PCC*. Indexes to the calendars of Wills proved in both the Exchequer Court and the PCY between 1731 and 1858 (pre-1731 Wills are in process of being added) and a separate index to 54 Peculiar jurisdictions, are available online on a commercial website; copies of the documents can be ordered on the same site.

Registered copies of Wills (but not of letters of administration - see p.207) from all deaneries and the PCY were written into large ledgers with numbered pages; copies of these ledgers on microfilm are what you will look at if you visit the Borthwick Institute in person. Other dioceses (and the PCC) followed the same practice: **be aware that copy Wills are secondary sources and can contain errors and omissions** - some names may be misinterpreted from the original, others are omitted, and occasionally it is obvious that a line has been left out. **The PCC Wills online are the registered copies, not the original documents**.

Bear in mind that:

♦   there were variations in the manner in which the two provinces dealt with probate matters but many books describe only practices in the southern one; this can be very misleading.

♦   indexes to probate records vary greatly in size, composition and quality. One may have thousands of entries, covering a whole county (especially where this is co-terminous with an archdeaconry); another, for a peculiar, could include only half a dozen entries but may include the very one you seek.

♦   an index may include Wills only; grants of administration (Admons) only; or the two combined - always check. In many books, all Wills are listed first, followed by any Admons.

♦   indexes may be in manuscript form and held in a record office; card indexes; printed (book) indexes which are more widely available; on CD or on the internet.

♦   **an index is only as good as its compiler(s); most will contain errors and omissions**.

♦   **between 1653 and 1660 almost all Wills were proved in the PCC but some manorial courts continued to grant probate throughout. This fact is often overlooked.**

Before visiting a record office it pays to ascertain in advance the extent of its probate holdings and whether indexes or documents are available online. **Never assume that a county record office holds Wills for the whole, or even part, of the county it covers**. Some will hold all the documents (or microform copies), others none. *Lichfield Record Office*, for instance, as a diocesan record office holds the probate documentation for Derbyshire, Staffordshire and parts of Shropshire and Warwickshire. Yorkshire's probate records are split between four record offices in three historic counties but none of the three repositories often referred to as 'county' record offices (*Wakefield, Northallerton* and *Beverley*) holds original probate material before 1858. The bulk of Yorkshire's probate records are held at the Borthwick Institute for Archives in York (the diocesan registry) but researchers who have not done their homework arrive here to find that records for the parishes they require are held in *Leeds, Durham* or *Preston*. The situation in London and Middlesex is similarly complicated, with multiple courts and record offices involved.

A single index to all Wills and Admons proved in *Chester diocesan consistory court* between 1492 and 1857 is available online and copies may be ordered online or by post. If searching the alphabetical indexes in printed book form to Wills and Admons in the diocese of Chester, which are available in many libraries, be careful because estates worth less than £40 were filed separately and, from 1660 to 1800, indexed separately in the printed volumes so you need to search two indexes in each book. Also be aware that the printed indexes contain entries from much of Lancashire, which was in the diocese of Chester, but these are not included on the internet site because the records are now held in Preston, not Chester.

This all sounds very confusing and, to a degree, it is. However, as always, this chapter is not designed to be a definitive guide to Wills and where they may be found. It is intended to demonstrate some of the potential pitfalls but also to alert you to the range of exciting possibilities which Wills and their associated documents can offer. There are plenty of books and websites which provide detailed advice on where to look for Wills, once you have accepted the basic point made here that you may well need to look in more than one place. Do not be put off searching; you will never regret the effort expended in tracking down what can be a source of invaluable information.

ACT BOOKS AND ADMONS (LETTERS OF ADMINISTRATION)

Act Books (which, if they survive, contain details of day to day business in probate courts) are often ignored by family historians - especially before 1733 when most of them are in Latin - but they can contain vital information which cannot easily be found elsewhere and the Latin tends to be formulaic so it is easy to learn how to pick out the relevant information from the entries.

There were over 300 probate courts in England and Wales (deanery/ archdeaconry/consistory/peculiars/PCY/PCC and others) and each would have had its own Act Books. In some Dioceses, like York, the Act Books contain both grants of probate and Admons; in others, like Canterbury, there are separate Act Books for probate grants and Admons. Always check which system was used in the diocese in which you are interested.

Grants of probate noted in the Act Book should contain the date of the grant (see p.101 for difficulties with *eodem die* and it is important to note that, after 1733, where the entry begins *on the same day* you need to work backwards through the entries to locate the date as there may be 10 or more entries with the same date); the name of the testator and where they lived; to whom administration of the Will was granted (usually the executors); whether an inventory was exhibited; and the approximate value of the estate. Often the surname of the testator is given in the margin, making entries relatively easy to locate.

Letters of Administration (usually abbreviated to Admon), taken out when a person dies intestate, are a grant to someone, often the widow or next-of-kin, sometimes a creditor, to administer the estate of the deceased. Whilst not generally as informative as a Will, Admons can provide useful information.

The Admon for *John Turton* is granted to *Margaret Turton otherwise Adamson now the wife of Edward Adamson his widow,* making it clear that she has remarried and providing her present surname, which could otherwise be difficult to locate. An Inventory is exhibited and the estate is valued at under £20.

Admon of the goods of *William Roberts* is granted to *Joseph Roberts his brother and next-of-kin*, establishing a relationship and making it likely (though by no means certain) that there is no widow and no children.

Children named in Wills and Admons are usually subject to *curation* or *tuition* bonds (see p.210) and these will usually be found in the relevant Act Book in close proximity to the grant. In the example on page 210, curation was granted to the mother but be aware that, particularly in the case of a male child, curation/tuition was often granted to a male (commonly but not always a relative), rather than to the mother.

Another useful piece of information often found in the Act Books comes when the person is said to be *late of ... but dying at. Late of* can reveal where a person used to live (perhaps before moving in with a relative in old age or before a move from country to town) and *dying at* may provide an unexpected place of burial. Some entries provide even more information: *William Coldwell*, for whom a grant of probate was issued in 1837, was *form[erly] of Sheffield, afterwards of London but late of Liverpool, County of Lancaster* and *Charles Edwin Beddoe*, for whom letters of administration were granted in 1854, was *formerly of Bradford Co: York but late of New York, U.S. of North America.*

How long should you search after the death of an ancestor to ascertain if a Will was proved or letters of administration were granted? *Burn's Ecclesiastical Law* says that *testaments* [Wills] *ought to be insinuated to the official or commissary of the bishop of the diocese within four months next after the testator's death* but this did not always happen (see p.210).

Most Wills went to probate within a year of the testator's dying but some did not. If you think that there should be a Will but you cannot locate one soon after a man's death investigate what happened to his widow. **Delayed probates were common** when a husband left a life interest in his estate (real or personal) to his wife, with everything passing to his children on her death or remarriage. In such cases, applying for probate was often left until one of these two events occurred. Where minors were involved, applying for probate was sometimes delayed until the child reached the age of 21.

If there was a grant it did not always follow that the terms of the Will or the Admon were implemented immediately. *Rp[t] (respited)* alongside an entry means that a delay was being permitted before an inventory was produced or a statement of accounts made. In some cases, a second or even a third grant was necessary before an estate was finally settled: executors might die, disappear, or renounce (be unwilling to act); a Will could leave a life interest to one relative and, on their death, order distribution among a dozen others; legatees might be overseas and it could take months to locate them; relatives sometimes appeared 'out of the blue' and contested the Will; or one part of a man's estate might be administered separately (often when probate was originally granted in the diocese where he lived but he also held goods or property in another).

With the above in mind, there are plenty of instances of later grants of letters of administration being made at least 50 years after the death of the original testator. Not many equal that of *Elizabeth Atkinson*, widow. Administration of her Will was granted in April 1783 to her executrix, *Ann Wilson*, but the Prerogative Court of York (PCY) Act Book contains a marginal note: Administration of Goods unadministered passed at the Principal Registry 4 February 1891.

It pays to search all possible probate documentation. In some dioceses, indexes or calendars refer you to registered copy Wills (see p.206). These give details of the Will, the witnesses and the date of probate. Many researchers probe no deeper than this and so miss out on additional information. Ask to see the original documents and you will often find not only the Will or letters of administration but the bonds sworn by the executors (with their current place of residence). Particularly in the 17th and 18th centuries, there may well be an inventory of the deceased's goods and perhaps the accounts of the executors or administrators, detailing their expenses which they are claiming from the estate. **When requesting copies, it is advisable to specify that you require copies of all the relevant paperwork, not just the Will**. In many record offices all the documents are on microform but there are still a few where you can unwrap the original pieces of parchment, rolled and tied by a clerk several centuries ago, and know that you are handling the same sheet that your ancestor held.

In the PCY in April 1783: *Last Will and Testament of William Rhodes late of Wentbridge parish of Badsworth gentleman passed the Seal of this Court being first proved 27 September 1777 and Admon of his Goods (with said Will annexed) left unadministered by two executors (now deceased) granted to Elizabeth Rhodes Widow Mother and Curatrix or Guardian of Elizabeth and Abigail Rhodes. Third executor renouncing, having never acted.*

On the same day, *curation* (guardianship) of the two girls, aged *above 15 years and 13 years*, was granted to the mother. If either had been under 13 (15 if a boy) *tuition*, as opposed to *curation*, should have been granted. Watch out for the phrases *Administration with Will annexed* (often abbreviated to *AcT* [Testament]) and *A de bon n.* (Administration of goods not administered) as these often refer to a second grant.

It can pay to investigate what is obviously a cluster of entries for one surname as it was a fairly common practice to tie up various 'loose ends' with one visit to the probate court. The calendar of York Wills has, on 11 April 1783, three entries for the *Nelson* family:

Seth Nelson	*Ramsden Green*, Essex	PCY	*Admon*
Thomas Nelson	*Hatton*, Warwick[shire]clerk	PCY	*AcT*
Seth Nelson	*Askham Richard*, Yorkshire, gent.		*A de bon n.*

The PCY Act Book reveals that the Essex *Seth* and Warwickshire *Thomas* were brothers, both deceased. *Seth*, executor and residuary legatee for his brother *Thomas*, died intestate, and administration of both estates is granted to *Sarah Nelson, Seth*'s widow. *Thomas*'s Will had first been proved 13 years earlier in the PCC and both men lived in counties within that Archdiocese; the third entry explains why the grants are in the PCY.

On the same day, in Ainsty Deanery, *Administration of the goods of Seth Nelson late of Askham Richard deceased intestate not administered by Rosamond Nelson widow now also deceased granted to Ann Perkins spinster granddaughter and one of the next of kin (Henry Perkins grandson having renounced).*

Seth of *Askham Richard* had married in 1696 and died in 1721. *Thomas* and *Seth* were his sons (aged 14 and 10 when he died) and *Ann* and *Henry Perkins* were the children of his eldest daughter. When *Sarah Nelson* applied to administer the goods, held in Yorkshire, of her late husband and his brother, the unsettled affairs of her father-in-law, who had died 60 years earlier, were attended to at the same time, the grants between them revealing a wealth of information covering three generations (see p.259).

In 1853 administration of the estate of *Joshua Earnshaw* was granted in the PCY, together with the tuition of his granddaughter *Ruth Crossland*. The

Act Book reveals that both grants were to *Dan Crossland the paternal grandfather ... of Ruth Crossland ... under the age of election to wit of the age of two years without father, mother, brother, sister* but that she did have an uncle and an aunt, *children of Joshua, being resident abroad beyond the seas*.

In January 1855 an entry in the calendar at York notes that letters of administration were granted in the PCY for *Walter Black formerly of the town of Nottingham afterwards of Chatham co. Kent but late of Van Dieman's Land in Australia, a soldier*. While this is in itself an unusually informative calendar entry, in addition the Act Book reveals that *Walter* was a bachelor, with no parent living, and the grant was made to *Rebecca wife of Thomas Millott sister and one of the next of kin (James Black and Charles Godbehere Black brothers and only remaining next of kin having renounced)*.

Comments such as this, similar statements in Wills, and places of residence given on bonds, are often the only clue as to the whereabouts of people who have vanished from their home parishes.

INVENTORIES

A present day executor, applying for probate or letters of administration, is expected to produce, among other things, *particulars of all property and assets left by the deceased* but, unless it seems likely that there will be a dispute over specific items, a rough estimate of the value of the assets is usually acceptable and detailed inventories are rare.

Executors from the Middle Ages to 1782 (after which date inventories were no longer required by law) had a more difficult task as they attempted to comply with the law which said, *At the time of probate or administration granted, it is required that the executor or administrator produce an inventory of the goods chattels and credits of the deceased; and ... maketh oath, that he will exhibit such inventory into the court.* Between two and four appraisers were generally appointed - frequently creditors, neighbours or relatives of the deceased - to take stock of what possessions were involved but *goods, chattels and credits* was a loose description. Law manuals provided examples of inventories and what should be included in them but, as in so many other fields, what was recorded depended very much on the individual appraisers.

If you are fortunate enough to find an ancestral inventory it can provide you with invaluable information about the rooms in your ancestor's house, and its contents, how he earned his living, and his financial status; but be careful how you interpret it. Do not assume that an inventory includes everything which your ancestor owned or possessed. Certain things, including real estate and items which would automatically pass to the heir (heirlooms), were excluded by law.

£.s.d. (POUNDS, SHILLINGS & PENCE: LIBRAE, SOLIDI & DENARII)

Decimal currency was introduced in the British Isles (with the exception of the Republic of Ireland) in 1971 and we are now so accustomed to it that it is very easy to overlook the fact that, before that date, a very different monetary system was in operation. **Remember that amounts of money quoted in written documents, including inventories, Wills, and account books of all types (see p.251), will be in 'old money'.**

Some knowledge of the system used before 1971 is essential to enable you to work out, for example, how much your ancestor was paid in poor relief in a year (see p.251-2) or how much his goods were worth in an inventory. Anyone under the age of forty can be excused for not understanding pre-decimal currency but it came as a shock, on asking several friends older than that, to find that they had difficulty remembering. I admit to making errors in adding up columns of pre-decimal figures before suddenly realizing that I was treating them as if they were post-decimal. **Be warned, it is all too easy, particularly when a column includes only pounds and shillings and the £ sign and shilling letter are at the top of the page, to add, for example, 10.19 and 23.18 and write down £33.37 instead of £34-17s-0d** - I know, I have done it.

The pre-decimal figures you need to remember are:

One shilling (written as 1s or 1/-) = *12 pennies* (pence)
Twenty shillings = £1
240 pennies (pence) – £1
One guinea = £1-1s (the sale of livestock is often still quoted in guineas)
One penny (1d): the penny was one of the most commonly used coins.
It could be divided into:
a halfpenny (½d)
a farthing (¼d) = ¼ of a penny

Unlikely as it may seem today, a penny and its fractions often occur in documents. A 1743 inventory values 29 wine glasses at *3s 7½d*; in the 1800 Land Tax Assessment for *Luttons Ambo*, one-third of the 27 occupiers of land were assessed to pay sums ending in *½d*; and at *Thornton in Lonsdale* church in 1735 a brief (see p.103) for *Embsay Church* raised *4¼d*.

Until about the late 16th century in England and the 18th century in Scotland, amounts of money were often quoted in Roman numerals (see p.101) and *l* or *li* (libra is Latin for pound) *after* the amount was commonly used instead of the £ sign. The £ symbol developed from the capital letter L in roundhand, with a bar across to show that it was an abbreviation (of libra).

TNA has a currency converter on www.nationalarchives.gov.uk/currency .

GOODS AND CHATTELS

Ecclesiastical law defined 'goods' as *all the testator's cattle, as bulls, cows, oxen, sheep, horses, swine, and all poultry, household stuff, money, plate, jewels, corn, hay, wood severed from the ground, and such like moveables.* This seems straightforward until you look into the arguments which arose and realise that no two lawyers agreed on its interpretation. Usually, cut timber was included in the inventory but growing trees were not; corn (cut or uncut) was - because the deceased had worked sowing and harvesting it - but uncut grass (for hay) and fruit on trees was not. The authorities disagreed on vegetables, one saying they should not be included *because they cannot be taken without digging and breaking the soil*, another arguing that, as the deceased had planted them, they should go in.

'Chattels', real or personal, were even more confusing as they included *all goods, moveable and immoveable; except such as are in the nature of freehold, or parcel of it.* Real estate, be it land or a house, was not included in inventories (although leases were) and disagreements raged over fixtures and fittings, as to whether they were part of the freehold or should be listed. In general, glass, panelling, doors, keys, window shutters and staircases were regarded as part of the freehold but hangings, tapestries, iron fireplace backs and ladders (often used as stairs) were not. Many appraisers, aware that the executors could find themselves in serious trouble if there was not enough money to pay legacies from the Will and it could be proved that the inventory was not a full and accurate one, took the trouble to list everything but some wrote down as little as possible. Generally speaking, the earlier the inventory, the more detail will be given.

The majority of appraisers seem to have worked through a house room by room, examining downstairs first and then upstairs (if there was one), followed by any outbuildings. Some listed every item in each room separately with its own value, others gave *goods in the parlour* with one total value and yet others merely named *goods in the house* with a value. It is a matter of luck which type of appraiser assessed your ancestor's belongings. Where specific bequests had been made in a Will, these may be listed separately, as in *Ann Moseley*'s 1704 inventory which included *Goods in the houseplace which are bequeathed to Thomas Moseley a Cupard, two Coffers, Iron Pott ... bedd in the parler and its furniture,* but cursorily dismissed everything else as *the rest of the things in the house ... all sorts of husbandry ware* and *things unseen and forgotten. All sorts of old lumber* is another phrase beloved of appraisers.

Most inventories will put a value on the *purse and apparell* of the deceased and may also include details of debts owed by, or credits due to, the deceased, which can make a significant difference to the estate. *Elizabeth Litton*, dying in 1713, left personal estate of *£10.17s 6d* and debts of *£9. 14s 6d* so, once the debts were paid and funeral costs and other expenses had been met, her daughter would be lucky to inherit a few shillings.

A true and perfect Inventory of all the goods
Cattell and Chatells of John Litton late of
Snelston in the County of Derby Clark decea-
sed valued & appraised the 20th day of November
1662 by Tho: Gaunt of Knyveton gent Edw-
ard Coxon & Nicholas Redfearne of Snelston
aforesaid yeomen & Wm Salt of Thorpe as
followeth:

		£	s	d
Impris [in the first place]his wearing apparell & money in his purse		1	0	0
In the house				
Item	three little pewter dishes, 1 salt, 1 candlestick, 1 sawcer, 2 pewter porringers & 1 ould flagon	0	4	6
Item	three Kettles & 1 brass pott	0	16	0
Item	one Cupboard & dishboard	0	15	0
Item	one short Table, forms and settles	0	5	4
Item	Two Chaires	0	1	6
Item	the Landiron, fireshovell, tongs and potrackes	0	2	2
In the Chamber over the house				
Item	one bedstidd with the beddinge & Curtains now of it & belonging to it	1	0	0
Item	one other ould bedstidd & trundle-bed, with the ould bedclothes now upon it, belonginge to it, vallued at	0	13	4
Item	one ould Chest there	0	1	6
Item	three pairs of course sheetes	0	6	8
In an other little Chamber				
Item	one Chest, one old Cofer, & a box	0	7	6
Item	a little ould table & frame & an ould cheese cratch	0	2	6
Item	All his Bookes	2	10	0
Item	5 little Cheeses	0	3	8
Item	2 ould Kymnells, 2 old wheeles, & 3 little milkinge kitts	0	3	0
Item	4 Kyne vallued at	13	6	8
Item	three mares & a little foale	8	0	0
Item	one Sow & 8 Piggs	1	0	0
Item	one hogge swyne	1	0	0
Item	the Hay to keepe the Kyne	2	13	4
Item	the Corne in the barne unthrashed	1	10	0
Item	3 little dayes workes of winter corn	2	10	0
Item	one Cart, & the Cart saddle	1	0	0
Item	3 paire of horse geares	0	3	0
	Summa tot huius Invent.	39	16	2

Apraised by us: Tho: Gaunt, Edward Coxon, Nicholas Redferne, William Salt

214

Another *Elizabeth Litton*, dying in 1710, left *£77 1s 8d* of which *£70* was *Money due* [to her] *upon a Mortgage but supposed to be desperate* (which meant that there was little chance of its being collected by her heirs). Compare a Will with the total value of the personal estate given in its accompanying inventory and it may be clear that the legatees named in the former would be lucky to receive any, never mind all, of what they expected.

Do not forget that many elderly people ended their lives living with their children so only their own personal possessions will be listed. When *Thomas Glover*, a webster living with his daughter and son-in-law, died in 1682 his inventory consisted of: *two loomes a warp Stocke a Ringe and a Rathe and a pin wheele* (tools of his trade)*; geeres and slayes* (loom parts)*; one cowe* but no furniture or bedding as that would belong to his son-in-law.

Many people had more than one occupation, often revealed by their inventories. Farmers and their families often did spinning and weaving as a side-line (as did injured miners who could no longer work underground); innkeepers might also be butchers (those with a convenient field where drovers could rest their cattle or sheep for the night often took payment in kind); joiners could be brewers 'on the side'. Whatever their occupation, many families kept a few animals for their own use. Do not make the mistake of thinking that the presence of cows, in particular, necessarily indicates a farming family. Cleric *John Litton* in 1662 (see p.214) had *four cows, three mares and a foal, one hog, one sow and eight piggs (piglets)*; *Thomas Glover*, the webster mentioned earlier, had *one cow*, as did town dweller *William Litton* in 1724 (together with *a parcel of hay*), and as late as the 1840s and 1850s many of the inventories taken in *Marsden*, Yorkshire, list *one or two cows*.

How likely are you to find a surviving inventory? During what has been called 'the golden age of inventories', from about 1660-1775, when they were usually filed with the Will or Admon, they survive in large numbers. There are plenty before 1660 but their survival is patchy and varies from diocese to diocese. In the Prerogative Court of Canterbury, the Exchequer and Prerogative Courts of York, and many diocesan courts, detailed inventories declined markedly after 1775, from which date an estimate of the estate's value, given under oath, was usually considered sufficient. Thereafter they tend to be taken (or survive) only if there were complications such as a disputed Will or the heirs being under age. In some Peculiars and Manorial Courts (like *Marsden* in Yorkshire) they continued to be taken until 1857. They were usually taken within a few weeks of the death but, as with Wills, some were made years later; *Ann Perkins*, applying in April 1783 to administer the estate of her grandfather who had died in 1721 (see p.210) was ordered to submit an inventory within six months, which must have caused problems.

Most inventories will be found filed with their Wills or Admons, but not always noted in the calendars or indexes. In some record offices there are separate indexes for inventories, and sometimes one will survive where the

Will does not, so it is always worth checking. Remember to ask if there are any publications containing details or analyses of local ones as many have been compiled by individuals or societies.

WILLS OF CLERGYMEN

Separate rules (often varying between dioceses) governed the pre-1858 Wills of Anglican clergymen, and there were far more ordained clergymen than most people realise. In many dioceses their Wills were proved in the consistory (bishop's) court. Where this was the principal probate court there should be few problems. In dioceses which had archdeaconry courts, where the majority of Wills were proved, and a consistory court, it can be easy to overlook the fact that Wills of most clergymen are to be found in the latter's records. Where the diocese covered parts of several counties these may be held in a different record office to archdeaconry Wills so, if you suspect a clergyman ancestor, make sure you check these records. Most Suffolk clergymen's Wills are to be found in consistory court records in Norwich (Norfolk) and other dioceses, including Lichfield, Lincoln and Salisbury, each covered several counties. Wills of bishops, even if they held no goods or property outside their own diocese, should be proved in the relevant Prerogative Court in Canterbury (PCC) or York (PCY).

Some dioceses distinguished between the Wills of *beneficed clergymen* (principally *rectors, vicars and perpetual curates*) and *unbeneficed clergymen* (those ordained but holding no living, which included *chaplains and curates paid by beneficed clergymen*). In the Diocese of York Wills of the former were proved in the Chancery Court of York (and are listed in a separate index); those of the latter in the Exchequer Court; those holding a benefice within a Peculiar jurisdiction, and having no property elsewhere, in the relevant Peculiar court. It is all too easy to search the main series of Wills (which includes diocesan Wills, PCY Wills and Admons) and to overlook the Chancery Court index and Peculiars. The administration of *Robert Warburton, Rector of Holtby*, can be found in the peculiar jurisdiction of *Howden and Howdenshire* because *Holtby* came within its jurisdiction, despite being in a different Riding and miles away from the rest of the peculiar. It pays to make sure which ecclesiastical jurisdiction covered any place where your ancestors lived or died.

As with other testators, if *bona notabilia* (*considerable goods*: in most dioceses those worth more than £5, £10 in London) in more than one diocese were involved, a higher court, generally the relevant Prerogative Court, had to be used.

WILLS OF THOSE DYING OVERSEAS

Wills of those dying overseas, or at sea, were normally proved in PCC (accompanied by the abbreviation *Pts - short for [died in] Foreign Parts*).

Many 'text-books' present this as an unbreakable rule but there are some exceptions, especially where personal estate only, and not real estate (land), was involved. The PCY, which was often unwilling to accept the superior jurisdiction of the PCC, contains some Wills for overseas testators whose English interests lay wholly within the northern province. Many Wills of people dying overseas (or in Scotland or Ireland) were proved in the PCC (or Edinburgh or Armagh) with a second grant, usually a few weeks later, in the PCY, with a copy of the Will attached. That for *Robert Lang* of *Largs* in Ayrshire, registered in *Edinburgh* in August 1849 and proved in *York* in November, covered 47 A3 pages, with a note appended that copying (by hand) the 24 sheets cost *£4.8s.5d* - the equivalent of about *£200* today. *William Lean's* Will, proved in the PCC in November 1856 and in the PCY in December described him as *formerly of Gwennap co. Cornwall but late of Cronebane Mines parish of Castlemacadam co. Wicklow, Ireland, mine agent.*

Such copies are particularly common in the 19th century, up to 1858. Sometimes it is easy to see the reason for this second grant, because the deceased has Yorkshire connections, but often there is no apparent link with the northern province. It has been suggested that, for merchants and plantation owners, it may have been to cover the possibility of goods they owned being on board ships in ports such as *Hull* and *Liverpool*. Whatever the reason, if you have easier access to records in York than London or elsewhere, it may pay you to look there first.

If you cannot find a Will in PCC for someone you think was living overseas, make sure they did not die after landing in England during their final journey home. *Philip Howell*, clerk, made his Will, detailing personal estate only, in *Bristol* (in the Province of Canterbury) and he died there in 1805. Probate was granted at York in 1806 (for *Philip Howell*, gentleman - remember that a rise up the social scale on death or marriage was common practice) because his widow was domiciled in Yorkshire. His Will made no mention of overseas connections (or property) but the probate grant describes him as *late of the Island of Jamaica but dying [in his passage* - crossed out] *at Bristol.*

WILLS OF SOLDIERS AND SAILORS

Wills of soldiers and sailors are usually to be found in the PCC but those of some mariners in the 18th century were proved in the *Archdeaconry Court of London*, whose records are in the Guildhall Library, and there may be a few in other courts. There are a number of indexes available to PCC and Archdeaconry Court of London Wills. Always read the introduction to ascertain what is included in these. The Index to PCC Wills and Administrations 1701-1749, as its title says, includes both - but the series of volumes edited by *Anthony Camp* covering 1750-1800 and *Cliff Webb's* index to Archdeaconry Court of London Wills 1700-1807 include Wills only, not Admons. Copies of Wills or Admons are often found in TNA attached to records concerning servicemen; it is worth checking here as well as in the PCC and local court records.

Admons for soldiers and sailors are often granted in local archdeaconry or deanery courts rather than in the PCC. They were applied for so that relatives could claim wages owed to the deceased or, in the case of sailors and marines, his share of any prize money and they frequently contain valuable genealogical information.

In Yorkshire, in September 1815, letters of administration for *James Peele heretofore of Birstal but late a Private soldier in His Majesty's 33rd Regiment of Foot and slain at the battle of Waterloo a Widower without Children deceased Intestate* were granted, in the *Deanery Court of Pontefract*, to his father *John* (his estate, i.e. his effects, being under £50); in 1816 *Joseph Atkinson* was granted administration in the *Ainsty Deanery* for his son *James Atkinson formerly of Leeds but late a Private of the 34th Regiment of Foot stationed in the East Indies* ... (estate under £40); and in 1817 *John Armstrong* took out administration in the PCY for the effects of his brother *Thomas Armstrong late of Hilsea Hospital or Barracks near Portsmouth County of Hants (sic) Private Marine* ... (estate under £300).

These entries were extracted from the Act Books (which give brief details of grants of probate and administrations). Bonds and other surviving documents often provide additional information, particularly occupations, so it pays to look at them. In the case of *John Swallow*, they prove that secondary sources, such as Act Books, can be suspect. On 15 April 1806 an entry in the *Doncaster Deanery* Act Book states that *Administration of the goods of John Swallow late a sailor on board His Majesty's ship* Tartar *a bachelor died Intestate was granted to Thomas Swallow and Mary wife of Thomas Crookes his brother and sister and only next of kin (Ellin wife of Charles Simpson heretofore Ellin Snowball widow his mother having renounced)* with his estate being worth under £100. This reads as if his mother was previously married to a *Mr Snowball*. The renunciation bond makes it clear that she was *Ellin Swallow* - perhaps it was snowing in April 1806 and the clerk's mind was not wholly on his job. The bonds also supply the information that *John's* family were living in *Rotherham* where brother *Thomas* was a saddle and collar maker, brother-in-law *Thomas Crookes* a stationer and step-father *Charles Simpson* a boat builder.

BENEFICIARIES, EXECUTORS & WITNESSES

You may not be able to locate a Will or letters of administration relating to your ancestors but do not discount the possibility that they may appear in the probate documents of relatives, friends, neighbours or business associates. They may be mentioned as beneficiaries, creditors, executors, trustees or witnesses. It pays to look at Wills relating to anyone bearing the same surname in the same area as your ancestor and to search for probate documents for the family of his wife. The appearance of land, money and even titles in a family can often be explained by marriage to a brotherless heiress.

Tracing references in Wills outside the direct family can be difficult but well worth the effort. Ask record offices or local family history societies whether printed volumes (perhaps including transcripts of Wills for a given area) or indexes exist to help you. Some societies are compiling Wills Beneficiaries Indexes. Always read the relevant entry carefully - a few indexes have been completed from original records; others depend on entries submitted by individual members from their records, so are more of a lucky dip; many are still in their early stages and, as yet, cover only a limited period. Most contain all names mentioned in the Will but a few include only surnames which are different to that of the testator. As well as beneficiaries, witnesses and executors are generally named.

WITNESSES

In general, a Will had to be *duly published in the presence of two sufficient witnesses at the least* (*Grey*'s **Ecclesiastical Law** 1735); three if the Will was a nuncupative (oral) one and in certain other cases. Until June 1752 witnesses could be beneficiaries in a Will which they witnessed. *Abbotside Wills 1552-1688* and *Swaledale Wills and Inventories 1522-1600* (both in the *Yorkshire Archaeological Society's Record Series*) deal with probate documents from rural districts in the Yorkshire Dales and show clearly that, in isolated communities at least, Wills were frequently both written and witnessed by principal beneficiaries. In Derbyshire, *Anne Lytton*'s Will in 1688 divided her goods between her son and daughters and *I give to Mary Skelton for her care and trouble during my sickness five shillings.* The Will was witnessed by *Anthony Trollope* (who wrote it) and *Mary Skelton*, who were presumably the only people present at Anne's sickbed.

Mary's bequest was no doubt justified but there were many cases where undue pressure was brought to bear on testators by witnesses, to include them as beneficiaries, so **an Act of Parliament, effective from 24 June 1752** and applying to any Will made after that date, **forbade witnesses to a Will to benefit from it**.

Mary could just about sign her name but many witnesses made their marks. The majority of Wills today are arranged through solicitors, to avoid possible legal complications, but, particularly in the 18th century and earlier, many were written (in decidedly non-legal language - see p.203), and witnessed by friends or neighbours and you may find examples of your ancestor's handwriting in such a Will. You may even find him described, like *John Forster of Askrigg* in the 1670s, as a scrivener, and a study of Abbotside Wills makes it clear that *John* was responsible for writing many of the local Wills and inventories.

Executors (executrix if female), whose task is to make sure that the terms of the Will are carried out, **are commonly beneficiaries**. Wives and unmarried daughters living at home were frequently named as executrix[es], often 'supported' by a male relative or business associate. Under ecclesiastical law (which applied until 1858 except in Scotland) the only people who could not generally serve as executors were agnostics, Roman Catholics, and craftsmen who regularly worked overseas. There was no lower age limit - infants (a term applied to those under 17 or 21 years of age, depending on the period) could be executors with a tutor, guardian or suitable adult appointed to carry out their duties until they reached their majority. If the testator's wife was pregnant when he died, the unborn child could theoretically be named an executor.

In most cases, where the Will was straightforward and there were no disputes over the terms, the executors' duties would generally not prove too onerous and, if they were not principal beneficiaries, they often received a small bequest in the Will *for their pains*. In the *City of York*, at least, some men appear to have acted as executors for the local gentry, as banks and solicitors do today, so do not assume that executors are related, or even connected, to the testator.

Executors could claim expenses from the estate, providing that they filed proper accounts. Where these accounts survive, they can reveal a great deal of information about the testator and his affairs. In 1751 *Robert Wigin*, one of the executors of *Henry Finney* late of *Houghton* (see p.9) in the parish of *Castleford*, handed in his accounts, covering five closely-written foolscap sides of paper. They begin with *Meat for funeral 15/-; wine for same 15/-; bisketts £1-9-1; Shroud and making 16/-; Coffin 15/-; Clark for Buryal fees 2-0s* and go on to name many local people with whom *Mr Wigin* had dealings. A seven page inventory accompanies the accounts. Two and a half pages deal with *Mr Finney*'s *goods* (and the prices they sold for); the rest list *debts paid, debts standing out and supposed to be good, and debts desperate* (unlikely to be paid), some of them dating back twenty years and naming more than a hundred people living in the West Riding at the time. Gems like this are few and far between and tend to survive more often in cases involving disputed Wills.

DISPUTED WILLS

Objecting to the terms of a Will, and going to court (ecclesiastical before 1858, civil after that) in an attempt to overturn them, has always happened. The main reasons cited for disputing a Will include questions as to the mental capacity of the testator; whether undue influence or duress was used to persuade the testator to include certain clauses; claims that the Will was invalid for some reason - often that it had not been signed and witnessed correctly by two independent witnesses or (after 1752) that a witness was a beneficiary; claims of fraud (that the testator had been tricked into signing the Will or that the executors had not paid out legacies).

If you find evidence of a disputed Will involving an ancestor (often indicated in the PCC indexes, but not the PCY ones, with the words *by decree* or *by sent*[ence] next to the name of the deceased), or anyone from the same area, ascertain if the 'cause papers' relating to the case survive as they can be a goldmine for the family historian. Such cases often involved statements being taken from a large number of witnesses, who usually began by stating their name, occupation, age, residence and connection to the deceased (relative/nurse/ servant/neighbour). When *Thomas Cust*, in 1754, claimed the right to administer his late uncle's estate in opposition to his aunt (his uncle's sister) because she had been for three years in a state of *Lunacy distraction or Madness* and had suicidal tendencies, doctors, servants and relatives all bore witness to her disturbed state of mind. Unfortunately, as with many of the cases, the verdict of the court is not given.

DEATH DUTY REGISTERS

Death Duty Registers, covering the period 1796-1903, can provide additional information relating to some estates in England and Wales, including the value of the estate, details of relationships, who was entitled to legacies and what amount each person actually received, and (before 1858) in which court the Will was proved. Be aware, however, that the records are not very user-friendly. The records are held at TNA at Kew; currently details for 1796-1811 (for courts other than the PCC) are available on the **/documentsonline/** section of the TNA website and the indexes covering 1796-1903 are available on a commercial website; these dates will change as more records are added to the databases. Similar, if not as detailed, Estate Duty Office Registers are held by the National Register of Archives in Scotland.

RESOLUTIONS:

I will always search for a Will or Letters of Administration for my ancestor, whether he was a gentleman or an agricultural labourer.
I will remember that before 1858 probate was dealt with by an ecclesiastical court.
I will read any introductory material on the site before using an online Wills Index.

CHAPTER 20

PEOPLE ON THE MOVE

Most of the records dealt with in earlier chapters are full of pitfalls which you need either to avoid or escape from. This chapter is more concerned with the possibilities which may arise when you search the records dealing with the movement of people within, to or from the British Isles from the 17th to the 19th centuries.

Passports for foreign travel have been in existence since at least the 17th century but passports as we know them today, as an essential identity document needed before leaving or entering a country, date only from the early 20th century. A modern-day passport will usually include stamps from all the countries visited and enable anyone looking through it to work out where the holder has travelled in the last few years. A settlement certificate (see below) served as a passport for our ancestors wishing to move around the country looking for work but who might at some point need poor relief.

DID YOUR ANCESTORS MOVE?

The once widely-held belief that one's ancestors were born, married and died in one place, and never moved away from it (cited as one of the original pitfalls), can be largely discounted. *Norman Tebbit*'s remark, made in 1981, *I grew up ... with our unemployed father. He did not riot, he got on his bike and looked for work* could, with the substitution of *feet* for *bike,* sum up the situation in which working men have always found themselves. Economic necessity - how to obtain enough money, in the days before any social security provision was made by the state, to feed and clothe their families and put a roof over their heads - was usually the factor which dominated their lives. If they failed to find employment close to home, many would travel far afield looking for work.

Those who stayed close to home can be as difficult to pin down as those who migrated hundreds of miles. Agricultural labourers, until the late 18th century the most common occupation, were often hired for a year at a time. They would go to the annual fairs, frequently held in the nearest market town, and hire themselves out for the best wage on offer. This might mean a move to a farm a few hundred yards away from last year's job but it could be in a different village and parish and even be in another county (many market towns were situated very close to county boundaries). If a man appears to have his children baptised in one parish but there is a gap of, say, three years in an otherwise regular sequence, it often pays to check neighbouring parishes for another child; similarly, if the father suddenly appears in a parish but is not baptised there, cast round the area and do not forget to look over the county boundary.

For every family which stayed on the same farm, or lived in one village for close on 500 years (since parish registers began), there was another which moved, be it five hundred yards or five thousand miles. Even those families which remain rooted in one spot usually had members who wandered farther afield. Since the mid-19th century, when census returns started to include places of birth, it is often possible to track down such migrants, whether they emigrated to other parts of the world or moved a few yards into another parish or another county. **The 1881 census statistics**, revealing that close on one million people, out of the 26 million then living in Great Britain, had been born elsewhere (including 767,261 in Ireland; 27,468 in the United States and 4,814 'at sea'), **give an idea of the scale of long-distance movement**; the extent of short-distance movement was infinitely greater.

Finding where your ancestors came from, or went to, before the 19th century is rarely easy. Monumental (Memorial) Inscriptions, with references to family members dying far away from their home base (see p.176); Wills, naming children as being last heard of *abroad, overseas, in foreign parts*, in *India*, or in America or Australasia; family papers, including letters written from, and photographs taken in, other parts of the country or world, can all provide evidence of movement.

Clues may be found in parish registers, particularly *'Dade style'* ones between 1770 and 1812, which can include names and places of residence for all four grandparents. The example cited in Chapter 12 of *Matthew Browne* of *York*, born in 1774, demonstrates that people did move considerable distances. His paternal grandfather (a gardener) came from *York*; his paternal grandmother (daughter of a fruiterer) from *Cheshunt* in Hertfordshire; his maternal grandfather (a currier) from *Bakewell* and his maternal grandmother from *Hayfield*, both in Derbyshire. Registers from several parishes in the city of York reveal the scale of movement of those with military connections (see p.260).

THE SETTLEMENT SYSTEM

The documentation connected with poor law administration is probably the most likely source for information about your ancestors' movements. In a nutshell, in England and Wales until 1834 a parish was responsible for the maintenance of its own poor, whether or not they were living in that parish when they applied for poor relief (money or food to help them survive). A system of *settlement examinations* (to ascertain to which parish a person properly belonged and to make sure that that parish would bear responsibility if the person or family fell on hard times), *settlement certificates* (which those leaving their parish of legal settlement to live elsewhere were supposed to carry with them and hand to the officers of their 'new' parish as an insurance policy), and *removal orders* was developed. Anne Cole's *An Introduction to Poor Law Documents before 1834* (FFHS: 2nd edition 2000) describes the system, the documents, and other sources where information on the poor may be found. For post-1834 Poor Law Records in England and Wales see the four Gibson Guides on *Poor Law Unions*.

WHERE MIGHT YOU FIND THE RECORDS?

Where such documentation survives in England and Wales, it will often be found among the parish chest material in county or diocesan record offices. Some offices hold name indexes to their settlement and removal papers; these indexes may be found online on the relevant record office's website but very little of the actual documentation is as yet online. It is always worth contacting the RO to ask if any poor law material has been published in any format, possibly by the local FHS.

The survival rate of pre-1834 papers relating to poor relief varies widely from county to county, and even from parish to parish within a county. Of 23 historic parishes in the city of York, with records held at the Borthwick Institute for Archives, only nine are listed as having any settlement/removal documents and, for several of these, a few 19th century documents are all that remain. Of the 30 existent settlement/removal documents, covering 1728-1849, which survive for the parish of *Holy Trinity Goodramgate in York*, more than half relate to movement between parishes within York and the same is true of other towns and cities which included more than one parish.

Remember that in some counties, principally in the north of England where parishes could cover thousands of acres, local government was often organised by township rather than by parish with each township within a parish having its own overseers, system of poor relief and records. If an ancestor, living at a distance, names a large town, particularly in census returns, as their place of birth this should be treated with caution. If a man says he was born in *Halifax* in Yorkshire, an immense parish with 23 townships, does he mean the *parish* or the *township*? The odds are that he means the *parish* (see p.69). All the *townships* have at least some surviving parish chest material, presently held at *Calderdale Archives* in *Halifax*, and searching the records for *Halifax township* alone could lead to your missing a vital piece of evidence which is to be found in a neighbouring township's records.

Always ascertain whether all records relating to a parish, particularly parish registers and parish chest material, are held in the same record office. *Harrogate (Christ Church)*, historically in the West Riding of Yorkshire but currently in North Yorkshire, has parish registers and some vestry minutes in the West Yorkshire Archive office in *Leeds* but the parish chest, including much poor law material, is in the North Yorkshire Record Office in *Northallerton* (deposited after 1974 as local government documentation) and the Quarter Sessions Records, which contain much information relating to settlement and removal, will be found in the West Yorkshire Archive Office in *Wakefield*. Our ancestors may not be the only ones who need to be 'people on the move'.

Vagrants' passes, often stating where a person was examined as to their settlement and sometimes providing details of the route by which they were sent back to their place of settlement, may be found in various record repositories, including the parish chest of the vagrant's eventual destination (see p.235), or parish or local government records in counties through which they passed (for example, details of vagrants' passes involving people from the northern counties can be found in Wiltshire County Treasurer's Finance Papers). Many of them were the wives and children of soldiers and sailors, being sent 'home' after their husbands had embarked at a port for service overseas. Churchwardens' and overseers' accounts frequently include the financial costs incurred by a parish or township in moving people along. The outlay could be considerable, particularly if the parish was on a direct route from ports used by the army, or from London.

The Acts establishing the system of poor law administration were often loosely drafted, full of loopholes, and with the wording open to interpretation. The increasing complexity of the legislation, and the possible financial consequences for parish officers and local government officials, is evidenced by *Burn*'s ***Justice of the Peace and Parish Officer*** which, in its 17th (1793) edition, under the heading **Poor**, contains 430 pages dealing with settlement and removal alone, including numerous examples of court judgements where the law had been questioned. The extent to which the laws in force at any given time were carried out depended very much on the individuals - overseers of the poor, constables, justices of the peace, even churchwardens - whose responsibility it was to operate the system. Humanitarian ones might bend the rules to suit individual cases; others would stick to the letter of the law even if it meant breaking up families.

Remember that they were always dealing with their own and fellow parishioners' money, usually raised via parish rates. Their funds were limited and they had to feed, clothe, house and find work for their own poor so the more they could limit the numbers, the better; dealing with vagrants, or other parishes' poor, was to be avoided if at all possible. In very general terms, overseers were responsible for moving people with settlement certificates; constables for vagrants and rogues and vagabonds.

Paperwork began to accumulate (in England and Wales) following the Act of Settlement of 1662 (officially, ***an Act for the better Releife of the Poore of this Kingdom***) but, for several decades, few records survive apart from references in the account books of various parish or township officers. Some idea of the scale of people moving around can be gained from the accounts of the parish of *Pannal* where, between 1661 and 1663, at least 76 un-named people with travel passes were given financial aid. Some of them are merely noted as being given *relief and lodging for one night*, and presumably then had to walk to the adjoining parishes of *Knaresborough*, *Spofforth* or

Hampsthwaite, but those described as cripples, and many women and children, were taken on horseback or by cart.

The cart mentioned above may have been a local vehicle but the *cripple cart* - used to convey people often long distances to their parish of settlement - was a familiar sight on the roads in the 17th and 18th centuries. Contracts were issued to operate such carts and there was constant bickering between parishes and townships, particularly those on major highways, over the costs involved and how much each parish should pay for the 'taxi service'. West Riding Quarter Sessions records reveal details of quarrels, particularly between parishes on the *Doncaster* to *Ferrybridge* stretch of the Great North Road, where smaller parishes felt that they were being charged too much.

RIGHTS OF SETTLEMENT AND SETTLEMENT EXAMINATIONS

Almost everyone born in England and Wales began with a settlement in their place of birth but this was usually over-ridden when a settlement by inhabitancy was acquired. *Inhabitancy* covered a wide range of options - 11 being listed in *Burn* - the most common being marriage (for women); serving an apprenticeship (seven years, possible from the age of seven); being hired and in service for a full year (the amount of litigation generated as parishes argued as to what constituted a full year brings home the lengths many would go to to prevent workers gaining a settlement); renting or owning property of a certain value (another fruitful source of dispute); paying parish rates; or serving as a parish officer.

Settlement examinations (usually conducted when a person either applied, or seemed likely to apply, for parish relief or was picked up begging) tend to be the most informative of the documents and are the only ones likely to include ages for adults. Examinations like that of *Nicholas Kennedy*, a livery-lace weaver aged 40, apprehended begging in *Sandy* in Bedfordshire in 1787 and removed to *St Mary Castlegate in York* on the strength of a settlement gained some ten years previously when he had been hired there for one year (and served 1¼ years) explain why parishes kept such a strict eye on hirings and firings.

Until 1795 anyone who had entered a parish without the proper paperwork (unless they had managed to remain there unchallenged for 40 days) could, in theory, be removed to their last place of settlement. After 22 June 1795 this could not be done *until he shall have become actually chargeable* and applied for parish relief. Problems occur with 'foreigners', which in England and Wales included Scots and Irish, because they had no settlement in the country by birth and, as many were itinerant or seasonal workers (or soldiers), they often failed to obtain one by other means. They were sometimes ordered to be removed to a suitable place to enter Scotland, cross to Ireland or leave the country but might well be escorted to the parish boundary and left there so tracing their movements can be very difficult.

226

Where a foreigner's wife and family was involved, the wife might be allowed to retain her previous settlement.   Thus in 1769 the removal of *Margaret wife of Charles Grimmer and a Male Infant Child aged about one month, Charles Grimmer having no legal settlement in England having lately run away and left her* was ordered from *Holy Trinity Goodramgate in York* to *Water Fulford*, a few miles away, *her last legal Place of Settlement before Marriage.*

Even if you believe that an ancestor was born in a parish and remained there all his life it can still pay to check the parish chest; documents may reveal that he moved away and came back or that his legal settlement was elsewhere. *George Radford*, a labourer aged 26, was born in *Elmton* in Derbyshire. In June 1808, when he was examined, he was living there with his wife and family, baptising his children in the parish church, but his examination revealed that he had *performed several years service in different places*, of which the most recent which qualified for a settlement (taking precedence over his birthplace) was with *Francis Bagshaw* of *Langwith*. If *George* required parish relief, there was liable to be a dispute as to whose responsibility he was.   He says *he has heard and believes that the said Francis Bagshaw's House stands part in the parish of Upper Langwith* [in Derbyshire] *and part in Nether Langwith* [in the parish of *Cuckney* in Nottinghamshire], *That the room that Examinant used to sleep in is in that part which stands in Nether Langwith.* The family remained in *Elmton* but did *Langwith* or *Cuckney* at some point have to pay for his upkeep? Answering the question could involve making searches in record offices in both counties.

The practice of permitting someone claiming relief to remain in a parish, with their parish of settlement paying for them to be maintained there, was a very common one. *George Knowles*, although baptised in the parish of *St Michael le Belfrey in York* in 1775, gained his settlement there because of his apprenticeship, beginning in 1790, to *Thomas Braithwaite*, who resided in the parish, and *for the last six years of his apprenticeship he resided and slept at the house of Thomas Braithwaite.* When, in 1849, the overseers of *Holy Trinity Goodramgate* wanted to return him, as an elderly pauper, to *St Michael* it was recorded that for more than twenty years, while residing in *Holy Trinity*, he had been relieved by *St Michael* with sums varying from *2s 6d* to *1s 6d* per week. In 1820 (see p.268) *George* had been elected a freeman of the City of York so do not make the mistake of assuming that those in need of relief were always from the labouring classes - illness, accident or bad luck could force unexpected people to ask for help.

Cities like *London*, *Norwich* and *York*, with a number of churches, often had duplicate dedications. London had eight churches called *All Hallows* and more than 10 dedicated to *St Mary*; *Norwich* had three dedicated to *St John* and four to *St Peter*. *York* had three churches dedicated to the *Holy Trinity* and three to *St Mary*, each distinguished by adding a street name. In 1819 *Mary Price* was picked up begging in *Grantham* in Lincolnshire and removed to *York* because she said, in her examination, that she had *served one year with Mr John Smith under a yearly hiring in the parish of St Mary.* A note on her removal order says: *There are several parishes of St Mary in the City of York: the vagrant cannot be received as she cannot state which of them is the place of her settlement.* Was *Mary* shuffled between the three until *St Mary Castlegate* (amongst whose papers her removal order survives) finally accepted responsibility for her? There is no mention as to whether she was single, married or widowed, no indication of her age and no trace of a baptism or marriage in *St Mary Castlegate.* Other cities presumably encountered the same problem.

MEN AND OCCUPATIONS

FAMILY HISTORY AND LOCAL HISTORY

Family history and local history go hand-in-hand and nowhere are the two more closely linked than when you are trying to find out why your ancestor suddenly appears in a parish and lives and dies there, without leaving a clue as to whence he came. You may be fortunate enough to find settlement documentation in the parish chest which will answer your questions but often you will be left wondering why he chose that time and place to surface.

Learning something about the history of the area where he (and possibly his family) appears, what occupations were common there, who the local landowners were, which manor courts existed, and whether a new industry was established around the time of his arrival, may provide clues which enable you to discover where he originated. The same works in reverse: if a family disappears from the records, ascertain whether an industry declined, an employer moved his workforce to another area, an enclosure act (see p.267) or a succession of bad harvests displaced the agricultural workers.

Why did *John Ethell*, son of a Yorkshire farm labourer, move to Kent around 1810? He did so because he was a carpenter and shipwright in *Hull* who heard of opportunities to work in the naval dockyards at *Chatham* and *Gillingham* building ships for the Napoleonic Wars. He settled in Kent and his descendants still live there.

Around 1750 *Thomas Bourne* died at *Neston* in Cheshire, leaving a wife and four young sons. He was a tenant of *Lord Crewe* whose steward granted the bereaved family tenancy of a smaller farm on another of his estates at *Barthomley*, some 35 miles away. Descendants remained in that area for two hundred years.

The ship *Two Friends* sailed from *Hull* on 7 March 1774 and arrived in *Halifax, Nova Scotia*, on 9 May carrying, among many other Yorkshiremen: *John Fawceit* farmer aged 29, his wife *Jane* aged 28 and four year old daughter *Mary*, emigrating because *rent raised too high*; *William Hodgson*, husbandman aged 22 *to seek a better livelihood*; *Robert Fawent*, sailclothmaker aged 30 *on business as agent*; and *Thomas Harrison*, who gave as his reason for going *rents raised by William Weddell* (see p.230).

In 1816, in *Northwich*, Cheshire, Methodist Minister *Joseph Meek* baptised eight of his children on the same day, giving their dates of birth between 1805 and 1816 and their places of birth as *Ponder Cawfield*, North Britain (Scotland); *Inverness; Thirsk, Malton, Driffield* (2) and *Whitby* (all in Yorkshire); and *Northwich*. *Joseph Meek* married *Frances Smith* at *West Heslerton* in Yorkshire in 1804. Look in the IGI and you will find all eight baptisms recorded, mostly in Wesleyan Methodist Chapels, in the years when the births occurred (see Double Baptisms p.114). The IGI provides the baptisms of three further children: 1818 in *Bacup*, Lancashire; 1820 in *Ashton under Lyne*, Lancashire and 1822 in *Belper*, Derbyshire. Methodist ministers moved every few years. *Joseph Meek* moved at least 10 times during the 17 years when his wife is known to have been bearing children and he presumably thought it advisable in 1816 to keep a record of where his children to date had been born. A likely 'pitfall' here: the birthplaces of most of the children given in 1816 'match' where they were baptised but the two children born in *Driffield* were baptised in *Bridlington* (although there was a Wesleyan Chapel in *Driffield*); and a 'possibility' as the eldest child, whose birthplace has not been identified, was baptised at *St Vigeans* in Angus - it pays to check all possible sources.

These were all people who, before the full impact of the industrial revolution changed the pattern of migration for ever, moved considerable distances for very different reasons and without leaving documentary evidence in the English poor law system. So how was it possible to locate where they were born? An 1851 census entry provided the clue for *John Ethell*; a document written in 1846 by *Thomas*'s youngest son for the *Bourne* family; a chapel register for *Joseph Meek*; and *Peter Wilson Coldham*'s book **Emigrants from England to the American Colonies 1773-1776** (1988) for the others.

EMIGRATION

The 1770s saw a marked increase in the numbers leaving England for North America. Most of those recorded give only the county from which they came so how is it possible for their descendants to find further information? The IGI is one possibility but if that fails (and many had very common names) turn to local history. By the 1770s the enclosure movement (conversion of the open field system into compact landholdings - see p.267) was in full swing in most areas and ascertaining which villages were involved in enclosure and the subsequent rise in rents (which many labourers could not afford to pay), in the months before the emigrant ship sailed may provide vital clues. Details of enclosure awards should be found in the record office covering the relevant area. A few of those departing made a final dig at their landlords which might help you. *William Weddell*, the landlord 'named and blamed' by *Thomas Harrison* (see p.229) was the owner of *Newby Hall* near *Ripon* in Yorkshire so *Thomas*'s baptism may be found in *Ripon* parish registers.

Following the **1834 Poor Law Amendment Act**, the Poor Law Commissioners, many Boards of Guardians and parish officials in England and Wales provided 'assisted passages' to enable the poor to emigrate - it was cheaper to pay for (or at least to contribute to) a ticket than to maintain someone on long-term poor relief. This practice, together with the highland clearances in Scotland (beginning around 1750) and the poor living conditions in Ireland, coupled with the potato famine in the 1840s, saw hundreds of thousands emigrating firstly to north America and later to Australasia. Local newspapers in the mid-19th century often carried advertisements, particularly from shipping companies, stating when a particular ship would be sailing for Canada, Australia or New Zealand and painting a rosy picture of life there.

Bear in mind the thousands of members of the LDS Church who emigrated to America from Liverpool during the second half of the 19th and early part of the 20th centuries, together with many thousands more from Scandinavia who entered England via *Hull*, crossed the country by train, and sailed from *Liverpool*; also the close to one million Jews from Eastern Europe who followed the same route between about 1880 and 1920. Some of the 'emigrants' from both groups decided to remain in England.

ESTATE WORKERS

Landlords were often seen as 'the villains of the piece' but many did their best for their tenants (see the *Bourne* family p.228). If you suspect that your ancestors were tenants on a large estate it is worth trying to locate the estate papers, which may contain lists of tenants and other employees, ranging from stewards, butlers, footmen, and maids to land agents, gardeners and gamekeepers, and finding out if any work has been done locally on them. Many of the gentry and aristocracy owned land in several parts of the country and the papers will commonly be held either at their main seat or in a record office close to it. The *Vernon archive* in Chester includes a set of detailed mid-18th century maps for the family's estates, principally those in Cheshire and Derbyshire, but including one for *Widdrington* in Northumberland, which name their tenants. West Yorkshire Archives in Leeds holds papers relating to many estates including those of: the *Earls of Harewood* in Yorkshire, Buckinghamshire, Essex, London and the West Indies; the *Earls of Mexborough* in Yorkshire, Derbyshire, Nottinghamshire and Northumberland; the *Gascoigne of Parlington* family in Yorkshire, Scotland and Ireland; the *Newby Hall* archives, with papers from the *Compton, Vyner, Robinson* and *Weddell* families and their estates in Yorkshire, Cheshire, Gloucestershire, Lincolnshire, London and Worcestershire.

Employees could be transferred between estates, or might accompany the family on their journeyings around the country, to another estate, to London or to a spa town. Some might find a spouse on another family estate; others stay with a daughter of the family when she married and moved elsewhere; elderly ones retire and be given the right to live in a cottage on one of the estates; ambitious ones change employers and end up on the other side of the country. Only if they leave the family's employ and fall upon hard times are you likely to find such people in poor law records. Gamekeepers, most commonly found in the northern counties and Scotland, and in East Anglia where they were responsible for the coney (rabbit) warrens, can cause particular problems because they were often employed on an estate well away from where they grew up, to avoid any possibility of their turning a blind eye to poaching by friends or relatives.

TRADE AND INDUSTRY

Those employed in some trades could also often find themselves on the move. The industrial revolution created hundreds of thousands of jobs for workers in the new manufactories and mines. At the same time, the factories had to be built and housing provided for both employers and employees. Stone masons, bricklayers, joiners, plasterers - not occupations normally associated with mobility - went where the work was. Members of an *Ethell* family, well-established in *Birmingham* as decorators and paper hangers, disappeared in the early years of the 19th century and reappeared twenty years later with children born in *London*, where they had been plying their trade.

Hatting used to be a widespread cottage industry. With mechanisation, smaller firms, which largely employed outworkers, were absorbed into bigger units. *Christy's*, which expanded in this way and became one of the country's largest hat-making firms, centred its manufacturing into some five locations. As is sometimes the case for large firms today, staff mobility became a job requirement and workers were moved, often large distances, at the whim of the employer. There seems to have been a particularly close connection between *Christy's* works in Gloucestershire and Cheshire, running throughout the 19th century. The 1851 and 1881 censuses both reveal hatters from *Frampton Cotterell* in Gloucestershire living and working in *Stockport* in Cheshire and nearby in *Denton, Gorton* and *Heaton Norris* in Lancashire.

In June 1816, following Luddite riots in Leicestershire, *John Heathcoat*, often called the founder of the machine-made lace trade, left *Loughborough* and moved to *Tiverton*, in Devon, to establish a new factory there. Up to 500 of his workers and their families followed him, most walking the 200 miles. His brother *Thomas*, and two of his former partners, established lace mills in the *Barnstaple* area of Devon and people born in Leicestershire and Nottinghamshire can be found scattered around Somerset and North Devon in the census returns of 1841-1861.

In the same year, *lace-makers* from *Nottingham* moved to *Calais* in France and established a successful lace-making industry there. The 1848 revolution in France obliged most of the *Lacemakers of Calais* to return to England and many of them (more than 700 in 1848 alone) then emigrated to Australia (although not as lacemakers). Details of those who emigrated are available on a number of websites.

At the same time, *framework knitters* (a home-based industry), particularly in Leicestershire and Nottinghamshire, were suffering severe hardship due to the development of lace-making machines; many emigrated to America and to South Africa and, again, there are plenty of websites which provide details.

In 1870 *Wilson Cammell & Co.* (later part of *Cammell Laird* shipbuilders) opened a factory in *Dronfield*, Derbyshire, manufacturing rails for railways worldwide; workers from their *Sheffield* factory moved to *Dronfield* in 1873. The *Dronfield* factory was closed, for economic reasons, in 1882 and a new one opened in *Workington* in Cumberland. Some families moved with the factory and can be traced in census returns, moving from Yorkshire to Derbyshire to Cumberland.

Fishermen sailed round the coasts of Britain. From Yorkshire men followed the herring north to harbours in Durham, Northumberland and as far as Scotland, or sailed south to East Anglia, London, Kent and along the south coast to Devon and beyond. Devon men sailed west to Cornwall and up to Bristol or east along the south coast.

MINERS

Mineral mining of all sorts was another industry whose workers moved around. Tin miners from Cornwall; lead miners from Derbyshire, Durham, Yorkshire, Wales and Scotland; copper miners from the Lake District, can all be found criss-crossing the country, leaving an area where a seam ran out and finding work where a new one was discovered. They, together with ironstone miners from the Midlands, can all be found flocking to the coal fields of northeast England and south Wales as they were developed in the 19th century. Some also went to help with constructing the railways - particularly in areas where tunnels had to be dug. The availability of the 1881 census on CD and online made it much easier to track families who moved long distances during the 19th century, to understand their reasons and to realise the scale of such migration.

Local history again goes hand-in-hand with family history. Living in Yorkshire in 1881, for instance, there were 32,000 people from Derbyshire; 30,000 from Norfolk and Suffolk; 25,000 from Staffordshire and 11,000 from Warwickshire. I quote these counties because I know from my own research that ironstone mining in the Midlands was in serious decline and East Anglia was suffering from agricultural depression. Meanwhile, the coalfields and iron and steel industries of the northeast were expanding rapidly and thousands of families, whatever their previous occupations, were flocking here to become coal miners or metal workers. My husband's great-grandfather originated from *Wednesbury* and his wife from *Darlaston* both in Staffordshire. He was a miner who moved north as the Yorkshire coalfield expanded and ironstone mining (his previous occupation) declined. In 1881 of the 25,000 people living in Yorkshire but born in Staffordshire, 1,121 of them were in the pit village of *Normanton* and of these 90 were from *Wednesbury* and *Darlaston*.

NAVIGATORS (NAVVIES)

The word *navigator* first came into use in the 1770s and generally meant a canal cutter. During the canal era (1760-1840) gangs of workers, many drawn from labourers and vagrants displaced by enclosure awards, and augmented by Scottish and Irish migrants, moved around the country building canals. In 1832, according to the OED, the shortened form *navvy* was first used and, for the next half-century, was applied almost entirely to those building the railway network throughout the United Kingdom. There is a common perception that most navies were Irish but studying the population of some of the camps or 'shanty towns' in census returns provides a rather different picture.

Particularly in the north of England, where lines were being constructed across open moorland and no accommodation was available nearby, some provision had to be made for the workers and 'shanty towns' housing hundreds of men were built and some families moved in. When the 1871 census was taken some 6,000 men in Yorkshire and Cumberland were working on the *Settle and Carlisle Railway*, with 2,000 of them engaged in building the *Ribblehead Viaduct* (which took almost five years to complete). There were a number of settlements on the surrounding moors. One at *Mossdale*, near *Hawes*, housed several hundred people from 30 of the 39 English counties, from South Wales, Scotland and Ireland, principally in 19 'railway huts'. The population included, as well as navvies and their families, blacksmiths, joiners, stonemasons and representatives of many other occupations. The navvy 'village' at *Batty Green* (near the viaduct) had a population of 2,000 and boasted a school and schoolmaster, a missionary, and a library. So many people died, from accidents and disease, that the railway company paid for the extension of the churchyard at *Chapel-le-Dale* and around 200 men, women and children from the 'village' are buried here. When work on a line was finished, settlements were abandoned and in time vanished but their names may survive on certificates and in parish registers.

If you have lost track of ancestors who may have been involved in building the railways it could be worth ascertaining when work laying the major lines was taking place and looking for records in that area. Many of the more experienced navvies were employed by contractors and moved around the country, following the work, so you may find an ancestor from Cornwall working in London in the 1830s, East Anglia in the 1840s, South Wales in the

1850s, the Midlands in the 1860s or Yorkshire in the 1870s. There are many books and online sites which give a detailed chronology of when the various lines, tunnels and viaducts were constructed.

ON THE MOVE

The coming of the railways was the cause of an unprecedented movement of people. The population of *Crewe* in Cheshire (see p.9) grew from around 1,000 in 1841 to 5,000 in 1851 because of the arrival of the railway after 1842. The census reveals that some of them came from elsewhere in Cheshire but many were from further afield with a number from other early railway centres like *Northampton, Swindon* and *York*.

Boys travelled hundreds of miles to public schools; *students* converged on *Oxford* and *Cambridge* universities; *journeymen* (having completed their apprenticeships) tramped the country looking for work. Some occupations - *pedlars, carriers, any branch of the armed forces, travelling players* (often referred to as comedians or tragedians, depending on whether they performed comedies or tragedies); *coachmen, drovers* - by their very nature will generally involve men (and often their families) moving around the country. *Clergymen, missionaries* (not all of whom went overseas – see p.233), *medical men, lawyers, schoolteachers, merchants* will often take up posts far from where they were born. Far more people were on the move than is generally realised.

MARRIED WOMEN

Equality of the sexes (to whatever degree you think this has been achieved) is a modern development. Women and children tended to suffer most from the settlement and removal system because they could rarely acquire a settlement in their own right but automatically took that of their husband or father. *Robert Burton* wrote, in his **Anatomy of Melancholy** in 1621 *England is a paradise for women and hell for horses* but it is doubtful whether many women, seen at the time and for centuries to come as little better than chattels to their husbands or fathers, would have agreed with him. The Settlement Acts, beginning in 1662, brought untold misery to countless women who were shuffled round Britain, like pieces on a chessboard, often with children in tow. Do not make the mistake of assuming that a married woman, before the late 19th century, was treated as an individual in her own right. Despite the fact that the documentation you find is in her name and is going to affect her future, you will often learn more about her husband than about her.

After 1662, if a married woman, whether under duress from parish officers to move on or simply needing financial assistance to return home, was obliged to travel alone, with or without children, you may find yourself with a detailed snapshot of a short period in her life but no idea of where she came from or where she ended up. When a woman married she took her husband's place of settlement and forfeited any previous settlement she had gained in her own right by birth or inhabitancy. If her husband died, deserted her, could not afford to maintain her or disappeared overseas with the army or navy, she could find herself sent to his place of settlement, which could well be in a county she had never visited and where she knew no-one.

A settlement certificate for a woman in her own right is comparatively rare; those which do exist almost always relate to spinsters or widows. Removal orders will often not specify whether a woman travelling alone is, or has been, married. Her parish of birth is sometimes stated but do not assume that the surname on the order is the one she bore at baptism. Ages of adults may be included in settlement examinations, rarely elsewhere, but ages of children are commonly given.

The cases of *Anna and Hannah Greenwood* (see **Beggars**) illustrate just how little control most women had over their own destinies; how much long-distance movement took place; and the amount of detail which may be included in the documentation available. One girl, leaving the *Isles of Scilly* to work on the mainland, ended up many years later being examined at *Frittenden* in Kent, having worked gradually eastwards across the south of England, gaining and losing several husbands (and settlements) en route, all set out in her examination.

BEGGARS

Anna Greenwood, apprehended for begging in *Shaw*, Berkshire, in November 1780, is a perfect example of a 'detailed snapshot'. In her examination she claimed a settlement in *Bramham*, Yorkshire which her husband, *Thomas Greenwood*, had gained by service. A removal order and vagrancy pass, issued on 22 November, and annotated in each parish in which she halted on her journey north, details her two-week journey. On 22 November the constable of *Shaw* was to 'convey the said vagabond' to *St Aldate's parish* in *Oxford*; *St Aldate*'s constable passed her to *St Thomas's parish* also in *Oxford*; on 25 November *St Thomas*'s sent her on to *Woolvercot* (2½ miles north of *Oxford*); the same day that parish conveyed her to *Aynho* in Northamptonshire; on 28 November *Aynho* passed her to *Adderbury* in Oxfordshire; on 29 November *Adderbury* sent her to *Mollington* in Warwickshire; on 1 December she went from *Mollington* to *Witherly* in Leicestershire; on 4 December from there to *Measham* in Derbyshire; on 5 December to *Sheffield* in Yorkshire (see extract on p.236) and thence to *Bramham*, where the settlement examination and removal order survive. There would have been a duplicate copy of the removal order filed at *Shaw*. It is worth checking *Anna*'s route on a map to gain an idea of how far she travelled each day.

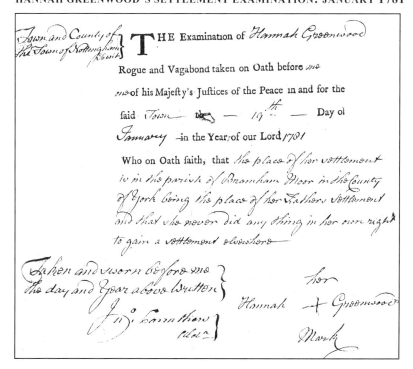

HANNAH GREENWOOD'S SETTLEMENT EXAMINATION: JANUARY 1781

On 19 January 1781 her daughter, *Hannah* was arrested for begging in *Nottingham,* examined (see p. 236) and started her journey to *Bramham*, said to be the place of her father's settlement, via *Arnold*. Mother and daughter may have met in *Bramham* but neither of them appears to have remained there. *Anna* did not marry there and *Hannah* was not born there; their sole connection with *Bramham* seems to have been that *Thomas Greenwood* once worked there for a year. Neither removal order gives ages or any indication of *Thomas*'s occupation or whether he was still alive.

HANNAH GREENWOOD'S REMOVAL ORDER: JANUARY 1781

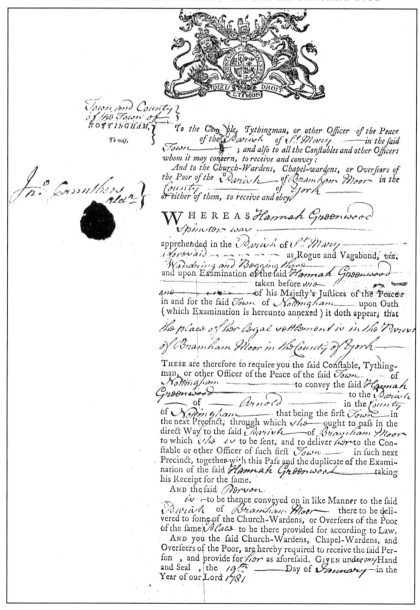

Examples taken from the records of *St Mary Castlegate* in *York*, a parish with strong military connections, show that being married to a soldier, sailor or militiaman was not an easy life, especially if he was sent overseas.

Maria Mobs, apprehended for begging in February 1781 in *Little Brickhill* in Buckinghamshire, said in her examination that she had been born in *Winchester*, Hampshire, but had married *John Mob*s, a soldier in the Yorkshire Volunteers, whose settlement was in the parish of *St Mary Castlegate* in *York*. To *York* she was sent, hundreds of miles from her birthplace. *Mob(b)s* is a surname almost unknown in Yorkshire, occurring much more frequently in counties surrounding Buckinghamshire, so Maria was forced to walk (unless she was lucky enough to hitch a ride on a cart - see p.226) some 160 miles to *York*, a strange city, from which she soon disappeared, probably retracing her steps to her own, or her husband's, family and liable to find herself in the house of correction and being whipped if she was apprehended begging again.

The same parish on 15 March 1814 ordered that *Elizabeth, wife of William Dorrington*, a private in the 4th or Royal Irish Dragoon Guards, together with her daughters, both aged under seven, be removed to *Harlow* in Essex (his place of settlement). The order was suspended because *Elizabeth* was heavily pregnant (her son was born on 18 April and baptised eight days later) but reinstated on 19 July, with an invoice for £9 3s 0d to be sent to *Harlow* to recover the money *St Mary's* had spent maintaining her. Her husband, meanwhile, was (from army records) in barracks in *Edinburgh*, his regiment having returned to *York* from the Peninsula in mid-1812 and moved to *Edinburgh* around the time *Elizabeth*'s removal order was made. *Dorrington* is a common surname in Essex but, again, almost unknown in Yorkshire. *William* was discharged from the regiment in May 1817: did he find his wife and children waiting for him in Essex?

Finally, the story of *Mary Hopkirk* serves as a reminder that all possible sources should be searched and that a removal may only be temporary. In 1798 an order was issued for *Mary, pregnant wife of Adam Hopkirk, a mariner absent from her in HM Service for three years*, together with two children under seven, to be removed from *York* to *Sunderland*, County Durham. (*Adam* was probably one of the men who became a mariner as a result of the 1795 Quota Act, under which each county had to provide a stated number of volunteers for the navy.) The order does not say whether *Sunderland* was *Adam*'s birthplace or his previous place of work and gives no indication of *Mary*'s origins. Fortunately, the parish register of *St Mary Castlegate*, which includes baptisms for two of the couple's children in 1793 and 1803, is a *Dade* register which names both grandfathers. *Adam* is described on each occasion as a tailor, and his father is a baker from *Sunderland*. *Mary* was born at *Kelfield*, south of *York*. *Mary*'s removal order, triggered by her pregnancy, reveals both *Adam*'s naval service and that *Mary* was being sent to his home town, to bear a child which was presumably not his. The parish register makes no mention of *Adam*'s naval career or *Mary*'s 'mistake' but shows them back together in *York* in 1803 with *Adam* having reverted to tailoring. What happened to Mary between 1798 and 1803?

CHILDREN

The number seven is often thought to be a 'lucky number' but to children caught up in the poor law system it must have seemed the opposite for within days of reaching their seventh birthday their lives could change completely and often not for the better.

In the eyes of the law, until the age of seven a child was regarded as a *nurse child*, in need of support from at least one of its parents or relatives. A legitimate child took the settlement of its father; an illegitimate one generally that of its mother, but from the age of seven a child was deemed capable of gaining a settlement of its own. This is why many early settlement and removal documents, whilst not giving exact ages for children, do distinguish between those under and over the age of seven. *Anne Cole*'s **Poor Law Documents Before 1834** gives half a dozen scenarios which could result in families being split up and children (particularly if they were illegitimate, orphaned or step-children) being removed from one, or both, parents, or from the only homes they knew, at the age of seven or, in some circumstances, even younger. In 1738, for example, following the examination of their mother *Hannah Lofthouse*, the removal of her children, *Mary* aged 4 and *Jane* aged 4 months, both described as *Lofthouse alias Moor* was ordered from *York* to *Leeds* (where both children had been baptised as *Moor*). Other instances include a child aged 7 years and 11 days moved from Lincolnshire to Cumbria and two recently orphaned children sent from Cheshire (where they were born) to Nottinghamshire (their late father's place of settlement). Most 'children on the move', however, were orphans, foundlings and others whose parents could not afford to maintain them.

How many readers have an ancestor who suddenly appears in a parish, marries and remains there for generations but with no indication of where they came from originally? It is always worth considering whether they could have arrived as a 'parish apprentice' from many miles away, or via the Foundling Hospital (see Chapter 21) or other charity hospitals. Overseers of the poor, and governors of charity institutions, were responsible for finding apprenticeships for their own poor children but do not make the mistake of assuming that they found them masters close to home and family or friends. From the age of seven they could be apprenticed *to the sea service* (which, as well as the Royal Navy, covered shipwrights, fishermen and ship owners), to factory owners, farmers or mine owners.

239

A particularly common route taken by large numbers of pauper children was that from the poorhouses of *London*, the south-east of England, and East Anglia, to the mills and factories of the north of England and the north midlands. If you are trying to find where an ancestor originated, especially in the late 18th and early 19th centuries, it is worth looking into the history of the area where he settled to see if anything has been written on local industry and, in particular, on how the works were staffed. Sometimes an agreement will be found between a mill or factory owner and certain parishes to supply him with apprentices. *Francis Horner*, in 1815, quoted to the House of Commons a contract between a London parish and a Lancashire manufacturer which stipulated that *among every 20 sound children there should be one idiot.*

It can also pay to look into the family history of the millowner. *James Pattison*, who had established a silk mill at *Congleton* in Cheshire in the 1750s, had married *Mary Maxey*, whose father owned an estate at *Plumstead* in Kent and the parish register of *St Nicholas, Plumstead*, contains an entry in 1781 that it was *Agreed that all girls at the height of 4 feet at the age of 6 years are to be bound out apprentice to Nathaniel Pattison esq.* (*James*'s son) *at the silk mills at Congleton in Cheashire to be found with two suites of cloathes, a working suite and a Hollyday suite. Arthur Redford*, in **Labour Migration in England 1800-1850**, quotes apprentices also being sent to the *Congleton mills* in the early 1800s from *St Andrew's [Holborn]*. As the late *James Blundell*, who first brought this example to my attention, said, it would be an interesting exercise to compare the baptism registers of *Plumstead* and *Holborn* with the marriage register for *Astbury* (to which *Congleton* was a chapelry) to ascertain how many families, resident in Cheshire for at least two centuries, have Kentish or London ancestors.

Quarry Bank Mill, at *Styal* in Cheshire, founded by *Samuel Greg* in 1784 and now run by the National Trust as *a working Georgian cotton mill,* also imported apprentices from the midlands and south and visitors today can see both the Apprentice House where they lived and the mill where they worked, and gain an idea of what life must have been like for the children in what was considered a well-run mill. *Samuel Oldknow*, whose mill was at *Mellor*, on the Derbyshire /Cheshire border, in 1796 took on 35 boys and 33 girls from *Clerkenwell* in London as apprentices and regularly received children, particularly girls, from the Foundling Hospital. In 1792 the town of *Bury St Edmunds* in Suffolk sent 22 children (eight from the parish of *St James*, 14 from *St Mary*) as apprentices to Ackers & Co. in *Manchester*. The notorious *Litton* and *Cressbrook* mills in Derbyshire each had several hundred apprentices and *Robert Blincoe*'s **Memoirs**, published in the 1820s, and accounts in the **Ashton [under Lyne] Chronicle** in 1849, detail the horrendous conditions which the children endured. One account of life at *Cressbrook* cites children there from *St Giles [Holborn], Clerkenwell, Marylebone* and the *Duke of York's School* (established in 1801 for the maintenance and support of the children of Regular soldiers), as well as from *Birmingham* and *Bristol*. Pauper children could be sent anywhere in the country. Add to these examples the hundreds of cotton manufactories in Lancashire, woollen manufactories in Yorkshire, and coal mines in the north of England which similarly welcomed pauper apprentices and you should gain some idea of the scale of 'children on the move' from south to north.

SCOTLAND & IRELAND

In *Scotland*, details of parish poor relief both before and after their change of system in 1845 may be found in heritors (landowners) or kirk sessions records in the National Archives of Scotland but surviving documentation is sparse; post-1845 records will often be found in local archives.

Ireland had no national system of poor relief prior to the Irish Poor Law Act of 1838, which was heavily influenced by the English Poor Law Administration Act of 1834.

RESOLUTIONS:

I will remember that people have always moved, either voluntarily or under duress.

I will remember that women and children rarely had a choice as to whether they moved.

CHAPTER 21

THE FOUNDLING HOSPITAL AND ITS CHILDREN

RECORDS

The Foundling Hospital in London (and some of its Branch Hospitals) kept detailed records of the children who passed through their hands (27,000 of them between 1741 and 1954) and, if it can be established that an ancestor was in the Hospital, it is possible, with luck, to obtain a detailed picture of their early life (see Chapter 22). The Foundling Hospital records (some eight tons of them) are held at LMA (www.cityoflondon.gov.uk/lma), which issues a useful leaflet entitled *Finding Your Foundling*, and records of the Branch Hospitals may be found in the appropriate local record office. The baptism registers for the Hospital are in class RG 4 at TNA (with a copy in LMA) and are available on FamilySearch but note that there are gaps in the series - including 1758-1759, which would have included several thousand children (see **1756-1760** below) including *Thomas Ithill* (see Chapter 22).

ORIGINS

Thomas Coram, a retired sea-captain, established the Foundling Hospital in London in 1741 mainly to help orphaned, unwanted and abandoned children. Originally situated in *Hatton Garden*, it moved to a permanent home in *Bloomsbury Fields* in 1747 and, in 1926 (as the *Thomas Coram Foundation for Children*) it moved to Brunswick Square where today the *Foundling Museum* (well worth a visit) can be found.

1756-1760: INDISCRIMINATE ADMISSION

A limited number of children were admitted in its early years (about 1500 between 1741 and 1755), and that only after a check to make sure they were healthy, but by 1756 applications for admission were so great that the governors of the Hospital asked Parliament for financial assistance. Parliament gave this - on condition that the Hospital would accept all children offered to it, whatever their state of health. Between 1756 and 1760 (when Parliament withdrew its grant), during the so-called period of *Indiscriminate Admission*, the Foundling Hospital took in 14,934 children of whom two-thirds died in early infancy. Babies could either be abandoned (often with a note attached asking that they be delivered to the Foundling Hospital) or deposited in the basket at the entrance to the Hospital, when all the mother (or other person) had to do was to ring the bell to notify the gatekeeper that the basket was occupied and then disappear. Tokens (commonly half a coin, a piece of cloth or ribbon, scraps of paper or even pebbles) were often left with the baby both as a means of identification should a parent wish to reclaim the child at a later date and as proof that the baby had been handed in alive if the mother was later accused of infanticide (a hanging offence). Many parishes throughout England saw the indiscriminate admission policy as a convenient way of disposing of illegitimate children who might be a charge on their parishes. There was a sizeable trade in unwanted babies and no shortage of people prepared to transport them to London and deliver them to the Foundling Hospital. Certainly in Shropshire (from whence my own ancestor (see p.248) was sent to London at about one month old) parishes appear to have gathered together a number of illegitimate babies and sent them by cart to London. Where children were 'handed in' like this, as opposed to being left in the basket, a certificate was issued and these can sometimes be found among parish papers (annotated on the back with the original name of the baby and its mother's name).

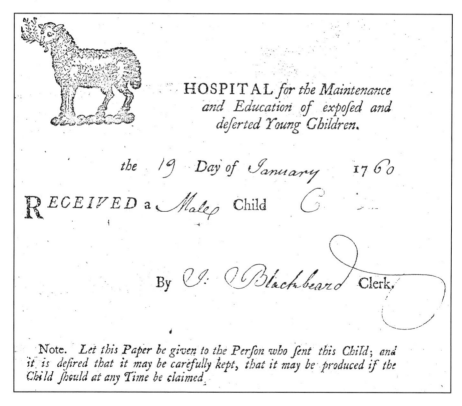

HOSPITAL *for the Maintenance and Education of expofed and deferted Young Children.*

the *19* Day of *January* 17 *60*

RECEIVED a *Male* Child *C*

By *J. Blackbeard* Clerk.

Note. *Let this Paper be given to the Perfon who fent this Child; and it is defired that it may be carefully kept, that it may be produced if the Child fhould at any Time be claimed.*

A FOUNDLING'S CHILDHOOD

All children were admitted at the Hospital in *London* and they were then immediately placed out to nurse with wet-nurses or foster-mothers in country districts (see below), generally until the age of five or six. At this point they

243

were returned to the Hospital in *London* and then apprenticed out (with the master being paid by the Hospital to take the child - the reverse of the normal process for apprenticeships), usually until the age of 21; most of the boys went out either to farmers or to manufactories or were sent into the army or navy, the majority of the girls went into domestic service or manufactories.

Obviously, during the period of indiscriminate admission, the number of women needed to foster and wet-nurse the foundlings increased markedly and the Hospital experienced some difficulty in finding enough suitable substitute-mothers. In the early days, and after 1760, districts in Surrey and Kent were mainly used to provide foster-parents but, in the intervening years, wet-nurses were drawn from a wide area including *Newbury, Reading* and *Twyford* in Berkshire; *Chalfont* and *Denham* in Buckinghamshire; *Epping* in Essex; *St Albans, Berkhamstead, Cheshunt, Great Gaddesden* and *Knebworth* in Hertfordshire; *Beckenham* and *Westerham* in Kent; *Edgware, Finchley, Hampton Court, Harrow* and *Isleworth* in Middlesex; *Camberwell, Chiswick, Deptford* and *Farnham* in Surrey; and extending as far afield as *Leek* in Staffordshire and *Hemsworth* in Yorkshire. *Hemsworth* was involved in taking foundlings from the very beginning. It was agreed in 1751 that the area between *Hemsworth* and *Doncaster is supposed to Nurse about Fifty Children* and they appear, from the records, mostly to have been well cared for; nevertheless the parish register between 1741 and 1773 records the burials of almost 100 young foundlings from the Hospital. Burials of children from the Foundling Hospital can be found in many parishes on the Great North Road between London and Yorkshire and on roads between London and the other branch hospitals and fostering areas.

In 1756 the Hospital agreed that, in addition to their 2/6d a week wages, nurses who successfully reared their children to the end of their first year should be paid a premium of 10/- and in February 1757 a rule was introduced that a nurse under whose care two children had died should not be entrusted with further children (a rule which still applied in 1935 when *Nichols and Wray*'s **History of the Foundling Hospital** was written).

BRANCH HOSPITALS

The number of children surviving infancy and needing to be channelled back through the Hospital and out to apprenticeships caused more problems. Branch Hospitals were established in various parts of the country where infants could be nursed in the surrounding area and older children could be more easily placed and superintended in apprenticeships. Most of the branch hospitals were in operation for only a few years during the 1760s and all were closed by 1773, when the 'bulge' caused by the years of indiscriminate admission had passed through the Hospital and Parliamentary financial aid had ceased. During that short period several thousand children passed through the hospitals at *Ackworth* (Yorkshire), *Shrewsbury* (Shropshire),

Chester (Cheshire), *Westerham* (Kent), *Aylesbury* (Buckinghamshire) and *Barnet* (Hertfordshire). It became customary to send a 'caravan' (covered wagon) of nurses from a given area to London to collect their infant charges and to use a similar system to gather the older children together and pass them to a branch hospital for distribution to masters as apprentices.

An incredible amount of correspondence between officials at the main Hospital, its Branch Hospitals, local inspectors, foster parents and children survives among the records, providing vivid pictures of the children's lives and of the amount of work that went into running the organisation. In October 1761, for example, *Mr McClellan* (apothecary at the Hospital from 1755 to 1797) was instructed to gather together a 'caravan' of children from the *Twyford* area in Berkshire and send them to the branch hospital at *Shrewsbury*. In his subsequent letter to the hospital he reported that he had travelled to *Twyford* and:

Very early on Friday morning (the weather being very rainy & most of the nurses living in very remote places scattered some miles distant from each other) in order to get the Children together time enough for the Carravan (sic) to return a small part of its journey homewards the same evening, I found it absolutely necessary to hire a guide & a horse. I went to Lawrence Waltham, Hurst and Sunning and from the outparts of those three villages got fourteen of the eldest of the Children (all in perfect good health) and sent them by their nurses to the Bell Inn at Twyford, where the Shrewsbury Carravan with four Nurses was in readiness to receive them; but judging it was not likely that four women could take the proper care of more than twelve children I sent the remaining two back again... After seeing that the Carravan was well defended from the Badness of the Weather by a good Covering, and that plenty of straw was laid at the bottom of it, I saw the Children put into it with some Biscuits for their use on the road and set out with their nurses on friday afternoon on their way to Henley, where it was intended they should lie that night... I delivered to the Carrier a List of the Numbers and Names of the Children committed to his care which are as follows:

8721 *David Calder*	7043 *Ann Shard*	7049 *Laurence Penny*
8559 *Edwd Abney*	7811 *Samuel Booth*	8349 *Marmaduke Allen*
6246 *Larpier Stepney*	7046 *Launcelot Sims*	7595 *Faith Wilson*
7990 *Mary Isham*	5644 *Ann Drummond*	7856 *Ann Carpenter*

The expenses of Mr McClennan's journey amounted to £1.19.0d, made up of:
16 shillings to the hire of horse for three days, his keeping and the payment of Turnpikes
5 shillings to the hire of a Guide and his horse
18 shillings to my own expenses.

Similar journeys documented in *Nichols and Wray's* book reveal just how widely foundlings, particularly during the 1760s, could be spread across the country; to quote two examples, in 1759 24 children were collected from the *Chertsey* area of Surrey and sent by two caravans to the Hospital at *Ackworth* and in 1764 20 children were collected from Surrey and sent to the Hospital in *Chester*.

The statistics for children aged 6 or more in the Hospitals and at Nurse on 31 December 1764 make interesting reading:

In the Hospital in London	*407*	*of which 387 are aged 6 years and upwards*
Ackworth	*568*	*of which 567 are aged 6 years and upwards*
Shrewsbury	*435*	*of which 433 are aged 6 years and upwards*
Westerham	*215*	*of which 177 are aged 6 years and upwards*
Chester	*59*	*of which 59 are aged 6 years and upwards*
Aylesbury	*52*	*of which 49 are aged 6 years and upwards*
Barnet	*40*	*of which 33 are aged 6 years and upwards*
At Nurse	*1,612*	*aged 6 years and upwards.*

The annual expense of maintaining each child was £7.10s.0d and the total cost came to £36,832.10s.0d.

Some 5,000 children survived to be sent out as apprentices during the 1760s, mainly in the Midlands and North of England, and many survived to marry and have children of their own. *Thomas Ethell/Ithell* (see Chapter 22) had three children and more than 40 grandchildren; nine marriages at *Sherburn-in-Elmet*, involving one partner stated to be from the hospital at *Ackworth* (see p.150) and where the couple remained in the parish, produced between them at least 45 children. As suggested in an earlier chapter, if you hit a brick wall it might be worth your while to look at the Foundling Hospital records. There are many 'untraceable' ancestors who can be traced at least as far back as their admission to the Foundling Hospital and many of their descendants who have good cause to be grateful to *Thomas Coram* and his determination to save the lives of unwanted children and give them a start in life.

CHAPTER 22

NEVER TAKE ANYTHING FOR GRANTED

Most family historians will admit to having an ancestor whom they regard as being their favourite or most interesting forebear. From the number of references to the Ethell/Ithell family in this book readers may easily deduce that, on both counts, Thomas Ithill is mine. Forty years after discovering his foundling origins I am still finding out more about him. Having, as I thought, dealt with his life and, in my own mind, closed the file in the 1970s, a serendipitous discovery in the 1990s and something I had overlooked until 2009 caused me to open it up again.

STAGE ONE: 1970s

THOMAS ITHILL NUMBER 13853

The life story of one foundling reveals some of the pitfalls and possibilities inherent in family history research, many of which are mentioned elsewhere in this book. See how many you can spot. Bear in mind that the original research was undertaken in the 1970s, when records were not so readily available as they are today.

At the age of 10 I was told by my great-great-aunt (always known as Auntie Ruth - see p.35) that the *Ethells* were descended from *George III* and his mistress, *Anna Lightfoot*. She had been told the story by her aunt born in 1849. Family legend said that a boy had been born to the couple in the late 1750s, given the surname *Ethell*, and sent to the Quaker School at *Ackworth* near *Pontefract* to be educated.

In 1968 *Jean Plaidy* published a novel, ***The Prince and the Quakeress,*** the story of a supposed affair between *George III* and *Hannah Lightfoot* and I became interested in family history. However, I discovered that the school at *Ackworth* was not founded until 1778 so I discounted the 'royal rumour' and started on the hard graft of tracing the *Ethell* family back from my great-grandmother, born an *Ethell*.

Via certificates, census returns and parish registers I tracked the family back to a small village in the East Riding of Yorkshire. Here my 4 x great-grandfather, *Thomas Ethell*, married *Deborah Rose* in *Scampston Chapel*, near *Rillington*, in 1782 (see page 248). The 1841 census stated that he was 85 and not born in Yorkshire and by the 1851 census he was dead. Over the next 18 months I extracted every *Ethell/Ithill* (because several parish register entries began with an *I*) entry from the GRO indexes for the period 1837-1871 (the 1871 census was released in the middle of my search), bought numerous certificates, and checked them all in census returns stretching from Kent to Northumberland.

With the exception of the Kent and Yorkshire/north-east entries (which I now know are all related and descended from *Thomas*), I traced all the entries back to three *Ethell* families in Shropshire, Staffordshire and Cheshire in the mid-18th century but failed to find a suitable *Thomas* in any of them. There were plenty of *Ithells* in Wales but, again, no *Thomas* who fitted the bill.

Then serendipity (making happy and unexpected discoveries by accident) took a hand. I paid 50p for a book entitled ***Ackworth School*** and discovered that for a few years in the mid-18th century the building, which in 1778 became *Ackworth School*, had been an annexe of the *London Foundling Hospital*. I wrote to the *Thomas Coram Foundation* (as the Foundling Hospital in London had become).

The Foundling Hospital Records were at that time held by the Greater London Council; their archivist searched all the classes of record listed on the LMA website (see p.242) for me and *Thomas* came alive. Extracts from her letters told of his early years:

4 September 1759 a male child about one month old requiring a wet nurse was admitted, being given the number 13853... The child was born in Prees Parish (Salop) August 3 1759... Number 13853 named Thomas Ithill was sent to nurse on 8 September 1759 with Mary Ward of St Mary Cray, under the Sevenoaks

248

Inspection of Doctor Lane… Thomas was transferred to Westerham Hospital on 21 April 1766… he was returned to London on 24 June 1766 and was inoculated for small pox the same month… Sent to Ackworth Hospital on 2 May 1768 he was apprenticed on 9 June 1768 to John Frear of Norton in the County of Yorkshire, a farmer, to be employed in husbandry.

Ackworth School in the 1970s still held all the records relating to the building's use as a Branch Hospital of the Foundling Hospital (they have since been deposited with the West Yorkshire Archive Service in *Wakefield*) and I was able to see the beautifully-kept register recording Thomas's admission, together with 15 other boys *sent to Ackworth by the Caravan last Monday*, and details of his apprenticeship to *John Frear* of *Norton* near *Malton* who was paid £4 to take *Thomas* and teach him *Husbandry*, on the same day as he was paid £6 to take *Elizabeth Buck* to instruct her in *Household Business* (the going 'apprenticeship rates' for a boy aged under 9 years and a girl aged under 10). Many foundlings ended up as little more than unpaid servants - and many more were ill-treated by their masters or died in accidents in factories - but Thomas survived.

This should have been the end of the story as most foundlings, by definition, have untraceable ancestries, but it was not. With *Thomas Ithill*'s admission paper to the Hospital was a piece of paper, 6½" wide by 3" deep, written in a poor hand, stating: *This is to sattisfi The under Taker of this plase that all Sides are Willing and The Child was Born in Prees Parish august the 3 1759 William Smith, franses ranalls, ann Smith*. Attached to the piece of paper is a scrap of flowered cotton material with the pattern in a dull purple.

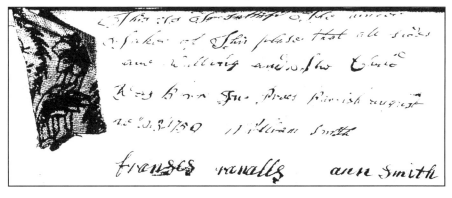

I checked the BTs for *Prees* and discovered no *Thomas Ithill* but there was a baptism on August 19 for *William, illegitimate son of Ann Smith*. I then searched the Bastardy Bonds for the parish and discovered one stating *Ann Smith of the Parish of Prees Singlewoman hath in her voluntary Examination declar'd herself to be now pregnant and with child and that the said Francis Reynolds* [of the neighbouring parish of *Hodnet*] *is the true and sole father thereof*. On checking the *Hodnet* PRs, *Francis Reynolds* proved to be married but childless. I then discovered that a child on entering the Foundling Hospital was baptised with names chosen by the Hospital, even if there was evidence of his name at birth and even if he had been baptised before admission. So *William Smith* became *Thomas Ithell*, presumably on the whim of an anonymous Hospital official.

As to the 'royal rumour', since I first wrote about it more than 30 years ago I have been contacted by a number of people with foundling ancestors and the same story. We can only think that some of the nurses/foster mothers tried to bolster the children's confidence by connecting them with a story which presumably had been current gossip around the time they were born.

Thomas married in *Scampston* (see p.248); baptised three children there; his wife *Deborah* died there in 1820 aged 69; he died there in 1842 aged 83 (his death registered by *Elizabeth Ethill* who I assumed was one of his many grandchildren), and that should have been his story told but, as I keep saying, never assume anything and never take anything for granted.

Stage 2: 1990

A Second Marriage

I have the surname *Ethell* registered with **The Guild of One-Name Studies**. All the *Ethells/Ithells* in the north east of England descend from *Thomas* and I have details of all of them up to at least 1871. In the 1841 census he was living in Scampston with a *James Parker* in the same house (see Stage 3) and he died there in 1842. It never occurred to me that he might have married for a second time - and that when I know that some 25% of marriages are second time around for at least one party.

The first clue to a possible second marriage came with the 1851 census entry for *Christiana Cordukes* nee *Neeshaw* (see Chapter 23: I encountered this entry only because I was helping a friend with his research - this is where serendipity again came in). Living with *Christiana* in *Huggate* was her mother, *Elizabeth Ithell*, widow, born in *Old Malton*, a lady who did not feature in my detailed records. In these I had a note of a marriage by licence in 1821 of a *Thomas Ethell* (no marital status given in the note) to *Elizabeth Neeshaw* at *St Michael's, New Malton*. I had always assumed this to be *Thomas*'s eldest (illegitimate) grandson. The Index to the **Archbishop of York's Marriage Bonds and Allegations 1820-1829** has an entry for *Thomas Ethell* of *Scampston* aged 21 and upwards to marry *Elizabeth Neeshaw* aged 21 and upwards but, until I saw the census entry, I had never checked the allegation and bond. These provided the vital information that he was a widower (and that *James Parker* stood as his bondsman). **Always check the original documentation and do not rely on an index, which is a finding aid but not a source.**

Who was *Elizabeth Neeshaw*? Looking at the *Rillington* PR I discovered that between 1812 and 1820 she had four children baptised at *Rillington* - the first two spelling her name as *Kneeshaw* (and being described as bastards), the others (born in *Rillington* Poorhouse) spelling her name as *Neshaw* (see p.256).

It seems likely that the marriage was an arranged one. Overseers of the Poor often 'persuaded' couples who were both either on, or likely to need, poor relief to marry as it simplified matters for them with one rent to pay instead of two. *Thomas*, aged 62, presumably needed a housekeeper and *Elizabeth*, with several illegitimate children, needed a roof over her head.

Thomas's second marriage does not appear to make any material difference to the *Ethell* family tree (because there is no evidence that *Thomas* was other than stepfather to the *Neeshaw* children). *Elizabeth* was not living with *Thomas* in 1841 but there could be any number of reasons for that so, once again, I let matters rest.

STAGE 3: 2009

THE PARISH CHEST

Despite making frequent references in this book to material which may be found in the Parish Chest I have to admit that I had never checked if any such material survived for the parish of *Rillington* or its Chapel at *Scampston* during *Thomas*'s lifetime. When I did finally look into it I discovered that *Thomas*'s story could be fleshed out still further. The *Rillington Overseers' Accounts* survive only for the years 1813-1823, and the *Churchwardens' Accounts* for 1814-1825, but those for the *Scampston Overseers* cover 1775-1848 and those for the *Chapel Wardens* 1737-1840. The ratepayers of *Scampston* were obliged to hand over one-third of their collected rates to *Rillington* (where the parish poorhouse was situated); the two sets of overseers presumably co-operated over their dealings with the poor, which may well account for the 1821 marriage between *Thomas Ethell* and *Elizabeth Neeshaw*.

Thomas Ithil made his only appearance in the *Chapelwardens' accounts* in 1789 when he was paid 3d for a Foumat (polecat) head. Certain animals - including badgers [also known as pates], foxes, hedgehogs, moles, polecats [foulmart], sparrows - were considered to be vermin and the parish would pay a small sum for every head of such an animal which was handed in. The names of some men appear regularly in the *Scampston* records as handing in foumat heads and, in a 60 year period, almost one hundred rewards were claimed (the man claiming for seven on one day had presumably found a nest).

Moving on to the *Overseers of the Poor Accounts* for *Scampston*, it becomes clear that *Thomas* spent much of the last 25 years of his life receiving poor relief. Affairs clearly began to go downhill in 1817 when he was paid relief *for 17 weeks at 1 shilling per week and 16 weeks at 6d per week.* His wife *Deborah* was ill and the accounts for that year record:

Paid for nursing Deborah Ithil   £4-0-2
Relieved Thomas Ithil at Different times   £0-14-6
Paid for coals and leading for Thomas Ithil   £0-19-10 ½
Paid Doctor for Attending Deborah Ithil (& another woman) £4-13-6.
The following year *Thomas Ethil* was relieved for 15 weeks at 2s 6d per week and in 1820 the chapelry paid for *Debrah*'s *(sic)* funeral.

The *Rillington Overseers' Accounts* list those who paid the parish rate and the amount collected from them; for the years 1821 and 1822 they also contain 'Disbursements' (sums paid out for poor relief) and in 1821 *Elizabeth Kneeshaw* was paid £5-10s-0d. It was in late September that year that she married *Thomas*.

For the next decade *Thomas* appears sporadically in the accounts; in 1823 he received £3-11-0; in 1824 his rent was paid; and in 1828 *relieved Thos. Ethil when ill 7s 6d.*

In 1830 *E. Eathel* was *relieved for 12 weeks at 1s 4d* and in 1832 *Thomas was paid 8 weeks at 2/6d, 1 week at 3/6d, 1 week at 2/6d.* To this point relief appears to have been intermittent, paid when he was ill and probably in winter when there was no labouring work available, but in 1833 he went on to full-time relief.

In 1833 and 1834 he received *40 weeks at 2/6d and 12 weeks at 3/-* (and in 1833 *relieved when ill 4/6d*). In 1835 he received *45 weeks at 2/6d and 7 weeks at 3/-* and in 1836 (the last year for which accounts survive) he was paid *2/6d* for each of *52 weeks.*

In June 1841 (when the census was taken) *Thomas Ethell* and *James Parker* were living in the same dwelling (with no trace of *Elizabeth* in the village). This is probably the same man who stood bondsman with *Thomas* for his marriage in 1821. From frequent references in the accounts to *James Parker* being paid to look after elderly or sick people, either until they died or went into *Rillington Poorhouse*, it seems likely that he was performing the same office for *Thomas* - but *Elizabeth Ethill* reappeared to register her husband's death in 1842.

Elizabeth was in Huggate in 1851 (living with her daughter who was six months pregnant) and died in 1860 in *Norton near Malton* (where *Thomas* had begun his working life in 1768 aged 8). Does the 1830 entry for her relief mean that she and *Thomas* were living apart? With her children (the youngest being 10) of an age to leave home had she (at about 35) had enough of nursing a man in his 70s? Where was she in 1841? Answer one question in family history and you almost invariably pose several more.

CHAPTER 23

A REFRESHER COURSE:

HOW MANY PITFALLS WOULD YOU HAVE SPOTTED?

CORDUKES OR CORDEUX?

Sometimes what you expect to be a simple piece of research drops you into so many pitfalls that you begin to doubt your own eyes. The *Cordukes* - or is it *Cordeux, Cardax, Cordox, Curdiks* or even *Curducks*? - family in Yorkshire serves as a refresher course on pitfalls in names, parish registers, bishop's transcripts, movement of families, handwriting, the IGI, census indexes, civil registration and online websites.

IS THE SURNAME UNCOMMON?

Never assume that, because a surname is uncommon in most areas, it is rare everywhere and no-one else will be researching it. In its area of origin it may be almost as common as *Smith* (see p.23-24). In the IGI, out of 873 entries for *Cordukes* and ten variants, 641 are in Yorkshire, mostly within a compact group of parishes in the centre of the county and almost certainly all connected at some point. **It is always worth checking any lists of names which people are researching**, in books, magazines or online and looking at the list of surnames being researched in depth by members of the *Guild of One-Name Studies* - there is always the possibility of 'connecting' with a fellow researcher.

WHERE DOES THE SURNAME ORIGINATE?

What is the area of origin of the name *Cordukes*? Some researchers apparently believe that, because the variant *Cordeux* looks French, the family is a Huguenot one coming over in the late 1600s; others that it is Flemish and arrived here with *Cornelius Vermuyden* in 1626 to drain the fens. If you look at the IGI, early Wills and marriage allegations you will find that the family was established in Yorkshire at least as early as 1570. **Do not fall into the trap of trying to hang a family with a foreign-looking or sounding name onto a convenient 16th or 17th century 'peg' with well-documented records**. Remember that most of the early post-Conquest English nobility (and their followers) were born in France or Flanders and bore French names.

WILLIAM & SARAH CORDUKES

In 1801, according to the marriage entry in the register of *Crambe, William Cordukes* married *Sarah Munkman* - but he signed the entry as *Cordeux*. **This variation between entry and signature is one of the problems most frequently encountered in post-1754 marriage registers** and, as said previously, it always pays to check both the name in the entry and the signature because they may differ by much more than this example, and many transcribers and indexers look only at the name in the entry and do not compare it with the signature.

William had been baptised at *Crambe* in 1772 as *William Cordux*, son of *Mw* [*Matthew*]. The incumbent believed in abbreviating male Christian names and occupations wherever possible and mothers' Christian names were not given. Working from microfilm, which is usually less easy to read than the original documents (especially before 1813), it was some time before I realised that there were two separate families being baptised with fathers *M[atthe]w* and *W[illia]m* – *Mw* and *Wm*, in a flowery 18th century hand, look remarkably similar and, if I had not been stopped in my tracks by two children baptised a month apart to what looked like *Wm*, I might have gone down completely the wrong line. *Mw* was described as *jnr* in several entries - there was another *Matthew* in the village at the time - but *Mw* was also a carpenter so did the incumbent mean *junior* or *joiner* (or both)? **Never take abbreviations at face value because you think you know what they stand for** - take time to study other entries and ascertain whether the writer has thought out his own shorthand system.

William (a carpenter) and *Sarah* had seven children, baptised in three different parishes. No children have been located between 1801, when they married, and 1808. This is not common – was *William* away from home or are there more baptisms in a parish not included in FamilySearch?

WILLIAM & CHRISTIANA CORDUKES

William, son of *William* and *Sarah*, born in 1816, married *Christiana Neeshaw* in 1840 in *Scampston* Chapel. As with his father (see above) the marriage entry is for *Cordukes* but he signs as *Cordeux*. His father is entered as *Curdeux*. *Christiana* is *Kneeshaw* in the entry but signs as *Neeshaw*.

William and Christiana had four sons (born in the 1840s) and a daughter. The daughter's birth is registered in 1851 but there appear to be no entries in the GRO indexes for any of the sons, under any of the known variants. Registration was not compulsory until 1875 (see p.85) but the non-registration of four sons, when their sister is registered, suggests either that *William* (who died within weeks of daughter *Rachel*'s birth) did not approve of the new system or that a new and keen registrar tracked down the infant *Rachel* (he was entitled to a fee for registering the birth - see p.80).

Fortunately, all the children were baptised at Huggate parish church - as *Enzah, Enos, Alfred* (correctly *Alvah* - the incumbent's knowledge of names used in the **Book of Genesis** appears to have failed him), *Laban*, and daughter *Rachel*. Look in the IGI; baptism dates match those in the PR but *Enzah* is given as son of *William and Mary* and *Laban* as son of *William and Ann*. Check the BTs, from which the IGI entries were taken, and *Mary* and *Ann* are indeed given as the mothers: in *Enzah*'s case the mother in the previous entry is a *Mary*, in *Laban*'s the succeeding one is an *Ann*. As any transcriber will tell you, it is easy to 'miscopy' a word from the line above or below, and it is apparent that in some cases the same care was not exercised over writing the BT as was usually granted to the PR.

Look at the original image for the family in the 1851 census and you will find the sons listed as *Henzah, Enos, Alvah and Labon* - the enumerator's attempt at four uncommon Christian names was considerably better than that of the transcriber for one commercial website who recorded them as *Herzah, Enos, Aloah and Jabon* and the surname as *Cordean*. If I had not already known where to find the family, I would never have been able to locate them via this site. Having submitted a correction, the entry will be annotated but will not make it any easier to locate the family in the index. The census entry reveals that *Christiana* was at home, with her four sons and her mother, *Elizabeth Ithell* (see p.250). *William Curdiks* (*sic*) was living, not with his family, but elsewhere in the village, as one of seven agricultural servants living in with farmer *George Clarkson*.

A surname index of the 1851 census might merely have revealed an *Ithell* on the same folio as several *Cordukes*. Only looking at the original image reveals the connection between the families. Most people, constructing a family tree from an index alone (as many family historians, despite warnings, still do), would have placed *William, Christiana* and their sons as a united family in the same household and ignored *Elizabeth Ithell*.

The divided household in 1851 does not alter the *Cordukes* pedigree but how many questions are left unanswered - why was *William* not at home on census night in 1851 (when his wife was six months pregnant) - marital breakdown or a rush job on the farm - and were the couple back together before he died four months later?

If you are tempted to believe that his death aged 35 supports the theory that our ancestors died young, his father had died the previous year aged *81* and his mother died 13 years later aged *82*. No amount of searching will produce a burial for *Christiana Cordukes* because, in 1854, she married *William Brown*. **Always be prepared for a woman, particularly one whose husband dies relatively young, remarrying and acquiring a new surname.** It is surprising how often this obvious solution to a missing female burial is overlooked. If the name is a common one, finding a second marriage (for male or female) may not be easy but, on the positive side, if it took place after 1837 it should give you the fathers' names which you may not know. For a woman, finding a census return in which children from her first marriage are described as *in laws*, or *step-children*, to the head of the household can be the clue you need to identify a second marriage.

CHRISTIANA CORDUKES AND HER SONS

In 1861 *Christiana* (born in *Rillington*) was in *Huggate* with her second husband, *William Brown* (born in *Chichester*, Sussex), *Enzah, Laban* and *Rachel* (described as *sons-in-law* and *daughter-in-law* to *William Brown* - see p.38) and two little *Browns*. *Enos* was a farm servant in *Thwing* and *Alva* (indexed as *Alan* but clearly *Alva* in the original image) was a plough boy in *Tibthorpe*.

By 1871 *William and Christiana Brown* had moved to *Whitwood Mere*, near *Castleford* - both claiming to be born there. It pays where possible to check several census returns (see p.68) as people, for whatever reason, may give different birthplaces. Three of the sons were living in *Wortley (Leeds)*; *Alva Corduks (sic)* and *Enos Cordukes* were both married and *Laban* was living with brother *Enos*. *Enzor (sic) Cordukes*, a tailor, was living in *Pocklington*. The move from village to urban area was a common one.

In 1881 *Enzah*, a tailor, was a patient in *Hull General Infirmary*; *Enos*, a gas stoker, was living near *Sheffield*; *Laban*, a mal(t)ster and painter, and *Alva* (indexed as *Aloa*), a labourer, had remained in the *Leeds* area. *Enzah* might still have escaped the net because he is not indexed under any known spelling of the surname - he is listed as *Euzah Corduker*. *Christiana* had died a few weeks before the census was taken.

ONLINE INDEXES

Online indexes, principally to civil registration and to census returns, can be invaluable but searching for 'interchangeable' surnames such as *Cordukes/Cordeux* and *Kneeshaw/Neeshaw* highlight that **it is essential always to read the introduction to any site and ascertain which system of indexing has been used** (see Chapter 5). Several sites index *Cordukes* and *Cordeux* separately; if you tick the *phonetic search* box you will often pull up a combination of the two names and other variants but beware of the site which offers you *Close variants* and *All variants* and provides the two versions only under *All variants*. (In the 1841 census *William and Sarah* are entered as *Cordukes*; *William* (their son) and *Christiana* as *Cordeux*, with both families living in the same village.) Note that many indexes give names in strictly alphabetical order and **remember that a difference of one letter in the spelling can make the difference between locating and missing an entry.** *Cordeux* (and *Corduex*) will come before *Cordukes* but *Curdeux* and *Curdiks* will come after both (and, on one site, *Cordux* comes under *Cardo*) and remember the *Cordean* transcription mentioned above. *Kneeshaw* will come before *Neeshaw*; *Kneshaw* comes after (not amongst) *Kneeshaw* and *Neshaw* is listed after *Neesham* (which is included as a variant). On one site,

Neshaw is indexed with *Nassau/Nassaw*. *Ethell* entries are listed together (*Ithell* are separate) but, on an alphabetical site, an *Ann Etthell* entry comes after *William Ethell* and is very easy to overlook.

A TALE OF TWO CLERGYMEN CALLED THOMAS NELSON

Here is a tale of two Anglican clergymen which contains both possibilities and pitfalls. They shared a name and a county of birth; were born within five years of each other; came from the same social stratum and, at one point, their families lived within half a mile of each other but I doubt that the two men ever met. It would, however, have been all too easy to confuse the two as I very nearly did.

Wills, quoted below, provide a vivid picture of the nepotism which prevailed in the Anglican Church and demonstrate how difficult it could be for anyone without money, connections or influence to obtain a 'good' living in the Church of England.

Thomas Nelson (1) was baptised at *Askham Richard* in the West Riding of Yorkshire in 1707 and died in Warwickshire in 1771. From his Will, proved in the Prerogative Court of Canterbury, with a copy annexed to letters of administration granted in the Prerogative Court of York in 1783, it was apparent that he was a clergyman, Rector of *Headbourne Worthy (alias Worthy Mortimer)* in the County of Southampton, Perpetual Curate of *Hatton* in Warwickshire and Rector of *Little Rollright* (*Rollright Parva*) in Oxfordshire (a pluralist with livings in three counties: see p.192). As he left a substantial bequest to *University College, Oxford*, it seemed likely that he had graduated from there, a fact confirmed by *Foster*'s **Alumni Oxonienses**, which stated that he was the son of *Seth Nelson* of *Ashcombe [Askham]*, had obtained his BA in 1730 and his MA in 1733 but gave no further details.

In 1731, a *Thomas Nelson* became *clerico stipendio* (paid curate) to *Henry Hudson, Vicar of Askham Bryan* (which is half a mile from *Askham Richard*), for four years at a salary of £30 per annum. So it appeared that *Thomas*'s first job was conveniently close to home. **Never make assumptions**. *Thomas (1)* was not ordained in *York* and he never held a benefice in *Yorkshire*.

The *Thomas Nelson (2)* who became curate at *Askham Bryan and Healaugh* turned out to be someone completely different, born in the North Riding in 1704, graduating from *Jesus College, Cambridge* in the late 1720s, moving on from *Askham Bryan* in 1735 to become Rector of *Fingall* in the North Riding and dying in 1786 with a memorial in the church at *Holtby* (see p. 216).

Without the Oxford connection, gleaned from the Will of *Thomas (1)*, it would have been very easy to confuse the two men, especially as the *Cambridge* entry for *Thomas (2)* just says 'of Yorkshire' and does not name his father. It does, however, name his wife and her father [*Catherine Preston* daughter of *Darcy Preston (of Askham Bryan)*], whom he married in *York*

Minster in March 1736/7. Marriages in York Minster between 1681 and 1753 are printed in **The Yorkshire Archaeological & Topographical Journal** Volumes II and III, with footnotes by *Robert H. Skaife*. The footnote for this marriage gives details of *Thomas*'s career, *Catherine*'s parentage, notes that she had a marriage portion of £1,000 (the equivalent of around £75,000 today) and gives a reference for her father's marriage, also in the Minster. This turns out to be *Darcy Preston*'s second marriage but the footnote gives details of his parentage. His mother was *Elizabeth*, daughter and heiress of *Darcy Conyers* of *Holtby* - which explains why the *Nelson* family came to hold the advowson of *Holtby*, where *Thomas Darcy Nelson* [son of *Thomas (2) and Catherine*] became Rector in 1775, and where *Thomas (2)* was buried in 1786.

Advowsons (the right to recommend a suitable person as incumbent - see p.190) could be bought and sold like property. They could similarly be bequeathed by Will. *Thomas (1)* and *Thomas Darcy Nelson,* son of *Thomas (2)* both willed their benefices to specified successors, and included plenty of genealogical detail. *Thomas Darcy Nelson*, making his Will in August 1793, left *the perpetual advowson of the Rectory of Holtby* to his sisters, *willing and directing that they do supply the vacancy in the said Rectory of Holtby which will be occasioned by my decease by presenting thereto my nephew Robert Warburton son of my late sister Mary in case he shall then be in Holy Orders and desirous of such presentation and capable of accepting the same.* His nephew was ordained as deacon and named as Curate of *Holtby* in October 1796 and as priest and Rector in July 1799 (three months after his uncle's death), a position which he held until his own death in 1845 (see p.216). *Thomas Darcy Nelson* is buried at *Holtby* aged 59, with no indication in the register of the manner of his death, but his **Alumni** entry says that he died suddenly at the *George Inn, York* and gives reference to an entry in the **Gentleman's Magazine.**

Thomas (1), in his 1770 Will, bequeaths one of his benefices, *Hatton* in Warwickshire. He refers to *the powers and authorities to me given* in the Will of the late *Mrs Jane Norcliffe* and to a *Trust Deed or bargain and sale* of 1744 and goes on: *in as much as my Nephew Mr Seth Pollard* (who also went to University College, Oxford) *named in her Will is dead I nominate appoint and recommend ... my esteemed Kinsman John Morfitt of Horseforth in the County of York Clerk who is married to the Sister of the said Seth Pollard* (their son also went to U.C., Oxford) *to be ... Curate Minister or Incumbent of the said Curacy Church Chapel or Donative of Hatton ... in my place ... my Executors shall deliver up to ... John Morfitt ... the Box and Writings in which are the Book and Papers relating thereto.* Definitely a family affair.

His executor (his brother *Seth*, living in Essex) was also to deliver *all my Papers and Accounts relating thereto* to his successor at *Headbourne Worthy* but *Thomas* did not have the right to nominate his successor here, where he had become Rector in 1759, because the advowson belonged to *University College, Oxford.*

In February 1738/9 Thomas had been given the task of sorting out the affairs of his mother and his brother *Richard.* On 24 February he applied for letters of administration for both estates, describing himself as *Clerk of University College, Oxford.* So he was still in *Oxford,* eight years after obtaining his BA. In the bonds accompanying his mother's Will and his brother's Admon a great deal of family information can be found (see also p.210). His father *Seth* had died intestate in 1721, when *Thomas* was 14, and his mother *Rosamond* was granted letters of administration. The accompanying inventory totalled £491 (£35,000). *Rosamond* died in January 1738/9, leaving a Will (describing herself as of *Little Askham,* i.e. *Askham Richard*) and naming her son *Richard* as sole executor. He died intestate four weeks later before applying for probate. Within a week, *Richard's* siblings: *Seth Nelson of Henrietta Street, Covent Garden, London, Mercer; Rose the wife of Henry Perkins gentleman; Ellen the wife of John Pollard gentleman and Anne Nelson spinster,* had renounced their rights to administer the estate (see p.209) in favour of their brother *Thomas Nelson,* clerk.

ENTRIES FROM *ALUMNI OXONIENSES* FOR THOMAS NELSON (1), SETH POLLARD AND JOHN MORFITT AND HIS SON

> **Nelson,** Thomas, s. Seth, of Ashcombe, Yorks, gent. UNIVERSITY COLL., matric. 16 Nov., 1726, aged 18 ; B.A. 1730, M.A. 1733.

> **Pollard,** Seth, s. John, of Horsforth, Yorks, gent. UNIVERSITY COLL., matric. 13 Dec., 1749, aged 14 ; B.A. 1753, M.A. 1756.

> **Morfitt,** John, s. John, of Osgoldby, co. York, gent. QUEEN'S COLL., matric. 10 March, 1736-7, aged 23.
> **Morfitt,** John, s. John, of Guiseley, co. York, cler. UNIVERSITY COLL., matric. 8 April, 1775, aged 17 ; bar.-at-law, Inner Temple, 1784.

ENTRY FROM *ALUMNI CANTABRIGIENSES* FOR THOMAS NELSON (2)

> **NELSON, THOMAS.** Adm. pens. at JESUS, June 2, 1722. Of Yorkshire. Matric. 1722; Scholar, 1722; B.A. 1725-6; M.A. 1729. C. of Askham Bryan and Healaugh, Yorks., 1731. R. of Fingall, 1735-86. Married Catherine, dau. of Darcy Preston, of York, Mar. 1, 1736-7. Died Mar. 29, 1786, aged 82. (A. Gray; *G. Mag.*; M. H. Peacock.)

CHAPTER 24

MISCELLANY

This section includes several topics which are not covered in depth in the preceding chapters because they are, in the main, covered by more specialist books and websites dedicated to the specific topic. Brief details and examples are included here in the hope that they may provide pointers to possibilities and pitfalls in the relevant areas.

THE ARMY

NEVER ASSUME THAT YOUR ANCESTOR JOINED HIS LOCAL REGIMENT.

With a few exceptions (like the *Atholl Highlanders* and the *Pals Battalions* in World War I who found their recruits locally) regiments had a 'home base' but gathered men for the ranks from far afield. Which regiment your ancestor joined, until the 19th century, was likely to depend on the arrival of a recruiting party, offering *the king's shilling,* at a time when he was feeling patriotic, drunk, or needed to leave the area in a hurry. During World War I many men joined a local regiment but remember that there was a great deal of movement of soldiers between regiments. *Henry Pettit* and *Samuel Shaw* (see p.262) were first cousins and both joined a *Yorkshire* Regiment but *Henry* was killed serving with the *Northumberland Fusiliers* and *Samuel* was wounded while fighting with *the 11th East Lancashire Regiment (the Accrington Pals).*

GARRISON TOWNS

Study the PRs of garrison towns (which had a permanent military presence), ranging from *Colchester* in Essex to *Berwick upon Tweed* in Northumberland and from *Devonport* in Devon to *Carlisle* in Cumberland and you should gain some idea of just how diverse were the origins of soldiers of the British army. In the early part of the 19th century about 40% of the army were said to have been born in Ireland, and many British regiments served tours of duty there.

The baptisms of soldiers' children in *Dade* registers (see Chapter 12) in the city of *York*, which was a garrison town, make it clear that those in the armed forces often travelled widely, finding brides either en route, from those widowed within the regiment, or among its followers. (For the serious repercussions which could ensue for an army or navy wife if her husband died or was sent overseas see page 238.) The grandfathers of *Elizabeth Geary*, baptised in *York* in 1788 to a Corporal in the 46th Regiment of Foot, came from *St Martin's in Birmingham* and *Ireland*; those of *John Zacharias Brown*, baptised in the same church the following year, son of a trumpeter in the 1st Regiment of Dragoons, from *Udestall in Germany* and *Tottenham in Suffolk*;

those of *Elizabeth Wright*, baptised in 1805, daughter of another trumpeter in the same regiment, from *Lichfield in Staffordshire* and *Broad Hambrey in Devon*. The naming of the regiment (in baptisms and burials) can be a boon when searching army records in TNA or online.

MILITIA

The militia who, under normal circumstances, could expect to serve for a limited period and usually within their local area found that during the period of the French Revolutionary and Napoleonic Wars they were sent farther afield and for longer. Parishes in York, which showed no hesitation in 'removing' servicemen's wives when their husbands were absent (see p.238) appear to have shown a little more compassion to those whose men were in the militia (but any whose husbands did not reappear when the militia returned were given short shrift). The East Yorkshire militia was in Sussex in 1796 (when several men married local girls in *Brighthelmstone*); the North Yorkshire militia was also in Sussex in 1808 when three men married in *Winchelsea* and again in 1811-1812 when 17 militiamen married in *Brighton* (as *Brighthelmstone* had been re-named). Militia regiments from many English counties were to be found spread along the south coast, especially in Kent and Sussex, to defend England against possible invasion. If you fail to find a marriage for an ancestor in this period it could be worth your while to ascertain whether he was in a county militia and where he was serving.

DEATHS IN THE CRIMEAN WAR

Until the passing of the ***Registration of Births, Deaths and Marriages (Army) Act of 1879*** (later replaced by the ***Registration of Births, Deaths and Marriages (Special Provisions) Act of 1957***) there was no provision for the deaths of those in the army dying overseas to be recorded at the GRO. Deaths of those dying in the Crimea may be found in regimental records or be inferred from their absence from later muster rolls and paylists.

Accounts of the Crimean War (from official despatches) can be found in *The London Gazette* (see p.269). A *Supplement* published on Friday, November 17 1854, *from reports just received*, includes names of those who took part in the *Charge of the Light Brigade* on 25th October, stating if they were *Killed or Missing, or Wounded (slightly, seriously or dangerously)*. Be aware that, as with most newspaper reports (see p. 270) it contains errors, omissions and mis-spellings so read it carefully if searching for news of an ancestor.

Henry Pettitt and *Samuel Shaw* (see p. 260) both died during the war but their deaths were recorded differently as *Henry* was killed in action (see below) but *Sam* died of wounds in England (see p.263). Note that different wording was used on certificates for those who were known to be *killed in action* and those who were *missing*.

FIRST WORLD WAR DEATH CERTIFICATES: KILLED IN ACTION & MISSING

CERTIFIED COPY OF AN ENTRY OF DEATH

Given at the GENERAL REGISTER
SOMERSET HOUSE, L
Application Number 581195

Registration of Births, Deaths and Marriages (Special Provisions) Act 1957

Death outside the United Kingdom

Return of Warrant Officers, Non-Commissioned Officers and Men of the Northumberland Fusiliers Killed in Action or who have Died whilst on Service Abroad in the War of 1914 to 1920.

Rgtl. No.	Rank	Name in Full (Surname First)	Age	Country of Birth	Date of Death	Place of Death	Cause of Death
22240	Private	PETTITT, Henry	29 5/12	England	16.8.1917	France	Killed in Action

CERTIFIED COPY OF AN ENTRY OF DEATH

Application Number P.S.S. 8.111.66

Registration of Births, Deaths and Marriages (Special Provisions) Act 1957

An Entry in the Army War Records of Deaths 1914-1921

Return of Warrant Officers, Non-Commissioned Officers and Men of The Royal Engineers Killed in Action or who have died whilst on Service Abroad in the War of 1914-1921

Rgtl. No	Rank	Name in Full (Surname First)	Age	Country of Birth	Date of Death	Place of Death	Cause of Death
110393 227th Fld. Coy	Sapper	WRIGHT Reginald	27	England	on or since 28.3.18	Missing . France	Officially considered dead

An Entry relating to the death of Reginald Wright

262

Note the differing dates given for the duration of the War. The designated period of the war, as far as the CWGC is concerned, was *4 August 1914 to 31 August 1921*. British Army Service Records (on a commercial website) and Medal Rolls (on TNA site on /**documentsonline**/ both cover 1914-1920.

THINGS MAY NOT BE AS THEY SEEM: CIVILIAN OR 'MILITARY' DEATH

Sam died of wounds in the *1ˢᵗ Eastern General Hospital* in *Cambridge* in May 1918 (according to his death certificate he was aged 29, in fact he was 25 but recorded on his commemorative bookmark as being in his 26ᵗʰ year - see p.70).

IN LOVING REMEMBRANCE OF
LC.-CPL.
SAMUEL SHAW,
E. LANCS.,

The beloved son of
Joseph and Martha Shaw,

Died in Cambridge Hospital,
May 6th, 1918,
Of Wounds received in France,

In his 26th year.

One of the best towards his mother.
Duty called and he was there
To do his best and take his share.
Now that the battle is over,
And Victory won at a cost,
We only remember a dear smiling face,
And think of the son we have lost.
We pictured his safe returning,
We longed to clasp his hand,
But God has postponed the meeting,
It will be in the better land.

8, Churchfields,
Glassboughton,
Castleford.

According to information supplied by the GRO some years ago, those who died of wounds in the UK were counted as civilian deaths (and appear in the main GRO indexes); those who were killed or 'missing' overseas were *Deaths outside the United Kingdom* (as on *Henry*'s copy death certificate issued to me in 1969) and they appear in the ***Miscellaneous Returns*** (see p.90). More recent certificates state *an Entry in the Army War Records of Deaths 1914-1921.* They should all appear in the ***GRO's Index to War Deaths 1914-1921*** (both *Henry* and *Sam* are in the Army (Other Ranks) section) and in ***Soldiers died in the Great War 1914-1919*** (published by HMSO in 1921) which gives details of their service, including regimental numbers and whether they served in more than one regiment (as both *Henry* and *Sam* did).

Those who died overseas are almost all commemorated either with a gravestone or on a war memorial in the region where they died. **The Commonwealth War Graves Commission website (CWGC.org) is a must for anyone with family in any of the services during the two World Wars.** Working in association with the CWGC (with a link from their site) is **The War Graves Photographic Project** which can supply digital images or hard copy of the headstones of most service personnel from both World Wars.

Those who died of wounds in this country may appear on a war memorial in their home town but may not have a military headstone. I have a copy of *Sam*'s death certificate but there are no surviving records of the military hospital where he died and a gap in the records of the cemetery where he is probably buried. Because he was in a famous regiment when he died, a local historian tried, and failed, to find details of a headstone or of a memorial inscription for him. He identified his date of death from ***Soldiers died*** …(see above) except that this records the date his death was registered, not his actual date of death. He approached the CWGC, assuming that *Sam* had slipped through the net, and, to cut a long story short, *Sam*'s name was added, some 90 years after his death, to the memorial nearest to where his regiment was serving when he died; not strictly accurate but commemorating him among comrades. Look at the *Addenda* panels attached to most ***Memorials to the Missing*** on the CWGC site and you will find that names are still being added today. See the *In From The Cold Project* online, which aims to record all those servicemen who 'fell off the radar'.

THE LABOUR CORPS: 1917-1921

The British Army's Labour Corps was formed in 1917, to support the front line troops by undertaking tasks such as moving stores, unloading ships, repairing roads, railways and canals, building defences (both at home and abroad) and keeping lines of communication open. The Corps consisted principally of soldiers who were unfit or too old for front line service, conscientious objectors, and those with minor disabilities. Foreign labourers and German Prisoners of War also served in the Corps. By the end of the war, some 400,000 men (11% of the strength of the army) were in the Corps and 9,000 had been killed. Many soldiers spent some time with the Labour Corps, before returning to the trenches. It could be worth checking if your ancestor was amongst them and maybe discovering where he served.

CHELSEA PENSIONERS

The term *Chelsea Pensioner* today applies to a resident of the Royal Hospital, Chelsea. However, between the late 17th and mid 20th centuries, there were far more *out-pensioners* than *in-pensioners* – 51 in 1703, 20,000+ in 1792, 36,000+ in 1815. The census returns contain many men described as *Chelsea Out-Pensioner* or merely as *Out-Pensioner*. The /**documentsonline**/ section of the TNA website gives details of where to find records of both *in-* and *out-pensioners*.

The Royal Hospital Kilmainham in Ireland was built in 1684 to provide accommodation and financial support for military pensioners. It closed in 1929. Records are divided between the National Archives of Ireland in Dublin and TNA.

**CWGC HEADSTONE ON RATHLIN ISLAND, CO. ANTRIM
FOR THREE SAILORS FROM HMS VIKNOR WHICH SANK
ON 13TH JANUARY 1915 WITH THE LOSS OF 293 LIVES**

DEEDS REGISTRIES

Registries of Deeds were established in the 18th century in Yorkshire (one for each Riding), Middlesex and Ireland. They were for the voluntary registration of deeds, conveyances, mortgages and other documents affecting land (including, in some cases, Wills). They dealt with freehold land and leases of more than 21 years (not with manorial land). The West Riding Registry of Deeds in Wakefield opened in 1704 and closed in 1970 (see p.45); the East Riding one in Beverley opened 1708, closed 1974; the North Riding one in Northallerton opened 1736, closed 1970; the Middlesex one (which did not include the City of London) opened 1709, closed 1940 and the Irish one in Dublin opened 1707 and still exists today. Records from the three Yorkshire Deeds Registries are held at the relevant CRO; those for Middlesex are in LMA and for Ireland are at Henrietta Street in Dublin. There are various projects to put the records online but all are in their early stages.

The West Yorkshire Deeds Registry registered 7 million deeds between 1704 and 1970, of which 1 million were registered between 1704 and 1837.

What you will usually see when researching is memorials of registered deeds. A memorial is essentially a synopsis of the deed, including the date (and time) of the registration; the names of all parties concerned, with their occupations or titles; and a description of the property.

The memorials can be very formulaic and wordy but the following abstract gives an idea of what information may be found:

On *16th January 1862 at two in the afternoon* a memorial of an indenture made on 12th December 1861 was registered, whereby *John Hinchliffe of Huntroyd in the Township of Upper Whitley in the County of York, farmer* acquired *all that Messuage or Dwellinghouse with the Cowhouse, Outbuildings and Garden adjoining or near thereto ... to a place called Sowood Head in the Township of Upper Whitley in the parish of Kirkheaton in the said County of York containing six perches or thereabouts ... and also all that close or parcel of land adjoining or near to the said Messuage or Dwellinghouse commonly called or known by the name of the Croft containing two roods and six perches ... which said premises were formerly in the occupation of John Jessop late of Francis Pickles and are now in the occupation of the said John Hinchliffe.*

John (see p.70) died in 1877 but the property remained in the family until 1887 when it changed hands. The parties named in the deed included ten of John's surviving children, all with places of residence and occupation, and, for the daughters, included the names of their husbands and whether they were widowed.

ENCLOSURE AND TITHE AWARDS AND MAPS

ENCLOSURE AWARDS: in England and Wales these record the enclosure and reallotment of open fields, commons and wastes in parishes and townships. Some awards were made by agreement but most were brought about by private or public Acts of Parliament. The award names local landowners and defines the extent and position of their landholding. From 1770 grants were often accompanied by a map.

An enclosure award for Ossett in 1810, describing the land allocated to *George Fligg* (landlord of *George Mercer* - see p.28), gives an idea of what you may learn from such documents:

Also I do set out, allot and award unto George Fligg All that Allotment or Parcel of Land situate in the East Field, containing 1 acre, 3 roods and 15 perches, bounded Eastward by an Allotment awarded to Hannah Rooke, Westward by an Allotment awarded to Joseph Ingham, Northward by an ancient Inclosure now or late belonging to Joshua Ingham and Southward by Wheatley Road. And I order and award, that the said George Fligg shall make and forever hereafter maintain good and sufficient fences on the Westward and Southward sides of the said Allotment. And I declare that the said Allotment is Copyhold (see p.29) *compounded for of the Manor of Wakefield.*

Enclosure awards were sometimes used as an opportunity to extinguish tithes (see p.192) by allocating land to the tithe owner in lieu of payments in cash or kind.

In many cases, tracks (later becoming roads) had to be made between allotments to enable landowners to reach their holdings. These were often long and straight and it is very easy to mistake them for Roman roads.

Copies of the awards will generally be found in ROs or libraries but some may still be found in private estate or manorial records. TNA holds copies of post-1845 awards.

TITHE AWARDS: the Tithe Commutation Act of 1836 commuted tithes to a money payment (for a definition of the tithes see p.192.). Among the documents created by this act, the most valuable to family historians are the schedules of apportionment which list landowners, tenants and fields in the tithe district (normally a parish or township) and the accompanying maps.

Do not assume that every parish/township will have a tithe award and accompanying documentation. **If an enclosure award had already commuted the tithes, there was often no need for a tithe award.**

Three copies were made of tithe maps and apportionments: one for the tithe commissioners (now held at TNA); one for the bishop (in either the diocesan registry or local RO); and one for the parish clerk (may be in the parish chest or local RO but not all survive).

FREEMEN

A Freeman is defined as one who possesses the rights and privileges (and sometimes duties) of a citizen (or a burgess). Today, most people are only aware of the term when someone is granted the honorary freedom of a town or city as a reward for services rendered. To our ancestors, becoming a Freeman could be essential before they could live and work in a town or city and the records created by their applications can reveal a great deal of genealogical information.

Records of Freemen date back to the 13th century in some cases. Cities which hold, often extensive, records of their Freemen include *London, Berwick-on-Tweed, Bristol, Chester, Coventry, Exeter, Newcastle-upon-Tyne, Norwich, Oxford, Preston* and *York*. Some lists of Freemen are available online and others have been published and are available in local libraries or record offices.

There were usually four ways in which a person could become a Freeman: by invitation; by purchase; by inheritance or by apprenticeship. The rules governing the granting of the freedom of a city, and the terminology used, varied from city to city. Not all cities invited people to become Freemen; buying the privilege was known as *by redemption* in London and *per ord[inem]* in York; *by patrimony* (inheritance), the right of children of a Freeman to claim freedom by birth, might extend freely to all children, be restricted to male children, or be free for the first child but require payment from younger siblings; *by apprenticeship* (or by servitude) involved the completion of an indentured apprenticeship of not less than five (commonly seven) years to a master craftsman, who was himself a Freeman of the city.

Examples from the **Register of York Freemen** show the types of information which may be found, detailing a daughter becoming free, movement for one family and a hundred years of genealogical information for another:

George Knowles (see p.227), translator, was apprenticed to *Thomas Braithwaite*, translator and became a Freeman in 1820.

In 1700/1 *John* son of *Thomas Lucas*, tallow chandler, became free and in 1725/6 *Jane*, daughter of *Thomas Lucas*, chandler and soap boiler, became free.

James Lund, joiner, apprenticed to *Robert Lonsdale*, joiner, became free in 1795. He moved to *Manchester* and, in 1830, *George Lund* of Manchester, calico printer, son of *James Lund* of *Manchester*, joiner, became free.

It has recently become popular in some cities for those who can prove freedom by patrimony to claim it and the following example provides four generations in the male line for one family: *Matthew John Hare of 22 Falconer Street, salesman; son of John William Hare, carriage painter; son of William Hare, taylor, deceased; son of Matthew John Hare, tailor, deceased, free 26 May 1903*. A later claim, by a daughter of the 1903 Freeman, adds the information that the original *Matthew John* was apprenticed to *Thomas Waind*, tailor, and became free in 1820.

NEWSPAPERS

THE LONDON GAZETTE

The London Gazette is the Official Newspaper of Record for the United Kingdom.

It has been published continuously since 1665 and is now available to search online at www.londongazette.co.uk   It contains a remarkable amount of information relevant to family historians including:

details of naturalizations and changes of name by Deed Poll (see p.25-26 for examples of the type of information available).

all official dispatches when the country is at war (see p.261 concerning the Crimean War).

commissions and subsequent promotions in the Armed Forces.

awards of honours and military medals.

The London Gazette includes materials of nationwide interest and publications [notices] specific to England and Wales; the Edinburgh Gazette and the Belfast Gazette similarly carry information of nationwide interest but include publications specific to Scotland and Northern Ireland respectively.

BRITISH LIBRARY NEWSPAPER COLLECTION

The British Library Newspaper Collection is currently housed at Colindale in London but this facility will close by the end of 2012. Current intention is to move the newspapers into storage at Boston Spa in Yorkshire, with digital and microform access being provided at the British Library's site at St Pancras.

An increasing number of newspapers is becoming available online. The British Library (with commercial partners) has put a selection of *British Newspapers 1800-1900* online and also the *Burney Collection of 17th and 18th century newspapers* (including those published in London). *The Times Digital Archive (1785-1985)* is another very valuable resource. These are all subscription websites but some subscribing libraries and other institutions may provide free access to local residents and institutional members.

British Newspapers Online (www.britishpapers.co.uk) contains a complete list of all local papers currently being published, together with addresses and websites.

Local newspapers are included in the BLNC but be aware that the collection will usually include only the 'lead' edition. *The Harrogate Advertiser*, for example, is the lead title in a series of six newspapers covering, among other places, *Ripon, Knaresborough and Wetherby*. Each newspaper contains news relevant to the area, but also includes local news specific to the town concerned; to access these local editions it may well be necessary to contact the publishers (via the website mentioned above).

During the late 19th and the first half of the 20th century local papers often covered the funerals of local people and included a list of mourners present (often including their relationship to the deceased); these can be a goldmine of information for family historians.

NEWSPAPER REPORTS – TRUE OR FALSE?

Newspapers, by their very nature, are prone to inaccuracies in their reporting of events. The following examples demonstrate both how misleading - and how illuminating - reports can be:

1. In 1846, a senior assistant at Greenwich Observatory (who had lost his job because the news of his incestuous relationship with his daughter had reached the ears of the Astronomer Royal) and his daughter were accused of concealing the birth of their incestuous child and then of murdering it. They were both found not guilty. Following the verdict, as reported in the **Kentish Mercury** newspaper, *one of the gaol officials came into court to know whether there was any other charge against the prisoners: ... he was informed there was not and that the male prisoner might instantly depart. The female prisoner... on the following morning was conveyed to some refuge, THERE TO REMAIN UNTIL SHE HAD GIVEN BIRTH TO ANOTHER CHILD OF WHICH SHE IS AGAIN PREGNANT BY HER FILTHY INCESTUOUS PARENT* (capital letters as used in the newspaper report). The reporter was clearly incensed by the situation, **The Times** found the incest abhorrent, several newspapers described the case as almost without a parallel in the history of this country, but the fact remained that, in the eyes of the civil law, no crime had been committed (see p. 37).

2. On 4th October 1886 *William Megson*, a colliery blacksmith, died from injuries received in an explosion at *Altofts* colliery. His death certificate reads: *Burnt and injured by explosion of Coal Dust ignited by blasting Stone with Gunpowder... Lived 40 hours.*

The explosion took place at 3pm on Saturday 2nd October but a full inquest could not be held until 16th December when all the bodies had been recovered (see p.90). The explosion killed 22 men and 53 horses. The first reports in the **Yorkshire Post** referred to *William* as **J.** *Megson a blacksmith, a married man, of Altofts;* the report of a preliminary inquest named him as **George** *Megson blacksmith of Silkstone Row identified by his wife Anne.*

3. On 21st August 1894, according to his death certificate, based on the coroner's certificate, **Alfred** *Dews* was executed in Her Majesty's Prison, Armley – *dislocation of the neck by hanging under sentence of law* – except that his correct name was **Albert** *Dews*. **The Yorkshire Post** named him correctly both when he was arrested in May and executed in August.

4. Brothers *James Thomas McDuff* and *John McDuff* had started work at *Burnhope Colliery*, Co. Durham, in early November 1910. On Wednesday 9th November they were involved in an explosion, which killed one brother and

injured the other. The **Consett Guardian**, a weekly paper, reported the incident on 11th November, writing that *a man named John Thomas McDuff lost his life in a shocking manner. McDuff, along with a brother named James, both belonging Lanchester, were engaged in shot-firing operations ... It is stated that John Thomas ... was killed outright ... A later report states that James McDuff, who never regained consciousness, died on Wednesday afternoon. In accordance with custom the pit was laid idle.*

The following week's paper, reporting on the inquest, correctly identified *James Thomas McDuff* as having been killed and *John McDuff* as having been injured.

THE GENTLEMAN'S MAGAZINE (first published in 1731 and continuing in the same format until the mid-19th century) was a monthly magazine, not a newspaper, but its contents - including reports (from home and overseas); articles on a wide range of topics; letters to the editor; items of gossip; details of births, marriages and deaths, of ecclesiastical preferments and military and civil promotions - are very similar to those of a modern day newspaper. The obituaries below (from the *May 1792* issue, so presumably referring to deaths in March or April) give a flavour of what can be found:

> 13. At her houſe in **Aſſembly**-row, Mile-end, Miſs Dorothy Smith.
>
> At Weſton-hall, co. Stafford, in the prime of life, Francis Lycett, gent. His death proceeded from a fall down ſtairs on the 8th inſtant, at the Falcon, in Stone (owing to one of his ſpurs unfortunately catching in his great coat), by which his ſkull was ſo dreadfully fractured that he languiſhed till the 13th, when he expired, to the great affliction of his family.
>
> 15. At Jura, one of the Hebrides, aged 98, Donald M'Crain; and, two days after, his wife, Catherine Lindſay, aged 108. Theſe two remarkable people were ſtout and active till a ſhort time preceding their deaths. The woman, to the aſtoniſhment of all the country, gained her harveſt-fee in the years 1788 and 1789.
>
> Rev. Mr. Vaux, rector of Courteenhall, near Northampton. The rectory, worth 200l. a-year, is in the gift of the Crown.
>
> 16. At his houſe at Hampſtead, aged about 64, of the gout, Mr. Edward Stokes, attorney, of New inn, agent to Lord Liſburn, in whoſe vault at Enfield, as impropriator of the great tithes of that pariſh, he was depoſited on the 23d inſtant.

CHAPTER 25

THE FINAL CHAPTER AND THE LAST RESOLUTIONS

When I wrote the original articles, I received many letters (in the days before e-mail was widely available) with comments ranging from *I enjoy your articles although they often make my head spin and even make me feel like giving up* to *Many of the pointers I've heard you give in talks but I find a salutary reminder never goes amiss.* Up-dating and expanding the articles for this book has made me realise how both correspondents felt. **Please** do not be deterred by anything you may read and also accept the fact that a certain amount of duplication (which occurs in some chapters and particularly in this one) can serve as a useful reminder of something you have read but forgotten.

Serendipity making fortunate discoveries by accident, crops up frequently with family historians (see Chapter 22 for three instances). The possibility that a vital piece of information might suddenly appear out of the blue, keeps many of us going as we fall into, and climb out of, pitfalls. There can be few family historians who have not experienced at least one instance of this phenomenon in their researches.

Many correspondents provided valuable information from their own research (for which I was most grateful and much of which has been incorporated into this book). Following the comment on page 86 that not all children were given a Christian name before being registered I was told that, in the remote rural area around *Longnor* in Staffordshire in the 1850s and 1860s, a *very considerable number* were not named (the local registrar had been interested enough to search the records).

Never take anything for granted has been my constant refrain throughout this book. Remember, whether you are dealing with original records, modern transcripts, indexes, databases, websites or your own family tree, that they were all put together by humans - and humans make mistakes.

The rapidly increasing amount of information available on the internet has opened up endless possibilities for family historians but do bear in mind that the information on many websites has been put there by individuals and much of it has not been verified by reference to the original records or secondary sources. The words *I've done my family tree on the computer* send a cold shiver down the spines of long-established researchers because they know that accepting anything at face value, without recourse to the original source, can be dangerous and can drop you into a very deep pitfall.

Several experienced researchers have generously sent details of their own proven researches to online enquirers, only to find later that the enquirer has put the research online as their own work but managed to incorporate errors into it. Imagine how galling it is for the original researcher to point out the error to another person further 'down the line', only to be told that they are wrong because *that's what it says on the internet.* **It is recommended that**

you exercise caution when giving out details of your research to an unknown online enquirer.

Many a family tree constructed by using FamilySearch or the IGI has come crashing down when a check in the original parish register reveals that the person at its head died under the age of eight (see p.55).

Ancestors supposedly missing from the 1881 census might have been located if the searcher had read the instructions and realised that the indexes covering this census in its various forms (online, on CD, on microfiche) vary in their formats. There are hundreds of people under the name of *Wright* in Yorkshire; of these, 16 spelt their name as *Right* so are listed separately in the microfiche index. If using the latter, would you have remembered to check both names and, when searching the GRO indexes, would you have searched *Wright, Wraight, Right, Rite* and so on? Failing to find an expected *Catterick* in the 1881 census would you have looked under *Patrick*, where two were found using a wildcard and a 'soundex' program (see p.57).

Do not forget that many of your ancestors were illiterate and some had strong regional accents (or no teeth) which made them very difficult for the enumerator, registrar or incumbent to understand or interpret.

The scribe had to write clearly (and with plenty of ink on his pen) and if he did not it is all too easy for a stroke to become invisible on microfilm or fiche and for *Fireman* to be indexed as *Tireman*, *Bettany* to be misread as *Bellamy* or *Walter* to be seen as *Waller*. The fact that my marriage appeared in the GRO indexes under *Littar* (see p.21) is evidence that bad handwriting can still cause problems today.

In the first chapter I urge readers not to be discouraged by all the pitfalls they will read about and not to go looking for trouble because most people will encounter only one or two of the problems mentioned in their own research - and, in any case, forewarned is forearmed. I still remember the chairman of a family history society who had never considered that his grandparents might have married less than nine months before the birth of their first child and who, consequently, had been 'stuck' for some considerable time (they married well after the birth). The friend who could not accept a *Whittaker* with double *tt* instead of one (see p.18) was upstaged by the correspondent who had found 28 different spellings for the surname *Rochester*. Then there was my husband's great-grandfather, from all accounts a staunch Anglican, who was buried in the Nonconformist part of the cemetery because his son, who arranged the funeral, was a Primitive Methodist. These are all matters which could be easily resolved with a little flexibility of mind but which could have been major hurdles if the researchers had not become aware of the possible pitfalls.

What about the possibilities? How many readers have made contact with unknown relatives because they have put the surnames they are researching online or into a family history society journal? Many years ago a family historian in Kent read of my interest in the surname *Ethell* and mentioned it to a colleague of that name. The colleague turned out to be a descendant of *Thomas Ethell*'s elder son, *John*, (see p.228) and he supplied me with a great deal of information about his branch of the family. Following a mention of this serendipity in a family history magazine, I received a letter from a lady also in Kent who proved to be a first cousin once removed of the earlier contact. Sixteen years between the two links, a bit more information to add to the tree, and the possibility that there are more cousins out there somewhere.

Then there's *Thomas Chamberlain* (see p.66-67). For thirty years I believed that his absence from home on the night of the 1851 census meant simply that he was working away from home, until a correspondent sent me all the paperwork proving that in 1851 he was a convict in Australia who managed somehow to return home at the end of his sentence. Several of his children and his nephews and nieces later emigrated to Australia and New Zealand. Australasian death certificates, usually so much more detailed than English ones, include (like Scottish ones) the names of both parents together with mother's maiden name and father's occupation. In addition you may learn the place of burial and, if you are lucky, where the person was born, where and whom they married, the names, ages and sex of living children and how long they had been in Australasia (but see below).

As so often in family history, what should have been written down and what was actually recorded often fail to coincide. A great deal depended on whether the person who registered the death knew much about the deceased (and the one useful fact generally omitted from NZ certificates, but included on Australian ones, is who the informant was). When *John Chamberlain* died in New Zealand in 1894, the only information additional to that found on an English certificate was his place of burial, his county of birth (Warwickshire, England) and the length of time he had lived in New Zealand (30 years); when his widow died in 1911 I learnt from her certificate the names of her parents (including mother's maiden name and father's occupation); her place of burial; that she was born in Scotland and had been in New Zealand for 50 years; she had married John Chamberlain in Victoria; was aged 40 when she married and had three living children, a son aged 47 and two daughters aged 45 and 36. It is tempting to believe that her death was registered by one of her children and his by an 'outsider'.

It is noticeable on both certificates that a high proportion of the answers to questions which required numbers to be given end in 0. In any document - parish registers, marriage bonds, certificates, census returns - it pays to be cautious about accepting such answers as accurate. Many informants would know only approximately how old a person was and how long they had lived in their present country or at their current address; more often than not *about 30 years* would be written down as *30* and a *guesstimate* would become a *fact*.

RESOLUTIONS FOR FAMILY HISTORIANS

I will remember that family history is a hobby.
I will resolve to enjoy my researches and will try to help other family historians to do the same.

I will read the introduction to any book, microfiche or computer program.
Failure to do this can, at best, waste your time and, at worst, bring your research to a dead end. The introduction to a published parish register may warn you that part of the register is missing; that a page was torn out because it contained an interesting signature (like *Ashbourne* in Derbyshire which 'lost' a page which Charles I had signed); or that the church was closed for repairs so parishioners had temporarily to use a neighbouring church. If you rely on the index, without realising that the register is defective, your ancestor can disappear into a black hole.

I will be aware that the spelling of names has always been fluid.
This applies to every sort of record and every kind of name - surnames, Christian names, place-names and relationship names. For example, the surname *Ankers* can appear as itself but also as *Anchors, Ankiss* or *Hankers, Litton* occurs as *Letton* and *Lytton* and one Cheshire incumbent wrote *Matwigon*, which turned out to be *McGuigan*. *Jacobus* is Latin for either *Jacob* or *James*; many incumbents had difficulty with *Francis* or *Frances* and you need to check carefully that the correct spelling for the sex has been used (see pp.55 & 98) and remember that *Gulielmus* is the Latin for *William*. In Staffordshire, *Alton* (Towers) was previously *Alveton*; in Rutland *Oakham* was often spelt *Okeham*; and in Yorkshire, *Whitkirk* was originally *Whitechurch*. *Stepson* has been in use for centuries but until the mid-19th century *son-in-law* was commonly used to describe this relationship.

I will double-check the accuracy of any information I find or am given before accepting it.
Family stories generally contain some truth but have often been exaggerated or transposed to a different generation. I was sent a family tree, compiled largely from the IGI, which had used Bishop's Transcripts for the parish concerned. This credited one man (wife unknown) with nine children, some of whom were born too close together for comfort. On checking the parish registers, which contained more information, it became obvious that there were two men involved, with four of the children belonging to *Robert senior*, four to *Robert junior* and one not specified. A following generation on the same tree showed only seven out of 10 children, because there are some Bishop's Transcripts missing.

I will treat printed pedigrees with caution.
Some compilers omitted any mention of members of the family who had dropped down the social scale, others created an imaginary link to an armigerous family or made genuine mistakes because of the lack of material available to them.

I will accept that my ancestors did not always tell the truth.
This does not necessarily mean that they were being deliberately untruthful. Often they would not know that they were giving incorrect information to the minister, registrar or census enumerator. If they could not read or write, they might not know their exact age; be unaware of where they were born, especially if they had moved away when very young; or not know that the man whose surname they bore was their stepfather. On the other hand, they might have claimed to be 21 so that they could marry without parental consent; lied about their place of birth because they feared that they might be uprooted and sent back to their parish of settlement; or invented a father because they did not want to admit to being illegitimate.

I will not believe that modern technology holds the answers to all my problems.
Incredibly, there are some people who think that the internet can produce their family tree at the press of a button. On the other hand there are those who manage very happily without access to a computer. Most family historians fall somewhere between the two - using a computer or the internet to seek out information but verifying their findings in the original records.

I will seriously consider joining one or more family history societies (if I am not already a member).
My local society will enable me to meet like-minded people with whom I can share ideas and give and receive encouragement as well as enabling me to listen to speakers, receive a journal, consult their library and take part in family history projects. The society or societies covering the area or areas from where my ancestors came will enable me to tap into local sources of knowledge and possibly link up with other people researching either the same name or, if I am fortunate, the same family. If I develop an interest in one particular name, I will check whether it is registered with the *Guild of One-Name Studies* (and if not, will consider registering it).

I will make provision in my Will for my genealogical research.
A sentence in your Will, or a codicil added to it, requesting that your research be handed over to a friend or relative, a local library or family history society (if pertinent to the area), or to the Society of Genealogists might prevent the destruction of years of work. Spouses and children do not always share one's interest in family history and there are horror stories of a lifetime's research ending up on a bonfire, in the dustbin or in thin air when the computer programs were wiped.

Family history is like a game of snakes and ladders. Pitfalls are snakes, possibilities are ladders, but most squares represent steady progress towards your final goal - just like family history!